Praise for
The Madagascar Manifesto Series

"When I reviewed the first volume in this series, *Child of the Light*, I compared it to the masterpieces of Italian neo-realistic cinema that dealt with WWII and its aftermath, with a layer of the fantastic interwoven. However, volume two, *Child of the Journey*, resembles in its gritty verisimilitude more a Lina Wertmuller spectacle of degradation and inhumanity, while the concluding book, *Children of the Dusk*, ventures into some really strange Conrad-Ballard territory. Taken together, the trilogy moves ingeniously from the personal to the political to the personal again, forsaking the center of the global maelstrom for a murky yet fascinating backwater.

"Berliner and Guthridge plumb the psychological depths of Nazism, the mystical glories of the Kaballah, and the arrogancies of Western colonialism with subtlety and craft. Their Manifesto is a blueprint for a world different from ours on the surface, yet utterly congruent beneath."
— Paul Di Filippo, *Asimov's SF Magazine*

"The last segment of the Madagascar Manifesto trilogy is as poignant, terrifying and grandly moving as the two preceding it. I know of no other work dealing with the Holocaust that treats this defining event of the twentieth century with such imagination and such brilliant inventiveness linked to deeply respectful scholarship. Rounded off so splendidly in *Children of the Dusk*, the Manifesto should now take its place among the very few works of our time that truly deserve the title epic."
— Peter S. Beagle, author of *The Last Unicorn*

Praise for Child of the Light

"Beautifully Done." — *Kirkus Review*

"Superb historical verisimilitude." — Chicago *Sun-Times*

"The fantasy in the novel seems absolutely natural, the supernatural weft in the mimetic warp. The horrors of Nazi Germany, which in lesser hands might have seemed overfamiliar, are made fresh by the unique perspective of these victims and by an acute eye for the telling detail.
"At one point, Miriam thinks of her famous uncle, Walter Rathenau, 'It would unnerve her too, if she were forced to look into the face of his humanness.' So this book should unnerve its readers with its all too human face."
— Paul Di Filippo, *Asimov's SF Magazine*

"To those who read [*Child of the Light*], it will be a powerful, perhaps unforgettable experience."
— Orson Scott Card author of *Ender's War*

"A shocking yet warmly human story. Very much worth reading."
— Marion Zimmer Bradley, author of *Mists of Avalon*

"A truly remarkable and moving book unique in its blending of inescapable fact, informed speculation, and fantasy. As believable as the nightmare truth of the holocaust. It has been said by South American writers that such magical realism is the only way to deal fictionally with the brutal history of this continent; perhaps *Child of the Light* will open similar avenues into Hitler's Germany."
— Peter S. Beagle, author of *The Last Unicorn*

"A rich and marvelous book." — Greg Bear, author of *Moving Mars*

"Gorgeously written, profoundly moving—a book that has all of the virtues of good mainstream fiction and adds that special kind of insight into the human condition that's only possible through the introduction of a fantastic element. I'm wary of collaborations, but for once here's a book that probably *is* too good for one author to have pulled it off on his or her own. A masterpiece."
— Robert J. Sawyer, author of *The Terminal Experiment*

Praise for Children of the Dusk

"What a story! …vivid, almost magical, set in an alien place with unique characters embarked on equally alien and divergent goals. It was very readable, calling me back every time I had to lay it aside, in fact costing me one very late night, although there were some parts I would have preferred reading in the sunlight.
"I think it's a real winner." — Larry Bond, author of *Vortex*

"*Children of the Dusk* is a highly unusual and frightening depiction of a little-known aspect of the Holocaust, filled with startling details and eerie atmosphere."
— Kevin J. Anderson, author of *Dune: House Atriedes.*

The Madagascar Manifesto

Child of the Light

Child of the Journey

Children of the Dusk

The Madagascar Manifesto

Child of the Light

Child of the Journey

Children of the Dusk

by Janet Berliner &
George Guthridge

Meisha Merlin Publishing
Decatur, Georgia

This book is a work of fiction. While names of certain historical figures are used, the actions, situations, and events depicted are products of the authors' imaginations. Any similarity to actual persons or events is purely coincidental.

The Madagascar Manifesto consists of the novels *Child of the Light* (White Wolf Publishing, 1995), *Child of the Journey* (White Wolf Publishing, 1996), and *Children of the Dusk* (White Wolf Publishing, 1997). An earlier novel, also called *Child of the Light* (St. Martin's Press, 1992), contains a significant portion of the text of the White Wolf editions of *Child of the Light* and *Child of the Journey*. However, the works were reorganized and expanded for publication by White Wolf.

The text of this edition has been modified from the White Wolf publication to eliminate transitional duplication, primarily between *Child of the Journey* and *Children of the Dusk*.

Copyright © 2002 by Janet Berliner-Gluckman and George Guthridge. All rights reserved.

No part of this book may be reproduced in any form, with the exception of short quotes embodied in critical essays or reviews, without express written permission from the publisher.

An MM Publishing Book
Published by:
Meisha Merlin Publishing, Inc.
PO Box 7
Decatur, GA 30031

http://www.MeishaMerlin.com

Cover and Interior Design by Robert L. Fleck.
Cover Illustration copyright © 2002 by Robert L. Fleck

ISBN: Hard cover   1-892065-57-6
       Soft cover   1-892065-58-4

First printing: February 2002

1 3 5 7 9 8 6 4 2

for the survivors

Acknowledgements

In the creation of a novel—particularly one which is intended to be historically accurate while at the same time being entertaining—a multitude of people contribute in both large and small measure. We would like to thank a few of those people here.

Two names deserve special attention.

First, without the willingness of Janet's mother, Thea Cowan, to relive the memories of Berlin between the Wars, this book would have been devoid of humanity. May she rest in peace.

Second, without the assistance, patience, and occasional bull-headedness of Robert L. "Cowboy Bob" Fleck, the sky would have tumbled before this book was finished.

Thank you to Laurie Harper of Sebastian Agency, for being everything one could hope for in a friend and an agent. Thanks to Stephe Pagel for believing in the Madagascar Manifesto enough to do this book. Thank you to Rob Hatch, Staley Krauss, and everyone else at White Wolf who took part in the initial paperback publication.

In addition to her unending debt to her mother, Janet wishes to recognize the formative contributions of Professor Samuel Draper. She also wishes to thank her friends Risa Aratyr, Rich Dansky, and Dave Smeds for their help, as well as her family for their support.

George extends his special thanks to Noi. He also wishes to thank Kay Addrisi, Eseta Sherman, and George Harper for their valuable contributions.

Foreword

The Madagascar Manifesto is not a work of idle fantasy. Nor is it a story purely of horror. While most of the events described in these novels are products of the authors' imaginations, they are set amidst the true history of our world. Painstakingly researched, written, rewritten, and rewritten again, the work took more than fifteen years before all three volumes finally saw publication. To Janet and George it was worth all of the effort when the final volume, Children of the Dusk, received recognition in the form of the Bram Stoker Award for Superior Achievement in a Novel in 1998.

The work began after Janet and George met at Norwescon, a popular science fiction convention, in 1982. At that convention, where they were both panelists, they agreed to collaborate on "something." About a month later, Janet received in the mail a single paragraph from George, who said that he liked the paragraph but didn't know where to go with it. Janet took that paragraph and expanded it to a few pages before sending it back to George.

What developed was a novella, called "The Song of the Shofar," set in a rainforest on Madagascar. The story sold to the science fiction magazine Far Frontiers, but was later returned unpublished because, the editor said, it was too strong for his expected audience.

Janet and George agreed that "Shofar" could easily be expanded into a novel, so they worked their way backward to find the root of the story, eventually discovering that their tale began in Berlin at the end of World War I.

The Manifesto draws on the family history of Janet Berliner, whose grandfather, in fact, co-owned a cigar shop on Friedrich Ebert Strasse with his gentile friend. While James Abraham had no sons—where Jacob Freund in the novels did—both the real man and the fictional character were recipients of the Iron Cross for valorous service in the German Army during the First World War.

James Abraham, with his wife and two daughters, escaped Germany barely ahead of the Nazi tide and fled to South Africa, one of the few countries in the world that would accept the Jews who left Europe (the United States, by comparison, allowed only a handful of Jewish immigrants during that time, aside from the physicists and chemists we needed to improve our weapons capability). There, Janet was born to the Abraham's youngest daughter, Thea, on Erev Yom Kippur in the Hebrew year 5700.

In contrast, George Guthridge is the son of Americans of mostly German ancestry. For several years during George's boyhood, his family lived in Germany, where his military father was stationed. The rest of the time, George grew up in the Pacific Northwest. He became a world-renowned educator for his work with Eskimo children in Alaska, where he has lived for the past 20 years. He has also found a great deal of recognition for his short fiction, including two Nebula Award finalist stories and one Hugo Award finalist. By strange coincidence, or perhaps fate, George's birthday coincides with Israeli Independence Day.

The Madagascar Plan, the cornerstone of the alternative history used in the Madagascar Manifesto, was a true proposal originated around the time of the French Revolution by one of Napoleon's advisors. During the period in which Hitler was playing the role of reasoned statesman to the world outside Germany, the Madagascar Plan resurfaced and was seriously debated even in the U.S. Congress as a possible "solution to the Jewish question."

While the Madagascar Manifesto is a work of fiction, it is also a reflection of some of the realities of our world which we usually prefer not to see. It is not light reading, but its rewards are an understanding of what is bright and what is dark in all of us.

The original novella, "Song of the Shofar," can be found along with several other stories extrapolated from the Madagascar Manifesto, in the collection Exotic Locals. Information about this and other works by the authors can be found on the BerlinerPhiles web site at http://members.aol.com/berlphil/.

Child

of the

Light

Part I

"But every shadow is in the final analysis also child of the light, and only he who has experienced light and dark, war and peace, ascent and descent, has really lived."
— Stefan Zweig
Die Welt von Gestern
(*The World of Yesterday*)

Chapter 1

Berlin
December 1918

Nine-year-old Solomon Freund removed his glasses and pressed his face against the wrought-iron bars of his open bedroom window. Without the wire rims digging into his nose he felt more comfortable, but no less impatient. He had been at the window since sundown, waiting for the evening star, the wishing star, to take its place beside the moon, and watching the soldier guarding the fur shop that adjoined the Freund-Weisser tobacco shop across the street.

The star had not yet appeared, the soldier had lost his appeal, and Solomon had grown weary of waiting.

Earlier, his sister, Recha, had cored apples for the sauce that went with the potato pancakes his mother was making for tonight's birthday-Chanukah-Christmas celebration with the Weisser family upstairs; he had grated the potatoes. Now he could hear the *latkes* sizzling in the heavy frying pan his mother kept salted and greased for her specialty. The smell of browning butter wafted into his room and his stomach growled in anticipation. The soldier must be cold, and hungry, too, he thought.

He glanced up at the ceiling that separated him from his best friend, Erich Weisser. Here, on the ground floor, the Chanukah Menorah had been lit and the smell of butter and applesauce filled the air; up in the Weissers' second-story flat, there was the scent of pine and the glow of Christmas candles—and Erich, furious that once again his parents had said no to his birthday and Christmas wish: a dog of his own. He *needed* a dog, he said, the way Sol *needed* glasses. Besides, he said, Sol could talk to his sister when he got lonely. Whom did *he* have? At least if he had a dog he would have someone to talk to, he said. Strange how he always talked about dogs as if they were people. He swore he could talk to them and that they answered him—which wasn't all that crazy, Sol thought, not if their friend Beadle Cohen was right and anything the mind could conceive of was possible.

It didn't matter. What *did* matter was that Erich get over his sulk by the time the party started.

What a party this was going to be—the first night of Chanukah, Christmas Eve, Erich's tenth birthday. Best of all, Papa was back from the Front for good, recovered from influenza without infecting the rest of the family.

A true miracle, Mama called it.

Maybe the glow of Christmas and Chanukah candles together would make another miracle and stop Erich's papa from drinking too much tonight. Then he would not make all those snide comments about Jews, and Frau Weisser would not go on about all the things she wanted and could not have, all the while looking at Mama accusingly, as if she—and not Herr Weisser's gambling—were responsible for their reduced circumstances. Herr Weisser would keep off Erich's back, and—

Across the street, the soldier shook his fist at the moon.

Was he blaming the moon for keeping him from his family on this Christmas Eve? Sol replaced his glasses and waited to see if any of the people milling around Friedrich Ebert Strasse had noticed the soldier's strange action.

Nobody seemed to care.

A crowd had gathered at the corner, around a hurdy-gurdy man grinding out a polka on his barrel organ. Several beer-drunk locals had grabbed their fat, frumpish wives and begun to dance. Two women in ragtag coats begged at the door of the butcher shop whose shelves had long since held only black-market horse meat and a skinned cat or two; a couple of street vendors hawked indoor fireworks and sugar-coated ginger cookies. They stepped delicately around the beggars to approach a passing coterie of laughing Fraüleins in their fashionable calf-length holiday skirts. Having sampled the spicy cookies, the ladies boldly offered a taste to a trio of cadets walking stiffly upright to balance the weight of their gold-mounted Pickelhauben helmets.

The cadets ignored them and continued to make their way toward a group of men in uniform who stood at the far corner, beneath skeletal trees. Arms crossed, they listened to a Freikorps band play a solemn Lohengrin medley.

The scene held endless fascination for Sol. It was as if his entire pewter soldier collection had come alive in the street: Cuirassiers in armored breastplates, Death's Head Hussars, Foot Artillery, Hasans—

He thought about his little army, so proud and smart in the closet he carefully kept locked. Though he knew that daydreaming could bring the voices again and leave him shaking, he let his mind drift. He resisted the urge to imagine himself in the Great War. Papa had said the fighting had been too terrible to contemplate—and no glory in it, despite the Kaiser's decrees to the contrary—so Solomon imagined himself...*saw* himself...among his soldiers outside Paris forty-five years earlier, the great city surrounded, he with saber in hand, leading a heroic charge against a *mitrailleusse* machine gun. Bullets whizzed past his ears. He called out encouragement to his men and they in turn invoked the name of the Fatherland. The French abandoned their posts and scattered before the brave Prussians racing through the field.

The battle froze as if caught in a photograph. Everyone stopped running. The artillery bursts stayed in place, as though the sky were permanently bruised, yet light, a different light, flashed before Sol's eyes, spangling like a foil pinwheel. The flashes brightened, got bigger...seemed to swallow him. He no longer saw either the battlefield or the street of Berlin. Only a cobalt-blue twilight surrounded him—the world without form, without substance. He tried to shut his eyes, but the glow held him. A man's voice cried out from the twilight—shrill, plaintive, filled with pain:

"*Is this your season of madness, Solomon Freund? Is this your season of sadness?*"

A *real* machine gun rattled, cutting off the twilight voice—another of the voices he had been hearing off and on for at least as long as he'd been wearing glasses...which seemed like forever.

Solomon blinked. The cobalt-blue light dissipated as the music and the strollers along Friedrich Ebert Strasse paused. Rifle fire filled the momentary silence. Couldn't people, he wondered, trembling and angry with himself for hearing another of the voices again, at least stop shooting for the holidays? Sometimes he had a hard time remembering what things were like before the start of the Communist revolution. Seven weeks was not forever, but it was too long to be confined to the apartment house, where he had been since the Great War ended and the revolt in Berlin's streets began.

"Snipers!" A man dressed as St. Nicholas ran down the street, waving his arms. "They've positioned themselves atop the Brandenburg Gate!"

Two or three people turned and stared in the direction of the Siegesallee—the Victory Alley. Then the music began again, the barrel organ and the Freikorps band, and people continued to saunter down the boulevard as if they had heard and seen nothing more unusual than a man shooting wooden ducks at a carnival stand.

The shooting must have something to do with the Kiel sailors holed up in the Imperial Palace, Sol decided, vaguely remembering a discussion between his father and Herr Weisser about some mutinous sailors who had sacked the Royal Palace, "under the guise of socialism," whatever that meant.

Grownups often said things he and Erich didn't understand, he thought. Like Papa, getting agitated about Herr Lubov, the furrier, calling his shop *Das Ostleute Haus* because *Ostleute* meant "people of the East." The Lubovs were rumored to be Communist sympathizers who waved what Papa called "the red flag of revolt." Then he and Mama turned right around and talked about Rosa Luxemburg as if she were a heroine in a book—yet she was one of the founders of the new Communist Party in Germany. It was all just too confusing!

Taking a deep breath to calm himself and put the twilight voice from his mind, he refocused his attention on the soldier.

One by one, as dusk turned into night, shopkeepers doused their lights and closed up for the day. Finally, all the stores were dark except the furrier's. Mannequins dressed in sable and centered in blue-white light stared at Sol from behind the plate-glass windows. He squinted, distorting the image until the windows across the street became the irises of a Persian cat, a royal Eastern princess whose gleaming eyes hid ambition and avarice. *Prinzessin Ostleute.*

Intensified shooting again pulled him back to reality. He gripped the wrought-iron grill and leaned away from his open window, as much to give his nose a chance to warm up as to remove himself from the sound of the guns.

Staying home and playing with Erich all day had been fun at first, but he was beginning to miss school, and he and Erich were getting on each other's nerves. They needed something special to do, something different, like going back to the hideaway they had discovered just before all the trouble started. They had been sent down to clean the shop's cellar, a job that in the past had been done by hired help. While moving a crate to one side, they had noticed a rusty drain-grate that led into a section of ancient brick sewer, sealed off from Berlin's modern system. Though fetid and damp, the sewer ran beneath both the furrier's and their shop, and made a perfect hideaway.

Best of all, it was *their* sewer. Their secret.

"Tonight will be like old times," Sol's mother said.

He turned to look at her. She stood framed in the doorway of his room, wiping her hands on her apron. Her face was flushed, her hairline damp from the heat of the kitchen.

"Come, Sol. You must be hungry. Wash your hands and face and help me carry the food upstairs."

Sol glanced at his hands. "I'm starving."

"Wash," his mother said. "Even if you think you're clean."

Frowning, Sol moved away from the window.

His mother laughed. "Watch out—your face might stay ugly," she said. "And close that window, Solly, or there'll be icicles on your bed when we come home. Already in here it's like Siberia."

Chapter 2

"Aren't you going to help us put this on the tree?" Erich's mother held out a handful of tinsel.

Erich shook his head and went on rocking in the chair he had placed as far away from the tree as possible. He hated Christmas. Mama knew that! He hated his birthday, too, because it was Christmas Eve and he always lost out. He had liked them both all right until he was about six, when his parents started lumping everything together, cheating him, giving him one present instead of two. Sure, the present was bigger, but that still meant he only had one package to open.

"Here, Friedrich, you do it. I have other things to do before they come."

Inge Weisser handed the tinsel to her husband. He took it from her and threw it at the tree. "There! Is that good enough for them?"

"What do you mean *for them?* It's for *us,* Friedrich, and for the boy."

"Jews—what do they know about Christmas! Not even a tree in the shop—*he* wouldn't allow it—"

It's almost as though he wishes Herr Freund had died in the trenches, Erich thought. One of these days he's going to forget himself in front of Herr Freund and say something even Sol's papa—for all his niceness—cannot excuse, and then what will happen to us?

"I hear them coming up the stairs." His mother set her face in a smile and looked at her husband as if she hoped it were contagious. "Quick, Erich, open the door."

He let the Freunds in and for a while it was like old times. The two families sat on the Weissers' astrakhan rug, among stray tinsel and pine needles. There were warmed schnapps, potato pancakes, and easy laughter in front of a roaring fire. And songs—not religious ones of Jesus or God particularly—just non-secular, happy, holiday ones.

When the stories began about the children when they were little and Germany was at peace, Recha climbed onto her father's lap and snuggled against him. "Tell us about when *you* were little, Papa."

Jacob Freund smiled. Reaching into his pocket, he took out a tiny, four-sided brass top. "This *dreidel* is even older than I am. Can you imagine that, children? My grandfather brought it all the way from Russia."

Erich and Sol grinned at each other. This was their favorite story, the one about Sol's great grandfather Moshe, who was both a rabbi and a horse thief. Why didn't *he* have an interesting family like that, Erich thought.

Holding the *dreidel,* Jacob said, "We'll never be sure which of his two occupations made it necessary for him to leave Russia in the middle of the night, but—"

"Couldn't you spare us the story of your illustrious ancestors just this one time?"

Friedrich Weisser downed another schnapps and Erich felt as if a cold wind had blown through the room. There were hours to go before midnight and the opening of presents. An argument now would spoil everything.

"I'm first," he said, hoping to avert a quarrel. Taking the *dreidel* from Herr Freund's hand, he spun it hard. *"Nun, gimel, he, shin,"* he chanted, repeating the letters of the Hebrew alphabet that were engraved on the old brass surface of the *dreidel*. He had learned the words from the Freunds; maybe being the first to say them tonight would make up for his father's rudeness.

Recha, whose eyelids had begun to droop, got her second wind. She climbed off her father's lap and joined in the game, yelling loudly as the top slowed down and she, too, tried to guess which letter would be visible when the spinning stopped and the *dreidel* finally lay still.

"Ridiculous game!" Herr Weisser placed his rough hand over the top and stopped its spinning.

Ella Freund's face hardened. "All right, children," she said, standing up. "It's getting late. I think it's time to leave."

"Don't be so sensitive, Ellie." Her husband took out a fresh cigar. "Fred's just had a little too much schnapps. He doesn't mean anything by it."

Oh doesn't he, Erich thought, watching his father pace up and down the room.

"You Jews all think you're so special—" Friedrich Weisser stopped in his tracks and glared at Herr Freund.

He's done it! He's gone too far, Erich thought. "Let's go to my room, Sol," he whispered, embarrassed for his father. "You, too, Recha, if you like."

"Recha?" Sol asked.

Erich saw the worried look on Sol's face. True, Erich hardly ever voluntarily included Recha in anything—not that he didn't like her, but she *was* only seven.

"Come, Friedrich!" Jacob Freund said, his voice firm. "You don't really mean any of that. We are friends, all of us. Old friends." He put out his hand. "Let us put an end to this at once. For all of our sakes."

"Papa, please—"

Erich was cut short by a knock at the front door.

"The beadle." Frau Freund looked flustered. "I forgot. I invited him for a glass of schnapps. I didn't think you would mind—"

"Well, I do mind!" Friedrich Weisser jammed the cork into the bottle. "And so does my good wife!"

"Sol." Erich tugged at Sol's arm, pulling him toward his bedroom. "I have something for you."

"Bring it out here."

"No. It's private. Come now, before—"

There was a second knock at the door, louder this time.

"Do I let him in?" Ella Freund asked quietly. Sol's father gave her an *it's not our home* look.

"Please, Papa, he's a nice man. Let him come in," Erich said. He could feel that his face had turned red.

"Go on, go on!" His papa waved his hand. "Open the door. But only one drink—"

As graciously as if she had sent him a gilt-edged invitation, Frau Weisser ushered Beadle Cohen into her home. He was a short, rotund man with thinning hair and a limp that got better or worse depending on the weather. His built-in barometer, he called it, impressing the boys no end with the accuracy of his predictions. He spent all of his time around the synagogue, where he was a glorified janitor, or surrounded by musty books which he foisted upon the mostly unwilling boys who attended the Hebrew School attached to the *shul.*

Sol was one of the exceptions—not only willing but anxious to get his hands on as many books as he could. He loved to read. Most of all he loved to discuss what he had read with the beadle, who made no bones about either his poverty or his intellect. He had a particular fondness for Sol and, strangely enough, for Erich, who was not much of a reader—certainly not of Jewish literature. Often, when Erich was through with sports, he would walk past the Hebrew school and wait for Sol so they could walk home together. Sometimes the beadle would walk with them. He made a point of talking about things like astronomy, which interested Erich as well as Sol.

"Happy Chanukah." The beadle accepted a glass of schnapps and an invitation to be seated. "And a merry Christmas, too." He sipped at the drink with obvious enjoyment. "So kind of you to include me. Most kind."

"We have potato pancakes left over, if you're hungry," Sol's mother said.

"Hungry? One needs to be hungry to eat *latkes,* especially Ella Freund's *latkes?*" The beadle glanced down at his stomach and laughed. "But I can't stay long. I have other stops to make."

Erich saw a look of relief on his friend's face. He felt the same way; he wanted the beadle to stay, but who knew how long Papa would control himself?

"I have no gifts for the adults," the beadle said, "but I was able to manage a little something for each of the children. Recha!" He dug in his pocket and pulled out an old sepia photograph. "Because you love to dance, I brought you a photograph of Anna Pavlova. This was taken when she was just your age. Now she's the most famous ballerina in the whole world."

Recha took the photograph and stared at it, her dark eyes sparkling.

"Say thank you to Beadle Cohen." Ella Freund smiled at her daughter.

"Thank you, Beadle Cohen." Recha performed a little curtsy.

"I'd prefer a kiss, right here." Pretending great seriousness, the beadle pointed at his cheek.

Recha obliged.

"Would it be too much to ask for one on the other cheek, too?" The beadle was enjoying himself.

Recha shook her head and, instead, kissed the photograph.

"Well, I suppose that will have to do," the beadle said, with mock sadness. "Erich! I believe today is also your birthday. Happy birthday, my boy."

Erich saw his papa's expression harden. Hurry up, beadle, he thought. There's not much time left.

"One day you will get that dog you want so badly," the beadle said, "and you will have to know how to look after him. I talked to a man I know who knows *everything* about dogs. He gave me this for you." He pulled a worn leather leash out of his pocket and held it out to Erich.

"This is foolishness," Herr Weisser said. "I have told the boy he cannot have a dog. He nags me about it enough, now he will double his efforts. We cannot have that. The way he embarrasses me, telling people he knows what dogs are thinking—!"

"But Papa—"

"No!"

The beadle stood up. Stuffing the leash into his pocket, he gave the boys a broad wink. "Perhaps I can find a temporary use for it," he said. "Thank you for your hospitality."

"Your *latkes,* beadle." Ella Freund emerged from the kitchen with a plate in her hands.

"Perhaps you will be kind enough to repeat the offer some other time."

The beadle seemed calm enough, but Erich knew he was upset. Why else would he have forgotten to give Sol his present? Papa always spoiled everything, and *he* had to make excuses!

"Look, I'm sorry, Sol," Erich said, as soon as they were in his room. "My father, he..."

"Not your fault." Sol sounded close to tears.

"Here!" Erich handed Sol the dog collar he had kept hidden under the bed. "I made this for you—for us—in leather craft at school. We'll have a puppy soon. It'll be just ours, yours and mine, and no one else will even be allowed to pet him...'cept maybe Recha, sometimes."

"Boys, come out of the bedroom. Everything is all right," Jacob Freund called from the hallway. "We're all friends again."

"We'd better go—" Sol began.

"Don't you like it?"

"It's great, Erich. But—"

"I don't know when or how, but we'll do it, Sol," Erich said. "If we stick together, we can get whatever we want. We're blood brothers, right?" Remembering something he had seen in a film, he held up his arm, wrist toward Sol, who touched his wrist to Erich's and reached for the collar with his other hand.

"Wait!" Erich placed the collar carefully around their arms and closed it tightly. "Nothing can separate us now!"

"Ow! You made it too tight!"

"Okay, pull! One, two, three."

Laughing, the boys tugged in opposite directions and the collar dropped to the floor. Sol picked it up, examined it briefly, and stuffed it into his pocket. "Thanks."

"*Solll!*" Recha wailed outside the door. "Sol!"

Patting his pocket, Sol opened the door to a tearful Recha.

"You always leave me out. Always."

Sol crouched and gave his sister a hug. She was okay—for a girl, Erich thought. "What happened in there, Recha?" he asked.

Recha handed her brother a book bound in soft black leather. "Beadle Cohen went away. He left this for you."

Sol took the book and read the title out loud. "*Toledot ha-Ari. Life of the Ari*...the Lion. Look, Erich, it's the biography of Isaac ben Solomon Luria!"

Erich had no idea who that was but he could see that his friend was pleased.

Sol's mother came walking down the hallway toward them. "He said to tell you he was given this very book when he was your age," she told Sol. "He wants you to have it. Your papa said you were much too young to understand anything about the Kabbalah, but our beadle is a stubborn man. The Lurianic Kabbalah must be part of your education, he says, and to understand the philosophy you must first understand the man."

The book was small enough to fit in Sol's pocket with the dog collar. Erich saw him slip it inside and pat his pants. "I tried reading this once," Sol said. "It's about a man who saw things inside his head that other people couldn't see. He was a mystic, whatever that is."

"Ask your papa," Erich said.

"I did. He said, 'leave the study of mysticism to the *Hasids*—'" Sol looked at Erich and laughed. "They're *very* religious," he explained, "like the Pope and the Cardinals—"

"Beadle Cohen says that when you are ready, the understanding will come." His mother took Recha's hand and led the little girl back into the living room. Sol started to follow but Erich stopped him.

"When we get the dog, we'll keep it in the sewer," he whispered. "We'll take turns going down to feed him and—"

"Boys!" his papa called out pleasantly. "We've decided to start opening the presents early."

Erich looked at Sol, raised his wrist one more time, and grinned. "Brothers," he said again. "Forever and ever."

Chapter 3

"Liebknecht and Luxemburg! Both killed!" Jacob Freund removed his glasses and dangled them from his fingers over the newspaper headlines. "What is Germany coming to?"

Though this was one of those rare times that all the members of the Freund and Weisser families were in the shop together, Sol knew from his papa's tone that he was thinking aloud and did not expect an answer to his question.

"How did they die, Papa?" he asked from the back of the shop. Since the table was occupied, he and Erich were playing chess on the linoleum floor.

"What does it matter how," Friedrich Weisser said. "Dead is dead! Things will quiet down and we can get back to business."

"Ella, more and more I think you and the children should go to your sister. You'll be safer in Amsterdam with Herta." Jacob Freund sounded agitated.

"Look here, Recha." Ella Freund pointedly ignored her husband and gestured at the newspaper. "It says here this pretty little girl loves to dance, just like you." She leaned closer to the paper. "Miriam Rathenau, granddaughter of industrialist Emil Rathenau, is being sent to the United States to study the new modern forms of dance that have become so popular over there," she read aloud. "Poor thing. Her parents were killed in an automobile accident."

"Such a poor little thing I should like to be," Frau Weisser said. "They say her father left her a fortune in art in Switzerland, and it's just waiting for her to be old enough to collect it."

"Is money all you can think of, Inge? The child's an orphan—"

Sol stopped listening. Not that he didn't feel sorry for the girl, but right now he felt sorrier for himself. He was tired of staring out of his window and of reading about Isaac ben Solomon Luria. He was even more tired of listening to the four adults bicker about things that seemed entirely unimportant, or talk endlessly of danger and revolution. Already it was past the middle of

January and there was no end in sight. He would probably never see the inside of a classroom again—

Erich sat up so abruptly that he knocked over his king's rook. He did not seem to notice it, though he usually went to great lengths not to lose his castles, even sacrificing knights and bishops. His face was turned toward the door, his head cocked like that of a bird. The adults went on talking; Erich gestured, palms close to the floor, as though wishing he could will the conversation to stop. It was interrupting his concentration—whatever it was he was listening to.

"Erich?" Sol asked in a low breath.

Erich shook his head and went on listening.

Then he leaned conspiratorially across the chessboard. His blue eyes shone with excitement. "We need to go. *Now.* Make up some excuse."

"Why! Go where!" Sol whispered.

Again Erich shook his head.

"*You* make up the excuse," Sol said.

But Erich was back to listening to something outside. Besides, Sol knew why he would have to be the one to ask. Herr Weisser inevitably denied any request Erich made, no matter how innocent or rational. It was a matter of course. Oddly, despite his obvious feelings concerning anything Jewish, the father always responded to Sol's opinions and requests, as though the boy were an extension of the man to whom, like it or not, Herr Weisser was indebted. *He respects intelligence,* Sol's mother had said once of the shop's co-owner.

He's stupid, Erich had insisted when Sol relayed his mother's remark. Sol argued that no one should say such a thing about one's papa, but Erich would not be deterred. Stupid and...*and* selfish, Erich added.

"Do something." Erich poked Sol's forearm.

"I need to go...for extra lessons." Sol stood and held up his Luria book.

"You're going to the Grünewald? Now?" Sol's mother asked, wiping her hands on her apron as though ridding herself of imaginary dough.

"Yes. Me too," Erich piped in, rising so quickly that he bumped over more chess pieces. "Beadle Cohen promised to explain more about Mister Einstein's ideas."

"That damn beadle...teaching *my* boy," Herr Weisser muttered. "...Jewish science."

"You want instruction outside of school," Inge Weisser said, "you should go see Father...," she looked at her husband as if for confirmation about the name, "Father Dahns."

"Fast as he is, the boy should be looking for someone to teach him track-and-field," Herr Weisser said. "Not thinking about stars and psychics and God knows what else."

"*Physics,*" Erich said, then added as if in afterthought: "Papa."

Herr Weisser's features clouded as he looked at his son, yet Sol could see light in the man's eyes. *It's true what Mama said,* he thought. *He does admire intelligence—just doesn't want to admit it. Particularly in Erich's case.*

"I'm going," Erich said stiffly.

"You be careful on the trolley," Sol's mother said to the boys.

"Of course, Mama." Sol leaned forward to peck her cheek, a motion guaranteed, he knew, to get him *almost* anything.

Erich hurried outside. Sol put the chessmen away, avoiding the adults' eyes for fear they might change their minds, and backed through the door, smiling a simpering smile.

"I hate lying," Sol said as they hustled down the sidewalk, dodging passers-by. "Especially where Luria is concerned." He patted the book in his pocket to assure himself it was still there.

"Some things are more important than lying." Erich trotted across the street at a diagonal, Sol beside him. They rounded a corner and Erich gestured for Sol to follow him down an alley, a look of fear and anticipation apparent in Erich's face. He stopped behind a pyramid of garbage cans.

"There." He pointed down toward where the alley ended in a brick wall. "You see?"

Tied beneath a lattice of small filthy windows was a bull terrier, whimpering. Beside him stood a stack of crates crammed with chickens, clucking uproariously. A calico cat lay on the top crate, asleep in the slant of sunlight, seemingly oblivious to the birds below.

"The pup called to me," Erich said.

"Sure he did. Three blocks away. Next you'll be telling me that the Kaiser sends you mental messages from Holland."

Erich eyed him sternly. "Don't mock me, Solomon. Just because you can't—"

A barrel-chested man in a bloodstained apron emerged from the building. He carried a cleaver. A cigarette dangled from his lip as if it were glued there. He opened a cage and gripped a chicken by the neck. While it hung flapping he chopped the twine that had kept the cat tied against the crate, and lifted the animal by its collar. It dangled forlornly, as though surrendered to its fate. Holding both animals, the man went inside, kicking the door closed with his heel.

"Butcher," Erich said.

"I know that. I'm not stupid," Sol said.

"Not stupid. Just not smart." Erich sat down, his back against a garbage can. "Not smart *here*. In your heart." He tapped his chest with his forefinger. "Peer between the cans. Watch the pup. I'll show you what I can do. I won't even look at him."

Erich closed his eyes; his face tightened. Sol could tell he was thinking hard.

As if it had received some kind of message, the pup began mewling, straining so much against its rope that the forepaws scrabbled ineffectually against the pavement.

"His name's Bull," Erich said.

"I suppose he told you that."

"He's telling me...a lot of things."

"Like what."

"*Private* things," Erich said. "If I told you, he wouldn't trust me."

"He smells us, is all."

"All he can smell is death, right now." Erich stood and crept around the garbage cans, keeping close to the wall.

"If you can speak to him so easily," Sol said, "teach him to untie the rope himself."

Erich waved him off and continued on. Sol went around the cans but feared going further. "That butcher comes out and finds you with his dog, he'll chop you up instead," he whispered.

"You want me just to let Bull be someone's dinner?"

The comment caught Solomon so off guard that he consciously closed his mouth. He hadn't thought about the reality. Maybe Erich's right, he thought. Maybe I *am* smart yet stupid.

He ran to help his friend.

"Hurry up!" he whispered, as Erich fumbled with the knot. Erich bundled the dog into his arms and raced back toward the street. Sol looked at the thin rope...at the chicken cages.

He tied one end of the rope to the shop door and the other to the crates, which he unlatched but did not open. When the butcher opened the shop door, he would free the chickens himself. Life—and death—must go on, but perhaps having to chase after his chickens would make him think twice about stuffing so many into a cage.

Besides, Sol thought, why should only the dog go free?

Chapter 4

"This is crazy," Sol said, looking at the puppy Erich held wrapped in a piece of old blanket they had found in another alley. "We'll get...*caught.*"

He had started to say *scolded,* but knew it would spark Erich's always-sarcastic laughter. What did a scolding matter, when a puppy was at stake?

His back against the tobacco shop, Erich craned his neck and peered in through the door's window. "Your papa's busy with a customer. I can't see anyone else inside," he whispered.

"What if they're in the cellar?"

"They're probably over at the apartment. Go on, now. Do what we planned."

"What *you* planned," Sol said morosely, but opened the door. The bell jangled. Smiling deferentially to his father, he stepped inside. He did his best to block the view between the door and the curtain that led to the cellar stairs. Jacob Freund was busy showing a derby-hatted man a silver cigar-guillotine. He did not look toward the boys as Erich stole in behind Sol and disappeared behind the curtain.

"The beadle had other business, so we came right back. We'll be downstairs cleaning up," Sol announced.

His father nodded, gave him a cursory smile, and went back to his customer. A silver guillotine, Sol knew, would easily equal the value of whatever other products his father sold this day—or for the week, for that matter. Sol was angry with himself for having interrupted.

He went behind the curtain but paused at the cellar door. He wanted to go down there and yet he did not. If his papa or Herr Weisser caught them playing in the sewer, they would be punished and he would be right back where he had been for so many weeks—in his room—alone.

By the time he descended the steps into the cellar, however, he could hardly wait to push aside the crate they had left guarding the entrance to the sewer.

Their *magical* place, fearful yet inviting...especially after all the months cooped up across the street.

While Erich stood holding and kissing the puppy, the dog squirming against the confinement, Sol heaved the crate away from the sewer's grate. It was blood-brown with corrosion and recessed into a limestone floor discolored by a century of cellar moisture seeping into the drain. Taking hold of the crowbar they had hidden there, he jammed it beneath the lip of the grate and, using the tool as a lever, pressed down on it with all his might. The grate did not budge.

"Hurry up!" Erich said, hopping from one foot to the other as though he needed to use a bathroom. "Get the thing open."

"I can't!"

"*I* always open it easily," Erich said.

"You do it, then! I'll hold the dog." Solomon was getting annoyed. He was confident of his brains but not his muscle, which was why he usually left feats of strength to Erich, even though Erich was the smaller of the two.

Footsteps sounded above them.

"The customer's leaving. Wonder if he bought the guillotine," Sol said.

"Someone else," Erich said. "Coming *into* the shop."

They kept quiet and listened. There was movement in the shop upstairs, more footsteps, the faint echo of raised voices.

"Your papa," Sol said. "Hope to doesn't come down here for supplies."

Erich glanced anxiously toward the cellar steps, then sharply nodded toward the crowbar. "Get it done." His lips looked tight.

Holding down the crowbar with his foot, Sol gripped the edge of the grate and, grunting with the effort, began to lift. This time the grate creaked open. He gave it one last push and it thudded back against the limestone wall. After making sure the wire stems of his glasses were snugged behind his ears, he lowered himself into the hole.

The cylindrical sewer was three meters deep—a long drop. The last time they had come down, the boys had worked two bricks loose from each side of the sewer wall, at midpoint, and jammed in a two-by-four to serve as a step. Still, it was further down than Sol remembered. His feet dangled in mid-air and panic seized him. What if—. His toes found the board and he reached for the dog. The action was premature. He lost his balance and had to jump onto the partially dismantled packing crates they had used to cover the slick sewer floor.

The blackness smelled stale. He stayed crouched, his ears keened to the sound of dripping water and his eyes searching the darkness for—

For what?

Chiding himself for being afraid, he climbed onto the board. Balancing precariously, he reached up for the dog. He smiled as he dropped back down and cradled the puppy against his cheek. It felt warm and alive and somehow reassuring. When it licked his nose, he laughed and scratched it behind the ear.

"Watch out below," Erich whispered. Quick-footed as he was quick-tempered, he lowered himself onto the two-by-four, dropped deftly, and sprang to his feet.

"Give me that." Erich took the dog. He kissed the puppy on the nose and held the animal up at eye level to admire it. "The pup doesn't like the dark," he said. "Why didn't you light the candle?"

"Haven't had a chance," Sol said, choosing to ignore Erich's supposed knowledge of the workings of puppies' minds.

Served Erich right if he had to wait! Who did he think he was, treating everything like a military operation, with each of them allotted specific, immutable tasks—assigned by Erich, of course.

Scowling, Sol grabbed the jar of matches from the shelf they had fashioned by attaching the bottom of a cardboard box to coat-hanger wire and jamming the ends into cracks between the mildewed bricks. The candle on the shelf was burned down to a wick and melted wax. Beneath the shelf hung a sailor's bag containing such treasures as some of Sol's books and his extra harmonica, the gunsight Erich had found, the dried frog Erich had put in Ursula Müller's hair. From the bag Sol reluctantly retrieved the glass-encased *Yahrzeit* candle he had hoped never to use.

It took five matches before one of them yielded a flame. When he finally got the candle lit, it guttered and flickered. He had not wanted to bring it down here in the first place; a *Yahrzeit* candle was only meant to be used to commemorate the anniversary of the death of a close family member. That was its purpose. That, and that alone; to burn until there was no more candle. To mourn the dead. But because it was encased in a glass holder and fatter than an ordinary candle, Erich insisted it was far more practical for their purposes than the skinny Christmas candles at his house. True, a single *Yahrzeit* candle burned for a whole night and day—but Sol, for one, had no intention of being down here that long.

He stared beyond the small circle of light he had created, into the sewer's nether realms where anything could be lurking. He could not see the walls or the sewer's other entrance, which was a padlocked grate that led into the furrier's sub-basement.

"Erich?"

"What!"

"I—" Solomon, about to share his feelings about the darkness, changed his mind. "Will the puppy be all right here?"

"Why shouldn't he be?" Erich stooped and righted one of the packing crates. He lined it with the blanket and set the puppy inside. "We'll stuff some old rags in the grates so if he whines no one will hear. We'll visit him every day." He stroked the puppy's head. The dog was standing with its forepaws on the edge of the box, its tiny tail wagging. "Won't we, boy!"

"What if we can't get down to see him every day or if our papas see—"

"They won't be able to see anything. We'll put the boxes back over the grate." Erich pursed his lips and made little kissy sounds in front of the dog. "He'll be a real scrapper when he grows up. Like me. Right, Bull?" He scratched the puppy under the chin. "Better bring our own collar with you next time we come down."

"If we're staying down here for a while, we'd better close the grate," Sol said, conceding the argument. "If one of our papas comes down to the cellar—"

"I guess you're right." Erich stopped playing with the puppy. "Give me a boost."

Solomon braced himself and cupped his hands in readiness. He was not enjoying himself. The *Yahrzeit* candle bothered him, Erich's attitude bothered him, and he felt bad about leaving the puppy alone in the sewer. The candle would go out eventually and the little thing would be scared. Hungry, too. What if they came back and found it dead and stiff and covered with mildew?

Eyeing the open drain like an acrobat about to somersault toward an oncoming trapeze bar, Erich placed one foot in Sol's hands and hoisted himself onto the two-by-four. With Sol holding his legs to steady him, he poked his head and shoulders through the hole in the cellar floor. Then, snaking his hand through, he patted around for the crowbar.

"Whatever you do, don't let go, *Spatz.*"

"Maybe you'll grow longer if I leave you hanging for a while. Maybe then you'll stop calling me 'Sparrow.'"

"I might do that if you ever stop feeding the little buggers." Erich inserted the crowbar through the slats of the grate, and tugged.

The grate creaked but did not move.

"Damn this! What did you do to it?" He tugged harder, his body straining with the effort.

"Do to it? Nothing," Sol said. He had developed a crick in his neck from trying to see upward. "There! You've got it! No! Wait—something's wrong!"

Something *was* wrong—Sol could feel it. But what? He watched the grate come away from the wall and move to an upright position. As it teetered, he saw the problem.

Erich was balancing himself by holding onto the lip of the hole. His hand—

"Let go!"

Even as Sol yelled, he knew it was too late. The grate clunked down, followed a split-second later by the thud of the crowbar hitting the boards on the sewer floor.

Erich's scream died to a choking gurgle as he pawed at the grate. Light, slanting through the bars, cast pale stripes across his face, and blood curled down his arm. He kicked spastically.

"Erich!" Not knowing what else to do, Solomon held onto Erich's legs.

"Help me!" Erich screamed hysterically.

"Papa!" Sol shouted, as Erich stopped to take a breath between convulsive sobs. "Papa, help us!"

He waited, listening for footsteps, for a voice. At his feet, the puppy softly whimpered.

"Papa!"

A woman's voice answered him, floating out of the sewer's darkness.

Oh God, let me die. I did not know...I did not know.

Chapter 5

"It hurts! Sol, help me!" Erich tried to take a deep breath between sobs, but the pain was too great. "M-my hand. It's st-stuck! The crowbar! Open the grate. It hurts—it hurts!"

Sol let go of his legs. Erich could vaguely hear Sol rummaging around below. His own body weight was dragging him down, wrenching at his armpit. Oh God, he thought. What if my hand busts right off and my fingers stay up there and—

He heard himself screaming again. His heart was beating so hard, he knew it was about to burst open and fly right out of his body. He forced himself to stop screaming.

"Erich? Are you alive? Answer me!"

Sol's voice came from somewhere outside of Erich's cocoon of pain.

"I'll get there!" Sol was yelling desperately. "I'm trying to pull myself up!"

Why is he crying! Erich wondered, feeling a strange numbness creep over him. Why doesn't he just reach up here and help me? He doesn't have the strength and balance to get past you and shift the grate, some other part of him answered.

"Papa!" Sol shouted again.

Erich could hear him clawing at the slimy walls of the cellar. "Papa!" he screamed, in unison with his friend.

"Solomon? Erich? For God's sake, boys, where are you? What's happened?"

"Papa! Down here!" Sol shouted. "Erich's hurt!"

"Herr Freund! Help me, please!"

"Gott in Himmel!" Jacob's voice pleading for God's help came from directly above Erich's head. "I have to find something heavy to pry open this grate. I'll be as quick as I can, boys!"

There was the sound of running footsteps up and down the stairs. Then Herr Freund's voice again. "A moment and you'll be out."

Within seconds, he pried open the grate and hauled Erich out of the sewer like a sack of potatoes. "My hand!" Sobbing, he cupped his injured hand with his good one and blew on it. The ridge where the edge of the grate had flattened his fingers was like raw meat after his mama pounded it in the kitchen. The flesh around the ridge was puffed and red and swollen. He felt sick to his stomach.

"Friedrich!" Jacob Freund called. "Come down here. Your son has been hurt."

He cradled Erich gently and led him to the stairs.

"Wait!" Erich said. "Sol n-needs help getting out."

Herr Freund set Erich down gingerly on the bottom step and went back to the grating. "Here, take hold of me," he told Sol.

He reached into the drain and pulled Sol up through the hole. Sol collapsed onto his knees beside Erich. "You're alive—you're alive!" He was crying.

"He's alive," Jacob said quietly.

"Thank you, Papa!" Sol said. "Thank you. Oh God...what if Erich had died...and nobody knew where we were...and—!"

Jacob put his arm around his son. "Did you think I didn't know about this place? And the dog?"

"You saw?" Erich whispered.

Jacob nodded. "I didn't have the heart to say anything—"

"Erich! What have you done now?" Erich's papa shouted, charging down the stairs and almost tripping over his son. *"Mein Gott,* your hand! Did Solomon do this? I'll—"

"The boys got into the sewer—"

"The sewer!" Breathing hard, his papa bent over Erich. "Idiot! This will break your mama's heart!" He turned to Jacob. "It's all your fault. You should have sealed the drain!"

"Calm down, Friedrich. It was an accident," Jacob Freund said. "Let's leave recriminations for later, shall we, and attend to your son. We must get him to the hospital."

"It hurts, Papa," Erich said, trying not to cry and keeping a tight grip on his injured hand.

His father helped him to his feet. "Let's go," he said. "But I promise you, when I get back I'm going to seal that place so tight not even a cockroach will be able to get in!"

"I'll take care of it," Jacob said softly. "Now go. And don't worry about the dog, Erich, I'll—"

"Dog? What dog!"

Erich cringed at the look on his papa's face.

"A puppy," Herr Freund said matter-of-factly. "The boys have a puppy down—"

"You insist on disobeying me!" Erich's father shouted.

"Friedrich! This is not the time for anger! I told you, I will take care of everything."

"*Nein!*" Erich's father shouted. "Nein! Nein! Nein! *You* take him to the hospital. I'm going to take care of this grate, right now, this minute—"

"Sol! Don't let him seal Bull in there!"

Erich had begun to shake uncontrollably.

"The boy's going into shock," Herr Freund said. "He must be kept warm." He took off his jacket and wrapped it around Erich.

"He's having one of his seizures, Papa," Erich heard Sol say.

Suddenly Erich felt as if a giant fist had punched him in the small of his back. He heard himself scream as his head jerked back tautly and his body arched into a hard bow. He heard his teeth chattering, felt something soft being wedged between his lips. Pinpoints of light exploded in his head and he saw trees layered upon more trees, thick and lush, like a jungle, and a moon—yellow and full and round. The edges of the moon began to melt, coating the leaves in moon-wax....

He lay in a tumbled heap at the bottom of the stairs. There was pain coming from somewhere; he could feel it, yet it was distanced from him as if it belonged to somebody else. He could not understand why he was lying there, when he felt so strong. He tried to get up but the energy was trapped in his body—

"Erich?" Solomon bent over him.

"A moon," Erich whispered. "I saw a moon...melting like a candle. And trees...everywhere." He tried to reach for Sol. "I was scared—"

Sol pressed his wrist against Erich's. "Blood brothers," he said, sobbing.

Chapter 6

Right there, Jacob Freund took the boy in his arms and rocked him. For a moment, Erich appeared to relax. Then he arched his back again, and shuddered convulsively. His eyes were wide open, his pupils so small that Sol expected them to disappear altogether. Instead, his eyes rolled upward. All Sol could see were the whites before they closed and Erich passed out.

Still Herr Weisser stood by, doing nothing.

"Either get help, or hold your boy and *I* will get help," Sol's father said. "Your son is in shock. He must be taken to the hospital."

"Is he going to be all right, Papa?" Solomon asked.

His father nodded. "I told you already, Solomon. He is going to be fine. Fine."

"May I go to the hospital with him?"

"You not only may," his father said, "you must." He laid Erich down on the floor and headed up the stairs. "I'll find help," he called down. "The two of you bring Erich up here. Keep him covered until I get back."

Sol and Herr Weisser labored up the stairs with their inert burden. They placed him on the floor with one jacket over him and another under his head like a pillow. After a few minutes of pacing, Erich's father grew impatient.

"You stupid boys," he said. To Sol's horror, he appeared to be working himself up into one of his tempers. "You have no sense, either of you." He paused for a second, then went on, voice rising as it grew louder. "You watch Erich. I'm going downstairs. I'll make sure this never happens again, you can be certain of that."

He stomped downstairs. Sol heard the yelping of the puppy, punctuated by the scraping of a large crates being moved, until, what seemed like hours later, his father returned to the shop. He was followed inside by two burly men. One was shouldering a stretcher, the other carried two blankets and a medical bag.

"There was a shooting near the Reichstag, so there was no ambulance available. No taxis either when you need one." Jacob clutched the door jamb for support while he struggled to catch his breath. "We had run halfway back from the hospital before—" He stopped and looked around, frowning as if he had just noticed that Friedrich was nowhere to be seen. "Where's Herr Weisser?"

"Down there," Sol said, pointing toward the cellar steps. "He...he's sealing up the sewer."

His father sighed loudly and shook his head. Marching to the top of the stairs, he yelled down to his partner to come upstairs at once.

Face red from whatever physical effort he had been making, Herr Weisser appeared at the top of the stairs. "Well, Freund, you certainly took your time," he said ungraciously.

Jacob's own face reddened, and he opened his mouth as if to make an angry retort, but apparently thought better of it. "There were no taxis or ambulances available," he said quietly. "Herr Wohmann kindly stopped and brought us here on his wagon. He is waiting to take us to the hospital."

Sol looked up. Through the open doorway, he saw horses pawing uneasily. The closer nag had her head turned back, trying to look around her blinders at the leather-vested vegetable dealer on the back of the wagon, rearranging baskets, apparently making room for them.

"A *hamster* wagon!" Friedrich Weisser sounded outraged. His eyes had narrowed in a look of compressed fury. "I'm not going anywhere on a damn *hamster* wagon." He glanced toward the cellar curtain. "You take him, Jacob. I'll tend to...matters...here."

"For God's sake, Friedrich!" Jacob Freund stared at his partner with stunned incomprehension as the men took the boy from his father and laid him on the stretcher. With Jacob's help from below and Wohmann's from above, they hoisted it and themselves onto the wagon. They had reached down to pull Sol up when a taxi rounded the corner.

"Taxi!" Jacob called out. It came to a screeching halt behind the vegetable wagon.

Dangling halfway between the ground and the top of the wagon, Sol felt suddenly lightheaded. It was as if the reality of Erich's injury were only now taking hold of him. The hands holding him let go and he dropped to the ground, landing unsteadily on his feet.

"A taxi will be faster," Jacob said to the attendants. "Do you think it will harm the boy to move him again?"

"It won't help him," the burly one said. But he nodded at the other man and, together, they reversed the process and settled Erich, sans stretcher, onto the back seat. When they had folded the stretcher and placed it somehow in the trunk of the taxi, Solomon and one of the men squeezed in beside the boy, leaving the other medic and Jacob to maneuver themselves into the front seat beside the driver. Friedrich Weisser was nowhere to be seen.

"What about the father?" one of the medics asked.

"We have waited too long already," Sol's father said. His features looked strained. "Let's go."

Obediently but none too smoothly, the taxi driver pulled the car away from the curb. Jolted by the abrupt movement, Erich opened his eyes. Though he was wrapped in a blanket, he was shaking and seemed to be chilled. There was not enough light in the taxi for Sol to see if his pupils were still tiny pinpoints or if they had returned to normal.

The shaking worsened.

"Hope it's not another convulsion. Could affect the brain, too many convulsions," the attendant next to Sol said, almost absently. His white jacket rubbed against Sol; it smelled of disinfectant and ether. "Has he ever had anything like this before today, Herr Freund?"

"The boy has epilepsy."

"Aha!"

"Not 'Aha,'" Jacob said, "He has small seizures. Not even seizures, really. Small episodes. I'm told the doctor calls them lightning seizures. He never passes out or anything. Just kind of shudders and then gets really sleepy."

The medic had wrapped Erich's fingers in cotton and gauze which was rapidly reddening. Sol watched, fascinated but queasy. The blood was seeping through and spreading like red ink on a blotter. He felt dizzy, as if everything hung at the edge of his consciousness. The voices around him sounded hollow, and his own thoughts felt apart from him. *Don't faint,* he told himself. *Don't look at the blood.*

He forced himself to look straight ahead. He could see the reflection of his father's eyes in the windshield. They looked old and tired. He took a deep breath and looked outside, as though needing to get away, at least until his mind and stomach settled.

They were on a side street, headed toward Unter den Linden. People and traffic moved past as if in a world he no longer inhabited. He wanted to put his head between his legs. Or worse, vomit. He was supposed to be helping his friend, but instead felt sick. What a baby he was, a baby sparrow, like Erich said; too helpless to fly.

He removed his glasses, put his head against the seat-back and tried to keep from passing out. His skin felt cold and clammy, and the world outside seemed to be composed of dots, like the French pointillist painting in the book his mother had shown him during one of the "culture sessions" she insisted upon. His heart was racing. He thought he saw people lined up for a block behind a milk cart, empty bottles in their hands waiting to be refilled.

He could not look away, and suddenly he was no longer in the taxi. He was in the queue. "Last week I waited for six hours," the elderly man behind him in line grumbled, talking to no one in particular. Sol turned around. The gray of the man's woolen beret seemed to bring out the deeply etched lines in his face. "Should have sent one of my grandchildren," he said, putting a beefy hand on Sol's shoulder. "Damn *goyim*," he muttered, watching the policeman near the cart screen the people in line and pull some out to the back of the line.

"Careful," the man behind him warned. "They hear you, we may never get milk. My daughter has children to feed."

There was heavy activity in front as people made a social event of their milk purchases and Jews were rerouted to the back of the line to make room for *real* Germans. Sol looked down at the strange canvas shoes he was wearing and began moving in place, faster and faster, like someone trying to stay warm or treading water. The sidewalk seemed to slip beneath him, like a conveyor belt. He was running in place when several boys in lederhosen trotted by, a familiar face among them.

"Erich!" Sol called out.

His friend halted. "We're off to Luna Park," he said. "They've added a new hall of mirrors to the Panoptikum. Come with us."

Sol shook his head. His feet kept moving. "I have to buy milk," he said, puffing with the effort.

"No problem," Erich said. "Give me the money. I'll get it for you."

Sol gave Erich the two bottles and a fistful of marks.

Erich and the other boys disappeared, to return in what seemed to be an instant, Erich holding a filled bottle in each hand. He held them just out of Sol's reach. "Here they are. Now let's go to Luna Park."

"Can't," Sol said, stretching for the bottles. "Mama—"

"Ma-ma, Ma-ma," Erich mimicked in a baby voice. He swung one of the bottles menacingly over the curb. "You coming with us, or are you going home with *one?*"

"I told you, I—"

Glass and milk splattered. Sol jerked backward to avoid both...and found himself pressing hard against the seat of the taxi, which was slowing as it neared the hospital. Light filtered through the car's window, foggy with the breath of its occupants.

"Moon...melting moon," Erich whispered, eyes open wide and staring upward. "Jungle..." Fur glistening wetly, two black-and-white long-muzzled monkeys hunched over him.

Sol blinked hard and put on his glasses. Quickly, the image vanished. No monkeys...only the attendants. *A dream*, he told himself. *Only a bad dream.*

But then, why was he still frightened?

Chapter 7

May 1922

Solomon kicked off his shoes and stretched out on top of his eiderdown. He was so tired—and shaken. A few minutes of sleep and he would start studying again, he promised himself. In less than two months it would be his bar mitzvah. He had studying for that and schoolwork and—

His eyes closed.

"Studying dreams, again, *Spatz?*"

"Wha—who—oh, it's you." Sol could feel sweat running down the back of his neck. He shifted his position slightly and glanced at the bed to make sure there were no damp patches. Erich knew nothing about the bedwetting; Sol wanted to keep it that way.

"Still having nightmares?" Erich narrowed his eyes and stared at Sol.

Sol nodded. "What about you?"

"The Bull dream," Erich said. "If it's the last thing I do, I'll pay my father back—"

It had been three and a half years since the accident and, though they were less frequent, the nightmares had not stopped. The day after the accident, groggy with painkillers, Erich swore he could hear Bull gurgling as Herr Weisser drowned him in the canal. He had been dreaming about it ever since. Sol's nightmares were also always the same: Erich screaming; Erich hanging limply from the grate, blood curling down his arm; the woman begging God to let her die; and the monkeys—always the monkeys. Superimposed over all of it, swollen and bloody and bruised, Erich's three crushed fingers—

He looked at Erich's hand, at the pale flesh and the scars, red and raised, like symbiotic vines that had wound themselves around his fingers and taken root. Eventually the scars would turn white, the doctor said. Whiter than the flesh—

"Want to go for a walk—feed the birds—make trouble?" Erich asked.

"Have to study."

Erich perched on the edge of the bed. "Look, *Spatz,* I have an idea. Remember when Karl almost drowned at the swimming meet? Remember how he was terrified of water after that, until they *made* him go swimming again?"

"What's that got to do with me?"

"Saturday, you and your papa went to synagogue and I was helping in the shop. I got into the furrier's sub-basement—"

"How?"

"I have my ways." He took a key chain from his hip pocket. Attached to the chain was a small book-shaped leather pouch which Sol knew contained Erich's lock picks. "There's a padlocked sewer-entrance down there—"

"You went inside!"

"I went looking for that woman you told me about." He raised his voice and mimicked a woman's voice. *"Oh God, let me die. I did not know...I did not know."*

A thin shiver ran down Sol's spine—the kind his mama said meant a goose had walked on his grave. The nightmares, the fear—how foolish he had been! Maybe there had never been a woman's voice! He should have thought of this before, after the accident and Erich's grand mal seizure, when the doctor told them about some of the strange things that happened to people who had seizures. Sometimes they could not remember anything about what had happened before and after the seizure, and sometimes—during the seizure—they spoke in tongues. Erich's seizure must have been coming on when he was hanging from the grating. He could have mimicked a woman, like now, Sol thought. The sound could easily have been distorted by the sewer's weird acoustics.

Since Erich hated talking about his seizures, Sol decided to keep his latest theory about the voice to himself—at least for now. "You didn't go down by yourself," he said.

"Yes, I did." Erich looked at him and relented. "No. I didn't go down. But we're going down there tonight. I've decided."

Sol got up and walked over to his window. Two workmen were erecting an awning above the entrance into what had been the furrier's basement and was now about to become a cabaret. From where he stood, he could not see the steps leading down; the awning looked like it was at street level.

Once down those steps and through the door, there was a circular flight of metal stairs. After the basement—the cabaret—came a low-ceilinged sub-basement, on the same level as the cellar beneath the tobacco shop. And beneath both shops...the sewer.

"Forget it," Sol said. "We're not going down there."

"You're afraid." Erich joined him at the window.

"Am not!" Sol knew he didn't sound convincing. Even if it had been Erich's voice playing tricks on him, they boys had promised on their honor never to play in sewers again—and their fathers had welded the tobacco shop's grate down just in case. "Our papas will kill us if they catch us. The watchman could see us—"

"The construction-crew watchman won't be there tonight." Erich's eyes shone expectantly. "I saw him earlier this afternoon outside a Schultheiss. He was holding a quart of Pilsner and bragging to some girl about how his crew is so ahead of schedule he's been assigned to another project."

"I still don't think..."

"Tell you what." Erich sounded as if he'd just had an idea, but judging from the look on his face, Sol suspected his friend had worked out the answers to all of Sol's possible objectives ahead of time. "Bet your pewter soldiers against my bike there's no woman in the sewer."

Erich's voice had that *it's no use arguing about this one* tone to it that Solomon knew only too well.

"You might as well hand over the soldiers right now. Voices come attached to bodies. If there ever was a real woman in the sewer, Papa would've found her."

Erich's face darkened in anger and Sol guessed his friend was thinking about Bull. Neither of them were sure what Herr Weisser had done with the puppy; he had refused to talk to them about it. But Erich knew. Or so he said.

"I have to hear her...the woman...or you lose." Erich dangled the lockpick pouch in front of Solomon's face.

"That's dumb! Your bike against my soldiers? Dumb!"

Erich grinned and pushed a hand through his sandy hair. "I only bet on sure things. The voice was all in your mind. The trouble with you is, you read too much."

Sol watched the sparrows pecking at cracks in the sidewalk. They were not nearly as bad as the pigeons everyone hated—Berlin's second-worst enemy, the city council called them. What perversity kept him feeding the sparrows, he did not know. Habit, maybe. He had been taking them bags of crumbs since Recha was a baby. There were times, he thought, when he wished they would repay him by flying overhead and decorating his friend's hair. That would cure Erich of some of his arrogance!

The cabaret's awning slapped and heaved in the breeze. Startled, the sparrows took wing. The black, red, and gold striped canvas billowed like a flag honoring the Republic; beneath it, newly installed hand and guard rails—painted the hue of ripe bananas—shone in the weak afternoon light. A door veneered with sculpted ceramics had replaced the mass of rusted iron and enormous locks and bolts that had formerly marked the entrance. It led into a basement likewise transformed, for the furriers had moved all their inventory—wardrobe crates, odorous with mothballs and filled with coats of leopard, mink, and seal—from there to the building's upper two levels.

During the past month, he and Erich had watched the nightclub take shape. Sol enjoyed listening to the sawing and hammering, and he liked the smell of the new lumber. Leather-aproned carpenters and chalk-faced plasterers scuttled up and down the steps. He and Erich snickered at the effeminate gray-haired decorator in purple plus-fours who stood on the sidewalk, frenetically waving his arms whenever things seemed to be going wrong. Any day now, according to Solomon's mother, trucks would arrive with furniture—God should only grant her such elegant things as she had heard were coming, she said.

The door of the tobacco shop opened and Sol's father stepped out.

Jacob Freund was a thin, bespectacled man whose neck, constricted in his high starched collar, made him look rather like a rooster. He shielded his eyes from the sun and gestured to Sol to come outside.

"See. Even your papa thinks you should get some fresh air," Erich said, coming up behind Sol. "Let's go outside. You can study after supper. There will be plenty of time before we meet to go down there."

"I haven't agreed to go, yet," Sol said, though by now he knew—and so did Erich—that it was as good as done.

Chapter 8

"Well, boys—it seems as if it's actually going to happen." Jacob put a hand lightly on each of the boys' shoulders as they joined him on the sidewalk outside the shop. He smiled, and the crows' feet around his eyes deepened.

"Do you really think the nightclub will help the furriers all that much, Herr Freund?" Erich asked.

"It's bound to."

All of Berlin's businesses had been hurt by the rising inflation that had seized the city following the war, especially luxury shops like Das Ostleute Haus. Frau Rathenau's offer to buy their basement and sub-basement had been a double blessing. Not only would the money help keep the furrier shop afloat, Sol's father explained, but the kinds of people who would frequent the cabaret were also those who could afford life's other amenities.

"It will help the whole street." There was a soberly thankful tone to Jacob's voice. "Our business is sure to boom, not to mention that the cabaret will afford us the opportunity to meet and mingle with people such as the Rathenaus and their peers." He looked seriously at Erich and then at Solomon. "People whose decisions spell the future not only of Berlin but of the entire Fatherland—"

The pounding of a hammer interrupted him as a workman, standing on a ladder at the bottom of the basement stairs, unceremoniously nailed up a rectangular, mahogany-stained plaque above the door. The edges of the plaque were trimmed with a delicate gilt band, and the graceful lettering stood out black and bold:

KAVERNE

The sign gave Solomon a sense of satisfaction. He was proud of his neighborhood. Most of the store owners had moved to the more residential areas; he was glad his family had not—especially now. A cabaret, right here on his street! Papa said most of Berlin's nightclubs had sprung up after the war, when the Kaiser's *Tanzverbot*—the anti-dancing edict—was lifted. They were clustered along Leipziger Strasse, near the Kaiserhof Hotel and the

Prussian State Theater. Many of them were known for the decadence of their patrons, whose outrageous behavior made for meaty reading in the weekend papers.

Frau Rathenau's purchase of the furrier's basement had made the newspapers, too. A columnist for *Der Weltspiegel,* Berlin's most widely read Sunday entertainment insert, had quoted her as saying that she had deliberately chosen to open her nightclub away from the riffraff. Kaverne was, she had said, part of her "...crusade to bring respectability to Berlin's entertainment industry." The columnist had suggested that the real purpose of the cabaret was to showcase the talents of her granddaughter—Foreign Minister Walter Rathenau's niece, Miriam, who had recently returned from America.

"I'll be back, boys. Don't go away...I have something to show you." Jacob released the boys and went back into his shop.

"If we don't go down tonight, we may never get there," Erich said as soon as Sol's father was out of earshot. "If you're too scared, I'll go alone. Once the cabaret opens, there's no way we'll get in."

"I told you, I'm scared of getting caught, not of going down there," Sol said, gesturing emphatically.

"I'll bet there's a woman's body behind one of the walls at the end of the sewer," Erich said, as if trying to goad him into agreeing. "Maybe someone sealed her up back there, like the guy in that Poe story Herr Schoenfelder made us read."

In one of their many discussions about the subject, the boys had decided the sewer had probably once been a dungeon and that there were all kinds of bones shored up behind the wall. The idea of finding them might thrill his friend, Sol thought, but it was not his idea of a good time. "I still don't think—"

"If you're worried about the bet, forget it," Erich said. As if signaling for silence, he held up his crushed hand. "Tonight. We'll meet at—" He pulled up his sweater sleeve and checked his watch. "Midnight," he said, obviously carried away by his own sense of melodrama.

If only one of their papas had sealed off that sub-basement, Sol thought again, feeling less sure of his theory that the voice he had heard was Erich's. Something awful could be waiting for them down in that brick bowel.

"I—" Sol clamped his lips shut as the bell over the door of the tobacco shop jangled and his father re-emerged, waving a card embossed with calligraphy.

"You see?" His father ran a thin, long-nailed finger along the lettering as if to prove the invitation were indeed a reality, then placed it carefully in the breast pocket of his three-piece suit. "Already our foot is in the door. Oma Rathenau has invited all of us, the Freunds and the Weissers, to a private dinner party in celebration of the cabaret's opening. Good thing she is not as stingy as her husband was. He would never have invited us!"

Though Sol had never met the Rathenau family, he had seen them occasionally at synagogue—not Walther, who did not deny he was a Jew but never went to *shul*—but Mathilde, Walther's mother, his father, Emil, and his younger sister. He knew that Emil, who'd died when Sol was little, had built an empire after using a small loan to buy the German rights to the Edison invention; everyone knew that.

"Mathilde Rathenau is the grand dame of the Allgemeine Elektrizitats Gesellschaft—the General Electric Company combine," Jacob Freund said. "She will insist on preserving the integrity of the Rathenau name. You watch. There will be only genteel people at her nightclub." He patted his pocket with pride. "Two weeks from tonight we shall dine with the cream of Berlin."

"I dine with the cream of Berlin every evening," Ella Freund said, coming out of the shop. "Now why don't you take care of the customers, Jacob, while I put supper on the table. You're welcome to join us, Erich."

The boy shook his head and mumbled his thanks. "Have to go. See you later, Sol."

"Later, he will be at his studies," Sol's mother said. "Why don't you two take a walk or something. Wake him up, Erich. He has a lot to do before bedtime. Have you practiced your cello?"

"Not yet, Mama."

"You had better not neglect your music." She turned to Jacob. "Have you told him?"

"Told me what, Mama?"

"To express our thanks to Mathilde Rathenau, Recha will dance and you will play your cello at the opening of the cabaret."

"But I'm not good enough to play for those people—"

"We do not ask you to be a genius—simply that you show you are a cultured young man."

Cultured, schmultured, Sol thought, a sick feeling settling in his stomach. Was it not enough that he loved music? Did he have to be forced to make a fool of himself in front of—what was it his father had called them, "...*the cream of Berlin?*"

Erich decided he did not have to leave quite yet, so the boys continued watching the construction. At the first sign of dusk, the workers started packing up their tools.

"Now," Sol said, making a decision. "We go down now or forget it."

"Are you crazy? It's light enough for them to see us!"

"They're used to us. If we wander in like we're just curious, they'll probably ignore us."

"You really mean it, don't you?" Erich looked dumbfounded. "Listen, you don't have to punish *me* just because your parents want you to make an idiot of yourself with your cello."

"Never mind about the cello. Do you want to do it—or not?" Sol enjoyed the shift in power. Suddenly he, and not Erich, was in command.

Sol was right. Nobody noticed them as they wandered into the half-finished cabaret and down into the sub-basement.

"Over here." Erich knelt beside the padlocked drain.

"Well, open it." With a little luck, Sol thought, the padlock will be too rusty to budge and we won't have to go into the sewer.

However, it took Erich no time at all to pry the lock open. The grate was as heavy as the one in the tobacco shop, but Erich opened it easily.

"I'll go first," Sol said, deciding he might as well go all the way with his playing the leader. Besides, he was a lot taller than Erich; the drop would be shorter for him and he could help his friend down.

The sewer smelled damp and fetid. Hardly any light filtered down, but Erich's pocket, which always seemed to hold an endless array of surprises, yielded a candle.

"See, I told you." Erich lit the candle and held it up to extend the circle of light. "There's nothing here."

Erich's voice was a little tremulous. The place didn't exactly hold pleasant memories for him either, Sol reminded himself. And his friend was right. There was nothing down here—except slime and mold, he thought, touching the wall and wiping his fingers on his pants.

Herr Weisser had cleared out everything except the dismantled packing crates. Sol sat down and heaved a sigh of relief.

Erich laughed. "Did you really expect to find some woman hiding out? Lucky for you I took back the bet or you'd owe me one set of pewter soldiers. I'm going to search for bones. You coming?"

"Not yet." Sol was convinced now that his theory about Erich's voice was correct, but he was playing the game. He could soon hear Erich scratching around the bricks.

"Oh God, let me die!"

Sol went rigid with fear.

"I did not know...I did not know."

He waited, holding his breath. Then a man with a strange accent whispered something about blood, and another, his voice old and worn, rambled on about lice and corpses and cold, and pleaded for borscht to quiet his belly-pains.

"Erich!"

"What is it?" Erich held up the candle. "Bogey man get you?"

Sol didn't answer. He knew without asking that Erich had not heard them—not the woman, or the man whispering, or the other one, who spoke of death and of hunger. They were speaking to him, to Solomon, in voices only he could hear.

Chapter 9

Two weeks later, dressed and ready for the private opening of the cabaret, Sol returned to the sewer. He and Erich had come back several times together, but this was the first time Sol had come alone. They had left the padlock in place but unlocked, so he had no trouble opening the grate and climbing down. Though he had brought a candle, he did not light it.

He sat in the blackness and listened.

The voices would come, he knew that now. What he did not know was why he was stupid enough to come back, or why he would worsen the terror by sitting in the dark. He considered himself the brains of the Weisser-Freund team. Some brains!

Then again, he decided, he had reason to hide tonight. Not only did he loathe performing, he was terrible at it. And he got stage fright. But no amount of begging had changed his parents' minds about his cello performance at tonight's function. "The children of a cultured household," Jacob said, "must understand music and be ready and eager to perform at a moment's notice." It was tradition, he said; though why people should suffer for tradition's sake was never adequately explained. After hearing Gregor Piatigorsky play, he could harbor no illusions about his own ability. Gregor, who had fled Russia by swimming the Sbruch River, holding his cello over his head while border guards shot at him, had performed in the Freund's music room, and had played like an angel.

If Sol lived to be a hundred, he would never play that well, nor would he forget his mortification when his father insisted he perform for Gregor. He had squeaked and sawed through part of Haydn's *Concerto in D Major*, bowed—cheeks burning at the guests' tolerant smiles—and retired to his bedroom before bursting into tears.

Tonight would be worse. One of the honored guests was Walther Rathenau, Germany's newly appointed Foreign Minister and heir to the Rathenau fortune.

He gazed forlornly up into the darkness, toward the cabaret. If only he had refused to play for Gregor, there would be no issue now—

A baby began to shriek.

Sol shuddered violently and jammed his hands over his ears.

The wailing grew louder.

Pressing his back against the bricks, he kicked his legs as if to drive away the sound. It made him think of the lambs at the slaughterhouse he had visited before Passover a few years ago, of a lost kitten, of an infant too young to put words to whatever terror it was feeling.

Hearing voices, words, that was one thing. But this was really crazy. "Go away!" he shouted. "Leave me alone."

He took his hands away from his ears. The crying had died to a sob and soon only his own breathing rasped in the darkness. He took a deep breath, let it out slowly, and thought about lighting the candle, but the dark was almost comforting—like when he removed his glasses and images were out of focus—his own special, personal world. It was the silence that was making him suffer: he kept expecting it to fill with voices. If some outside noise would only restore a sense of reality to the sewer, he would feel better.

Sitting perfectly still, he looked up through the sewer's opening into the sub-basement. With over a hundred guests in the cabaret upstairs, the music, at least, should be filtering down from above. There—he could hear it now; first the melodious cry of a violin, then the tinkle of a piano. A timpani joined in.

Someone, probably a waiter, dropped a tray and, instinctively, Sol ducked.

Elbows on knees and head down, he examined his choices. He could stay in a hideaway that had probably once been part of a medieval torture chamber or enter a modern torture chamber, complete with audience and an instrument of terror—his cello.

"Solomon?"

"Erich?" Sol rose to help his friend descend by guiding his feet to the two-by-twelve they had installed as a step at this—the cabaret—end. "Am I ever glad it's you."

"Expecting one of your ghosts?" Erich hopped down. Using the cigarette lighter he had taken from the shop, he lit a candle he had stolen from the Seifenvogel laundry opposite Bellevue Station. "Your papa sent me to look for you. He's pretty upset that you aren't there yet," he said.

"I'm not exactly happy myself," Sol said, though now that Erich was here he felt a little stupid at his reaction to what was probably only a stray kitten up in the sub-basement.

He transferred his gaze to Erich, saw what his friend was wearing, and suppressed the urge to laugh. His amusement did not escape his friend.

"None of this was my idea." Erich touched his slicked-back hair. He had on pressed trousers, a white shirt with starched, rounded collar, and his father's silk paisley cravat. "At least I'm at the party, not hiding in the dark like a cockroach."

"You're not at the party. You're here with me."

"You know what I mean!" Erich raised the candle and looked at Solomon's face. "You been crying?"

"Of course not!" Sol stared down at the crate boards on the floor.

"Worrying about ghosts again? Guess I was wrong—I shouldn't have talked you into coming back down here. God, you're a baby!"

Shoving past Sol, Erich walked over to a clothes rod they had set up. Dangling from a coat hanger were a white shirt, a black tie, and suspenders: the uniform of his Freikorps-Youth unit.

"Pull yourself together, *Spatz*," He picked lint and dust off the outfit. "Fears are for queers."

"It's the cello. You know how much I hate performing. I can't go up there. I just can't!"

"Then don't perform," Erich said coolly. "If your papa says you have to play, tell him to—" He paused. "Just tell him no."

"Easy for you to say. You do whatever you want these days."

"That's right." Erich clenched his fist and narrowed his eyes. "They say I can't have a dog? I'll have any dog I want, and Papa won't be able to stop me. No one's ever again going to drown something *I* own. And no one tells me what to do! Like they said I couldn't join the Freikorps, 'Not until you're fifteen!'" He did a whining imitation of his mother. "What an idiot."

"You shouldn't talk about your mother like that," Sol muttered. Erich had secretly joined the Freikorps the morning after he and Sol picked the lock of the cabaret and re-entered the sewer that first time. Since then, he seemed to think of himself as older, wiser, more daring than ever, as if joining the movement had turned him into some kind of hero.

"I wish she could see me in this." Erich was admiring his uniform again.

"Your mother?"

Erich eyed Solomon with disdain. "Miriam. Rathenau's niece. She's really something." He made a slurping noise as if he were about to wolf down a piece of his mother's plum cake. Setting down the candle, he slid the suspenders off the shirt and held it across his chest. "Girls love uniforms."

"Clean uniforms, maybe. I wish you'd wash that thing. It stinks of dogs."

"One of the bitches at the camp just had puppies." Erich's voice was heavy with longing. "They'll keep the perfect ones and destroy the rest. If it weren't for my parents..."

"*You'd* take a reject?"

Staring off into the shadows, Erich did not seem to notice the implied insult. "I could give one of the puppies to Rathenau's niece. Papa said her dog died in the accident that killed her parents. Can you see me arriving at Miriam Rathenau's house in my uniform? With a puppy...maybe even two?"

His friend talked about girls as though he were Romeo, Sol thought, but if he had to choose between a dog and a girl, he would almost certainly choose the animal. "She probably wouldn't even speak to you if you went there dressed in that thing," he said.

"Her uncle financed a Freikorps unit during the war. Everyone knows that."

"That was before things changed. Besides, you're in the Freikorps-*Youth*. That's different. People in her part of society look down on you. The *Berliner Tageblatt* called you and your pals 'Pawns in short pants.'"

"Who cares about that conservative rag!"

"Which of your precious Freikorps leaders said *that?*" Sol asked. Erich parroted them more and more. "Your parents read the *Tageblatt,* you know."

"I told you, they're idiots."

"Maybe you're the idiot."

For a moment there was fierce anger in Erich's eyes. Then he said, "Just forget it." He replaced the suspenders on the hanger. "Want to go to the matinee tomorrow? *The Cabinet of Doctor Caligari* is playing at the Marmorhaus."

Sol shook his head. "I don't know why you enjoy films about murder and madness. I'd rather save my money for one of Elizabeth Bergner's plays."

"You really are a baby! No wonder you don't care about meeting Miriam Rathenau. You wouldn't know what to do with her."

"And you do?"

Before Erich could answer, a girl began singing in the cabaret.

"*Glühwürmchen, Glühwürmchen, glimm're...*" Shine little glowworm, glimmer, glimmer...

"Glowworm" was one of Sol's favorite songs. The composer, Paul Lincke, often visited his two spinster nieces late at night in their flat in the building next door to the Freunds to try out his latest melodies on them. The sound of their old piano would fill Sol's room. When he fell asleep to the strains of *Lady Moon,* his dreams were enchanted. But Lincke's music had never sounded like this—innocent, earthy, a firefly love song that filled Sol with feelings he did not understand.

The song ended to applause. "That was *her* singing," Erich said. "I'm going back up. I'll tell your papa I couldn't find you, but you don't know what you're missing!"

Sol tried to imagine what Rathenau's niece looked like. If she were half as wonderful as her voice—

"Some day I'll be a man and wear what I want and do what I want all the time," Erich said in a hoarse whisper. "Papa won't be able to order me around anymore." He boosted himself onto the plank and crawled up through the drain.

Sol stepped onto the board and poked his head through the hole. Erich, guided by the light seeping through the gap beneath the door upstairs, was climbing the steps to the cabaret. Miriam Rathenau had begun a second song. If he stayed in the sewer, Sol thought, the voices would return—and even if they did not, the fear would. He spat on his fingers, snuffed the candle, and crawled out. Closing the grate behind him, he ascended the steps and stretched out on his stomach across the top several stairs.

With his cheek pressed against the top landing, he tried to peer through the gap beneath the door.

Finding it hard to focus, he pushed his glasses as high as he could up his nose and held them there with his index finger. Now he could see plush red carpet, a metal table leg, three pairs of trousers resting on shiny black shoes, and white high heels festooned with seed pearls. But nothing resembling a beautiful young girl.

He stood and inched open the door.

"*Wenn der weisse Flieder, wieder blüht,*" Miriam Rathenau sang. "When the white lilac blooms again...." She held the microphone lightly with one hand. The other was slightly raised. There was about her a combination of delicacy and boldness—her face expressive, her body graceful and lean.

Something inside Solomon exploded. Standing there in the middle of the dance floor beneath a spotlight, the girl created a new universe for him. For an instant nothing existed except white tights, a form-fitting tunic, a knee-length swirl of pale pink niñon. Gradually he began to notice other things: the rose-colored shawl that draped her shoulders; her dark hair, pinned in a dancer's chignon and decorated with a spray of white lilac; the piano player, dressed in sequined tails and top hat and smiling up at her from the Blüthner baby grand.

It wasn't until she turned her head slightly to return the piano player's smile that reality intruded. Until that moment she had been facing Sol, and though he knew he was hidden in the dark of the stairway, he had felt she was singing for him alone.

He looked around the cabaret. Twenty tables ringed the dance floor. Each was set with an ecru tablecloth and a spray of lilac. It was easy to see his mother's hand in the decorating, for while some of the flowers were white, most were that shade between pink and white that was her favorite. Fine crystal, silverware, and gold-rimmed china gleamed beneath chandeliers fit for the palace of the Kaiser. Waiters in black tie and tails moved among the guests, offering a fish course. Silver platters were laden with exquisitely poached salmon, filet of sole, and sturgeon embellished with olive-green capers; there was even beluga caviar, sprinkled with chopped eggs and served on tiny rounds of pumpernickel.

The guests were arrayed in diamonds and lace, taffeta and ostrich feathers. White tuxedos trimmed in magenta vied for attention with chiffon and brocade cut from patterns designed to conceal or reveal secrets of the flesh. Smoke from cigarettes in silver holders curled into the glow of the spotlight. Everyone eyed Miriam Rathenau with rapt attention.

Erich was no exception. He and his parents were seated at Walther Rathenau's table, but right now it was not the Foreign Minister who impressed him. Face alive with nervous energy and anticipation, eyes bright, Erich focused on Miriam Rathenau as if he also felt she were performing only for him.

Chapter 10

"*Wenn der weisse Flieder wieder.*" Miriam paused and dropped her voice. "*Blüht,*" she ended softly.

She curtsied and listened to the applause.

With a few exceptions, it was what she had expected from an audience that measured its responses with care even after a virtuoso performance at the Berlin Opera. They were boring, the Germans, always controlled and disciplined—so unlike the Americans, with their wild enthusiasms and their appreciation for anything the least bit extraordinary.

Well, let them try to be neutral about this next number, she thought. She nodded to the piano player, who struck up a lively tune, his fingers springing across the keys.

Smiling, she flung aside her shawl and broke into a modified cancan, whirling, kicking—low at first, then higher—until her foot was above her head...repeating the routine until, with a suddenness calculated to send an ache through the groin of the shy-looking young man who had just crept into the room, the music ended and she dropped into a split.

The boy stared at her with his mouth open, as if she were a fairy princess and he the frog prince. The audience, less restrained, clapped louder; someone even called, "Brava!"

Resting easily in the split, Miriam touched one knee with her forehead, bent the other leg under her and used it to propel herself back onto her feet.

The boy seated at her Uncle Walther's table, apparently unable to contain himself, jumped to his feet and began clapping wildly.

Her uncle raised a black eyebrow in apparent amusement at the boy's excitement, and smiled at her. Easing his narrow shoulders against the back of the chair, he stroked his goatee, removed his cigar from his mouth, and blew a perfect smoke ring into the air. Despite his obvious pride in his niece, he took the time to flick a stray piece of ash from the sleeve of his finely tailored evening suit and replaced the cigar in his mouth before applauding.

After curtsying a second time, Miriam threaded her way to her uncle's table. She was almost there when her grandmother held out a gloved hand and touched her arm.

"You have given me much pleasure, my child. You never knew your Uncle Walther's brother. He died when he was fourteen...a little younger than you are now. He had the same delicacy you have...the same way of holding his head—"

As if contact with her granddaughter's young body had made her feel young and beautiful again and she no longer needed to hide her wrinkles, the elderly woman removed her gloves. Her hands were heavy with diamonds. Miriam glanced at them and then back into her grandmother's eyes. They held a sadness that spoke of more than the death of her asthmatic second son.

Miriam smiled prettily and bent to hug her grandmother. "Thank you, Oma. What a wonderful way to welcome me home from the United States."

"The delight is all mine, Miriam. Now go and have fun. That young man at your table will burst if you don't get there soon."

The band had begun to play and couples were gravitating toward the dance floor as Miriam approached her uncle's table. The boy's mother said something to him and, with a sickly, silly grin, he bowed formally and pulled out a chair for Miriam.

Wondering how he had injured his hand, she started to sit. Her uncle half-rose expectantly and, knowing what he wanted, she leaned over and kissed his cheek. Then she took her seat and smiled her thanks to the boy.

"I'm Erich Weisser." He beamed as he scooted his chair closer to hers.

"Hello, Erich Weisser." She looked toward the other boy. "And who's he? Your brother?"

"My best friend, *Spatz.*"

"*Spatz?* What kind of name is that?"

Erich laughed nervously. "I call him 'Sparrow' because he's always feeding the darn things. His name's Solomon Freund. His sister Recha is the one over there at the table next to us, staring at you. Those are his parents next to her."

"Why aren't they sitting with us?" Miriam smiled across at the young girl named Recha, who appeared transfixed.

"There wasn't room for all of us at this table so our papas—" He hesitated.

"They did what?"

"Rolled dice for who'd get to sit here," Erich said.

Though Miriam tried not to laugh, she could not help herself. "Did you hear that, Uncle Walther? They—"

"Don't say anything. Please." Erich's face was red.

Miriam stopped. She really hadn't meant to embarrass the boy. It was just so typical—so German!

Stretching out her hand, she introduced herself to Erich's parents and exchanged a few pleasantries with them. That ought to make the boy feel better, she thought, not particularly taken by Herr and Frau Weisser. The woman looked nervous; the man, at best, uncomfortable. His nose was red, as if he had been drinking too much, and his eyes were hard. Clearly, they were not enjoying themselves.

She glanced sideways at the boy; he had his father's square jaw but, unlike either of his parents, he had light hair and was quite good looking.

She turned her attention back to the Freunds. Recha's mother was removing a lace handkerchief from her evening bag and handing it to the girl. While she blew her nose, her father tugged nervously at his shirt cuffs and glanced anxiously about the room as if he thought the blowing might be offensive. Sol's mother leaned over and whispered something in her husband's ear. His eyes flashed angrily behind his thick lenses as he turned toward the frog prince, who had finally stepped all the way into the room.

By now, the waiters had begun to ladle out the entrée of sauerbraten and dumplings, which her uncle had requested. It was plebeian fare, but he had declared himself tired of foreign foods after his recent journey across the Atlantic. Reluctantly, for she missed America, whose chefs ironically prided themselves on producing superb European cuisine, Miriam lifted her fork.

"Your friend looks lonely," she said. "Why not ask him to sit with us?"

"Later. " Erich spoke without conviction. "Right now he's got stage fright. His papa wants his little sparrow to entertain us."

Miriam looked from one boy to the other. How very different they seemed! She liked Erich's Aryan good looks but there was something about Sparrow—

What had Erich said the boy's real name was? Solomon. Solomon Freund...wise friend. He looked more like his nickname, a sparrow hoping for tidbits of congeniality, for someone to reach out a hand or offer a crust of conversation and draw him in among the crowd. Something about him reminded her of the boys in her ballet class—not homosexual, but sensitive. That appealed to her as well; he seemed forlorn as he stood gazing at the cello that stood like a sentinel amid the shadows in the corner of the room. By the looks of him, he would rather face a firing squad than perform in public, and seemed about to retreat down the stairs.

"I'm going to ask him to join us," she told Erich.

She got up and walked toward Solomon, but she was too late. His father had seen him and was holding up a hand in a gesture that warned Sol to stay where he was. Pushing himself from the table, he gave a peremptory bow to the guests near him and made his way toward his son. Smiling and nodding in greeting to several guests who glanced up curiously, he guided Sol through the doorway.

Miriam followed them. Herr Freund had left the door slightly ajar. She pushed at it gently, let herself through, and found herself standing in the shadows at the top of a flight of stairs. There appeared to be a storage room at the bottom of the steps, and she could hear voices.

She went down just far enough to be able to see Solomon and his father; they stood under a dangling naked light bulb.

"Sit down." Herr Freund gestured toward a wooden box next to a pair of ancient, discolored laundry sinks.

Sol did as he was told. The bare light swung to and fro as, scowling, his father stood over him.

"So, and where have you been?" Jacob clicked open an engraved gold watchcase that hung from a chain across his waist. "You're such an important fellow that you need not show up on time for a party at which our Foreign Minister is present?"

Sol started to answer, apparently thought better of it, and sat with his eyes downcast.

Jacob put a foot on an adjacent box. "Poor Miriam Rathenau had to do an encore for which she was quite unprepared."

Unprepared! She controlled a giggle as Herr Freund wiped dust from his shoes with a handkerchief he took from his trouser pocket. The popular Reichsbanner handkerchief in the breast pocket of his pinstriped *Shabbas* suit was doubtless just for show, Miriam thought. The way Germans felt about their country, only a lout would soil a cloth that resembled the flag of the Fatherland.

"She looked prepared to me, Papa," Sol said in a low, weak voice. He reached for a rag on a packing crate and brushed the dust from his own shoes.

"Don't argue with me!" Jacob removed his glasses and, squinting angrily at Sol, wiped the lenses clean, refolded the handkerchief, and placed it back in his pocket. "She's a mature girl—too mature for her years—so she carried it off."

"Yes, Papa."

"It is rude to keep anyone waiting, you know that. But it is idiotic, Solomon Freund, to offend such as Walther Rathenau—and not just for business reasons."

"I know Herr Rathenau is an important man." Sol fidgeted, his head still lowered.

"Not merely an important man. An important Jew."

"You are an important Jew, Papa." Solomon looked up. "You won the Iron Cross, First Class."

"Ah, the Iron Cross!" Jacob chuckled sadly as he dusted off a box with his hand and sat down. "For that you would consider me another Rathenau? Look at me, Solomon." He turned his palms up in supplication. "I'm an ordinary Jew, forty-nine years old, a Berlin seller of tobacco. Hardly a Walther Rathenau."

Even at that distance, Miriam could sense that a sadness had displaced Herr Freund's wrath.

"One of every six German Jews fought in the Great War, Solomon. One out of six! That means almost every young male German Jew served the Fatherland."

He paused, and when he spoke again his voice had taken on the quality of a man immersed in memory.

"A third of us were decorated, another twelve thousand died. So I was not alone—or special. When we stood in formation to receive our medals, the names of the Gentile recipients were read alphabetically, then came the Jews. That's how it went in every platoon and company in the army. We Jews who had fought and lived, and we who had fought and died—all those to be decorated—we were all at the bottom of the lists." He put a trembling hand on Solomon's shoulder. "That is why the respect and friendship of a man like Walther Rathenau, himself a Jew, is so important—so your surname will never be at the bottom of a list."

"But isn't the Foreign Minister only half-Jewish?" Sol asked.

"There is no such thing," Jacob Freund said, looking directly at his son, "as being half-Jewish."

A long silence followed as Solomon stared into his father's eyes. He seemed unnerved by his father's sudden vulnerability. Miriam thought about her uncle, the only older man she really knew. He had always seemed to her to be larger than life despite his small stature. She realized it would unnerve her too, if she were forced to look into the face of his humanness.

"I think you understand what I have been trying to say," Solomon's father said quietly, standing up. "Let us go upstairs."

Quickly Miriam scooted back into the cabaret and waited near the door for father and son to re-enter. They did so together. Then Jacob moved ahead though the crowd.

Crossing the dance floor, he removed the cello from its mahogany case and placed it against a chair where it could easily be reached. He stood before the band and raised his hands for quiet. There seemed a calmness, a surety in his actions, as though he, and not her uncle, were the honored guest—as if this were his party.

"We of the Freund family are honored to be the friends and guests of Walther Rathenau, our esteemed Foreign Minister, of his esteemed mother, Mathilde, and his lovely and talented niece, Miriam." Jacob bowed slightly to each in turn. "In our house we like to listen to our two children perform together." He watched Sol take the cello bow from its case and snap the lid shut. "Recha sings and dances, and Solomon accompanies her. Our little Recha has become the darling, if I may say so, of the Berlin Singakademia."

Jacob waited for the brief round of applause to end. "Both of our children were to perform tonight in small repayment to you, Frau Rathenau," he bowed in Oma's direction, "for the wonderful companionship and dinner we have so enjoyed. Unfortunately, Recha has a cold. Therefore, Solomon will do a solo."

He looked at Sol, who bowed slightly and managed a weak smile.

"Solomon has not had quite the musical training Recha has enjoyed, but we should all remember that, in the world of music, unlike in business," Jacob nodded toward Friedrich Weisser, "or even in politics," a nod toward Rathenau, "the very act of performing is often at least as important as the product." Gesturing toward Sol, Jacob stepped aside. "So now, it is with great pride that I give you my son...."

Walking as if his knees had turned to liquid, Solomon clutched the neck of the cello and moved into the spotlight. He bowed to the audience.

Feeling a mixture of empathy and amusement, Miriam waited for the first note. When it came, she was relieved to find herself not entirely unimpressed. His playing was tenuous, but the emotion was there, the caring which, for her, shifted technique to secondary importance. She closed her eyes and let the sweet strains of Haydn flow around her. When it was over, she opened her eyes and applauded loudly. She would introduce herself to Solomon and tell him that he was not nearly as poor a performer as he seemed to think.

She rose and walked toward him, but was not quick enough. Apparently terrified that he might be required to give an encore, he bowed and fled the room. Disappointed, Miriam headed back to her table.

"I really enjoyed that," she said to Erich, who had once again jumped up to pull out her chair. "Please ask him to come back."

"He won't."

Erich sat down. He had a strange expression on his face, like a swimmer on the verge of diving into icy water.

"He'd come back if...if...you asked him," the boy said. "We could go for a walk...maybe...until he calms down...and then look for him together—"

"I'm starving. I have to eat something first or I'll faint right into your arms in the street," Miriam said, teasing. She wondered if Erich always stammered like that when he felt embarrassed. Or perhaps it was only when he did not feel in control of a situation, she thought. She had met men like that—grown men who had wanted her and were embarrassed by feeling that way about a fifteen-year-old.

"L-later? All right."

Seeing his crestfallen expression, Miriam relented. She took a slice of dark pumpernickel from a silver basket and bit into it hungrily. "Don't they feed the entertainers in Germany, Uncle Walther?" She motioned at the bare tablecloth in front of her.

"My profound apologies, Fraülein Rathenau," Erich's mother said. "I will rectify the situation immediately. You were—"

"Don't take me seriously, Frau...Weisser." At the last moment, she remembered the woman's name. "This will do just fine, thank you—as long as you save me some of those nonpareils they're serving with dessert. I crave them."

She took a second slice of bread and stood up.

"Let's take that walk, Erich."

Her uncle looked at Erich. "How old are you, son?"

"Fif—" Erich looked at his parents. "Thirteen, sir." He blushed.

"Just once around the block." The Foreign Minister barely suppressed a smile.

Miriam smiled openly at him. "Just once around the block. Promise!"

Erich led the way up the metal stairs, which gave Miriam a chance to see his outfit from the rear and to hope that he had not chosen it himself. Must have been his parents, she decided, wondering why she sometimes disliked people so intensely on first sight. She did not know Herr or Frau Weisser, yet something about them made her uncomfortable: the mother, obsequious and angry; the father arrogant, yet betrayed by a weakness around the mouth.

As soon as they were in the street, Miriam felt better. No matter how many German aristocrats she met, how many celebrities, she never felt quite comfortable being herself. They had a way of watching and judging, as if they measured everything anyone did on a scale of one-to-ten—one if you were Jewish, ten if you were an Aryan Berliner; anything else had to be earned, if that were even possible!

"Did they feed you, Konnie?" she called to her uncle's driver, who was lounging against their limousine, smoking a cigarette.

"Ja, Fraülein Rathenau. Thank you for inquiring." He quickly crushed the cigarette underfoot and stood up straight.

"Relax." Miriam waved her hand. "We're not leaving yet."

A few of her grandmother's guests, taking the air at the top of the steps, looked in her direction. Several other people craned their necks, trying to see into the cabaret. They glanced at her and at the limousine and, whispering and pointing, moved on. At the corner of the street, surrounded by a dozen locals, a barrel-organ man was grinding away.

Miriam stood for a moment and listened. Then she executed a few dancing steps and grabbed Erich's hand. "Listen. He's playing 'Glowworm'. I never get enough of that song."

She lifted Erich's hand so that she could see it more clearly in the lamplight.

"Kiss it better!" she said. Impulsively, she kissed the red scars. "Tell me about it one day?"

Before he could answer, she let go and danced in the direction of the music.

"Glühwürmchen, Glühwürmchen, glimm're—"

She stopped abruptly. She had not realized she was singing aloud. People were staring at her—not that she cared, but it was not exactly smart to draw attention to herself like that, at night, in the middle of the street.

Someone started to applaud and others joined in.

"More!" a man yelled. "More!"

"Play, barrel-organ man!" another shouted. "Bring out the beer. We're going to have a real Saturday night party now!"

The barrel-organ man grinned widely and patted the head of his monkey; it seemed to be grinning too. The stiff-necked upper crust could keep their genteel appreciation, Miriam thought as she curtsied and began to sing. This was more like it; this was the real thing.

Chapter 11

The clop of a leather dice-cup and the clicking of ivory dice against the glass counter lured Erich and Sol away from their Sunday job in the basement of their fathers' tobacco shop. From the top of the curtained-off basement stairs, they watched their fathers' customers come and go, hoping for a big sale that would provide them with pocket money for the week.

The two men playing dice asked for a box of Solomons, one of Herr Freund's first creations—a blend of cherry and Martinique tobaccos. After getting odds on the Dempsey-Hülering fight, they let the dice determine which man would pay for the purchase. Not for the first time, Erich wondered if there would ever be a cigar named after him, and dismissed the thought. Papa was and always would be nothing more than a junior partner in Herr Freund's shop.

If he were certain of nothing else, Erich thought angrily, he was sure of one thing: he was not going to play second fiddle to anyone—not even if, as was true for Papa, there was justice in it. After all, Herr Freund was the original owner of the shop.

He glanced at Sol and then back at Herr Freund, who was quietly restocking the shelves. Their parents had it all worked out—after all, the two boys were such good friends. What could be more natural than the two of them taking over ownership of the shop one day? Not me, he thought. He was destined for better things. Last night at the cabaret—and being with Miriam—had convinced him of that.

Not that this place was so bad; it was actually fun because of the gambling license, which many of the more elegant tobacconists had.

Like all other Berlin stores, Die Zigarrenkiste, "The Cigar Box," was officially closed on Sundays. But the cost of maintaining the gambling license was high, the rent on the shop exorbitant; in these days of encroaching inflation, Herr Freund said, shopkeepers could ill afford to close for an hour, much less a day. There were always high rollers seeking action, dapper men craving good cigars, and finely fashionable women wanting cigarettes to complement new outfits. Any of them might stop by their favorite tobacconist-bookie on Sundays "to see if the lights were on."

The shop was perfectly located, close to the train depot, the embassies, restaurants, and outdoor cafés, and surrounded by clothing and jewelry stores. Sunday strollers ambled along the wide boulevards of Unter den Linden, past Embassy Row, and on toward Pariser Platz. They turned into Friedrich Ebert Strasse at the Brandenburg Gate, meandered past the Academy of Arts, the Tiergarten, and the zoo, and stopped to window-shop at the various stores that dotted the route to their fashionable destinations. It seemed quite natural that, on the pretext of saying hello, they should drop into Die Zigarrenkiste for a quick gambling fix and their weekend smoking supplies.

The men purchased cigars singly or in cedar boxes; they carried them home like chocolate soldiers in wooden coffins, transferred them to humidors, and gave the boxes to their children to use as treasure chests. For weekdays, they bought less expensive cigars; but on Friday and Saturday evenings at the theater and after large Sunday dinners, only Havanas would do.

Berlin's upper crust ladies also frequented the shop. Erich loved to watch them make their selections. They purchased one or two at a time, agonizing over their choices. Right now, Turkish and Egyptian cigarettes were all the rage. Since most of the ladies smoked out of fashion rather than habit, nothing else would do but that their cigarettes be specially ordered: embossed with their own names or initials—or those of their tobacconist—or colored to match their outfits or their eyes.

On days when his own gambling losses were excessive, Erich's father complained about the expense of stocking goods to suit the whims of the rich. Papa could rant and rave all he liked, Erich thought, it did not take a mathematical genius to figure out that the profit was worth the investment. The bookie operation was no sure thing, so the shop's real profit lay neither in that nor in tobacco. Tobacco's accouterments, that was where the real money came from: gold and silver cigarette holders encrusted with gems that matched jeweled hatpins and tiepins; cigarette cases initialed or inscribed to husbands or wives or lovers; ivory and enameled guillotines for snipping cigar tips.

"Aren't as many customers as usual," Sol whispered.

"Maybe there'd be more customers if your papa weren't so stubborn," Erich said, referring to his father's contention that his partner was allowing street merchants to take profits rightfully theirs. *Why not,* Papa said, *cater to those who prefer the dreams brought by cocaine and morphine.*

And why not, Erich thought. It was legal, and would boost the shop's declining revenues. But Herr Freund inevitably dismissed the topic with words that brooked no further discussion. "We will leave such transactions to lesser men."

"Business will pick up after Kaverne opens," Sol said.

"Depends on how good the cabaret is. Papa says if Oma Rathenau thinks the rich will flock to her place just because *she* opened it, she's in for a surprise."

"My papa says they'll all come—the rich and famous."

"Your papa says a lot of things. People might come once, but after that Frau Rathenau has to make them *want* to come. They want excitement, not just elegance anymore."

Erich lifted his head and shoulders the way his new Freikorps-Youth leader, Otto Hempel, did when he was about to deliver a speech. Why couldn't *his* father look like that, Erich thought. Better yet, why couldn't he *be* like that. While his father was working here in the shop during the war, drinking and playing the horses, Otto Hempel was helping von Hindenburg decimate the Russians at Tannenberg, earning a field commission for gallantry. He had told them about it one night around the campfire, silver hair shining in the firelight. He had commanded the battery that fired those first shells of liquid chlorine in Poland, only to have it fail to volatilize in the frigid conditions. He had helped coordinate the mustard-gas attack at Ypres, only to have the victory that could have won the war snatched away because no one believed him about the new weapon's wonderful potential.

Now *there* was a hero—and he looked the part, too. Said his hair had turned silver from the ardors of the battlefield.

Erich glanced at himself in a cigarette case Herr Freund had left lying on the counter to be polished. He turned it this way and that, imagining himself with a head of silver hair and a row of medals.

"Give people what they think they want, then make sure they keep wanting what you give them," he said to Sol. "Some cabarets have naked waitresses. Men can touch them...anywhere they want."

Sol lifted his head and looked at Erich, who quickly put down his makeshift mirror. "Where did you hear that? At one of your stupid campfires?"

Erich narrowed his eyes. "You watch what you say about my camp."

"Then you watch what you say about my papa. He knows what he's doing." Sol raised himself to his full height and looked down at Erich.

Erich clenched his fist. "If you really want to know, Miriam told me." He opened his hand, but kept his fighting stance.

"I suppose that's what you talked about in front of her uncle and everyone."

"After you and your squeaky cello disappeared, Miriam walked with me to...to...the Tiergarten and back."

"Herr Rathenau would never let her walk with you or anyone else unchaperoned. Not at night—"

Erich gave a derisive snort and leaned back haughtily against the wall. "That's what *you* think. Go ahead, ask her! We went for a walk and—"

"She didn't tell you those things, about the cabarets," Sol said, but in a softer tone.

"Well, something like that." Erich took a bent cigarette from his pocket. "Want to go outside with me and smoke this?" He straightened the cigarette, then dabbed saliva on the paper to help hold it together where it had torn.

"You said we wouldn't take any more. Remember, you were the one who got sick—"

"I took them for Miriam." Erich pulled several more cigarettes from his pockets, most of them damaged.

"Her parents let her *smoke?*"

"They're dead, remember? She lives with her uncle." He thought about the way Miriam had looked, dancing in the lamplight. Funny how he wanted to tell Sol about that and didn't want to, both at the same time. He rolled one of the cigarettes between his fingers and remembered how she had taken his hand, *that* one, and kissed it. "Boy, I sure would like to do things to her."

"What things?"

"You know. Things."

"She wouldn't even let someone like you hold her hand."

"Bet she already kissed me."

"Liar!"

Erich felt his face redden. He shoved Sol against the wall. Sol swung wildly, managing a glancing blow off Erich's temple before Erich surged in with body punches.

"Be quiet, children!" Sol's father called out. "Look who has stopped outside. Herr Rathenau himself."

The boys dropped their guard and started into the shop, but Sol's father shooed them back into the alcove. Sol peeked around the curtain. "To see him twice in two days," he said in awe.

"Did he come in the limousine or the convertible?" Erich tried to see over Sol's shoulder. "Is Miriam with him? Maybe she suggested he come so she could see me," he whispered excitedly. His heart pounded at the possibility of being with Miriam again.

"Stop breathing down my neck." Sol shifted slightly so they could both have a clear view of the door.

The bell above the shop door jangled. With a theatrical wave of his hand, Herr Freund ushered in the Foreign Minister. Rathenau entered—alone. He wore a gray suit and maroon cravat and carried a walking stick under his arm. A huge diamond twinkled in its knob.

"How nice to see you again, Herr Freund."

The statesman surveyed the shop, breathing deeply as though savoring the rich aroma of tobacco that permeated the air.

Herr Freund slipped behind the counter and quickly removed the dice cups. "How might I serve you, Herr Rathenau?"

Now that the counter was between them, his tone was comfortable. Erich understood that feeling of putting something tangible between himself and someone to whom he felt in some way inferior; he had often wished he could do it with his Freikorps-Youth leader. He recognized the defensive gesture that allowed clerk and customer to maintain their separate worlds across the barrier of Meerschaum pipes and open cigar boxes and glass.

"A couple of cigars, to begin with," Rathenau said. "I'm to accompany my mother to the Schauspielhaus tonight. A troupe from Frankfurt is attempting *Faust*...mediocre talent, I'm told, but exuberant. Give me something light but full-bodied. Perhaps it'll help me forget that I'm allowing myself to sit through yet another butchering of Goethe."

Erich watched Herr Freund select two fine Havanas. Herr Rathenau paid for them with a banknote, then indicated he would take another, for immediate use.

"Perhaps you would honor me by accepting one of these." Reaching under the glass, Herr Freund produced a single cigar. He twirled it in his fingers, breathed in its aroma, and placed it on a small velvet pad, which he passed to the Foreign Minister.

"Something new?" Herr Rathenau asked.

"I have named a cigar for my son and a gold-tipped cigarillo for my daughter. We were about to name one for my partner's son."

"About time," Erich whispered, surprised.

"With your permission, however," Herr Freund said, "we should like to name this latest...a Rathenau."

Furious at having lost out to the Foreign Minister, Erich watched Herr Freund clip the cigar and light it. "Too early in the day to soak the tip in cognac," the tobacconist said, tossing the end in a trash basket and handing Rathenau the cigar.

I hope you choke on it, Erich thought, as the Foreign Minister moistened his lips with his tongue and rotated the cigar in his mouth, relishing it as one might a fine brandy.

"Excellent—and I am deeply touched by your tribute." Herr Rathenau raised his brows in appreciation, patted Jacob on the shoulder and blew a stream of smoke toward the ceiling's ceramic friezes. "You have proven yourself to be a seller of smokes without equal. And now, as to my main reason for stopping by—"

Herr Freund's smile remained fixed. He leaned forward, hands on the glass, shirt sleeves rolled up, the glow from the overhead lamps shining dully on the bald spot where his hairline receded.

"As I implied," Rathenau said, "I did not come simply for cigars. I came to see the boy."

"I was right." Erich poked Sol playfully in the ribs. "Miriam must have asked him to come."

"Is that you, Solomon, hiding back there?" Rathenau asked. "Come on out."

The boys exchanged startled glances.

"Go on!" Erich shoved his friend a little too hard and Sol practically fell into the shop.

"That was some performance you gave last night," the Foreign Minister said.

"I know I was awful, sir."

Erich secretly applauded Sol's honesty. Apparently Herr Freund felt otherwise, because his face tightened.

"Well, you're no virtuoso, but Miri liked your Haydn. Judging by your degree of discomfort with performing, however—" Rathenau smiled and put an arm around Solomon's shoulders—"I rather suspect you might be persuaded to give up playing in public."

Seeing them side by side, Erich was struck with how diminutive the man was; Rathenau had been seated at the party, and his stature and bearing had lent him an illusion of height.

"Sir?" Sol frowned, his face a study in puzzlement.

The statesman released him and laughed out loud. "Just teasing, young man. You did a fine job, under trying conditions. It is not easy to follow an act like my Miriam's."

He glanced curiously toward the curtain.

"Ah, young Weisser!" Rathenau looked directly at Erich and chuckled. "Took a fancy to my young lady, did you not?"

Erich had been holding the edge of the curtain and peeking around it. Feeling as if he had been reprimanded for staying suspiciously long in the bathroom, he jerked his head back behind the curtain. He would not go out there now, he decided, even if they tried to drag him out.

Then he heard Rathenau say, "I have taken a liking to your Solomon, as has my niece," and he was filled with such hurt that he stepped back against the wall as though someone had pushed him. His face burned and his heart thudded ferociously.

"With your permission, Herr Freund, I would like your son to join me for lunch today at the Adlon." The Foreign Minister's voice dropped toward the end of the sentence. "I have no son of my own, and probably never will have. I was impressed by his effort last night and I wish to reward him—"

Pretend Sol's a dog, Erich told himself. Send him a message. *Get him to invite me. Don't go without me.*

"You *liked* my performance?" Sol sounded amazed.

"Sol—" Jacob Freund said.

Erich crawled forward and, parting the curtain just enough to peek out, saw Rathenau hold up a hand in a gesture of forbearance. "Quite all right, my friend. The boy is naturally confused."

The Foreign Minister reached out and touched Sol's cheek. Erich put his hand against his own face.

"I shall explain myself further at luncheon, young man," Rathenau said, "unless, of course, you have other plans. Or perhaps you'd simply rather not come."

"Oh, no...I mean yes...I'd love to come, but—"

"But?" Herr Freund sounded dumbfounded.

"Herr Foreign Minister," Sol said, almost too softly to be heard, "...could...do you think...could my friend, Erich, come with us?"

The Foreign Minister eyed Sol's father, who returned the look without a sign of emotion. There it was, Erich thought. What Papa called the attitudinal interchange between classes. Herr Freund, the impassive merchant; Rathenau, his statesman's gaze bespeaking loftier aspirations and ideals than the sale of cigars, even to customers of wealth and power.

"Solomon will be honored to go with you, Herr Rathenau," Herr Freund said, his expressionless voice and face masking what Erich was sure must be a racing pulse. He remembered what he had heard the night he'd awakened and his mother was crying and his father was shouting, *That Jew is humble-ambitious, I tell you. Humble-ambitious!*

"What time should we have him ready?" Sol's father asked.

Have *them* ready, Erich corrected. Surely Rathenau would include him in the luncheon, now that Sol had asked—

"We have established that it is all right with you, Herr Freund," the Foreign Minister said. "Now let us hear from the boy."

Not *boys*. Erich felt his heart plummet and he chided himself for ever having admired the Foreign Minister.

"I am...honored," Sol mumbled. His hand trembled as he pushed his glasses back up onto the bridge of his nose.

Ask him again, Erich begged mentally.

"Good. I shall call for you at—" Rathenau opened his watch— "shall we say twelve?"

Father and son nodded in unison. Herr Freund walked around the counter and opened the door for Rathenau. Sol looked back, grimaced, and followed the two men into the street.

Erich crept along behind the counter for a better look. The statesman's chauffeur, a massive, homely man, leaned comfortably against the limousine. When he heard the bell above the door, he straightened up. He smoothed back his hair, which hung to his collar, slicked it beneath his cap, and held open the car door. Rathenau ducked inside and slid open the glass panel that separated the front seat from the back. Then he leaned against the plush, fawn-colored leather upholstery, gloved hands resting on the head of his walking stick, and his horseless carriage rolled away.

Thinks he's a king but he is just a little man with too much money and power, Erich thought. Like Papa says they all are.

"You see?" No longer impassive, Sol's father gripped his son by the arms. "All that practicing paid off. I told you it would!"

"He can't truly want me to play for him again, can he?"

"Who knows what he wants? Just that he *wants* is what's important." He put an arm across Solomon's shoulders. "You're a good boy, Solomon Freund, the best, but you listen to me. I know your intentions are good, but if Herr Rathenau wanted Erich to go with you, he would have said as much without your prompting." He patted Sol on the rump as if to give him a running start across the street to the apartment. "Go! Get ready!"

Sol glanced into the shop and shrugged his shoulders. His body said, *I tried*. "Must I take my cello, Papa?"

"Questions, always so many questions. No, my son. No cello." Herr Freund took out the long black key attached to a silver chain dangling from his belt loop, and shut the door.

In disbelief, Erich listened to the key rasp in the lock.

"Papa, you're locking Erich in!"

There was a second metallic scraping, and Jacob pulled open the door. Erich waited until Herr Freund had stepped back before he exited the shop. Keeping his gaze on the merchant, he eased around him as if around a large cat.

"I'm sorry, my boy. It seems we forgot you in all the excitement." Jacob smiled.

"Just forget you forgot!" Hands in pockets, Erich backed several steps up the street before turning and stalking away.

"Erich?" Solomon called tentatively.

Erich kept walking. No use going home, he thought. Papa would be mulling over his racing forms, downing sherry like beer to compensate for not having enough money to go to Mariendorf and bet on the trotters. Once he heard Rathenau had chosen to take Sol to lunch instead of Erich, he would start complaining again, and yelling, and his mother would cry. Why did they always have to be so predictable?

He headed toward the Tiergarten, remembering how Miriam had smiled and put her arm through his when they had heard the barrel-organ man playing "Glowworm." She had kissed him—sort of—and he had kissed her back—almost.

Well, he would show them.

There would be no almosts anymore.

Chapter 12

"Hello, Konnie." Miriam smiled at her uncle's chauffeur. "Thanks for coming to get me. Where's my uncle?"

"He and that young man are still at the Adlon, Fraülein—"

"*Miriam,* please! Which young man?"

"Young Herr Freund, Fraülein Rathenau." The chauffeur opened the rear door of the limousine.

Trying to cure the Germans of their excessive formality was an exercise in futility, Miriam thought, throwing her tennis racquet onto the back seat. But she was not about to stop trying—not until someone could give her a satisfying explanation of why people who had known each other for most of their lives still called each other Frau and Herr.

"Thanks again for the lesson, Vladimir." She waved to her tennis instructor, who was standing halfway between the court and the curb, staring at her. "See you on Wednesday. Don't forget to bring some of *Mashenka* for me to read next time."

Ignoring Konnie's disapproving look and the open door, she got into the front seat of the limousine.

"My uncle took Solomon Freund to the Adlon for lunch?" She thought about the doe-eyed boy with the cello. He had never come back to the party, so she had not been able to tell him how she had felt about the Haydn. "Did he take the other boy, too? His friend—Erich?"

The chauffeur shook his head and started the car. "Home, Fraülein?" He glanced sidelong at the tennis dress she had brought back from America.

"I think not," she said impulsively. "Where are you picking up Uncle Walther after his walk?"

"At young Herr Freund's home."

"Then that's where we'll go. I'll wait there with you."

The chauffeur gave her another disapproving look. "Do you not wish to change?"

"No, Konnie. Thank you. This will do perfectly well."

Uncle Walther would not exactly approve of her being seen in public like this, she thought, but she was not breaking any laws. Besides, he was enough of a renegade himself that he generally forgave her those kinds of trespasses. He tried to be stern, but the indulgent twinkle in his eyes betrayed his pride in her independent spirit.

As they made their way into the city, Miriam thought about the two boys—Erich and Solomon. Romantically, they were much too young for her, of course, but they were the most interesting boys she had met since her return to Berlin. She was used to young men like Vladimir falling all over her; it was flattering, but dull. There were lots of Russians in the ballet company in New York. They were attractive, but so serious about themselves. Vlad was no different, except that he was a writer, or wanted to be, instead of a dancer.

They were rounding a corner several blocks from Friedrich Ebert Strasse when Miriam spotted Erich waiting to cross the street.

"Stop the car!" She rolled down the window. "Erich! Erich Weisser! Come over here."

Erich looked up, squinted in her direction, and blushed.

"Here!" she called out again. "We'll give you a lift home."

She pushed open the door and beckoned. He darted across to the car and slid in beside her.

"We're going to pick up my uncle," she said. "Why didn't you go with them?" Oh Lord, she thought, seeing the expression on Erich's face. "Next time we'll all go," she added, hoping to alleviate some of the embarrassment she had caused. Konnie pulled up in front of the tobacco shop. "We could wait for them at your place," she said to Erich. "Didn't you tell me you lived above the Freunds?"

"Yes, but...but..." Erich stopped stammering, and looked angry as he took a breath. "My parents aren't home."

Miriam started to ask why that mattered. This is Berlin, she reminded herself. Here, parents expected children to be little Victorians, even if they themselves were anything but. "Okay. Then let's wait in the car."

"That's our shop over there, remember?" Erich pointed at the cigar shop.

Perfect, Miriam thought. She had forgotten about that. Now she could buy her uncle some of his favorite tobacco as a surprise. "Let's wait in there, then," she said.

"The lights are out."

"So?"

"Herr Freund hasn't come back yet. It's locked up." He stopped, as if he'd had an idea. "Come."

"Shall I wait here, Fraülein Rathenau?" Konnie asked.

"Whatever you like, Konnie." She thought about it. "Why don't you come back in, say, half an hour. They should be back by then."

She and Erich got out of the car and headed toward the shop. When they were at the door, he pulled out a key chain from his hip pocket and opened the oblong leather pouch attached to it.

"Don't you have a key?" Miriam asked.

Erich took out a pick and shook his head. "Have to pick the lock," he mumbled.

"Why do you carry lock picks?"

He shrugged. "Just because."

Like in the movies, Miriam thought, enjoying herself until it occurred to her that someone might think they were breaking into the shop—which they were, in a manner of speaking. "Hurry up!" She pictured her uncle's face if he arrived and found them being questioned by the police.

"It's open." Erich pushed at the door, and the bell above it jangled. "Quick—inside." He let the door close behind them.

"It's too dark in here. Put on a light, will you?"

Erich hesitated.

"Come on. I want to buy some tobacco for my uncle."

The boy walked across the store and turned on a single light near a red velvet curtain. She followed him and pulled the curtain aside. It led to a stairway, going down.

"Have you ever smoked?" Erich asked, from behind the counter.

Miriam shook her head. He reached under the counter, pulled out a cigarette, lit it and handed it to her. She drew on it and started to cough. Laughing, he took it from her.

"That is not funny," she said, though she could not help but laugh, too. "Let me try again." She took a second draw. Her head started to spin; she felt dizzy, like when she had tried champagne for the first time. The taste in her mouth was dry and musty. "Tastes like old shoes," she said. "See."

Leaning toward him, she kissed him on the lips. He stood there with such a shocked expression on his face that she could not resist. Putting her arms around him, she kissed him again.

A bell jangled and the shop was flooded with light.

"What do you think you're doing!"

Miriam whirled around to see Herr Weisser striding toward them.

"Smoking, kissing, breaking into the shop! What kind of a girl are you?"

Jacob Freund came in behind his partner. "Calm down, Friedrich. Please."

Herr Weisser turned to face him. "Calm down? Look at her! Acting like a street walker, and you tell me to calm down. I told my wife last night—already, you were making eyes at my boy—these rich Jews, I told her. They're not to be trusted!"

"Friedrich! Control yourself!" Herr Freund, obviously mortified by his partner's outburst, took off his glasses and began to clean them.

"I'm sorry, Herr Weisser." Miriam spoke slowly, struggling to mask her anger. She was bristling at the insults.

"Sorry? That's a thirteen-year-old boy and you say you're sorry?"

Miriam glanced over at Erich. He was standing against the shelves, his face red and angry. "Papa, we were—"

"I can see what you were doing!" his father bellowed. "You! Fancy lady! Sit down!" He turned to glare at his son. "You! Go home and wait for me!"

Erich did not move.

Warily Miriam made her way to the small round table that held an ebony-and-ivory chess set, and sat down on one of two identical spindle-backed chairs. While she waited for her uncle, there was nothing she could do but sit and listen to Herr Weisser carry on about her corrupting his precious son. The whole thing was ridiculous! Erich was nice, but he was hardly an angel who needed this kind of protection.

If only Uncle would get here. He would set things to rights. She was always happy to see him, but never more than she would be this time. Clearly, she was in trouble, but since the most reprehensible thing she had done was not discourage Erich from breaking into his own shop, she would be forgiven. Well, maybe she *had* encouraged him just a little....

Feeling far less grown-up than she had when she'd arrived, she decided that when her uncle came, she would allow herself to be led away without a glance in the Freunds' direction. She would find another time to talk to Sol about his music. In fact, she would not even meet his gaze or smile, lest he or his father think her coquettish—though why it mattered she had no idea.

Chapter 13

Sol looked around the dining room of the Adlon Men's Club. He should have tried harder to have his friend included, he thought, but he would make up for it; he would remember every detail, from the Foreign Minister's custom-tailored dress-suit and broad crimson sash, to the room itself, elegantly set, Spartan, crowded with the rich and powerful. He was proud, and more than a little astonished, at having been included in this milieu, but the rigidity—the lack of *Gemütlichkeit*—troubled him. Surrounded by the quiet buzz of intense conversation between men whose faces he recognized from *Der Weltspiegel* and the Movietone News, he felt small and embarrassed. A dose of the cabaret's magic—women and flowers and music—might lend a more festive air to the room, he thought. Everyone seemed so serious!

"The Idle Inn is more fun," Rathenau said, apparently reading the expression on Sol's face. "I prefer the Biergarten and would rather break bread with common men, but there is much unofficial business of State transacted here on Sundays."

At a table next to them, a man raised his glass of drinking water. "To your good health, gentlemen." He and the others at his table gargled their water and spat it into their finger bowls.

Sol mumbled something about never before having realized the bowls' proper purpose, and Rathenau laughed. "An end-of-the-meal fashion established by the Kaiser," he whispered. "I wouldn't suggest you do it elsewhere. Your hosts might not understand."

During the course of their meal, a variety of people had stopped at the table. Rathenau introduced him to each one. Earlier, walking toward the dining room, he had cautioned Sol to give more attention to listening than to eating. "Disregard anti-Semitic slurs," he had said. "Hear what they're saying *behind* the bigotry. Don't overlook a single nuance or inflection...and don't forget a word you hear."

Forget! As long as he lived, he would remember this day. These were men who could open doors for him—and for Erich—with a word or a wave of the hand. Not that it was all that important for him; he was going to be a scholar—study, teach maybe. But Erich...he was going to be "something big!" Anyway, that's what he said. With the right education, the right clothes, the right connections, you could do anything, Papa said, and these were surely the right connections—here in this room.

"Come along, Sol." The Foreign Minister led him into the lobby of the hotel. "Bear with me. I have some business to conduct as we leave. Then we'll take a *Spaziergang*—a stroll. Konnie will pick me up at your flat."

Sol followed him across the lounge toward two men seated in wing chairs, smoking and reading newspapers. A third man, dressed in the blue and gold of an officer's uniform, sat reading in the corner, his back to them and his boots on a hassock.

"I tell you it's a disgrace," one of the men said as they approached.

The other, blond, with a Tartar mustache that only partially concealed a scar along the edge of his mouth, looked up and nodded. Rathenau extended his hand. "Good to see you again, Auwi."

The second man, a rotund fellow with steel gray eyes and the downturned mouth of a carp, leaped to his feet and shook hands with the Foreign Minister.

"Glad you're here, George." Rathenau looked at Sol. "Solomon Freund, I'd like you to meet George Viereck, literary executor for the Kaiser, and," he nodded toward the seated man, "The Kaiser's son, Prinz August Wilhelm. 'Auwi' to his friends."

The Prince raised a desultory hand in greeting. Viereck pumped Solomon's hand so heartily that Sol found himself backing up.

"I think you'll recognize this lazy old soldier over here," Rathenau said.

A pasty, doggy-cheeked face sporting a drooping white mustache peered out from around the side of his chair.

Solomon swallowed thickly.

Field Marshal von Hindenburg!

Von Hindenburg cast a rheumy eye at Sol, cleared his throat, and reopened the weekend edition of the *Börsen Zeitung*. "Protégé, Herr Minister?" he asked. "Send him out on the balcony to wave to the masses like Jackie Coogan. You're his countryman, George. Is the Coogan boy really so talented, or is our city simply in love with youth for youth's sake?"

"I'm afraid neither Prinz Wilhelm nor the Feldmarschall is in a very good mood." Viereck's German was edged with an American accent. "The price of newspapers has gone up again. I remember when a single mark bought a quart of Fauwenhauser."

"Third time this week," the prince said sourly. "All this babbling and squabbling, inflation out of control—" he slapped the paper—

"revolutionaries and reactionaries running amok, foreigners and Jews and post-war profiteers stealing the country from under us!"

Stung by the racial slur, Sol looked to Rathenau for guidance. The Foreign Minister flashed him a look that said *stay calm*.

"We Germans were like the woman in the Aladdin story, too quick to give away the old lamp." Von Hindenburg cleared his throat huskily and adjusted his purple sash. Four starfish-shaped medals gleamed upon a chest once more massive than his belly.

"The Kaiser's greatest wish is to return and march with the workers against the government," Viereck said.

The American looked from Solomon to von Hindenburg, who drew his bushy brows together in an exaggerated frown. "Can the boy be trusted?" the general asked in a rough voice. "He has the features of a Jew."

You have the jowls of a bloodhound, Sol thought, stiffening.

"He *is* a Jew. Therefore I trust him as I do my own judgment," Rathenau said. "Fully."

"You think too highly of Jews, Herr Foreign Minister," von Hindenburg said.

"Perhaps not highly enough," Rathenau replied in an even tone.

Solomon lowered his gaze. For a while he had felt invisible; now he was certain everyone in the room was staring at him. He pretended to examine one of the massive tapestries hanging on the wall.

For all the times Sol had walked past the Adlon, this was the first time he had been inside. The outside was simple, a plain building with long wrought-iron windows, but the inside—tapestries and floor-to-ceiling shelves filled with leather-bound books, crimson curtains, walls wainscoted in mahogany and vaulted ceilings buttressed by elaborate plaster trellises. Words like *putsch* and *purge* and *anarchy* seemed to float in the air and he would not have been surprised to find the Kaiser walking across the candelabra-lit lounge.

"The Kaiser cannot regain the crown, he knows that," he heard the prince say. "He seeks only *Heldentod*, the hero's death he was previously denied."

So the Kaiser had desired *Heldentod* after all! Sol could hardly wait to tell Erich. Other boys at school had claimed the Kaiser was a coward. At the expense of several black eyes and split lips, Sol and Erich had insisted otherwise.

"Our beloved Wilhelm shall have his wish," von Hindenburg said. "I shall serve as scapegoat for our military humiliations and the sheep shall flock to someone—perhaps Walther here—who will lead Germany if not to higher heights then at least to solidarity."

He snapped his fingers and a waiter appeared with a tray of brandy snifters and a decanter. "Let us drink to solidarity," von Hindenburg said.

The four men drank, and Sol was filled with awe at how calmly and quickly history could be rechanneled.

Within moments he was out on the street, following Rathenau, who moved silently and at an energetic pace.

Sol's notions of a *Spaziergang* underwent a dramatic change. His father's penchant was for leisurely constitutionals along well-worn paths, conversing as he walked or pausing at benches to rest and argue a particular point, while Rathenau hiked wordlessly along Wilhelmstrasse, as if allowing the city's penury and seething anger to be his mouthpiece.

His senses opened by the Adlon luncheon, Sol took in everything with a tourist's unease: the farmers and fishmongers near the Ministry of Justice, hawking wilted wildflowers, lettuce, and oily, overpriced herring; the air, filled with grit and the stench of exhaust; the buildings' gray austerity. The streets seemed more littered with garbage and more asprawl with drunks and other dispossessed than he recalled: *Schieber*—foreign blackmarketeers—worked every street corner; political saviors wearing red cockades or black armbands stood on principles and soap crates, embracing immutable ideals Sol was sure they would be willing to discard for a meal or a few hundred marks; scurrying urchins poked and pleaded, offering shoeshines, sisters, the wisdom of white powders, the serenity of a syringe.

There were women, too, posing as ladies while promising to raise skirts but not prices, offering heavenly communions to be consummated in the privacy of the nearest alley.

"What this nation needs is a generation of *reasonable* Nationalists—Gentiles *and* Jews—willing to work together for God and good government...the dream of a true democracy," Rathenau said. He slapped his walking stick against his palm. He was walking so fast that Solomon had to run lightly to keep pace with him. "Europe has a history of vesting absolute power in one individual. I intend to position myself to block that sort of thing from happening again."

He halted. Putting his hands on Sol's shoulders, he looked down into the boy's eyes. "As I watched your performance last night, you reminded me so much of myself," he said. "Struggling. Forced to play solo. You are the new generation, Sol. With my help you may not have to accept, as I had to, that, in Germany, Jews will always be second-class citizens."

As suddenly as he had taken hold of Solomon, he let go. "Constant vigilance is exhausting, Solomon," he said, in a tired voice. "There are times I want to lie down and pull Berlin's sidewalks over me."

Sol looked down at his feet. How many weary men's spirits lay beneath the city? Perhaps theirs were the voices he heard, he thought, wondering fleetingly what the Foreign Minister might say about the voices and sounds in the sewer.

"Back in '18, I decided to retire," the Foreign Minister said softly, moving on. "I've a summer house in Bavaria—"

"Papa showed me pictures of it in *Der Weltspiegel*," Sol said.

"I intended to live there, away from all this. Fortunately for Germany—though unfortunately for me, since it thwarted my retirement plans—I decided to have the bedrooms repapered. One afternoon, the paper hanger and I talked as he worked. After listening to him, I realized that, with people like him around, my role in our country's history remained incomplete."

They rounded the corner at the Reichschancellery and headed down Friedrich Ebert Strasse. The cigar store was half a block away.

"The man proposed that Germany depopulate the African island of Madagascar and repopulate it with European Jews," Rathenau went on. "'The solution to the Jewish problem,' he said, 'is to pen them like wild dogs, tame them, and use what assets and abilities they possess for the good of humanity.'"

Until now, Sol had done what he did when his parents spoke Yiddish, a language he only partially understood: he had allowed the conversation to flow around him like a piece of music he had never heard before. Usually, if he relaxed into it that way, the pieces became a cohesive whole. However, what the Foreign Minister was saying now made no sense at all.

"He wanted to send the Jews to Madagascar? He must have been crazy!"

"I thought so too, and had him removed from the premises," the Foreign Minister said. "Shortly after that, I heard that he'd entered politics, and now Bavaria's National-Socialists support his ideas—"

Shouting interrupted him. Sol stared in the direction of the voices. Down the block, Erich was backing out of the shop.

Chapter 14

"You may be my son, but your actions are that of an imbecile!" Herr Weisser yelled. He was standing in the doorway of the shop, shaking his fist at Erich.

"Leave me alone, Papa!"

Erich turned, dashed across the street without any regard for traffic, and disappeared into the apartment house.

Herr Weisser, his face red with rage, fell silent. Apparently, Sol thought, he had run out of effective yet moderate epithets to hurl at his son.

"Maybe we should detour through Leipzigerplatz before going inside," Rathenau said.

Solomon shook his head. Once Friedrich and Erich started arguing, it would take longer than a stroll through the plaza for their tempers to cool. "Erich probably tried to sneak another dog into the apartment," he said, wondering why Herr Weisser had gone back into the shop instead of following his son.

"That much trouble over a dog?"

"Herr Weisser has agreed to let Erich keep a small dog in the apartment, but Erich says the little ones are toys. It's worse since he's joined the Freikorps-Youth—"

Sol stopped and, with a sick feeling, glanced up at Rathenau. During the waning months of the war, the Foreign Minister had financed a Freikorps unit, a movement that had begun before the war with Wandervögel—birds of passage—boys and girls who enjoyed outdoor activities. Some of those young men had been part of Rathenau's corps, but the years of fighting had hardened their idealism into hatred. In Sol's opinion, the post-war Freikorps-Youth was a step further down. A big step. Many of the boys were homeless ruffians, easily influenced; and the leaders, Jew-haters.

Judging by the set look on his face, the Foreign Minister had heard all right—and taken note. Sol practiced the truth in his head: *It just slipped out.*

I didn't mean to kill your chances with Miriam. At least he had not told Herr Rathenau that his friend talked to dogs. This was bad enough, but that would really have done it!

"Anyway, they fight about dogs," he said weakly as they entered the shop.

"Calm down, Friedrich, for God's sake," his papa was saying. "Why make a national tragedy out of it? They're just children."

They? Sol thought, wondering what Papa meant. Then he saw Miriam seated in the corner, her hands demurely folded on the table. He could see her face clearly now. She was even more beautiful than he had thought at first, and younger, nearer to fifteen than seventeen. Her eyes were a startling violet, and though her chignon was almost black, her skin had the bone-china delicacy that usually went with auburn hair.

"Miriam! What's going on? What are you doing here?" Rathenau looked from her to Herr Weisser, who was glaring at her as if she had two heads.

Jumping up, she ran over to him and threw her arms around his waist. "They're making such a fuss, Uncle Walther!" The action pulled up her tennis skirt; Sol tried not to stare too hard at her tanned legs.

"Fuss? Smoking, kissing!" Friedrich spun around toward her uncle. "Is that what they taught your niece in America?"

"I asked Konnie to bring me along when he told me you wanted him to pick you up here," Miriam said. "I wanted to surprise you. Erich was here, and we talked—"

"Talked?" Friedrich looked flushed. "You two broke into our shop!"

"Erich was showing me his lock picks," Miriam said.

"Showing *off,* you mean, and you encouraged him! And what did you two do once you were in?" Friedrich pointed at her. "For shame!"

Rathenau took hold of Weisser's hand and, looking less than amused, drew down the man's arm. "Such a small matter, Herr Weisser. Don't upset yourself so. We should all remember that when the trivial becomes important, the important becomes trivial. Why don't we go to your parlor, have coffee and a cigar, and talk this out like gentlemen."

"Talk! That's all you Jews are good at."

Sol saw Papa pale as he stepped in front of Herr Weisser and silenced his partner with an ominous glare. Rathenau's face hardened, and his knuckles tightened around his walking stick as if he wanted to thrash Friedrich Weisser. Taking Miriam by the arm, he said softly, "I guess this is a family matter after all. Come, child."

"At least let me call a taxi for you." Sol's father did not take his gaze off Weisser.

"My chauffeur will be here momentarily." Rathenau reached out and shook Sol's father's hand. "Things will work out. We'll get together...another day."

"So! He's gone!" Jacob Freund said to his partner after Rathenau stepped outside. "Shame on you, Friedrich! They say he may become Germany's president, and you treat him like dirt. What the children did was foolish, but—"

"You're an imbecile yourself if you think such behavior trivial. If you had seen them, behaving like that in my shop!"

"Our shop, Friedrich," Jacob said.

Sol watched his father carefully. His voice was gentle, yet it clearly indicated that Herr Weisser had overstepped both business and personal propriety. The business, begun by his father a dozen years before the war, involved a seventy-thirty split between the two men. Herr Weisser had been a bicycling *hamster*—an impoverished peddler who went out to the countryside each morning for produce to hawk—before Papa took him into the business, first as *Shabbas* help, and permanently when Papa had volunteered to fight for his country and needed someone to run the shop.

"Why don't we do as Herr Rathenau suggested? Let's go home—your home if you prefer. We'll drink a good strong cup of coffee. Talk."

"For all the good it will do," Friedrich said, but he began locking up the store.

In the apartment's parlor, Friedrich told his wife what had happened, and the argument was renewed. Sol, to his surprise, was not sent out of the room. He sat quietly listening to the two men: his own father, rational and positive, trying to make his friend see that he had overreacted; Friedrich, his voice raised, maligning the Rathenau family at every opportunity.

The two men had reached an impasse when Recha and Sol's mother, apparently hearing the commotion, came upstairs from the Freund flat. Mama wiped her hands on her apron. "What is the matter?" Her house dress smelled of baked bread. Her golden hair was pulled back in a bun and perspiration traced a path through a white splotch of flour on her temple. "I heard shouting." The lines around her eyes deepened with concern as she looked from her son to her husband. When Jacob started to explain the situation, Recha interrupted.

"What's so bad about kissing? It's in all the movies!"

Her father placed his hand against the small of her back and propelled her into the kitchen. "And stay there," he said.

"Forever?" the child wailed.

Jacob smiled fondly and swung his daughter off her feet. His breath came out in a huff, the way it did when he lifted a heavy crate; he set her down awkwardly, looking at her as if he realized for the first time that this spindly-limbed young lady was no longer a toddler.

"You think you're twenty again, Papa!" Mama said.

Both men chuckled and Solomon relaxed. For once he was glad he had a sister. Thanks to her, the tension seemed broken. *Now Papa will take out his snuff box,* Sol thought affectionately.

His father did not disappoint him. Pinching a little snuff between thumb and index finger, he sniffed it up and sneezed loudly several times. He blew his nose on a large white handkerchief, leaving a residue of brown snuff-stain.

"Time to take care of my son." Herr Weisser stood up and opened his hand to indicate a spanking.

"Take it easy on him, will you?" Sol's papa said, the hint of a smile on his face. "He didn't do anything any healthy boy doesn't want to do."

"Maybe you'd better come along, Jacob," Herr Weisser said, "or I'm likely to lose my temper all over again."

They are just like Erich and me, Sol thought as the two men delegated their anger to that crevice they reserved for such breaks in friendship and went together to look for Erich. After checking his bedroom, they tried the library.

Erich was there, rummaging through the drawers of his father's massive mahogany desk, strewing papers all over the hand-polished parquet floor. A vase of meticulously arranged white gladioli teetered atop the desk. Erich made no effort to keep it from falling and it crashed to the floor.

"Clean that up! Now!" his father ordered.

"C'mon, I'll help you." Sol bent and began to gather up the broken porcelain from amid the water and flowers.

Erich glared down at Sol, then continued rummaging. His eyes shone with such fury that Sol stepped backwards and bumped into Friedrich Weisser.

"Mein Gott!" Erich's father said in a tone of utter disbelief. "He's after my revolver."

"And when I find it I'll use it."

Losing all semblance of control, Friedrich Weisser hurtled forward and pushed Erich away from the desk. "Just who did you hope to shoot?" He spoke so quietly he could hardly be heard. "Me, your mother, our friends? Yourself?"

Erich steadied himself. "I hate you," he said in the same quiet voice. He held up his injured hand as if to slap his father. "You hear me, I—"

He shuddered, a slight tremor, and then blinked in surprise. Sol realized his friend had suffered another of the lightning seizures. He held his breath, but as most often happened, the slight seizure came and went so swiftly as to be almost indiscernible.

"Now you listen to me!" Erich's father took his son by the lapels. "If you ever—"

With his good hand, Erich peeled his father's fingers off his shirt. Sol watched Friedrich Weisser stand unmoving as Erich reached behind himself and, still holding up the injured hand like an icon, opened the door. For a moment, they just stood there as if posing for some ill-conceived photograph.

"Hamster," Erich said in a quiet, ugly tone. He turned and left the room. One door slammed as he left the apartment; another as he left the building.

His father started after him, but Jacob Freund gently restrained his friend. "Let him be. He'll be back."

Friedrich Weisser sat down heavily in one of the library chairs. Suddenly he looked to Sol like a very old man. "He'll never return. Not really. In body, perhaps, but never as my son."

Chapter 15

As dawn approached, Sol lay awake listening for the opening and shutting of doors and for the creaking of the apartment house's worn wooden stairs. If only I had been able to talk Rathenau into taking Erich along to the Adlon or had refused to go without Erich, he thought. Maybe none of the trouble would have happened. And mentioning the Freikorps-Youth to Rathenau! He felt guilty about that too, even if Erich did not know of the betrayal.

He had to find Erich and make him come home.

There were only two places Erich could have gone—the Freikorps camp or the sewer. Looking for him at the camp would be foolish and dangerous, especially at night; on the other hand, the last thing Sol wanted to do was go to their hideout, where the voices waited.

Still, anything was better than just lying in bed feeling bad.

He rose, dressed quickly, and crept into the kitchen. The key to the shop was in its usual place, hanging from a hook on the wall. He put it in his pocket. Erich could pick his way in through the cabaret, but Sol could not. The shop was his only hope. Once inside, he would go down to the basement and call to Erich through the tobacco-shop grate. Then Erich could let him in through the nightclub by opening the door from the inside. As soon as this crisis was over, he would ask his friend to teach him his lock-picking secrets. That would please Erich...make him feel superior.

Feeling much better, he poured himself a glass of milk and ate a piece of his mother's marble cake before wrapping up a slice for Erich, along with some cheese and liverwurst and two pieces of bread. Holding the package in one hand and his shoes in the other, he turned to leave.

"Going on a picnic?" his father asked from the shadows.

Sol started to put the package down on the counter.

"I won't keep you from sneaking food to him, nor will I say a word to Herr Weisser. But if you do this thing, you do so against my wishes. Whether or not you believe it, helping that boy defy his papa may not be in his best interests. Herr Weisser is not always right, we both know that. He is a difficult man. But Erich has to learn that he's not yet grown up—"

"But, Papa—"

"No arguments, Sol. Do what you must. However, if you go, I shall put you over my knee when you come home and spank you until my arm aches too much for me to lift it."

The emotionlessness of his father's voice bespoke his sincerity. This is all Erich's fault, Sol told himself. He gets out of line, and I am damned if I do and damned if I don't.

He hesitated. Then, trembling, he crept outside quietly, wanting to run but knowing the noise would upset Papa all the more.

Sol's plan to get into the sewer worked perfectly. Erich was there, heard him at once, and let him in through the cabaret. In their hideaway, a single candle was burnt down almost to its holder. It was too dark to see for sure, but judging by the sound of his friend's voice, he had been crying. He was wearing his uniform.

"Go home, Erich," Sol said. "Your papa will forgive you."

Erich seated himself cross-legged on the flooring crates, his hands sagged in his lap. "He'll forgive me, all right. He always does. But who needs forgiveness? I'm going to live in the camp. They'll let me stay there permanently if I promise to care for the dogs."

"Dogs can't take the place of family."

"For me they can."

Solomon handed the food package to Erich, who immediately devoured the cake.

"He just stood there looking at me," Erich said after a time. He put the cheese and meats in one of the knapsacks the boys kept among their other things in the hideout. "Never came after me or really tried to stop me from leaving. Some papa *he* is!" He wiped a tear from his cheek and glanced at Solomon as though daring his friend to comment on his crying. "Well, I know where I'm not wanted. Some of the other boys are already living at the campsite, even though we're only supposed to use it for meetings."

"Those are boys without families."

"And some who don't want families. They're the ones I want to be with." He whirled the knapsack around to his back and slipped his arms through the straps. "Come with me, Sol. You'll love it there."

"Don't be dumb! Everyone knows how your leaders feel about Jews."

Erich waved his hand airily. "That's just talk. The real toughs have joined a new unit, the Storm Troopers or something, and won't have anything to do with us."

"Forget it."

"*Your* loss." Erich picked up the candle and, apparently unconcerned that he was leaving his friend in darkness, hoisted himself onto the two-by-twelve and struggled up through the drain. He looked down at Solomon from outside the sewer; the candle cast shards of light across his face, and to Sol's surprise there was hurt in his eyes. Then he was gone.

Sol leaned against the damp wall and felt the darkness suffuse him. Exiting the sewer required only a grope and a quick climb, but the events of the past twenty-four hours had sapped his energy. He closed his eyes, painfully remembering the hope for his future—God and good government—that had fluttered in his imagination like a small bright bird as Rathenau ushered him along Wilhelmstrasse. Now the Foreign Minister and his niece were gone from him, probably forever. And the Weissers...would things ever be the same between the two families?

And what about Erich? Had he lost his best friend, too?

Oh God, let me die. A woman's voice. *I did not know...I did not know.*

Sol lurched away from the wall, flailing his arms in search of the two-by-twelve. He clutched at the plank, too distraught to scramble up, and peered around desperately in the dark. "You did not know *what?*" His words emerged as a strained croak.

My mother dug ginger roots with her bare hands.

An old man's voice, and a woman's, a different one, heavy with accent. *Looks like sweetbreads, eh Margabrook? Hungry enough to eat it?*

Lice, the old man said quietly. *Lice. Let the dead dream their dreams in peace.*

"Who *are* you!" Sol yelled in frustration, his voice resounding through the sewer. As it died away, the infant shrieked at him from the sewer's far reaches, followed by laughter and a low growling.

Snarling and snapping, something moved toward him.

A chill crept up his back and turned into a trickle of sweat. Spurred by terror, he fought to get up on the plank, kicking wildly in an effort to boost himself. His feet found the side of the sewer but failed to gain purchase on the slick bricks.

The breathing drew closer.

He gained the plank. Below him the breathing resonated strong and regular as a bellows.

His hands beat at the darkness. "Get away from me!"

Gripping the plank he frantically arched his back, straining to reach the drain. Somehow he found the power to stand. Balancing precariously he slid his hands up along the slime of the wall toward the edge of the hole and pulled himself through with an ease and strength he did not know he possessed. Then he slammed down the grate and pushed his sweat-soaked hair away from his forehead.

The creature was caged. He was safe...but from what? Would he ever understand?

What is the price of five sparrows, Solomon?

"Erich?" Sol whispered.

Laughter answered him—Erich's laughter.

The sound flooded the sub-basement with a horror far more terrifying in its familiarity than whatever unknown thing lurked beneath the grate. In some deep-down part of him that made no sense, he knew with absolute certainty that the laughter was Erich's—and that it was not human.

Chapter 16

A ginger cat meandered from the shadows and into the amber light the street lamp cast on the cracked sidewalk. Arching its back as if trying to gain warmth from the lamplight, the cat cocked its head slightly and waited as though expecting to be petted.

After glancing around to assure himself that no one would witness his avoiding the animal, Erich crossed the street and did not look back to see if the cat were still watching. Much as he loved dogs, he mistrusted cats. He had never been able to reconcile his pleasure in their sleekness and independence with their lack of loyalty.

After pulling up his shirt collar against the unexpectedly damp wind that caught him as he left the lee of the buildings, he rubbed his neck, trying to work out his exhaustion and tension. He glanced at his watch. Half past six. He had been walking for over an hour. If only he had taken Hawk, his bicycle, he would be in his camp bunk by now, dreaming of roller-skating with Miriam in the Grünewald or of sitting with her in the Schauspielhaus, watching her while she watched Rudolph Valentino play *The Sheik*—though he could not understand why she thought his effeminate looks so wonderful. As far as he was concerned, only dog and horror movies were worth seeing.

Except with Miriam.

So what, he thought, if he'd only seen her twice! He knew what he wanted, and he would take her anywhere...not that he had much chance of ever seeing her again after Papa's outburst. If only the Foreign Minister had taken *him* to luncheon too, none of this mess would have happened! What made Solomon so special? Like Papa said: Jews of a feather...

Still, it was not Solomon's fault, so he should not be angry at his friend—especially since Sol had come down to the sewer, at night yet, to make sure he was all right. Rathenau and Papa, they were the ones who had caused the problem. A rich fool and a stupid *hamster*. No wonder Herr Freund treated Papa like an underling.

He clamped his lips together and clenched his fists, fighting to harden himself against the squirrelly feeling that always formed after a fight with his father. Go home, Erich, it said. Forget what your father did and take your punishment like a man. You're smart and tough even if he isn't. You will find a way to fix things with Miriam.

The next realization followed just as inevitably. His father would not punish him. Too many hours had elapsed. The time for yelling was over; by now Papa was bound to be sleeping off a sherry sulk. Awakened, he would listen silently as Erich stammered an apology, then with a sluggish wave of his hand send him to his bedroom. After an hour or two he would come in to say he understood. And would accept. And forgive.

Who did he think he was—God?

Anger rose in Erich again, like a pot of frustration boiling over a stove whose flame would not go out. If he tried to remove the pot, his fingers would burn; if he did not, it would boil over. Again.

Abruptly, he cut through an alley toward Lutherstrasse. He would walk past the rectory and see if a light were on. Not knock or anything. But maybe Father Dahns would be outside watering the tulips before morning Mass. He would know what to do. After all, was not that what *real* Fathers were for—to fix things?

Once Mass began he could slip down the back stairs and nap for an hour among the pews stored in the basement. He knew the building well, catechism classes having been a mix of piety and hide-and-seek while Father Dahns— elderly, always smiling—alternately scolded and blessed.

Erich had loved the Mass, with its colors and mysticism, but had stopped attending two years ago. How could he confess that he adored the pageantry more than God, if indeed there were a God? After Papa's shouting, Mama's tears, and Father Dahn's questioning, amid the smiles, about Herr Weisser's own absence from church, there had come Papa's mute, angry acquiescence...and, for Erich, Sundays in the stockroom.

No. On second thought, he had better not talk to Father Dahns; it was just too complicated. Besides, he was *not* going back, no matter what Father Dahns said, not even if Papa found him and begged or beat him.

He felt in his pocket and discovered a few coins, enough to take a tram to Wannsee and the Youth camp. If only he had enough to go really far away, someplace where Papa would never find him. Munich, maybe—the camp leaders called it Heaven. Or maybe hike and camp all over Germany, as the Wandervögel had before the war.

I am as much to blame as anyone, he thought, stumbling along and blinking bleary eyes at the neon lights of the El Dorado nightclub. *Always trying to be the big shot.*

In the half-light of the overcast morning, he could see people lounging near the infamous club, smoking and laughing, waiting for the doors to open. Inside, it was said, men danced with men and kissed each other right in the open and, in darkened corners, rubbed each other's penises. Why would men do such things? Nah, it was nonsense—rumors concocted to draw people away from the Tauentzienstrasse, where women with whips and laced-up boots turned good German men into sex slaves. Like in that movie he had sneaked into—*Goddess, Whore, and Woman.* Not even Sol knew he had seen it.

Well, maybe not actually seen it, but almost. The usher had found him soon after the opening credits, so he had not really seen much and, truth to tell, he had not been sorry to be thrown out. Ugh! No wonder the papers called the film "criminal, sensational, erotic, sadistic." Erotic was one thing. He liked that word—liked how it made him feel warm inside. But the sadistic stuff—did human beings honestly do those things?

Erich avoided the figures outside the El Dorado as if they were alley cats. Afraid to turn his back on them, he moved in a wide semi-circle, fighting an urge to run as some of them looked his way and smirked. Clear of them, he swiveled and, fear chilling his exposed back, started to hurry away.

"Want a lesson, *Schatzie?*" A blowzy blonde leaned out of the shadows. She sucked deeply on a silver cigarette holder as long as a reed and blew a stream of smoke his way. "What do you say, baby-face? I'll make bacon and eggs for breakfast." Apparently mistaking his shock and curiosity for interest, she held out a languorous arm, gloved in elbow-length white lace.

Erich shook his head and, knapsack slapping against his back, dashed down one alley and rounded a corner. Bacon and eggs sounded awfully good, but thanks to Solomon he was not starving. Slowing, he licked the vestiges of Frau Freund's double chocolate icing from his fingers. That damn Solomon! Getting mad at him was easy; staying mad was impossible. He was always so *nice.*

He looked around to get his bearings, then tried another alley. It proved to be a dead-end littered with garbage and peopled by rats. Maybe he should take a tram back to the flat and forget the whole thing like Papa would—or at least he could pretend to. He ran back to the main street and found he had circled back to the alley corner, near the prostitute. He turned in another direction in the alleys' maze.

When he saw the blinking of the El Dorado neon toward the end of the next alley, he congratulated himself on how cleverly he had circumnavigated the woman. He could see three figures swathed in shadow near the nightclub's back door, but could think of no way to avoid them. With renewed bravado he decided to walk by and pretend not to notice them or what they were doing—whatever that turned out to be.

Whistling softly, he plunged his hands into his pockets and started forward. He had taken no more than a few steps when a man called to him.

"Over here. Join us—there's always room for one more."

Gorge rising in panic, Erich stopped in his tracks. He stared in the direction of the voice. Otto Hempel was slurring his words slightly. Like Papa, when he's had too much to drink, Erich thought. Nonetheless, there was no mistaking the voice—or the silver hair.

Run, he told himself. *Get away.*

But the same combination of fascination and horror he had experienced in the movie theater kept his feet planted as firmly as if he had taken root on Lutherstrasse.

"A shy one, huh? Rather just watch, would you?" The Youth-group leader laughed softly. "Well, that's all right too. But why not move closer? I'd like to see your face."

Leaning against the building, Hempel placed one hand against the back of the head of a blond youth kneeling in front of him. His other hand held what appeared to be a riding crop. A uniform jacket lay crumpled on the sidewalk, beside his feet. Near the jacket, head lowered and bare to the waist, was a second boy about Erich's age.

Raising his hand high in the air, Hempel whipped down hard on the youth's bare shoulder. The boy whimpered but did not cry out.

"Don't!" Erich's shout emerged as a gargled whisper through the bile in his throat. Finally able to move, he started toward the youth and held out his hand to help him to his feet.

The boy shook him off. "Get away!" He stared up at Erich, his eyes filled with hatred. "Find your own. This one's ours!"

"More! Beg for more." Hempel's voice was husky.

"More!"

Even in the half-light, Erich could see thick red welts forming where the crop had bitten into the boy's skin, crisscrossing each other as again and again the crop came down. Then Hempel groaned loudly and, tossing the whip aside, pressed down on the blond head with both hands. He moved against the boy's head with short, purposeful jabs.

Crawling forward, the second youth joined his friend and knelt at Hempel's feet.

Feeling sicker than he ever had in his life, Erich turned and ran blindly down Lutherstrasse. Where he was going did not matter—home, Munich, the camp—as long as he put distance between himself and what he had just seen.

Chapter 17

"Solomon. Wake up."

"It can't be time." Sol groaned. He had tossed and turned until well beyond daylight, hopelessly trying to make sense of Erich's overreaction and of the horrible voices and sounds in the sewer. He felt as if he had only just closed his eyes. "Erich hasn't—"

He started to say that Erich had not banged on the floor upstairs the way he did every morning so they could walk to the *Gymnasium* together. Then he remembered it was Saturday—*Shabbas*—the day Erich went to school without him. He had slept right through his friend's morning noises.

"Must I go to synagogue?" Sol asked, knowing full well what the answer would be, especially so close to his bar mitzvah. "I hate missing school."

"Hate is not a word to be used so lightly," his father said. "Besides, there are schools and there are schools. At times one becomes more important than the other. If we allowed you to go to school on *Shabbas,* it would make trouble for those Jewish children whose parents forbid it." He opened the curtains and stared out the window. "Already it's too late for us to get to the morning study group. You were sleeping so soundly, your mother and I decided not to wake you. Now get a move on. I intend to be there in time for services. These days, fewer and fewer people come to *shul*—they will need me to make a *minyan* for morning services."

"Are Mama and Recha coming?"

"Mama has a headache. Recha must stay with her."

Pushing aside his eiderdown, Sol swung his legs over the side of the bed. It gave him a sense of pride to think that once he had been bar mitzvahed, he could help make up the *minyan*—the ten men needed before a service could be conducted. For now, though, he counted only as the son of Jacob Freund.

Picking up Sol's glasses, which lay lenses down on the night stand, Jacob breathed on them and rubbed them vigorously with the edge of Sol's sheet.

"Still angry with me about that spanking I gave you last weekend?" He handed Sol the glasses.

Sol put a hand on his behind.

Jacob Freund smiled sadly. "Some lessons can only be learned when pressure is brought to bear. You will have to make many more...painful, shall we say...decisions in your life. Teaching you cause and effect is part of my job."

"But—"

His papa silenced him with a wave of the hand. "But? There are no *buts*. We both did what we had to do—you felt you had to help your friend, I felt you were doing yourself and his family an injustice by encouraging the estrangement between Erich and his papa. Now get dressed. It will do us good to sit together under the eyes of God."

As he was getting ready, Sol replayed the events of the week. His being with Herr Rathenau. Erich threatening his papa. The monster snapping at his heels in the sewer and the inhuman laughter that, somehow, incomprehensibly, was Erich's. Except for his luncheon with the Foreign Minister, the events seemed less like reality than the ghoulish, neo-Gothic movies playing all over Berlin: *Dr. Caligari*—and *The Golem*, which had Judaic implications.

Erich had been acting very peculiarly the whole week. His moodiness was nothing new, nor was his quick temper, but at least he had shared things before. This week, he had been uncommunicative, refusing to talk about where he had gone after he left the sewer, not answering when Sol why he had not gone to live at the camp after all. He had not even talked about Miriam and, if that were not strange enough, he had stayed in his room listening to music, and reading. *Erich, reading!*

Half an hour later, Sol and his father were on their way to the Zoo Station to take the S-Bahn to the Grünewald—a concession to the late hour, since they usually obeyed the Sabbath law and walked all the way. Even from the station, it was a fair walk to the synagogue, which lay nestled among the oaks and chestnut trees that proliferated in the lush suburb. Berlin's most affluent citizens, including Walther Rathenau, had villas there, and Erich's camp was only a couple of kilometers away, a short rowboat ride across the Wannsee.

What if Erich had played truant from school, as he often did, and they came across him strutting down the road in his uniform?

The idea was enough to make Sol genuinely anxious to get to *shul*. Anything was better than the possibility of having to explain Erich's uniform to Papa. Even if he would soon be considered a man in the eyes of God, the contemplation of such a thing sent his stomach going into the kind of loop it did on the roller coaster at Luna Park. Perhaps if he gave himself up to the sense of peace that pervaded the synagogue, God would see fit to send him some rationale for the events of the past week.

"We should hurry, Papa, or we'll be late."

His father smiled and increased his pace. Minutes later they were in the foyer of the synagogue, greeting the beadle at the door and donning their *yarmulkes*. Skullcaps in place, they slipped into their assigned seats near the *bimah,* the pulpit.

Sol craned his neck and looked upstairs where the women sat, just in case Miriam had come to services. There were rarely women at morning services, even on Saturdays. They came mostly on Friday nights and holidays, when services were as much a social as a religious event. As Papa had often explained, even an Orthodox temple like this was not designed simply for prayer; it was a gathering place for Jews, a center of safety where they could exchange ideas—a meeting place. While the men did their socializing on the steps of the temple, in the community room, and on the grounds, many of the women—restricted from the acts of ritual in the synagogue, though not less dedicated to God—were not quite as disciplined. Like most boys, until he had begun his bar mitzvah studies Sol had prayed upstairs with his mother and sister. He did not quite understand why the men and women were separated, but he had rather liked it up there in the balcony, where he could watch the sunlight on the stained-glass roof of the tiny *shul* and look down proudly on the congregation of men wearing hand-embroidered skullcaps and wrapped in *tallis,* silk shawls that covered the shoulders of their *Shabbas* suits. They bent over prayer books and sang in deep and varied voices to their God and the God of their fathers. While the men repeated the ancient words that gave them such extraordinary comfort, he would listen as the women quietly gossiped, commented on each other's hats, decried the behavior of their children, and defended themselves against the shushes of the more devout women who had come to pray.

When Sol was sure Miriam was not there, he opened his prayer book. The Hebrew letters swam around on the page as if defying him to set them in place. He had the feeling someone was staring at him, and it was all he could do not to swivel around and look up again.

Deciding that he might as well practice his Hebrew, he concentrated on the Service. As always, once he gave himself over to it, he enjoyed the songs and the familiarity of the prayers. Even the sermon did not bore him, and by half past ten, having wished the rabbi and various members of the congregation a good Sabbath, he was almost sorry to be going home.

"Aren't we staying for the *Oneg Shabbat?*" he asked, referring to the bread and wine served after Sabbath Services.

"Not today," Jacob said. "We have been indoors enough. It's such beautiful weather. We shall walk home through the Tiergarten."

The day may have been beautiful in his father's prayer-misted eyes; in truth it was typically overcast. Even so, Sol enjoyed walking, especially in the Tiergarten when the smell of oncoming rain heightened the scent of the trees and masked the city's noxious odors. He liked to watch men in their double-breasted suits move arm-in-arm with their fashionable ladies toward the restaurants that dotted the Tiergarten's western edge. Sometimes he made bets with himself about which of them would end up at The Cigar Box, just beyond.

Surrounded by city and smoke, Berliners considered the two-hundred-hectare park their Eden, a notion the boys shared. They loved the arboretum and zoo, the restaurants and lake and open fields. There was plenty of room for playing ball, for roller skating and riding bicycles. On lazier days they filled their pockets with acorns and chestnuts or simply watched the passengers riding past in open-topped, double-decker buses that rang their way from Potsdamer Platz to Pariser Platz and the Brandenburg Gate. Sometimes they lay near the lake on a palette of daisies and pansies and watched the young lovers who drifted by in rowboats, walked hand-in-hand along the narrow pathways, or monopolized benches that prostitutes considered their private domain.

Sol felt good strolling with his father in companionable silence up the Konigsallee, each in his own way enjoying the rare opportunity of unhurried time together. Perhaps when they reached the Tiergarten, he would broach the subject of Erich's unfathomable anger. Perhaps even confide in Papa about the sewer.

Jacob Freund slowed to indulge in a pinch of snuff. "Our city is all business and energy," he said. "Men must have cigars to consummate business deals, and women cigarettes to contemplate how to spend the money their husbands make. On weekends they smoke to assure themselves the past week has been successful and that next week shall be even more successful. It is a good arrangement, an excellent legacy for you someday, Solomon, despite these inflationary times. For Erich, too."

He smiled. "You know how his father came to be with me? I advertised for help on Saturdays. He was hired to be our *Shabbas* goy, our Sabbath Gentile, as Mama called him. By the time I was inducted, he knew the business...I thought running it while I was away would stabilize him. Six years, it has been...."

Sol had heard the story many times. He nodded and mumbled once in a while as if he were listening, and returned to thinking about the events of the past week. He was pleased to be forgiven for the fuss he had made about playing the cello. As for the spanking, Papa had told him that was a matter of a lesson to be learned rather than punishment. They had not talked much about Rathenau or the luncheon—

What about Rathenau? Sol asked himself, as they passed the small local police station. Would there be more luncheons? Would the statesman keep his promise to make him a member-in-training of a generation of German

Jews committed "to God and good government"? Or had Erich—and Miriam—ruined that?

"See that man? Chances are, even he buys a cigar now and then." Jacob pointed at a house being constructed across the street, next to the trolley stop. A bricklayer in coveralls lifted his peaked cap and grinned down at two women in nurses' uniforms who had stopped beneath his scaffolding.

"How goes it, Helene?" the workman shouted, balancing precariously.

The shorter of the two women smiled and waved. "Fine, Krischbin!" She had her hands cupped near her mouth to be heard above the late-morning traffic. "Still slapping up bricks, I see. You must like it up there."

"Who's your friend with the big blue eyes?"

The women grinned at each other. The second woman laughed and straightened her gray skirt. "Fräulein Steubenrauch," she called out. "Judith."

"Steubenrauch, huh! Related to the general?"

The women nodded and Krischbin looked impressed. "I did a job for him once. Liked him well enough. But his son was—" The man touched his temple as if to indicate derangement. "Fancied himself a revolutionary. Kept talking to me about joining his organization and helping to rid the Fatherland of—"

The woman's face soured. "Hans is just a boy."

"He has a mean mouth," the man said. "You should—"

A Daimler Benz neared, drowning out his words.

Sol pulled at his father's sleeve. "In the car, Papa—it's Herr Rathenau!"

"And why not? His house is practically around the corner from *shul*. For shame he is never seen in synagogue when he lives so close. It might do the girl good, too, to be taken there once in a while."

Sol imagined Miriam dancing the cancan on her way to services, making partners of the birch trees, their trunks encased in silver leotards. As the car cruised past them, he waved, but the Foreign Minister was not looking his way.

"Do you think he will ever bring Miriam to see us again, Papa?"

A second convertible, this one with the top down and carrying three young men, closed on Rathenau's car as it slowed for the S-curve.

"Maybe someday. For now, he'll probably seclude her at his estate or send her to his sister in Switzerland. A word in the wrong ear, and Berlin will buzz with talk of Jewish immorality. Herr Rathenau can ill afford that kind of—"

Screeching tires interrupted him. The second car was overtaking Rathenau's, forcing it to the side of the road. The Foreign Minister, looking angered, shook his walking stick. They're in for it now, Sol thought, staring in disbelief at the rudeness of the rowdy occupants of the other car.

One of the youths—all three of whom were wearing leather jackets and caps—leaned toward Rathenau's car. Probably to apologize, Sol thought, looking at the young man's healthy, open face and reassuring smile.

"No!" Fräulein Steubenrauch screamed.

Tucking a machine pistol in his armpit to steady it, the young man fired point-blank at the statesman, who threw back his arms and collapsed.

"*Um Gottes Willen.*" Jacob knocked Solomon to the sidewalk and landed on top of the him. "*Don't move!*"

From beneath his father, Sol blinked up at a crazy-tilting, slow-motion world. He could see the workman gesturing frantically at the nurses as he flattened himself on the swaying scaffolding.

Another of the leather-coated men stood upright. Clinging to the top of the windshield, he threw an egg-shaped object. It bounced on the tonneau and fell from the roof of the enclosed rear compartment of Rathenau's car into the street, where it lay spinning.

As the larger car started to roar away onto Wallotstrasse, the man tossed a second grenade, arm swinging with a follow-through.

The bomb went through Rathenau's open window and landed in the back seat. Konrad, screaming for help, tacked crazily to the left and pulled up on the tramlines near the entrance to Erdener Strasse.

"Herr Rathenau!" Sol yelled.

An explosion erupted. Rathenau's car seemed to rise and jump forward. The body in the back tossed upward like one of Recha's rag dolls, and Sol heard himself screaming.

Shrieking, Helene left her friend and ran toward Rathenau's car. She climbed in and bent over the Foreign Minister. Sol imagined him slumped, gazing toward the gray sky, mouth open, face covered with blood.

Konrad mashed gears and sent the Daimler squealing in reverse. He jammed the gears again, did a screeching U-turn onto the wrong side of the street, and raced away in the direction of the police station.

"They've killed him, Papa!"

Jacob Freund rolled off his son and sat on hands and knees, watching in shock as the workman climbed from his scaffolding and helped Fraülein Steubenrauch to her feet. As Sol started to stand, Jacob grabbed him by the lapels and pulled Sol's face close to his own, which was chalk-white.

"I wish you long life." His words were the ones Jews use to cover that moment of shock when death reminds you that you are not immortal.

"I wish you long life too, Papa!" Sol desperately wanted to cry, but no tears came. "Herr Rathenau, Papa! Wasn't he a good man?"

Shaking with fury, Jacob held Sol's cheeks, fingernails digging into the skin. "There is nothing Rathenau can do for us anymore," he said in a hoarse whisper, "but there *is* one thing you can do for him. Remember this day. Remember that we Jews can never be safe from our enemies. And may God help you, Solomon Freund, if you ever forget!"

Sobbing, Sol struggled to free himself. He watched Fraülein Steubenrauch stumble across the tram tracks and stagger in a daze down the street. Seeing the unexploded grenade lying on the pavement like a *dreidel,* he jerked from his father's grasp and ran toward her, waving frantically. "Get back!"

The world roared.

Instinctively he threw himself against the curb, sobbing with fear and sorrow as bits of metal and dirt rained against the back of his jacket.

Then silence filled the morning as if a storm had abruptly stopped. Summoning his courage he turned his head and saw the woman sprawled, twisting and squirming, on the pavement.

"Please don't be dead." He crawled toward her.

She momentarily lifted herself with her arms, blinking as though she were waking. Her nurse's uniform was shredded, her face and shoulders splotched with blood.

"I convinced myself they wouldn't do it," her lips told Sol. "I could have...have...warned Herr Rathenau, but I was afraid to get involved. I was afraid...." She laid her cheek against the pavement as if it were a goose-down pillow, and sighed.

Whimpering, Sol picked up one of the cartridge cases scattered along the street. "Don't be...dead." He held it out to her between forefinger and thumb, like an offering.

She looked up at him, her cobalt-blue eyes shining with tears. He felt himself swimming inside them, drawn into her dying. Filled with terror, he felt something rise from her and fight to enter his body as she shuddered, sighed, and lay still. He began to shake.

"There was nothing either of us could do," his father said, coming up behind Sol. Stooping he took the woman's pulse. Then, releasing her wrist, he held Sol in his arms. When Sol's sobs had quieted, Jacob shrugged off the jacket of his *Shabbas* suit and draped it over her. He glanced around anxiously as police-car klaxons rang through the Grünewald.

"This is no place for a Jew to be found." He took Sol's hand and led him away. "May God rest her soul."

"Something happened to me, Papa!" Sol was sobbing. "I could feel—"

A fog enveloped his mind. In a world that seemed a dream, he was aware of a taxi, its door yawning. The glass that separated passenger from driver seemed to hold an image of Walther Rathenau, composed and elegant and gracious as they threaded their way toward the Adlon; and superimposed upon that was a vision of the statesman, slumped over and covered with blood. When they stopped on Friedrich Ebert Strasse, he recognized the shop and the need to vomit.

"Have you heard the news?" Friedrich Weisser asked as they entered the cigar store.

"We saw it all," Jacob said.

"Saw it! My word!" Friedrich wiped his hands on his apron, his eyes sparkling with envy. "Is it possible? They say the chauffeur miraculously wasn't hurt by the grenade."

"There were two grenades."

"Two! Nothing about *that* on the radio."

Sol's mother came hurrying across the street, her shawl fluttering. "Jacob! Solomon! I've been so worried!"

"We're fine, Ella. Sol's dazed. But fine."

"We must close the shop," Friedrich Weisser said. "The radio said people are already entering the streets to demonstrate against the murder. There could be looting."

"Yes. Close the shop," Jacob said. "Who is demonstrating?"

"Workers from the factories. They say they'll be marching four deep within the hour—"

"We must join them."

Ella Freund touched her husband's arm. "But there could be danger. They will never miss us if we mourn him here, at home."

"We shall join them nevertheless," Jacob said. "All of us."

His wife turned away. "You men are all the same. If Walther Rathenau, may he rest in peace, had listened to his mother, he would be alive. They say she did everything she could to stop him from becoming Foreign Minister. She knew his life would be in danger."

Sol heard the conversation but could not respond to it. Once in the apartment, he came out of his stupor. He felt strange. Angry. Sad. He knew something had happened, something more than the obvious tragedy, but he did not know what. He was grateful when his mother suggested they do something normal, like wash up and eat lunch, yet he felt guilty that he was hungry.

"It's nearly one," she said. "Who knows when we'll get home?"

Apparently sensing his son's discomfort, Jacob looked across the table at Sol. "Life must go on," he told Solomon. "Eat your soup."

Sol did so, and was washing the bowl when he heard Herr Weisser yelling. Please, no more trouble, he thought, opening the front door. Erich stood in the main foyer, in uniform. He *wants* his papa to get angry, Sol thought, remembering what Erich had said about his father. What he cannot stand is his papa's weakness. Why can't Herr Weisser see that?

"So! Now you're wearing your defiance," Herr Weisser said. "Go to your room and change. I'll give you," Friedrich glanced at his watch, "two minutes."

Erich climbed to the next landing and looked down over the banister. His voice sounded choked with anger, though whether at himself or at his father, Sol could not tell. "I'm not going anywhere. Especially not with you."

Visibly controlling his temper, Friedrich went up the stairs and, bending before his son, straightened the boy's Freikorps tie. "They've shot Herr

Rathenau. There's a demonstration. We do business in this city. We cannot afford not to pay our respects...all of us."

Erich pulled away and went up further. He's dead—that's all that matters to me. *Rathenau, old Walther, shall have a timely halter!*" he sang, insolently and off-key, staring at Sol, who had seen the German youth song printed in the *Social Democrat.*

Please don't sing the rest, Erich, Sol begged silently, remembering the last lines: *Shoot down Walther Rathenau...The Goddamned swine of a Jewish sow.*

"Shoot—" Erich began.

Something's boiling over in him, Sol thought. Something that's been brewing all week.

Face reddening, Friedrich started after the boy, but Frau Weisser gently caught her husband by the wrist and slightly, darkly, shook her head. Sol heard Erich race up the remaining stairs, unlock the apartment, and slam the door behind himself.

"It's not my place to interfere between parents and son, but we're all involved." Jacob climbed a step and reached out a hand to his friends. "We will always be involved with one another. What the boy has done is despicable. You must make him come with us. Can't you see he's crying out for you to be strong?"

"You knew about this uniform he wears?" Herr Weisser asked Solomon, raising his hand.

Sol backed away, sure he was going to be struck. "He told me not to tell."

"You knew, yet said nothing!" Then a look of vapid acceptance came over Friedrich. "You are not to blame, Solomon." He shook his head sadly. "It is that *boy* up there. I keep telling myself—" he was speaking to Jacob now— "it is because of the seizures, but we cannot blame everything on those. I cannot remember when Erich was not rebellious. My papa used to tell me, 'Life is not always cause and effect, despite what your so-called science claims.' I should have listened to his advice. I should have understood." He took his wife's hand. "We go now, Mama. The boy can do as he wishes. He always has."

Without waiting for Erich, the five of them went down the stairs, out the main door and into the June sun, which had broken through the clouds. Before long, they were part of a spontaneous, giant procession snaking silently up Unter den Linden toward the Reichstag. Already, people said, Rathenau was being brought there to lie in state.

Gone were the ladies in expensive hats and the riders who used the grassy sides of the boulevard to exercise themselves and their horses, gone the men in top hats and the children and toy poodles.

The workers owned the boulevard. They marched, faces set and in silence, alongside street-corner hooligans, politicians, and prostitutes. Like an orderly lynch mob, they moved steadily forward, four and then six abreast as people joined from every alley and side street.

Above the crowd, the black-red-gold banners of the Republic waved in the breeze alongside the red banners of socialism. Politics were set aside for the first time in over a decade as Berlin mourned a statesman who had begun to set into motion his personal dream of a better Germany through negotiation.

"He was so much the aristocrat," Friedrich Weisser said, his mouth close to Jacob's ear. In order to talk to his partner, he had to lean over Solomon, who marched between the two men. "I never realized he had such a following among the working class."

"In a year, they will claim he was purely a man of the people." Jacob Freund was staring straight ahead. "They will even conveniently forget he was a Jew."

For the first time in his life, Sol felt his father's bitterness as his own. "In a year," Sol said, "they will blame his murder on the Jews."

Chapter 18

"It's been some time since your bar mitzvah, Sol," Beadle Cohen said. "I have missed you. Will you be returning for advanced Judaic studies?"

Sol rubbed his temples, hoping to ease his headache. Bar mitzvah boys went two ways: some swore they would never read another word of Hebrew or Judaica in their lives; others, suddenly filled with sentiment, expressed the intention of becoming rabbis or Hebrew scholars and never doing anything else. Unsure of how he felt, he had devoted what little time he had—when not studying or working for Papa—to reading and rereading his growing library of books on Jewish mysticism.

He had come to no conclusions, except to decide that, for the time being, he fell somewhere between the cracks.

As a bar mitzvah gift, the beadle, already responsible for the library of mystical books in Sol's room, had given him the *Book of Formation* and the first book of the Lurianic Kabbalah. Both were inscribed with his usual message: "When you are ready, you will understand."

Thus far, all Sol understood was that Luria believed Jews were born with a consciousness of their heritage—a sort of untapped well of accumulated experience and knowledge.

"Beadle Cohen, I need your guidance. I know I want to continue learning," he said, "but I don't really want to be part of a set traditional program."

As always, the beadle got straight to the point. "You don't look well. Is there something I can do to help you?"

Sol paced around the beadle's study—wondering where and how to begin—suppressing the urge to shout, scream, throw something across the room. He was moody and depressed most of the time, struggling with unaccountable angers, convinced he was being haunted by the soul of the woman who had practically died in his arms, and fighting blinding headaches. The voices came more and more, repeating words and phrases that made no sense.

"I have nightmares," he said slowly. "I see Erich hanging from the grating. I hear...sounds. Strange, ugly laughter that is Erich's, but isn't human."

Except for the bar mitzvah, which Erich had attended despite the pressure of his Freikorps-Youth friends, Sol had seen little of his friend since Rathenau's death. He knew that the Weissers had finally given Erich permission to belong to the group, and he had watched Erich's uniformed comings and goings, but they had not done anything together. They had not even gone to the hideout, which was just as well. He was still trying to escape his memories of the assassination and of Erich's ugly behavior that day.

"I keep thinking Rathenau's assassins are after me...."

"Tillessen, von Salomon, and the Techow brothers are in prison," the beadle said.

Sol knew that. And Kern and Fischer, the ringleaders of what had proven to be a conspiracy, had been tracked down, too. One was shot to death; the other committed suicide. Yet in his nightly imaginings, they came to his window, holding knives and grenades, looking for the boy-witness.

"I get headaches," he said. "I hear voices...one woman cries out *'Oh God, let me die. I did not know...I did not know.'* Another talks of *sweetbreads* to someone called Margabrook who speaks to her of lice and the dreams of dead men."

Haltingly he told the beadle about the sounds in the sewer, and about the feeling that something had entered him, taken possession of him as he had looked into the eyes of the dying woman.

The beadle listened without interruption. "Ever see flashes of light?" he asked when Sol fell silent.

Sol nodded. "Right before the headaches come. The doctor says it's part of them."

"That is one possibility. There are others. You have read *The Book of Formation?*"

Again Sol nodded. Terrified, searching for answers, he had read and reread it. The more he came to understand, the more afraid he became.

"Solomon ben Luria was a mystic and a prophet," the beadle said. "He knew the past and had visions of the future. They were always presaged by brilliant flashes of light."

"I see nothing. I just hear voices, over and over—"

"Give it time, Sol."

"Are you saying—"

"God has the answers. The only help I can offer is to suggest possibilities."

"For example?"

"Are you sure you want to hear this, Solomon?" The beadle looked extremely serious. When Sol nodded, the beadle sighed in resignation and said, "All right, then. I'll tell you what I think. I have known you for a long time, Sol, and I do not say this lightly. I believe it is entirely possible that, like Ben

Luria, you are a visionary. I also believe you have a dybbuk in you, and that it is muddying your abilities. When...if...the dybbuk leaves you, everything will become clear."

"I don't what any...any *thing* in me," Sol said, then mentally backed away, embarrassed even to countenance such an outrageous possibility. Like most Jewish boys, he had heard of dybbuks—vaguely—some kind of soul that was unable to transmigrate to a higher world because the person had sinned against humanity.

"I just think I'm going crazy," he said. "Am I? Tell me...*please!*

"Sometimes," the beadle said, "dybbuks seek refuge in the bodies of living persons, causing instability, speaking foreign words through their mouths."

"You're saying that *that's* what is wrong with me?" Sol asked, dazed.

"Perhaps."

"Well, get rid of it! It's affecting my schoolwork. It's affecting my whole life! My parents are worried—and I don't blame them. I can't talk to them about something like... How could I possibly tell them!" Exasperated, he put his head in his hands.

The beadle waited for Sol to calm down. "Sometimes a rabbi can exorcise a dybbuk," he said at last. "But that is not always the right answer. You are strong, Solomon. For those who are strong, a dybbuk can open doors into worlds that other men cannot enter. Eventually it will depart as it came—unbidden—and then you will understand its message. Go home and think about it."

Leaving the question of his studies unanswered, Sol went home. That night, lying in bed, he wished he had opened himself up to the beadle sooner. He had almost forgotten how much he treasured their discussions. The man was the only person he knew who was not afraid to acknowledge the difference between rhetoric and original thought. He really listened, debated each point, gave of his knowledge, yet left the conclusions open so that Sol never felt like a young know-nothing fool when he expressed his views.

It was amazing, Sol thought, how quickly life could change. Bedtime had once been the best part of his day. In bed, it had no longer mattered that when he took off his glasses he could not see things in sharp focus. He had liked the way his lace curtains clothed the night sky in crisscross patterns and the way the moon looked dressed in lace. He had even made up stories about moon men and about beautiful princesses held captive in lunar craters.

But, as with so many other things in his life, the death of Walther Rathenau had altered all that. Reality had conspired to draw aside the lace curtains in his life. These days, after his parents made sure he was in bed and closed the door, his inclination was to reach for his glasses; as he watched the clouds chase each other across the moon, his head was filled with thoughts of the Adlon luncheon and of assassins who lusted after blood and power, instead of Hessian princes who fought moon men with swords bejeweled with stars. More often than not, he fell asleep with his glasses on, even on nights like this when he could see the full moon with clarity. Ringed with dark clouds, it was set in a night filled with questions. Why did God allow assassins? Why am I a Jew first and a German second? Falling asleep was no longer an easy drifting, but a time for doubts and fear—and headaches—

He felt a sharp stab of pain in his left temple. Groaning he pressed his knuckles into the pain. There was another stab of pain and a flash of light which dissolved into pinpoints floating in the night like fireflies. A cobalt-blue glow superimposed itself over the darkness and he huddled, terrified, under his eiderdown.

Don't think about it, Margabrook. Just drink the tea, he heard a woman say, her voice familiar.

Best you get rid of it now, Peta, a man said. Sol knew the voice well. *If you don't acknowledge the soldiers' twisted idea of a joke, who knows what they will put in the teapot the next time.*

Then the lights...and the headache...were gone. All that was left was the blue glow and, emerging out of it——

——*a paraffin lamp casts a lavender shadow across a rude table in the center of a one-room wooden shack.* Snow blows through gaps in the wall-boards. Beyond a single small window, curled edges of snowdrifts mass like breaking waves. Smoke veils the ceiling. A man in a ragged army overcoat and woolen scarf huddles close to a brazier's red coals. Frostbite has scabbed and pockmarked his dark sunken cheeks. His eyes are dull, his hands wrapped in bloodstained gauze. An emaciated woman wearing an old blanket, an ancient carbine slung across her back, steps from the shadows in the corner and leans over him. Carefully she unwinds the gauze from one of his hands. The fingers are gangrenous stumps.

Eyeing the old man angrily, the woman uses the edge of her blanket as a pot holder and removes the cast-iron teapot from the brazier's grate. She raises the lid of the teapot and looks inside.

Her face hardens.

"You've seen worse," the old man mutters. Lifting the edge of his coat, he unsheathes and hands her the bayonet that was strapped to his leg. "Pick out the thing and save the tea."

She has started to pour the contents of the teapot into the snow through a large crack between two of the unplaned floorboards. Apparently deciding the old man is right, she takes the knife and clanks it around inside the pot.

"What a waste." She pulls out a steaming thumb, stuck through with the knife. "Looks like sweetbreads, eh Margabrook?" She swipes the knife against the brazier. The thumb slides off the blade and onto the floor; she pokes at it like a child worrying a snail.

"Doesn't matter what it looks like," the old man says. "Don't even think about putting it in your mouth. Between us, we get enough food to stay alive."

"So what."

"You'll hate yourself."

"The only thing worth hating is hunger." The woman reinserts the bayonet and turns the thumb over to scrutinize it. "You Nazis! *Your* mandate is hatred. *Mine* is survival."

"Nazi? No! But I *am* German, and proud of it." He lowers his voice. "I joined the Nazis because, like you, I thought survival was everything. I have learned. It is what survives in *here* that counts." He thumps his chest with a gauze-wrapped fist. "Retain what little dignity the world still accords you, Peta. Forget what the others out there have become and leave that thing alone."

"You don't know what hunger is," she says. "When you had nothing to eat, you fed on idealism. I've had none of that with which to fill my belly or heart."

Unbuttoning his coat, the old man takes out a tin cup and holds it up. The woman fills it and her own cup from the teapot, gulps down her tea, and pours herself a second cup.

"What I'd give for fresh goat's milk," he says, touching palsied fingers to his lips as if complimenting the chef. "You city dwellers know nothing of such delicacies. My mother milked the goats every morning—"

An explosion rattles the shack and snow billows through the cracks. The old man shakes his head sadly and returns to his tea, ignoring the yellow and red starbursts that bruise what sky can be seen through the window. "Again the steppes test us," he says, putting down his cup.

The woman unslings the carbine and checks the bolt, dry-firing the weapon three times. "Here, put on your *Kopfschützer,* old man." She hands him a balaclava. Having pulled one over her own head, she helps him up. "Make sure there's enough paper stuffed inside or your ears will fall off from the cold, like Hansie's did."

On crippled feet he hobbles to the door and waits for her to open it. A gust of wind pulls it from her hand and slams it against the outer wall of the hut.

Facing them is a long gentle slope ending in what appears to be a frozen lake shining like a silver platter beneath thick low clouds. Except for clumps of rushes, feathery with ice and sticking up here and there at windblown angles, the area seems without vegetation—a white treeless waste. Along the edge of the lake, white-clad infantry move like phantoms before a line of tanks. Bursts of smoke from the armored vehicles are followed seconds later by the sharp crack of firing and sprays of snow farther up the hill.

At the crest of the hill, behind a breastwork of what looks like ice-covered logs, a group of men crank howitzer barrels into position. Others pull white canvas tarpaulins off mortars and machine guns. From that distance, the men and machinery look like a collection of animated pewter miniatures.

"I've had goat's milk." As she surveys the battle scene, the woman speaks as if their conversation has never been interrupted. "I have eaten and drunk almost anything you can name."

"Your family was wealthy?"

Through knee-deep snow they crunch uphill toward the gunnery. From all over the hill, people like them emerge from huts and, like disconnected threads, move toward the battlement.

"Non-practicing Jews and Party members like us managed some luxuries," she says. "Unfortunately, Papa had reservations about the Party and talked too much. Someone informed on him. They convened a Kolhosp court and accused us of being exploiters of the poor—*Kurkuls*. My parents were sent to help dig the Baltic Sea-White Sea Canal, or so we children were told."

Her expression softens as she speaks of her parents. Now it hardens again. "They disappeared. The Komsomol sent my brothers and me to a collective and assigned us to the worst of the subunits—the crocodiles."

The man nods, saying nothing.

"They said we who gobbled the bread of the Soviets had to meet harvest quotas. We were villagers and townspeople competing against farmers and even they could not meet the quota, because whenever they did, it was raised."

She halts in front of a pair of boots sticking out of a snowdrift. "These will keep the chilblains away from my toes." She tugs at them. "Come on. Help me."

The old man bends to help. They both pull, but nothing budges.

"If we failed to meet the quota, we were put on the *chorna doshka*, the blacklist." Gasping, she lets loose of the boots. "Our rations were halved. Not until the Soviet is satisfied! they'd tell us. Nurse the fields. Nurture them. Fill up on the conscience of the collective!"

"Bastards," the old man says. "I was much luckier than you. I grew up in the Oberharz, in Hahenklee, right next door to Paul Lincke's house. Once he even walked to Goslar with us, to watch the figures dance around the old town Glockenspiel. He said they should be dancing to *his* music. Often my friends and I watched the cable car carry tourists around Bad Lauterberg and or watched them eat cake in the cafés. Before going home, we dug in the garbage for leftovers. When the tourists stopped coming, we roasted crickets and field mice and picked gooseberries and wild mushrooms. We thought ourselves kings--except for those who died because they could not tell toadstools from *Steinpilze*."

"They say seven-hundred thousand have died in the Ukraine," the woman says. "God only knows how many of those starved to death! We thought it a blessing when you Nazis came to liberate our village. We thought you'd put us in ghettos and leave us alone."

She looks up; the howitzers are returning fire. "Lend me your ax," she says.

The old man ignores her demand. "When this war started, I was too old to enlist. Like an idiot, I pulled strings and became a soldier for the Reich! I was assigned to an extermination center in eastern Poland. Would you believe I thought I'd be killing lice? *Lice!*"

"You're an old fool, Margabrook."

"Daily there came new truckloads of Jews. They were asked for volunteers who could operate heavy equipment. The endloaders were assigned to dig graves. Each hour we shot so many people we had to soak our rifle barrels in cold water to cool them." He snorted sarcastically. "The Jews dying by the hundreds, and we worried about rust! At twilight, when the graves were filled and covered, our Untersturmführer made the endloader operators lie on the mounds, heads together and feet outward like daisy petals. Then he shot them in the stomach and watched them bleed to death. A flower of death to commemorate man's capacity for evil."

"I suppose that is why you won't carry a carbine, even here at the Front?"

"There are no real Fronts. This is a world without Fronts. Only backstabbing and lies...lies," he repeats softly.

"You're right, old man. Now give me your ax or I will take it from you."

He touches her arm and points at the breastworks. "Let the dead dream their dreams in peace. Look at them. A wall of dead soldiers masquerading as logs to protect their living comrades in a treeless land."

He steps closer to the battlement. The woman follows.

"Don't give in...as I did." He stares at the frozen bodies. Icy limbs protrude in impossibly contorted positions. Faces are molded into snow-covered masks.

The woman shrugs. "Stalin starves people, Hitler shoots them, we use them as logs. What's the difference?" When he doesn't answer, she turns back toward the boots. "The hatchet, please, old man. I am younger and stronger than you are, and I intend to survive. I want those boots. When the rest of you run out of paper to wrap your feet in, mine will be warm."

He hands her the hatchet. "Three days now the clouds have held." Knee-deep in snow, the old man looks up at the sky. A worker next to him grabs hold of a corpse and flops it down as if it is a sandbag. The old man glances at it, then at a row of fresh bodies. The setting sun—its palette congealed blood and military uniforms—decorates the dead with ribbons of russet and gold.

With the woman's first determined swing, one of the soldier's legs cracks like a large dry stick——

Sol sat upright. His heart was pounding madly, but his headache was gone. So were the blue glow and the voices. All that remained was the stillness of midnight.

He recalled that the beadle had spoken of visions. Could this...he shook his head and lay down again. A nightmare, he decided. He had fallen asleep while trying to analyze the voices, and his night-mind, encroaching upon his wakeful efforts, had created faces, bodies, a story to match some of the voices: the woman's, talking of sweetbreads; the old man, Margabrook, speaking of lice and saying, "Let the dead dream their dreams in peace."

He shuddered, remembering the boiled thumb.

Think about something else.

Miriam.

He looked over at the framed photograph Erich had given him as his bar mitzvah gift, wrapped in a square of mauve silk. He still had not figured out how Erich acquired the photograph of Miriam, but he was glad he had it. He smiled, remembering how she had winked at him during the most serious moment of his bar mitzvah speech. Later, just before he intoned the blessing over the long *Challah,* the slightly sweet, plaited bread that looked like a woman's shining braid, she had pushed her way through to him and kissed his cheek. He had felt so benign about everybody that day, as if writing his speech and thanking them all for their love had been a tonic. Take one spoonful morning and night for three days and the world will look better.

He snuggled into his pillow. If he could just figure out how to feel that way every day, he thought.

Chapter 19

Camouflaged with the green and brown facial pastes the Youth leaders had given them, Erich and some of the other boys from the group hid behind a hedge and spied on the last of the day's Wannsee picnickers. Night had long since fallen. Moonlight lay upon the lake, and still the people lingered, gathering their foodstuffs, folding blankets, and slipping into their clothes.

It was the boys' assignment to watch and report, though for what reason Erich could not figure out. There was all too much about the Youth group that he could not understand these days, though nothing as much as the experience near Lutherstrasse, which had spoiled things for him more than anyone would ever understand. Anyone, that is, except Solomon, who was the one person he could never tell about it. No more than he could ever again convince himself that Rittmeister Otto Hempel was his ideal.

Worst of all was what seeing the Rittmeister that night had done to his relationship with the other boys at the camp. He had never really been close to them, but he'd never felt completely felt estranged, either. Now he found it harder and harder to relate to them at all. Except for the stuff about the Jews, his belief in the original ideas of the Wandervögel remained unshaken. For that reason, he shut his mouth when they talked of the perfection of their hero, Otto Hempel, and when they downgraded Erich because of his friendship with Solomon—though with all his faults, Sol was a prince compared with these boys.

"I'm hungry," one of the younger boys said, staring in the direction of the nearest picnic basket. "You'd think they'd throw some of that food away."

"I'll check the garbage cans," a second boy said.

Erich put a restraining hand on his arm. "They're not supposed to see us. You're a soldier. You can go without food till later."

"We've been crawling around for hours just watching. It's boring. Aren't we supposed to do something to the people?"

The whine in the boy's voice was beginning to irritate Erich. He would have said something, but one of the older boys got in first. "Quit whining, kid. Good question, though. Anyone know why we're here?"

"We're doing what we were told to do. That's enough," someone answered.

"Says who?"

Another boy joined them in the underbrush. His eyes, accented by the ragged lines of paste, gleamed in the moonlight. "Come and look," he said. "They're dressing at the naked beach!"

Not naked beach, nudist beach, you idiot, Erich thought. He glanced through the woods toward the whitewashed fence that demarcated the nudist beach from the family picnic area. "Why would you want to watch people putting their clothes *on?*"

"When the women have their skirts but not their tops on, it makes their...," the boy cupped his hands over his chest, "stand out."

Though he had no interest in seeing unclothed people, Erich understood the boy's fascination. He had spied through and over the fence dozens of times. Everyone he knew had, even Solomon. The first times had been exciting, but the truth was that he found little erotic about assorted naked women lounging around, displaying their lumps and sags, or men with their penises flopping around like cooked noodles. What he did like was watching the women dress. That made his heart beat wildly in his throat. When a woman was naked, his interest waned within moments, but when she dressed herself, the result was just the opposite. He wondered if the other boys felt that way, but feared to ask, lest they laugh at him for being abnormal.

"They're hard, aren't they?" one of the boys asked.

"Titties?" The boy's friend sounded incredulous. "They're soft. Like pillows."

"They bleed, you know," one of the boys added. "Girls bleed. Women, too."

"Once a month," Erich said, feeling obliged to contribute. "Down here." He patted his crotch, proud to dispel the belief he knew some boys had—that the bleeding happened at the breasts, the reason for brassieres.

The possibility of the female phenomenon was debated, but Erich was not listening. A bitch's keening had floated toward him from their camp across the lake. Grace's voice. Crying in pain, her pregnancy bothering her again. He did not look around, as he once would have, to see if the other boys had heard her too. He had accepted long ago that he was attuned to the canine mind in a way that no one else was. He could feel not only the animals' thoughts, but their emotions. If he mentioned any of that to the other boys, all they would do was laugh at him, like the time he had asked, as circumspectly as possible, about the sexual habits of the Rittmeister, who was most of the boys' favorite leader.

Probably does it to *lots* of women, the boys agreed.

What about with...boys? Erich had asked.

Maybe you want to put a straw up your penis or a stick up your butt and let him watch, they had said, laughing uproariously. Maybe you want to kiss his wiener or put *that* in your butt!

Erich had flown in with his fists, but the others ganged up against him. He had grabbed a burning log and started swinging, and they had backed off. No one had challenged him since, but the laughter continued to haunt...and hurt. He could not abide being laughed at in the first place, but *again*, by the same boys, especially when he knew he was right...that was unthinkable. As for putting a straw up one's penis, supposedly the ultimate in sexual satisfaction, he could no more imagine himself like that than he could imagine willingly tolerating their derision.

Grace's mental cry for help came again, less urgent now but equally disquieting. She was a beautiful shepherd, or *shepherdess*, as he preferred to say. He spent as much time as possible with her, often to the detriment of learning woodsman skills or practicing his javelin throwing, at which he had become adept. Whenever the leaders began deprecating the Jews, or praising the contributions of the Storm Troopers or the National Socialists, he would sit stroking her, staring into the campfire and listening to her voice, her inner being. Or he would put his head against her silky coat, pretending to look for fleas and concentrating on her so hard that he heard the minds of her unborn pups.

"Let's find some food or go see the naked people," the smallest boy said, careful to eliminate the whine from his voice.

After minor discussion about whether they should leave their present posts, the boys set off, spreading out among the trees as they had been taught. Erich looked back once at the traditional picnickers departing the park, envious of family outings that were pleasant, fun, concluded without battles that inevitably took place when he and his parents spent any time together. Then he moved forward with the others.

When the boys reached the fence, they found the nudist area empty. They gathered to decide whether to raid the garbage cans, as was customary, or simply to return to camp.

Then, drifting out from the edge of the lake came a woman's laughter, musical, tinkling. A young man and woman ran from the shadows, a gray French poodle prancing alongside them on a leash. The man put his arms around the woman's waist and pulled her off the ground, twirling once as, her arms around his neck, he kissed her, the dog struggling to keep up with the choreography.

Back on her feet, the woman tied the end of the leash to a sun-umbrella post, pulled off her sweater, and unhooked her brassiere. The man stripped off his shirt and trousers and placed them neatly in a pile next to her tumble of clothing. The moonlight bathed his white back and buttocks. Sitting down, she shed her white shorts and reached up as if to tug on his penis. He dodged her hand, laughed, and pulled her to her feet.

"I know him," the oldest boy said. "His name's Stein. A stinking crop-crippled Jew."

Erich cringed at the boy's use of one of the Rittmeister's favorite phrases. With a sense of impending disaster, he watched the couple race hand-in-hand toward the beach and plunge into the water, leaving the dog to yip sadly at having been left alone.

"Just look at them," the same boy said. "Dirtying our lake. If only the Rittmeister were here. Bet he'd teach them a thing or two!"

The boys looked at one another expectantly. The sudden quiet chilled Erich. "Let's steal their clothes," he said, to alleviate the tension and prevent some worse idea from taking form.

He grabbed hold of the fence, pulled himself over, and stood on the other side for a moment, wondering if this was such a good idea. Before the other boys had a chance to huddle and decide on a more dangerous plan, he snatched up the clothes and sprinted into the trees. He tossed the things among the branches—the boyfriend would have a scratchy climb among rough bark and needles, but could retrieve everything—and, feeling the brassiere's satin lining, turned to watch the others coming toward him, ready to show them his trophy.

They were fanned out amid the shadows. The poodle increased its yipping, warning its owners instead of begging to be let loose, but the couple was too busy splashing each other and kissing to hear the change of tone in his bark.

The youngest boy seized the leash and tugged the poodle after him. The dog, its legs splayed, tried desperately to pull away. Another boy ran over, holding a garbage can lid like a shield, and slammed it down against the animal. The dog squealed and collapsed, its legs kicking. Fear and pain raced up Erich's neck and down to his ankles.

"Hey there!" the man yelled as he came tearing toward them from the water. "Stop that!"

The smaller of the two boys grabbed the poodle by the tail and pulled it beneath the trees. The one with the lid slammed it down again. Erich and the poodle shrieked simultaneously with the pain of the impact. For a moment Erich felt too dazed to react. Then he stumbled toward the animal and its attacker, aware in his peripheral vision that two of the other boys were hurling rocks at the man, who was running naked from the lake. Through stunned senses, he saw him halt, arms raised against the stones, while the woman huddled in the water, trying to cover herself.

He was almost at the poodle's side when one of the boys yanked another garbage lid from its can and hold it up, blocking Erich's way. "We all know how you feel about Jews!" the boy said. "Are you with them or with us?"

Erich pushed against the lid, but his strength, like the poodle's, had ebbed. He felt defenseless against the boy and his two rock-throwing friends who had raced over to join the fight.

"He's a Jew dog, Erich!" one of them yelled.

Another boy spat on the ground. "A *French* Jew dog!"

A rock bounced off a tree trunk as the man returned the rock-barrage, but the boys had lost interest in him and were concentrating on Erich and the dog. One held the dog's collar, another the hind legs, while a third continued to beat down with the lid.

"Cut the damn mutt's legs off!" someone shouted. "That's what the Rittmeister would do!"

A jackknife blade snapped open, glinting in the moonlight, and the boy with the knife knelt over the poodle. Though the boy had his back to him, Erich could see the blood-hunger in his eyes.

I'm seeing through the dog's eyes! Erich thought.

Knowing that the action was not going to increase his popularity with the other boys, yet having to defend the dog—and thus himself—he picked up one of the lids that had been dropped nearby. Lunging, he pushed it against the face of the boy with the knife, so startling him that he dropped the weapon. Erich tried to get it, but he was too late. Someone picked it up and slashed down at the dog. The poodle howled, and pain sliced through Erich, sending him reeling.

"Again!" the boy at the collar said. The dog twisted savagely. "Cut him again, Albert!"

The knife slashed down and Erich collapsed to his knees. *Bite!* his mind cried out to the dog. *Bite, for all you're worth.*

Something warm filled his mouth.

"It bit my hand!" one of the boys wailed. "The son of a bitch bit me!"

The others abandoned their attack on Erich and turned to look. One of them stepped forward and kicked at the dog with his hiking boot. Erich felt the kick in his ribs. Just as he thought he would faint from the pain, two cars pulled up. A party of loud merrymakers exited the cars, heading their way. The pounding stopped. He staggered to his feet and stumbled toward the fence. Knowing he was too weak to climb, he sat down in the grass and fought to catch his breath as he watched the last of the boys scatter, hooting, into the deeper shadows. The man and woman were kneeling over the dog, she shrieking.

Sobbing with equal parts of pain and shame, Erich crawled to the lake. He washed the taste of blood from his mouth and, using handfuls of sand as soap, cleansed the paint from his skin. He was ready to leave, when he felt another dog call to him, this time from across the lake.

"Grace," he whispered.

She too was in pain, though not from death but from birth. He must go to her. The problem was, if she were in desperate straits, he would need help, and he would sooner die than ask the leaders—or certainly the other boys—for anything tonight.

Which left only Solomon.

Chapter 20

Something clunked against the window frame.

Sol was immediately wide awake and terrified. He pulled the edge of his eiderdown close to his throat and waited for a face to appear, plastered against the pane and framed by the night—Rathenau's perhaps, a bloodstained Reichsbanner handkerchief covering his shattered jaw as he demanded to be led to the sewer where the dead lived.

Moving as little as possible, Sol crept his fingers along the night table in search of the lamp. Not that he really wanted to flood the room with light and turn himself into an icon, unable to see out while the night saw in.

"Solomon!" A loud hoarse whisper.

Erich.

Shaking, Sol threw off the covers and padded to the window. Cupping his hands against the sides of his face to reduce the glare of moonlight, he squinted toward the scrawny blue-spruce hedge that demarcated the lot of the apartment building from the sidewalk. Erich crouched near the hedge corner where they had played in the days before they had found their sewer hideout.

Wondering fleetingly what had become of the toys they'd had then—his war ambulances, specially ordered from Planck's in Frankfurt, Erich's hand-carved hook-and-ladder, the miniature human figures he and Erich fought over—Sol opened the window and thrust out his head.

Erich waved furiously. "Come down!" He went over and shut the apartment building door—evidently he had just come from within—then jumped over the hedge and grabbed up his bicycle, which was lying on the sidewalk. Mounting, he motioned again for Sol to join him.

"What is it? Tell me!" Sol cursed under his breath. He sensed trouble. Erich seemed to be less and less the boy with whom he had grown up. Everything might have been so different if he had come along to the Adlon, Sol thought sadly and with a renewed pang of guilt at not having tried harder to persuade Rathenau to include Erich in the invitation.

"We're still blood brothers, aren't we?" Erich raised his wrist in the old gesture. "Come down. It's important!"

Sol pulled himself into his trousers, a corded sweater, and a pair of old shoes. He put on his cap and took a rucksack from the crowded shelf that held his schoolbooks and his pewter Hessian soldiers. Tucking his jacket under his arm, he poked his head into the hall and stared at his parents' door.

No, he decided, returning to the window; if his parents heard him, this adventure would be over before it started. He was tired of kowtowing to Erich's demands, yet he felt flattered when his friend insisted on including him in his unlikely adventures.

The sill was wide and he was able to balance in a squat while he shut the window behind him. Tossing down the rucksack and jacket, he launched himself two meters to the ground and landed briefly on his feet before his knees gave out and he tumbled onto the dirt.

"Hurry!" Erich stood with one leg in the hedge, urging Sol forward. "It's Grace. She's about to have her pups—and there's no one to help her. I heard her crying. Something's gone wrong."

"You *heard* her? All the way from Wannsee?"

"You have to help, *Spatz. Please,* Sol."

"You want me to go with you to Wannsee? To the *camp?*"

"I don't really understand the Jew-hating and the awful things they say, honestly I don't."

"If you don't understand, why parrot them?"

"I'm going to change things, Sol!" Erich's voice was tense. "When I'm a leader I won't let them do those things. Our group used to be different. We weren't like those others who do things—"

"Things?"

Sol had heard about those "things"—the initiation rites, like the older ones peeing on the younger ones to delineate authority; like demanding that they give up loyalty to everything but the group.

"Come on! *Please!*" Erich trundled the bike onto the street and, one foot on the curb for support, kept it steady.

Sol mounted the handlebars. Erich's bike was a second-hand Machnow Herr Weisser picked up at an auction over on Muhldamm. Erich had painted the bike red and black, the new colors of his Freikorps unit. Sol had no bike of his own. His mother felt they were too dangerous in a city.

Erich shoved away from the curve. The bike wobbled as he fought to balance it, and Sol.

They passed the open square of Potsdamer Platz and wound through the Kurfurstendamm's more squalid section, where soap-streaked windows, spiderwebbed with shadows, were made lurid by the moonlight. Dilapidated marquees announced burlesque shows. Handwritten signs pasted on shop windows advertised going-out-of-business sales. Butcher shops boasted of specials on high-quality meat—Grade A cats and dogs, more than likely, Sol was sure. Homeless huddled in doorways or lay curled on the pavement. Whores with black, slicked-down *windstoss*—pixy-cut—haircuts and throats heavy with Charleston beads leaned against *Litfass-Saulen*, adding their bodies to the peeling advertisements pasted around the thick, two-meter posts. The women exchanged gossip and cigarettes with homosexuals sporting sheepskin jackets, striped sailors' shirts, and tan dungarees.

Life in the city was unkind, Sol thought, yet at that moment he felt far less frightened by the loiterers than by the friend he had known most of his life. Lately he hardly knew Erich at all.

"Queers! I hate them." Erich picked up speed. "They should all be shot."

With seemingly superhuman balance he steered the bike with the palm of his crushed hand and, reaching under Sol's left arm, held an object before Sol's nose. His thumb was hooked through the trigger guard of Herr Weisser's pistol. The weapon looked very large and very silver beneath the street lamp.

Sol swallowed in fear. "You stole it?"

"No. I wrote my beloved papa a letter," Erich said, his head down as he pedaled, "explaining that I thought I should inherit it a little early!" He straightened and, thrusting out his lower lip, blew a breath up over his sweaty face.

"You make me sick when you talk like that." Sol looked at his friend in disgust. "Good thing you can't fire it."

"The hell I can't."

"I thought your papa said he had taken out the firing pin, after...." Sol did not feel like finishing.

"I made a new firing pin on the metal lathe at school...out of a Groschen nail. *And* I've got bullets...."

"What were you really angry about that night?" Sol asked. "We've never talked about it."

"Papa, mostly. He's so...*weak*. And Miriam...that whole thing was so unfair. Rathenau not inviting me, I mean. It makes me mad, sometimes. It's like you people have a special club and there's no way in—"

"You people?" Sol felt his stomach forming another knot.

"Don't get mad at me," Erich said. "I just mean that it's as if you have this club and the rules are that you help each other—like we do at camp. It's a club, too—"

A club where you help each other to hate better, Sol thought, glancing uneasily at the people they passed. Judging by his friend's anxiety to get through this part of town as fast as possible, Erich's bragging about roaming Berlin's alleys after midnight was doubtless just that—bragging. Like saying he had slipped a hand beneath the tie-strings of Ursula Müller's underwear. His evenings out probably consisted of nothing more than beer, song, and knockwurst around a Freikorps campfire.

"Slow down!" Sol shouted as the handlebar nut rammed into him.

Erich pedaled faster. They rode on in silence through the city, past an abandoned Bolle Wagen, the milk cart's giant ladle and pails of milk and buttermilk gone with the nag that had once pulled it daily to Sol's neighborhood. According to the *Tageblatt*, when the nag collapsed, hungry Berliners fought its owner and each other for the horse meat and the warm, protein-rich blood.

At last they entered Zehlendorf and headed toward the Grünewald. Three-and-a-half kilometers long and fifty meters wide, the Kurfurstendamm stretched from Kaiser Wilhelm-Gedachtnis Kirche all the way to Koenigsallee. At its eastern end were some of Berlin's most elegant shops; at its western end stood the graceful suburban homes of Zehlendorf. In between was the city's sordid section.

Sol felt a stab of resentment and loss. Although many Jewish businessmen and industrialists lived in the two suburbs, this was a world he would never inhabit. Among the shadowy lushness of oaks and chestnut trees, slender white-stemmed birches stood guard, shining silver, like armored lords before the moon. Except for the occasional Audi or Model-T puttering past them, or the prestigious Buick that swerved to avoid their unexpected presence, the streets were deserted. Twice, flashlights lanced toward the road—probably watchmen determining what creaky machine would dare disturb the sleep of their employers.

He imagined being married to Miriam, living in a villa and surveying the tree-lined avenue from behind a tall window. Erich could be Otto von Bismarck, a royal guest with a taste for fine wines and rare books. The three of them would be out riding near Jagdschloss Grünewald, their headquarters for the hunt.

But such imaginings served only to deepen his sense of loss. The time had come, he thought, to accept the fact that the door Walther Rathenau briefly cracked open was forever shut.

Chapter 21

By the time Erich steered into Wannsee Park and dumped the bike, his chest felt tight with the effort of pedaling, and his breath was coming in short harsh huffs. He looked around uneasily, in case the other boys were still on this side of the lake, saw that the picnic area was empty, and sprinted across the sand to the edge of the Wannsee.

Beside the small dock was the beach for swimmers and, beneath the trees, an open-air restaurant with signs that listed rules for picnickers. The largest one read: "Families May Brew Their Own Coffee Here."

"See those willows?" Erich whispered when Sol joined him. He pointed across the lake. "That's where we're going."

"I know—" Sol did not sound happy. "What was that ride? 'Joy in Hardship' lesson one?"

His Youth camp's motto was "Strength through joy in nature." Sol consistently called it, "joy in hardship." Before the war, the cluster of Spartan three-sided huts had been an apolitical Wandervögel camp for children who liked nature, hiking and singing around a campfire. Now the Freikorps ran it.

Erich squinted toward the willows. Shouldn't have dragged Sol into this, he thought, praying that none of the really tough guys had decided to spend the night at the camp. Even if some of the boys had decided to go home, there were always two or three who had run away from their families and had nowhere else to go, and at least one leader who stayed to guard the camp. If he and Sol were caught hanging around, it would simply be a question of who was in the most trouble—Sol, or himself for bringing Sol there.

Crouching, Erich crept along the beach. "We'll have to row across." He pointed toward a rowboat beached at the fence that enclosed Wannsee Park. "But first swear you'll never tell anyone about tonight. If you do, I'll turn you into a vampire, just like—*blaah!*" He jumped on Sol, teeth bared and fingers curved like claws. "Just like Nosferatu!"

"Idiot!" Sol shoved him away. "I won't tell. What's the big secret, anyway?"

"Shake on it." Erich clasped Sol's hand in the Wandervögel handshake. He felt a momentary resistance and stared deeply into his friend's eyes. Then Sol grinned and Erich felt his grip harden. "I better never find out you broke your word," he said.

They pushed the boat onto the moon-dappled water. As Erich rowed, Sol clutched the oarlocks to help keep them from creaking. "We should have wrapped the oars in silk," he whispered, apparently beginning to get caught up in the adventure. "That's what Hessian spies—"

Erich put a finger to his lips and glanced over at a sleeping fisherman whose canoe bobbed gently in the water. Watching people fish sure wasn't interesting, as it used to be. Not since Berlin banned the used of grenades.

When they reached the other side they tied the boat to a branch and crept into the foliage, wilder and denser on this side of the lake and still wet from the previous evening's rain. By the time Erich parted the last set of branches and peered into one of the huts, he was as damp as if he had been walking in a drizzle.

"Do you see her?" he whispered, examining the tiered bunks inside, three on each side. A few of them held sleeping figures.

"I see *them!*"

"Shsh!" Erich clamped a hand over Sol's mouth and pointed toward a young sentry who sat, hunched over and asleep, beside a blackened fire pit.

Sol sputtered and backed away. "I didn't think anyone would be here," he whispered. "I should go home."

"Alone? Out there?" Erich started crawling through the undergrowth. He felt Sol's hand on his shoulder, holding him back. "We're crawling around some woods in the dark, looking for a pregnant mutt—"

"Don't call her that!"

"We're in danger of being beaten up by your buddies and our families are probably worried sick," Sol said, ignoring him. "But that's okay because we're here to see your favorite dog."

"Please, Sol," Erich said. "She's the top of the Thuringia strain, the camp mascot, *and* pregnant. I asked for one of her puppies but they said no because they'd taken her all the way to Holland, to Doorn, to mate her."

"They mated her with one of the *Kaiser's* dogs?"

"Not just *one* of the Kaiser's dogs—last year's German Grand Champion. Remember that Movietone segment about the Sieger Dog Show? Remember Harras von der Juch? That's the sire."

"If she is so valuable, how come one of your leaders didn't stay around to take care of her?"

"They're stupid, that's why."

Sol could not fail to be impressed, Erich thought as he started crawling again. In front of him, twigs crackled softly as he moving ahead. Grace, mated to Harras, the offspring of Etzel von Oeringen, son of Nores of the *Kriminalpoletzei!* Then again, what did Sol know? *He* couldn't commune with dogs or rattle off their family lines as if they were his own.

Well, Sol *did* know Etzel, but everyone knew the dog that had been taken to America and became the star of the Strongheart movies, each of which Erich had seen close to a dozen times. He was saving for another movie marathon when the new German shepherd film came to Berlin, the one starring Rin Tin Tin, a dog bred in the trenches during the war.

"Why did we come here?" Sol asked. "I mean, *really?*"

"I *told* you. I heard her calling. Also, I want one of her pups," Erich answered truthfully. "If we're there when she gives birth, they'll never know."

"What if they catch us stealing?" Sol sounded scared.

"They'll scream at me, discipline me—threaten to cut my nuts off and feed them to the squirrels." He looked at Sol. "With you they might not just threaten."

"Because I'm Jewish?" Sol narrowed his eyes in anger.

"Because you're not Freikorps."

Sol backed away but Erich grabbed him. "Just kidding." He knew his voice lacked conviction. "That's where Grace is supposed to be." He pointed to a tiny hut whose front was covered with chicken wire. "But I know she's not there. She...escaped. When that kid watching her fell asleep."

"Maybe she's resigned from the Freikorps," Sol said.

"I'll find her." Erich led Sol behind the other huts and along the far side of the camp until they reached the biggest hut. The outside of its rear wall looked like the heavily decorated chest of a general; nearly a hundred sports medallions hung alongside four javelins. Beneath them, sheltered from the weather by an overhang, were shelves cluttered with badminton rackets and nets, soccer balls, shot-puts, medicine balls, and an array of black track shoes.

"That's mine." Erich pointed at the longest javelin. It was white, with two red stripes taped near the center. The chrome tip was honed to a gleaming point. "Isn't she a beauty?"

"Yes, but where's the *dog?*"

Feeling more than a little hurt by Sol's quick dismissal of his javelin, Erich concentrated. Suddenly he bounded away from the hut and toward an enormous weeping willow on the west side of the camp, its canopy so full it touched the ground. He waited for Sol to catch up before he held the branches apart.

He was shocked at what he saw.

Though Grace could not have chosen a more pastoral sanctuary, she looked anything but the consort of a German champion. She raised her head to see who had intruded upon her. Then, as if the action had completely enervated her, she laid her head back down on the ground. Her head appeared abnormally extended, her ribs were prominent, her abdomen sagged.

Moonlight, seeping through the willow, mottled her coat, which looked gray and lifeless. In the lee of her belly, their eyes closed to slits, their tiny paws curled and vulnerable, lay two pink hairless pups, covered with bloody mucous and forest duff.

A third pup lay to one side, swaddled in a bluish membrane and still attached to its mother.

Feebly Grace wriggled her mouth closer to the umbilical cord so that she could chew through it. As she moved her head her throat spasmed. She gagged and jerked in what was obviously terrible pain.

"Erich?"

"She's going to die." Erich felt a lump in his throat, and tears were right near the surface.

Again the dog picked up her head. This time she held it rigid; her eyes bulged, her throat convulsed. A stream of bloody vomit gushed from her mouth. Her head slumped and she lay staring, through sad dark eyes, at the willow trunk.

Erich wanted to rush to Grace, stroke her, comfort her; at the same time, he was afraid to touch her—afraid, and nauseated. She used to be so beautiful. He pictured Miriam lying there, pregnant and...ugly. When they were married he would tell her, *no children!*

"For God's sake, Erich, what is *that?*"

Sol clutched Erich's shoulder and pointed at a distended sac that lay on the dog's hind side. Pink and quivering and slicked with blood, the sac looked like an oversized fleshy larvae—an oval reddish mass stippled with spongy-looking knobs.

Shaking, Erich knelt to examine the sac. Grace looked at him, and shivered.

"What's happened to her?" Sol whispered.

"I think this came out of her." Erich pulled a face.

"Ugh! What *is* it?"

"I don't know," Erich said slowly, "I have this feeling...I think...she wants us to put it back in."

"No!" Sol's face was ashen. "We'll kill her. We don't know anything about that stuff."

Carefully, Erich lifted the membrane-covered pup and pulled off the film. His stomach clenched and he had to breathe deeply to keep from throwing up. "We should go for help, but we can't. If I bring back a leader and he finds out you're a Jew, we're both in *bad* trouble—"

"And if the others find out about Grace being here, you'll never get a puppy," Sol said, a cynical tone in his voice.

Erich gently set the whelp next to its mother. "Remember what I told you about some of the camps?" He paused, wanting Sol's full attention. "There's no guessing what they would do to you."

Sol huddled next to Grace. "So what do we do now?"

"We'll need hot water, clean towels—like in the films." Erich rose to his feet. "Here, guard yourself with this." Acting a lot more casual than he felt, he threw his father's gun on the ground near Sol's feet. "I won't be long."

He hurried through the tall grass. Behind him he could hear Sol speaking to Grace in the soothing tones his parents used when he was ill. What, he wondered, had really made the leaders bring hatred into the camp?

What was so bad about Jews, anyway?

Take Sol—he'd never had a problem with Sol being a Jew. But then Sol was different. He was just...Sol. *Spatz.* A sparrow.

The leaders had said that Germans should follow Martin Luther's suggestion. Seize all Jewish property and send the Jews to mines and quarries and logging camps.

Now there was a stupid idea. The Jews *he* knew weren't exactly the most *physical* people in the world.

Dismissing the subject, as he usually did, he crept around the camp looking for things he needed or might need. He found a pot and poured in water from the drinking barrel, letting the liquid run over his hand so it would not ting against the metal and wake someone up. The top bunk of the empty hut nearest the willow turned out to be strewn with bedcovers and camping gear—some cry-baby who'd had second thoughts about staying the night, Erich figured. He flung two blankets and a couple of dirty towels over his shoulder; he got lucky and found a flashlight, which he put in his hip pocket together with a sewing kit and a fishing leader. Then he sprinted back to the willow.

"Couldn't get *hot* water. This'll have to work." He tried to sound confident. This birthing business was awfully complicated. *C'mon, Grace,* he begged silently. *Tell me what to do.*

"What are we going to do?" Sol asked, echoing Erich's plea to the dog.

Erich hoped Grace would commune with him, but—nothing. "She's too weak. We'll have to decide as we go. If only I could remember what the Rittmeister wrote about whelping!"

They spread one blanket on the ground, maneuvered the animals onto it, and covered them with the other. Grace did not resist. There was a dead weight and a rank wet odor to her, and her skin felt clammy and coarse.

"She's feverish," Erich said. "Feel her nose—it's hot and dry." He drew the blankets around her, forming a cocoon for the pups. "Hold her still!" He folded part of a blanket forward to expose her hindquarters. "This is going to hurt her."

Sol cradled the dog's head in his lap and leaned over to brace the torso with his hands. Erich turned on the flashlight and wedged it in the crook of the willow. It cast a weak circle of light over the dog.

Kneeling beside Grace, Erich plunged his hands and then a towel into the water pot. "Don't even breathe, Solomon." He began to clean the sac. "Just hold her."

The dog's eyes were filled with apprehension and pain; she was shivering slightly, but she did not struggle.

"I've got her," Sol said.

"I know. I know. We have to be careful. I think it's her uter-in." He felt sick as he softly put his fingers on the 'thing.'

Think about something else. He glanced at Sol, whose face was set in a stoic expression. *Bet he's thinking about something he read in a book. That's his answer to everything.*

As gently as he could, Erich continued to work. He pictured his own bookshelf at home. Though he pretended he never read—mostly to annoy Sol—he owned many books about dogs and uniforms and Imperial history. He could quote passages verbatim from lots of them. His favorite was *The German Shepherd Dog in Word and Picture* by Rittmeister Max von Stephanitz, the "father" of the German shepherd. Through controlled breeding, he had produced a master-breed based on efficiency *and* beauty. According to him, the German shepherd was not a means to an end but an end in itself.

"You got her, Sol?" Erich tentatively patted the uter-in with the dry towel. Why had none of his books taught him what to do in a situation like this? With the back of his wrist he wiped away the sweat that beaded his forehead. "Here goes. It can't be that different from stuffing a chicken. I've seen my mother do that plenty of times."

Taking a deep breath he began to ease the organ inside. It had come out of her, so it had to fit back in, but it seemed too big—awkward and shapeless, like a pile of raw sweetbreads.

"Steady," Sol told him.

"I'm doing the best I can!"

"Sorry."

Sol stroked the dog, as if hoping to relax her tense muscles.

"That's my lady." Erich tried to keep his voice quiet and gentle but the dog stirred beneath his touch. "Oh God." He lowered his head and examined the part of the organ that remained in his hands, though he had no idea what he was looking for. "I must have done something wrong."

"Careful!"

Raising his gaze but not his head, Erich glared at Sol. "I *am* being careful. Just hold her! If something goes wrong it's *your* fault."

"*My* fault?" Sol glared back, then looked away.

Watch yourself, Erich thought. *All you need now is for Sol to leave.*

Whining deep in her throat, the dog shivered, trembled, and began to whimper.

"There." Erich sat back and wiped his forehead again with a blood-covered hand. "I think it's in." He took the large needle and a loop of transparent leader from his breast pocket. "This was the thickest stuff I could find." He held up and scrutinized the loop before threading the needle.

"What's that for?"

"To sew her up, stupid."

"You'll kill her."

"Just hold her and keep quiet. If I don't sew her up, the ...the...*thing*—it might come out again."

Sol bent his head. *"Baruch ata Adonai..."* he whispered, gripping wads of her shoulder muscle in his hands. "Blessed art Thou, O Lord our God, King of the Universe, who knows and does good things—"

"Now what are you jabbering about!"

"A prayer. For the dog."

Erich adjusted the flashlight so the beam was truer, hunkered down behind the dog, and began to work the needle. "You people have prayers for dogs?" He hoped Sol's God would hear even if Grace were not Jewish.

The animal's breathing became raspy and ragged. Growling she tried to bring her head around and scrunch her backside away from the pain. She fought to rise as Sol held her down. "Papa says there are prayers for everything," Sol said, "but it's okay to make them up, too, long as you don't *ask* for things—just give praise and thanks, and believe."

"Finished." Erich exhaled loudly, arched his back and stretched. Maybe a little more praying wouldn't hurt, he thought, too embarrassed to say as much. He washed his hands. "Let's clean the pups." Folding aside a blanket corner, he picked up the tiny mewling creature he'd handled earlier and scratched it gently behind the ear. Grace lay unmoving, her head in Solomon's lap. Erich reached over and stroked her muzzle. "You're okay now," he said. "Uncle Erich saved you."

"I helped." Sol maneuvered his elbow so Erich would have trouble petting the dog. "I did a lot!"

"In an emergency, *Spatz*—" Erich pushed Sol's arm aside-"you're about as useful as a blind man on a battlefield."

Sol looked darkly petulant. "You always do that," he said in an injured voice. "Insult me. Take all the credit when things go right and blame me when they don't."

Erich set down the pup and lurched to his feet. He clenched his fists. Sol was right, he thought, feeling foolish. He lowered his guard and put a hand on Sol's shoulder. "Just kidding. You know I didn't mean it."

"Yes, you did. Go ahead—you might as well hit me."

Erich looked down at his mangled hand. Despite it, he was an expert boxer; his friend never stood a chance against him in a fist fight. Yet when it came to words, Sol was the expert. He was like a conscience, Erich thought. Too quick with questions, too accurate and truthful with analyses. No wonder the other boys at school avoided him.

"You said it yourself, remember?" Sol jerked his head up angrily. "You said, 'She's going to die'!"

Furiously, frustrated beyond words, Erich punched down, hitting his friend with such force that Sol was slammed against the tree.

Grace's head, abruptly released from the protection of Sol's lap, bounced lightly and lay still. Sol rolled over, groaning as he clutched his temple and his glasses.

"Goddamn four eyes!" Erich hopped around, his knuckles pressed against his lips.

"Feeling better now?" Sol muttered, taking off his spectacles and squinting at them in the weak light. They were bent but intact. He straightened the wire rims a little and put them on again.

Erich blew on his knuckles and fought the pain. If only Sol would lose his temper! That damn self-control of his was the most annoying thing of all. "You think you're a man because you've had a bar mitzvah! Hell, you haven't even undressed a girl, let alone—"

"Neither have you."

"Well, I could have. Ursula Müller wanted me to."

"She'd let anyone."

"Not a Jew, she wouldn't!"

Sol rose, apparently ready to resume the fight regardless of the inevitable outcome.

Though he was angry with himself for his outburst, Erich flexed his muscles. Then something wet and warm soaked his ankle. He looked down, horrified, to see Grace spasm. Her eyes were wide with terror. Blood gushed from her mouth and over his shoes.

"We've got to try to help her!" Erich collapsed over the dog, his arms around her neck. "Sol, please!"

"Take back what you said."

"Go to hell."

"I'll go, all right—back home." Sol stepped away and parted the branches.

"You know I didn't mean it," Erich said quickly.

Sol hesitated and Erich knew his friend would stay. Funny how you could love someone, need him, and be infuriated by him at the same time.

"Try pouring water down her throat," Solomon said. "It might help break the fever."

The thought was logical enough but Erich did not want logic; he wanted a miracle. Again and again he begged her to live. He cuddled and covered her; he poured water across his hands and patted her nose. When she did not respond, he reached inside the blanket and drew out the other two puppies.

"If she notices them she'll want to live," he said.

Standing in the moonlight, he toweled the tiny heads. Then his hands opened and he let the puppies fall, one at a time, onto the blanket.

"They're dead, Solomon!"

Sol touched the pups and nodded, saying nothing. A strangling sound from Grace pulled Erich to his knees beside her.

"They're just pups, don't you see?" He lifted a dead whelp by the scruff of its neck. "You can have more! Look, there's another one here." He ransacked the folds of the blanket and drew out the live pup. "We're here, girl. Me and the pup."

Sobbing, he rubbed Grace's nose with her pup. Sol placed a consoling hand on his friend's shoulder.

Erich shook it off. "Don't touch me! Don't touch the dog, either, or—"

He spotted the gun, still lying where he had thrown it. Without thinking about what he was doing, or why he was doing it, he grabbed hold of the pistol and pointed it at Sol.

His friend backed away, arms up, face constricted with fear.

What am I doing? Erich stared in disbelief at the pistol, wondering how the thing could possibly have gotten into his hands. There was a dull pressure at the base of his skull, then an electric charge that made him arch his back involuntarily.

He rose up onto his toes as the thin, hot sensation ran the length of his spine, split in two, surged to his heels—and raced up again. He jerked involuntarily, groping for something to hold on to, but the force was too great and darkness spilled over him like paint.

He staggered forward, stumbled, tried to keep himself from falling into the blackness that was pulling him down into some bottomless abyss.

The choice was not his to make.

He felt the gun drop from his hand; felt the darkness envelop him; felt, rather than heard, himself scream.

Chapter 22

Erich's scream hit Sol in the solar plexus with the force of a fist. He scrambled to his feet. All he could think of was that the pistol must have gone off accidentally. But then why hadn't he heard a shot?

He grabbed the flashlight from its perch in the willow and shone it directly at Erich. His friend had fallen onto the blanket; his fingers clutched at the air and his head lurched from side to side.

Trying not to panic, Sol recalled the only other time he had seen Erich having a full-blown seizure—after the accident in the sewer. His usual lightning seizures were over before anyone could fully react. A trembling or a simple spasm. A split-second rigidity. A gasp, during which, Erich said, he felt as if he were falling off a cliff—into darkness.

But this....

Sol sighed with relief as Erich stopped convulsing and opened his eyes. Turning awkwardly onto his side, Erich wrapped his arms around Grace's neck and pulled her head into his lap. "I...I loved you s-so much," he stammered, his voice broken, high-pitched. "We were a *t-team.*" He kissed her muzzle, neck, ear.

Grace gave a guttural sound, like a deep-throated purring. Erich released her head. She slipped onto the ground like a heavy sack and lay staring at him, her legs moving against the dirt as if she knew her destiny and wanted to crawl away from it.

Erich stared blankly up into the branches. Without moving his body, he patted the blanket. "Men don't l-let their friends s-suffer." He stopped. His hand ceased moving. Balling the fingers of both hands into fists, he turned onto his side and began to sob. He stroked the dog as he wept.

Suddenly he swayed to his feet.

The action drew Sol out of the strange inertia he had been feeling and he darted forward, hoping to grab Erich and keep him from falling again. Erich easily shoved him away. Then he pushed between the branches and disappeared among the moonlit grasses and alders.

Now what? Sol thought, his heart thudding. There was no telling what Erich might do next. So what alternatives did that leave him? He could find his way home, but if something happened to Erich, he would never forgive himself. Besides, leaving meant taking the boat, which would infuriate Erich and possibly antagonize him permanently. He could not risk finding a camp leader, but many doctors lived in the Grünewald.

Wondering briefly why Erich's scream had not brought someone crashing through the trees from the campsite, he turned his attention to Grace. Even given Erich's emotional state, he was right about one thing: the dog needed to be released from her misery. At least he had not tried to shoot the dog. Gunfire would surely have brought trouble.

Sol checked the surviving pup. Asleep. Every now and again it quivered violently, as if the memory of its birth-throes intruded on its dreams. How sweet and small and defenseless it looked. He stroked it gently with the side of his finger.

Feeling powerless to change whatever course of events Erich was putting into motion, he looked around for something useful to do. He would bury the two dead puppies, he decided. He moved outside the umbrella of the willow and, using his hands and the heel of his shoe, fashioned a shallow grave beside a patch of wild strawberries. He placed the puppies inside, covered them with soil, and matted it down. Feeling the need of ceremony, he bent and smelled a flower whose center was white as snow and whose edges were tinged with red. He plucked it, and a second one, and laid them both on top of the grave. Bowing his head, he began a few words of prayer.

"What do you think you're doing!" Naked to the waist, Erich sprang toward Sol through the grass, his javelin raised overhead.

Terrified, Sol backed away and dashed wildly past the willow. Behind him, an animal's scream shattered the night. He stopped running and listened, but already the screaming had ended. All he could hear was his own pulse thundering in his ears.

He trudged back to the willow and carefully, quietly, parted the branches. The scene made him gag.

Erich had rammed the javelin through Grace's left eye. Blood and something black oozed from the socket as the dog twisted and jerked against the shaft, which Erich held firmly, leaning his weight against it. "I love you," he said. "I love you."

Except for the small sound of her haunches thudding against the earth as she struggled to free herself, Grace made no noise. Her mouth opened and closed.

She slumped, shuddered, and lay still. As blood drained from her mouth, Sol thought of the Kabbalistic belief that animals, too, had souls.

In the silence, a cricket chirped.

Erich tugged the javelin from the wound. It made a sucking sound. He dropped it, clutched his head, and fell to his knees, eyes open wide.

This was no lightning seizure, Sol thought, panicking. Either his friend was having a grand mal seizure or this was his grotesque idea of a joke.

"Erich?"

His friend did not respond. Instead he began to shake as if with uncontrolled fury. His lips were pulled back, his teeth exposed. With each exhalation, his nostrils opened and closed like overworked valves. Then he toppled forward and lay jerking.

Have to do *something!* Block the mouth open if Erich ever has a bad attack, Papa had said. Otherwise he might bite his tongue in two. But block it with what?

He reached for the javelin, but the bloody tip made him retch. Seeing a stick close to the willow trunk, he leaned forward to pick it up.

The stick proved to be a root, stuck firmly in the ground.

He pulled at a willow branch. It bent resiliently. Frustrated, he returned to yanking at the root; it ran from the ground like a cable being unearthed. In desperation he lowered his head and gnawed at the wood. Something syrupy sweet oozed into his mouth, but he could not rip through the sinewy pulp.

Angrily thrusting aside the root, he reached for the javelin—and spotted the pistol. Though he had never touched a revolver before, he unloaded it easily and rolled Erich over. His friend was bathed in sweat, twitching. Saliva drooled from his mouth.

The barrel proved to be too short to fit neatly between Erich's lips, so Sol crammed the chamber in. He took a deep breath to calm himself, then with the edge of the blanket toweled Erich's face.

Suddenly Erich gripped Sol's shirt as if for support and arched his torso into a taut bow. His eyes rolled up until only the whites showed. Releasing Sol, he stretched out his arms and emitted a choking snarl. The gun fell from his lips. He reached upward with rigid fingers, muttered a stream of unintelligible syllables, and sagged in Solomon's arms.

Slowly he opened his eyes. "There was a jungle." His voice rasped and he licked his lips as though his mouth were parched. "A clearing in a jungle. And overhead, a moon. It was...melting." His tone was in some way accusative but he did not resist when Sol eased him onto the ground and covered him with the stained blanket. "You were there, Solomon. I saw you." Erich's face was pale and he seemed sleepy and disoriented. "I saw you." He was shivering.

Sol sat back, feeling flushed and wondering if it were his turn to faint. His head exploded with light and it ached so badly he could hardly see through the blue glow——

——an arm dangles from the battlement of bodies, its wrist blue and icy, its black hair frozen and stiff. Thousands of bodies—thousands of dead soldiers—are the bricks and mortar in a breastworks five bodies thick.

The woman, Peat, crouches beside the breastworks, her carbine poked through an aiming hole at white-clad infantry ascending the hill. Some of them are crossing the slope laterally at a crouch, some are crawling, others stoop to fire at her position.

She pops off several rounds. Down the hill, a soldier clutches his head and topples. She sits on her haunches and watches the old man labor to drag yet another body toward her.

"I could use a bowl of semolina soup." He lets the body drop.

"Phfui! Food for pigs!" She positions the body, readying it to be hoisted to a worker on the higher tier. "No matter how much you sift semolina, it's like eating sand."

Above them, the worker grabs hold of the corpse and flops it down like a sandbag.

"Three days now the clouds have held," the old man says. "One more hour and we will have survived another day. Maybe your God does hold you Jews in special favor."

"You think Jehovah is maintaining our cloud cover?" Laughing, the woman rams a cleaning patch down the barrel of her carbine and reloads the magazine. "Perhaps we could get Him to send in a few yaks or Siberian ponies!" She stares down the hill. "Here come more people they don't care about. Look at them. Penal troops this time, I think. Surely no one believes they're real soldiers!"

The old man peers through the aiming hole.

"Dissidents," he says. "Children of White Russians and probably a lot of Jews like you, who never knew what it was to be Jewish until...Senseless! Germans shooting Russians, Russians shooting Russians, Jews shooting Jews, and in the end it's the winter that will kill us all." He looks along the line of people working behind the barricade. "What are you doing here, Peat, shooting at your own kind!"

"Thank our revered Russian traitor, General Vlasov. That bastard saved Moscow, then switched sides. He's over at the hut—waiting to inspect his *troops!*" She turns her head and spits into the snow. "When he defected, he promised the Ukrainian Jews the return of their families and a homeland in Madagascar. If we fought for Hitler at the Russian Front, he said, the German forces would be free to finish taking London."

She tightens her jaw and fires three times. No one falls. Behind them, mortars begin to pop; far down the hill small fountains of snow and the roar of explosions confirm the shells.

The old man plugs his ears with his fingers. "You believed him?" he shouts.

She says no more until the firing has lessened. Pulling his hands from his head, she shouts, "I chose to believe!"

"Like you chose—" He stops in mid-sentence and stares down at her boots.

"I might have liked that soldier had he lived," she says softly. "But he didn't, and I will. Go back to the hut." Her blanket is flapping wildly in the wind. She tightens it around herself. "Warm your old bones at the brazier, Margabrook. Just don't throw out the meat I left to thaw in the hut. I don't want it to refreeze."

The old man recoils in horror. "God help us both."

He reaches out his hand. The woman seems to know what he wants. She reloads the rifle and hands it to him, then she follows him toward the hut. A man wearing the uniform and medals of a general stands in the doorway.

Margabrook falls to his knees in the snow.

"They will kill you, old man," the woman says, but she does not stop him when he lifts the rifle.

The shriek of incoming shells muffle the rest of her words and the sound of her carbine as it is fired again and again. The man in the doorway clutches his belly. He takes several steps into the snow, staggers, falls.

Margabrook drops the rifle. He is crying. The tears freeze instantly on his eyelashes.

"My eyes!" he screams—

"You'll tell no one!" Erich demanded, sitting up, his voice strong again.

Startled, Sol looked up. His headache had gone, along with the flashes of light and the eerie blue glow. "I...I think I just had a vision, Erich." He remembered what the beadle had said about Solomon ben Luria. "There was this—"

"The hell with your visions! I'm talking about Grace and about me. You'll tell no one what happened. Ever! Or that I cried and acted...weird!"

Gripping the javelin, he staggered to his feet and pointed the tip at Sol's chest.

"Whatever pleases you," Sol said. "Just put that thing down."

"Promise you won't tell!"

"Promise."

"Damn right, or you'll be one dead bar mitzvah boy." Eyes wild, Erich squatted and, still threatening Sol with the javelin, found the pistol.

"Look—you had a seizure. You're not yourself. Leave the gun alone. You might shoot yourself...or me."

A look of dismay gripped Erich's features as he checked the revolver. "The bullets! You stole them."

"I didn't steal them. I—"

"I never thought you'd do something like that!" Erich thrust the spear close to Sol's throat—and pulled back, eyes narrowed.

With a sick, sinking feeling, Solomon retrieved the cartridges from among the forest duff and handed them to Erich. There were soft clicks as Erich inserted the rounds.

"I *saw* you in that jungle clearing." With each word, Erich shook the pistol barrel as though scolding a child. "While I was having the seizure-thing. I *saw* you as clearly as I'm seeing you now!" He motioned with the pistol. "Come here, *bar* mitzvah *boy.*"

Erich stuck the javelin in the ground and, keeping the pistol pointed toward Solomon, stooped and rubbed his damaged hand in Grace's blood.

"Here!" he commanded.

Sol stepped forward fearfully. "You're acting crazy. I'm your friend, remember?"

Erich smeared blood all over Sol's cheeks. "That's why I'm doing this." He looked Sol straight in the eye. "I know you didn't *mean* to cause the...seizures, or make me see what I did."

Sol pulled away from Erich. He wasn't afraid anymore, just angry at himself for having submitted so readily to his earlier fear. "Cause them? How could *I* cause them? I'm not God!"

"It's because of you and your ghosts," Erich said angrily. "I saw a jungle and heard a baby crying. There was a kind of scroll and big rocks...like gravestones."

Sol wiped his cheek with the back of his hand and looked at the streak of blood he had wiped off. With his tongue he tasted a salty tear as it reached the corner of his mouth. Something was terribly wrong with his friend, but what?

"Something was snarling," Erich said. "I couldn't see what it was. But I could see you. You were there, watching." He leaned closer to Sol and squinted, an artist admiring his work. "We're on the warpath now. Just like in the movies. Whatever it was, we'll fight it. *Together.* But no more seizures. You got that? Now—your specs." He took the glasses off Sol's face and smeared them with the dog's blood. "There, I've cleansed *them* too."

He handed them back and Sol put them on. He squinched up his nose, forcing the glasses down enough so he could see a little, albeit poorly. The world was a blur of light and shadow. Vaguely he saw Erich stoop and, bloodying his fingers again, make circles on his own cheeks and forehead.

"Now help me bury Grace," Erich said, "and if you know what's good for you, you'll keep your crazy visions to yourself."

Grace was big and the ground was hard. Digging a shallow grave for the puppies with his hands was one thing; this was another. Erich, on his hands and knees scraping at the ground with the pistol handle, apparently came to the same conclusion. After a few minutes, he stood up.

"Let's just cover her." He piled the bloodied blankets and one of the towels on top of the dead dog.

Gratefully Sol stood up. Soon all traces of the dog were buried beneath a dense pile of undergrowth, topped off by some branches and twigs that Erich found a few feet away.

"I think I should say a prayer," Sol said softly, pushing his anger and confusion aside.

"Why?" Erich wrapped the live puppy in the remaining towel and put it in Sol's rucksack. He slipped his arms through the rucksack straps. "Dead is dead."

Chapter 23

Erich could not remember ever having felt so tired and thirsty, not even after long hikes with a heavy pack or running multiple wind sprints in preparation for his first javelin competition, near Oranienburg. Had he suffered a grand mal seizure? Did it affect everyone like this—first a sense of enormous strength, as though he could conquer the world, then debilitating fatigue?

The closest he had come to the aftermath of this seizure was the way he had felt after wandering around the city that night before someone had the good sense to shoot that power monger, His Highness Herr Rathenau.

He glanced over at Sol—stumbling half-blind toward the boat, tripping over rocks and limbs—and felt bad. Funny how he could think things like that when Sol was not around, and feel no hint of conscience. Never mind conscience; when he was with the other Freikorps boys, thoughts like that gave him status.

Happy to wait for Solomon to catch up, he untied the boat, dropped in the javelin and climbed in. He had not meant to hurt Sol physically or emotionally, he thought, so why had he done it? Because Sol made it so easy for him? *I blame Sol every time something happens that I cannot control, because Sol always forgives.* One day he would go too far; Sol would declare him a fool and move on and there would be no apologizing, no understanding.

Erich sighed and shook his head. "Rinse off your glasses and get in," he said when Sol was within earshot.

Sol peered at him over his smeared spectacles and took hold of the boat's gunwale.

"Go on—rinse them," Erich said.

"Don't know if I want to." Sol climbed into the boat. "It's a pleasure not to have to see your ugly face." He swished his glasses in the water, dried them off on his shirt and tried to adjust them. They ended up even more lopsided than before.

"Take off your war paint too, if you want," Erich said. "I'm leaving *mine* on."

Solomon leaned over the boat to wet his face, sat up without washing, and squinted curiously at Erich through the dripping lenses.

"Here." Erich pushed the oar handles toward him.

"Me? Row?"

Erich nodded. "You row well."

Sol positioned himself on the middle seat, his back to Erich. "You were crazy back there, you know," he said over his shoulder.

Erich slipped off the rucksack, put it in his lap and lay back, head on the bow as he gazed at the moon. Sol did row well, he thought, pushing the memory of the seizure away. The boat moved straight and true, leaving a wake in the moon's reflection.

When they neared the other shore, Erich put a hand on Sol's shoulder. "It was because of the seizure," he said. "Shake?"

They gripped hands and gazed into one another's eyes, but Erich remained unsatisfied. He grabbed Sol's arm and rubbed his wrist against Sol's. "We're brothers in blood now."

"We've been blood brothers for ages, remember?"

Erich stood up. Despite the boat's sudden rocking, he jumped deftly into the lake, holding the rucksack above his head. The cold thigh-high water refreshed him. He felt a new surge of energy and heaved the javelin toward the sandy beach. "Now," he said, sloshing toward the shore, "we're also brothers in blood."

While Solomon nosed the boat to the dock and tied up, Erich found the spear, jogged over to the bike and waited impatiently for his friend to cross the beach. Deciding Sol was fine and he had done enough penance, he hopped onto Hawk. Yelling, "Race you back home!" he took off with such power that the front tire lifted off the ground. The seizure and Grace's death seemed like a bad dream. He was feeling good again.

Whooping loudly he hoisted the javelin like a spear.

"Wait for me!" Sol shouted.

Erich glanced back. Laughing he rode in circles around the oaks and birches—then pedaled off into the shadows.

"Damn you, Erich!" Sol yelled. "Where are you!"

Erich walked the bike out from behind the foliage. Remounting with a kind of insolent ease, he leaned over the handlebars and thrust his face directly in front of Sol's. "Start running. We're brothers all the way now. That means *you* have to get in shape, like *me.*" He lifted a foot onto the higher pedal as if to ram the bike into Sol, who backstepped rapidly, turned, and made for the street.

"Are you or are you not going to give me a ride home!" he demanded as Erich rapidly caught up with him.

"Home?" Spear lifted, Erich let out a loud war-whoop, like the ones in Wild West films.

Glowering, Solomon trudged off toward the Kurfurstendamm. "Some friend you are."

"*Some friend you are,*" Erich mimicked, making made another whirlwind circle. Then he steered down the street and returned at high speed, skidding to a halt at Sol's feet. "*I* don't want to go home yet!"

His friend kept walking resolutely, not looking back even when Erich nosed the front wheel up behind him. "Don't go," Erich said.

"Why not? You can manage fine without me!"

"I'll let you ride the bike home if you'll stay around a little longer." Erich made his voice sound low and contrite.

Sol turned and smiled as if in disbelief.

The reaction did not surprise Erich in the least; he knew he guarded his possessions somewhat too jealously. "Honest—you can ride Hawk all the way back," he said.

"We really should go home, Erich. I'm tired, you've been...ill and," Sol glanced at the rucksack, "that puppy's probably dying of hunger."

Oh Lord, Erich thought. He had forgotten all about the puppy. He had an idea. They were not more than minutes away from the Rathenau estate. Miriam and her grandmother were living there. This was as good a time as any to sneak in. The old lady would be fast asleep. He would give Miriam the puppy and....

Sol mounted the bike. "We'll do whatever you want for a little while longer and then go home, okay? Get on."

"I'll run." Erich glanced at his biceps with satisfaction. "That way!" He pointed in the direction of the estate.

"Bet we're headed to Miriam Rathenau's," Sol said.

"Very good, Solomon." Javelin in hand Erich glided along with the fluid ease of a warrior. "Only took you a year and a century to figure that out."

He fell silent and looked back over his shoulder. Sol was frowning, as if trying to solve an obtuse mathematical problem.

"Erich, what really happened that night before Herr Rathenau...when you ran away?"

Erich did not answer. He was not ready to talk to Solomon or anyone else about that night.

"Mind your own business." Erich clenched his fist. "I told you. I slept at the camp and went to see Miriam the next day to get the photograph for your bar mitzvah present." *And she let me in for all of ten minutes,* Erich thought angrily, keeping that information to himself.

"She won't let you in this time," Sol said, "not covered in dirt and blood."

Erich looked down at his chest and arms, flexed his muscles, and lifted his blood-smeared face in a statuesque pose. "I guess some water wouldn't hurt," he said reluctantly. "Their dogs will go nuts if we try to get in while I'm painted up like this."

"*Guard* dogs?"

"Don't worry, I'll take care of them." *Better than I took care of Grace,* he told himself angrily.

The boys were almost upon the estate when they spotted a pump. They took turns at the handle, using Erich's shirt as a washcloth.

"Did you scrub behind your ears, Solomon?" Erich said in a maternal falsetto, stuffing the shirt under a hedge. "No sense keeping this. Let's go."

The Rathenau house was constructed of limestone and surrounded by a tall stone wall. Square turrets latticed with ivied trellises were surmounted by mock parapets scalloped with friezes. Ornate cornices shadowed many of the narrow leaded windows, and moonlight glinted off the circular stained glass set above the front portico. A golden flagpole rose over the roof.

"That's Miriam's room." Erich stuck his arm through the side gate's iron grating and pointed toward the far turret. There, beyond a trellised balcony, white curtains draped French windows.

"You're something, Erich! You wouldn't walk in Rathenau's honor, yet you have the nerve to come here."

"Why should I care about her uncle? I didn't even like him."

"You didn't even know him."

"What difference does it make!" Erich took hold of the grate and peered through as if between the bars of a cell. "Tonight's the night, Fraülein Rathenau."

"Not while I—"

"Relax! I just meant I'm going to promise to take her to Luna Park."

There was loud barking and growling as two sleek shadows raced across the grounds and lunged at the gate.

"Down, Princess." Erich kept his voice silky as the Doberman and the Russian wolfhound snapped and snarled and thrust their muzzles between the bars. "Down, Piccadilly."

"Piccadilly?" Sol's tone was a mix of terror and disbelief.

"Something to do with your pal the Rat's hatred of England." Erich knew his disrespect would aggravate Solomon. "There's a circus or something over there by that name." He reached out and, closing his eyes and tensing, let his hand slowly descend between the bars. "Easy girls."

The dogs quieted and Erich stroked the terrible heads, wishing with all his heart he were petting a living, breathing Grace. "We can go in now." He wondered how long it would take for him to stop feeling queasy about what had happened at the camp.

"You're sure?"

"Course I'm sure." He was already climbing the gate.

"I could wait here for you—"

"Please, Solomon."

Looking forlorn, Solomon began to climb. He crossed the iron spearheads that rose from the gate top and dropped to the turf at Erich's urging. The dogs circled and sniffed him.

"Lead on, Princess," Erich whispered. "Let's go."

Together, he and the dogs raced across the lawn toward the west-end turret. He started up the ivy and rose-laced trellis. "We go hand-over-hand along the eave, then drop to her balcony," he said to Solomon. "It's not much of a drop. If you stretch, you'll be able to touch the balcony rail with your toes."

"How do we get back down?"

"With difficulty. Or else sneak through the house."

"You're insane."

"So is the world—or that's what my dear papa keeps telling me." Erich dropped quietly as he could onto the balcony's hexagonal tiles.

"I'll stay here," Sol said from the terrace. "Who's in the house besides Miriam?"

"Her grandmother." Erich squatted beside the French doors and tried to peer in through the curtains, which were too sheer to block the view completely. "Some other relatives, too. I don't know who. They were there when I was here before. I think they came in from all over Europe after the Rat kicked it."

"He was *assassinated.* And please don't call him that!"

"I keep telling you—dead is dead! Anyhow, there's also a whole platoon of maids and valets and gardeners."

He rapped lightly on the door. The sound seemed to shimmer in the air like something tangible.

"I'm going back!" Sol said.

"Stay...please!" Heart pounding in his ears, Erich pressed his face against the door's edge. A small night lamp stood on a vanity neatly arrayed with silver-handled brushes. Moonlight swam in the vanity mirror. He could see the corner of a bed with a pink coverlet. He rapped on the door again, a little louder.

"Maybe they've gone away," Sol whispered.

Erich had about decided the same thing when a light blazed and Miriam emerged, looking as if she had thrown off the bedcovers in the middle of a dream. Her face shone like ivory, an effect intensified by the edging of cream-colored lace around the neck and sleeves of her peignoir and by the tumble of long dark hair that framed her face and shoulders. He caught sight of the silhouette of her breasts.

If only he were older...richer...taller—

If only he were Jewish.

Frightened by the intensity of his feelings, he twisted his head to look for Sol. The action sent him off-balance, and he grabbed the balcony rail.

"Something wrong?" Sol asked. "Another seizure?"

Erich twisted his head around to answer, but Sol shook his head and held a finger to his lips. Then he ducked behind the corner and Erich turned back to see Miriam staring at him through the glass door.

Chapter 24

"Who's there?" Miriam called out, more curious than afraid.

She pulled on a pink robe, framed along the collar and cuffs with vanilla fur, and walked toward the balcony door. With the light on in the room, she could barely make out a dark shape outside the door; she could see a circle of moisture where his nose, or perhaps his mouth, had been pressed up against the glass.

Quickly she doubled back and switched off the light she had turned on when the rapping at her door had wakened her.

"Erich?"

She stifled her laughter for fear of hurting his feelings. Before going to bed she had drawn aside the thin, gauze curtain that usually covered the door and separated her from the moonlight. Oma called it a privacy curtain and insisted it should be kept drawn, which had always seemed ludicrous to Miriam. Her room was, after all, not in the middle of a traffic pattern. Every now and then her fantasies included a handsome beau climbing the trellis to her balcony, a Scarlet Pimpernel in a red velvet jacket, lace at his neck and a plumed hat set jauntily on his head—not this bare-chested hopeful Romeo-with-a-rucksack who stood out there now.

"What on earth are you doing here in the middle of the night!" She opened the door and looked past him, down at the trellis. "Where's Sol?"

Erich shrugged. "Not here."

Miriam frowned. There were little lies and big lies, and times when both were necessary. What she could not abide was a *wasted* lie. A pointless one. Someone else had been out there, and who else but Sol would consent to come out with Erich at this time of night?

Boldly, though awkwardly, Erich leaned toward her as though to kiss her on the lips. Miriam pushed him away. "You know you shouldn't be here. You especially shouldn't be here doing *that.*"

"You liked it at the shop."

"Maybe I did like it," she said honestly. "Just don't do it." She had liked it all right, but not enough to be the booty in a bet, which was probably what this was all about. Still, she had to admit she was enjoying the idea that Erich—and Sol—had braved the dogs and the trellis to get to her.

"How did you get past the dogs? I thought I heard them barking. And why aren't you wearing a shirt?"

"I can handle dogs." Erich took a step backward and looked over the rail as if to see the animals below.

"You're lucky they didn't attack you! Well, now that you're here and in one piece, you want to tell me why?"

Erich grinned, and she felt foolish. Talk about giving someone a—what did they call it in America?—a straight line.

"Brought you a present," Erich said.

"My birthday's not till the end of September."

"It's an un-birthday present."

Removing the rucksack from his shoulders, he reached inside and took out a tiny puppy. He held it by the nape of the neck, its legs dangling.

A stuffed dog—from Erich? She might have expected that from Sol, but not Erich. A snake, an alligator, a live dog maybe, but not— She reached for it.

"Here!" she said. "No! Take it away!"

At the point of tears, she thrust it back at him. This was no stuffed dog; it was living, breathing. Like Susie—

"What's the matter? I haven't done anything wrong."

"I'm sorry," Miriam whispered. "It's just that my parents were taking my English sheep dog to the veterinarian when they were—" She took a sharp breath. "Well, you know."

But he did not know, she was aware. Not about the fire or her fears. How could she explain to this too-young boy that she wanted a dog more than anything else in the world, yet was terrified that owning one would cause her to lose someone she loved?

Erich kissed the puppy on the nose. *"Her* mother's dead, too. T-take her...go on. Please." A sense of worried begging shone in Erich's eyes.

A rustling from the trellis provided Miriam with the distraction she needed. She stepped toward it and was about to say something more about Sol when the guard dogs growled.

"They're just jealous," Erich said, too quickly. He waved a hand near the trellis as if shooing away a fly.

Signaling his friend, Miriam thought. Hope the dogs don't tear Sol apart. "Those dogs *are* jealous." She decided not to mention Sol again. Sooner or later, she would find out what was going on.

"She needs to be fed," Erich said.

"Who? Oh, you mean the puppy." Miriam reached out tentatively and stroked the dog; it was soft—and warm. "Look at your tiny paws." She wished she had the courage to hold it.

"She's going to be a beauty," Erich said. "I bet you and I love dogs more than anyone else in Berlin."

Miriam steeled her resolve. Carefully, as if the animal were made of eggshells, she took the dog from Erich. "You're right, I do love them, but—" Frustrated with herself, she sighed deeply. "I can't accept the gift, Erich. I just...can't."

"Sure you can."

"No!"

She handed the puppy back to him. He kissed it on the nose again and rewrapped it with the towel. She watched him place it in the corner of the balcony and did not retreat when he stepped forward and took her awkwardly in his arms. For a moment, not wanting to think about the puppy, she gave in to his boyish embrace, then pushed him away.

"Stop it. If anyone sees us—"

"No one will see."

She felt a mixture of agitation and pleasure as he put his arms around her again. "Please, Erich. Don't." He kissed her throat insistently. "This is stupid." She tried to ignore the warmth creeping through her. "We're asking for trouble."

She pulled roughly away and did her best to glare at him.

"I'm sorry." His bravado was gone and he sounded on the verge of tears.

He is just a boy on the edge of manhood, Miriam thought. And she did like him—a lot. Well, maybe she didn't *like* him all that much—he was too mixed up and too...Aryan. What she liked was the person he *could* become, if he discarded the arrogant set of his shoulders—if the slight hardness around his mouth when he was refused disappeared—

If! Ifs didn't count, she knew that. Like the "if" at work right now: *if* he didn't give her that warm feeling when he looked at her, when he touched her, she would have sent him away at once. In fact, she would have had nothing to do with him in the first place.

Relenting, though only slightly, she placed his arm around her shoulder and kissed him on the cheek. He was barely taller than she as she leaned into him. Barely taller, Gentile, too-young...but still, *if*—

She felt his arm tighten around her. Oh, hell! She stared up at the moon. What did it matter; she was not exactly going to marry him!

Turning to face Erich, she closed her eyes and let herself enjoy their first real kiss. Just one, she told herself, and then she would go back to bed.

Chapter 25

The rose vines irritated Sol's cheek, and his forehead itched. The dogs panted, circled, whined, rose on hind legs to paw the ivy. Moonlight and silence veiled the balcony.

Around the corner from the balcony, he went further down the trellis. The wolfhound growled and the Doberman climbed onto the latticework in bright, angry anticipation. Sol cursed softly.

Above him, Miriam gave a small sigh.

Definitely not his idea of a good time. Erich was up there playing Romeo, while he was playing—what? Monkey?

Carefully he maneuvered closer to the corner and peeked around. Miriam's head was cocked flirtatiously to one side while Erich held her. Earlier, his heart had skipped a beat when she had insisted that he, Sol, was here too. Now he could feel his heart turn inside-out with a quite different emotion. What was it? Anger?

He knew what Papa would call it. Jealousy.

Fighting tears, he dropped from the trellis. The dogs, apparently sensing that he had discarded his fear of them, left him alone. They continued to whine and stare up at the balcony.

Grateful for that, at least, Sol charged through the gardens and climbed the gate. He picked up the bike, shivered with fury and slammed it down. Never again did he want to touch anything belonging to Erich Weisser.

If it weren't for Papa, he told himself, there wouldn't be any Erich Weisser hanging around the store, tormenting people, treating Miriam Rathenau as if she belonged to him. The Weissers would still be hawking vegetables and speaking *Plattdeutsch*.

He chided himself for being so small-minded. Yet as he began to walk, all he could think of was how to get back at Erich for everything—but especially for dragging him out to the estate and then dismissing him with that imperious wave of his. He felt stupid for having fallen for Erich's friendship routine one more time, so stupid that even the Grünewald's mansions and chateaus, set among manicured gardens and neatly trimmed trees, seemed to mock him with their mien of regal repose.

Leaving the Grünewald, he found himself outside the Goethe *Gymnasium*, at the corner of Westfalische and Eisenzahn. The streets were empty, as were his pockets. No way to take a taxi or tram, and by the time he walked home, Papa would be awake.

Then he remembered. The money in his shoe! His mother had put it there. For emergencies, she had said, God forbid you should ever need it.

Sitting on the curb, he removed his shoe and worked the lining of the instep free. There, protected by a bit of chamois, was the ten-mark note that had initially given his arch a callus.

He retied his shoe and, with a feeling of slow, suffocating desperation, unfolded the money. Even if he could get home before Papa arose, he would have to try and stay awake all day under his teacher's scrutiny. Worse, Erich would be in school. Sleep or no, Erich would go to school just so he could brag about what he had done with Miriam. A knot of admirers had surrounded him all morning after he told everyone that Ursula Müller had offered to drop her drawers for him.

Liar!

And I was right there among them, eager as the others, wanting to believe him.

Curling his fingers around the money, he made a decision. He was probably the only student at Goethe who had never skipped a class. As Erich would say, there was a first time for everything. Assuming Papa was not wise to the fact that he had been out almost all night, he would pretend to go to school—only never arrive.

A bus turned onto Eisenzahn Strasse. Rising to board it, he wondered if he shouldn't avoid going home altogether. No, that would worry his parents too much. Being caught playing hooky might earn him a paddling. He could handle that. He could not handle the pain of deliberately hurting Mama and Papa.

A few hours later, having catnapped at home, Sol trundled off to school—with his mother's blessing and without Erich, who "will be a little late for school today," as Frau Weisser had come down to inform Sol.

Avoiding the usual route, Sol made his way into the center of the city. He had decided to spend the day at Luna Park, but it did not open this early. While he stood among the crowds of the Tauenzien Strasse, yawning and bleary-eyed, his attention was caught by one of the KadeWe's window displays—a window devoted to Käthe Kruse dolls. The window dresser had seated them like an audience around a life-sized model of Grog, Berlin's most famous clown.

"*Schö-ö-ön*—beautiful," Sol thought he heard the department store dummy say, although its mouth did not move.

"*Schö-ö-on,*" he repeated, completing the famous circus routine. Snapping his mouth shut and feeling foolish, he looked around. Too little sleep, he thought, excusing himself. As if it were not bad enough to hear voices in an abandoned sewer, now he was hearing a clown mannequin talk! The live Grog only left Circus Busch at Christmas to work department stores and other places where crowds gathered.

"*Schö-ö-ön.*" With slow marionette motion the mannequin lifted a hand in an awkward greeting, its mouth fixed in a rictus-grin.

Sol stood staring at the colorful marble eyes, ignoring the hoi polloi on their way to coffee, cake, and gossip at Kranzler's, and forcing them to walk around him. Was it Grog? A mechanical man? He might have stood there all day, had a man with an umbrella not bumped into him and shouted at him, breaking the spell.

Feeling a sudden need to get away, he turned and ran past the counter at Aschinger's where he had intended to stop for a bowl of their inexpensive pea soup and sausage, which would have held him until he got to the sourpickle barrel at Luna Park.

"*Das ist die Berliner Luft..,*" a barrel organ man—the oldest one Solomon had ever seen—played outside Kranzler's. Sol slowed down to listen and to watch the animal perched on a stool beside the hurdy gurdy. Black and white, with jade-green eyes, the tethered animal looked like a cross between a large monkey and a teddy bear.

The man played on, head lolled to one side as if his neck were broken. He was toothless, and a great bib of creased wrinkled flesh hung below his chin. But his music was beautiful. A Paul Lincke medley filtered through the air and Solomon swayed, mesmerized--

The man's eyes popped open, revealing milky unseeing pupils.

"*Lieber Leierkasten Mann, sieh mich nicht so traurig an,*" Sol said. "Dear barrel organ man, don't look at me so mournfully."

The animal reached down and closed the man's eyelids. Wondering why German children had a verse for everything, Sol stretched to offer the animal a Groschen.

The animal emitted a weird wail that sounded like someone sliding a hand up and down the scale of a saxophone, and snatched the coin. Sol lurched back in pain, clutching his hand. He looked at his palm, then at the animal in frightened disbelief. A gouge brimming with blood ran the length of his lifeline.

"Gotcha, did he, boy?" The blind man laughed. "He does that with people he doesn't like."

The animal leaped onto the old man's back and curled across his shoulders, looking like a fluffy winter wrap.

"What *is* it!" Half in horror, half in fascination, Sol held his palm to his lips. He had a feeling he had seen something like the animal before. But where?

"It's an indri," the hurdy gurdy man said. "A type of lemur. The name means—'behold!'" His lolled to the other side and he began cackling. "A Frenchie went into the jungles of Madagascar looking for the cynocephalus—a mythical dog-headed boy. When the Natives pointed out one of these little fellows, they shouted, 'Indri! Indri!' to get the man's attention. So that's how it got its name." He hawked deep in his throat and spat a brown stream of tobacco juice onto the street—and onto Solomon's shoes.

"Are you a dog-headed boy, Solomon?" the old man asked as Sol backed away in terror.

"You *know* me?"

"I know everyone who's anyone in Berlin—even if *you* don't know who you are."

Shaking his head against what *had* to be a nightmare, Sol turned and began running toward the Zoo Station. Behind him, the indri caterwauled and the old man shouted, "Well, are you a dog-headed boy? Is that what your dreams say?" and cackled insanely.

Boarding an open-topped bus and too afraid to look back, Solomon followed a long-legged prostitute in a short skirt and leather boots up the stairs and to the front seat. She placed her whip across her knees and patted the seat beside her.

"Don't worry," she said. "I like 'em young, but it's been a hard night. I couldn't lift my whip even if you begged me."

Embarrassed and upset, Sol looked around the bus. The seat next to the woman was the only empty one left. He sat down and examined his hand. It was stinging, but already the bleeding had begun to stop. He would probably get blood poisoning and die, he thought, sitting up stiff and straight and trying not to think too clearly—for fear something might make sense and he would discover he was not dreaming.

While he watched the city pass in a blur, the woman next to him drifted into sleep, her head against his shoulder. The bus bounced them both around as it negotiated the three-and-a-half kilometers to Halensee at the upper end of the Ku'damm. The journey seemed interminable; Sol could hardly wait to see the Halensee Bridge.

Directly below that lay Luna Park.

"Hallensee! Luna Park!"

Sol disengaged himself from the sleeping woman and disembarked.

"Achtung...Achtung! Hier spricht Berlin! Attention...attention! This is Berlin speaking!" Alfred Braun's voice boomed through the loudspeakers of the Funkturm. The radio tower was Berlin's tallest building and loomed high over the city, the bridge and the park.

"Luna Park!" yelled the main-gate barker, using a megaphone so his voice would carry from the amusement park below the bridge. Anxiety rippled through Sol; was today, he wondered, one of those during which people could take their clothes off in the Park?

At least the barker was clothed, so probably this was a regular day after all.

"Open seven days a week! Ride the carousel and the Ferris wheel! Risk your lives on the roller coaster! Win prizes!"

"Achtung!"

"Luna Park! Open seven days—"

"Achtung!"

Blinking and slack-muscled from sleeplessness, Sol staggered down the hill to the Park. The barker's hand emerged as if disembodied and took one of the notes Sol had changed—when? Last night? Sol couldn't recall.

"Luftballons. Nur ein Sechser." Inside the gate, a man holding a rainbow of balloons in a deformed, white-fleshed hand gripped Sol's arm. "Balloons. Only five pfennig."

Sol shook loose and ran into the Park. When he stared back over his shoulder he saw the man was wearing a white glove and grinning like a clown.

Trying to clean his glasses, Sol staggered among the booths.

"Wheel of Fortune. Three turns, three winners."

"Glühwürmchen, Glühwürmchen...."

The song drew Sol away from the booths to the carousel. Around and around it whirled while the song played over and over, a giant music box without a stopping mechanism. He thought he saw a dark-haired girl in a cream-colored peignoir on the other side, sitting on a white horse and reaching for the brass ring that dangled from a rope amid the galloping circle of wooden steeds.

But the carousel was empty, its animals riderless.

He rubbed his eyes. Whatever had possessed him to skip school!

"Berg und Tal Bahn!" a barker shrieked, offering Sol a roller coaster ride.

"Three turns, three winners!" another called from the closest booth. "Win an ostrich feather for Mama!"

The roller coaster went up and down and the carousel kept turning around and his head spun and the ground tilted—

"A stuffed doggie for your Fräulein. Every time a winner!"

"Three turns, three—"

"Visit the Panoptikum, the Hall of Mirrors. See yourself as you really are!"

Yes, Sol thought. Yes! That was what he wanted, what he needed—to see himself as he really was. He paid and stumbled through the door. The mirrors leered and wavered, but it was dark inside, and cool. If he could just lie down for a while. Here, where the carousel was muted.

He sagged in a corner, his back against a mirror and, sighing, let his eyes close.

"Up! Out! What do you think this is, a hotel?"

A huge hand held fast to Sol's lapels and a bearded barker in a pinstriped coat pulled him to his feet. His glasses slipped off his nose and he struggled to rescue them. When he looked up, the man grinned at him and dissolved. Images appeared in a convex mirror, tall as the Funkturm. A goatee, the white flesh of a deformed hand, Erich and Miriam—arms around each other, pointing and laughing—

"Glühwürmchen...."

Sol could hear the strains of the carousel's calliope, pulling him back outside, away from the laughing images in the mirror. He glanced at the door, wondering how he was going to find the strength to get out of here and make his way home. He looked back at the mirror, afraid he might see a manifestation of the dybbuk.

A thin convex version of himself stared back at him. Nothing but a jealous and tired thirteen-year-old who was more than ready to go home.

Chapter 26

October, 1924

Miriam surveyed the disarray of her room. Her navy-blue private school uniform lay crumpled on the floor. Her suitcases, half-packed, stood beside the door. Make-up was strewn all over her vanity.

"Here, Killi," she said, close to tears. Obediently, the shepherd came over and nuzzled her. "You'll like being with Vlad," she told the dog, more for her own sake than for the animal's. How she'd battled Erich about calling a female dog Achilles, she thought. The name, he'd insisted, had come to him out of the moonlight, so even if this was a bitch, no other name would do. Sad as she felt, she could not help but smile at the memory of Erich's appearance on her balcony that night with the puppy, his fumbling attempts at caresses, his pride in saying *bitch,* as if it made him older and taller to say it out loud in her presence.

That night was really the beginning of their friendship.

Why was it she found beginnings so easy and endings so difficult, she wondered. She picked up her journal from the top of her suitcase. There were so many memories.

She stopped herself, calling upon her pragmatic streak. There was much to be done before the train left for Paris; she could not allow sentiment to distract her, at least not until she picked up the boys en route to the train station.

Mentally she ticked off her list. Finish packing. Hand Killi over to Vlad, who had agreed to make things easier for her by meeting her at the cigar shop—

Dammit, what did Sol and Erich expect her to do now that she had graduated from school—hang around until they grew up too? Her choices were clear enough. Go back to America, enroll at the University here in Berlin, or do what she was doing—join a dance company and start trying to earn her own living.

Not that she had ever wanted for anything, not even last year during the worst of inflation, when an egg cost eight hundred marks and even middle-class Jews like Sol were forever having to stand in long Gentile-first lines for milk and other staples. She wished her grandmother could live forever, but the truth was that, even if Oma died, she would not lack for money. Perhaps with her funds, she could assure that Sol would never again have to stand in lines. The estate would be hers, and Oma's jewelry and money—and the trust fund in Switzerland. Oma was there right now, making sure everything was in order before joining her in Paris.

Eventually it would all be hers, but that wasn't the same as earning it herself. Besides, she loved performing, and she had a right to her own life. Time to leave; time to get on with it.

Good intentions notwithstanding, she sat down on the bed and opened her journal, a gift from Sol for her sixteenth birthday. It bulged with mementos. Ticket stubs. A dark curl she had kept from the day she'd had her hair bobbed. Photographs: Vladimir holding a tennis racket, his eyes telling her he'd had a different game in mind for a long time; Oma, her arms filled with freshly cut roses, her shoulders bent with the weight of her sorrow for her sons—

And the boys. Always the boys—alone, together, she and Erich, she and Sol, the three of them—

The boys would be men when she came back. If she came back.

She leafed through the pages, stopping here and there as a word, a sentence, a pressed flower triggered memories of the last two years. Sol, his nose buried in a book; Erich in his ridiculous uniform. Erich and Sol under a tree in the park, picnicking on Braunschweiger and Pickart bread and arguing about Adolph Hitler's jail sentence for his part in the Munich Beer Hall Putsch—

She opened the journal at random.

Wedged between two pages was a letter from Sol, written to her the day after he had talked to her. In it, he spoke about his visions, about his fears for the Jews, about his dream of spending his life studying and interpreting the mystics in ways everyone could understand, and about his visions...*I remember the day Erich hurt his hand,* he wrote. *We were taking him to the hospital in a taxi. I was exhausted, and terribly upset. I thought I had fallen asleep in the car and dreamed about standing in line for hour after hour to buy two bottles of milk for Mama. In the dream, the milk cost a fistful of money; in the dream, Jews had to stay at the back of the line until all non-Jews had been served. And then, as we all know, it happened. Really happened. I wonder how many other things I have "dreamed" in that way will turn out to be visions of the future. Not too many, I hope, for few of my dreams are pleasant.*

On the same page, and on half-a-dozen of the following ones, she had pasted photographs of the three of them at Luna Park. She read the captions. *Erich protecting me on the roller coaster. Erich being romantic on the Ferris* wheel. Me, hugging the music box Sol won—after a lot of trying—at the pfennig-toss. How jealous Erich had been over that!

She took the music box off her vanity and placed it next to her handbag. She was leaving enough behind; she could surely afford to take a few things for no reason other than sentiment. The memory made her smile, and she opened the lid and listened to "Glowworm."

So sweet, those boys. She closed the music box.

Again she opened the journal but this time there was nothing random about her choice of page. She ran her finger along an electric-blue peacock feather. Pulling it off the page, she attached it with a hat pin to the soft felt cloche she had picked for the journey—the same one she had worn on the ferry to Pfaueninsel—Peacock Island—that Saturday....

She and Erich had gone to the island alone, leaving Sol to his renewed studies with the beadle. She had probably learned more about Erich that day than before or since, she thought as she picked up her journal and skimmed what she had written. They had talked about Sol's visions and about Erich's views of the world and the Great War. At first, listening to him, she had thought him against war, but she had slowly come to realize that he imagined himself as a member of the German nobility, willing to sacrifice himself for his king or his lady and doing battle for both to prove his heroism. What had surprised her was his clear perception of his own shortcomings—his need to control others and the temper that would not allow him to live up to his conception of what he would like himself to be.

And what he could be! Miriam thought. A pressed lilac blossom fell from the journal and fluttered onto the bed, wafer thin and diaphanous—like the dress she had worn in celebration of free-love advocate Isadora Duncan and her marriage to the Russian poet, Sergei Esenin. She had packed the dress. She would wear it on some stage somewhere, when she needed to be close to Sol and Erich.

She riffled through the pages and found her description of the day she had worn the dress. The limousine ride to Wiesbaden, the three of them, Achilles, and the ever-obliging Konnie. A picnic in the park....

Erich stood stiffly upright and held the rough army blanket to one side like a toreador's cape. Sol grinned, put down the picnic basket and took out his harmonica, which he kept wrapped in one of his father's Reichsbanner handkerchiefs.

"Play the 'Toreador's Song'," Miriam said, positioning herself.

Sol played—badly—but that didn't matter. It was drizzling slightly—that didn't matter either. Miriam could feel the rhythm through the thin strains of the harmonica. She stamped her feet, swirled, charged the cape again and again. At her side, watching them, was a small statue of Pan. She danced around him, paying tribute to Isadora, her free-flowing movements inspired by Sol and Erich, and by the music of friendship. Erich watched, forgetting to move the blanket and lusting after her body. She liked that. Most of all she liked the way Sol watched her, loving her being.

"I'm starving." Erich threw the blanket on the ground and reached for the picnic basket.

But Sol played on and she danced just for him. When the song was over, he shook the harmonica and put it back in his pocket. Smiling, he walked over to a blooming lilac, plucked a flower, and presented it to her.

"The star must have flowers," he said.

Not to be outdone, Erich pulled off a whole branch. Soon they were plucking the blossoms and throwing them at each other, tumbling around on the blanket like puppies.

Later, emptying out the picnic basket, she found blossoms among the crumbs....

How carefully she had orchestrated that day—and others too. Like the time she had arranged to meet the boys in front of the Siegessäule for an on-site debate about the stupidity of putting up a *victory* monument after a defeat. Or the time the three of them had pedaled all the way to the Grünewald, she and Sol together on a borrowed bicycle-made-for-two, to visit the estate of a close friend of her family.

They had entered the estate through wine vaults so enormous that they pedaled through the rooms. In the vaults they used the bikes for a jousting tournament, Erich proclaiming himself Tannhäuser and Miriam the Lady Venus. Sol astonished himself by winning and Erich astonished her by laughing in appreciation of his friend's skill. What fun they'd had among the dusty bottles, playing hide-and-seek in the darkened cellar...until Sol's ghosts came. She remembered his face, pinched and drawn, as he turned away from Erich's attempts to cajole him back into the spirit of the game.

Beginning to feel maudlin she snapped the journal shut, but not before she allowed herself a final memory—

She flipped to her last journal entry.

Wedged into the page, not yet pasted in, was a photo of Erich and Sol taken at the estate less than a month ago. The three of them had been sitting holding hands amid the dying roses of an Indian summer day. As dusk turned the sky pink she had told them of her decision to leave Berlin. First one and then the other, unembarrassed by the other's presence, swore to wait for her.

"I can't marry both of you," she had said.

"Ja, but would you if you could?" Erich had asked.

"I would."

He had plucked three long grasses and wound one around her ring finger and another around his own. The third one he handed to Sol. "Now, say 'I do!' and the three of us will be joined forever."

Sol, his eyes dark and intense, looked at her and then at Erich. Tossing aside the strand of grass, he had released her hand and walked away to stand by himself. She had wanted to go to him and comfort him, but Erich had held her back with a look that almost frightened her...and the moment passed—

"Almost time to leave, Fräulein Rathenau," Konrad called from downstairs. "May I collect your suitcases?"

Panicked, Miriam looked at her watch. "Give me another fifteen minutes, Konnie."

She threw the rest of her things in the cases and slipped into her clothes. In fifteen minutes, exactly, Konrad was back.

"I...I will miss you, Fräulein Rathenau." His usually implacable face wore a saddened expression.

Impulsively, Miriam hugged him. "And I, you, Konnie. Will you be here when I return?"

His face scarlet, Konrad nodded. "Your grandmother has been kind enough to give me a retainer. I shall stay here and take care of things as...best I can. I am not so young anymore and it would have been difficult...."

He stopped, as if embarrassed by his sudden garrulousness. He picked up the smallest of her cases and tucked it under his arm, lifted the other two as if they weighed nothing, and left the room. Achilles followed him to the door, then stopped and turned around as if waiting for her to come. She picked up her handbag, hat, and gloves, and glanced around one more time. Swallowing hard, she left the room and went quickly down the stairs and out the front door.

"Shall I wait right here?" Konrad asked when they drove up to the shop.

Miriam got out of the car and nodded. Taking Achilles by the leash, she tethered her to a pole outside the shop.

Sol sat at the table, the *Book of Formation* open in front of him. When he saw her, he simply stared.

"You look beautiful, Miriam." Jacob Freund stepped from behind the counter. "You will doubtless turn Paris on its ear."

Miriam had already said her farewells to him and to Sol's mother and sister. She had said less fond farewells to Erich's parents, who had long since forgiven her—or so they said—for "corrupting" their son. Despite their forgiveness, there had never been any love lost among the three of them.

"Where's Erich?" she asked. "We don't have much time. As soon as Vlad gets here I have to go."

"Why don't I tell him to hurry?" Herr Freund said.

"Thank you, Herr Freund," Miriam said.

"There is one condition," Jacob Freund said seriously. He opened his arms and smiled. "An extra hug for an old man, if you please."

"That's easy." Miriam was happy to oblige. She liked Sol's mother and sister, but her fondness for them did not equal the way she felt about Jacob. She really did love him, she thought, enjoying the smell of tobacco and Aqua Velva as he put his arms around her.

"Hey—come back with that!"

Miriam and Jacob whirled around to see Sol give chase to a little boy in uniform. Sol did not get very far, for he bumped head-on into Vladimir, who had stooped to pet Achilles.

"Thieves!" Jacob muttered. "There are more of those these days than customers." He glanced over at the table. "If my son does not start paying more attention, there will soon be no more pieces left." He walked over to the ivory chess set. "The ivory queen is missing!" He shrugged. "Ah well! The ebony one has been gone for months."

"I'm sorry, Papa." Sol limped back into the store.

"Today I forgive you," Jacob Freund said. "You have reason to be distracted. Tomorrow, you will not be as easily forgiven. Leave your books at home, Solomon. There will be plenty of time for you to read those things when you are older. Ah, here's Erich at last."

Miriam looked up to see Erich crossing the street. Please, Erich, she prayed. No more fuss about Achilles. They had already argued enough. First Erich had said he wanted to take the dog to the camp. Sol reminded him that the animal could not be kenneled there, since Erich had stolen it from the camp in the first place—a fact Miriam had not known. A compromise was reached; come the new year, Vlad would move onto the estate to act as caretaker— and to finish writing his novel. The dog would belong to Erich but would remain at the estate, where he could visit her any time he pleased.

"Erich! Hurry—there's not much time!" Miriam called out from the doorway.

Erich stopped in mid-street. He lifted his hand in a tentative wave and, ignoring the traffic, turned around and rushed back into the apartment building.

"What now?" Sol said.

"Maybe we had better go and find out or I'll miss my train." By now they were all gathered on the sidewalk and she was, once again, precariously close to tears. "Vlad, go. Please." She raised herself up on her toes, kissed him quickly on the cheek, and dropped to her haunches next to Achilles. "Don't forget me, Killi." She hugged the dog.

Quickly, without looking back, she crossed the street, Sol close behind her. They ran into the building, up the stairs, and into the Weisser flat.

"I was going to put it on for you, but...I've changed my mind." Erich stood at the window of his room, his back to them. His uniform was laid out on his bed. Miriam sat down heavily and stared at it. "You hate it—don't you!" He did not turn around.

"I hate what it stands for," Miriam said quietly.

"I'm going to change all that." Erich's voice was deadly calm. "You wait and see if I don't." He looked back out the window. "I'm not going to spend my life in that cigar shop, waiting on people who think they're better than I am." His face hardened. "Go now—both of you!"

"Erich—"

He turned to face her. "You'll come home, Miriam." His voice was still calm, and surprisingly soft. "I will be here."

"Will you write?"

"I'll—try. I'm not much good at that."

She wanted to kiss him one more time, but she did not. "I may never come back." Her voice was almost a whisper.

"You'll be back." Erich was looking at Sol. "One day, Miri, you'll have to make a choice—"

"Perhaps I will choose someone else," she said.

He smiled, though the smile did not reach his eyes. "I don't think so," he said quietly. "It will always be the three of us, tied together..." He let his voice trail off and turned back to the window. "You'd better go."

When they were in the limo, Miriam took Sol's hand. They had not spoken since leaving Erich's room.

"Perhaps I should not come to the station either," Sol said.

Miriam tightened her grip on his hand. We have never embraced, you and I, she thought, hearing the echo of Erich's words. *One day, Miri, you'll have to make a choice...the three of us.*

"Will you miss me, Sol?"

"Would I miss my right arm if they cut it off?"

"Will *you* write?"

"Do you want me to?"

She laughed softly. "Would I miss my right arm if they cut it off?"

With a sureness that surprised her, he put his arms around her and kissed her. She returned his kiss, tentatively at first, then with a warmth that shocked her.

"I've never said this before because I didn't want you to laugh at me." He sat back against the leather, but did not release her from his embrace. "But now...I love you, Miri. I always will."

She leaned against him, filled with a sense of wonder at how right this felt.

"Always," she said softly, "sounds like a very long time."

Part II

"I have and know no other blood than German, no other voice, no other people than German. Banish me from German soil, I will remain German, and nothing changes.... My People and each of my friends have the right and the duty to correct me, should they find me inadequate."

— Walther Rathenau
Foreign Minister 1922,
letter January 23, 1916.

Chapter 27

September, 1933

Sol looked from the profusion of geraniums bordering the patio of the Tiergarten café to the trees beyond. Already it was September. The trees were almost bare and the earth was a carpet of leaves and acorns. To him it seemed only yesterday that the scent of May lilacs hung in the air.

"Beautiful, isn't it!" He looked across the table at Erich and wondered what had happened to the years.

"The Führer loves nature, doesn't he, girls?" Erich leaned down and petted his two German shepherds. Achilles, lying like a bunched blanket against his legs, lifted her head and gave a contented *ruuff*. Taurus, the younger dog, sitting with ears perked, appeared not to respond to the affection except to shake her head, dog tag clicking, after Erich was through.

"He's probably much too busy at the Reichstag to make time for oaks and elms." Sol was hard-pressed to keep the edge of sarcasm out of his voice.

"He'll be here," Erich said.

"I'm not waiting much longer."

Erich pounded the metal table with his fist. "Dammit, Solomon, he'll *be* here!"

"*Schlemiel!*" Sol grabbed hold of the tankards of beer. "You wouldn't want to stain your precious uniform, would you?"

Erich's face reddened. He gripped the table edge as if he were about to vault it like a gymnastics horse. "I've warned you not to speak Yiddish in public," he whispered, glancing at the threesome who had just arrived and stood waiting to be seated. "Even one word is dangerous!" He lowered his voice still further. "You're pushing your luck, Solomon."

Sol looked at the threesome—an elegantly dressed couple and a tall silver-haired man in a blue-serge suit who stood behind them, a hard feral smile on his face. He kept one hand possessively on the woman's shoulder and the other on the man's while he surveyed the Biergarten.

"Who's the one with the silver hair?" Sol asked. "Anybody important?"

"Important, no. Dangerous, yes!" Erich whispered. "That's Otto Hempel. He's only an Untersturmführer, but he's SS. I don't have the power to protect you from people like that even if I do outrank him." Erich clutched Sol's wrist. "Watch out. *Please.*"

"I'll hold my tongue if you hold your temper." Sol pulled his hand away. "Maybe you should befriend Hempel. You serve the same king, after all."

Erich ignored Sol's mocking tone. "The only people he wants to get close to, other than the High Command, are boys—bent over with their pants down. Goddamned queers are worse than whores." His voice was laced with disgust. "I hate immoral people!"

He glowered and sipped his beer. Sol watched Achilles wolf down a bockwurst that had rolled off the table during Erich's outburst. Taurus took no notice. Like Erich and me, Sol thought. Erich, so quick to seize any opportunity that he claims will help our families weather the Nazi storm, while I wait and watch.

Deciding to give the Chancellor ten more minutes, he listened to the threesome's conversation.

"They're all the same." The woman was addressing the shorter man. "Take that French philosopher, Bergson, and that renegade Jew—whatshisname?—the one who emigrated recently?" She tossed the tail of her narrow boa angrily around her neck.

"Einstein?" The man sounded bored.

"Right. The one who said you can bend light or something? I mean, who cares? Only a Jew would be interested in such foolishness. So what do the other Jews do? Give him a chair at the university. Does he stay there? No! Takes off for North America. To tell them our secrets, no doubt. *Our* secrets. *German* secrets."

"Eavesdropping again, Solomon?" Erich asked. "I think you look upon it as sport—though from the sounds of it, you'd be better off not listening."

"Same old argument," Sol said impatiently. "Always the Jews. We've conspired with the Communists to create *Kultur-Bolshevismus*. We're trying to rot Germany's moral fiber by corrupting its scientific and artistic institutions. Such absurdity would almost be funny if so many people didn't take it seriously."

He gave a sad smile as the woman started in on the architect Walter Gropius and the Bauhaus Movement.

"Just don't listen," Erich said. "Don't be a masochist."

"How can I help but listen?"

"All that glass and concrete," the woman said. "The building has no character. Much like you, my darling!" She removed a shoe and, balancing on one foot, dumped out a stone. "As for your wonderful ideas! Let's go for a walk, he says. It might improve your temperament! Ridiculous! Walking is for Jews and peasants. Besides, there's nothing wrong with my temperament that a good *man* couldn't cure!"

"What can it matter to you how something's built?" the shorter man asked in an even tone, as if the intimation that his manhood left something to be desired was unworthy of his attention.

"It matters because it's decadent!" The woman held onto her anger like a cat with a bird in its mouth. "Like those vulgar American skyscrapers. You can't tell the front from the back."

"Cubism and the concept of the multi-sided universe are simply reflections of the times."

"Nonsense! Your fancy theories reflect nothing but radicals and Jews, wanting to change everything. Like the roof of that monstrosity—the Bauhaus! It's flat, for God's sake! A flat roof in the Fatherland! It's unChristian! UnGerman!"

"Not to mention impractical, since it's likely to collapse under the first snow," the SS man added.

"That's right. *You* tell him, Otto," she said to the second lieutenant. "If Franz won't listen to reason, maybe *you* can make him understand."

"Perhaps you should calm yourself, Helga, before you bring on another migraine," Hempel said. "As for me, I do my best not to think." He raised his hand and snapped his fingers for a waitress. "It muddies the emotions."

The waitress, a girl of no more than seventeen, offered a choice of tables, one within view of Erich and Sol, the other in a prime spot around the corner and overlooking the lake with its weeping willows, swans, and blanket-wrapped boaters. The woman, appearing to seethe from her companion's treatment of her, indicated a preference for the table closer to Sol and Erich. Seating herself in Erich's line of vision, she arched an eyebrow, smiled, and draped her calf-length skirt so her ankles were seen to best advantage.

Sol looked from her to Erich and tried to assess him through her eyes. The young first lieutenant did look handsome in his uniform. Were it not for the mutilated hand, he would appear the perfect Aryan, as if he had stepped from one of the State-financed propaganda films at the Marmorhaus. The ribbons above his breast pocket added just the right touch of color, even though they represented completion of Abwehr military-security instruction and not gallantry in action. The neat mustache that graced his lip had surely stirred the heart of many a Fraülein on the parade field and at sports rallies in the Oranienburg grain fields.

"Ever have a woman like that?" Erich picked up his beer, toasted his admirer, and drank deeply.

Sol shook his head. "Have you?"

"She's no beer-and-bockwurst lay, I'll tell you that. You might try it some time. Do you good."

"Me?" Sol laughed.

"Why not? You're good-looking enough, in a Semitic kind of way. Lots of misguided women go for the dark brooding type. You can't spend the rest of your life moping after Miriam." He paused and his eyes darkened. "Have you heard from her lately?"

Sol shook his head. "I did write and tell her about the estate, but that was three months ago. Maybe more. Perhaps she never received the letter."

"Or perhaps she just doesn't care anymore. How long has it been since you heard from her—at least three years."

"We've both had birthday cards."

Erich laughed. "I'm sure Vladimir has too. She has a new life, Solomon. Face it. Do yourself a favor and get yourself one of those." He nodded in the direction of his admirer. "How old do you think she is? Forty? Forty-five?"

Sol shrugged, knowing that whatever he said would give Erich the opportunity for some acidic reply. When it came to Sol's shyness, Erich seemed unforgiving. As for his comments about Miriam, Erich's philandering was no indication that he had forgotten her, Sol thought. Different people used different ways to protect themselves; for Sol it was isolation, for Erich, just the opposite. That didn't mean a thing.

The woman leaned back, gave her order to the waitress, and made a limp-wristed motion with her hand. "Send the Gypsy to read our tea leaves. I wish to see if life has any excitement in store for me."

"I'm afraid she's unavailable, Fraülein," the girl said apologetically. "She says there is too much wind upon the water today for her power to be effective."

"Ridiculous!" The woman darted her gaze across the lake. "Not so much as a breeze. You bring her out here!"

"I'm sorry," the girl replied. She lowered her voice. "You know how stubborn the lesser peoples can be, Fraülein."

The waitress departed for the kitchen. With a defeated sigh, the woman sat back on the white wicker chair. Glancing toward Erich, she pushed at her auburn hair, then shook her fashionable center-parting back in place. Her gaze roamed from his eyes to his ribbons and down his shirt buttons; she recrossed her legs, pointing a slim foot in his direction, her red patent-leather shoe as covert an invitation as a lighthouse beacon. "If the Gypsy is unavailable, perhaps *he* could read my tea leaves," she said in a voice just loud enough to make certain Erich heard.

Franz took her hand and pressed it to his lips. "You are a wicked creature. Such a taste for soldiers."

The taller man leaned over and quietly said something to the woman. She stiffened. When she looked back at Erich, her eyes had narrowed.

"A well-preserved forty, I'd say," Erich whispered. "They're best about that age...no games, and they work hard at it."

"Seems your SS friend has changed her mind."

"She knows what she likes." Erich settled back confidently. "She'll come around."

Other than dogs, Sol thought, the only two things that seemed to arouse his friend were conquests and contacts. The right ones. Erich's Reichsakademie studies had been but a means to an end, like his interest in mathematics and physics—derived from recognition of his excellence, not from fascination with the subjects themselves.

"Such women excite me." Erich's voice was suddenly husky. "They know everyone who's anyone, and ultimately they talk. The SA Storm Troopers can keep their barrel-chested wives and simple-minded whores. I'll stick with the cream. By the time I leave here, I'll have her key and telephone number."

"Doubtless you'll use both."

"Shsh!" Erich's brows drew together and a look of concentration entered his eyes. He set down his beer and turned toward the graveled path that serpentined through the woods. "Did you hear that?"

"Hear what?"

"Them! Him! I told you he'd come."

Sol listened for the crunch of boots on gravel. He could hear nothing, but then Erich frequently sensed sounds and movement before others did. After his Freikorps unit became part of the Hitler Youth, his superior woodsman skills had earned him a two-week intensive camp in the Black Forest. He was an excellent tracker, as good and sometimes even better than the dogs he worked with so closely and loved so much; they too had senses beyond human ken.

Erich gripped Sol's wrist. "I've never seen him up close before. My God, this is a day, Solomon!"

Solomon. These days it was always "Solomon," as if Erich were deliberate distancing himself from the old days. Just as Herr Weisser had become "sir" to Erich ever since their big blow-up after Rathenau's murder. No hint of disrespect, only a coldness, as if Erich were no longer an integral part of the Weisser household or of the cigar shop, with its Jewish co-owners. Yet he insisted that he had come to hate the Hitler Youth and was bent on moving up in the Party proper precisely *for* the sake of family and friends.

There was a missing puzzle piece somewhere, Sol thought. He could feel his friend's sincerity when he said things like that. And yet—

"Can you hear him? I told you he'd come!"

Jittery as a first-day kindergartner, Erich smoothed his hair, straightened his tie, picked lint from his lapels.

Sol saw the SS man sit up even straighter than before and turn his head toward the trees. Now Sol heard voices, one resonating louder than the rest, demanding attention with the deep throaty insistence of a cello. He listened, torn between curiosity—he had never seen the Chancellor at close range like this—and the strong urge to run.

Chapter 28

Sol watched Hitler and three paunchy Storm Troopers saunter into the open. A white terrier pranced at the Chancellor's side. While Achilles simply looked from the terrier to Hitler and lifted her brows with lazy disdain, Taurus emitted a low growl. The little dog immediately cowered behind its master's legs. Almost imperceptibly, Hitler glanced down. He shifted his gaze to the tables and looked around with the air of a man who had arrived at a popular restaurant to find his regularly reserved table taken. Then he stared over the heads of the café customers, out across the lake, as though absorbed in a vision only he could discern.

"Führer, *wir folgen Dir!*" The woman, Helga, shouted words lifted from a popular election poster: "Führer. We follow you!"

The Chancellor bowed slightly to acknowledge her adoration.

"*Mitt Gottes Willen,*" Erich added softly. Rising to his feet, he clicked his heels and saluted Helga's small compact hero. "With God's will."

Hitler and his entourage lifted their arms in an answering stiff-armed salute, which induced most of the customers to shout *"Heil!"* and raise their arms in return.

The Chancellor was the last to lower his arm. Rumor had it that he took special pride in maintaining the salute for lengthy periods in front of female admirers, as if doing so proved his virility. He had apparently issued a standing challenge to any Storm Trooper who believed he could hold the salute longer than his Führer.

Grateful to the few who merely gestured in desultory fashion, Sol kept his arm lowered. Hitler looked his way. Fortunately, the Chancellor's attention was not on him, but on Erich's dogs. After looking with disgust at Achilles, Hitler fixed his gaze on Taurus.

"A beautiful dog. A fine, proud bearing. Good lineage?" He moved toward their table.

"The best, mein Führer," Erich replied. "Descended from the German grand champion."

"In animals, as in people, breeding is everything." Hitler's gaze roamed the audience. When he was sure he had their attention, he lifted his finger like a schoolmaster and said, "Genetic purity creates strength of character." As if it were being scolded, the terrier backed under the nearest table. "Your animal's name?"

"Achilles. And this—"

"I was not referring to the old one, Herr Oberleutnant."

"—is Taurus. Achilles' offspring."

Sol saw anger flare in Erich's eyes.

"Taurus!" Hitler patted Taurus on the head; she did not respond to the display of affection. "Born in May?"

"The fourteenth."

"And your name?"

"Weisser." Again Erich lifted himself into military bearing. An odd expression crossed his features. "Erich Alois Weisser. I had my name legally changed to honor your father."

The bastard doesn't miss a move, Sol thought, stunned by his friend's audacity. There was a certain appeal in Erich's lying to someone who told so many lies, but why this particular lie? Why work this hard at impressing a man he purported to despise?

What had happened to Erich's unwillingness to compromise that had caused them so much pain when they were boys?

He had finagled his way into the Reichsakademie despite his hand and come back from his training camp in the Black Forest full of tales of the people he had met there—men in counter-espionage whose mere hints about the training center in Oranienburg had been enough to convince him not to ask too many questions. He was, he had told Sol many times, thankful to be in the security division, where he could acquire power and correct abuses without inflicting pain. As for his being taken with the Nazi Party, he insisted he saw its potential for bringing Germany out of the *De*pression and, like everyone else, desperately wanted to see an end to that, as well as to *re*pression. Recently, he had managed to get a promotion and to maneuver his Abwehr canine unit into headquarters security. *I'm not guarding Goebbels, I've penned him,* he had said when the orders came through. *I intend to use him before he uses us.*

To Sol it sounded too easy; all too terribly familiar.

"Weisser." The Führer mulled the word like a fine cognac. "A good German name. A good German dog. I shall remember you."

"Maybe I was not born too late after all," Erich said, as the Chancellor patted him on the shoulder and stepped away. He looked as if he'd been touched by a god and rendered immortal.

Examining the newly appointed Chancellor as objectively as he could, Sol tried to see what it was about him that commanded such worship. He looked nothing if not ordinary in his oft-photographed, belted trench coat: a nose too large for his face; eyes, blue and clear and seemingly without guile or, more accurately, without expression at all.

A Storm Trooper pulled up a chair for Hitler and the Chancellor sat down. "You must all read Schopenhauer," he told his entourage as if continuing a lecture cut short by his emergence from the woods. "Detailed knowledge of his philosophy must be required of all Germans. My dear Schopenhauer teaches us that although all forms of life are bound together by misery and misfortune, we higher forms must struggle against, and separate ourselves from, the lower." His hands fluttered as he spoke, not with the careful theatrics with which he endowed his Reichstag-balcony speeches but, Sol thought, like the wings of an injured bird. "His books, with their affirmation of the strength and triumph of the will, kept me going"—another flutter of the hands—"no, kept me *alive,* during those terrible days in the trenches, when we dined on rats and died from typhus and influenza and were up to our knees in mud."

Again he lifted the index finger. "Yes! Everyone will read Schopenhauer."

He patted the terrier and looked at the two Brownshirts. They stood at parade rest, watching the woods as though they expected trouble from that quarter. "You may leave," he told them. He waved in the direction of the woods. "Anywhere I go in our beloved Fatherland, I'm among friends."

The men looked startled but did as they were told. At once, Hitler called over the waitress.

"Bring me apple-peel tea and the Gypsy."

She looked nervously in Helga's direction before obeying.

"I told you he would be here today to consult the Gypsy," Erich said, a little sheepishly.

"It's all so..." Sol searched for the right word. "Absurd."

"Like your voices and your visions, Solomon? Perhaps you and he should both attend the Psychoanalytic Institute. I hear Freud's old students are paying people to come for analysis."

What entitles you to be a judge of sanity, you and your dog fixation, Sol thought, glaring at his friend. Saying you feel *married* to your canine unit. Sorrowing openly over Rin Tin Tin when he died in Jean Harlow's arms. If that weren't something for Freud! As for his own voices and visions, and the dybbuk he had believed in so fully, that was over...the stuff of childhood. According to his readings and to the beadle, the practical necessities of adult life had stunted his development as a mystic, forcing the dybbuk into inactivity; he preferred a less complex answer.

The waitress trundled out a serving cart, its wheels creaking across the flagstones and interrupting Sol's introspection. Lemon cakes glittery with colored sugar and edged with frosting graced a large cut-glass plate; a porcelain teapot wobbled precariously, threatening to knock down two china cups nestled on a stack of cake plates and saucers.

"The Gypsy will be out momentarily, mein Führer." The waitress placed a cup and saucer and the teapot on Hitler's table.

He took hold of her hand, looked at it, and smiled. "They told me young girls were painting swastikas on their fingernails."

The girl smiled back at him proudly.

"Find out why that Gypsy bitch is keeping me waiting." He dropped eight sugar cubes into his tea with a fine waiter's precision. "Tell her I have a good mind to—"

"A good mind to what?"

The Gypsy's voice was soft and sweet, not so much lacking in respect as filled with a surprising familiarity. She wore a simple, long black knitted dress, cut low in the front to reveal enormous breasts. Her feet were bare. The scalloped edge of a red lace shawl framed a mass of curly black hair and draped her ample shoulders, lending her broad-hipped and overweight body the voluptuous innocence of a Rubens model. She looked at Hitler with dark eyes that hinted of humor, sensuality, and a depth of understanding. Sol felt drawn to her.

"He often consults her in private," Erich whispered. "When he has a specific and immediate problem, he comes here."

"How did you know he would be here today?"

"A contact—"

"Sit!" The Chancellor pointed toward the chair beside him.

The woman glanced sidelong at the chair and, with the barest hint of disdain, took Hitler's cup.

"She doesn't seem to be treating him with reverence," Sol said.

"He makes no secret of the fact that he hates Gypsies almost as much as Jews." Erich's whisper was tense.

Apparently Hitler also found the Gypsy lacking in servility. Lifting the teapot he thrust it toward her face. "*This* is indicative of the life of Adolph Hitler. Not some little teacup." He slapped the teacup from her hands, sending it crashing to the flagstones. She knelt to pick up the shards.

"My apologies, Herr Chancellor." Her tone mocked him. "By all means, swirl the leaves in the teapot."

Using both hands, he swirled it around. Then, red in the face, he poured the remaining tea onto the flagstones. The Gypsy started as the hot tea splashed her, but she took the pot from his outstretched hand. Tipping it slightly, she examined its interior from this angle and that.

"Well?"

Motioning him forward, the woman placed her lips near his ear and murmured words unintelligible to anyone but the Chancellor.

He lurched upright and, rigid with rage, grabbed the ends of her shawl. "How dare you!" He crossed the corners of the shawl as if choking her would force her words back down her throat. "My Reich shall live a millennium!" Face fiery red and jugular engorged, he released her.

Coughing, the Gypsy started to rise. At once, the silver-haired second lieutenant glided from his table and seized her from behind, his forearms across the front and back of her neck in a choke hold. As he forced her head up, she gagged in pain.

Looking down into her fear-filled eyes, he blew her a kiss.

"Gypsies and the Jews, they are one and the same," Helga said loudly. "They give us nothing and take all we have in return."

Hitler's eyes were shut, his face drawn tight with wrath as he raised a fist above the table. Sol waited for the hand to bang down, sealing the Gypsy's fate, but the Chancellor unclenched his fist and, fingers quivering with fury, pressed his palm against the table. "Let her go. And I thank you for your trouble."

"No trouble." Hempel released her. "I live to serve."

Hitler peered down at the Gypsy, his eyes little more than slits. "We shall begin again."

He looked up in the direction of the waitress, who hurried indoors. She emerged almost at once, carrying a fresh pot of tea. The Chancellor took it from her. "This time," he said, "no mistakes. Speak the truth, and in specifics."

Slowly and deliberately he tilted the teapot and poured the searing hot tea onto the flagstones directly beneath the Gypsy's dress, scalding her bare feet and ankles. She screamed in pain and backed away—into the arms of Otto Hempel. Without a moment's hesitation, he yanked her into an empty chair and gripped her arms so she could not clutch at her scalded flesh.

The onlookers gasped and Sol felt his stomach clench. Achilles gained her feet and Taurus moved up under Erich's arm. An angry sound began in Taurus' throat. Erich, his face scarlet, did not seem to sense the danger. Sol tugged at his friend's shirt. Erich glanced at him and patted Taurus, who immediately quieted.

Absorbed by the drama, the audience pressed closer. Several of them rose from their chairs, apparently more eager than afraid, more participant than spectator.

The Führer held up a hand and smiled reassuringly.

Like a master magician, he looked down at the woman through eyes that seemed capable of mesmerizing stone. "Think *past* the pain," he told her. "Be German, not Gypsy. Love your land and your Führer so much that human frailty ceases to exist." He held the teapot, slightly tipped, over the woman's lap. "Concentrate."

Hitler tipped the teapot further. The woman stopped moaning and set her face hard.

"You will see your way to the truth? Remember there is always more tea." The Gypsy nodded. "No more lies," she said hoarsely.

He swiveled the pot around and handed it to her. Eyes bright with tears, she examined the contents. Her face went vapid. She looked from the teapot to the Führer, her chin trembling, her eyes filled with terror. When she spoke, her words were incoherent.

"Tell me!"

The woman's breathing became raw and rapid. She peered back into the teapot, squinted up at Hitler and, quivering, shook her head. "Mein Führer...." Her voice trailed off.

"Say it!" Hempel put his arms across her throat and tilted up her head. She nodded and he released her, shoving down her shoulders in his disgust.

"I saw...power." She was bent over. Gasping. "Your power." Sobs punctuated her words. "Two...Berlins. One here...in the east. One...in the west."

"A Berlin in the Americas!" Hitler's eyes gleamed. He waved off Hempel when the Gypsy, shaking her head and attempting to stand, sagged to the flagstones. "And why should it be otherwise?" the Führer asked his audience. "Did English religious fanatics carve a nation from that wilderness? No! *German* brains and *German* backs! A Berlin in each hemisphere. It is," he formed a fist, "our destiny! A world made whole by German blood!"

Helga's feverish applause broke the ensuing silence, and soon the other watchers joined in. Everyone except Solomon and Erich, who sat with one hand on the head of each dog, staring blankly toward his Führer.

Papa was right, Sol thought. The Chancellor was deranged and dangerous not only because of his delusions, but because he believed the myth he had created.

Helga believed it. So, it seemed, did Erich. More dangerous yet, Hitler placed people in the power structure who believed it, too. Goebbels was a perfect example, which, of course, was why Hitler had elevated him to Gauleiter of Berlin. He had been nothing but a scrawny government clerk and failed novelist with a penchant for pornography shops and sleazy cabarets; now he was making speeches from the Reichstag steps. Sol himself had heard the man call the Rathenau assassination a blessing, had seen someone walk from the crowd and slap the Gauleiter's face with a black glove, shouting, "It isn't for garbage like you that we murdered him!"

Since then the assassins had been granted sainthood in the Nazi hagiography.

Only the Jews and the Gypsies remained sinners.

Sol touched Erich's sleeve, but his friend shrugged off the hand. "The man's nothing but a bully," Sol whispered.

Here was a man who, within four months of taking power, had managed to eradicate virtually every vestige of democracy in Germany, including the

Nationalist Party that had supported his candidacy. In less than a year, Hitler had gone from losing an election by six million votes to gaining over fifty percent of the Reichstag seats. Bully or no, it would be nothing short of insanity to take him on alone. One did not, after all, use stones to fight tanks. Not unless one happened to be David.

"It makes me sick to see him act that way," Erich said bitterly. "But as long as Germans demand a scapegoat for the war and the Depression, as long as the SA and SS hold the reins of power, Hitler must play the brute."

Solomon dabbed beer from his lips and set the wadded napkin on the table. "Are you so sure it's an act?"

Erich sadly shook his head. "God, I hope so."

The emotion in Erich's eyes told of a need to talk things out, but this was hardly the place. "I have to get back to the shop," Sol said. "You coming? We've seen almost nothing of you since you moved into your flat."

"I...I can't." Erich's lips tightened. "That damn Goebbels stepped up the time schedule for the headquarters' move. The estate's still being renovated. We moved Goebbels' office furniture yesterday. Tonight I move in the dogs."

He paused, as if he had just thought of something. "Listen, Sol. I'm not giving up my flat, but I won't be able to use it much now that Goebbels has stepped up security. It's yours if you want to—"

"Use it for assignations? Thanks anyway," Sol said. In a way, he envied Erich being out on his own. There was no way he could leave; his parents needed him too much.

"It's incredible, the tensions I'm under, Solomon," Erich said. "Hurry up and wait, hurry up and wait. We don't even have kennels. There are no documents to guard, no personnel...*nothing!* Why must we start before we're really prepared?"

He put a hand on Sol's forearm. The momentary look of need in his eyes caused Sol a passing moment of guilt at his constant examinations of Erich's motives.

"I asked you here because I needed to have a drink with someone *real*. And to relax, just for a minute." Erich downed his beer and raised his hand to signal the waitress. "Let's have another."

"I'm sorry, truly I am," Sol said quietly, "but the urge to throw something at that man—preferably my fist, for all the good it would do—is just too strong."

Sol felt very conspicuous, and very Jewish. What was he doing here? It was Friday afternoon, and *Shabbas* would soon begin. His place was at home with his family. He stood up. "I have to leave."

"Wir folgen Dir! Wir folgen Dir!"

The cry rang out, punctuated by cheers as the SS man, noticing the Gypsy trying to crawl away, used his shoe to push her past the fence. The Chancellor's terrier growled and scampered over to tug at the hem of her dress.

"Careful with her." Hitler grinned. "I may need her again ...in a millennium."

For as long as the Chancellor needed her, the Gypsy was safe from everything except his tantrums—and not for a moment longer. Would it be the same with the Jews, Sol wondered, or would hatred ultimately prove to be stronger than Hitler's need for what Walther Rathenau had called Jewish assets and abilities? The phrase was Rathenau's, the delusion Hitler's.

The Gypsy pulled herself away from the terrier and rose laboriously to her feet. As she limped toward the woods, a pianist in the main part of the restaurant struck up a *Lady Moon* medley from the recent Paul Lincke revival. Sol felt ashamed and embarrassed. He had desperately wanted to go to her aid earlier, but to do so would have been both foolish and dangerous.

As if a performance were over and the post-show party had begun, the milieu abruptly changed to cocktails and light laughter. Hitler sauntered among the crowd, making casual conversation and shaking hands. The terrier bounded from table to table, for scraps fed by people eager to please anything the Führer loved.

Without another word to Erich, who sat in the midst of the festivities unemotional as a corpse, Sol slipped away from the Biergarten. Taking the long way around Hitler, he headed for the trees to find the Gypsy and offer her what help he could. He had hardly gone beyond the first line of trees when he came upon her. She lay beneath an oak, sobbing, her head on a pile of leaves. Her dress was pulled up to her knee; he could see angry red patches on her calf.

Sol stooped and placed a consoling hand on her shoulder. "Those are ugly burns," he said. "You need medical attention."

Sitting up, she peeled a leaf from her cheek and looked at him through narrowed eyes. The tree's branches cast fingers of shadow across the blotches where her mascara had run. "I can help myself." Pulling down her dress, she turned her head and stared toward the Biergarten.

Sol followed her gaze and saw Erich approaching at a run, the dogs at his heels.

"What do *you* want with me?" she asked when he was near enough to hear her.

"I wish to get you medical assistance." Erich stooped as if to examine her.

She batted his hand away and, wincing, covered her legs with her skirt. "What you *wish* is to convince yourself that your beloved Hitler didn't hurt me."

"I didn't come here to be insulted," Erich said testily.

"I didn't invite you to come." She spat on the ground. "Leave! Go back to your idealism!"

Visibly fighting for self-control, Erich looked at his watch. "The dogs and I are due at the barracks in twenty minutes. Do you or don't you want my help?"

"No."

"Then that's how it will be." Erich shook Sol's hand with a kind of military stiffness. "Tell Recha and your parents I said hello. I hope your father feels better." He nodded toward the woman. "If he decides she needs help, I'll pay the bill."

Hand raised in farewell, he walked into the woods.

"I have perturbed your friend, Solomon," the Gypsy said.

A shock ran through Sol as the Gypsy spoke his name. Then he laughed at himself. How easily the simple was overlooked! She had obviously heard Erich call him by name.

He squatted beside her.

She squinted as she peered into his face. The scrutiny made him uncomfortable. "I know you, Solomon Freund," she said. "I am a dancer in the dwelling place of dreams."

She looked down at her leg, which had already begun to blister. Removing her shawl, she wrapped it loosely around the burn. Closing her eyes, she began to rock, as if to relieve the pain.

Sol bent closer.

Her eyes snapped open. "You will not escape your dreams, Solomon."

"It is one thing for you to know my name. But you seem to know all about me." Sol backed against the oak.

"Over the years, my sleep spoke." She lifted a painted brow. "My dreams divulged. You're older, stronger now, Solomon." Her voice was soft, vibrant, and when she reached out with trembling fingers and touched Sol's cheeks, her eyes were moist, though whether with joy or grief he wasn't sure. "When your visions return, respect them. Even fear them. But listen to them, Sol. Listen. And learn."

He was stunned by her words and the extent of her emotion.

"Listen and learn," she said again. Removing the shawl from her leg and, grunting in agony, she managed to stand. When he moved to steady her, she pushed him away. "Leave me now," she told him. "I have to go back alone."

"Go back? To the Biergarten? That's crazy!"

"Do not concern yourself with me, little sparrow," she said softly. "There are paths we each must walk. Mine lies in that direction, yours...."

"Could we—"

"Meet again? I think not." Head down, she limped off.

Sol let her go. The truth was, he was afraid of hearing anything more of what she had to say. Hands balled into fists in his pockets, he made his way through the Tiergarten, his route a palette of memories splashed on a canvas of autumn leaves, his mind an amusement park where the thin strains of a calliope echoed the pianist's lively rendition of Lincke's melodies. *Shine little glowworm*, it mocked. Shine on this fool who for a decade has thought himself free of the voices, believing them sealed in the sewer, left behind except in memory when Kaverne closed after Rathenau's murder. *Glow and glimmer* on the nightmares that will not, after all, die childhood's natural, gradual death.

Still shaken by the afternoon's events and by the Gypsy's knowledge of him, he reached the Zoological Gardens, near the Bahnhof Zoo Station.

In a gazebo decorated with lights, a woodwind quintet was playing Schubert for passers-by. Sparrows twittered in the trees; grebes, with dusk approaching, called a warning from the ponds. Men and women in trench coats strolled arm-in-arm toward Lochau, the intimate café as famous in its own way as Kranzler's for its coffee-cake conversations. In the Hansaviertel—where the rich frittered away their days—wealth, fame, and love always seemed possible, as though the wealthy could mold hope into reality out of the gray air. How often he and Erich and Miriam had wandered here, talking of the future and of a pre-war past that, of the three, only she clearly remembered. How often they had hiked and bicycled to the Reichstag! How often he had watched Miriam stare wistfully at the Siegessäule and say that the lady with the golden wreath, her arm lifted high over the city, made her long for New York.

A train hooted its way into the Zoo Station as Sol trudged through the gate that separated the gardens from the street. He stood for a moment to watch with growing loneliness as people detrained—men with satchels, women lugging hatboxes and children, all of them with somewhere to go and circumnavigating him as they might a pole or a tree.

"Solomon? Sol?"

Miriam's voice sang out his name, its cadence lilting above the street noise. Sol dipped inward for its source, into the well of visions in the sewer and nightmares in his bed, certain that now he was dreaming in the streets.

Chapter 29

"Need help with your suitcase, pretty lady?"

Miriam shook her head at the overweight, overcoated man. He had sat in the seat across from her all the way from Paris, and again during the journey from Frankfurt, where she had changed trains for the last part of the trip home. Though he had stared fixedly at her ankles, he had made no previous attempt to talk to her. Her suitcase was heavy and she was tempted to let him help her as far as the taxi rank and worry about getting rid of him later. Not that she could afford a taxi, but what the hell.

Apparently sensing her hesitation, the man stepped closer. The look of delighted anticipation in his eyes quickly changed her mind, and she shook her head again. "Thank you, I can manage," she said politely but firmly.

He made no effort to hide his disappointment.

For the thousandth time Miriam wondered why she hadn't contacted Sol or Erich. They had never been far from the periphery of her consciousness in the nine years she'd been away. She had written to Erich a couple of times and he had always responded, but through Sol. Eventually, she gave up the effort except for a birthday card once a year which he dutifully reciprocated, never so much as adding anything but his name.

Sol was a different story. They corresponded regularly at first. His letters had been a great source of pleasure and comfort for her, especially after her grandmother died. Through him she learned that Erich had given up his veterinarian apprenticeship in favor of an appointment to the Reichsakademie. As of Sol's last letter three years ago, Erich was hopelessly devoted to dogs, making progress in the Abwehr, and conquering attractive, influential women. At the time, Sol was enrolled at the Language Institute, studying the Talmud and the Kabbalah, and helping in the tobacco shop. In deference to practicality, he was also studying bookkeeping and accounting.

When she sold the last of her grandmother's jewelry and her life began to sour, she stopped writing to Sol. Running through the money so fast was her own fault, she thought. Somehow she'd convinced herself that the well was bottomless.

There followed three years of silence, then she'd received the letter that had brought her back here. She dug it out of her handbag and read the beginning again:

29 *Junie,* 1933

Meine Liebe Miriam,

It has been so long—so very long—since I last heard from you. When half-a-dozen of my letters went unanswered, I at first worried that perhaps something terrible might have happened to you. Finally, I decided that you were simply too busy with your new and glamorous life and that the best thing I could do was send you warm thoughts, keep loving you, and pray that someday our lives would once again intertwine.

Now, I have heard news that I feel I must impart to you. Forgive me, I hate to be the bearer of bad tidings, but someone had to tell you—they are gaining more power every day, if not every minute. Some time ago, Erich told me that it was the good Dr. Goebbels' intention to conscript your home and use it as his headquarters—mostly, I fear, because it is far enough away from Wallotstrasse and the ever-vigilant SS that his bedroom activities with every willing star-struck blonde in Berlin will be overlooked.

Whatever the reason, I begged Erich to intercede on your behalf, as I did last year when—as I wrote and told you—I found out that the most valuable of the paintings and furniture in the house were appropriated. Whether or not Erich could have done anything to help without significant injury to himself is something I cannot judge.

I do know that by early October the move into your estate will be well underway—if not completed....

Miriam folded up the letter and put it in her bag. She knew its contents by heart. The letter had taken more than three months to find her; three days later she had booked her ticket home.

Standing alone on the steps of the station, she asked herself why she had really stopped writing to Sol—and answered herself in the same way she had done for three years. In Erich's case, it was annoyance; in Sol's, she had found herself unable to reply. She wanted the ink of her adolescence to blur...wanted her future to be a tabula rasa. The past, which held the pain of youth's broken promises, needed to be relegated to the past.

She laughed at herself.

Those were fine thoughts, or at least pragmatic, but the truth was she wanted to see Sol *and* Erich. Wanted? No, longed! Dammit, she missed them both. Loved them both. Her love for Erich, she had long since decided, was perverse. When she thought of him, she felt aroused; loving him was stupid but exciting, like walking by a river during an electric storm. Worse yet, he made her dislike herself.

Sol?

Sol was mist and rainbows and the smell of Frau Freund's *latkes*.

Thinking about those made her remember her hollow stomach, growling with hunger. She hadn't eaten anything more nourishing than a sweet roll in days.

She inhaled deeply, but the smell around her was hardly that of potato pancakes; as usual, Berlin's sidewalks were splotched with dog droppings. Still, it was Berlin. Whatever else that meant, she was home.

Dropping her suitcase at her side, she massaged her shoulder and congratulated herself for having had the good sense to leave the rest of her things to another ex-member of her troupe. She leaned sideways to pick up the case again and noticed a young man across the street. He was standing motionless in the path of the other passengers, who had crossed over and were moving around him as if he were a tree that had taken root in the sidewalk.

Come on, Miriam, don't be an idiot, she told herself, aware of her pounding heart. Nevertheless, she squinted to see more clearly in the encroaching dusk.

"Solomon! Sol Fr—!" She stopped. It was too much to ask of the Fates and, besides, *Freund* was too Jewish a name to yell.

The young man turned his head in her direction but did not react. Embarrassed, she changed her gesture into a wave and smiled as if she had recognized someone behind him. She was beginning to feel like an absolute idiot. Such happy coincidences were the stuff of dreams.

Then again, she'd made a fool of herself before, she thought as he took one step, and another, until he was running toward her.

"My God, it *is* you!" Sol grinned widely as he dodged a car.

"Who did you think it was? A ghost?"

She opened her arms and he embraced her, lifting her up and whirling her around.

"Miriam Rathenau at your service, sir." She laughed and held onto her hat.

"You look wonderful." He let go and stepped back to admire her.

And you *feel* wonderful, she thought. "What do you think?" She executed a pirouette. "Is Berlin ready for my return?"

"If the city's not, I am."

She smiled at his open appreciation. The worse she felt, the more carefully she dressed, as if looking good worked some inner magic that forced her to take a more optimistic view of her life. She had put on a stylish calf-length tweed skirt and matching jacket. Her legs were stockinged in black silk, and a white silk blouse and cloche cap completed the outfit. Aside from a tall feather, the cap resembled a Pilgrim's bonnet and would have looked very proper had she not turned the edge up saucily on one side.

"Can it really be you?" Sol made no attempt to hide his pleasure. "You were a girl when you left Berlin."

"I'm twenty-six, Sol."

"Well, you look seventeen, at most."

"I'd *love* to believe you, darling, but you need to have your eyes checked."

For an instant she sensed a change in Sol, as if she had said something tactless. Then he said quickly, "I feel like I should spout poetry or say something philosophical to mark the occasion."

"You could give me a kiss for starters." She smiled. "And maybe carry a disgustingly heavy suitcase?" She folded her arms around his neck and stood on her toes.

To her surprise, his lips tasted of beer; his kiss was warm, but that of a brother. He was a man now, not the tentative boy she had left behind; tall and handsome, with that kind of brooding intensity in his eyes that many women found irresistible. Was there someone else in his life, some other woman—a wife? She glanced at his left hand.

The extent of her relief at seeing a ringless finger shocked her.

"You've come home...for good?" he asked

"For good or bad. Depends on your point of view." She linked her arm through his and he lifted her case with the other. "In answer to the question in your eyes, my Sol, yes, I received your letter. I got it a few days ago." She stopped. There would be time for all that, and for asking about Erich. "Could we be serious later?" she asked.

Sol looked relieved. "Been in Paris all this time...I mean, since your last letter?"

"Paris, Amsterdam, Zurich...everywhere." She waved as if to include the universe in her experience.

Sol looked at her slim waist. "Aren't world travelers supposed to get fat from sampling all sorts of delicacies?"

"Me, fat? Never! Matter of fact, you could take me to your parents for a *Shabbas* meal. It will be my first in...too long."

She laughed and nuzzled her head against his shoulder. Clutching the post of a street lamp, she swung around it at a tilt.

"It's so good to be back, Sol! So good to be with someone I know." She looked toward the Brandenburg Gate. "We share so many memories."

"Mother and Recha were sure you had become the toast of Europe. When we stopped hearing from you, we decided you had gone to Hollywood and married Errol Flynn or someone. We kept expecting to see you on the Movietone News, wearing furs and posing for photographers."

"Why an American?" She pouted coyly and once again tucked her arm through his. "Why not Willy Fritsch? I'm sure I could have dazzled him into a trip down the aisle. But I've simply been too busy to take time off to marry a star!" More seriously, she added, "Actually, for the past three years I've been with a dance company from Stuttgart."

"The Stuttgart Ballet?"

"I wish. You see before you the star of that traveling talent showcase, *La Varieté Nouvelle.*" Star ballerina of third-rate theaters, she thought as she bowed grandly to hide her unease. "Danced excerpts from every great ballet on Europe's worst stages, for a lot of applause and little else. Did a bit of everything. Lehar. Lincke. *Giselle,* the Sugar Plum Fairy, you name it."

"Even so, Recha's such a balletomane I swear she gets programs from Siberia. We should have seen your name *somewhere.*"

"I used a stage name." Again Miriam waved her hand in the broad gesture that encompassed fate and the universe. "Every time I handed someone a portfolio of my American performances, they looked duly impressed—and slammed the door in my face. Eventually I realized that people were afraid my name would attract Nazi attention. All I had to do at *Nouvelle* was audition, so I became Mimi de Rau. Like it?"

"Mimi, you make me sad and dreamy," he sang softly.

"Chevalier you're not." Miriam laughed with delight. "I am *très Parisienne, n'est pas?* So, verree Frrench." She rolled her 'rrs' and tried to look like a seductress.

"So, has the company come to perform in Berlin, Fraülein de Rau?" Sol asked as they reached the apartment house.

"Hardly!" She gazed up at the barred windows. "We made the mistake of performing in Munich. The Chamber of Culture shut us down." She frowned at the Minister of Propaganda's latest lunacy: a few weeks before, Goebbels had formed the Chamber *to protect the public from non-Aryan influences in the arts.*

"The company's director was Jewish?"

"No, but they decided he was because of his nose. Next they'll be *measuring* everyone's noses."

Though Sol laughed as he held open the door, he did not sound amused. He had doubtless heard the rumors that the nose-caliper test was a reality in some places and that circumcision examinations were a possible next step. "Failure to fit accepted parameters" and "Jewish tendencies" had become familiar catch-phrases.

"If you don't have work here, why did you come back?"

Miriam reached in her purse. After some digging, she produced a large latchkey. "I came across the keys to Uncle Walther's house the day we were notified the company was being disbanded, which was also the day your letter found me. The front door key fell off the ring and into my hand. I took it as an omen."

"Think of it this way—you would rattle around like a ghost if you lived in that mansion...alone."

"Good old Solomon—always finding something positive, even in evil. If I could afford to live there, I could also afford servants, Solomon." She kissed an index finger and pressed it to his lips, then turned her palms up in mock despair. "But that's all moot, isn't it. I'm penniless. Can you love a Poor Little Match Girl?"

"You're not bitter about the estate?" Sol sounded shocked.

"Bitter? No. Furious! But later, Sol, please."

"Just one question. Didn't your grandmother leave you anything?"

"Everything she had left, which was mostly jewelry. Didn't take me long to spend it. You know me—used to the good life!"

"What about your trust fund?"

"Gone. After Oma's death, I found out inflation had eaten up most of her fortune. The Nazis took what was left. She and I lived on the trust. I couldn't deny her anything, Sol. She was old, and used to a certain way of life. I just figured, when it was gone, it was gone. I probably should have sold the estate years ago but, to cut a long story short, Princess Miriam 'Mimi de Rau' Rathenau has been paying for her own bread and butter—and precious little jam."

Sol put down the suitcase and gave her a hug. "I can't promise you butter, but you are always welcome to whatever bread we have."

She kissed his cheek. He reddened slightly. After fishing in his pockets for the key, he opened the front door.

"Mutti? Recha? You'll never guess who's here!"

No one answered. Sol peered into the music and sitting rooms. "They must still be in the food lines."

"Hello?" Miriam called. "Herr Freund?"

Sol sent Miriam a cautionary look and signaled her into the library. The room had two tall narrow windows. The one nearest the door was trimmed in Dutch curtains and spilled light onto a table cluttered with papers. The other was covered by a shade.

Seated near a corner, facing the darkened window and slowly rocking back and forth, was Jacob Freund.

"Oh my God!" Miriam thought of Jacob Freund as she had remembered him. Gentle. Dapper. Resolute.

This couldn't be the same man.

Jacob stared straight ahead, face set as though sculpted. Though not yet sixty he looked eighty. His cheeks were sunken, his cheekbones protruded. He stared toward the window shade through eyes that, clouded with film, seemed distended from their sockets. His hair was white and butchered; liver spots mottled his scalp. His right hand lay motionless on the blanket across his lap. His left forearm was on the rocker's arm. A silk ribbon dangled from his left hand, which hung as if it had no bones; attached to the ribbon, moving like a pendulum with each slight twitch of his hand, was an Iron Cross.

Try as she would, Miriam could not stem the tears. "Is he always...like this?"

"It comes and goes." Solomon put his hands on the old man's shoulders.

"Miriam Rathenau's here, Papa."

The chair continued its rhythm. Sol motioned Miriam aside.

"His eyes.... Is he *blind*, Sol?"

"He has chosen to be blind."

She looked at Sol in horror. He gripped her arms as if he wanted, needed to hold her. "Accept it," he said. "I have." He stared at the carpet. "At least I think I have."

They waited helplessly for a response or any sign of recognition from Sol's father. When none came, Sol guided Miriam into the kitchen. He poured them each a buttermilk.

Miriam turned and stood in the archway, staring at the old man.

"Seems like everything is a rare treat these days." Sol handed her the beverage. "It's hard to buy anything, what with 'We do not serve Jews' signs going up everywhere. At first it was only, 'Don't buy from Jews'...."

"What do you mean 'chosen'?" Miriam kept her eyes on Jacob as she drank. "How can he have *chosen* to be blind?"

"His eyesight's been failing for years but he can still see—with glasses. However, he refuses to get another pair. He says there's nothing left he wants to see."

"Then he's not completely—"

"Not yet." Sol's voice faltered. "He broke his glasses the day von Hindenburg appointed Hitler as Chancellor."

Nine months ago, Miriam thought. Some people give birth to sweet-smelling babies; we Germans bear tyrants.

"That evening," Sol said, "Papa placed his glasses under the chair and rocked back, crushing them. Since then his condition has worsened rapidly—"

"What's the prognosis?"

"The last doctor who came said it was acute depression, complicated by what we've known for some time. He has *retinitis pigmentosa*. Basically, a splash of melanin on the back of the retina." He struggled to finish. "I'm afraid it's degenerative."

"There must be something...other doctors..."

"There's nothing we can do. It's getting harder and harder to find a doctor willing to come to a Jewish household."

"There must be Jewish doctors."

Sol shook his head. "Most have left the country. The rest have to employ constant watchfulness to preserve their own safety, for all our sakes."

"He just sits and rocks?"

"Sometimes he putters around the house, but he doesn't go to the shop anymore. I've taken over for him. Mother helps with the books. I'm a linguist, not an accountant, despite all those classes."

"You're a student, Sol. It's all you should ever have to do."

Sol wiped off her buttermilk mustache and she chuckled despite herself. They eased into the table's corner-bench and deliberately talked of pleasant things—sunsets in the Alps, where she had learned to ski, and of how she had performed an excerpt from *The Dying Swan* in a rainstorm on a Rhine tourist barge. As they washed and put away the glasses, she asked him to come with her to the villa.

"Why torture yourself?"

"I want to see what dust has gathered and what insults the sparrows have deposited. We'll be back before dark, in time to celebrate *Shabbas,*" she told him. "Promise."

Still, he hesitated. "Why not wait until tomorrow? You'll be more rested."

"What is it, Sol? What's really bothering you? We both know they have taken what's mine. I've had to face that. There is something else. Isn't there."

"Miri." Sol took her hand. "When we—Erich and I—heard about this, we talked about it. He was very upset. He said he would do what he could to stop it, but he doesn't have that kind of power."

"Erich..."

"We have to talk about him. He's there, Miri. At the estate. In charge of guarding it for Goebbels—"

"No!" She hadn't meant to shout but the word rang out like an alarm. She lowered her voice. "Why Erich? Explain it to me."

"He'll have to do that himself. I just wanted you to know. We could bump into him—"

Miriam glanced in Jacob Freund's direction. "Let's go. Now!"

Outside, they stood hand-in-hand as Solomon flagged a taxi. "I need to find work," Miriam said as they slid inside. "A cabaret, anything, it doesn't matter."

Sol gave directions to the driver. She leaned close to the window and looked across the street at the cabaret's faded awning. "If only Oma had not closed Kaverne."

If only, she thought, wondering if her life would always be filled with those two words.

Suddenly all she wanted was for this day to end. Her emotional bucket was filled to overflowing; she envied the taxi driver his isolation, closed off from them by a glass partition and separated from the outside by glass and metal. It had all been too much. The news about the house, the company disbanding, the long train rides back to a hate-filled city that had once been home. Seeing Sol was wonderful, but Jacob...When she'd insisted on going to the villa *now,* she'd failed to realize how tired she was. She wasn't at all sure she could handle anything more; under the circumstances, she was especially not sure she could handle seeing Erich again.

She glanced at Solomon, grateful that he understood her need for silence. With any luck, Erich wouldn't be at the estate—

Luck hasn't exactly been your middle name of late, she reminded herself. Her only hope of making it through this day was to set aside her feelings. There would be time enough to examine those. For now, the best thing she could do was to act and react, and leave the thinking—and the feeling—for tomorrow.

Chapter 30

The cab rounded the last S-curve before the estate. Heart racing, Miriam waited for the villa to come into view. Even had the place still been hers, she reminded herself, she could not afford to park so much as a dog in the driveway. It took wealth to maintain an estate, not just income—all of which was moot, since she had neither. Her uncle had kept the place immaculate. The lawn was always manicured, the chestnut that shaded the west chimney pruned, the ivy that covered the gate and guardwall-ironwork trimmed. There never seemed to be an end to the work that needed to be done. The east wall re-grouted, the trim of the front-door canopy touched up. Always something.

The cab stopped and she stepped out. While Solomon paid the driver, she walked over to the east gate and gripped the bars, inhaling the richness of newly mown grass. The place was even more beautiful than she remembered. There was so much to the villa she had taken for granted. Red-and-black brickwork graced each corner and set off the entryways. The wrought-iron grills over the windows nicely contrasted with the limestone. The black, red, and gold cobblestones in the crescent-shaped driveway had been chosen to match the colors of the Weimar Republic.

She remembered the wording of Uncle's will. *Meine Vorfahren und ich selbst haben sich von deutschem Boden und deutschem Geistgenärt...my forefathers and I myself have nourished ourselves from German earth and spirit...should death of inheritee occur before liquidation of my estate, the grounds and buildings shall revert to the German people, to serve as a showplace for art and artifacts by Germans of Jewish descent....*

On the roof, a man in a carpenter's apron hoisted a flag from the flagpole on the southeastern turret. The cloth unfurled in the breeze.

Red, with a white circle and a black swastika.

"Take that down!" Shaking the gate, she thrust an arm between the bars. "You hear me, you bastard? Take it down!"

She dug into her handbag for the keys to the estate and tried each of them in the lock. None worked.

"Stop it, Miri." Sol took hold of her arm. "They are not going to fit. You can be sure they've changed all the locks." He pointed toward two workmen opening the western gate for an army truck. "If someone sees you, we could be turned in."

"Turned in? This is *my* home!"

"This *was* your home!"

Furious, Miriam shrugged off his hand and hurled the keys through the bars of the gate. They clinked as they landed.

Covering her mouth with her hand, she watched a tar sprayer enter the other gate and move along the driveway, suffusing the air with stench. A yellow steamroller with a puffing exhaust followed, its driver waving frantically and shouting invectives at the workmen as if he were in charge of smoothing out the broad boulevard of the Unter den Linden during rush hour.

"I won't believe Erich is a part of this!"

Sol's dark eyes held an answering reflection of her own hatred and helplessness. She put her arms around his neck and laid her head against his chest. This time, when he held her close, she could feel his love for her. She breathed in the smell of him. Please don't let go of me, she thought. Outside of myself, you are all I have left.

The stuttering of an engine right behind her made her turn her head. A motorcyclist in leather helmet and goggles crested the hill and roared past. The rider, bent low for aerodynamics, seemed almost part of the machine.

He glanced sideways toward her and did a double-take, changed his balance, and throttled down. The engine screamed in protest. Jamming down a boot, he swung the machine in a shrieking U-turn, bumped over the curb and skidded to a halt in a cloud of dust.

Sol pulled Miriam back against the gate.

Gunning the engine, the rider raised his goggles.

"Erich! Are you crazy?" Sol shouted. "You almost killed us!"

Miriam said nothing. Her heart was pounding as much from the rush of adrenaline as from her first sight of Erich in nine years. For a moment she forgot about the house, the Nazis—the real world—and stared at this man who, together with Sol, had occupied so many of her thoughts. Except for the area the goggles had protected, his face was grimed with dirt and exhaust. Still, she'd have recognized him anywhere. He never really had looked like a boy, she thought. More like a miniature man waiting to catch up with himself.

"So! The prodigal has returned, and more beautiful than ever."

He smiled, obviously pleased with the drama of his entrance. Turning off the cycle, he put down the kickstand and draped an arm across the handlebars. His body seemed charged with the power of his machine, the supple muscularity of his torso evident even in his leather jacket. Like a confident warrior on a steed, Miriam thought, glancing at Sol. He looked jealous, and angry with himself. Damn Hitler and all his barbarians! Damn *you,* Erich, for the weakness at the back of my knees.

Deliberately she put aside who he had been and looked at what he had become—at his army motorcycle and the swastika on his sleeve. "How dare you take my house!"

"Me?" He seemed taken aback.

She glared at him. "You and yours!"

With the back of his hand, Erich wiped sweat and dirt from his face. *"They* took your house while you were cavorting around Europe. You should have sold the estate years ago!"

Should have? Who was he to tell her that! Her grief over Oma's death, and her desire to keep the villa in the family despite the downturns in her finances and career, had made her procrastinate, but that did not excuse these Nazi thieves. "Why didn't you stop them?" Miriam asked quietly.

"I tried." Erich looked uncomfortable. "I confronted Goebbels."

His brows were pulled down, his need to rationalize clear. Though she could not think of a single thing to justify his association with these madmen, Miriam held herself in check. Let him bury himself with his own words, she thought, over her weak-kneed reaction to seeing him again.

"I looked into the situation myself." Erich's face wore an expression of deep concern but she believed none of it. "I demanded to see papers. Almost lost my commission because of it, but I saw them." He slapped the cycle to make his point. "I even went to an attorney. It was all there in the new laws, spelled out in their usual mumbo-jumbo—their right to appropriate whatever they wanted for the good of the Fatherland. I had to apologize—*officially* apologize," his voice rose, "to that goddamn cripple. He's been watching me like an alley cat ever since."

"It all boils down to one thing, Miri," Sol said wearily. "Empty Jewish houses don't stay empty very long."

"I wish them dead. Every last one of them." Miriam felt like a bomb, ready to explode. Grief, love, her initial delight at being in Berlin, even her feelings for Solomon—gone, all of it. There was room for nothing but anger.

"I'll keep trying, Miriam. Anything's possible, I suppose, even with the Nazis." Erich lowered his voice as he said the word. "They control the courts, but they are not above the law of the jungle. Goebbels is under fire for his earlier Bolshevik writings. He may be more approachable now." He lifted her hand and, looking into her eyes, brought her fingers to his lips. "How about formulating our battle plan over dinner? There's a new Italian place. They serve exquisite eggplant parmigiana, the wine cellar's superb, the violist plays a wonderful Albinoni sonata...."

"When?" She was toying with him, looking for a way to pierce his arrogance.

He pulled back his jacket wristband and looked at his watch. "Would an hour from now be too soon?"

"No, Erich. It can't be too soon." She forced herself to smile at him and to ignore Sol's obvious discomfort.

"I can't make it any sooner. I'm sorry, my love."

"Good. An hour, then, and I'll have my house back."

His smile dissipated. "Really, Miriam! This isn't a game—"

"Of course it isn't a goddamn game!" She was half-shouting, hysteria driving her.

Erich glanced anxiously across the villa grounds. The tar sprayer and steamroller had stopped and the men were looking in his direction. "Control yourself." His tone was low and anxious. "This is hardly the place for—"

"For *them!*" She shook her fist at the workmen.

Sol placed his hands on her shoulders and drew her away. "You'll get it all back."

Erich gripped the handlebars, put his machine in neutral, and walked it clear of the gate. "My idealist friend! Your little universe in perfect harmony!" He put down the kickstand. "You really do believe all of the wrongs of the world will be redressed."

He stopped, as if he sensed something beyond the hill. After a moment she heard dogs barking and gears grinding, and an army deuce-and-a-half crested the rise and came grumbling toward them. Sticking out of rubber-rimmed portholes in the truck's canvas canopy were several yelping German shepherds.

Erich took a key from his pocket and stepped up to the gate. "I have to see to the dogs," he said over his shoulder, nearly shouting to be heard above the din of the animals and the engine. "Look, I gained a certain advantage with the Führer today. Maybe I can go to him about the house."

"Sure," Miriam said sourly, her anger renewed by seeing him with a key that fit. "He'll break a leg for a Jew."

"You never know." Erich unlocked the gate and swung the left side wide. He returned to unlatch the foot bolt of the right half and push it open. "The Chancellor sees benefits where his underlings see obstacles."

Like a huge lumbering animal oblivious to anything in its path, the truck closed in on them, huffing and spitting exhaust as it pulled toward the gate. Sol pulled Miriam out of the way. Erich signaled and the truck snorted and rolled into the drive, making its way toward the azalea garden. She watched forlornly as it plowed across the lawn, its tires pulling up long divots.

"As long as Hitler holds the reins of power but weaklings like Himmler and Goebbels and Röhm are in the harnesses, the country's running on feeble legs...the Führer knows that," Erich said.

"The Führer apparently knows everything," she replied, debating walking onto the estate while the gates were open.

Before she had made up her mind, Erich shut them. When he reached out between the bars as if to touch her shoulder, she made no attempt to draw closer to him. She felt nothing, nothing at all.

"I'll be back when I've shown the trainers where to bed down the dogs."

He turned and ran after the truck. It rumbled down the hill separating the front lawn from the gardens; he rushed down the stairs between the marble lions and past the rose beds.

"Do you know him?" Miriam asked. "Know him at all?"

"Erich Alois Weisser!" Sol's voice was laced with disgust.

"Alois?"

"Hitler's father's name. That's what he meant by 'advantage with the Führer!' He told his precious leader he had already changed it. Now he'll have to find a way to pre-date the documents."

The tar sprayer started up with a growl. The steamroller's engine rumbled and the machines resumed their steady pace toward the east gate. The truck, it seemed, had needed to enter before the tar was laid down. Schedules had overlapped in a rare display of inefficiency. Whole minutes had been wasted, Miriam thought bitterly. Erich should inform the Führer so he could have those responsible shot.

"Erich Alois Weisser," Miriam said. "Why not!" Ultimately, she thought, environment and background won out against rebellion, especially here in Germany. "He's always wanted to be some other person, to have lived in some other time. Why keep his surname? He's never been his father's son."

"Don't torture yourself like this. Let's leave."

"No. Pamper my masochism." Crossing her arms, she continued staring at the villa.

The tar sprayer neared the gate, and the driver, a huge man with a concave, rubicund face, climbed from the cab. "You can see it when we're finished," he said, shooing them away as if they were stray animals or waifs. "I know you're curious, but off with you now. We don't want anyone holding us up or getting injured."

She ignored him. "You were there, weren't you?" she asked Sol. "The night Erich gave me the dog."

"I left when you and Erich—"

"Why didn't you stay...why were you there at all?"

Sol took off his glasses and cleaned them with his handkerchief. "I don't know, Miri," he said slowly. "I always found it hard to say no to Erich." He put his arm around her. "As for why I left—I guess I couldn't imagine why you'd want me there."

She mustered up a smile. "Will you ever know your own worth?"

He laughed gently. *"I* knew. The question in my mind was, did *you?* Now we really must leave. Erich's right about one thing. It is dangerous, our being here."

You were so right, Uncle Walther, she thought, remembering what he had said the evening after Friedrich Weisser's ridiculous over-reaction to finding her kissing Erich. *Keep your eye on young Solomon Freund. You may not think so now, but I tell you his spirit is much like your own. He will not be defeated easily.*

"You're not afraid, are you?" she asked.

"Yes. And if you're not, you should be. Erich thinks I'm oblivious to the real world, and in a way he's right. But I am not stupid. There are times when fear is the only expedient means of self-preservation."

She could feel tears very near the surface. How could a day be so tender yet so terrible?

"I'm ready to leave," she said. "But I'll be back—shaking the gate and shouting until Goebbels himself has to deal with me."

Chapter 31

"Miriam! Here's someone you might remember," Erich called out, returning to the gate with Killi at his heels.

He saw Sol steer Miriam to the crest of the hill. She shook him off and they looked around and stood unmoving for a moment. Then they turned their backs and disappeared over the rise.

"Come back. Please." Erich grasped the bars of the gate and let Achilles' leash slip from his wrist. Wearing a red cape with a swastika emblazoned on it, the shepherd wandered up the driveway.

"She doesn't l-love us any more, K-Killi!"

He had asked Sol to write and tell Miriam that he had taken Achilles; she had not even asked about the dog. He had imagined her running back to the gate, stooping, opening her arms—to the dog, and to him for looking after Achilles so well. Instead...

He eyed the dog, which was circling around a scattering of keys someone had dropped on the driveway—sniffing and whining, growling, backing away.

It's so easy for them to blame everything on the Nazis, he thought. Because they're Jews...

In mid-thought he mentally castigated himself. Now he was beginning to sound like Goebbels! But Solomon and Miriam—! "They don't understand," he said under his breath, to Achilles. He and the dogs were in *military* security. Abwehr—not something foul, like the Gestapo. Didn't his friends know that? Couldn't they see the difference?

He and the shepherds *had* to wear the trappings. That simple. "Only a j-job," he said. He did not believe the Party line. He hated anti-Semites. They reminded him of...Papa.

In nearly a dozen years he hadn't used that word.

Tired of Achilles acting like a foolish pup over a bunch of keys, he silently commanded her to return. She did so instantly, crawling forward on her belly to allow him to stroke her huge smooth head. But he found, for once, that he could not enjoy the dog. He kept imagining what his friends were saying about him. Miriam, in that hysterical anger only women seemed capable of, telling Solomon, "He wears their uniform, he represents them!"

Solomon, in that quiet voice of his, the one that meant business, replying, "He claims he can use them, but he is fooling himself. They are the ones with the power. They are using *him!*"

He felt blood rush to his face. As though he truly had heard their words, he seized his sleeve, pinching the Nazi insignia between his fingers, ready to tear it off. His eyes moistened from the fury of his frustration. "One day you'll thank God you have a friend on the inside!"

Feeling enormous fatigue he sat down next to Achilles. He was sorry about the house, he really was. On the other hand, he had worked so hard for Miriam! Well, maybe not exactly for Miriam, but she had always been in his mind. For *her* he had worked to get himself and the canine unit into the center of things, where no one could dislodge them—where he could do some *good*. For people like the beadle, too.

He slapped the leash against his palm, remembering with a sad inner smile he remembered the Christmas Day Beadle Cohen had come around again, to present him with the leash behind the apartment building.

If only Goebbels and his goddamn greed had not interfered! Then Miriam might have appreciated his efforts or at least feigned interest. He wanted her to see how his unit worked together, dog and trainer in a wonderfully transcendent Gestalt. The team was at a point where neither verbal commands nor hand signals were necessary. By the time the trainer issued a command, the dog was underway. Almost impossible to believe, and yet, through love and discipline, he had achieved it. Even the two misfits at the estate, the affenpinscher and Hempel's wolfhound, were good dogs. Or could be with the right training.

No one could deny the achievement. Not even Goebbels or Himmler. Once the dogs were absolutely ready, he would wangle an audience with the Führer. Hitler would have to be impressed—man and animal thinking as one. Then maybe the High Command would be more amenable to the plight of Miriam...Weisser.

He snorted. Taking himself seriously again! What could he be thinking? Did he need her so much? Or just want her.

Achilles growled, up again, nervous, looking through the gate, toward the hill. He tied her leash around a bar and stepped outside, admitting to himself that he wished his friends would return. But he heard—and sensed—nothing from beyond the rise.

Maybe it was for the best that they not come back, at least for now, he decided. Killi was not young anymore and she tended to get jealous of anyone who had his attention. Miri might not understand that, even though the dog wouldn't attack without provocation.

None of the dogs would hurt a fly—except on command.

Chapter 32

December, 1935

If he could not do this, the years of believing in his psychic connection with dogs were a farce. He was a farce. *Give me this,* Erich said to himself as if in prayer. *A birthday present. For Bull and Grace. For the years of feeling their pain as they died.*

Muffled in protective gear and standing at "six-o'clock" on the field of attack, he watched the twelve shepherds. They sat in a tight circle, facing outward, eyes bright with excitement as they waited for the attack command.

Peering between the wires of the facial shield, he did a final visual check of the other trainers. They stood at varying intervals from the dogs, each man covered with thick padding and a mask. Feet braced, each stood ready to absorb the lunge of seventy-five pounds of canine fury; each was one position to the left on the clock from where his animal would attack—close to the dog once the attack began, yet not the dog's prey.

Only Corporal Krayller was with his own dog.

Krayller was a huge man, yet Erich knew he was almost certainly having difficulty controlling the tiny, feisty Affenpinscher. The two of them were in the center of the circle, the hub of the wheel of dogs, where they would remain throughout the exercise. Once the attack commenced, Krayller's terrier would assume a role perfectly suited to its size and temperament; for now, however, it was forced to remain absolutely still.

For this particular maneuver, which Erich called Zodiac, the field of battle was broken into a clock, each of the twelve shepherds securing the position respective to its name. Thus, Aquarius was responsible for attacking the one o'clock position, Taurus the five o'clock, Pisces the nine. The central position, however, required persistence rather than power—a dog agile and quick-tempered enough to keep its eyes on everything and capable of issuing a warning if the enemy compromised the circular perimeter. And so the Affenpinscher.

Never before, Erich thought, had he asked—expected—so much of his dogs or of his trainers. *The attack command is to be mental and given from a considerable distance.* He was not even sure it was possible, especially since the dogs' attention would be divided between target and trainer, though the maneuver had proven successful when the dogs received visual, not mental, commands.

Since the beginning of the month he had also begun incorporating a new tactic into the strategy, one calculated to approximate a surprise attack. Regardless of how far from the hub each aggressor was, the dogs were to hit all twelve targets at the same time. They would have to function as the perfect team he believed them to be, as aware of each other's timing as they were of their masters' wishes.

Get the exercise right, he thought, and you will all get the day off tomorrow, and maybe a second day as well. Maybe the Party felt Christmas was symbolic of the Christian yoke that had held down the Fatherland's true potential for too long, but that philosophy had not yet been accepted by the masses.

The trainers looked at him. Waiting. He took a deep breath, let it out slowly. Concentrated. The white light filled his mind. When he could see nothing else, he thought of the eyes of the shepherd.

He nodded.

Zodiac!

The shepherds moved out, slinking among the dead flower gardens, crawling across the snow-crusted lawn. Keeping down, silent, lethal. Hardly a breath in the frosty air.

Soundlessly, simultaneously the animals seized the targets. Going first for hands that held sticks or pistols, then for the crotch. The men went down under the onslaught but the dogs continued the attack, tearing at the padding. Not so much as a growl—the only sounds those of the targets, beating muffled arms against the dogs.

In the real world of trained dogs and defense, the bite would be so painful that an unprotected target would be nearly paralyzed, Erich knew. He held one hand instinctively over his groin, as thankful for the padding as he was of the dogs' performance.

Again he took a deep breath, let it out slowly. Nodded.

Return!

Twelve shepherds backed off twelve fallen men, the dogs creeping backward, ever watchful of their assailants, like a film run in reverse.

Heart pounding with happiness, Erich picked himself up. Nodded. Concentrated—

City!

Seemingly the friendless, loneliest strays in the world, the dogs meandered back toward their targets. Some of the shepherds lay down, head between forepaws, others sat up and begged, others held out a paw—ready to shake. Some whimpered, some panted.

None growled.

Twelve tails wagged, ticking like metronomes.

Twelve men reached to pet an animal, feed it, shoo it away.

And were attacked, as silently as before. The dogs' pent-up fury kindled in their eyes and the froth of their mouths as they tore at the crotch—then at the throat.

Return!

Again benign, but watchful. Ever...watchful.

Center.

The dogs slowly retreated a few steps and eyed their adversaries carefully. Looking back now and again to make sure they were not being followed, they padded back to the terrier and resumed their initial position in the closely knit circle.

"Got it!" Erich cried. "Yes! Yes! Perfect!"

Trainers' caps and shouts of joy soared as the men ran to congratulate their charges, who stayed where they were. Unlike their masters, Erich thought proudly, they were obeying the fact that no orders to break ranks had been given.

Someone applauded from the part of the driveway that slanted down to the garage beneath the villa. Erich turned to see Hempel smiling approvingly.

"Bravo, Herr Rittmeister!"

Only twelve more days with the bastard! The transfer Hempel had requested was confirmed. Twelve days until Epiphany.

Erich smiled at the irony. What a grand gift for himself—and for his men, who hated the first lieutenant almost as much as Erich did—to have Hempel leave on the anniversary of the day that celebrated the coming of the Wise Men to the Christ child. SS Lieutenant Otto Hempel—soon to be Captain Hempel, commander of one of Himmler's units that rounded up dissidents and other undesirables.

As far as Erich was concerned, Herr War Hero Hempel could command the licking of the Führer's feces.

Ignoring the first lieutenant, Erich went over to Taurus. Apparently aware of how well she and the other dogs had done, she was panting with pride and wagging her tail—no deception this time. Erich knelt beside her, hugging her and stroking her broad, thickly muscled back.

Her ears perked up, the wagging ceased and she looked over Erich's shoulder. Her vigilance was not necessary to tell him that Hempel had walked around the retaining wall and was crossing the lawn. The hairs on the back of his neck warned him as much.

"Simply superb." Hempel stuck his cigarette back in his mouth and, bending, extended a hand.

Erich took no notice of the hand except to avert his head from Hempel's brandy-breath. "Drinking again, Obersturmführer?"

Compensating for Erich's lack of response, Hempel patted the head of the enormous gray-and-white wolfhound leashed at his side, as if that were what he had intended to do all along. Erich disliked the dog, not because he disliked the breed—a lithe, silken-coated cross between an Arabian greyhound and a Russian collie—but because of Hempel.

"Yes, really superb," Hempel said. "All except that stinking affenpinscher."

"His name's Grog," Erich said. "They all have names. I would think you'd know that by now." He rose and began leading Taurus to the dog-runs. "Good job!" he called to the other trainers. "Street security tomorrow and Wednesday."

They grinned. "Street security" meant keeping their homes free of foreign insurgents—except, maybe, St. Nicholas. Only those unlucky enough to have pulled guard duty would be required to come to the estate during the next two days.

"Grog," Hempel said. "Fits him well, unfortunately. A clown at the center of the zodiac. I tell you, he simply has no presence." He thrust out the leash he was holding, forcing the wolfhound forward as though against its will. "Wagner is perfect for that post."

The dog, long and lean, bred for speed rather than vigilance, looked up at Erich with doleful eyes.

"Wagner is SS," Hempel said, "and the SS are destined to be at the center of everything."

Always the same argument. The terrier was not what really concerned Hempel. It was just that he—The Great Otto Hempel—had no part in the production. How many times, Erich wondered, had he almost told Hempel that he *knew?* Knew that the same sophomoric antagonism he had displayed these past two years on the estate had put him on a collision course with his superiors after Ypres?...and that the only war wound he had suffered was an emotional one, when his predilection for young recruits—for very young recruits—had surfaced and he had been drummed from the service?

So what if Hempel had helped quell the Communist insurrection in Berlin! His new commission had come not from service to the Fatherland but from service to Goebbels, as lackey.

Erich chained Taurus to her dog-run and brought her food and fresh water. He took no overt notice of Hempel, who nonetheless continued to follow him around, mumbling about the affenpinscher. Erich reminded himself that this was not the time to have it out with Hempel.

Right now, his duty was to his dogs and to his men. Darkness was descending, and he knew they wanted to get home. He had them form ranks, thanked them for a good day's work and announced, "For their efforts, each dog shall receive a bonus of one extra pound of meat! Dis-*missed!* Tell your families I said...hello."

The men laughed at his oblique Christmas reference. Slipping out of their protective gear they ran to pet their dogs a last time, and headed down to their lockers.

Then all but Ferman were gone. He had drawn Christmas Eve duty. Resolutely the little man—whom Erich had nicknamed "Fermi" after the Italian physicist because of his high forehead and dark hair—came out of the garage and trudged toward the guard house at the east gate, helmet on and Karabiner 90 slung over his shoulder.

Erich thought of Hawk, lying abandoned in the garage. On impulse, he decided to exercise Achilles. He would ride Hawk, he thought—he rarely rode the bicycle anymore, even though he had repainted and modified it to look like an adult's bike. A romp with his old friend would be fun.

The dog had the first kennel, the one nearest the house. He unhooked her from her chain and attached one of the long leashes for running that hung like equine tack over a railing at the end of the kennel. The dog licked his face and snuggled into him. He put his arms around her. He loved the feel of her, the warmth and fur and muscle, and he loved giving her what she seemed to desire most—affection and the freedom to run.

Sensing a presence behind him, he looked up. Hempel stood next to the elm, smoking, looking at the sky.

"I'm taking Achilles," Erich said. "She needs a good run."

Immediately he was annoyed at himself for explaining his actions to a subordinate officer, especially when it was Hempel.

Hempel drew on his cigarette. The end glowed briefly brighter. "A good limp-along might be more accurate," he said.

Erich rose to his feet, stiff with anger. "Your attitude is intolerable!"

Hempel ground out his cigarette, took a bottle from the crook of the tree and drank from it. "My apologies, Herr Rittmeister. The comment was inexcusable." He patted the wolfhound. "Sometimes my anxiety to embrace my true destiny makes me careless toward anything that is old, that represents the past. We are the first of the new world, are we not? And yet one cannot forget…" His voice became bitter, and he stopped talking.

The admission startled Erich. Tensing, he stood, expecting trouble, but Hempel just looped the wolfhound's leash around the rail and, straightening, extended his right hand as he offered Erich the bottle with the left. "We should bury the hatchet. We serve the same master, after all."

Against his better judgment, Erich shook hands. A chill seized him; the hand was strong but cold as stone.

"A toast," Hempel said.

Erich took the bottle. "To the Führer," he said brusquely, and handed the bottle back to Hempel.

The lieutenant drained what was left. "To the SS! The soul of the Fatherland." He flipped the empty into the hedge. "I remember that first

Christmas after the war, when I joined the Freikorps and we fought to keep Berlin from falling to the Bolsheviks. How black things were!" His facial muscles tightened. "Now nothing can keep us down. Nothing!" Eyes gleaming, he looked at Erich. "Hitler and Himmler and others of vision have shown us the German phoenix can rise from the ashes and become supreme."

Erich itched to get away. Even Hempel's contempt was more palatable than standing here listening to platitudes about the Fatherland's greatness and the wonderful men who were leading her to world supremacy.

"Four days ago, at the SS Yuletide bonfire, I saw the future," Hempel continued. "Reichsführer Himmler himself invited me to Wewelsburg."

Erich tried not to show surprise. Wewelsburg was the SS high temple—a moldering, Westphalia cliff-top castle recently overhauled by detention-camp inmates. It was there, seated with his SS knights at an Arthurian round table, that Himmler held court. If Hempel had received a personal invitation to attend the Solstice celebration there, the climax of the Nazi calendar, he had more prestige in the SS hierarchy than Erich had realized.

"Anyone who has seen it must believe in our cause! We sang and the flames created by the burning pages of all those books filled the darkness." Hempel looked up into the night. "And I knew I had a soul." His voice cracked from the intensity of his emotion. "They say we sense the primitive when we gaze into flames—that we claim the past. I did not see the past, I saw the future. I saw our destiny. We will burn the world clean of impurities. It was as if the flames were calling to me."

Achilles began to growl but Erich barely noticed. Hempel's sense of certainty was so crystalline that he felt drawn, not to the man but to the dream. He looked for the Christmas star. No matter how much he hated Hempel and everything he stood for, he understood the man's desire. The difference between them was a matter of choice, and degree.

Hempel shook his head in amazement. "When I looked beyond the flames, I saw the Reichsführer, fire glinting in his glasses, and I knew. He smiled at me and I knew I was...blessed."

"So your loyalty, your commitment, is to Himmler rather than Goebbels?"

"Allow me to tell you about commitment, Herr Rittmeister." Hempel's feral smile returned. "The bonfire burned through the night. We stood there, without coats, at parade rest, from midnight until dawn. No one ordered us to. It was simply *right*. There were a hundred and forty-four of us—all personally selected by the Reichsführer for the ceremony—and not a man moved, even when it began to sleet, until the sun broke through the clouds. I felt...purified. Redeemed."

He pulled out and lit another cigarette.

"Then Reichsführer Himmler said he had something to show me. He looked at me as if I had been transformed—which indeed I had—and led me inside, up to the Supreme Leaders' Hall. Not a word from him once we were inside the castle. Not a word."

Hempel shook his head in wonder. "I've seen a thousand castle rooms, but nothing that compares to that one in Wewelsburg. Circular, with windows that made the dawn-light look almost mystical. The swastika chiseled into the vaulted ceiling." He arched his hand to show Erich.

"Around the wall were twelve pedestals, each with an urn. I'd heard they existed, and now I was in their presence!" He sounded breathless with the wonder of it. "They are there to hold, as each man dies, the incinerated coat of arms of Himmler's twelve most trustworthy knights."

Gently he took hold of Erich's shoulders. "I shall achieve that immortality. With your help."

As gently as they had been placed, Erich removed the hands.

"My help?"

"You and your dogs. They're special. We both know that. The canine equivalent of what we Germans shall be in a generation. One people. One mind. One soul." He made a fist, then said in a husky voice, "But they're not SS. They never will be as long as you are in charge of them."

As if she understood the words, Achilles' growling became more pronounced; Erich's once benign mood became a growing fury that twisted in him like a rope. There would, he thought, be no pleasant bicycle ride tonight.

Chapter 33

Damning himself for wanting Miriam's approval—even after his success with the dogs—Erich shouldered his way toward her dressing room. People not associated with the show normally were not allowed backstage, but he came to see her at least twice a week and was used to making his way relatively unnoticed between the performers and props crowded in the cabaret's stage wings. His presence usually aroused nothing more than an occasional leer.

Tonight, however, he was carrying a pineapple, its aroma unmistakable even in the wine- and sweat-filled air. He could probably buy any chorine for the price of one slice of the coveted fruit, he thought bitterly. Certainly the fruit gained him attention, such as might have been given a Yank overtly carrying nylons. If anything, his gift was even more appealing here, where desire was the stock-in-trade. The cabaret's name was, after all, Ananas: *Pineapple*.

A long-legged chorus girl dressed in little more than feathers and flesh emerged from the storeroom that served as the main dressing room. Eyeing him, his uniform with its new captain's bars, and the pineapple with open and equal admiration, the girl bent to smell the fruit.

"Which tastes better, you or the pineapple?" She tickled him under the chin and laughed when he batted her hand away. "Wish you were waiting for me, Poopsie." She wiggled her bottom. "That one won't give you ice in winter, you know."

She was pretty enough, but he couldn't manage a smile; the woman disappeared in a flurry of dyed ostrich feathers.

He could see Miriam's dressing room from where he stood. Though she knew he was coming, the door was closed. The paint had peeled where a star once marked it, leaving only two faded points. Everything in the club was tawdry and cheap. Everything, he told himself, except that goddamn Miriam. Which was doubtless why he continued to make an idiot of himself, bringing testimonials of love—and despair—to heap at her feet.

Striding to the door, he raised his hand to knock, decided the hell with that and turned the handle.

Miriam sat before a cracked mirror framed with tiny, flame-shaped light bulbs. Some cast a pink glow; other filaments glared from plain glass. The mirror was decorated with faded sienna photos, bits of ribbon, ragged feathers and splashes of make-up.

"Know how to knock?" she asked Erich's reflection.

She picked up her mascara, spat in it and mixed it vigorously with the small brush she used to apply it to her lashes. As she leaned forward to put on a layer of eye shadow with the tip of a finger, one of the narrow rhinestone straps that held up her dress slid down her shoulder. The dress was little more than a silk slip, black and flimsy, an illusion as thin as stardom's hope. Erich had to stifle the urge to unzip the back and slide his hands beneath her arms and over her breasts—to make love to her, now, at once, on the grimy carpet if need be.

"What do you want?" she asked brusquely, without turning.

"I came to warn you."

"About yourself?"

She stood and, placing each foot in turn on the chair, adjusted the seams of her black lace stockings. Her dress was slit up to her thigh on one side, and he could see the edge of black lace panties.

"Say what you have to say, then leave me alone." She slipped into silver shoes and straightened the dress against her hips. "I'm tired of you bothering me, and I'm just plain tired—period. I'm here until four in the morning and up at ten to help in the shop. I eat on the run, take the trolley here to dance for the animals…I have no time for what you want. Nor," she looked right at him, "would I take the time if I had it."

"You don't have to live with the Freunds or work in the shop." He set the pineapple on the vanity. "I've offered to get you a place of your own."

As always, she ignored his offer to take care of her. Lifting the pineapple by its green topknot, she thrust it back into his hands. "Why don't you try this on one of the other girls? They may be stupid enough to confuse exotic with erotic."

Her tone was cold and uncompromising. In the two years since her return to Berlin, she had yet to give him one gentle look, one pleasant word. She had been, at best, polite until he had told her finally that he could do nothing about her estate. Surely she knew he had tried his best. He had broached the subject with those few individuals he knew who dared speak frankly to the Führer. Professor Gerdy Troost, widow of Hitler's favorite architect. The Harvard-educated eccentric Ernst Hanfstaengel, who had drawn and published, with Hitler's consent, caricatures criticizing the Führer. Leni Riefenstahl, the actress turned film maker.

Of the three, only Fraülein Riefenstahl had agreed to look into the matter. She had met him over a cognac to inform him quietly, "You pursue this, and your Miriam Rathenau could lose a lot more than her estate, and so could you. Goebbels would rather have that house than all his harlots."

Clearly Leni was right, Erich thought. The house was not the issue, not anymore. The danger to Miriam, and to Solomon and his family, was growing more evident by the day. Somehow he had to take care of them, but how? He could try to help them get out of the country, but that would ensure his losing Miriam. Not that he had ever really found her again since her return to Berlin.

Damn little Jewess! Who was she anyway? Nothing but a saucy ex-debutante who thought herself better than everyone else. Which was probably why he wanted her—because she considered herself inaccessible. Jews were so stubborn! And foolish!

What if she or the Freunds did something stupid and were arrested? Only God, if indeed He existed, could withstand an SS interrogation. Even if talking meant implicating him—and just knowing him was enough to do that—he would want them to save themselves. Add to that his reputation as an officer, an Abwehr member no less, who had criticized the Reich and who openly worshipped the niece of the man who exemplified everything the Reich detested....

No matter what he did, Erich thought, he could only lose.

Feeling awkward and angry, he continued to hold the pineapple on his open palm. "Tomorrow is Christmas, Miriam. If you don't want this, give it to...to someone." He was thinking of the Freunds and his parents but was unwilling to mention them by name.

"Tomorrow is Christmas! That's what you crawled in here to tell me? Wonderful. I'll mark my calendar and make sure there's room at the inn."

He lowered the pineapple. If any other woman dared treat him like this, he'd give her a boot in the backside and send her out the nearest door. "You must be careful, Miriam."

"What are you, my protector? I'm told you beat up one of Himmler's cronies after the show the other night because he made a comment about me. Sounds like you should be the one to be warned. Your dear friends may not appreciate your solicitude."

"I am not concerned with what—"

Someone rapped twice on the door, stopping him from adding more lies to the ones he had already told himself. He had been about to tell her that he didn't care what others in the Party thought of him—that, unlike them, he could never be a racist. He alone among his classmates in the Bavarian camp and in the Berlin-Tegel classrooms was different. Was Solomon not his friend? He knew most of the others in the Party were not fit fodder for pigs, but that would change as the Führer rose above his petty need for scapegoats.

"Duty calls." She lifted an index finger. "In the future, if you want to talk to me come to the shop. You do remember where it is, don't you?"

"You know I don't go there."

"More shame on you, Oberleutnant Weisser." She spoke with such venom, he recoiled as if from a snake bite. Then, frowning at his uniform, she corrected herself. "Forgive me. I see it is Rittmeister Weisser. That little choreography of your name-change paid off, did it?"

"This warning isn't something to shrug off, or laugh at." He put a hand on her forearm as she opened the door.

Her glance at his hand contained only contempt.

He let go of her, feeling ashamed. Why was it that the lower he seemed in her eyes, the more he wanted her? "The cabaret scene's under fire by the National Socialists. There could be trouble. Real trouble."

"You're telling me nothing new."

Her gaze strayed to the pineapple and, for an instant, she looked hungry. Women! Why couldn't she be like the rest, capable of love at any time as long as there was some price tag attached?

"Don't you know that we're part of the Jewish conspiracy to pervert the purity of Germany's young men?" she asked. "Their strength and virtue might become so drained they could no longer lift blackjacks and billy clubs against old women and rabbis. We must not corrupt you boys with elegance such as this." She gestured toward the dirt-encrusted pipes that crisscrossed the room. "We must save ourselves for true-hearts like Herr Himmler, and pray that Goebbels—the darling—will honor us with a visit."

"They wouldn't come here."

"Oh? Göring already has. Twice. Our manager led everyone in a standing ovation. I wonder if that fool even entertained the possibility that Henri was mocking him! I wouldn't be at all surprised if Goebbels showed up too. He does hate to be outdone. Wouldn't it be wonderful if he got a hard-on watching Rathenau's niece strut her little butt!"

"Stop it!" Furious beyond caution, he gripped her arms. "You have to leave this place. It's dangerous, immoral, not for you."

"Where else can a dancer with Jewish blood find work these days?" She jerked free of his hold. "As your mistress? While you're earning your keep playing footsie with the Nazis, I could take in laundry, and while you're entertaining the officers' wives, I could earn pin money in one of those cabarets where they have sex on-stage. Would that turn you on?"

To taunt him, she took a wide-legged stance and placed her hands on her hips. *"Zieh dich aus, Petronella, zieh dich aus,"* she sang. "Get undressed, Petronella, get undressed." She had Trude Hersterberg, the most famous of the stars who satirized Berlin's penchant for nudity, down pat.

Erich's head pounded. It frightened him, this side of her.

"I could fornicate with one of your shepherds onstage. Now that would be unique! Pisces and a Jew going at it while you Nazis applaud and Goebbels stomps his clubfoot!"

Stunned by her outburst, he let go of her. Without another word she walked from the room, not with the saucy hip-swing some of the other performers affected, but with the grace he remembered from long ago. At the end of the hall, where a red curtain hung in an archway whose plaster was badly chipped, she turned and blew him a kiss. "Happy birthday, Erich."

He stood in the dimly lit passage, damning her again—and himself for allowing her to stir him so. Only he seemed to bring out this side of her. It was as if she were punishing him for not having been born a Jew or for not being foolish or philosophical enough to scrape off his foreskin and cover his head with it like a caul, seeing only what his culture wanted him to see...thinking its hooded thoughts.

He could feel the anger rising in him, as it always did after yet another defeat at Miriam's hands. The time had come to stop treating her like the princess she pretended to be. Why should he have to feel like this whenever she rejected him. He wasn't a leper, unclean and unworthy. His approach had been wrong, that was all. She was always pushing him toward the edge. Tormenting him. Pushing him to be more insistent. He could see her now, fighting him and fucking him with equal abandon.

Sometimes he stood outside the cigar shop, watching her with Solomon and envying their ease with one another as they arranged cases and swept the floor and waited on people. With Solomon, the Freunds, sometimes even with his own parents, she laughed freely, her spirit one of dogged optimism. She was also like that with those customers who could no longer afford real Havanas or Cubans and bought cigars made of cabbage leaves soaked in a solution of nicotine.

He had seen Solomon walk her to the trolley, watched them exchange smiles as she boarded. Their umbrella of shared warmth made him feel small and cold, an uncovered child curled up asleep on a drafty floor.

Not that he was jealous of Solomon, he assured himself—even given the probability that Solomon and Miriam were sharing a bed.

After all, he did not lack women. On the contrary; the wealthier and more powerful their husbands were, the more the wives seemed to want him. Because it pleased him to do so, he made them beg for what they wanted. Lately, however, the more they writhed and moaned, the more he loathed them, and himself. He slept little, and usually alone, falling asleep to dream of Solomon's hand on Miriam's pubis, his mouth on her breasts.

"You shouldn't be back here now." A balding, thickly sweatered dwarf lifted a broom like a quarter-staff and shook it at him. "It's show time."

Erich shoved the pineapple into the dwarf's arms and pushed past him into the nightclub. The place was crowded, a-throb with a four-four beat.

Faded, water-stained green and white awnings sagged from black poles; a pink, plaster Venus de Milo wearing a maroon brassiere decorated the bar. Men in ratty suits and overalls, some cradling bar girls in short leather skirts and silk stockings, lounged beside tables covered with green and white tablecloths. The air was heavy with smoke and stank of sweat.

Onstage, a clown wearing a green-and-red shirt, baggy pants, and a wolf's mask which sported a bulbous nose, boasted of his days as a waiter at Luna Park. "There I was on Naked Days, in my formal attire," he said, eyeing the derrière feathers of a blonde-wigged Red Riding Hood who came prancing onstage, "while Berlin's best families romped nude around me."

As if determined to make up for lost time, he took hold of the blonde, knelt beside her, and began working his nose under her feathers and into her ample posterior. Wide-eyed, the girl jumped forward with a startled "Oooh!" The audience screamed its approval, cheering and whistling and stomping in time to the music.

Appearing to gather her resolve, Red Riding Hood turned and confronted the beast with her only weapon. She opened her cape, and wriggled. A St. Nicholas beard covered her pubis, and her red brassiere, studded with jingling bells, had holes that revealed blinking green nipples. The drooling wolf's pants burst open and a prosthetic penis the length of a broomstick sprang up, a Christmas bow tied behind the knob.

Daintily she tugged at the ribbon, and a banner unfurled under his wolfhood. It read: *"Sieg Heil."*

The crowd roared and the curtains closed. Knowing Werner Fink, on loan from Katakombe on Bellevuestrasse while that club was being revamped, would be on next, the audience grew silent. They had come to see the infamous *conférencier* half in the hopes that they would be there on the inevitable night of his arrest, for why and how he had survived this long remained a mystery.

Fink stepped out between the curtains and threaded toward a table. The spotlight followed him. He was a pasty-faced man with heavily mascaraed eyes and hair slicked with black shoe polish.

Standing there in his black shirt and tie and too-small black jacket, he surveyed the audience.

"We were closed yesterday, and if we are too open today, tomorrow we may be closed again."

Laughter followed Fink's famous opening lines; several men in the audience raised their mugs and shouted, *"Prosit!"* Erich, who liked Fink, wondered if the man had avoided arrest precisely because he was so outrageous. It might be useful to keep that in mind.

The *conférencier* made his way to center stage. "No, I'm not Jewish." He placed a white-gloved hand to his forehead. "I only *look* intelligent."

The drummer hit the cymbal. Mugs were lowered and the laughter became more restrained. A man in the uniform of the SS, seated at a table to the far left of the stage, stood up, his face a study in disgust. He clicked his heels, saluted smartly, and strode out of the nightclub. Erich quickly took the man's chair.

Fink stared out over the stage lights. Cupping his hands like a megaphone, he asked, "CAN YOU HEAR ME ALL RIGHT? ANYONE OUT THERE WHO'S NOT HARD OF THINKING?"

Erich was close enough to the stage to smell the sweat of the performers and to see the spray of saliva that emerged from Fink's mouth as he continued his diatribe. However, the awning overhead was ripped and hung annoyingly in his face, disturbing his vision. He slapped it aside.

"Just tear it down." The swarthy man seated at the table placed the elbow of his grimy leather jacket on the table and revolved his black cigar with his tongue, chewing rather than smoking it. Picking a clump of sodden tobacco off his lip, he frowned and wiped his hand on his grease-spotted white shirt. Coarse black hair poked out of an old workman's cap, and a two-day growth of beard completed the picture of a man of the masses.

In the subdued applause that followed, the man said, "The name's Brecht. Bertolt Brecht."

Before Erich could give his name, Fink's rapid-fire delivery filled the room. "I love black shirts." He opened his jacket and puffed out his chest. "Brown ones, too. I salute them!" Raising his hand in the Nazi salute, he looked from his hand to the floor and back again, and said, "That's how deep we're in the shit."

While Fink bowed to polite applause, a dancer who doubled as a waitress sauntered over to Erich's table. He ordered Berliner Weisse mit Schuss, champagne-beer with a shot of raspberry syrup. When she brought the glasses she bent and placed a napkin on his thigh, giving him ample view of her cleavage. He knew he was expected to slip folded money between her breasts. He glanced away. She gave him a hard smile, swiped at the table with a bar rag and walked off.

"I can tell you from personal experience," Brecht said, "that one has more honey in her pants than a Bremen beehive."

"Not interested."

"Chacun à son goût—to each his own." Brecht sipped his white beer. "Me, I come for the sequins and sex. There's no art to the shows anymore, except for Fink, and I hear he's hanging on by his fingernails." He eyed Erich's uniform suspiciously. "I suppose you're another of those who has come to write him up so he can be punished by the keepers of order."

Is that what he looked like to Brecht? A keeper of order? How laughable! His dogs...*they* were the *real* keepers of order, capable equally of killing upon demand and loving without reservation.

"Just here for the main attraction," he told Brecht.

Brecht shook his head. "Now there is wasted talent."

Erich had heard of Brecht, some poet or playwright who hung around cabarets like a pig around a corncrib. People of such so-called occupations were worthless; as waffle-brained as Solomon, except that they had the bad taste to air their souls in public.

"In case you haven't heard, I'm not to be called a *conférencier* anymore," Fink went on. "The government says I'm an *Ansager* because that *other* word is too French. So many changes! Government, language, the newspaper on the bottom of my bird cage, my face if I'm not careful. Change everywhere except in my pocket! Only one thing never changes—the beauty of our very own Mimi de Rau!"

As he backed into the wings, the curtains swung open. Reclining on an ottoman and haloed in red light was "Mimi," kohl-eyed and wearing a spangling headdress roped with fake jewels. From her ears hung brass baubles. Erich recognized them even if the rest of the audience did not. They were matching *dreidels,* like the ones the Freund and Weisser children had spun each Chanukah until the world went mad.

"*Sei lieb zu mir,*" she sang, her voice sultry while her earrings told the world in her own small way that life had spun her around once too often. "*Komm nicht wie ein Dieb zu mir....*"

Erich could feel the crowd's pulse quicken as people responded to her version of "Mean to Me," the popular Dietrich song. "Be kind to me. Don't come like a thief to me...."

"Time was when a talent like that would have embraced the audience. Now she merely entrances them," Brecht said.

"Go to hell."

"Already have. It rang with the tramp of jackboots, so I have returned here to Limbo, where the entertainment's better. Take the lady on stage, for example. There's a Christmas treat. Voice like an angel, body waiting to be unwrapped."

Knocking over the beer, Erich grabbed Brecht's throat so fast that it appeared the playwright's cigar must shoot from his mouth. For an instant the men stared at each other, Erich with his mangled hand raised to slap the playwright, Brecht with his eyes bulging.

Brecht took the cigar from between his lips. "Meant no insult, friend." Despite its being unlit, he thumped the cigar on the ashtray as if to dislodge imaginary ash.

Erich released him. Embarrassed, he stared at the table. The man was not out of line. "Look, I'm—"

"Sorry? Don't be." Brecht rubbed his neck. "The Fatherland has too much to be sorry for already."

"*Sei lieb...zu...mir.*"

Miriam's song, plaintive and sensual, floated to its conclusion amid a burst of applause.

She rose slowly and drifted forward, arms outstretched as though to embrace a lover. Erich looked around the audience with cynical detachment. Strange how the only time she did not stir him was when she was performing. The red stage lights were intended to make her look wanton, but the effect was both illusion and delusion, for her demeanor made it apparent she was untouchable. That knowledge seemed to enflame most spectators, yet the more the other men wanted her the less enticing he found her. It was only when he and she were alone, or when he was alone and she was alive in his fantasies, that he could not control his childhood desire of wanting her to love him. Not just screw him. Love him.

Chapter 34

Miriam stood quietly at the microphone, waiting for the applause to die down. She had one more song to do before a big production number that did not include her. During her first two songs, she habitually took little notice of the audience, viewing them as heads of cabbages, featureless and brainless. By now, individuals began to take form. The regulars, there to pinch the bottoms of the waitresses and to drink as much as they could in as little time as possible. Goebbels' spies, probably playing with themselves in the dark under the tables. Bertolt Brecht, always at the same table, always with the same laconic expression.

She looked over at Brecht, and winked. He winked back. It was their private nightly tradition, an acknowledgment that they admired each other's work and talents.

Erich, sitting tonight at Brecht's table, turned red. So he had noticed the exchange, she thought. Good. Maybe that would finally keep him away from her. How much more overt did she have to become before he'd give up the challenge of getting her into bed?

She took hold of the microphone and faced Brecht.

"This song is my tribute to you, Bertolt." She smiled at the playwright. The orchestra began the overture from *Threepenny Opera* and segued neatly into *Mack the Knife*.

Listen to the words, Erich, she thought, and began to sing.

At the end of the song, the curtains swung shut, draping around her. When they reopened, she stepped onto the stage apron and descended the stairs that led to the floor. She had to mingle with the patrons at least once each night; part of her job. It helped when Brecht was there. She simply headed for his table and had a drink with him.

"Going to drink with your Jew-lover friend?" One of three boys seated at the table next to Brecht's took hold of her arm as she tried to walk past. His tone was friendly, conversational, but his free hand was tapping the beat of the music on a pistol lying on the table. "I'm talking about that one there. The Rittmeister." He nodded toward Erich. "C'mon, *Judsche*. Try some real men. It'll make you feel like a German."

Miriam looked at Erich, sensing his body tighten with coiled fury. Hadn't he once boasted to her about his Oriental fighting lessons? Said he took them and guerrilla tactics from Otto Braun himself, who had, as Li Te, fought alongside Mao throughout the Long March. Well, use what you learned, damn it!

The youth stared coldly at Erich, his hatred apparent. "You have run with the wrong dogs too long, Weisser."

"Who sent you here?" Erich's voice was deadly calm, barely audible beneath the music.

"Never mind who sent us!" another said. "We'll fuck 'The Star' after you do. Three at once! Cork all three holes at the same time!"

"Do what you want with the whores." Erich still sounded reasonable, rational. "No one touches Miss de Rau."

"Shoot the Jew-lover, Klaus," his buddy said. "Who cares who he is!"

But the boy holstered his pistol. "We've done our job. Let's go." He spat on the floor and stood up. "If you love the Fatherland," he said, "you'll stay away from this pigsty in the future...or we'll burn it down around you."

"Like you did the Reichstag?" Brecht was seemingly beyond caring what the boys might do next.

"That was the Communists."

"Jews."

"Foreigners."

Shaking, as angry as she was afraid, Miriam watched the boys go out the door, a Machiavellian chorus of avenging angels. Whatever it was that had happened to German society that February night the Hollander, van der Lubbe, torched the congressional building, she was certain it would take a cataclysm to assuage it.

"Jewmongers!" one of the boys screamed before following his friends into the street.

He flipped a wine bottle over his shoulder. The sound of smashing glass coincided with the crash of the cabaret door as it slammed shut behind him.

Stooping awkwardly in her tight dress, Miriam picked up a champagne glass and a bottle from one of the front tables. Leaning across Brecht's table, she said to Erich, "You brought them here. They came for *you*. The rest of us were only diversions." She filled the glass.

"They would have come anyway. I warned you."

She glanced up at the stage. Oblivious to the drama on the floor, a circle of ersatz Ziegfield girls in scarlet ostrich feathers strutted around the stage. Forming a crescent, they opened their feathers to reveal g-strings and tasseled nipples.

"Yes, perhaps they would have come," she said, staring at Erich. "But not tonight."

Turning from him she lifted her glass as if it were a chalice.

The girls took their final bow. The music stopped. The applause quieted.

"I had a friend once," she told the audience. "Today was his birthday. I wish to sing his favorite Christmas carol."

Erich grabbed her arm. "Haven't you had enough for one night? You could be arrested for blasphemy."

"This has nothing to do with you," she said. "Erich *Joachim* Weisser was my friend. I'm singing this for him."

Twisting from his grasp, she raised her head. *"Stille Nacht,"* she sang. *"Heilige Nacht...."*

As her voice filled the room she prayed—that someday God would replace bullets and broken glass with love.

Chapter 35

Erich pushed money at the taxi driver and stepped out into the wind. Alois. Joachim. *Names*. Didn't *she* use a stage name? Was she so unperceptive that she didn't realize his being in the Party was as much an act as hers? Women! Not one of them worth the price of a pineapple.

He looked up at the bedroom Goebbels occupied when he was too "busy" to go home to his wife and family. Surely on Christmas Eve...

The light was on. Above the villa shone an icy star, as if to remind Erich that Adolph Hitler, the twentieth-century Messiah, had ordered him to keep an eye on the Gauleiter, who remained suspect in the Chancellor's eyes. The way Goebbels behaved, like probably sending those youths to Ananas, made it hard to believe the man was educated. It was as if the osteomyelitic inflammation of the bone marrow that had caused his foot to be deformed had also attacked his brain, wiping out any semblance of normal behavior.

Even now, the Gauleiter had probably passed out with his head between some prostitute's legs.

To hell with him, and Hitler—and women. Erich pulled his collar up against the wind and followed the path around to the dogs. Only they were worth anything. He could hear them as he approached, barking and howling at the moonless sky, as restless as he.

He shook the chain-link fence he'd had erected along the west end to separate the sloped, circular dog-runs from the rest of the grounds, and the dogs came charging. When they reached the ends of their chains, they were jerked from their feet, only to circle and charge again. Their ferocity sent a welcome chill up his spine.

"Password!" The bolt of a carbine rammed home and an overcoated helmeted soldier with the broad shoulders of a Greco-Roman wrestler hustled from the shadows; the affenpinscher yipped and ran in such circles at the end of its leash that it became entangled and had to roll over to extricate itself.

"*Tannenbaum,*" Erich said. "And Merry Christmas, Oberschütze."

"Oh, it's you, sir." Krayller lowered the 98 from his shoulder and grinned down at his monkey terrier's antics. The dog was barely bigger than its master's hamhock-sized hand; he loved it like a father might an infant. "Merry Christmas."

Putting the rifle butt against the ground, Krayller stooped to pet the dog, which rolled over to have its belly tickled. "I'll let you in, sir."

"I thought Holten-Pflug had drawn the midnight shift."

"Well, their new baby and all—"

"You're quite the altruist, Johann."

As Erich walked through the gate, he smiled at Krayller's affection for the little dog.

"What's the meaning of all the commotion?" Hempel strode toward them, a bottle in one hand, in the other a Mann—connected to his holster by a black braid. Though he was clearly inebriated, the alcohol seemed to have tightened rather than loosened his rigidity. He did not stop walking until his nose almost touched Erich's.

"Have we disturbed the Gauleiter's...holy night?" Erich asked, not backing up.

"Don't be impudent."

Hempel raised the gun. Erich brushed it aside nonchalantly. Touching Krayller's shoulder, he sent the lance-corporal back to his post. With a flourish he probably would not have exhibited had Hempel not been present, the corporal clicked his heels together and, saluting, bellowed "Heil Hitler!" loud enough to be heard in the upstairs bedrooms if not throughout the rest of the Grünewald.

"Someday his impudence will get him shot." Hempel reholstered his gun. "The way he mollycoddles that excuse for a dog! It's unmanly." He paused, then added in a low voice, "Like a man who would rather fuck than fight for his country when she is at war."

"Like Doktor Goebbels, Herr Obersturmführer?" Erich glanced again at the bedroom light, wondering if by some quirk he would have to defend Goebbels in order to put down Hempel. "And is the nation at war?"

Hempel's smile did not waver. "I'm referring to you, Herr Rittmeister. The Fatherland will always be at war, if not from without then from within." His gaze flickered with contempt, but perhaps sensing Erich's clenched fist, he took a step back. "I mean nothing derogatory, Herr Rittmeister. It's just that we've much in common, you and the Oberschütze and I—bachelors who are married, as the best of German men should be, to ideals rather than to wives or to our mothers. I hate to see any man prostitute his possibilities. I'd as soon see Krayller dead...nothing personal against him, you understand."

"As you said," Erich glared up into his adversary's face, "our country is at risk, from within and without. You are to be commended for helping Herr Goebbels in his efforts *within*—" Erich pointed toward the villa. "But just as you do whatever you must, it is the duty of myself and my men, and whatever dogs we feel best belong in the unit, to keep these grounds patrolled. That is what you need to understand. As far as I'm concerned, that is all you need to understand."

He waited for Hempel to back off, but the man did not move. "Anything else we need to agree to tonight?" Erich asked.

"All we have ever asked is that you keep the dogs quiet when we are," again the smile, "in conference."

"You're speaking for Herr Goebbels?"

"I have always spoken for Herr Goebbels." Hands in pockets, Hempel walked over to the scarecrow elm, where he had an undisturbed view of the Gauleiter's window.

Always his insistence about his closeness to Goebbels, Erich thought as he strode toward the kennels. Well, bad as Goebbels was, at least he was man enough to prefer women over boys. Greeting him, the shepherds yelped with delight and tugged at their chains. He wanted to pet Achilles, but instead he unhooked and leashed up Taurus. Killi reminded him too much of Miriam and her stubborn rage. What would he have done if those youths had raped her? What could he have done?

Involuntarily he remembered an experience he had tried to bury. One Easter, while motorcycling down for field training in Bavaria, he had witnessed the aftermath of a rape—the people of a village walking past a naked woman sitting on a wagon tongue in an alley, crying. No one went to her aid; they simply averted their eyes. A Jew, obviously. *And I did nothing either*, he thought, just roared away, speeding deep into the Black Forest, the wind—surely it was the wind—making his eyes water.

She could have been Miriam...*could have been Miriam*...

That night, as he camped alone beneath the stars, those words echoed in his head like a song. He kept asking himself why he had done nothing. By morning he had neither answers nor sleep. When the sleepless nights continued during the bivouac, he requested a pass to attend the Passion Play at Oberammergau. Maybe Father Dahns had been right all along. Perhaps religion did hold answers or, if not, then at least clues to the secrets.

As Christ was nailed to the cross, an elderly woman behind him whispered, "Mein Hitler," and the response, increasingly louder, quickly serpentined through the audience.

Soon each character in the play had a German counterpart. Even Bethlehem, which the audience took to be Berlin. Mutterings and murmurs and lisped whispers hovered about him like prayers breathed by dark angels. He left after the first curtain call, when the rest of the audience rose in ovation.

Was Miriam blind to everything beyond the stage lights? Was that why she insisted on putting herself in danger, like staying in that damn cabaret and singing, of all things, a Christmas carol?

"The shepherds do need a responsible leader, Herr Rittmeister," Hempel said, coming forward. "Human as well as canine. Nothing personal, you understand, but they lack proper orientation. As you do. You've run with the wrong pack too long."

Erich saw in Hempel's eyes the same haughty disdain for others he had witnessed in the youth at Ananas.

You have run with the wrong pack too long—

"*You* sent those animals to the club! Not Goebbels." Erich felt the rope of his gut twist tighter. They were your *boys!*"

"And why not? You *must* learn—"

Erich's fury exploded. *Get him, Taurus. Tear the son of a bitch to pieces.*

Taurus lunged for the lieutenant. For an instant, Erich hesitated—just long enough for Hempel to know the attack was no accident. Then he grabbed her collar and tugged her away.

The lieutenant lay on the ground, shaking. His wolfhound whined and licked his face.

Erich stared down in horror. He had allowed—instructed—Taurus to attack an officer. He should stoop and help the man. Apologize.

He could not bring himself to commit such hypocrisy. Instead, after mentally commanding Taurus to sit, he leaned over just enough to remove the Mann from Hempel's holster. The braid on the handle felt slick and soft. Looking more closely he realized it was human hair. Nauseated, he unhooked the braid and pitched it and the pistol into the hedge.

The lieutenant groaned and opened his eyes. As he sat up, he gave Erich a perverse, suave smile.

"How kind of you, Herr Rittmeister, and how crass of me. I forgot it was your birthday and did not buy you a gift. And here you are giving me such a priceless one." He fingered blood-rimmed teeth marks on the back of his hand. "I do believe you have given me incentive for doing anything I wish to you and your brood."

Fist clenched, Erich stood over him. "The hell I have."

"Something's already in the works, Herr Rittmeister. When the dogs are fully trained, I will have them." His smile broadened. "But not now. Not yet."

"Stick to buggering boys." Fuming, Erich strode down the section of drive that ran to the garage, Taurus trotting alongside. *She has tasted blood,* Erich thought. *The worst thing that could happen to a guard dog.* Would that make her too emotionally unstable for duty? If so, he would cover for her; that was what partners were for.

He opened one of the garage doors and switched on the light. The place was dank and smelled of oil. Two rows of vehicles, civilian cars and military jeeps and cycles, faced one another beneath the bare bulb. The cars that were still Konrad's responsibility, Rathenau's limousine and the Daimler, were parked on each side of Goebbels' SSK Mercedes Benz. Beside the limo hulked the Gauleiter's pride, a Minerva Landaulet imported from Belgium. Next to the Daimler an empty parking space awaited the prize Goebbels wanted: a Sears, from the American catalogue.

Erich had never touched the Daimler. Now, running a gloved hand across the smooth curve of its fender, he thought of Miriam, sheathed in black silk, singing before the floodlights. He banged his fist down. Why must she always demean him! Why did he keep pushing? He should not even be associating with her, or with Solomon—especially after tonight's episode at Ananas. Any fool could see their ties were a danger to him, and to them...more so, now that he and Hempel had declared open warfare.

He cursed himself for allowing Hempel to goad him like that. If Hempel filed charges—not that he could prove anything—things could get messy. The man's past was an open secret; his own could as easily become one. Any of his Abwehr superiors could insist he cut all ties with his impure past. Burying it could literally mean burying Miriam and the Freunds.

He shuddered.

Trading his overcoat for a flight jacket and the leather helmet he kept in one of the lockers along the east wall, he climbed onto his cycle. He kick-started it with such force that he almost toppled the machine, and raced the engine without regard for Goebbels' comfort. He roared out of the door and up the incline, waving at Krayller to open the gate.

With Taurus loping next to him, Erich wound his motorcycle through the Grünewald and past the Tiergarten. He had gone through Potsdamer Platz and was cruising up Friedrich Ebert Strasse, throttled down and coasting in neutral, by the time he acknowledged to himself he wasn't running from something as much as to something: he wanted to go home.

He slowed to a halt in front of the cigar shop. It looked dark and forlorn, and the lights of Das Ostleute Haus bathed him in blue. Snow had begun to fall. He gripped his lapels together against the cold and stared at the elongated reflections the street lamps cast as the pavement gave itself over to white. Across the street, the curb and the ragged blue-spruce hedge seemed like a line someone had drawn in the powder, daring him to cross. But he was not ready—yet.

A woman in a fur coat stepped around the corner and into the blue light. For a split second it seemed as if one of the furrier's mannequins had come alive. Then he saw the whip and the high-heeled boots so capable of trampling across a man's conscience. The fury and nervous near-exhaustion he had thought he had shed on the Ku'damm returned to suffocate him.

"Evening, soldier." The woman lifted her gaze seductively.

Taurus, panting from the run, went rigid and bared her teeth. No sound. Her affect was one of silent, mean cunning.

The woman backed away. "Some animal you've got there." Fear in her voice.

He switched off the engine but held onto the handlebars as he strained to see into the Freund-Weisser apartments.

Twirling her whip, the woman circled Taurus and stepped saucily toward Erich. "Want to be my slave? Or perhaps I should be yours? I don't mind pain if the money's right."

"How much are you willing to pay?" Erich asked in an off-hand tone, not looking at her.

"Pay?" She laughed and tried a new approach. "Don't want to be alone on Christmas Eve, do you, Sugar Plum?"

"That's exactly what I do want."

Still gripping the cycle, he stared into the darkness, imagining Miriam kissing Solomon's fingers, easing his hand down over her breast and belly to her thighs, she sliding her fingers down his chest. Damn her! Those three in the alley behind the El Dorado had gloried in whoredom, yet even in his mind's eye he could not force Miriam to compromise herself.

"What's wrong, honey? Cat got your tongue?"

She took a feather from her coat and drew it across the nape of his neck. Giggling, she slipped a hand in his coat, reaching for his crotch. He debated having her get on her knees to service him—power-prayer, he called it—but pulled away.

He wanted to wish his mother a Merry Christmas and maybe drink a schnapps with his father. He could stand the old man for that long. Except Miriam might hear him upstairs and think he had come around because of her, he thought, knowing full well that he was making excuses and that Miriam could not possibly distinguish his footsteps from those of any stranger.

"Prefer boys?" the prostitute asked.

"Bitch!"

Letting go of the cycle, Erich backhanded her as hard as he could. The machine fell with a crash. Dropping the whip, the woman put her fingers tentatively against her cheek. Erich slapped her again. Hard. As she stumbled and landed on her knees, Taurus leapt. She sank her teeth into the wrist, just above her glove. When the whore's flesh broke against her canines, Taurus quietly hunkered down. Belly tensed and shoulder muscles rippling, she swallowed and bit deeper.

Blood ran down the whore's arm and she screamed, her face contorted with terror, her acne-scarred cheeks as death-white as rotted carp flesh. An electric tingling rolled down Erich's spine. He stiffened. The street lamp took on the form of a lopsided moon, and a feeling that he was surrounded by greenery and gloom suffused him. He felt hot, sweaty. Then, just as abruptly, he was cold again, looking down on the whore and thinking how ludicrous women really were.

For all their power, life rendered them as helpless as men.

Chapter 36

Berlin was alive with lights.

The New Year, the Führer had assured everyone, would ring in greater times for the New Order, and so the Reich was beribboned and pulsing with music and laughter.

Solomon waited outside Ananas for Miriam to finish her performance. Around him, couples clung to one another as they reeled along the pavement, many with half-finished bottles of champagne in hand. He tried to feel their joy, but he could not see or feel beyond their swastika armbands—their emblems of hope and the coming happiness. He kept to the shadows, estranged from the crowds yet part of them—like a man dining alone in a fine restaurant, aware of the quality food but unable to enjoy it because he had no one with whom to share the meal.

He wished Miriam would hurry. Since the Christmas Eve incident on Friedrich Ebert Strasse, he had walked her home every night rather than having her take the trolley. According to the papers, an overcoated, enormous-nosed Jew had attacked one Gisela Haas while she was out collecting money for the poor. *Der Stürmer,* the most viciously and openly anti-Semitic of the papers, compared her wounds to those inflicted by Peter Stumpf, the self-confessed werewolf convicted of lycanthropy in Cologne in 1598 and flayed alive on All-Hallows Eve. It was suggested that perhaps the Jew was seeking a virgin's menstrual blood for another satanic rite to be perpetrated against the Holy Child.

Such nonsense! Not that the truth was relevant; only the danger to Miriam was. The heritage of the family who owned the cigar shop was no secret, nor was hers. Audiences at Ananas knew she was Jewish. Fink, now the cabaret's manager, did what he could to defuse the jeers and shield her from the bottles that were occasionally thrown while she performed, but it was up to Solomon to keep her safe. If she walked in the streets unescorted, it was just a matter of time before something happened to her.

Miriam emerged at last, slipping furtively through the cabaret's service entrance. She held her coat close, like protective armor, and smiled at the sight of him.

"How do you always manage to look happy?" Sol bent and kissed her, wondering for the thousandth time what miracle had finally brought her to him.

"Shouldn't I be? The past is gone. Buried. No sense dwelling on its ugliness." She looped her arm through his.

"You have a God-given talent for optimism." The way her eyes reflected the holiday lights overhead enchanted him.

Right before Chanukah, a week before Christmas Eve, she had come to his bedroom with the ease and familiarity of a wife. Her attitude was perfect, for had she been hesitant, he might have kept his distance, and had she been too bold, he would have been overly concerned with his performance. He had consummated the sexual act only once before, with a prostitute Erich goaded him into buying. It had been a dismal failure, too ephemeral to constitute reality, and he had continued to think of himself as a virgin.

With Miriam, lovemaking was a glorious event. Like children holding hands at the ocean's edge, they laughed and splashed and leaped over waves, daring each other to go together into deeper and deeper water, and he did not even care that his parents and Recha might hear them.

Nodding and smiling at passers-by like any Gentile couple, they walked home along Leipziger Strasse, past Wertheim's. Like the KadeWe's square-block delicatessen, perhaps the world's largest, Wertheim's was for all practical purposes off-limits to Jews. The Depression had again brought scarcity to the Fatherland, so Aryans—real Germans—were to be fed and clothed first.

Thank God people still found money for tobacco, Sol thought, seeing the crowd that milled outside Die Zigarrenkiste. "Looks like Herr Weisser was right," he said. "He insisted business would be good tonight, so we should turn up the lights and stay open late. 'What good is a holiday brandy without a fine cigar.'"

Miriam laughed at his imitation of Herr Weisser. "See, you worry needlessly about leaving him to handle the shop."

Sol hugged her, slipping his hands inside her coat so he could hold her more tightly.

She was right; he worried too much. Like his father, he feared things might not be done correctly unless he did them himself. He needed to rely more not only on Miriam and Herr Weisser but also on his mother and Frau Weisser. On Papa too, perhaps. Lately there were days when Papa's melancholia—he laughed at himself for his use of the illness' archaic name, as though that romanticized it and thus lessened its reality—released its grip. At those times, Jacob was able and willing to help with small tasks. Since Christmas Eve, when Miriam came home from Ananas so distraught and

Sol held her through the night as she cried, Jacob kept the curtains and window open when he rocked. He wanted, he said, to hear all the horror outside, and did not seem to mind the chill that seized the room.

Sol checked his watch as they neared the crowd. Three in the morning. "Herr Weisser has extended his midnight special. He enjoys spreading happiness on nights like this."

"I think the general idea is for the customers to do the spreading...of their money."

Sol laughed but his laughter died in the air. Grabbing Miriam's hand, he rushed forward. Something was very wrong. The crowd was static, gawking. Nobody was going inside the shop, no one coming out, and the door of the shop was open, its glass shattered.

"I don't care who they are, people ought not to be treated like that," said a hefty woman on the crowd's outskirts.

"Nonsense, Luise." The skinny man beside her was on tiptoes, straining to see. "They've been cheating people for years. Don't you listen to what the Führer says?"

The man swore at Sol as he and Miriam shoved past and entered the shop. "All his fault," someone said.

"No. He was a nice man. I liked him."

"Money-sucking Jews. We should rid Germany of the lot of them."

The inside of the shop was a shambles. Display cases lay overturned and broken on top of merchandise that would never again be salable. Herr Weisser, his face red and swollen and splotched with darkening bruises, lay amid strewn money and broken glass. His head was on his wife's lap. Leaning against the upside-down cash register, she wept and stroked his cheek.

Friedrich lifted a hand when he saw Solomon, then his head lolled and his hand fell to the floor.

"Fred offered them money. They wouldn't take it," Inge Weisser said. "They said it was tainted. Jew money. Can you believe, they called him a Jew? They beat him, kicked him. Four of them held his arms and legs and two others...two others...oh God! They dropped the cash register on him." She put her head in her hands. "It's his ribs. I think one has punctured a lung."

"A Jew they called me!" Friedrich Weisser wheezed and then caught his breath. "Me! A Jew!"

"If I had only been here," Inge Weisser told Sol. "I would have told them the truth, that they had the wrong—"

As if realizing what she was saying, and to whom, Frau Weisser covered her mouth with her hand. *She is determined to blame this on us*, Sol thought angrily as two burly men carrying a makeshift stretcher shouldered their way into the shop.

"I've been here before," one of them said, glancing around. "People like these never learn." He shook his head. "Waste of our time, if you ask me."

"What are we supposed to do? Leave the old man to die? He could be your father."

They knelt and eased Friedrich Weisser onto the stretcher. He whimpered. "Cover me with cheese and charge admission," he said through compressed lips.

His bitter humor made Sol wince. Weissenberg, the Weimar-Berlin healer considered by many to be a saint, had claimed he could resurrect the recent dead by applying cheese curds to a body. When cheese and corpse began to stink and the police stepped in, he ranted that his impending miracle had been circumvented by police interference.

"Anyone else hurt?" Sol asked Frau Weisser.

She shook her head. "Your mother was here when they came, but she's safe."

"Mama? Where is she!"

"At the apartment. She got away." There was a biting edge to Inge's voice. "Left my Friedrich to those animals!"

"I'll go and find her," Miriam said softly, touching Sol's arm as if to quiet his nerves.

Sol followed the stretcher out the door. Inge clung to her husband's hand.

"I'm sorry, Freddie. You said we should insist they send her away, but I wouldn't listen," she said. "That Miriam and her cabaret dancing! First we lost Erich because of her, now they came to finish what they started at the nightclub on Christmas Eve!"

"Did they mention me, Frau Weisser?" Miriam's voice was tight.

After a moment's hesitation, Inge Weisser shook her head. "Not exactly, but...but you may be sure they were after you!"

Miriam's shoulders sagged, and she looked very pale.

"Please, Frau Weisser," Sol said. "I know how upset you are, but watch what you're saying."

"I am watching! I'm watching my Friedrich here! Where were you when the Brownshirts arrived? Out on your nightly stroll!"

Sol leaned over Friedrich. "I'll find a way to get in touch with Erich—"

"No!" Herr Weisser's voice was amazingly strong. "I don't want to see him." He stopped and closed his eyes before he went on. "He did not come. Not even for Christmas...or for his birthday."

Sol patted the man's meaty hand. "I must check on Mama, then I'll come to the infirmary. You'll be all right."

"He'll be fine. We'll all be fine, won't we Solomon-the-Wise! Especially your papa over there!" Frau Weisser spat on the street. "My Friedrich might die, but Jacob Freund will be fine!"

Solomon looked sadly at the woman he had known most of his life, realizing he did not know her at all.

Chapter 37

Miriam put her arms around Sol's waist and her cheek against his back. She leaned against him for a moment, warming him, then took his hand and led him to the apartment like a child.

They found his parents and sister in the library. His mother stood in the corner, body pressed against the wall as if only it stood between her and collapse. Her left cheek was badly bruised. Recha, dressed in a white pleated floor-length gown, sat with her head tilted against the rocker back, staring at the ceiling. Her father stood behind the chair, gripping its scroll tops and staring blankly out the window toward the store front.

"Thank God you're all right, Mama," Solomon said.

"They called me a whore, Sol. Me! A whore!" His mother twisted a blond curl around and around her finger. Her voice was soft. Toneless. She was not crying. "They said any Gentile who was in partnership with Jews certainly copulated with them. As God is my witness, I didn't deny our—Him—but I didn't argue with them either. I wanted to live, Solly. For you and Papa and Recha."

"Anti-Semitic garbage talk." Jacob's chin was stubbornly lifted, his voice stronger than Solomon had heard it in years.

"They thought I was Frau Weisser and that Friedrich was Jacob. One of them hit me, then they told me to get out." She was twisting her hair with both hands now.

"I just sat here," Jacob said. "What kind of man would do that while his wife and best friend—"

"I'll have it cut." Ella Freund pulled her curls down in front of her eyes. "And dyed. What do you think, Sol? Recha? Miri? How would I look with black hair?" She posed like a little girl pleading forgiveness for some silly infraction of family rules.

Recha rose from the rocking chair and faced her mother. "You will look beautiful, *Mutti*," she said quietly.

"She's right," Miriam added. Hoping her voice had not betrayed her concern, she kissed Ella Freund's cheek. The woman smiled, her face strangely calm. She had the look of a piece of fragile porcelain, as if she could shatter from the slightest touch.

Sol looked gratefully at Miriam. She could see her own fear mirrored in his face.

"I sat and rocked!" Jacob lashed out at the chair with his foot. In his near-blindness he missed and kicked again, knocking the chair on its side. Kicking at it a third time, he splintered two spindles.

Recha put her arms around him. He twisted, then allowed his body to slacken. "They'll be back," he said. "What then? Shall I sit and smile while they rape my wife and daughter and plunder my shop whenever they choose? Or should I sell them pencils so they can write their names on our souls."

"I could take money from the till and go to Fenzik's," Sol's mother said. "He cuts hair so well."

"There could be a thousand tills, Ellie." Jacob Freund spoke in a measured tone. "You still could not go there. Fenzik's has been off-limits to us for a year. Jew hair, eyes, flesh. We have become Jewish shadows."

Recha kept her arms around her father. "You'll see, Papa. After the holidays, things will calm down."

Miriam silently applauded Recha's optimism as she watched Jacob Freund gently push his daughter away and shuffle toward the hall. His footsteps faded, stopped, returned. He was right, she thought. They had all become Jewish shadows, she thought, true children of the light.

"Pack!"

He dropped two battered suitcases at his wife's feet.

"Pack?" she asked. "Are we going to Mainz for a vacation?"

"You're leaving. You and Recha. Getting out. That's the least I can do for you."

He turned and plodded back toward the bedroom. Ella hurried after him. "I'll cut it myself, Jacob. And dye it too. Black as the Queen of Sheba's I'll make it."

"Pack!"

"Will you go too, Papa?" Solomon asked.

Jacob stood in the archway, one hand against the wall. "I've gone too many kilometers in that rocker to run now. Recha and *Mutti* will go to Amsterdam tonight, to your Aunt Hertl's." He glanced at Miriam. "She should go too."

"If Solomon stays, I stay." Miriam looked quickly at Sol. She was too involved with him even to think of leaving. No matter what.

"I'm staying too," Recha said. She picked up an ermine cape that lay on the desk and draped it around herself as if it could protect her from what was happening.

Waltzing up to Recha, Frau Freund whirled her around. "You too, my sweet," she sang, as if at a party. "We'll cut and dye your hair as well. Then Papa won't send us away!"

"Neither of you will touch your hair," Jacob said. "These days it is a blessing to look like *goyim*. It will help on your trip."

"Ernst says that with my looks, if I legally change my name and move in with him, no one need know," Recha said.

"That you are Jewish?" Jacob was picking up the rocker. Now he lifted it off the floor and set it down, face rigid with rage. "My daughter would deny her heritage so easily?"

Recha backed up. "I have no intention of denying anything, Papa, not in the long run. But Ernst says I'm destined to become a star. A star, Papa! He's the best in the business. He should know."

"He knows what is in a father's heart? He knows what is in the mind of God, who made you one of His Chosen People?" He raised his arm as if to strike her. Sol stepped between them, ready to take the blow.

"Please, Papa," Recha said.

The arm Jacob had raised faltered, and he lowered it. Recha picked up her cape and fondled it, as if it were a living thing.

"I wish I did not love you so much," Jacob said, gripping the chair. "Do this thing for me, Recha." He closed his eyes as if in prayer. "Take your mother to her sister, to safety. For almost three years I have sat here, thinking myself half-blind and sick because the world is blind and sick. But it is my beloved wife who is not well. I have made her that way, too dependent on hope. Take her to your aunt, then do whatever you must."

Recha had been so proud when her agent gave her the ermine, Miriam thought, remembering the day, a few months ago, when the girl signed the contract to pose for Mercedes advertisements. The golden-haired sylph who had sniffled her way through the evening at Kaverne, so in awe of Miriam, had blossomed into a beauty. Her bootpolish-brown eyes had attracted the producer of UFA films and landed her a bit part in *The Blue Angel*. Her parts since then were small but important, as she put it. She had begun to be noticed. Miriam remembered Recha's confidence about an affair with a rich playboy associated with the film industry. He smoked opium and could make love only if the lights were on; he believed the dark brought out the devil in a woman. Rachel Roland, as Recha called herself, was all grown up, and entitled to make her own choices.

Or was she? Wasn't it her duty to go with her mother, who appeared to be verging of some kind of breakdown?

Recha trembled and looked at the floor. Sol started to move to her, but she lifted her hands and moved away from him, as if she were so filled with despair and the knowledge of separation that she wanted no one to touch her. "I love you, Papa."

"I know you do."

He gazed at her quietly, then lowered himself to his knees and drew back the ancient Oriental rug. Using the fingers of one hand to feel the nubs of the numbers while he worked the dial with the other, he opened the safe he had recessed into the floor. He removed several bundles of paper. Lifting out a tray, he reached further down and took out a wad of currency and a leather pouch.

"Here are your birth certificates, what money and jewels we have left, and a few odds and ends of sentimental value." He held them out, waiting for someone to take them.

Recha did so. "The final audition for the *Lady Moon* revival is this weekend, Papa. It's a major role. Ernst will kill me..."

"Would you rather the Nazis killed you...and your mother?"

"I'll have Ernst talk the studio into a late call," Recha said after a lengthy silence. "I'll take Mama to *Tante* Hertl. But I'm coming back when she's settled. Life is dangerous, Papa, but I intend to live it as fully as I can. The mistakes I make will be my own."

"Even if they are fatal ones?"

"Especially those."

The comment brought silence. They packed in silence, closed the apartment door silently behind themselves, walked somberly to the station. New Year's Eve was not a popular night for travel. On one hand, it meant seats might be available; on the other, it meant the Freunds would be conspicuous. Recha was elected to purchase the tickets while the rest waited near the train, which was huffing steam by the time they arrived.

Relatively few people boarded the gray-brown Amsterdam-bound train. Miriam stood with Sol and his parents, terrified that Recha would have difficulty buying tickets. She heaved a sigh of relief when she saw the young woman run toward them along the platform, waving two tickets.

"No trouble," she called out breathlessly. "The clerk recognized me. He was too busy trying to get my autograph and make a date with me to look at our passports."

Jacob caught her in his arms and held her close. "It might not be quite so easy at the border," he said. "Remember—none of what you're carrying is as valuable as life itself."

She patted her coat. The lining hid a false pocket which held the family jewels. She had been instructed to use them for her mother's needs, and for bribes if necessary. In the coat were her great grandmother's pearl brooch, her mother's diamond rings, her grandmother's tourmaline that she considered her own.

"The tourmaline goes last, Papa."

"Maybe nothing will have to go." Jacob put his arm around his wife's shoulders and kissed her. The train hooted. "*Mutti* is in your hands, and she is our most precious jewel," he said softly.

"I don't understand why I have to go all the way to Amsterdam to have my hair cut and dyed," Ella Freund whispered. "You are sending us away, Jacob. Why are you sending us away?"

"Papa and Sol will come to Amsterdam in a week or so," Miriam said. "Me, too." She tried to look cheerful as she helped Sol's mother on board. Not that Ella would notice, she thought, fighting tears. The rational, practical person who had been the strength of her family had been displaced by a stranger...an elderly, pathetic victim of the times.

"Promise you'll come?" Ella Freund leaned precariously from the top step.

"Promise," Jacob Freund answered.

"No tears, now," Recha said, her eyes brimming.

"No tears," Sol said.

Miriam's head was against his shoulder and she held tightly to his hand in an effort to control her emotions. The engineer sent a last steam blast echoing through the station, and the train began to move. Miriam and Sol walked alongside the cars, together with other people likewise in motion, offering good-byes and good wishes.

"Be happy," Miriam called. "Remember, life's a passing dream, not—"

"Not a dress rehearsal!" Recha said.

Within seconds, all that remained were those left behind and a series of disembodied arms and hands waving as the train chugged away. Miriam and Sol watched until it was lost in the collage of Berlin buildings, while Jacob stared across the track as if the train were still there. He seemed startled when Solomon put an arm across his shoulders to steer him from the depot.

Back at the apartment, Jacob wandered into the library while Miriam went into the kitchen to make coffee. The place was strewn with possessions left over from the heat of packing. After she and Sol sat quietly together for a while, they set about folding and putting away the clothes. Among a heap of Recha's lingerie they discovered a packet of family photographs. The top one was a picture of Sol beside his cello.

Were we ever really that young? Miriam wondered, watching him snap the packet shut and remembering again the party at the cabaret—the night she had first seen Solomon.

When everything had been tidied up, she and Sol went to the library to return the photographs to the safe. They had reached the archway before either of them saw Sol's father.

Jacob Freund sat in his rocker. His Iron Cross dangled from his hand and he stared at the wall. He wore his *tallis* and *yalmulke*. Both the prayer shawl and skullcap looked sadly out of place.

"Papa?" Sol sounded like a little boy.

Jacob curled his fingers around the medal and, putting it in his vest pocket, took out his gold watch and held it up for Solomon to see. "I've prayed for your mother and sister's safe journey. The time for prayer is over. Be a good boy and get my spare glasses from the accessories box in the shop cellar. I'm so blind without them I cannot even see the hour hand! The whole world is a blur."

He smiled but there was something dark about his face, as though his skin were underlain with shadow.

"I'm on my way, Papa."

"On second thought, let the three of us go together."

Miriam took Jacob's one arm and Sol the other. They helped him make his way slowly out of the building and across the street. A bit of glass fell from the broken door as Sol opened it and turned on the lights.

A cold calm lay inside; even the air seemed brittle.

They let go of Jacob and he walked around the shop, moving as if through a house unused for decades and filled with memories that could shatter like crystal if anything were disturbed. The cash register lay on its side like a wounded animal. He stooped, but did not touch it.

"Stay with your papa," Miriam told Solomon. "I know where to find his glasses."

She had never been downstairs alone. It seemed to yawn open as she drew aside the curtain and started down. The flooring that once had separated the basement and cellar had been removed decades if not centuries ago. In the small weak light, the storeroom seemed narrow and abnormally deep.

She descended softly, the wood quietly creaking. Reaching the bottom stairs, she stretched to the shelving rather than take the final step, and felt through the accessories box until she located the glasses. Her forehead was damp as she started backward up the stairs.

Nothing to be afraid of, she told herself. Even Sol doesn't hear voices down here anymore. Still, she found herself listening for the wail of an infant and for a woman crying, *"Oh God, let me die!"*

A steady drip-drip-drip resounded through the cellar, drawing her attention toward the sewer. Her throat tightened and her hands shook violently. A cold sweat seized her as she watched cellar-seep as dark as blood serpentine toward the grate.

She lurched up the stairs and tore aside the curtain that separated her from the shop.

A skinny figure stood there, motionless.

"Papa?"

Jacob's face held the solemnity of *Yiskor*, the prayers for the dead that Jews repeated every *Shabbas* in synagogue. "So much to be done. We must have the shop running smoothly by the time Friedrich returns." Jacob took his glasses from her.

"Why don't we all go to Amsterdam. There are other shops—in countries where we need not fear for our lives."

"This time the Nazi rabble came in the night," Jacob replied. "Until now, that has been their way. Soon they will expose themselves in the daylight. Then we will know the beginning of the end is upon us. We must be here, awaiting them with our eyes open."

"But *why*, Herr Freund? Why must we stay here? I don't understand. We Jews can't win—"

"We are Germans first, Miriam," Herr Freund said quietly. "If we run away, they will never learn that."

He moved slowly toward Solomon, clasped his son's hand as if to shake it and put his other hand on Sol's shoulder.

"Every day for twenty-three years we have served this city," Jacob said. "Tomorrow shall be no different."

Chapter 38

August, 1936

Wondering why anyone would object to taking a ferry across the Havel to Pfaueninsel—Peacock Island—Erich ambled across the pontoon bridge the Wehrmacht had erected for the convenience of Dr. Goebbels' guests.

Achilles tugged at her harness, a firm chest brace such as a blind man might wear. Erich kept her heeled at his side. He felt proud of himself and of the dog, despite her advanced years. Her coat was dull, her ears sagged, and her canines were yellow and crooked, but she was after all over ninety in human years. She was hard of hearing, and every now and then he had to repeat a command which in earlier years would have brought instant obedience. Still, for an old dog she was in superb shape and capable of inflicting enormous damage—sow-bellied or not. Most of the time she was alert and carried herself well. Not as well as Taurus, of course. Nor could she handle his mental commands as easily. Sometimes the messages were obeyed; sometimes not. He knew he should have brought Taurus tonight, but Achilles was his only hope for a connection to Miriam, and to their shared memories of the island.

They had come to the island together once—she sixteen, her head filled with fairy tales, he determined to be her hero. She had played princess to his Prince Charming as they flirted in the Garden of Palms, danced to the music of King Wilhelm's organ, kissed next to a wooden cabinet that one of the court designers had whimsically shaped like a bamboo hut.

Remembering that day, and hoping she would too, he had slipped her name to someone on the entertainment committee. She had refused to see him since the disturbance at Ananas where she was now waiting tables—she who used to be the stellar attraction. The only time he saw her was during his brief visits to his parents. He went to catch a glimpse of Miri.

Tonight, she would surely talk to him. He would introduce her to Leni Riefenstahl. They had much in common. Both in the arts, both started out as dancers. Leni was making two documentaries about the Olympic Games. Maybe she would use Miri.

He stopped himself. He was dreaming. A woman who said publicly that when the Führer arrived, the rays of the sun crossed the Hitler sky, would hardly employ a Jewess. She was more likely to put a gorilla to work. Her film, *The Eternal Forest*, for example. About survival of the fittest, it starred ancient Gauls born to worship forest gods and die where wild boar roamed. They clothed themselves in animal skins, drank mead from a ram's horn.

A strange but fascinating woman. Erich wondered what Leni would choose to film tonight. This party was slated to be quite a bash. Everyone from Hess to the Duke of Hamilton was coming. Solomon would say: "And how many Jews?"

He had to admit, he missed Solomon's directness. It was getting dangerous to be seen around a Jew, but that would change. Soon. There would be no more mistakes like the one that had nearly killed his father; there would be no more beatings. The Games had seen to that. Only yesterday, he had spent the day taking down *Juden Unerwünscht*—Jews unwanted—signs. For all their racism, some signs were humorous. Like the one, combining official warning with someone's painted scrawl, that he had put in the trunk of the Rathenau limousine, which he was now driving:

CAUTION!
SHARP CURVE
Jews Drive 200

Just a memento. Even Solomon would understand, surely. No matter what Solomon said, those signs would never go up again. Not after what Hitler and his cronies told the foreign press. The press would report that the rumors were nonsense, that the charming and brilliant Adolph Hitler was Germany's savior, that sometimes the Berlin sky was hazy with skywriting proclaiming peace and good will. "Germany's Golden Age," they announced, led by an "astute, gracious, energetic leader."

Thus heralded, Hitler and his people would dare not go back to what they had been. Thank God.

Erich walked slowly across the bridge, strolling so that he did not over-eager to investigate the fashionable women and the men in serge suits and uniforms who sauntered on the other side. He did not wish to appear unused to mingling with such an assembly. The guest list was varied enough to have pleased even the eclectic fantasies of King Friedrich Wilhelm II, who had designed the island as a playground for his mistress, the Countess Lichtenau.

Doubtless, the king would have been delighted to find his *Lustschloss*—Pleasure Palace—filled with foreign dignitaries and members of the old nobility. His "Swiss cottage" in the park, among the tulip trees and Weymouth pines he had imported from the United States, was a fitting setting for drink and discussions between foreign diplomats and generals. The "dairy" and "guest house" were perfect for assignations, as was the Greek temple that stood among Lebanon cedars whose girths measured two-and-a-half meters? What better place for Olympic athletes to live out their fantasies?

He stepped off the bridge and onto the island. Thousands of muted yellow lights shaped like tiny flames adorned the trees. Dancing girls carrying flaming torches lit the footpaths; dressed as pages, they guided the guests to their evening of enchantment. Their full-sleeved satin shirts, tight black pants, and powdered wigs were a touch of genius, combining the theme of the Olympics with the aura of aristocracy.

Erich scanned their faces, looking for Miriam. The island's muster of peacocks, so protected by the law that even pocketing a fallen pinfeather was forbidden, preened around three outdoor dance arenas. Couples waltzed and tangoed, applauding each tune with white-gloved hands and applauding again when, as if rehearsed, the peacocks spread their feathers and screeched. Refreshment pavilions offered lobster, pheasant, and caviar. Waiters in red and black tuxedos trimmed in gold poured streams of champagne. For those with more plebeian tastes, there were cauldrons of hot beer soup.

He took a glass of champagne and sipped it. Fascinated by the people, he failed to see Goebbels approaching.

"Toasting the Reich, Herr Rittmeister?"

He must have looked guilty, because Goebbels' thin face broke into the smile of a man who had scored a minor victory over someone he disliked. Erich's unit was guarding Nazi headquarters; he had no specific responsibilities on the island. Technically, though, he was still on duty and should not have been drinking.

Before Erich could think of an appropriate response, Magda Goebbels drew her husband away to watch the brewing of the potent punch known colloquially as "Warsaw Death."

Thank you, Magda, Erich thought, watching them walk away. They were one of the least attractive couples he had ever seen: Goebbels with his limp; she, a head taller, with a prominent nose and chin. Her appearance belied the suggestion that she had once been an actress of beauty, much like the women her Josef consorted with on the nights he was not pretending fanatical devotion to her and to their family.

"The hell with you, Herr Doktor!" Erich took a second glass from a silver tray and followed the crowd to a punchbowl filled with boiled brandy, lemon peel, cloves, and cinnamon. Across the top lay two crossed sabers crowned by a large flaming rum-soaked sugar cube.

The flames rose and the military men around him burst into songs of bravery and battlefield chivalry. If this were the new aristocracy, Erich thought, feeling pleased with himself, perhaps he had not been born too late after all.

A passing waiter took his glass and handed him a fresh drink.

The song began. "*Deutschland, Deutschland über Alles.*"

The crowd turned, Erich with it, to watch the Führer step off the bridge. His arm was around the shoulders of an Arab dressed in a flowing robe of white silk. Behind them came the rest of Hitler's party—Göring, Himmler, and the former prince whom many considered to be the true heir to Pfaueninsel, Augustus Wilhelm. Like Goebbels, all were dressed in formal evening attire.

"Heil Hitler!" Goebbels' voice rang out.

"Heil Hitler!" the crowd chanted, lifting their hands to salute their Führer.

Forgetting for a moment that he was holding Achilles' leash, Erich started to salute. Choking, the dog growled in protest.

"Sorry, old pal." Erich lowered his hand.

"Not saluting the Führer, Rittmeister?" Goebbels asked.

Making the only decision he could, Erich whispered a terse "Stay!" He dropped the leash and saluted.

At the edge of his peripheral vision, he sensed movement. He turned his head slightly.

A peacock, claiming ownership of the territory, fanned its feathers. It was accustomed to people but not to a German shepherd invading its territory. Dogs were not usually allowed on the island.

Achilles growled and assumed an attack stance.

"Steady, girl." Erich patted the dog and felt for her leash. Achilles did not seem to feel the affection. Her gaze was riveted on the peacock, her ears pricked up, her tail lifted and stiff.

The singing had died down and the Führer's voice could be heard. "I was misquoted by the press. I have nothing against Negroes," he was saying. "By all means let them compete. We are a democracy, are we not? What I did say is that, descended as they are from jungle peoples, they have an unfair physical advantage and a disadvantage emotionally, intellectually, and socially. Instead of representing the United States, they should be sent to Africa, where they belong."

"A simplistic solution, Herr Hitler." The man who had spoken stepped out of the shadows. His voice held an accent, Spanish perhaps, or Latin American, but the most outstanding thing about him was his clothing. He wore a white silk toreador's "suit-of-lights" trimmed with heavy gold brocade. Down his back and pinned to his hair was a long black pigtail and, on his head and drawn down toward his nose, the heavy *montero* of the bullfighter. Pinned to one shoulder and flowing into and over the crook of his arm was a black cape lined with red silk.

Forgetting all about Achilles, Erich stared in fascination. The man was outrageously handsome in a way Erich was sure no woman could resist.

"Simple, but not simplistic, Señor...Péron, is it?"

"Perón." The man corrected the accent, and made a slight bow. "And what of the Jews, Herr Hitler? Do you have an equally *simple* solution for the 'Jewish Question,' as I've heard it called?"

"There are many possible solutions."

"Name one I have not yet heard."

"Let me first remind you that the anti-Semitism people have ascribed to us is a thing of the past. You might not know it, but a Jew, one Hauptmann Fürstner, was responsible for building and organizing the Olympic Village."

"Yes," the man said, "but you have not answered me."

Reporters gathered around the two men scribbled furiously.

"Very well. Though I believe I can safely predict that in another decade or two what you call the Jewish Question will no longer concern anyone, I do have several suggestions. For one thing, they could be ordered to choose a homeland."

The "matador" smiled pleasantly. "I believe someone suggested Nigeria. However, the Nigerians might object to being displaced."

"There are other places. Madagascar, for example."

"Madagascar?"

"Why not? We could pack them off in ships and—"

"You are serious about this, Herr Hitler?"

"It would be convenient if they were all gathered in one place, would it not?"

"Convenient? For whom? And what of the Malagasy?"

"A hodgepodge at best. Negroes, Javanese—"

"I take it you would send *them* back to Africa and Java."

"Ja." The Chancellor glanced around, apparently growing bored with the discussion. "You there! Rittmeister...Alois, is it not? Enjoying yourself? I see you brought your old friend." He nodded toward Achilles.

"Ja, mein Führer!" Erich moved forward, pleased at having been singled out.

"That must once have been a fine animal—but might one of our beautiful young Fraüleins not be a more suitable constant companion for a virile young man?" The Chancellor turned to the man he had called Pérön. "The Rittmeister is in charge of a special canine corps. You would be amazed at how well his animals are trained. Not so, Herr Rittmeister?" He motioned at the press. "Tell them!"

Erich hesitated, less pleased. He was being patronized—the butt of Hitler's minor annoyance with the foreigner.

"Go on. Tell them!"

"I—" Erich's mind reeled. "Dogs have a number of military uses," he said quickly. "There are sentry-attack dogs, scout dogs, messenger dogs, wire-laying dogs, pack dogs, sledge dogs. We are trying to combine these types into one." He brought his fists slowly together to illustrate his point. "Imagine a single entity, a Gestalt, a team of dogs as capable of acting on their own initiative as they are of—"

"Tell them what you told me about the javelin," Goebbels interjected. "What did you call it—an art form."

"An art aerodynamically," Erich said, gaining confidence. "Thrown well, it arcs clean, without compromise, like an irrefutable argument—"

Goebbels took hold of Hitler's elbow. "The Rittmeister here won several Youth events. He is a local champion, shall we say."

Hitler jerked from Goebbels' hold. "All of Germany's new generation are champions!" He motioned with his fist as if pounding on an imaginary table. "In any other country, the Rittmeister here could easily have been the best! But here, we have a new Germany, of such depth and breadth of skill..."

He was beginning to lose control of his temper, Erich realized. He did tend to do that at parties. With the foreign press here in full force, the Führer would have to be closely watched.

One of the pages, unmindful of her audience, flung her flaming torch into the birdbath and threw herself into the arms of a young officer, who led her away. His attention distracted, Hitler moved on. The press followed him.

A tipsy, middle-aged woman in a pink gown and hair tinted to match gripped Erich's arm. "Seen my husband?"

"What does he look like?" Erich asked, more happy than not at having had the spotlight removed from him.

"Like a lecher!" She stumbled off into the shadows.

Magda Goebbels walked up to Erich. "They are all lechers." She did not look happy. "My husband said he wanted the girls to look svelte, not homespun, but these girls' behavior is indecent! Disgusting!"

Some of the girls were members of the State Opera's *corps de ballet*, but most, Erich knew, came from music halls and cabarets. Their morality seemed as flexible as their bodies. Already, couples headed for more secluded realms. Former torchbearers and officers, former torchbearers and foreign dignitaries, former torchbearers and men—whatever their description.

"If my Paul Josef spent less time with his movie star harlots, he might be less accepting of this behavior," Frau Goebbels said quietly. "Any time now, the Führer will lose his temper over this situation, you wait and see. It must be stopped. Can you not—"

She stopped talking, her attention diverted toward Achilles. Unleashed, the dog had begun to stalk a peacock standing like a lawn ornament, its long neck lifted and still. Muzzle thrust out and tail out straight, the dog eased forward.

The peacock screeched indignantly, looking for all the world like a false-eyelashed transvestite whose bottom had been pinched by the wrong person.

Quickly Erich tried to fill his mind with light, to visualize the dog's eyes and transfer a command: *Friend!*

Achilles pivoted mechanically toward the bird.

Play!

Achilles' body untensed. Scampering over to the bird, she nudged it as gently as a kitten testing a ball of string. The peacock strutted back, lifted its fan and emitted a sound that was more tease than screech.

Again the dog advanced and again the bird sidestepped, the beauty of its feathers and voice making the dog appear clumsy by contrast.

People began gathering. The Führer, smiling, nodded to the spectators, then toward his retinue of adjutants and aides, who apparently knew what he wanted of them. Without a word, they scurried in all directions, running into bushes and the pavilions, knocking over trays and tables, pulling people in varying states of undress into the open. Fists and feet and bottles flew.

A bottle hit the peacock. Screeching and stabbing with its beak, it attacked Achilles, who backed up, obviously perplexed.

"Those birds are sacrosanct!" the Führer screamed. "You should have commanded the dog to stay away from it!"

"I—" Erich stopped. No one, not even Adolph Hitler, would believe in the kind of communication he had with his animals. He grabbed for the leash. "Down!"

Achilles sat dead still.

Apparently sensing its advantage, the bird circled her.

"Stop that stupid dog!" Goebbels yelled, limping forward.

"Down!" Erich shouted again…too late. Achilles gave in to instinct. Erich could feel the animal's single-minded intensity and knew he had lost control; his only hope was that the peacock would back away.

But the bird was in full motion, protecting its territory from this strange four-legged invader. One more time it darted forward. One time too many.

It never had a chance. There was a squawking, and a flurry of feathers. Achilles' mouth was around its neck.

Goebbels picked up a tray that had fallen to the ground, held it like a moon-burnished shield, then threw it at the dog.

Achilles opened her mouth as if catch the tray, and dropped the bird, its wings beating feebly and head hanging limply to one side.

"Stay!" Erich commanded.

Growling, the dog stared at Goebbels' groin.

"Somebody shoot that beast!"

Erich grabbed the dog's harness. Achilles, done with her show of strength, became meekly obedient to Erich's command to heel.

"My fault for losing hold of her," Erich said.

"No one is at fault." Hitler stepped forward and leaned down to pet the dog. "She was simply overexcited by this idiotic event."

Erich breathed more easily.

Hitler leaned close to Erich and, smiling at those around him, said softly, "Now, Herr Rittmeister, you will shoot the dog."

Erich stared in disbelief. "But Herr Führer, you said—"

"I know perfectly well what I said. There is no blame. Nonetheless, there are times when the blameless must be destroyed."

Erich knelt next to Hitler and put his hands in Achilles' fur. He could smell the pungent, sour odor of age.

Briefly the tips of Hitler's fingers made contact with Erich's. "I have given you an order," the Führer said, continuing to fondle the dog. "Once I have made up my mind—" He paused. "I have plans for you, Rittmeister, but I must know you are strong enough to accept the fact that there is no room in the Reich for compassion."

Erich stared at the bright stones on the footpath and wondered what the party-goers were thinking. Many were stepping back, aware that something unusual was happening and wanting no part of it.

"Give me a pistol," Goebbels said, fuming.

"No!" Hitler stood up. "The Rittmeister shall do what must be done. His dog has outlived her usefulness." He took hold of Erich's arm. "I will watch. I order you not to look away or to display emotion."

A series of lightning seizures jolted Erich's body as he unholstered his pistol and released the safety. When they subsided, he cocked the pistol and took aim, his vision blurred by angry tears, his thoughts damning himself, Hitler, the Reich.

Forgive me, Achilles. I love you.

Knowing that the pain the dog would feel would seize him as well, he fired.

Achilles gave a cry that sounded like a human child, fell and lay still. Erich lowered the pistol and stared at his old friend. Red, raw muscle showed where the fur was suddenly missing. *Good-bye, old friend.*

He waited for the pain, welcoming it, but it did not come. He experienced neither guilt nor pain, only numbness. There was no room in him for anything except hatred.

"Now let us forget all of this unpleasantness and watch a more pleasant form of entertainment." Goebbels gave a passing glance to the dead animal. "Come, everyone, the bolero is about to begin."

Erich knelt beside Achilles, stroking her warm fur. Taking Magda by the arm, Goebbels led the way to the largest of the three arenas. Only Perón remained near Erich.

In the center of the arena and raised a meter off the ground was a small circular stage surrounded by twenty chairs, their backs toward the stage. Male dancers in tuxedos and white ruffled shirts emerged from behind a screen and straddled each chair. An equal number of violinists took their places beneath a circle of flickering gaslights.

A circular curtain was raised from the middle of the arena. Curled on the floor under a single gaslight was Miriam Rathenau, sheathed in black tights and leotard.

Softly, slowly, Ravel's music began. She uncoiled languorously, her face expressionless. Erich thought her the most desirable creature he had ever seen. She stretched, swayed—and resumed the fetal position.

Almost imperceptibly the music increased in tempo and volume. This time when the woman stretched, she remained on her knees. The audience's breathing quickened and the circle of male dancers half-stood and inched their chairs toward the raised stage.

Stopped.

Sighed.

Miriam raised her head and slowly came to her feet as the tempo of the music picked up. He glanced at the audience, then up at Perón, who was smiling. Women eyed their partners who, in turn, ogled Miriam.

The male dancers removed their tuxedo jackets, threw them aside and inched their chairs forward. The music and the audience and the circle of male dancers were a moving articulation of lust. One dancer, kicking over his chair, climbed up onto the stage. Another followed, and another. The three of them crawled toward her as she turned, lifting her leg higher and higher until it seemed she would surely fall or split herself.

And then the music stopped and the gaslight, flickering one last time, went out.

"Brava!" a man called out. "More!"

After a long silence, the applause began. Despite Miriam's bravura performance, it was, at best, restrained.

Perón bent down close to Erich's ear. "You Germans are a strange breed," he whispered. "On the same night, in the same place, you execute your friend and then view this celebration of life. Neither time have you shown emotion. In Buenos Aires, both would move us to tears."

Chapter 39

With the Games a thing of the past, Sol waited for the *Juden Unerwünscht* signs to go up again—like an expectant father waiting for the birth of a child he knows will be deformed. Every evening, before dinner, he went for a walk. Body throbbing with tension, he wandered Berlin, looking, listening, watching. Though he was accustomed to the noise and odor, tonight the city's sounds and smells assailed him as if the honking and engines and exhaust were somehow exaggerated. There seemed to be an undercurrent, an undefined heightening of the usual cacophony and stench, as if the city of which his family had been a part for eleven generations had become an enormous and unfamiliar factory producing machinery he neither recognized nor understood.

Something drove him out of the city. He had refused Erich's repeated offers to pay for a ticket to the Games, saying that if they disbanded the Oranienberg detention center before the Olympics, he would believe that the signs would stay down—that the worst was over. If that happened, he would buy as many tickets as his pockets could hold and hand them out to the Jews of Berlin. They would come to cheer, hold hands and sing *Deutschland über Alles*.

Sweating profusely from the effort, he walked five kilometers to the Olympia Stadium, to see for himself that all was as surely gone as the Olympic village organizer and builder, Captain Wolfgang Fürstner. Replaced at the last moment as village commandant because he was Jewish, he had calmly put a pistol in his mouth and pulled the trigger.

Still, the Games had been good for business. Foreign visitors bought marks at rates set especially low and, for the first time since Friedrich Weisser's beating, the shop made a nice profit.

Sol had avoided seeing the Games but there had been no avoiding the loudspeakers spread throughout the city. The triumphant cry of the predominantly German crowd calling out, "*Yessa O-vens! Yessa O-vens!*" rang in Solomon's ears as he watched the last of the dismantling process taking place at the stadium.

Though personally delighted by Jesse Owens' triumphs, Sol predicted they would bring nothing but trouble. Even a fool could tell that the Führer was livid over the American's victories. The world's cameras and journalists had recorded the festival of color and sound, the long blue banners showing the five Olympic rings, the red banners decorated with swastikas hung from poles fifteen meters high. The world pictured Berlin roped with evergreens and gold. Thanks to Movietone News, they had seen Hitler Youth bands, brown shirts and short pants scrupulously starched, move through Olympia Stadium's arch and onto the dull-red cinder track; they had heard snare drums rattling out marches and loudspeakers playing waltzes and quickstep marches. They had laughed at Hitler's heavy-handed architectural approximation of the grandeur of the Roman Coliseum, his unschooled vision of a new Berlin.

None of it meant anything. The truce was transient, the memories fleeting. Temporary—the operative word of the times.

The Games, the memories, the present—all vaguely moving shadows.

"O-VENS!"

"SIEG HEIL!"

"O-VENS!"

"SIEG HEIL!"

Head pounding, Solomon began the hike home. When his head and chest began to throb so hard that each step took his breath away, he left the Olympic Highway and hurried along the Konigsallee. Pain notwithstanding, he would be home in time for a whispered *Shabbat* Service around his mother's starched white linen tablecloth and candlesticks—his sister's most recent letter propped against them: *Mama's fine, I'm fine, when are you and Miriam coming so that you can be fine, too?*

Near the Imperial Palace, he had to stop. The noise that spilled from adjacent alleys and avenues engulfed him. Deafened him. Buffeted him as if it were alive.

Then, reflected in a department store window, he saw the sign that had entered his subconscious and registered its effect on his body before his conscious mind could deal with it:

Jews Not Welcome.

Crowds surged around him, smiling and unnoticing. Cars growled and windows leered, tall buildings wavered—and the pain worsened.

He walked on, holding his chest.

Heart attack. Twenty-eight years old, and about to drop dead.

By the time he reached Franzosische Strasse, his chest and throat felt constricted and an icy cold had enveloped him, bringing with it sweat and chills. The sidewalk seemed to roll beneath him, burning his feet.

It's really all gone, Sol thought desperately. The banners, the cheers, the drummers and athletes marching in revue, the doves and balloons and the promises of peace...the journalists, parroting Hitler's proclamation of a Golden Age not only for Germany but for the world.

The city had returned to normal.

A worker in a white painter's smock watched Sol curiously, then picked up a second sign. Expertly splaying out the edges with a yellow bristled brush, he slapped it up:

Shop Here! Jews Not Admitted!
We Guarantee Jewish Filth
Won't Defile This Establishment

The worker smiled and nodded, his face distorted like an image seen through a fish-eye lens. Sol took off his glasses and rapidly cleaned them. Sweat stung his eyes.

Around him, unconcerned, people moved at their normal pace.

He leaned against a brick wall that proclaimed *Death to all Jews*. The pain in his chest was a jackhammer. The city's noise roared in his ears like a animal. He made his way laboriously along the wall, sliding a hand along its rough surface. At the end of the wall he sank to his knees, teeth gritted in agony.

A white-haired shopkeeper dressed in the black robes of orthodoxy was taping a Jewish star on his shop window. "You all right?" He stepped away as though Sol were unclean.

"Must get home," Sol mumbled in Yiddish.

The man looked around furtively and then bent over Solomon. "Are you ill?" he asked anxiously. "In trouble? Get inside, man. Our enemies are everywhere."

Sol struggled to his feet. He stared at the *Mogen David* the man had pasted on the window; the Star of David bulged and receded as he struggled for breath and tried to focus.

"Why?" He pointed at it.

"Orders. They say they'll leave us in peace if we announce our heritage. So what if Gentiles don't buy from us, at least we'll keep our businesses."

"You believe that!"

"Please, be quiet!" Gathering his scissors and roll of tape, the shopkeeper withdrew into his store like a snail into its shell. When the door shut with a click, the city noise again became a carnivore—some ancient god escaped from back alleys.

Suddenly Solomon knew it for what it was.

Half running, half staggering, he reeled down the street, away from the beast of oncoming riot. His breaths came in gasps. His chest felt white-hot with pain. Auto horns roared in warning and people hurried, looking fearful as they made a path for a madman.

Father! Miriam!

Half an hour later Sol burst into the shop and slammed the door, its bell jangling. Clutching the accouterment cabinet, dripping sweat onto its glass, he fought for breath. His father was in the alcove of the basement stairs, holding the open curtain in his hand. He did not turn around.

"Make a star!" Sol cried. "Put it in the window. They're coming now! In the daylight! I can feel it!"

"What use is there in doing anything—now," Jacob muttered.

"I met another shopkeeper. He was—"

"Only two people besides our family knew that combination." Jacob's voice was low and hoarse. With a sweep of his hand, he indicated the open safe set in the alcove wall. It was empty.

Half a minute passed before Sol realized that they had been robbed and that he knew who had done it. Looking toward the ceiling friezes, he made a sound that was a mix of sobbing and laughter. "Should I summon the Weissers?" he asked sarcastically. "They really should be told."

Jacob wheeled around, his face contorted by fury. "Has my son learned so little? You won't find the Weissers home today. They've abandoned us! Taken what they could, sent away and squirreled away what they could, and abandoned us!"

Solomon heard a new sound inside his head. The wailing cry of a mourner. "I knew it!" he said. "I knew our families should have sat down together months ago and divided everything! One pfenning for you, one for us. One for you—"

"Stop it!"

"The Weissers could have had this case." Sol slapped the one that held the accouterments. "They would have liked that, don't you think? We could have had the one with the pipes. They could have taken the cigars, we the cigarettes. We would get Recha, they would get—"

Jacob raised his hand. "I said stop!" As if involuntarily, his hand continued its motion and he slapped Solomon across the cheek. He was staring, horrified, at his hand when Miriam dashed into the shop.

"Sol! I went upstairs to borrow some yeast from the Weissers. Their door is open and they're not home. I'm worried. There's some kind of commotion down near Leipzigerplatz. I heard someone say it's another food riot." She paused for breath and seemed to notice for the first time that something was amiss.

"I slapped my son, and for what?" Jacob said to no one in particular. "May God forgive me."

"It's not a food riot, Miriam." Sol put his hand on his father's should, his other on his cheek. "It's all right, Papa," he whispered. His chest still hurt, but it was a new hurt, one of loss more than of fear. Much more was gone than the four years' meager profits they had not dared place in the bank to be confiscated. So much more. The Weissers had been like second parents to him and Recha. Jacob and Friedrich had worked together for decades; Jacob gave Friedrich not only a start but a career.

What fundamental madness could cause this? The Nazis? Friedrich's beating? The Depression? All too simplistic.

Father and son looked at one another in terror as shouts and gunshots and sirens echoed from all directions. Then they watched from the door as a phalanx of Nazis moved toward them, striding up Friedrich Ebert Strasse with pistols and clubs and the trophies of rampage. A ruddy-faced Goliath, a swastika armband on one sleeve, a Red Cross armband on the other, marched at the apex of the mob. Whenever he signaled to the men and boys behind him, five or six would break off and enter shops. Sol could hear screams and shrieked prayers rise above the sounds of carnage.

"We must get a star up, Papa!" He scrambled for tape and scissors among the low drawers of the accouterment case.

Arms crossed, Miriam stood on the sidewalk, tears marking her cheeks. "They're destroying everything...all that is or might be Jewish."

"Even where there are stars?" Jacob held his glasses slightly away from his face in an effort to see farther.

"Everything."

"It is the end." He stumbled back inside the shop. There was about him the look of a man hollowed by despair. His face was utterly without emotion and his shoulders sagged as though time itself had bent and then broken his back. "I've seen the beginning of the end. Now I shall see the end. We have all become children of darkness."

He walked in a daze toward the alcove and, after wiping his glasses with his Reichsbanner handkerchief and replacing them on his nose, stood staring at the safe. In a monotone, he said, "The basement. Into the cellar, children."

"They'll come there to ransack the inventory," Sol said.

Jacob dug in a drawer and held up a hammer. "Perhaps, but you will be in the sewer."

The hair on the back of Sol's neck bristled. Some inner sense told him that the chest pains he had experienced had as much to do with whatever lay in the cellar as it did with the terror outside. Numb, he followed his father and Miriam downstairs—toward what? he wondered. His boyhood nightmares?

"We'll never break the weld in time, Papa."

"What choice do we have but to try?" Jacob searched along a top shelf and located the boys' crowbar. Miriam held it against the weld while Solomon, using it like a chisel, bashed against its neck with the hammer. Jacob stood guard at the steps, listening between the ringing of metal against metal.

"I think they're at the apartments! Hurry, my son!"

Solomon did not waste time replying. Ceasing to worry about the possibility of missing the crowbar neck and hitting Miriam's hands, he smashed down again and again with all his strength. Sparks flew, some scattering across the limestone before dissipating. Like glowworms, he thought, sweat running in rivulets down his temples and face. Fireflies come to dance on the dead.

"They're outside the shop, Solomon! Faster!"

The weld peeled apart in metal curlicues. Miriam's eyes were filled with fear, but she kept the bar steady, her whitened knuckles as strained as leather about to be pierced by an awl.

From above came laughter, then the sound of splintering glass.

"Break it, Solomon!" Jacob said hoarsely. "Break it now!"

There was the thumping of boots. Shouted orders. More laughter. The thud of a display case crashing to the floor.

"It won't break, Papa! There's not enough time."

"Baruch ato adonai," Jacob prayed. He added a prayer of his own. "May you grant my son the strength of Samson and the wisdom of the king whose name he bears."

Sol jammed the crowbar into the weld and, with Miriam's help, pried down. His muscles screamed and he could feel his veins, enlarged and pulsing in his neck and forehead.

Jacob hurried over and together they pushed down.

The weld gave with a crack. The grate faltered and slid sideways in its rim, and Sol thrust the crowbar back under the lip.

"If Erich's among them, he'll know we're in the sewer," Miriam said.

"If Erich's among them," Sol grunted as he used the crowbar to raise the grate enough to grip it with his fingertips, "then life's not worth living anyway."

The grate creaked and fell back against the wall.

"Go!" Jacob said. "Go!"

Sol lowered himself into the hole, found the two by four and dropped the final meter, landing on the rotted, dismantled packing crates. Jumping to his feet, he took hold of Miriam's legs as she lowered herself. They fell back together, and he heard her stifle a startled laugh.

"Your turn next, Papa."

On hands and knees, Jacob Freund looked down into the sewer, surveying its bracken walls in what little light the drain hole allowed. "A man of my years should leap down into such a nether world?" His tone was oddly flippant. "And who would shut the grate? Are we acrobats who can stand on one another's shoulders?"

"There's a board here, Papa!" Sol started to climb up.

The grate clanged down.

"Papa? What're you doing!"

Fingers through the grating, Jacob Freund looked down with kindly, gray, bespectacled eyes that revealed an acceptance of the world's cruelty. "This we do my way, children." He was whispering, yet his voice seemed to fill the sewer. "First I'm going to cover the grate with empty boxes, then I intend to go upstairs and offer those...those...offer them cigars to commemorate their victory over the helpless."

"But Herr Freund—" Miriam peered up into the drain. "Please, Papa! All of us, or none!"

Sol struggled to open the grate again but could not lift it; his father held it down. Even through the small slats, he could see the slight, wry smile on his father's lips.

"I came through the Great War with but a broken nose and an outbreak of cynicism," Jacob said. "I wish to do battle again. Alone. That is my right as head of this family. Now hush, both of you. Let a not-so-young man have his way."

"Papa...I love you."

"And I love you, Solomon Isaac Freund. No man could have asked for a finer son." He moved away from the grate. Moments later, just as Solomon jumped down from the board and shook his head in bewilderment, Jacob's face was above them once again. Poking his glasses between the slats, he let them drop. Solomon, catching them, looked up in confusion. "If I should die, make sure I'm buried wearing my spectacles," his father said. "I wish to see the face of our enemy when I point him out to God."

He looked at Solomon and Miriam and muttered, in Hebrew, "May God provide." He placed the boxes over the grate.

Chapter 40

Residuals of light danced before Solomon's eyes as he tried to accustom himself to the darkness. Clinging to Miriam, he listened to his father ascend the steps.

"Maybe the Nazis won't hurt him when they see that he's old and half blind," Miriam said.

She sounded unconvinced. Knowing words would only betray his own despair, Sol remained silent. Blackness reigned. It swirled around him, enveloping him in its shroud. The *plook...plook* of dripping water resounded through the sewer, and he thought he heard the scuttling of rats.

The place was colder than he remembered. He welcomed Miriam's embrace as much for its warmth as for its comfort. He tried to concentrate, to control his ragged breathing as the shortness of breath that had seized him on the streets returned to deflate his lungs. Pain settled on his chest like a great weight, but this was no heart attack...he knew that now. A sense of such foreboding filled him that he was sure Miriam must feel it too.

He let go of her and stared into the darkness. Waiting for the laughter, the voices, the images.

"I can hear them up there," Miriam whispered. "Why don't they leave!"

As if in answer to her words, the laughter came, rippling through the sewer.

"No! Go away!" Sol shouted.

"Be quiet, Solomon." Miriam placed a hand over Sol's mouth. "What is it? Are you in pain?" She removed her hand.

He shook her off, fighting the explosion of light in his head.

Miriam gripped his shoulder. "Don't let go of me again, Sol. I'm afraid."

"Me too." They embraced. Upstairs, there was faint scuffling. He could barely hear it above the pounding of his heart and the ghostly laughter that he knew did not come from the shop. Laughter that stopped when a cobalt-blue glow appeared at the end of the sewer and an image of a young black man began to take shape——

——*the black man's skin shines with a blue fire.* He is naked except for a small piece of torn blanket that covers his genitals. He sits perfectly still, staring outward, face expressionless. A white man, monocled and wearing a white, blood-stained laboratory smock, moves toward him, scalpel in hand——

"No!" Solomon reached toward the image. "They've come back!" he whispered, transfixed by a second image that materialized at the other end of the sewer.

——*a paraffin lamp casts a blue-black shadow across a rude table in the center of one-roomed wooden shack.* Snow blows through gaps in the wallboards. In one corner, a figure huddles close to a brazier's red coals, its smoke veiling the low ceiling—a man in a ragged army overcoat and woolen scarf; frostbite has scabbed and pockmarked his dark, sunken cheeks. His eyes are dull, his hands wrapped in blood-stained gauze. An emaciated woman wrapped in an old blanket, an ancient carbine slung across her back, leans over him. Carefully she unwraps the gauze from one of his hands. The fingers are gangrenous stumps——

I am losing my mind, Solomon thought. The riot, the emptied safe, the degradation—together they had caused him to snap.

A fit of shivering seized him, and with it came a voice.

——*Three days now the clouds have held,* an old man says. Standing knee-high in snow, he looks toward the sky. A worker next to him grabs hold of a corpse and flops it down as if it is a sandbag. The old man glances at it, then at a row of fresh bodies. The setting sun has cast ribbons of russet and gold out of congealed blood and military uniforms——

"Try to see it," Sol told Miriam, though he knew he was asking the impossible.

"What are you talking about!"

"Look!" He turned her around forcefully. "There! There is another! Can you not hear the music?"

——*gossamer veils of blue dust-moted light filter through a stained-glass window onto a man seated at a pipe organ.* He is blond and broad shouldered, and looks as athletic as he is musically talented. The Bach concerto he plays reverberates throughout the tall reaches of a rococo church that was obviously once a castle——

"Pull yourself together, Sol!" Miriam's voice was taut with terror. "There's nothing down here! Why don't you think about your papa! He's the one upstairs with...with...."

Papa! Sol blinked and drew a sharp breath as the vision vanished. Was that what the images were telling him—that if he stayed hidden down here, he was no better than the dybbuk?

Running his hands along the moss-slimed bricks, he made sure the board was properly emplaced and again boosted himself onto it. "I don't care what Papa said. I must go up and do what I can."

"Don't be a fool, Sol." Miriam tugged at his trousers. "You'll only make matters worse."

"Have you forgotten what those bastards did to Herr Weisser?"

Boots clumped down the stairs. Sol stood suspended between the board and the grating, unable to tell if what he was hearing were out there or inside his head.

"That can't be your father," Miriam whispered. "They are heavier boots..."

The footsteps reached the bottom of the stairs, and stopped.

Jars crashed, followed by what Sol supposed were boxes being pulled from shelves. He heard grunts and the tearing of cardboard. The boxes on top of the grate were sure to be next.

Then, from what seemed the top of the stairs came orders. "As much as you can carry...Havanas if you find any, and American cigarettes."

The boots went up the stairs, and down and up a second time. Then, silence.

"Sol, I smell smoke!"

Sol lifted his nose. His sense of smell had already begun to adapt to the sewer's noxious odors. "You sure?"

Miriam sniffed. "I think so."

"They must be burning whatever inventory they've chosen not to steal." The smoke had begun to penetrate his nostrils and sting his eyes. "We're going up." His matter-of-fact tone reflected his relief at having to deal with something tangible, no matter how dreadful. "We are not going to suffocate down here."

He climbed back down and dislodged the board. "If we go up this way we might be climbing right into a fire or...." Or into Nazi arms, he thought. "There's another drain beneath the furrier's. Maybe when the cabaret was sealed up the workmen didn't realize Erich and I had left the padlock open. It's worth a try."

They went along the sewer, fingers against the walls for guidance, and located the large board at the other end. After hoisting himself up, he helped Miriam.

The grating was unlocked.

"Push!" he told her.

As the grate opened, he remembered the time he and Erich had tried to pick the lock on the cabaret door. Sol had said he wanted to leave the place alone in honor of Rathenau's death; Erich had simply laughed and insisted. The lock had proved easy to jimmy, but they'd not been able to open the door. The workmen had apparently bolted it from the inside, for added security, and had exited through the furrier's upstairs, much to Erich's annoyance and Sol's relief.

He crawled out and helped Miriam through the drain.

Holding hands, they groped their way through the sub-basement and up the stairs to the deserted cabaret. Musty linen covered the tables. The chairs stacked up against them were netted with spider webs, and above them, from street level, the small stained-glass windows cast a green glow across the dance floor.

He felt an odd sense of wanting her to dance with him and pretend for a moment that dancing and music and love were as commonplace as hatred. Instead they hurried across the room, up the metal stairs, and unbolted and unlocked the entrance door.

It had begun to rain. Miriam started up the steps that led to the street. Sol held her back. He waited, listening for the tromp of boots, watching for them to appear at street level. When none appeared, they ascended to the street. It looked like a war zone. Sticks, bricks, and garbage lay everywhere. Glass from shattered windows gleamed in the waning light. From the direction of Unter den Linden came the sounds of ongoing riot.

Good Yomtov—happy holiday—he thought grimly as, heads down against the rain and the fear of being recognized, they raced to the shop. One of the windows had been knocked out, the other was cracked. The door hung lopsided on a single hinge. Smoke filled the room.

Sol pressed his arm against his mouth and nose, and indicated for Miriam to do the same. She stood in the center of the shop, peering over her arm, quietly crying. Her muffled sobs made him realize that, despite the day's horror, these were the first tears she had shed. She was amazing he thought, looking at her as he stumbled around in search of his father.

Display cases lay knocked over and shattered. Glass, cigars, cigarettes and smoking accouterments cluttered the floor. He backtracked to the door and, lowering his arm from his face, peered out at the carnage.

"Must have taken him outside," he said.

Miriam wiped her eyes and lowered her hand. "Maybe he's all right and went downstairs to put out the fire." She pointed at the ribbon of smoke seeping beneath the curtain of the alcove to the basement. "Most of the smoke is going out the door, so he shouldn't be suffering too badly from inhalation."

Sol hurried across the room and, with a growing sense of doom, he threw open the curtain.

Jacob Freund hung upside down, his feet attached to the overhead plumbing by a strand of thick wire. His eyes were open. His mouth had been gagged with a Nazi armband, and his Iron Cross dangled from his neck.

"Papa!" Sol felt the blood leave his face. He reached for his father, but his resolve gave way, and he sagged against the wall. "No! Oh, God, no!"

After a moment he took a deep breath and managed to stand upright. He wedged his fingers between the old man's neck and the twisted ribbon that had stopped the breathing. "May it go easier for you in the afterlife," he cried bitterly. "May your soul flourish in *Olam Haba.*"

He laid his cheek against his father's flesh. Already it was becoming cold.

Chapter 41

I truly loved Herr Freund. Tears rolling down Miriam's face. She turned from watching the rain—said to be sent by God when a good man died—to watching Solomon. He cut the body down from the rafter and placed it gently on the floor. Pulling up a stool from behind the counter, he removed his shoes, sat down, and wept.

Yes, my Solomon. Cry for your papa, and for us.

Obedient to Jewish tradition, she neither spoke nor attempted to comfort Solomon, allowing him opportunity to give fullest expression to his sorrow. Later, they would reminisce; it would comfort Sol and lend dignity to Papa.

She wiped away her tears; they would have to wait. The Freunds had taught her about life and, when Sol's grandparents passed away during the previous year, about the dignity of death. Her concern now must be for Sol's well-being.

She made a mental list of death rites. How inappropriate—and inconvenient, she thought, with a stab of guilt—that Jacob had died on the eve of one of Judaism's most joyous holidays, the Festival of the Harvest.

Tradition demanded that he be buried quickly, especially since tomorrow was Succot; the internment could not be on the first day of a festival. She would have to find a member of the sacred society organized by the Jewish community to take care of burials. Succot would pre-empt the traditional observance of *shiva*—the first week of mourning—and the month of mourning that usually followed, but she was not sure if it pre-empted the twelve Hebrew months of mourning for a parent, after which Sol would be forbidden to mourn overtly. She had to find food for the Meal of Comfort—bread, to differentiate the meal from a snack; an egg, to symbolize life's continuum—and food for tomorrow's Succot meal.

She remembered the year she and her family built a *succah* in the gardens at the estate. They erected the roof of the hut in the ancient way, with roots and plants, trying to make it as exposed and insecure as the huts the Jews had used during their forty years of wandering. Then they celebrated their trust in divine protection—Mama and Papa and her grandparents leading the family processional around the estate, branches of citron, palm, myrtle and willow held aloft to signify God's omnipresence. And now where was God! Hadn't He tested them enough?

She glanced across the street, and shivered. It had grown dark and the lamps were lit. The men who had done this could easily be waiting there, hiding in the darkness inside the apartment entrance.

Rites. Concentrate on rites, not fears. Complete the respect and honor due all people, even the dead. If she could not acquire a white robe for Jacob's burial, she would see to it that he was properly covered with his *tallis.*

She quietly repeated the prayer said upon taking leave of a mourner during *shiva:* May the Lord comfort you with all the mourners of Zion and Jerusalem.

Sol did not raise his head.

Somewhere, in some deep part of him, he would know where she had gone, that she had not deserted him—she thought, walking to the door of the shop. She had not sat *shiva* for Uncle Walther, her parents, or Oma; she was not raised that way. Some rites had made sense to her even then, like covering mirrors to avoid vanity and only reading books or chapters dealing with laws of mourning. Other rituals, though, had seemed irrelevant: bathing only for cleanliness, wearing the same clothes for a week. Having seen the comfort they took from ritual during their week of *shiva* for Sol's grandparents, she had begun to understand.

She reached for the door handle, but stepped back as a siren screamed—a sound as common to Berliners as the linden trees on the Avenue. A Mercedes with the familiar SS insignia painted on the door pulled up at the apartment building, and a tall SS man whose hair shone silver in the lamp light climbed from the car.

He stared at the shop, then turned toward the apartment building, where a Gestapo agent had appeared. The older man pointed at the shop. The younger nodded, returned to the car, and came away with a clipboard which held several sheets of paper. Judging by the way he ran his index finger down page after page, Miriam figured it was some kind of list. When he had flipped the last page over, the younger man nodded to his companion, and they both laughed. They waved as if at somebody in the apartments. Car doors slammed, and they drove away.

Miriam turned back into the shop. "Solomon," she said softly.

He looked up at her, his face stained with tears.

"I'm sorry, Sol. I wouldn't disturb you, but we have to go back." She knew not quite how—or how much—to tell him. "We have to go back into the sewer. They're still out there—the ones who..." She could not go on, despite the urgency.

"We have to take Papa with us." Sol stood up. "We can't leave him here."

"There's no time for that," Miriam said. "He would not want us to die for his body." She searched for the words that Solomon had taught her, the words that described the afterlife, where a man was judged and where his soul thrived. "He is in *Olam Haba.*"

The shop's cellar was too smoke-filled to allow them to descend that way, so after furtive glances up and down the street they returned to Kaverne. Like two small frightened children, they helped each other into the sewer. Please, let them not come looking for us, Miriam prayed as Sol closed the grate.

"There's no way to cover the grate, Miri." His voice was hoarse from weeping.

She nodded, though she knew he could not see her in the dark. When he sat down, she moved beside him and they held each other in silence until, finally, she could hear by his breathing that he had dozed off. Only then did she allow herself the luxury of more tears.

"*Bruqah!*" Sol shouted.

Miriam awakened into blackness. Her skin felt clammy; her clothes clung to her, and the darkness felt like oil against her face. She shifted her weight and soothed Sol, hoping to stop his nightmares.

"What do you want of me!" He shoved himself from her arms.

"*What do you want?*" the sewer echoed. "*You want...*"

"It's Miriam! I'm here, Sol!"

He found her hand and held it fast. "Tell me it isn't true. Any of it."

"Oh God, how I wish I could!"

"Papa!" He began to weep anew.

When the tears subsided, he said, "The images, Miri. They're still here. A voice kept saying, *Bruqah*, and another asked me over and over, 'Do you hold your seasons dear, Solomon Freund? Is this your season of sadness?'"

Letting go of him, she stood up and groped through the dark, trying to get her bearings.

"Go away!" he cried out.

"Solomon?"

"Miriam?"

She heard him sigh in frustration, and she wondered, as she had before, if his fear of the visions was tainted by his longing for them. Lately, when he talked about his childhood visions, he had tried to convince her, and himself, that the horrors of the sewer had been foreknowledge of what Berlin and the Fatherland would become. They were a barrier, he said, against the insanity.

Tonight she could understand his inability to function, but there had been other times when things mystical seemed to call to him more loudly than his need for her. What must it be like, she thought, living with scenes and voices you could not share? She tried to imagine what Sol had described to her, images seen as if through the aperture of a camera, widening until they crystallized into visions of terror. Laughter mingling with the music-box melody of "Glowworm" as an apparition clarified and dissolved—

"I'll be...all right," he said.

When he said nothing else, she found she needed the reassurance of his voice as a buffer against a silence broken only by dripping water. "How long do you think we've been down here?" she asked him.

"Hours. Who knows. What's it matter, anyway."

The voice came from below her, and she realized he was still sitting down.

"You think they're still out there?" she asked. "They must go home to sleep sometime. I—"

She could hear his breathing, and she made her way back to him. When she touched him, he put his head against her legs, his arms embracing her at the knees. "We will fix up the shop, Miri. And this place. We'll be safe down here. We'll make it comfortable, you'll see—"

Her hands found his chin and she tilted his head back, bent and awkwardly kissed him. "I'm going to go, now," she told him. "Sleep while I'm gone. I'll find help for us—for Papa...."

There was no point in finishing her sentence. She would have to do this alone, though for a few moments she would need his help.

He boosted her, and she climbed from the sewer without much difficulty. She did not know exactly what it was she meant to do, only that something needed to be done. They could not hide forever. The apartment was out of bounds until they were certain the men had found some other form of entertainment, she thought grimly. Burying Jacob was out of the question until a member of the sacred society was found or until Sol had calmed down enough to make rational decisions. But...something.

She entered the shop and made her way to the door, averting her eyes to avoid seeing Jacob's body.

The street, swept with driving rain, was deserted. She cursed the bell that jangled as she opened the door and shivered as a blast of rain and night air hit her. Leaving the door ajar, she went back inside to get her coat and the old boa she had taken to the shop in the hopes of selling it. Ever since she had lost her job at Ananas, she had looked at her few possessions as nothing more than eggs and milk and bread. Things had been better during the Games, but she had harbored no illusions about their remaining that way.

There was only one way they could hope to survive for the long term. They had to leave Germany. Any idea of staying and trying to put the shop to rights was crazy—but leaving required papers, or excellent forgeries.

She went out into the rain, walking fast but in no particular direction, not slowing even as she passed Ananas. The club's new owners had corrected the place's so-called abuses. Symbolic of peace and prosperity, an eagle clutching a swastika medallion in its claws blazed from the marquee like a beacon. Everything about it promised sanctuary—though not for her. Nowadays the place was almost always filled with military revelry.

The door opened and two men came out. One wore the uniform of the Abwehr. For a moment she thought it was Erich, though she knew he never frequented the club anymore. Chilled to the bone, she stepped into the street, silently acknowledging where it was her feet were taking her: to see the Rittmeister.

He was the only one who could help them. He could find a way to call off the SS, a way to bury Jacob Freund, a way to get them out of the country. Or at least the necessary papers. Or—

Angry at her desperation, she strode toward his apartment. He would have to help them! What choice did he have, after his father robbed them blind? He too had loved Jacob Freund, in whatever way he was capable of loving. Surely he could not refuse!

But he could, and she knew it.

After the Olympics, he had legally divested himself of his former surname, due to its association with the Jewish shop. *Erich Alois* he called himself now. If he could do that, she thought, he could certainly refuse to take any responsibility for their safety.

She was across the street from the building where Erich lived when she realized she would be unable to go inside after all. Anything was better than accepting help from Erich or, worse, having him refuse to help them.

Twenty meters away through the fog and drizzle, a rotund, heavy-jowled man wearing a fur-collared overcoat and carrying a walking stick had stopped beneath a street lamp and was staring toward her. Someone she knew? She squinted in his direction.

"*Wie viel!*" he called out. "How much?"

She smiled somberly. Must look quite a sight, she thought—the boa bedraggled, hair rain-soaked and plastered to her head. Small wonder he thought her a prostitute!

He rapidly approached. "Let's not waste time!" His accent clearly pegged him as British. "Answer me! I asked you how much!"

Impatience had turned his tone ugly.

"Sorry, *Schatzie,*" Miriam said. "I'm through for the night."

"Not good enough for you?" Putting down the tip of his walking stick to balance himself, he stepped across the water accumulating in the gutter and grabbed hold of her arm.

"Get away!" She tried to shake off his hand, but he tightened his grip.

"Look at you! Why would anyone pay good money for such a tramp! You should pay *me* to take you home."

He shoved her aside. Caught off-balance she stumbled and with a cry fell into the street. She huddled there, head down, sobbing softly and uncaring that she was forming a dam in the drainage.

The man laughed and reached down with his walking stick as if to help her lift herself. "Come on. I'll scrub you down and you can service me while I dine."

Miriam batted away the stick, climbed from the gutter with the dignity of a dancer recovering from a fall during a performance, and unsteadily gained her feet. Throwing the boa over her shoulder, she started across the street. The heel of her left shoe had been loosened by the fall and she walked awkwardly, but she held her head high and her face was set like stone against the slanting rain.

"A filet of sole for a superior performance."

"I would rather starve."

The man shook his stick. "Come back, or I'll report you to the Gestapo for soliciting! I know you're a Jew! I can smell it."

Miriam quickened her pace. It was enough to cause her heel, already weakened, to collapse. Even her dancer's training did not enable her to stay upright.

She hit the sidewalk clumsily, in a sprawl. She heard the man laugh as she drew herself up with her arms and unsteadily climbed to her feet. She bent over, balancing precariously on one foot as she tried to remove the broken shoe.

"I saw you from my window." Erich stepped into the light and reached to take hold of her shoulders before she toppled again.

She stepped away from him, nearly going down again in the process.

"That little otter's mine by first right, soldier." The man in the overcoat ambled toward them. "Go back to your flat. If you want to fuck her you'll have to wait your turn."

Erich stepped back, poised on the balls of his feet, eyeing the man coldly.

"Anyone can see she's Jewish." The man looked startled by Erich's officer insignia. "First come, first—"

"She doesn't have a trace of Jewish blood in her."

"Oh? Friend of yours, Herr Rittmeister? I'd be more careful of the company I keep if I were you."

"That's enough." Erich's voice was dangerously low.

"Whatever you say, Rittmeister. You want to tarnish your soul by protecting a Jewish whore, that's your business."

Without warning, Erich's foot snapped up. The Britain tried to block with his walking stick, but did not get it horizontal fast enough. The kick struck his abdomen, and the man's eyes bulged. He stared at Erich as though attempting to hold his breath, then bent over, clutching his midriff. Air issued through his lips. Erich hit him in the face with his fist. His ring, with its curled metal center, gouged the man's cheek, and he toppled.

How she'd like to place the stick across that fat neck and strangle the swine, she thought. Strangle them both! "You're quite the gentleman," she said angrily, furious at herself and the whole situation.

"I'll kill him if you want."

"Don't be an ass." She finally got her left shoe off, stepped over the fallen man and clumped through the puddles, hurrying away from Erich.

He caught up as she rounded the corner onto Mauerstrasse. "I don't know what you think you're doing wandering around the streets in the middle of the night," he said, taking her arm. "You'd better come with me before someone worse finds you."

She shook him off. "Leave me alone."

"You may be sure that man will go to the authorities. You'll be detained before you ever reach—"

"I couldn't care less."

"Don't be a fool, Miriam!"

Wheeling, she faced him. "What would you have me do? Register a complaint with the police? Go with you, perhaps even to the home you and your Nazi cronies stole from me?" Clasping her hands as though in prayer, she gazed into his eyes with the over-acted, maudlin look that until recently had so characterized romantic films. "Shall we summon a carriage and a team of four to whisk us away to your estate, my love? Maybe while we're there His Highness Gauleiter Goebbels will set our lives aright. Think that if I fuck him, he will give me back what has been stolen from us, or grant me clemency from hunger? Maybe he can do better than that. Maybe he or His Holiness Adolph Hitler can raise Jacob Freund from the dead!"

She broke into sobs.

"Jacob? What about Jacob! Dead?"

She nodded, and the world began to swim. Trying to keep from blacking out, she did not resist when he put an arm across her shoulders. He guided her into the building.

In the smoky Bierstube on the ground floor a trombone was blowing *oom-pah-pah* and people were laughing and clinking glasses. She forced herself up two steep stair flights, Erich holding her to keep her from collapsing. On the third-floor landing he pulled her to face him, clutching her hands with his, against his chest. "What's this about Jacob!"

"They...they hanged him. Oh, God." She felt dizzy again. "Brownshirts broke into the shop and...your parents...I need to lie down."

"My parents! They were attacked *again*?"

"They got away. Got away with—"

"Thank God for that." He inserted the key, kicked open the door, and maneuvered her inside. "And Solomon? Is he okay?"

"What do you care about Solomon!"

Erich helped her onto the bed and, pulling a blanket across her feet, looked at her quizzically. He appeared stunned, and she wondered if he were focused on an issue he had hoped never to have to examine too thoroughly. Then slowly he appeared to regain the control that she knew was as essential to him as breath itself. He finished covering her legs with the blanket, and leaned over her.

"Solomon," he said huskily, "is my brother."

She sensed it was the truth. At least for the moment.

Chapter 42

She's beautiful, Erich thought. *Even drenched, she's beautiful.*

Miriam held out her hands as if to stop the world from spinning, exhaled audibly and sat up, blinking. She rubbed her eyes and, shaking her head ruefully, put her hands over her face as if to shield herself from grief.

Gently Erich lifted her hands aside. Her eyes were downcast and her face looked haggard. "Dry your hair." He handed her a towel. "You'll feel better."

She sat with the towel against her left cheek, slowly rocking.

"The man outside. Did he hurt you?"

She shook her head. "Only my pride. At least, what's left of my pride." Her trembling increased. Tears rolled down her cheeks. He lifted the wet boa from her shoulders and threw it in the sink, thinking fleetingly that it looked like a drowned cat. Then he pulled up a chair and sat on it, backwards, facing her.

"I knew it would come to this!" He made a fist.

"There was an officer with a list. An SS officer."

"Silver-haired?"

She nodded disconsolately.

"That *bastard!*" He punched the air.

"There is more." From the strain in her face he knew she was on the verge of hysteria. He patted her wrist to calm her, but she jerked away. She took a deep breath. "Late this afternoon, Sol went out for a walk. I was at home. Your parents were minding the shop. Around sundown, Herr Freund and I went across the street to the shop and—and—"

He tilted the chair forward. "Tell me!"

She lifted the towel and began rubbing vigorously, wrathfully, at her hair, her features seized with anger. "Everything had been cleaned out...everything! Is that what you need to hear, Erich Alois? Your parents cleaned out the safe! They took every last pfennig and as many accouterments as they could!"

"Surely there's some mistake...."

Feeling suddenly, strangely empty, he tipped back in the chair.

His parents were imperfect, yes, but...*thieves?* Had all moral values been signed away with the 1918 Armistice? Betrayal, the Führer taught, was the province of Red revolutionaries, republicans...and Jews.

Especially the Jews.

His parents had stabbed the Freunds in the back; in time, they too would find some way to blame their misconduct on the Jews.

"Herr Freund made us hide in the sewer." Miriam's words were tumbling out now, and she was crying. "They destroyed the shop and...and strung him up in his own shop like a criminal, Erich...strangled him with his Iron Cross—"

She broke into convulsive sobs. He wanted to comfort her, but instead and backed away as if from something too hideous to contemplate. He felt as though he, personally, had killed Jacob Freund by provoking Otto Hempel's hatred and by being a part of the larger organization that condoned and encouraged such acts. A murderer, he thought, had no business giving solace to the orphans he had created. And then there were his parents.

"We *have* to get out of Germany," she said. Her voice had taken on a new urgency. "You're the only one who can help us, Erich...."

Angry and frustrated that all his dreaming about her had come to this, he walked to the balcony window and stared at the city's fog-blurred lights. Yes, he had to get them out, but how? Even if he could secure papers for them, getting them out of Germany wasn't enough. Right now there were neutral countries, but for how long?

Ultimately, Adolph Hitler would lay claim to them all.

"I'm deeply sorry, Miriam," he said softly. "Herr Freund was a good man. I wish—" He was about to say he wished his own father had been as moral. "He was...special. I promise I'll find a way to help you, but it's not going to be easy. I have to think about it...find a way, a safe way."

"But you will try to help?"

"As God is my witness. Whatever you need, I'll get. Papers, petitions, money. Whatever it takes. I'm no longer powerless in the Party," he assured her in a choked voice. "There is much I can do behind the scenes. I want to keep you safe."

She looked up at him. "If you're serious, why have you stood by for so long?" she asked between sobs. Her eyes revealed her need to accept his offer, no matter how much she mistrusted him.

He knelt beside her, elbows on the chair, and looked at her closely. "I don't blame you for the way you feel." When he reached out and touched her cheek, he saw her steel herself, but she did not draw away.

Exhausted, her face tear-stained, she still looked beautiful; only an enormous effort of will stopped him from trying to kiss her. Was Solomon, he wondered, similarly enslaved?

"You'll catch pneumonia if you stay in those wet things," he said, standing. He lifted off his desk top and set it against the wall; where the desk had been was a gold-rimmed porcelain bathtub. "You'll feel better after a bath and some food."

"I have to get back to Sol...."

"Solomon can take care of himself. You need to take care of *yourself* for a change. Please—while I think this through."

"I must get back." She no longer sounded defiant. "Herr Freund's body. What are we going to do with the—"

"Just rest. You'll be able to think better after you've had some sleep. I'll get you some food from downstairs. Sol will be all right for now. And he'll be a lot more all right if I can work things out."

He put a large kettle on each of the narrow stove's two burners. After placing a silk shirt and one of his robes on the bed, he gave her the most reassuring smile he could muster and headed down to the Bierstube.

Think! he told himself as he descended the stairs. There had to be some service he could render in exchange for the safety of his friends. Would he ever be rid of Hempel and his need for vengeance? Hempel was no fool; he knew just where and when to inflict pain, as if he had a talent for looking into the soul of his enemy. It was not happenstance that the mob had stormed down Friedrich Ebert Strasse. Brownshirt violence was seemingly random only in the particulars. Hempel, he was sure, had chosen the area carefully.

It would happen again. Unless he could get them out.

Why such emphasis on eradicating the Jews! he thought bitterly. They weren't responsible for what ailed the world, though some facts *were* irrefutable. Only one in a hundred Germans and one in five Berliners was Jewish, yet they dominated the giant Darmstädter, Deutche, and Dresdener banks; owned such huge department stores as Wertheim, Tietz, and KadeWe; and controlled the largest newspaper groups, Ullstein and Mosse. The question was not whether the Jews had power, but whether they wielded power for the good of the Reich.

In his opinion they had. People like Jacob Freud were proof of that. Until Adolph Hitler had insisted otherwise.

I too might have marched to the drum of the Party propaganda, had Pfaueninsel not happened. So perhaps Achilles did not die in vain.

Before entering the Bierstube, he took a deep breath to compose himself, and straightened his uniform.

He returned with a metwurst, a loaf of pumpernickel, a couple of cheeses including a small brie, a bottle of burgundy—hardly the meal he had envisioned serving Miriam the first time she came to his flat, he thought angrily. He found her sleeping, her hair turbaned, more towels on the floor, her shoulders bare and beautiful. No wonder, he thought, unable to stifle a sentimental smile, Lady Venus so easily entrapped Tannhäuser in her web of desire.

Removing his clothes, he slipped into the tub. Perhaps, like Napoleon, he could best contemplate conquests in the bath. What looked like one of her pubic hairs floated in the water. He wound it around his finger and, settling back, watched the lights of a barge moving along Landwehr Kanal, its filthy water a dumping place for refuse—and bodies; during the aborted Bolshevik Revolution, the Freikorps had dumped Rosa Luxemburg there after bludgeoning her to death. Four months in the canal before being found.

That was 1918. The same year he and Solomon found the sewer.

Poor *Spatz*. So naïve, so sure the world was rooted in good and not evil. He himself had known better, even then. They'd been born too late for the war—the real war—the one against moral decline. How he longed, even now, for the imperial purity of the Kaiserzeit, the pre-war Old Order. Peace, and respect for traditional values.

Chivalry and the Kaiserzeit had died the moment the Armistice went into effect, the eleventh hour of the eleventh day of the eleventh month of the year the Freikorps quelled a revolution and Friedrich Weisser drowned a terrier pup named Bull.

"I've got it!"

He sat up and with a perplexed cry, Miriam jolted upright in bed, the robe clutched against her throat. Smiling at his creativity, he stepped from the tub and wrapped a towel around his waist. How clever, he told himself as he sat down at the table, grinning at her; use that asset which made it so dangerous for her to stay in the Fatherland.

Her name. Her legacy from one of the last of the Old Order.

"I can get you out. Both of you."

"You're certain?"

He nodded. "I *will* help you...and Solomon."

"I know." She was trying to be patient, but he sensed her growing agitation.

"Getting you out of Germany is not enough. You must leave Europe. There's a South American here in Berlin." He hesitated, then decided there was no harm in mentioning the name. "An emissary to Italy—Perón's his name. He'll help. I'm sure he will."

"Juan Perón? I've known him for years. He was a friend of Uncle Walther's. They really liked each other."

"Well, he certainly seems to like you," Erich said, watching her face. Her tension seemed to have lessened. Apparently, he had managed to say the right thing. He wondered, with a pique of jealousy, about the wisdom of having thought of the Argentinean, feeling a vague unease about her exact relationship with the man. "Perón saw you dance at Pfaueninsel. He was enchanted. If he made an official request to have you perform in his country, Hitler would not refuse. But it will take time—"

"Sol must leave now!" Her voice was edged with panic. "He's cracking up, Erich. If he stays any longer, that sewer could become his tomb—if we're not arrested first."

"Then there's only one answer. Solomon must go to Amsterdam right away and join you in South America later. He's not the problem, you are. Papers for him shouldn't be impossible to arrange—I don't think he's on any list of known enemies of the Party—"

"He's a Jew!" she said bitterly.

"It can be done, Miri. But you're Walther Rathenau's niece—"

"Are you saying I'm on some kind of special list?"

"I don't know, but it's more than likely. Anyhow, the problem's more complicated than that." He looked at her seriously. "What I'm saying is that it will take time to make the arrangements for you. I must be careful, if I am to stay alive myself."

"And in the meantime?"

"In the meantime," he said, "Solomon leaves and you stay with me."

She laughed mirthlessly. "I see. I'm beginning to understand. You've dropped the name *Weisser*, now all you have to do is get rid of Solomon—"

"Stop it!"

"No, *you* stop! If you think I'm coming to live at the estate with you—"

He put a hand on her arm. "You couldn't, even if you...if I wanted you to. Not without renouncing your faith. But you can stay here safely, at least for a while. Fortunately, the landlady doesn't care who lives here, she just cares about the rent money. That way I'll look after you—but only as much as you want me to."

After a moment's silence Miriam nodded in acquiescence. "Thank you, Erich," she said simply. "Now I really must go."

"Stay in bed," Erich said gruffly. "You need to rest. I'll go and find Solomon."

"No." She rose from the bed and scooped up her clothes. *"I* have to go to him. Tell him myself."

"All right, then. But be ready for me when I come."

"When, Erich? I must know—"

"I told you, I don't know. Today, tomorrow, next week."

He thought for a moment. What he really wanted to say what that he didn't know the answer to that *either,* but as his mind began to reel, he realized he *could* do it. With luck, in a few hours. At least set the thing in motion.

"Tonight," he said definitively. "I'll send Konrad with the limousine. He can take Solomon to the train station and bring you here."

"Konrad," she said softly. The expression on her face told him that she was thinking of the other time Konrad drove her to the station, with Solomon in tow, only that time she was the one leaving, for Paris. "Won't that draw too much attention to us?"

"I don't think so," Erich said, his mind continuing to spin out the scenario and its possibilities. "Once you are living in my flat, it will be assumed that you are my mistress. Making a show of bringing you here at the same time as sending Solomon away will make sense to the Party. They know of your...friendship...with Solomon. My participation in both actions will be understood."

"If you say so," she said quietly. "I have no choice but to trust your judgment. It seems to me, however, that understanding does not necessarily constitute approval. I imagine they would be more likely to approve if you disposed of Sol is some other, less kindly way. Not so?"

"Not so," Erich said. But Miriam's question penetrated to the darkest regions of his soul. To keep from looking her directly in the eye, he turned to stare out of the window. He saw the lights of another barge moving through the fog. Probably carrying coal, he reflected, and more than likely headed for the Krupp furnaces. The munitions factories were working at full capacity. War was inevitable, people said, though surely not in *this* decade.

Well, let it come—whenever; he had his own war to wage.

He listened to the sounds from the bathroom, where Miriam was dressing to leave. Someday, somehow, he swore, he would have Adolph Hitler's head on a pike.

And Miriam Rathenau permanently in his bed.

Chapter 43

——*a sea, blue-black as ink.* On a cliff, silhouetted against the ocean, is a tall man whose hair is the color of foam. A second man squats in the grass, his dark skin deeply pockmarked.

The tall man has one end of a leather strap wound around his wrist; the other end is attached to a boy who crouches at the man's feet like a dog. His back is covered with the furry skin of an animal, and he wears a collar around his neck.

The man who is standing signals for quiet. The boy quivers visibly, shoulders tensed and face set in a fury as he strains against the leash. Kneeling, the tall man puts a hand on the boy's furry back and unhooks the leash clip from the collar.

Solomon! the boy cries. Bruqah!...Miriam!...Solomon! For God's sake, somebody help me!——

"Somebody help me," Sol mumbled as the vision dissipated and he awoke into the blackness of the sewer. His skin and clothes were soaked with the sweat and smell of terror, and the darkness around him pressed in on him like a live body.

He rolled over on the makeshift flooring and slid his hands up the slimy walls, struggling to stand. Papa! He must go upstairs and pray for Papa, and for himself; he must pray for Miri, and Recha, and Mama. In the darkness he found his old book bag, still hanging from the two-by-twelve after so many years. He hugged it to his chest as he rocked on his heels, crying——

——*the sea roars like a beast in heat as the boy bounds forward toward a corpse that hangs from the branch of a huge palm tree.* Above its head, a simian creature points a long finger.

Mihinana! the white-haired man commands, swacking the boy on the butt. Eat!——

Sol leaned forward, as if seeing more clearly would bring understanding, but the knot in his stomach simply tightened and the fog that clouded his mind thickened——

―――*the boy responds to the whip.* First on all fours, then on his feet, now flying through the air as he grips the corpse like a gibbon, legs hugging the waist. He swings upside-down with the body, sinking his teeth into the hip and shaking his head wildly as he fights to tear off a chunk of flesh. His eyes are wide open. Blood curls down his chin.

A guttural voice rings through the darkness: *"There is nowhere to run, Solomon Freund. Watch. Enjoy. As you hold your seasons dear, so you have no choice"*—

"What do you want of me!"

"What do you want?" the sewer echoed. *"You want...want..."*

A light from above erupted against Sol's face, and he jerked up his arms defensively.

"Go away." His voice was a rasp.

A whisper: *Is this your season of madness?*

"Yes!" Sold shouted at the twilight voice of his childhood. "Yes, I am mad. *Mad!*"

"Solomon, are you all right?"

"Miriam?"

Leaning down, she shone a flashlight around the sewer—like a mother assuring herself there was no tangible cause for her child's nightmare, Sol thought bitterly.

He let go of the book bag, as ashamed of the pleasure it had once brought him as he was of Miriam seeing him like this, and squinting upward, trying to focus. Her face floated behind the light. "I'm fine, I...what time is it?"

"Six o'clock."

"In the morning?"

"Yes." She sounded defensive, as if his question contained an accusation. In a way it had. He needed to know where she had been—and with whom.

"Papa!" he said, remembering. Papa was dead, his body lying in the shop—and he was concerned about where Miriam had been! How long would it take before he fully comprehended Papa's death? A week—a month—a year? And at what cost to his sanity?

What is the price of five sparrows, Solomon?

The voice came to him out of the sewer, as it had done so many years before.

"Eat," he heard again, but this time it was real. "You must come out of there." Miriam reached down as if to pull him out. "I have brought bread, and here's a hard-boiled egg."

"I'm going to Papa." He took hold of her hand and climbed into the sub-basement.

"Papa would wish you to keep up your strength." She had spread out a newspaper on the floor of the sub-basement and laid it out like a tablecloth.

On top of it, she had placed a metwurst, half a loaf of pumpernickel, a small brie, a half-empty bottle of burgundy.

From her pocket she took a precious egg wrapped in a face-cloth. He took the egg from her, broke it in two, and handed her back on half. "This food," he said. "Where did you get it?"

"Eat," she said. "When you are finished we have urgent things to talk about."

In deference to the pain in Miriam's eyes he broke off a small crust of bread and ate it with the egg. "God willing," he said, "whatever we must discuss can wait until sundown. For this one day, I will mourn for my father."

"And I will leave you to mourn in solitude," Miriam said. "But if I must interrupt...if I call out to you to come at once, do as I say."

When Sol did not answer, Miriam became insistent. "Promise me, Solomon," she said.

The urgency in her voice transferred itself to him through his pain. "I will," he said, nodding at her. "Now I must go to Papa."

He made his way up through the cabaret and into the shop. Once inside, he tore down the curtain that separated the shop from the basement steps, and covered his father's body. That done, he sat down on the stool and gave himself up to a day of prayer, and to memories of his father's goodness.

Time slid by, almost tangible, emollient and liquid as he sank ever deeper into dreams that were memories. Light played along the edges of his consciousness and began to turn slowly, a sparkling pinwheel that revolved, broke into shafts, became a world of gently tumbling crystals. "Season of madness," he thought he heard himself mutter, though he was uncertain if the words were outside his head or within it. He felt his chin droop forward and the muscles of his neck and shoulders go slack, and he entered a darkness tinged with gray, moiling fog.

For all the hours of the day, no other reality entered his consciousness. He would have sat there through the night had Miriam had come for him.

"The sun is setting," Miriam said. "You have been here all day, Sol." She took his hand. "It is Succot. Come. We will sanctify this holy day as best we can."

"I love you, Papa," he said softly. He looked at the Iron Cross that lay on his palm. He had been clutching it throughout the day, and its edges had ridged his skin. Turning to Miriam, he did his best to smile. "I love you too," he said.

She watched him find a box, layer it with tissue paper, and lay the medal on top.

"I want you to have this," he told her. "If anything ever happens to me, it is yours."

"Nothing—"

He placed his hand over her mouth. "If I am not here and you need help," he went on, "you must go to Erich. Despite everything, he is the only brother I have. It is tradition that a man take care of his brother's wife."

She took the box without further protest and gently kissed him on the cheek. There were tears in her eyes, though whether for Papa or because of his words to her, he did not know.

Silently, she led him to the meal she had set up on the floor of the cabaret's sub-basement. Covering her head with one of Jacob's old handkerchiefs, she lit a candle she had melted onto a saucer. When she had repeated the traditional blessing, she poured wine into a chipped coffee cup Jacob had kept at the back of the shop.

Sol lifted the wine, placed a hand on his head where his *yalmulke* should have been and sang softly, *"Baruch ato adonai, eluhainu melech ha-olam..."*

Remembering other holidays with his family and choked by tears, he could not finish the prayer.

"Now let us eat." Miriam took the cup from him.

"How can I fill my stomach when my father's body is—"

"Didn't God command us to give thanks, even during mourning?"

A strand of hair had fallen across her eyes. He pushed it back in place. "Is this the time for talking?" he asked. *Is this your season of madness?* he heard, as if in counterpoint to his own words.,

"While you were in there," she nodded toward the sewer entry, "I went to see Erich. The food we ate, it came from him."

Sol glanced toward the sewer. While he was in there, talking to ghosts, had she...He put his hands on her shoulders. "It's all right if you slept with him—"

"It's all right with *you*?" she said sharply.

"Stop it. Please. Not now."

"How can I stop anything, Solomon? In the name of Heaven, how? Sometimes I feel like walking into the Reichschancellery and spitting in the eye of the first SS officer I see, just to get it over with."

"I'm sorry, Miri. I did not mean to offend you." Sol waited a moment before continuing. Taking her hand in his, he said, "You have to come with me to Amsterdam, Miriam. We must find a way to leave together. If you stay here, Erich will never let you go."

She shook her head. "You may be able to get to Amsterdam without too many problems right now," she said, "but even Holland will not always be safe for either of us. Erich came up with a better idea. He's going to suggest to an Argentinean named Juan Perón that he ask Hitler for me do an official dance tour in South America. He feels that the Führer is unlikely to refuse the request."

"Why would this Perón do you a favor?"

"I've known him longer than I've known you. He was very fond of Uncle Walther—and me. He'll do it. I know he will. Once I'm there you will join me, you and Mama and Recha."

"Like Papa joined them in Holland? If you insist on South America, I'll leave when Hitler grants Perón's request. Not a moment sooner."

"No, Sol. You have to leave as soon as possible!" Suddenly she was in his arms, sobbing. "Why must you fight me, Solomon? Safety—that's all that matters, right now."

"What is Erich's plan for me?"

Quietly, she filled him in.

"And what happens to you in the interim?"

He could feel her stiffen. "Erich says it will be safest for me if I move into his flat while I wait for him to make the arrangements for me to leave."

Sol heard the echo of his own words. *You must go to Erich. Despite everything, he is the only brother I have. It is tradition that a man take care of his brother's wife.*

After a moment he said, trembling, "I will do what you wish on one condition."

"Anything—"

He put his finger to her lips and picked up the candle. Taking her hand, he led her up the stairs and into the cabaret. On the dusty dance floor, amid the pallor of green light beaming down through one of the few small stained-glass windows that remained unbroken, he lifted her knuckles to his lips and closed his eyes.

"There is a season for all things, Miri," he said, once again echoing the twilight voice. "Marry me."

"Here? Tonight? And who will be the rabbi?"

"God."

He opened his eyes and looked into hers, and saw her answer. Though he felt joyous, he held back, denying himself his emotions. If he gave in to his feelings, would God not punish him, what with Papa dead upstairs, Mama unstable, and Recha—

"I have no right to be happy," Miriam said, as if she could hear his thoughts. Her eyes shone with tears. "You say there is a season for all things. Perhaps, too, there is a reason for everything, one only God understands. If so, He will surely forgive me for a moment of joy."

What Sol felt at that moment was akin to the passion of cerebral discovery; he had not believed it possible to feel that way except from what lay between the bindings of a book. He had the impression that if he stood still long enough and stayed silent enough, the cabaret would disappear and they would be transported to some bygone era when the world was whole and where they had a chance for peace and contentment.

They stood among dusty muslin sheets, thrown carelessly over once-new tables and chairs surrounding an abandoned dance floor in a closed cabaret in a world without hope. Berlin, the Reich, their own emotions, Erich: to Sol, they all seemed like spokes of a wheel someone else had set in motion.

Like the wheels of Walther Rathenau's limousine, which could even now be headed toward the cabaret. He gave no credence to Miriam's words and hopes concerning the freedom South America afforded. He did not want to leave her, had not really believed she would accept his suggestion—no matter how obvious and necessary his immediate departure.

"The marriage will make the paperwork easier when I get to South America," she said.

"Is that the only reason we should marry?"

"What do you think?" she asked softly.

He slid his arms around her waist. "I think love is a better reason."

"And I do love you," she said.

He kissed her and discovered a new yielding to her lips. When the embrace ended, he glanced around the room and said, "Didn't I hear something about there being a wedding in here today?"

She squeezed his hands, and smiled. "Make two stacks of three tables each. I will be right back."

Fear touched him. "You're not going outside, are you?"

"Of course not," she said as affably and coyly as a girl at a prom. "Wait and see." She moved across the floor and into the shadows with her dancer's grace.

By the time Sol had the tables piled up in the center of the dance floor, Miriam returned, a rose-colored shawl over her shoulders. "Remember this? I wore it that first night in the cabaret—Miss Debutante, singing and dancing and expecting the world to applaud." She briefly curtsied.

"But where—"

"A different kind of tradition, Sol." She took off the shawl and draped it between the two table stacks. "Every performer leaves something behind in the dressing room, for luck. I was young, rich, and silly...I left the biggest and brightest thing I could think of. It was there, in the costume trunk. It's a bit musty, but at least the fish moths left it alone. Here, give me a hand."

"And do what?"

"We have to have a canopy, don't we? It wouldn't be a wedding without one."

"Does that mean you are accepting my proposal, Fraülein Rathenau?" he asked seriously.

"Let's just say I have given the matter due consideration, and I concur with your idea, Herr Freund."

Before he could say anything else she bounded off again, this time down the stairs leading to the sub-basement. He worked on the canopy, wondering what surprise she now had in store for him.

She returned with the burgundy and three dusty glasses.

Wriggling out of her slip, she wrapped it around one of the glasses and placed it under the canopy. "Now flowers, and..." She looked around in dismay. "Forget it. There's no way."

"Music? I'll be back."

He hurried down the stairs. When he returned, she twirled around to show him the lavender spray she had twisted into her hair. "Lilac. It's silk, but it'll do."

"And here's my contribution." He dug in his pocket and pulled out the harmonica he had retrieved from his old book bag. He blew in the mouth organ to clear it of dust and, with the instrument cupped lovingly in his hands, watched her sway as he softly played a Schubert melody.

When he had finished, he fished in his pocket, pulled out a cigar and removed their gold bands. "I went up through the sewer and..."

She put her fingers to his lips to hush him. "My God, Solomon Freund, you must have shopped for weeks! Don't tell anyone where you bought the rings." Glancing around suspiciously, she added, "Some of the fashionable women in this place might overhear and bribe the jeweler for duplicates."

Taking the wrapper-rings from his hand, she held them in her palm for a moment before returning the smaller of the two to him. The look in her eyes told him that to her it truly was a treasure.

He ushered her beneath the canopy and took her in his arms. "In the eyes of God, from this day on and for as long as we shall live, we are man and wife," he said huskily. Trembling, he slid the cigar band onto her finger. "I love you, Miriam. I always have, I always will."

"And I love you, Solomon Freund."

He held out his hand. As she slipped the ring on her finger, he brought down his heel sharp and hard onto the wrapped glass and felt it splinter underfoot. Then he kissed her.

As dusk faded and shadows lengthened, they held each other like children. When night came, so did Konrad.

"A few more minutes, please, Konnie," Miriam begged.

Sol knew that Konrad had never been able to refuse Miriam anything. Though he frowned and was clearly worried, he did not refuse her now. "It *can* only be a few minutes, Miss Miriam," he said, glancing at the wristwatch Miriam had brought him from America so many years before. "The train for Amsterdam leaves in half an hour, and you are expected at the flat."

He headed up the circular stairs. As he closed the door behind himself, Miriam glided into Solomon's arms. "One dance, my love," she whispered.

He held her so close, he thought she must break in two. Then, warmed by wine and passion, they ignored the storm clouds gathering outside and danced to imaginary violins playing Schubert and Strauss and Brahms for them alone.

But the storm would not be denied. Growing ever more ominous, it continued unabated on its predetermined course.

Child

of the

Journey

Part I

"What is the price of five sparrows? A couple of pennies? Not much more than that. Yet God does not forget a single one of them."
— Luke 12:6

Chapter 1

Berlin
April 1938

Was there any vestige left of the girl-woman who had enchanted the boys that night in Kaverne, Miriam wondered, or had the shadow of these last years erased it all?

Tilting her head, she inspected herself in the ornate mirror of her childhood. She had twisted her hair into a dancer's chignon and decorated it with a sprig of lilac, as she had done the night she first met Erich and Solomon. Leaning closer to the mirror, she inspected the inevitable fine lines that proved the passage of the years. She was more than twice the age now that she had been then. How was that possible, when only yesterday she had been fresh and young and fifteen?

Yesterday, and forever ago.

Time was a vagabond, at once a memory saboteur and a comforter, like an eiderdown that keeps you cozy and warm while it makes you weep and your skin itch.

Here, alone in her old room at what had once been her family estate, she felt relatively safe. She was aware of the comings and goings of Erich's Abwehr colleagues, and of occasional visits by Hermann Göring and Paul Joseph Goebbels, but when she stood on her balcony and stared out across the gardens, she saw only the quietly suburban, upper-crust veneer of the Grünewald. Erich kept to his own quarters, rarely intruding upon her privacy except by invitation, and she had plenty of time for solitude.

An excess of time, probably, judging by how often she caught herself avoiding the present and dwelling on a past that was, at least for the moment, lost to her, and a future that had become increasingly inaccessible.

As if venting her anger on it would somehow help, she picked up her hairbrush and flung it across the room. It thudded against the wall, bounced on the carpet, and lay there like the inanimate object it was.

The futility of the gesture served only to increase her misery. The last thing in the world she wanted to do was attend a party honoring Adolph

Hitler, she thought, contemplating her partially dressed image in the mirror. It would be delusional to believe that the Führer's birthday celebration would be anything but a stiff and formal dinner party, with nary a guest on the list who could provide her with either entertainment or intellectual stimulation.

So she had dallied too long. Now she was sure to be late, which would infuriate Erich, and cause the evening to turn out more unpleasant yet.

She retrieved her brush from the carpet and sat back down in front of the mirror, but instead of busying herself with the business of dressing, she allowed herself to drift sixteen years into the past, to a dinner party which had been anything but dull.

"Wenn der weisse Flieder wieder Blüht," she sang softly, reprising the song from her memories of that night at Kaverne, the cabaret her grandmother had built in the converted basement beneath a fur shop. It was an unusual place for a nightclub, across the street from the block of flats where Erich Weisser and Solomon Freund lived, and next door to their parents' cigar shop. Only she had not known any of that at the time. Nor would she have cared if she *had* known. They were around twelve, going on thirteen. Mere *boys*. She, on the other hand, had been fifteen, just back from dance training in America, her head filled with visions of stardom. Still, she knew enough to be grateful to her grandmother, Oma Rathenau, and to what the social gossips called her grandmother's crusade to bring respectability to Berlin's entertainment industry. Nor did she resent the suggestion that the real purpose of the cabaret was to showcase her talents. Why not? She was the old lady's granddaughter and the niece of Germany's newly appointed Foreign Minister, not to speak of being the heir to the Rathenau fortune.

What would her life have been like now, Miriam wondered, had she not performed at Kaverne's pre-opening dinner party? There might have been no Solomon in her life. There certainly would have been no Erich, for it was there that she had met both of them: Solomon, clutching his cello and dressed as if for his own bar mitzvah; and Erich, hair slicked-back, wearing pressed trousers, a white shirt with starched, rounded collar, and his father's silk paisley cravat.

From strangers, to acquaintances, from friends to intimates. It was a strange, wonderful, and terrifying progression, fraught with the best and the worst that human nature had to offer.

Enduring the customary pain that accompanied even the most fleeting reminder of Sol, she opened one of the drawers of the tiny porcelain music box he had won for her in the ring-toss booth at Luna Park.

"Glühwürmchen, Glühwürmchen, glimm're.... Shine little glowworm, glimmer, glimmer...." The Paul Lincke song was one of Solomon's favorites, the first of the two songs she sang at Kaverne. There, for the first time, she met Erich. It was not until later that night that she actually met Solomon, Erich's brother-in-blood and, now, her dearest husband-of-the-heart.

How disappointed she had felt at the tepid applause of the audience that night, though it was what she had learned to expect from the Germans, disciplined, and so unlike the Americans, with their wild enthusiasms and their appreciation for youth and beauty.

Smiling at her instantaneous fifteen-year-old rebellion against the self-control of her audience, *she remembered*....

...Tossing aside her shawl, she erupted into a cancan, whirling, kicking, repeating the routine until, with a suddenness calculated to send an ache through the groin of the shy-looking bespectacled young man who had just crept into the cabaret, and to shock the other boy who had risen to his feet and was clapping wildly, she dropped into a split. She was playing to him and to Solomon, and they both repaid her with naked adoration, staring at her as if she were the beautiful film star, Lilian Harvey, in the flesh.

Her diminutive uncle raised a black eyebrow and blew a perfect smoke ring into the air before applauding his favorite niece's performance. She smiled prettily at him and at her bejeweled old grandmother as the band began to play and couples gravitated toward the dance floor.

She approached her uncle's table. Having introduced herself to Erich's parents and exchanged a few pleasantries with them—the woman looked a little too nervous; the man, at best, uncomfortable, his nose red, as if he had been drinking too much, and his eyes hard—she glanced sideways at the boy. He was good-looking, not like either of his parents, yet he had his father's square jaw and his mother's light hair.

Miriam turned her attention to Solomon's family. His sister Recha looked like Goldilocks with a nose-cold. Her father looked nervous but proud, as did her mother, who had leaned over and whispered something in her husband's ear. His eyes flashed angrily behind his thick lenses as he turned toward Sol, who had finally stepped all the way into the room.

She looked from one boy to the other. How very different they seemed. She liked Erich's Aryan good looks but there was something about Solomon that appealed to the gentlest side of her. He looked sensitive. And *forlorn*.

Too late, she rose to speak to him, for he was following his father through the doorway.

Curious, Miriam followed them. Herr Freund had left the door slightly ajar. She pushed at it gently, let herself through, and found herself standing in the shadows at the top of a flight of stairs which led to a sub-basement.

She went down just far enough to be able to see Solomon and his father who stood arguing under a dangling naked light bulb.

Herr Freund clicked open an engraved gold watchcase that hung from a chain across his waist, wiped dust from his shoes with a Reichsbanner handkerchief he removed from the breast pocket of his pinstriped *Shabbas* suit, and reprimanded Solomon for keeping an important man like her uncle waiting. "Herr Rathenau is not merely an important man," Herr Freund said. "He is an important Jew."

"You are an important Jew, Papa." Solomon looked up. "You won the Iron Cross, First Class"....

She touched the Iron Cross that lay inside her music box, remembering how—a dozen years later—Solomon had removed it from the body of his dead father. Even now she gagged at the memory of the gentle and generous Jacob Freund, hanging upside-down in his own shop. Dead. Blue. Strangled with the war medal's cord...and her uncle also dead, victim of an assassin's grenade. Why were men of peace always targeted!

She clutched the Iron Cross in her palm, letting its sharp edges dig into her skin, the way Sol had done before he had handed it to her to keep in trust. For Sol it was an instrument of pride, of terror, of death. For her it was a reminder of Solomon and of all that she held most dear.

She shut that drawer of the music box and opened a second one. Carefully, as if it were made of butterfly wings, she took out her cigar-band wedding ring and slipped it onto her finger next to the ostentatious diamond Erich had given her. On an absolute basis she supposed it was quite extraordinary, but to her it was as synthetic as their mockery of a marriage.

If anything ever happens to me, go to Erich, Sol had told her. *It is tradition that a man take care of his brother's wife.*

She remembered the expression on Erich's face that childhood night in Kaverne, when she returned from eavesdropping on Solomon and his father. Strange, like a swimmer on the verge of diving into icy water. Stammering as he begged her to take a walk with him on the darkened streets outside. She had wondered if he always stammered under pressure, when he did not feel in control.

Her decision to do as he asked had been colored by the knowledge that Konnie, her chauffeur, was out next to the limousine, and would protect her.

Dear Konnie. After so many years of driving her uncle—driving her— around, he was at the beck and call of the boy she had teased that night.

That boy was a man now. A potent force in the Party—or so he told her. Still stammering when he lost control. But alive. As Konnie was alive. Not dead like her uncle and her grandmother, or half-alive, like her.

Like Sol.

She wound up the music box. "*Glühwürmchen, Glühwürmchen...*"

The barrel-organ man had played the song that night in the street, as if it were her theme song. She had executed a few dancing steps and grabbed Erich's hand. "Listen. He's playing 'Glowworm.' I never get enough of that song."

She had lifted Erich's hand to see it more clearly in the lamplight, kissed the red scars she had noticed earlier, and asked what had happened to cause them.

"M-my badge of courage?" He was blushing, though whether from pleasure at the touch of her lips kiss or out of embarrassment, she could not tell. "L-long time ago. An accident..."

Whatever else he had said was submerged in the sound of her own voice.

"Glühwürmchen, Glühwürmchen, glimm're—"

She had not realized she was singing aloud that night. People stared at her—not that she cared, but it wasn't exactly smart to draw attention to herself like that, in the middle of the street. Still she had danced toward the music.

Someone started to applaud and others joined in.

"More!" a man yelled. "More!"

"Play, barrel-organ man!" another shouted. "Bring out the beer. We're going to have a real Saturday night party!"

The barrel-organ man grinned widely and patted the head of his monkey; it seemed to be grinning too. The stiff-necked upper crust could keep their genteel appreciation, she thought as she curtsied and began to sing. This was more like it, she had thought; this was the real thing.

But that night wasn't real. Not anymore. So far in her past that it was like another life. Make-believe.

Tonight...was real.

"I made a deal with Erich, Sol," she whispered, holding her ring finger close to her cheek. "He may share my bed when he pleases, but I decide who shares my heart."

Erich's terms had been clear; he would make sure Solomon stayed alive in the camp if she publicly renounced Judaism and became Frau Erich Alois...in the eyes of the world, his loving wife.

Be alive, Solomon, she prayed. Oh God, be alive. I'm doing my part. Do yours, and we'll make it out of this God-forsaken country.

She replaced the cigar band in the music box and bent over to smell the roses from the Argentinean emissary, Juan Perón.

"He still sends them to you every time he is in Berlin, doesn't he?" Erich came up behind her. He sounded peeved.

"Yes, he does." He had since before Uncle Walther's death. She pictured Perón's face the last time she had seen him, watching her place a wreath under the plaque commemorating her uncle's assassins.

They had the courage of their convictions, the plaque read.

Men and women do what they must to survive, Perón's card told her, as if he felt the need to rationalize her actions for her. This, all the ugly things, were for Sol. Always for Sol. She was his protector, carrying his spirit, and the three of them—she, Erich, Solomon—were a triumvirate still, as they had been from the start. Only now Sol was in a camp and she was in a different kind of prison, wearing a traitor's hat.

"An Argentinean custom—courting another man's wife?"

Miriam stared at Erich in the mirror as he strolled out onto the balcony. Seeing him out there never failed to remind her of the time, eons ago, when he had climbed the rose trellis and watched her in her peignoir in front of this same mirror. And Solomon somewhere out there in the darkness, Erich's constant friend and support system. There—but too embarrassed to show himself, even when Erich made her the gift of a puppy.

Watching Erich kiss her.

Watching her let him.

She had insisted on having this bedroom before agreeing to move back to the estate. The move, he had said, would prove her sincerity to Hitler and Goebbels. Perhaps he secretly hoped that the move would placate her. The estate, hers by birthright after her uncle's and grandmother's death, had been stolen by the Nazis...and now, ironically, was hers again. To use, but not to own. And for a price.

She had allowed Erich to apply to have her status changed from Jew to Aryan.

To further placate her, he had indulged her trivial request for the bedroom. That was the trick to getting what she wanted: convince him an issue was trivial.

"Do I look beautiful enough for your precious Führer's party?"

"Almost perfect, my darling." Erich came inside.

"Almost perfect?" she said as flippantly as she could.

"Wear this and you'll look absolutely perfect." He put his hand in his pocket and took out a necklace. "Here."

He reached in front of her and centered a large sapphire above her décolletage. "It matches your eyes." He bent to kiss the back of her neck before fastening the delicate gold chain beneath her hair. "My God!" He stood back to look at her reflection. "You just get more lovely."

Heart thumping, she fingered the necklace. "Where did you find this? It belonged to..."

"Your Oma."

She clamped down on her rising rage and fought with the clasp, trying to open it. "I can't wear it!" she said, momentarily losing control. "I can't go tonight. You'll have to say I'm ill—"

"Don't be hysterical," he said coolly. "The necklace looks magnificent, and I've already made excuses for you once too often. It was an honor to be invited. This is important to me. To us."

To me and us, only a different *us*, she thought, knowing she had to pull herself together in case someone at the party had a message for her from the underground.

"I suppose I can't let my dressmaker down." She forced a half-smile. "She would never forgive me if I didn't show off her creation. She tells me it's going to be polka dots for the opera season, if Berlin still has an opera house by then."

"I've been meaning to ask why you go to Baden-Baden for your dresses. Are there no seamstresses here, in Berlin?"

"Of course there are. But I like Madame Pérrault. I've known her since I was a young girl." She stopped. She must be careful to say just enough and not too much. When Konnie drove her to Baden-Baden, they spent only minutes with the seamstress; the rest of the time was devoted to meeting with various members of the underground, for whom she acted as liaison here in Berlin.

"Remember Nabokov, my tennis instructor?" she asked him.

He nodded, his expression telling her that he had not forgotten his childish jealousy of what he took to be the man's obvious desire for young Miss Rathenau.

"This woman was his mistress," Miriam went on. "He deserted her when his first book came out, and she came to me for help. As you see, she is good at what she does."

She got up and showed off the full effect of the dress.

"You'll be the belle of the ball."

"The belly of the ball's more like it! I'm getting fat. I'm getting fat without my dancing. Maybe I should have had her make the dress in some simple fabric and fashion—something more suitable for a matron of the Reich."

Erich laughed. "You'll never look matronly, *Prinzessin*. Not even if you were...pregnant."

Miriam met his gaze in the mirror. Such an event was unlikely. They had not had intercourse for a couple of months, and it had been a fortnight since he had even slept with her, preferring his own bedroom for reasons she could not fathom. Whatever the cause, she was thankful.

Unable to pass up the opportunity for sarcasm, however, she added, "And if I were? How would you feel about that, Erich? After all, my blood is tainted no matter how many times I renounce my faith. Could you dare love a child that would be a *Mischling*—half-breed?"

The color rose in his cheeks, and she thought she had gone too far, but he simply shrugged and said quietly, "If you were carrying my child, I'd strut around like a Pfaueninsel peacock, and the hell with anyone worried about genealogy."

Miriam chuckled. "Peacock strutting is conduct unbecoming of an officer of the Reich." She wished there were more moments like this. He generally took himself and his damn Party so seriously, it was hard for her to recall if he had the capacity for anything else.

"It's good to hear you laugh," he said.

He reached for his cigarette case, clicked it open, and automatically offered her a smoke. When she shook her head, he took out one of the fashionable flat cigarettes he smoked on formal occasions, and lit it with the engraved lighter his parents had given him when they reopened the shop. He inhaled and blew several smoke rings. She watched them drift toward the ceiling.

"Time to go." He removed his formal jacket from the wardrobe.

Miriam stared at the armband, as if its white circle and red and black emblem were an adder about to strike.

"Our dear Gauleiter has already grown impatient and gone on without us," he said.

"Don't worry. As long as he had his schnapps, he won't care. Why on earth did you ask him to come here before the party anyway?"

"He keeps making such a point of telling me how much he misses living here at the estate. " He paused and glanced down at his arm. "I have to wear it," he said coldly.

She had not realized that she was still staring at the armband. "You like to wear it."

"Let's not start that again."

She turned back to the mirror and removed Oma's necklace. Fiddling with the row of minute pearl buttons that ran from her lace-edged décolletage to her waistline, she said, "I'm sorry, Erich. The necklace holds too many memories." She picked up the double pearl choker he had given her for her birthday and struggled with the clasp.

"Women! I give up." Erich sighed and helped her with the necklace. "Now we really do have to go."

Chapter 2

Less than half an hour later, Konrad pulled up outside Schloss Gehrhus. Two cars were ahead of them. Miriam watched as men in evening dress and women in gowns and furs stepped out. They wore the somber colors that were reputedly the Führer's preference, all but one, an ambassador's wife who had—or so Erich had told her—graced his bed upon more than one occasion. She was tall and angular, quite beautiful. A silver mink dangled from her arm. Her gown was midnight blue, beaded across the right shoulder in silver bugle beads and black sequins.

A little dressmaker in Baden-Baden, no doubt, Miriam thought cynically. Turning her head, she looked at the castle's façade. No sequins there. The architecture was severe, if not dull—more like Jagdschloss Grünewald, the famous hunting lodge, than a castle.

Inside, as she recalled from the visits of her youth, opulence gave lie to the exterior. The castle, built by one Dr. Pannwitz, personal attorney to his Majesty Kaiser Wilhelm II, had long been a gathering place for important people. Politicians, artists, scientists and diplomats from all over the world had met there, striding across its oriental carpets, exchanging confidences under its crystal chandeliers, dancing across the parquet floor of its two-storied mirrored ballroom. The Kaiser himself had been the first guest to enter the house, shortly before the outbreak of the Great War.

Konrad opened the car door.

"How long do we have to stay?" Miriam asked.

"As long as seems expedient," Erich said curtly. Apparently immediately regretting the brusqueness of his answer, he reached for her gloved hand. She pulled it away. "I'm sorry, *Prinzessin,*" he said. "I have much on my mind. And this is, after all, the Führer's birthday celebration."

On his actual birthday, on the twentieth of April, Hitler was at Berchtesgaden with Eva and his cronies. By his order, the streets of Berlin had been filled with open crates of oranges; the crates would be replenished all week.

Tonight, three days later, the leaders of his "master race" were gathering at Schloss Gehrhus to eat caviar and pheasant and drink champagne to his continued good health.

"How many celebrations does that madman need!" she asked.

Hoping that someone from the underground would be here with a message for her to pass along so she could rationalize her presence to herself, she allowed Konnie to help her from the car. She pulled her cape around her shoulders and followed Erich up the stone steps and into the entry hall. It was filled with people. Champagne flowed freely and flowers streamed over the balustrades, fresh roses and carnations from the estate which ranged across more than twelve thousand square meters.

"Doesn't such extravagance make you at all uncomfortable?" She tugged at her gloves.

"I can never walk in here without wanting to touch everything." He looked as excited as a sailor confronted by the infinite variety of Amsterdam's red-light district.

He lusts after the oriental carpets and mahogany balustrades, she thought. She took in the gilt-edged chairs and matching tapestry-covered walls, the vaulted ceilings carved with inlaid wood, the giant arrangements of agapanthus and gladioli in the entryway. From the dining hall she could hear *"Für Elise,"* one of Hitler's favorites, and the buzz of conversation.

"So you two lovebirds finally decided to grace us with your presence," Goebbels called out from across the foyer. Short and spare, he leaned toward them as he hoisted the inevitable glass of schnapps in a mock toast. "Perhaps now we can eat."

As he moved toward them, the chandelier caught the movement of the silver-haired man who had been standing against the wall in the shadows, behind the Gauleiter. Heart pounding, she thought she recognized the man responsible for giving orders outside the cigar shop, on the day of Jacob's death.

"We shall talk more later, Otto," Goebbels said, over his shoulder.

The tall man clicked his heels. "Certainly, Gauleiter. It will be my pleasure."

Hearing the voice, Miriam was certain that she was right. "Erich, that's—?" she began.

Goebbels was already at her side and she could say no more. She gave him the closest approximation she could manage of a smile, and instantly wished she had not when he offered her his arm. Erich was forced to escort Magda. Miriam could feel him watching her, feel his ridiculous jealousy. Apparently he could not help himself, no matter who the man was. He had even flinched when she so much as mentioned Nabokov with the least bit of affection in her voice.

The four of them wandered into the dining hall. According to Erich, there were fifty invited couples—one for each year of the Führer's life.

They seemed all to be here, examining place cards at eight small tables set for ten people apiece. The rest, including the Goebbels, who quickly excused themselves, floated toward the head table, where one seat remained conspicuously empty, waiting for a host who seldom arrived until the meal was well underway.

As drums rolled, a group of boys from the Adolf Hitler school, apprentices for the Hitler Elite Guard, entered the dining hall. Seven years in training, culminating in the honor of service to their Führer, Miriam thought, first as waiters at his birthday party, later in the SS or at some foreign Front.

The youths were assisted by pigtailed girls from the RAD—*the new human beings,* they were called—wearing white pinafores, orange kerchiefs and the royal blue shirts that marked them as new members. They were supervised by graduate black-uniformed Elite Guard members while the female graduates, distinguishable by their white shirts and ties, navy skirts and aprons, were relegated to the kitchen and the reception area.

The orchestra switched to Strauss.

"Prosit!" Erich lifted his glass and addressed the officer across from him, but his gaze was on Miriam.

Lift your glass, she told herself. Respond to the music. Smile. Eat. Look as if you want to be here. But though the meal was exquisitely prepared, she barely picked at her food. Even the dessert of raspberries and crème fraiche held no appeal.

"Champagne?"

"Thank you. Pour it for me. I'll be right back."

"Feeling all right, my dear? Like me to accompany you?" The officer's wife gave her an emphatic *You must be in the family way* glance.

Miriam dabbed at her lips with the linen serviette. "No thank you. Most kind of you, but I'm fine."

She left the room and was headed to the garden when she spotted a narrow staircase barred with a chain and a sign that warned her not to go beyond it. Picking up the candle-lantern that stood on the bottom step, she unhooked the chain and made her way up the stairs to the grand ballroom.

This was not her first visit to Schloss Gehrhus. She had been here before with her uncle at a diplomatic function honoring a group of visitors from South America. What a fuss they had made of her—the exquisite Miriam Rathenau! She had danced all night, up here, mostly with a handsome young diplomat-in-training, a South American attached to the Italian Embassy. Of course he was too old for her, but for a few days she had walked around with the glassy-eyed look of young love while her uncle teased her unmercifully, especially when roses arrived for her the following morning.

A week later, her uncle had informed her with mock-sadness that Juan Perón had left for Rome. In the throes of her first "desertion," she had sworn never to come back to the Schloss—especially not up here.

She placed the lantern on the floor and gave herself up to a harmless memory of a time long gone, and then to a time more recent. A time of hope for a safe future, when for a moment she had believed Erich's assurances, believed that he would be able to provide Sol with safe transit to Amsterdam.

Surrounded by mirrors and haunted by a harmonica, she closed her eyes and slowly waltzed, remembering the last bittersweet hours she had spent with Sol in the dust-covered remains of what had once been the Kaverne.

Sol had put his finger to her lips and picked up a candle. Taking her hand, he had led her up the stairs and into the cabaret. On the dusty dance floor, amid the pallor of greenish light beaming down through one of the few small, stained-glass windows that remained unbroken, he lifted her knuckles to his lips and closed his eyes.

"There is a season for all things, Miri," she remembered him saying. "They have turned this into a season of endings. Let us defy them and make it one of beginnings. Marry me."

"Here? Tonight? And who will be the rabbi?"

"God."

They had stood among dusty muslin sheets, thrown carelessly over once-new tables and chairs surrounding an abandoned dance floor in a closed cabaret in a world seemingly without hope, and uttered words that denied Berlin, the Reich, Erich, and hopelessness. They spoke of ultimately finding freedom and a life together in South America.

They spoke of marriage, and of enduring love.

She squeezed his hands, and smiled. "Make two stacks of three tables each. I'll be right back." By the time Sol had the tables piled up in the center of the dance floor, Miriam had returned, the rose-colored shawl that she had worn that first night in the cabaret retrieved from the costume trunk.

"We have to have a canopy, don't we? It wouldn't be a wedding without one."

Before he could say anything else she had left again, this time to retrieve a hidden bottle of burgundy and three dusty glasses.

Wriggling out of her slip, she wrapped it around one of the glasses, placed it under the canopy, and twirled around to show him the spray of lavender silk lilac she had twisted into her hair.

Now, standing in the Grand Ballroom of Schloss Gehrhus, she touched the fresh sprig of lilac in her hair. Her eyes misted with tears. In her mind's eye, she watched Solomon pull a harmonica from his pocket and blow into it to clear it of dust. She saw him cup the instrument lovingly in his hands, and felt him watch her sway as he softly played one of her favorite Schubert melodies.

When he had finished, he fished in his pocket, pulled out two cigars, and removed their gold bands—the ones she now kept hidden in her music box, among the gaudy jewelry she wore to impress Erich's fellow officers.

That night, as dusk faded and shadows lengthened, she and Solomon had held fast to each other and to their dream of a tomorrow. When night came, so did Konrad.

"The train for Amsterdam leaves in just over half an hour, and you are expected at the flat," Konnie had told her, glancing at the wristwatch she had brought him from America.

"One dance, my love."

She whispered the words to the walls of the empty ballroom, as she had to Solomon then.

Back then, warmed by wine and passion, she and Sol had danced to imaginary violins playing Schubert and Strauss and Brahms. Now she danced alone, not for want of a partner, but because the only partner she wanted was lost to her, perhaps forever, except in memory.

"May I have this dance?"

She looked up at Erich and graced him with one of her rare, open smiles. "You caught me," she said.

He bowed and took her in his arms. "Do you have any idea how beautiful you are, Miriam?"

"It's this room," she said softly. With a graceful sweep of her arm, she guided his gaze to the ballroom ceiling, two stories high, to the twenty floor-to-ceiling mirrors, each reflecting the soft glow of the lantern, to the moon, shining through the beveled French doors and adding its shadows to the fairy-tale glow.

"It's not simply the room, Fräulein," another voice said.

Miriam's sweeping gesture faltered and froze in mid-air as Erich whirled around to face the Führer, who stood at the top of the forbidden stairway, arms crossed in the familiar pose.

"Forgive me. You must be Frau Alois. Herr Rittmeister, where have you been hiding this extraordinary creature? May I have the pleasure?" He stepped toward them. "You don't mind, do you, Alois? After all, it is my birthday. It is only fair that I be allowed to dance with the most beautiful woman at my celebration."

Erich nodded and let go of Miriam's waist. He watched as Hitler pushed her stiffly around the floor to the strains of Strauss.

Somehow, she thought, I will get through this moment.

"I saw the light from outside and came up here first." The Führer wiped her sweat from his palms as the notes faded. "How fortunate that I did. You are a wonderful dancer. Now, however, we should join my other guests."

Asking forgiveness of Sol, Miriam held onto Hitler's arm and allowed herself to be ushered downstairs and into the dining hall. The band switched to *"Deutschland über Alles,"* and Erich saluted with the others.

"Hoch soll sie leben!" They toasted their Führer. "May he live well."

Smiling a pinched smile, Hitler acknowledged the repeated good wishes as he made his way to the main table. When he was seated, the orchestra renewed its evening of Strauss with "The Blue Danube."

"Why didn't anybody ever tell Strauss that the Danube is grey and dirty, not blue?" Miriam said irritably.

Erich was too busy watching Hitler to respond. The Führer was going through his ritual of consuming a quantity of tablets, probably Dr. Koster's strychnine and atropine anti-gas pills, which he took constantly to reduce the flatulence that reputedly plagued him.

Wishing he would choke on them, Miriam also watched the ritual. When it was over, Hitler leaned across the table and spoke to his Gauleiter who, face red with fury, whispered something to his wife and stood up.

After making his way to Erich's table, Goebbels said in an icy tone, "The Führer wishes to have you and your wife dine with him."

"No, Erich," Miriam whispered. She had done enough for him tonight, dancing with Hitler, smiling at the rest of his sick ménage, and not even a message from the underground to make her feel useful. "I—" She looked at his face and gave up.

This was not going to be one of the times to expect indulgences.

Chapter 3

"Please...be seated." Hitler waved at the chairs vacated by Dr. and Frau Goebbels. "Tell me more about this beautiful woman." His tone was genial. Expansive. "Can she really be the niece of that traitor Rathenau?"

"Walther Rathenau was—"

"Her adopted uncle," Erich said, finishing Miriam's sentence. "She was adopted by his sister and brother-in-law, mein Führer."

"Where are they, these people?"

"Dead, mein Führer."

"Just as well." Hitler scrutinized Miriam as if she were a piece of fruit and he a prospective customer making sure there were no bruises. "With your grace and beauty, you could be a wonderful tool for the Reich. I have been assured that you believe in our cause and reject that Jew's philosophies."

He turned to Erich. "Pity she is so dark, although they tell me that can be easily remedied these days—"

A drum roll announced the presentation of Hitler's birthday gift, a globe whose uneven surface outlined the world's topography. Erich was grateful for the interruption; he could feel the heat of Miriam's wrath rising from her like steam from a radiator. He held onto the hope that the distraction would remove the Führer's attention from her, but no sooner had the orchestra resumed playing than Hitler returned to the same topic.

"We must let the newspeople ascertain that she was adopted. Exposed to Jewish blood, but not possessed of any. I will make the necessary arrangements."

"Thank you, mein Führer, but we have already applied to the Reichs Department for Genealogical Research to invoke the 1934 edict you yourself wrote," Erich said.

"Good!" Hitler turned to Miriam. "I will contact Leni Riefenstahl and make sure she puts you in her next propaganda film."

There was only one way he was going to get Miriam to do this, Erich knew. Again he would have to use Solomon's safety as a bargaining tool. He would even offer to try again to "find" Sol. Good thing he had mailed that letter to Amsterdam, effectively stopping the flood of correspondence to Miriam. It had been tiresome intercepting everything, and even more tiresome having to change the telephone number at the old place. It was better now that they had moved to the estate; even if Sol forgave her, he would not attempt to contact Miriam there.

"What a pity she is not expecting a child." Hitler's voice had become shrill. Excited. People around them looked up and listened. "You are a Nazirite, the true Biblical figurehead of commitment."

The man was beginning to ramble, something he did frequently. His five-minute audiences were notorious for lasting hours; people left them exhausted and confused.

"Even the Christian God, you know, though spineless, ordained our triumphs." Hitler laughed, pleased with himself. "Ordained," he repeated. "Like my departure from art into politics. Have I ever told you, Alois, how that came to pass?"

His voice turned soft. Dreamy. "I was in a hospital, having been overcome by mustard-gas fumes on a train. While recovering from my ordeal, I heard voices, Alois. They told me what to do."

Mustard fumes! Voices! The man's as crazy as Solomon, Erich thought.

Another drum roll saved him from further speculation.

"It is time for the entertainment." Goebbels stood up to make the announcement. "Let us proceed outdoors."

"I must talk to you," Miriam whispered.

"Later."

"Now!"

"Talk, then." Erich dawdled behind the others, who were hurrying into the garden. He knew what had been planned. He had seen it all before, had taken part in a similar ceremony usually reserved for Midsummer Night.

"You must promise me something," Miriam said urgently. "I cannot make such a film!"

"Miriam." He was pleading with her. "How can I promise you that? You heard what he said."

"Who is he—God? I can't! I won't!"

"Think of Solomon if you will not think of me," Erich said.

"Is that a threat?"

"It's a statement of fact."

"What will happen if I refuse to do this thing? Will you let them take your *friend* from your Führer's precious camp and hang your *friend* in public?"

Erich searched for a lie by omission to pacify her, if only for the moment. Lies by omission were easier, less likely to ricochet.

"I must see for myself that Sol is all right," she said.

"We have been over this a thousand times." He spoke as patiently as he could. "You cannot go to Solomon. The danger to both of you is worse now."

"You mean danger to you," she said flatly.

"You're no fool, Miriam. The Führer's attention is on you—"

"*There* you are, Herr Rittmeister," Goebbels said. For once Erich was grateful for the Gauleiter's appearance on the scene. "I wish to speak to you for a minute."

"Certainly, Herr Minister."

The two men moved ahead of Miriam as they walked toward the lawns at the back of the Schloss Gehrhus estate.

"The Führer has told me to contact Riefenstahl regarding Miriam." Goebbels' voice remained icy. "I will, of course, do his bidding, but—"

"But what?" Erich sensed he was not going to like what was coming; he would have to watch his back more closely than ever.

"In my opinion, your wife's reformation needs something more. A doctor at the Sachsenhausen camp, Schmidt by name, has some interesting ideas. She is conducting experiments..." He paused, then quickly added, "I have suggested to the Führer that Miriam take part in those experiments."

"Experiments?" Erich tried not to sound afraid, but his voice was gravelly.

"Total blood transfusions." Goebbels smiled. "Don't look so shocked. After all, if Miriam were to be transfused with Aryan blood, no one would dispute her place beside you in the New Order."

"Isn't such an operation...dangerous?"

"We must all take risks for the Fatherland, Herr Rittmeister."

Goebbels veered to the right and the conversation ended.

Drawing on deep reserves of self-discipline, Erich set his face in a smile and waited for Miriam to catch up. He would have to worry about this new issue later, he decided, as, arm around her waist, he guided her toward a group of RAD girls and students from the Adolf Hitler School. They had gathered in a circle around a blazing fire.

To one side of them stood a woman dressed in the uniform of the RAD graduates. "The young people before you have formed a magic circle around the sacred flames. They have been taught that the highest honor they can receive is to lay down their lives for the Fatherland." Her voice was deep as a man's.

"From Rhineland Hills blaze upward and ascend," she said in a chant. "Let those of you with dreams of a heroic future dedicated to our Fatherland take hands and leap over the flames to prove your love for our Führer and for our cause."

Two-by-two, holding hands and laughing, the new human beings and students of the Adolf Hitler School leapt over the flames and ran into the woods.

"Could we please leave now, Erich?" Miriam asked, when only the flames and the adults remained.

Erich looked at her face. She had her eyes shut and looked as if she were about to faint. "Let us say our farewells," he said, leading her over to the Führer.

"Yes. Good night." Hitler waved his hand arbitrarily, as if he had already forgotten both of them.

"What will happen if I refuse to make the film?" Miriam asked on the way home.

"To whom?"

"To all of us. Me, you, Solomon?"

Omission, Erich reminded himself. But because he could not find a half truth that would serve the purpose, he said nothing.

As they drove along Brahmstrasse, away from Schloss Gehrhus and toward the Rathenau estate, he kept wanting to touch her hand. When he finally did, at least for the few minutes that it took to get to their destination, she did not pull away. Usually his displays of affection were met with neutrality, if not coldness. He was grateful for even so small a concession. Neither of them spoke again until she stood in the doorway of her bedroom.

"What about Solomon and your conscience?" she asked then, as if the conversation had not been broken.

There was no answer he could give her, so he simply kissed her lightly and retired to his quarters. He was barely in bed when a knock sounded on the door downstairs. Grumbling, he climbed from bed and drew on his robe, a garment given him by a youthful whore Goebbels had brought home for a week after his trip to Lisbon. The girl's name was *Toy*. He could recall that much because he not heard the name before or since, but he hardly remembered the girl herself. He did, however, love the black silk robe with its red fire-breathing dragon embroidered on the back. Most of all he loved it because it reminded him of Goebbels' anger upon discovering that Erich had bedded her. The man had threatened to chop her into dog meat for the kennels and had, in fact, given her to his guards...all twenty of them. Rumor had it she now was working the Elbe waterfront.

The knock came again, louder this time. Knotting the robe's sash, Erich descended the steps with a certain sense of urgency. Even now, after midnight, his men were putting the shepherds through obedience drills. At this hour, it could only be a trainer having problems with one of the dogs.

He glanced up at the crossed Nazi flags above the front door. The midnight sky peered in the tall front window; the mace-wielding suit of armor that stood in the corner, beside the aquarium he had recently acquired for Miriam's amusement, seemed to be waiting for him to open the door.

The knock came a third time.

"All right, all right! I'm coming!"

He opened the door a crack, then threw it wide open. A soldier stood there, a messenger. He saluted and handed Erich a sealed envelope. The letter had Hitler's personal blue seal.

Erich felt his blood run cold. Trembling, he slit open the envelope with his finger. What if Goebbels had talked Hitler into demanding that Miriam have the transfusion? What would he do? Hide her, promise again to send her away? What a waste that would be! Instead of using her talents, the Reich would lose out again. That seemed to be the leitmotiv of the Reich: abuse talent, beat out the brains of people who had so much to give, drive others into exile. If only Hitler, or that fat imbecile Göring, would wise up. The Führer had said in Erich's presence that the Jews and Gypsies would ultimately serve the state.

But as what? Fuel?

As long as Goebbels keeps seeing to it that I'm excluded from all important discussions with the Führer, he thought angrily, I will never know the answer.

"The Führer feels you're too emotionally tied to the situation," Goebbels had explained on one of his many returns to the mansion that had been his private brothel. "He's afraid you could not examine the issue with enough dispassion. But you can be sure we will keep your ideas concerning re-education of the Jews at the forefront of our discussions."

The soldier cleared his throat. Erich opened the envelope and focused on the paper with its official letterhead. He laughed. A promotion to major! Immediate, and at the Führer's personal behest.

It all was too good to be true. His moving from being in charge of security at the estate to running the place...that goddamn Otto Hempel out of his hair, transferred to helping run the detention camp outside Oranienburg...and now this!

"Happy birthday to you," he said. Paper in one hand and envelope in the other, he danced around the foyer. *"Hoch soll er leben_—"*

As if they had heard him, the dogs began to bark.

"Do you hear them? My dogs?" he asked the soldier. "It seems the Führer has finally understood that they could be a major force in a blitzkrieg operation. Think of it! A canine commando unit, trained to infiltrate and neutralize enemy advance units!"

The young man stared at him with a dazed expression. Erich smiled pleasantly at him. "It's late, soldier. Go home to bed."

The soldier saluted and half-ran toward his motorcycle, as if anxious to get away from this strange man who danced around hallways in a silk kimono.

Not ready to go back upstairs, Erich went outside. Though it was not yet May, an early warm spell had fooled the chestnut trees into blossoming. The scent was sweet, like a woman perfumed to please her man. If only Miriam...

He discarded the thought.

They had lived together at the estate for well over a year, and not once had she indicated even the slightest softening in her attitude toward him. Small wonder he could become erect with her only when he gave himself over to his anger...*to baser instincts*, he forced himself to admit. How had the Führer worded the edict? When it came to Jewish women, "the soldiers' baser instincts are not to be denied." It disgusted him. Potent only when he imagined himself raping her—what kind of lovemaking was that, even if he thought for a moment she was truly his? Was there no circumventing the reality of whom she belonged to, at least while Solomon was alive?

Nothing but a poor substitute for a sparrow such as Solomon Freund. What a price to pay for the love of one woman! He had no such problems with the rental ladies he brought to the apartment to service his needs, so, clearly, the fault lay with Miriam. Her bedroom seemed almost an arena for trial by combat, one he could win only by trampling down the sanctity of his beliefs like so much clover. The pride he felt in denying himself the God-given right as her husband, of taking her as often and as thoroughly as he pleased, brought him some satisfaction, but nothing, he was certain, to equal what he would feel when she eventually came to him of her own free will.

Some night she would be his. Completely. Without his having to degrade her in his mind while he took her. And without thought of what she or Solomon could gain by it. *Then* he would show her the lovemaking of which he was capable! Had not his capacity for multiple orgasms earned him the name Javelin Man among Frau Goebbels' socialite friends? Meanwhile, he would keep Miriam guessing, wondering why he was sleeping apart from her. For most women, rejection was an aphrodisiac. Why not for her?

Determined to continue in his current mode, he hurried toward the kennels. At least his dogs gave him what he needed—unqualified love and respect.

He wondered if dogs had a conscience, and then laughed at the absurdity of questioning a dog's morality. Such a thing could not possibly exist within their framework. They would not care if one of their fellows was in a place like Sachsenhausen, or even if their master were a human cur like Otto Hempel. What might it feel like to be truly amoral, to live only for obedience and food, for sleep and the praise of your master?

"Kinemann," he called out as he approached the kennels. "Could I see you for a moment?"

The trainer, a pudgy corporal, was kneeling next to Aries, holding her firmly by her collar. Though the dog appeared to be calm, Erich could sense the fury that rippled beneath her fur.

"The dogs are restless tonight," the trainer said.

"Any special reason?"

Kinemann looked at Erich strangely, as if he were not quite sure if he or the dog were being addressed. "I'm not certain, Sir."

As he had been able to do since early childhood, Erich tuned in to the dog's consciousness. She growled softly, a visceral rumble like an instrument tuning up for an overture.

Erich felt his anger mount. "The motorcycle disturbed her. This one's always been extremely sensitive," he said.

Erich knew that there was not enough space, even on this large estate, for the kind of kennels he would prefer—where the comings and goings of motorcars and bikes would not disturb trainer-shepherd concentration. He had performed miracles with the dogs, glad that Hitler himself knew enough to insist that each dog respond to the command of its individual trainer *and* to Erich, the officer in charge. That way, order could be maintained if the trainer were killed during a military action.

But that was not enough.

Given the right place, isolated, tall trees and meadows, the right combination of love and discipline, his shepherds could be trained to do almost anything.

Chapter 4

November 1938

Miriam glanced around Friedrich Ebert Strasse at the aftermath of *Kristallnacht*.

Seven months ago, she thought, *moonlight shone through the glass of Schloss Gehrhus. Now all windows everywhere are shattered.*

The sun shone on remnants of broken glass, still unswept after gangs of young Nazis, many of them driving cars, went on a rampage. *Cars,* for God's sake, she thought. They actually *drove* during the riot. Leaned out of motorcar windows to smash thousands of store fronts belonging to Jewish merchants and destroy hundreds of Jewish homes. Looting, robbing, killing. When would such carnage end!

How ironic that a young Polish Jew, Herschel Grynspan, had inadvertently sparked this recent night of so-called retribution. Distraught over the treatment his parents had received in Germany and intent on assassinating the German ambassador, Grynspan had murdered Ernst von Rath, a minor German official living at the Parisian consulate—only to find out, Konnie had told her, that von Rath was been under Gestapo scrutiny for *opposing* anti-Semitism.

According to news reports, Grynspan, under arrest in Paris, said, "Being a Jew is not a crime. I am not a dog. I have a right to live and the Jewish people have a right to exist on this earth. Wherever I have been, I have been chased like an animal."

"What a goddamn mess. About time you got here." Erich's father unlocked the door of the shop and signaled her inside. "I'll be leaving right away." He adjusted his tie and buttoned the waistcoat of his Sunday suit. "And you can tell your chauffeur this will be the last time you'll need him here. After what happened earlier this week, I've requested a security guard for the shop at night, and for Sundays."

At least the synagogue in her suburb, Grünewald, had not been desecrated, not yet. Still, with so many synagogues stoned and Berlin's main synagogue burned to the ground, she was worried about her friend, Beadle Cohen, the custodian-scholar who had taught Solomon so much about religion and about life.

"You don't need anyone else here on Sundays," she told Herr Weisser, afraid that acceptance on her part would endanger the already tenuous safe-house of the ancient sewer that ran beneath the tobacco shop and what had been the cabaret, below the furrier's next door. In the seven months that had passed since Hitler's birthday party at Schloss Gehrhus, she had provided sanctuary for an ever-increasing number of people.

Konnie was essential for her to continue such work. He was the only one she could trust to guard the shop while she guided transients through the deserted cabaret and into the sewer. After last Wednesday's terrors, there was sure to be increased demand for a place to hide until night claimed the streets.

Needing access to the sewer, she had traded on the fact that the Weissers also accorded her, their son's wife, no more status than an animal. She was right. They had jumped at her offer to be their unpaid Sunday Jew, to keep the shop open while they went to Mass and cleansed their souls. They equally readily agreed to let her stay on for the rest of the day while Friedrich played poker with the other newly affluent merchants of Friedrich Ebert Strasse, whose poker stakes also came from tills conveniently "neglected" by Jews.

As she had known it would be, her offer was irresistible: free labor from someone who knew the shop, someone it pleased them to denigrate. Six days a week she moved in the same circles as Goebbels and even the Führer; on Sunday she stepped down from her high-and-mighty pedestal and assumed her true identity—a Jew dancer turned shop girl after she had frittered away her fortune; the seducer of their beloved son and the reason he never visited, ashamed to face their disapproval for his poor matrimonial choice.

Miriam turned on the lights and readied herself for another ten hours at the shop. She glanced at herself in the counter glass as she removed the two crossed diamond hatpins she had placed in her hat as carefully as if she were going to a garden party. It was a navy-blue picture hat. The soft waves of her auburn hair were visible in front, but the rest had been pulled into a severe bun from which only tiny wisps escaped. The heron feathers that decorated the hat were the latest fashion, and the hue made her eyes look the color of iodine. Her dress was a low-cut navy woolen affair with a white lace collar and a fitted waist. Where her décolletage ended, she had clipped a lavender shell cameo; each of her high-heeled boots was decorated with a dozen tiny buttons. The boots, long out of fashion, reminded her of her grandmother.

She had told Erich she'd found the boots on the estate and the hat and dress on a pile of discarded clothes and furniture outside the home of the

Weintraub family, who had been transported from the apartments across the street the previous Saturday. The truth was, the clothing was a gift directly from Frau Weintraub in gratitude for being hidden downstairs in the sewer one Sunday. She had waited there to be spirited out through Kaverne in the early hours of the following morning. Where she was now was anybody's guess.

"I'm hungry," she told Konrad, who stood at the door staring impassively out on the street.

He nodded at the code and went to the car. When he returned, he carried a large shopping bag which held their food for the day. Without further discussion, he went downstairs to add that to the supplies they had already secreted in the sewer.

"I really am hungry," she said, when he came back upstairs.

"Me too. Should I go back down and bring up something for us?"

She shook her head. "There's little enough in the way of supplies. Whoever's there next will need it more than we do. You know what I'd really like? A Berliner *Bulette!*" Unlike many other Germans, who derided Americans for calling the beefsteak *ham*burger, Miriam knew that the sandwich had originated in Hamburg, New York. She had lived in the United States, touring the country and learning American dances, for four years following the Great War.

Reaching into her own shopping bag, she pulled out a bar of chocolate and a package that contained one of the new so-called unbreakable gramophone records. She had bought the old kind first and clumsily dropped it on the sidewalk; the record had shattered like a Jewish windowpane.

"How long should I go on believing Erich wants to protect Sol, Konnie?" She split the chocolate bar and handed him half. "Sometimes I think his protestations are about as solid as that record I dropped yesterday. For all I know, Solomon's dead...."

It had been two years since Erich learned that Sol had not made it out of Germany, that he was in a camp. Two years since, to protect Sol, she had consented to a marriage ceremony and moved into the estate with Erich. At first, thinking Sol safely in Amsterdam and believing that Erich was working on getting her out of the country—she had lived as a virtual prisoner in his apartment.

That was better, she thought; being at the estate hurt too much. At least at the flat they had made one person happy: Erich's landlady. She had been delighted with the extra money he had given her to keep her mouth shut.

"Don't worry, mein Herr," the landlady had said. "For my part, Satan can hump the Virgin Mary in this house, as long as the authorities stay away. I have nothing against Jews—only against *poor* Jews."

What might she have said had she known Erich was housing Walther Rathenau's only living relative!

Two figures approaching the shop distracted Miriam from her thoughts. When they got close, she saw that one of them was Beadle Cohen. He carried a satchel and held a boy by the hand, a gamin of about nine who wore black pants and a gray shirt, and whose eyes looked glassy. Blank. The look, she fearfully realized, of shock.

"We need help, Miriam," the beadle whispered without preamble. "This is Misha Czisça." Leaning forward, he whispered, "His parents, Rabbi Czisça and his wife...transported."

The beadle stopped and released the boy's hand. He bent down. Looking into the child's eyes, he said, "Listen to me, Misha. We do not know where your parents are, or if they are. You must do whatever Miriam and I tell you. Now go and sit on the linoleum behind the counter, where you will not be seen, and practice your Hebrew lettering. Before you know it, you will be thirteen. You cannot neglect your bar mitzvah studies."

The boy did not answer, nor did he move. He stood in the middle of the shop, dry-eyed, a picture of stoicism. In one hand he held a notebook and a pencil.

"The main temple has been destroyed. Mine will probably be next," the beadle said, standing up. "The boy and I must get out of Germany. I have papers that, with luck, will get me to Copenhagen." He lowered his voice. "Somehow I'll get the boy through, too."

"And then?"

The beadle smiled. *"L'shanah haba-a b'Yerushalayim."*

"Next year in Jerusalem." Miriam repeated the ancient words that symbolized the Jews' hope for a safe harbor where they would always be welcome.

"Perhaps the following year." The old twinkle momentarily returned to the beadle's eyes. "Via New York, I hope. I intend to get to Holland first—I'll have the best chance of a berth from the Port of Amsterdam. While I wait, I'll find Sol's mother and sister."

"Don't tell them about Sol," Miriam said, "not even Recha. She might let it slip."

The beadle looked puzzled. "Surely you correspond with them?"

"I did, while Sol was with me. When Erich told me that Sol was captured...his mother has been in such a precarious state, I thought the truth might—" She stopped.

What *was* the truth? At first she had rationalized that the news of Sol's internment would kill his mother, that Sol would be out soon, that they had not known Sol was en route to Amsterdam in the first place. And there was Erich. Her life with him was so public. She had crumpled page after page of attempts to explain why she was with Erich. No matter what she wrote, her words sounded like a hollow series of excuses for choosing a soft life. She had finally dashed off a note, saying simply that Sol was safe and that they should not expect to hear from him until, with God's help, they saw him. Her letter had crossed with one from Recha, his sister. She had seen Miriam on the Movietone News, flanked by Erich and Hitler, laying a wreath at the foot of the memorial to her uncle's assassins. Further correspondence from Miriam, Recha said, would be returned unopened.

She had written back twice. Recha remained good as her word. She had not written again. And telephoning? Out of the question. She couldn't. She simply couldn't.

"Come with us to Amsterdam," the beadle said. "I am sure it can be arranged."

Miriam shook her head and thought about another letter, the one Erich had agreed to have delivered to Sol at the camp. He had censored it, made her phrase it so it would seem that she had chosen to be with Erich because she loved him. By the time she had determined to find a way to send an uncensored letter to Sol, someone—according to Erich, it was probably Goebbels or Hempel—had arranged for Sol's transfer to another camp. Erich said he had been unable to ferret out which one, and she had tried, too, with equally fruitless results. Since Sol had no way to communicate with her, she might never know if she had succeeded in her attempt to convey the truth between the heartless lines Erich had forced her to write.

"I'm sorry, Beadle," she said. "If I stay, Sol has a chance."

The beadle took her arm. "I understand. We must each be true to ourselves." Unexpectedly, he kissed her cheek. "Now, to the business at hand. You said that if I ever needed help, to come to you. You said you could hide me." He looked at the boy. "I must ask you to hide *us*."

Miriam was happy to replace words with action. "Of course," she said. "At once. But you must leave the safe-house before first light, through the empty cabaret next door. We jimmied the cabaret door, so you can slip in or out if need be. The sewer is not exactly the Hotel Kemp—"

She saw the boy stiffen and stopped in mid-word, mentally slapping herself on the wrist for her own thoughtlessness. The Kempinski was practically next door to the temple the ruffians had destroyed, and to the boy's home. Any mention of it would naturally cause him more pain.

"Ah yes, the Kempinski," the beadle said, as if by saying the word out loud he was removing her guilt at her tactlessness. Or if not removing it, make it a shared guilt, "The price and the service are better here."

"You are right on both counts," Miriam said. "I'm forced to breakfast there tomorrow, my once-a-week concession to Erich's insistence that we be seen out regularly together in public, *like any other married couple.*" She was struck, as always, by life's inequities. Where was it written that this good man and this innocent child had to hide like rats underground, while she, by accident of a somewhat skewed birth, lived out her social exile in physical comfort? "You'll be safe here for one night," she said.

"One night it is." The beadle smiled sadly, and tapped a fingernail against a tattered manuscript he drew out from under his coat. "I will make it as worthwhile a night as possible. And you and I, Miss Rathenau...will meet again."

Miriam also smiled, picturing the beadle and his charge huddled beneath candlelight over Hebrew lettering; even now, the learning would go on.

She leaned toward him and kissed him on the cheek. "Yes, Beadle Cohen," she said, mostly for the boy. "We will meet again. Next year, in Jerusalem."

Chapter 5

Misha huddled under the train-station bench and occupied himself by squinting upward through the slats at the lights hanging from the high roof overhead. He cupped a grubby hand over one eye and then the other, noting the way the lights appeared to be moving when he did that, even though he knew they were not.

It was the only thing he could think of with which to occupy himself until the train left with the beadle on it. He had to consider what he was going to do next.

His course had seemed perfectly clear and simple to him sitting in the sewer, awake while the beadle slept: stay in Berlin and find Mama and Papa. Exactly how he was going to find them, or how he was going to stay warm and fed during his search had seemed irrelevant then. Now that his stomach was rumbling and he was shivering from the cold November draught blowing across him from the open railroad tracks, he was less sure of himself. It was not that he was any less determined to keep his promise to himself to find his parents, he told himself; it was just that, like Mama and Papa always told him, it was a big world out here and he was only a small boy.

Forgetting his game, he flattened himself on his belly and looked up and down the platform. Though the ticket inspector was on the steps, a whistle in his mouth, the beadle continued to rush up and down the platform, with complete disregard for his own safety, looking for the boy. In his hand he held the satchel that Misha knew contained what food had been left in the sewer, minus the few pieces of bread and chocolate he had secreted away in his pocket.

Misha took out the chocolate, smelled it, felt himself salivate, but resisted the temptation to nibble. He allowed himself a corner crust of bread, and replaced that, too, in his pocket. His hunger could wait to be appeased, It wasn't going anywhere. It would sit there like something alive, making noises inside his stomach, and eventually he would have to eat. But not now. Not yet.

"Misha," the beadle yelled. "Mishele. *Nu, komm schon.* Come already. Do not do this foolhardy thing."

It was cold and draughty so low down near the cement of the station platform. Misha wrapped himself up with his own arms and determined that, no matter what happened, he would not cry. Not now or ever again.

Dry-eyed and feeling like a traitor, he watched the beadle give up the search and, holding his hands palms-up in exasperation, board the train. "Goodbye, Beadle Cohen," he whispered. "I'm sorry to be a trouble to you."

The inspector gave three long blasts on his whistle. The train rattled its own warning, chugged forward a hiccup, and stopped. A swirl of steam rolled down the platform. Misha watched it hopefully. If it reached him, it would improve the look of his wrinkled black pants and gray shirt, and warm him up a little.

Three short blasts on the whistle, and the beadle was gone.

There's no time to panic, Misha told himself, pushing away the feeling of total isolation that threatened immobility. What he needed now was a plan. That much he had to have. He could not just wander around Berlin. For one thing, by tonight the robbers and destroyers could own the streets again; for another, it would be cold and probably raining. Maybe even snowing.

He stood up and dusted himself off. He would run, if he knew in what direction. As he reached the cherub clock, someone called his name.

"Papa?"

Heart beating wildly, Misha turned around. Herr Becker, the owner of the bakery around the corner from the temple, waved from across the platform. He was a gentle man who used to put old bread out at the back for people to take to the Zoo Gardens to feed the ducks and the swans. Misha's hunger tempted him to answer, but then he remembered that Herr Becker didn't feed the birds anymore. Now, even when the bread was old and hard, he *sold* it. Readymade toast, Mama used to joke.

Misha waved back and turned to run, as if he were late for an appointment.

"Why is a cute little boy like you running around this place on his own?" A fat man held Misha by the arm and spun him around. He had a nasty glint in his eye and stank roundly of herring and beer. "If you don't have any place to go, you can always come with me. I know someone who would love to take a bite out of you." He smiled, showing a row of rotting teeth.

Stories about Georg Haarmann, murderer and cannibal, rose to the surface of Misha's memory. A fat, no-neck, heavy-jowled man like this, Misha was sure, ugly as a bulldog. Bet this one kidnapped boys and girls, too, and cut them up, and cooked them and ate them. And it was all true. Twenty years ago, Papa said, but true. He thought his papa had said the man was dead, but—

He shook himself loose, stumbled, fell, got up and ran on, feet automatically running in the direction of home.

Several blocks from the station, he finally slowed down. He looked into the shattered glass of a Jewish shop window and caught his fractured image. He had to look pretty closely to see even a glimpse of Rabbi Czisça's neat young son. For the first time, he noticed the hole in his pants his falling onto the pavement had caused. Such a klutz, Papa used to say. Other people wish they had a third eye in their heads to improve their psychic abilities, or in their chests to add to their understanding. Not our son. He needs a third eye underfoot.

Less afraid now of being recognized, but feeling no less hungry or helpless, he continued in the direction of home. Or what used to be home. He was almost at the Kempinski corner before he admitted to himself that he was being followed. He glanced back over his shoulder.

The no-neck man grinned, making no secret of being in pursuit.

Less afraid now that he was out in the open, in the streets, Misha crossed the street at Kempinski corner, and hovered at a gap in the hedge that separated the building from the people who walked the sidewalk. Between the glass windows of Kempinski Café and the hedge lay an outdoor dining area. Stacks of square green iron tables and chairs stood unusably wet from the early morning rain that lay in puddles in the narrow corridor.

Suddenly he heard the echo of Miriam's voice: *I'm forced to breakfast there tomorrow.*

There was the Kempinski, and today was yesterday's tomorrow, Misha walked quickly through the break in the foliage. Perhaps God had sent him a piece of luck because he was doing what Papa always told him, and helping himself.

Sure enough, as he neared the cafe's plate-glass window he saw Fräulein Miriam and a uniformed man seated at the table nearest the light. She must have been cold, for her coat was thrown around her shoulders. With one hand she toyed with a bowl of fresh strawberries; her other had lay ungloved on her lap, beneath the table. The man's uniform was different from the ones the men who had taken his parents away had worn, but it still succeeded in reminding him of them. A covered wicker basket of bread lay untouched between them, and a pot of what he assumed must be coffee.

As if she felt his presence, Miriam looked up and turned her head. She seemed to be looking straight at him, yet she did not react. Perhaps the glare of sunlight on the glass was distorting her view, he thought, moving to a different position.

He waved at her, and pointed at the table, expecting to be beckoned inside. Miriam started slightly, looked straight at him briefly, and shook her head. She made a similar gesture with the hand that was out of sight, pointed down the street, indicating that he should leave, and clenched her fist.

Shocked, he walked on, past the entrance to the hotel. He glanced into the lobby, at the huge displays of flowers, the knots of tourists and business men in pin-striped suits, the uniformed black-booted officers with their Gestapo leathers.

He was at the corner when the same fat male hand spun him around.

He kicked out and felt his toes connect. No-neck yelped and momentarily released the boy.

Giving no thought to direction, Misha took off at high speed —and barreled straight into a tall man in black.

"Hey, there, young man," Konrad said, his hand lightly but firmly on Misha's shoulder. "Where's the fire?"

Misha glanced quickly around. He was standing between the entrance to the Kempinski and the street where Miriam was seated half-in half-out of the back of a shiny limousine. No-neck had disappeared, as had the uniformed man. Was the uniformed man, Misha wondered, the one called Erich, of whom Fräulein Miriam had spoken when she talked to Beadle Cohen?

"Get him into the car and let's go, Konnie," Miriam said. She slid across the back seat of the car and patted the seat beside her. "Get in, Misha. Quickly. I'm late for the shop. We can talk on the way and you can tell me why you aren't on the train." She paled. "Did something happen to the beadle?"

"He's fine, Fräulein Miriam," he said. "I ran away and he looked for me but I hid, and—"

"Thank God. Now get in the car."

"But...but—"

"No buts. Get in."

Totally confused by her mixed message, Misha copied the gesture she had made earlier. "You shooed me away," he said, "like the son of Rabbi Czisça was a...a street beggar."

"I'm sorry, child. I did what I had to do. I'll explain later, I promise."

Shaking his head, not knowing whether to be grateful or terrified, Misha climbed into the car. As Konrad started the car and pulled away from the car, Misha knelt on the seat and looked out of the back window. At once, Miriam's hand came up to steady him. Its warmth comforted him almost as much as the fact that the fat, no-neck man was nowhere in sight.

Chapter 6

Kosher or not, Solomon had grown to like Amsterdam's Javanese food. He liked the variety, and the manner in which it was served—in many small bowls, and with condiments as varied as raw fish and sliced bananas. Except he was tired of eating alone.

Tonight, he decided, his mother and Recha would join him at the little restaurant he frequented when he sought diversion from teaching and his own studies, which currently centered on the relationship between present mystical thought and that of the ancients. His latest obsession was with the Lost Tribe, and with the Falashas—Ethiopian Jews who lacked knowledge of Hebrew and the Talmud, and who had priests rather than rabbis.

He chose the long route home from the temple where he taught Hebrew school. As always, on his *Spaziergang,* he mulled over the latest news from Berlin. It had been a month since *Kristallnacht;* the temple buzzed with talk of an underground, of German rabbis transported to camps, of cantors and beadles whose services, should the men escape, might become available to Dutch congregations.

After his two years in Amsterdam, Berlin seemed at last to be losing its hold on him. He had spent the first year mourning his father, the second growing to think of Holland as home. He still mourned the loss of Miriam. At first, each minute was tinged with the anticipation of hearing from her, seeing her, especially after Hitler declared Holland to be neutral territory. When the letter he had been waiting for finally had arrived, his hands shook so much he could not open it.

Recha had no such reluctance. As if without thinking, she had read Miriam's letter aloud. "...I have come to realize that I love him."

"I don't believe it," Sol said. "I *won't* believe it."

"You had better believe it, Sol." Recha had handed him the letter.

How vigorously he had charged to Miriam's defense, refusing the evidence of his own eyes, insisting Erich had dictated the words.

Recha's counter-argument was irrefutable. She took him to see the Movietone News clip of Miriam honoring her uncle's assassins.

He went home and tore up the letter he had started to write, affirming his love. If he were to write at all, it must be to break the ties between them. He could not do it, not while the hope existed that she would change her mind. She had let go of him, but he was not ready to let go of her. Recently, to his amazement, though the ache remained, the pain had begun to lessen.

Then, three months later, her face stared up at him from the pages of the Sunday tabloid. She was dancing in Hitler's arms, "and not for the first time," the text said. Erich stood proudly by. The paper also reported that the niece of Walther Rathenau had renounced her heritage and married Major Erich Alois, "her childhood love."

After the tears, after the sorrowing, Sol no longer had any choices to make. In the beginning there had seemed to be a need for decision: run to her and pull her out of Erich's embrace, or stay here and wait for her to come to him. Slowly, surely, he had begun to realize that *he* had no choice because she had already made it. If she wanted to be in Berlin, with Erich, then she must have what she had chosen. There would always be times when he would wonder what she was feeling, if she had thought of him when she danced with Adolf Hitler, if she had buried him when she buried her heritage...just as there would be times, like now, when he wondered about Erich.

Had Erich really risen to such dizzying heights in the Party? Did he ever remember that he once had a brother in blood?

Turning away from the grassy walk along the canal, Sol descended the steps to a concrete platform, built next to the water. He sat down next to a narrow culvert opening, balanced Joseph Halévy's study of the Falashas on the inside of its curved edge, and leaned back.

At once he found himself bothered by the sunlight reflecting off the water. He took off his glasses, closed one eye, and tested his peripheral vision. His eyesight was definitely worsening. Ultimately he would learn to accept that, the way he had learned to accept all of the other inescapable things in his life, even the presence of the dybbuk, the wandering soul that had possessed him since that terrible day when he witnessed Walther Rathenau's assassination.

Eyes closed, Solomon recalled Beadle Cohen's words: *sometimes those souls seek refuge in the bodies of living persons, causing instability, speaking foreign words through their mouths.* Such lost souls, the beadle had maintained, were unable to transmigrate to a higher world because they had sinned against humanity.

But what sin had so absorbed Judith, the nurse whom the grenade had also killed, that her soul had sought a new vessel?

A flash of light exploded out of the water, and then another —cerebral fireworks, come to warn him that he should pay heed. A cobalt-blue glow followed. He shut his eyes and waited, feeling the sun warm his cheeks. Soon, he thought, letting his mind drift, it will be dusk and another day will be over. Meanwhile, in his mind's eye, he decided, he would watch another vision the voices brought. Some, at first, had been fascinating. Then many had turned ugly...because of his losing Miriam?

He watched, waited, like someone fearing an execution but anxious for the finality to begin.

He saw a cobalt-blue dusk, and an orange sun setting above the domed keep of a ruined castle. It was the Ethiopian vision again, the one that had sparked his interest in the Falashas——

——*A black man, lanky, rawboned, bald but for a bowl of hair at the crown of his skull, leans crouched against a castle wall.* His left shoulder is draped with a white cloak, caked with dust; a brown stallion grazes beside him, amid waist-high daisies. He seems so weary that only his spear shaft holds him up.

At the bottom of a grassy slope, a short distance below, is an elderly woman wearing bifocals and a safari hat wrapped and tied under her chin with a bright blue chiffon sash. She sits crossways in a motorcycle sidecar, her boots up on the main seat. As she watches him with the quick-eyed appreciation women usually reserve for new lovers, she makes quick, easy strokes on the pages of a combination sketch pad and graph-paper notebook balanced awkwardly across her lap. She draws him rapidly, not looking at the paper. Her wrinkled hands are the same hue as her khaki jacket and pants.

"Don't change your mind now, Zaehev Emanuel," she says in English, talking softly to herself. "This old girl's come too far for that."

A bee buzzes in front of her face. She swishes it away. When another lands on her lapel, she flicks it off with forefinger and thumb and, frowning, glances back over her shoulder. Thirty meters behind her, a dozen two-meter-high man-made beehives resembling banded sheaves of straw stand as if in formation. Smoke plumes from two of them, mixing with that of a campfire built between two stones. A small black man wrapped from head to ankles in a tattered robe squats beside the fire, pouring batter in a spiral onto a ceramic griddle. On the matted grass beside him sit an ebony jug and two bowls, plus several wicker baskets decorated with chevrons. Set into an hourglass-shaped basket is a metal dish holding bread rounds. They look like enormous uncooked *latkes*...potato pancakes.

"Can't you just *cook* instead of fiddling with your bees, Malifu?" she asks.

The man beside the griddle lifts a hand in acquiescence. He removes smoking torches from the base of each of the two pluming hives and shoves the sticks, base down, into the ground.

Suddenly it is night. A horse and rider, silhouetted by a full moon, amble down the hill. Stones click beneath the horse's hooves. The rider is carrying a spear perpendicular to the ground, as if he is a standard-bearer.

"It just might happen tonight." She sits up straighter, holding the pencil poised above the paper. "Just might happen."

The rider reaches the motorcycle. Slackening the reins, he rises to sniff the air. "Sandalwood incense and *injera*. Bread." He speaks in a strange, musical Hebrew. "Such odors could domesticate a man." He smiles wanly, obviously exhausted. "Hopefully, the smoke will attract a swarm to the hive. They do say it charms the bees." He looks around tentatively, as though seeing the scalloped, verdant valley for the first time.

"Malifu indicated that it doesn't look promising," she replies, also in Hebrew. "Getting more bees, I mean." She grunts as, with forearms and elbows, she pushes herself up from the sidecar and extends him a hand.

Leaning down, he clumsily kisses her knuckles. "I am honored you have journeyed so far to see one so lowly as I."

"The honor is all mine, Zaehev Emanuel."

"You know *my* name, while I—"

"Judith Bielman-O'Hearn. Judy." Having extricated herself from the sidecar, she brushes dust from her jacket.

"I trust your travels were pleasant, Miss Judith."

"Malifu guided me. He sat in the sidecar with his head down, gesturing wildly the whole way. I think he had his eyes shut most of the time. The trip was…" She grins, shrugs, opens her hands in supplication.

"Mountainous?"

"Eventful. One I shan't soon forget."

He laughs, swings a leg over the pommel, dismounts. "You were not," he ties the reins to a bush and lifts his eyes toward her, "followed?"

She answers with a shake of her head.

"Not even…" He undulates his hand in the air and makes a motor sound deep in his throat.

"I saw no airplanes, if that's what you mean."

"The beekeeper is a friend of yours?"

"Not exactly. He heard I was looking for someone from your village and offered to guide me here. He seems harmless enough."

"Doesn't everything? Even the airplanes, the first time we saw them." He moves toward the fire, swatting hard at the bees in front of his face, as if to rile them. "I hardly imagine you journeyed to Gojjam, the province of honey, to talk of innocence and insects…or even of airplanes."

Notebook in hand, she follows him to the fire.

"I have questions," she says, "but I also have *injera*. You must be terribly hungry." Her voice is sharp, as if in rebuke. "Honey wine, too. And coffee rich enough to melt the soul."

"You've driven all the way from Addis Ababa to feed me?"

He kneels beside Malifu, who has placed a black lid over the pan. The smaller man appears to stiffen. Shooing away flies, the horseman opens the lid of a vase-shaped wicker, reaches in, and withdraws a slab of honey translucent as amber. He wraps it in one of the breads as though in bunting.

"You want me to take a bite?" the woman asks. "To prove the food is not poisoned?"

He shakes his head and bites off a huge hunk. Strands of honey cling to his lips and chin. His sinewy muscles seem to slacken while he eats. As he devours half the sandwich, he sits on his haunches, arms draped across knees, eyes blank.

She brings a gray woolen blanket from the sidecar and spreads it out before him. He appears to take no notice. When she moves the black jug and one of the bowls onto the blanket, he ceases eating and, holding the honey-and-bread, removes a tiny golden spoon from his broad belt. Eagerly he plunges it into the bowl, scooping up a dollop of dark honey. This he places beneath his tongue. Then he withdraws the spoon, slowly and upside down, cleans it with his lips, and puts it back in his belt.

"I've never seen a man carry around a spoon before, especially one like that." She sets down her sketchpad and pours coffee into two small cups painted with silver leafwork on a blue field. "Does each man in your village carry one?"

His eyes shift to her. His smile holds neither humor nor suspicion.

"I'm sorry," she says. "I shouldn't pry. When I'm excited I sometimes overstep. I meant no harm."

"The spoon *is* very beautiful." He touches it as if to assure himself of its presence. Taking the cup she offers him, he says, "Perhaps it is all right to tell you that I am *not* the only man in my village to wear such a thing."

She curls two fingers into the bowl, scoops out a glob of honey, and places it beneath her tongue. "Would it be something a village boy might wear?"

He lifts his cup in a toast; she responds in kind. *"L'Chaim."*

"L'Chaim." She slurps, sets down the cup and picks up her sketch pad.

"They say the trick is not to swallow—but to *savor*," he tells her in a voice devoid of inflection. "But they are wrong. It is not a trick. It merely mixes the black," he bows slightly, then points his glass at her, "with the sweet." He nods toward her, makes as if to toast again, and drinks half the cup's contents. After several moments, during which she continues her work, he smacks his lips.

"My compliments to your gentle man," he says.

"He likes your coffee," she tells Malifu in English, raising her voice like someone speaking to a deaf person.

His back to her, Malifu lifts an index finger in answer and peeks under the griddle lid. He replaces it with a clang of metal against ceramic and blows mightily on his fingertips.

Emanuel chews off another chunk of bread and lays it down on the blanket; the honey—melting from the warmth of the *injera*, spreads among the fibers.

She has resumed sketching. "I understand you've fought the Italians for seven years," she says without looking at him.

"And will seven more, if necessary. And seven thereafter."

"Were you the only person in your village to go off to war?"

"This time." He sounds despondent.

"Malifu tells me you call yourself a *dejasmatch*—one who, in war, camps near the door of the Emperor's tent."

"I prefer to think of it as 'one who will not surrender.'"

"But surely you've no love for Selassie! What did he ever do for any of the Black Jews? Not even allow you to own land! Persecutions at every turn! Not that I don't admire you for fighting the Fascists, you understand."

"Am I to understand that you have come all this way to steal the worth of those seven years?"

"Fighting Mussolini—that makes sense! But vowing devotion to the monarchy that held Black Jews in servitude for fourteen centuries? Even the title—*dejasmatch*—is that not limited only to the Coptic aristocrat...the legendary Christian warrior-prince?"

After a moment he says quietly, "Perhaps when we Ethiopians found ourselves fighting tanks with ancient rifles and machine guns with spears, the slaughter was so great that most of the legendary Christian *dejasmatch* were cut down like Maskal daisies gathered with a scythe. Perhaps when my country capitulated to the Fascists, a list was drawn up of the surviving *dejasmatch,* or at least those willing to go on fighting. Perhaps—"

He pauses, as if gauging her response. When she remains silent, he smiles as if to concede her a minor victory and finishes his thought. "Perhaps," he says, "the scarcity of remaining *dejasmatch* left room at the bottom of the list for one who imagines he is also a Jew."——

"Is there room for an old Jew to sit down?"

The familiar voice came from behind Sol. He withdrew from the vision and turned around. Hoping. "My God—can it be?" He jumped to his feet and took the beadle in his arms. "You still smell like old books, you old Jew," he said. "What are you doing here?"

"Mostly looking for a place to rest my weary bones." The beadle grinned widely. "Your sister told me I would find you here. May I join you?" Groaning slightly, he lowered himself to the concrete. "As Miriam said of the sewer, it's not exactly the Hotel Kempinski, but it is cheap."

Heart pounding, Solomon sat down next to the beadle. What he really wanted was news of Miriam, but he could not bear even to speak her name. "Was your temple destroyed?" he asked.

The beadle shook his head. "Not yet, but I could see no reason to stay." He took a breath, as if he were about to say something more, then shut his mouth.

"Say it, Beadle Cohen. You were never a man to go out of your way for a mere exchange of pleasantries."

"When I arrived in Amsterdam a few hours ago, I went straight to the temple. I asked if anyone had heard of Ella and Recha Freund."

"Did you not ask after me?"

"I did not, and for very good reason. Until I spoke to your mother and sister, I thought you had been transported—"

Once again Sol jumped to his feet. "To a camp? What made you think that!"

"You are shouting, Solomon. Calm down—sit down! I am too old for this much excitement."

Obediently, Sol sat down.

"Erich has convinced Miriam that you are in a camp, Sol. She has no idea you ever reached Amsterdam—"

"But my letters!"

"Did you address them to the estate?"

"Of course not! I wrote almost daily, in care of Erich's apartment, until—" He stopped. "The estate?"

"They moved there soon after you left."

"And disconnected the phone at the flat," Sol said quietly, beginning to understand. Small wonder he had not been able to get in touch with her. Erich had seen to that—disconnected the phone, waylaid the letters. "So that is why she has done all those things—married Erich, renounced our faith."

"She thinks she is protecting you, Solomon."

"That son of a bitch," Sol said slowly. "That Nazi bastard."

He was pacing up and down the narrow concrete platform. He would call the estate at once. No. Erich might answer or find out about the call, which could endanger her life. The man was obviously capable of anything. He would go to her. On the next train. Pluck her out of the hands of that lying son of a—

"If you're thinking of going back, think it through again. Except for her work with the underground, she is quite safe—"

"The underground?"

Laboriously the beadle rose to his feet. "Erich's parents have reopened the shop. Miriam works there every Sunday—their Sunday Jew, she calls herself. The sewer is being used as a safe-house. I, myself, hid there for one night."

A sadness passed over his face, as of a memory he would rather forget.

"I must go there!" Sol said. "I should have known—!"

"You could not have known," the beadle said. "If you must go, you must, but see to it that you arrive there on a Sunday. It will be the easiest way, perhaps the only way, to make contact. Except when she is with Konrad, Erich keeps her pretty well confined to the estate."

Taking the beadle's arm, Sol led him up the steps, away from the water. "You'll stay with us for a while?" he asked.

The beadle nodded.

"And perhaps you will take over my teaching duties?"

The beadle nodded again.

"That is good," Sol said. "Because, God willing, I intend to be at that shop on Sunday—and I intend to come back…this time, with Miriam."

Chapter 7

Astonished at how easy it was to get into Berlin, at how little notice anyone took of him, Sol walked from the station to Friedrich Ebert Strasse. Getting out should only be that easy, he thought, but then getting into *prison* is easy too.

Getting out—getting to Amsterdam—he'd had phony letters and affidavits from Erich. Erich had provided everything, down to actual train tickets. He had even included a time-table in the package, and a book to read on the train.

Now, two years later, getting out would be much harder. This time he had real affidavits, but papers from a Hebrew School would carry little if any weight if there were trouble. He had brought affidavits for Miri, too, but she would need more than that. She was too visible a personality to be able to leave quietly.

It was ten o'clock in the morning. He had no intention of being in Germany any longer than he had to—a day at most—so he had brought nothing with him save what he could fit in the pockets of the heavy winter coat he had bought at a secondhand store before leaving Amsterdam. He was determined that, no matter what, by tomorrow morning he and Miriam would be on a train, headed back to the tenuous safety of Holland.

Everything else, the question of Erich, the problem of getting all of them out of the country—to South America or South Africa or South Australia, he did not care where—could wait until later.

Before he knew it, he was within sight of the shop. Herr Weisser stood alone in front of the door. Seeing him filled Sol with a burning hatred that almost—but not quite—equaled what Sol felt for their son. He tugged at the Homburg he had purchased along with the coat, crossed the street, and walked on.

He had forgotten how dreary Berlin was at this time of year.

The sky was gray. The wind whistled around the corners of the buildings, and the air smelled of soot from chimney smoke held in by the low clouds.

People en route to church walked with their heads down against the wind. Every now and then, a man or a woman with a dog stopped to let the animal do what it must. The occasional motorcar passed by, and once in a while a man with heavy black boots and a long woolen coat strode by, smelling of Gestapo as strongly as the air was scented with the threat of a late-November snowfall.

He circled the block several times, alert for the Rathenau limousine. It passed him at last. Konnie was at the wheel, alone in front. The back was too dark for him to see who sat there.

Don't let Erich be in that car, he prayed as the limousine slowed to a halt in front of the shop and Miriam stepped out. Despite his increased pulse rate, Sol tried to look at her dispassionately. Her movements were graceful and fluid; her coat was trimmed in white fur, to match her hat, and her boots were the latest fashion. As she leaned back into the car to get something she had apparently left on the seat, her coat pulled up and he could see her legs—trim as a girl's though without the slight muscularity of a dancer's calf.

She's thirty-two, he reminded himself. I have missed so much!

He watched her talk to Herr Weisser, watched him unlock the door and let her inside. Knowing he dared not go in until Weisser had left, and that he had probably already stood in one spot long enough to have aroused suspicion for loitering, he walked in the direction of the Tiergarten. He forced himself to keep moving away from the shop. When he could stand it no longer, he turned back. He walked faster and faster until he was running, and did not slow down until the shop came into view.

Konnie stood at the door, staring out into the street. Sol followed the direction of the chauffeur's gaze. He could see two people walking in the opposite direction. Squinting, he thought he recognized Frau Weisser's movements.

Konnie disappeared into the shop, reappeared, and went to the car. Moments later, he went back inside, this time carrying a shopping bag.

At the end of his patience, Sol approached the tobacco shop, *Die Zigarrenkiste.*

The familiar jangle of the bell over the door made his stomach tighten. Miriam stood with her back to him, reaching for something on a shelf high above her head.

Konrad saw him at once. "Herr—" He turned pale, then beamed as Sol put a finger to his lips.

Walking up to the counter, Sol pulled his hat down low and bent his head as if to examine the cigars that lay beneath the glass. *"Kan ek yets kopen, Mejevrou?"* he asked softly in Dutch. "Could I buy something, Miss?"

She turned around, startled in the way of someone whose thoughts have been a million kilometers away.

"Forgive me, sir, I don't speak—" she began.

He lifted his head. She stopped, grew so pale he thought she would faint, and began to cry.

At once he was behind the counter, his arm around her waist. Tightening the heel of his hand against the base of her spine, he arched her toward him and bent to kiss her. Her mouth tasted warm and moist. He kissed her face, drinking in her salty tears.

"You're alive...free!"

"I've been in Amsterdam all this time."

Miriam touched his face as if to assure herself that he was flesh and blood. She could not seem to stem the flow of tears down her cheeks. "Erich," she managed between sobs. "He...said you'd been arrested. Put in a camp." She took a deep breath. "He said the only hope I had of protecting you was to stay with him and do everything he said!"

Sol's thoughts must have been written on his face; as if she could read them, she looked at him seriously. "He could not force me to love him the way I love you."

"I know what happened," he said gently. "Beadle Cohen made it to Amsterdam. He told me."

"Why didn't you write? What you must have thought before you knew...."

"I did write...at first. Erich must have intercepted the letters. Later, I decided you had made a choice. You do have that right, you know."

"I am your *wife,* Sol. I made my choice a long time ago."

"We'll get out—this time together." Sol lowered his voice. "Can we talk here? Is it safe?"

As if in answer to his question, the doorbell jangled. He glanced at the curtain that separated the shop from the cellar stairs, and she nodded. "I'll be down as soon as I can."

He went down into the cellar and opened the grate that led down into the sewer. A child again, climbing down into the hideaway that had been his and Erich's secret place.

The sewer was cold and damp. He took off his coat and put it over his knees like a blanket. He waited.

There was a flash of light. A cobalt-blue glow infused the sewer. Let it be the Ethiopian vision, he thought. On the train from Amsterdam, he had decided that the woman, Judith, represented the dybbuk. Knowing that, he would watch more closely, listen more carefully. He had experienced visions since childhood. At first he had thought them disjointed, random, but slowly there had emerged common themes. Each had a person who might, like himself, be possessed by a dybbuk. Mention of a Jewish homeland on the African island of Madagascar—an idea similar, Herr Rathenau had once told him, to what the Nazis had long considered.

Eventually, Sol thought, giving himself over to the light, I will understand the visions' lessons...if indeed they have anything to teach——

——*stars sprinkle the cobalt-blue heavens.* They shine on beehives rising up like ancient columns and on a black man and a white woman who sit on a blanket spread out among daisies and wisps of smoke. The woman lies down on her side, props herself up on one arm and begins to sketch. The man remains on his haunches, forearms across knees—hands turned palms up; anguish etches his face.

"I want to be considered a *whole* Jew!" His voice is strained with emotion. "Can't they understand that?"

"You *are* a whole Jew." She sounds more clinical than concerned. "Only the Falasha think differently."

"They treat my people like lepers! Because of them, we have been forced to live in the honeycomb caves for a hundred generations. It is neither right nor fair!"

"Prejudice exists everywhere." She shakes her head sadly, folds the overleaves of her sketch pad down flat, and drops her pencil. "What *is* the name of your tribe, Emanuel?"

"*L'Am*—The People. Do not ask me where they are. As for *why* they are, if I knew, I would tell you that!" He covers his head with his hands. "When I was young, my nights were full of such questions, but I did not ask my elders for fear they did not know the answers." His voice has taken on a hollow, haunted tone. "One day a group of Falasha nomads camped near our caves, come to graze their goats. At night I could hear them praying. One night, when I could not sleep, I stole in among their tents. Their *kohamin*—the priest—spotted me. They threw me into a thorn bush. As I lay crying and bleeding, the priest spat on me. 'Hydra-headed Jew!' he shouted. 'Go home to your pagan gods!'"

"No doubt he was referring to the First Commandment—'Thou shalt have no other gods before Me'," the woman says.

"Does that Commandment not prove there are other, lesser gods? Yet they pretend otherwise! And our language—"

"What about your language, Emanuel?"

He stares at the cocoon of bread with its melting honey.

She leans toward him. "Tell me."

"The Falasha...they laugh at it. They call it 'The Language of the Bee.'"

"Yours is the language of the Song of Deborah."

"De-bo-rah." He pronounces the word as if it were music.

She places a loving hand on his arm. "Deborah means 'bee' in Old Hebrew," she says. "She was a prophetess—a judge who was instrumental in freeing the ancient Israelites from the Canaanites."

"I do not understand." He looks at her curiously, as though she is saying words he has never heard before.

"The Cushitic Falashas—we call them Black Jews—don't speak your language," she says. "Only musty scholars like myself and your people know Old Hebrew. The true language of liturgy, I call it, for it is free of the Aramaic influences that changed Hebrew forever." She gives him a gentle shake as if to break him from his mood. "Your tribe is blessed, Emanuel. Your...your *agony*, if you will, has preserved the past. Soon the whole world will know of your suffering and be grateful to you."

He furrows his forehead, then looks down at the ground as Malifu pads forward. The smaller man holds a huge dish quilted with *injera* layered with chunks of meat and light broth. The two men do not look at each other.

"The *wat*—stew—looks lovely," the woman tells Malifu, taking the dish from him. "Fetch the wine, please. Then tend to your bees. The hives *farthest away* need the most attention."

He bows; understood. He has not once looked at Emanuel. After he brings the wine, he wanders off amid the hives.

"*Tej*—honey wine...nectar of the gods." The woman grins and drinks deeply. "If nothing else, *this* proves the whole universe isn't monotheistic!"

Emanuel too drinks deeply, thoughtfully. "I prayed, after the Falasha threw me into the thorn bush like so much excrement. I wanted to understand why they had treated me in that manner. But Jehovah would not answer. At dawn, the goddess Anuket spoke to me out of the sun as I sat looking at the mountains and the hills lush with flowers. I knew it was she, for she wore a crown of feathers and carried her scepter and *ankh.*"

"Anuket—goddess of the Nile, nourisher of the fields." The woman takes notes in small, impeccably neat handwriting. "What other gods are important to you?"

"Her sister, Sati. Their husband, Khnum, god of the cataract."

"Anuket, Sati, Khnum." Her voice is breathless. "The Elephantine Triad. Does your tribe believe in any other Egyptian gods?"

"*Egyptian?*" He frowns and leans forward to peer over the top of her notebook.

"Any other *gods.*" She tears off a piece of bread, wraps it around a morsel of meat and, after popping it into her mouth, readies the pencil above the graph paper.

He puts his arms around a bent knee and looks toward the far horizon. "There is, of course, Ra, god of the sun."

"Is Ra greater than Jehovah?"

"Jehovah made the heavens and the earth. Therefore He created Ra. At least, as a child I thought so. That is what I was taught to believe. Now...I'm not sure."

For a while there is silence. In the tension silence can cause, the woman's face seems to lose its look of aged innocence. She stops writing and presses the pencil hard against the page; the tip breaks.

"Tell me, Emanuel," she says quietly, "do you believe that the gods are punishing you for leaving your village...that they have taken away your heritage, only to replace it with doubts?"

"I cannot understand why Jehovah sits by and winks at war. Had I not left home I would not have known the meaning of war and—"

"I, too, have doubts." The woman removes her hat and sets it down with trembling hands. She watches him eat more of the stew, jiggling the hot bread in his hand; there is a deep sadness in her eyes. "All these years of searching, Emanuel, and now that I have found you, I am no longer sure I should ever have begun the quest," she says finally.

"Quest? Explain, please." He leans close.

"Seventy-five years ago, a French professor named Joseph Halévy discovered the Falashas—African Jews who lacked knowledge of Hebrew and the Talmud, and who had priests rather than rabbis. The Lost Tribe, he called them. Probably descended from—"

"Menelik the First, son of Sheba. They all say so."

She nods. "All those centuries, living by the dictates and dreams of the Jewish people, yet unaware other Jews existed!" As if in an effort to calm herself, she selects and wraps another morsel, which she holds before Emanuel's mouth. "The finest portion, to honor the favored guest."

He opens his mouth for it like a bird.

"After the Italians invaded Ethiopia," she says, "we heard rumors of a tiny enclave of Jews who were *not* Falashas. A people who spoke Hebrew but did not follow Levite law concerning monotheism. Perhaps descended from Jews who were driven out of their colony at Elephantine, the Nile's southernmost cataract in Egypt, and never heard of again. Four *hundred* years," she looks at him soberly, "before the Christians' Messiah, and a century before the Hebrew language began to change." She starts to roll another bread-and-meat, then stops. "The destruction of the Jewish temple and the slaughter at Elephantine occurred," she says quietly, no longer looking at him, "when Khnum priests realized they were losing power and therefore bribed the commander of the Egyptian garrison."

She holds out the morsel, dangling it between forefinger and thumb. He cranes his neck around in order to take it between his lips. As he eats, he eyes her steadily. "So you wish to study us and make yourself as famous as the Frenchman."

She looks away. "I come from a country called Ireland, but I am a Jew with an African heart," she tells him. Her shoulders sag, and she runs her fingers through thinning hair. "I spent years among the Bushmen. Now I'm not sure who I am. Like you, in a way," she adds softly. "If I expose you to the world you will suffer less—but it will change you. Your people will never be the same. Having found you, I could fulfill *my* dream." She lifts her gaze and looks directly into his eyes; her expression is intense, searching, caring. "It would be better if that were your wish, too."

"I am most confused," he says.

She turns a page of the sketch pad to reveal an excellently rendered drawing of Emanuel squatted peasant-style beside the blanket. "This is *real.*" She holds up the sketch pad. *"This...you*...you are the living essence of my Jewish heritage. *My* needs are only a part of this. Everywhere, Jews are being forced to deny their heritage if they wish to survive."——

"You can come out now, Sol."

Miriam's voice pulled Sol out of the vision. He hoped it would not be one of the fragmentary ones that never returned. The people intrigued him—the woman with her sketch pad, the princely black man.

"It's safe for a little while," Miriam said. "You remember—the customers always seem to come in waves. I left Konrad up there. He will call me the moment someone approaches the shop."

Sol took a few seconds to allow the blue glow of the vision to dissipate. "I...fell asleep," he said. There would be time later to talk of the visions, he told himself, clambering out of the sewer to take Miriam in his arms.

They dared not turn on a light. He wanted to look at her, to drink her in as he might a good wine. Instead, he traced her features with his fingers—the slant of her eyes, the curve of her lips, the high cheekbones. He buried his face in her hair, inhaling its sweet, clean smell as if it were a field of freesias. "God, how I missed you," he whispered.

"We may only have minutes," she said, drawing away from his embrace. "We have plans to make."

"Let's just leave. Now. Walk away from here. Better yet, drive away in the limousine until we're close to the border."

"And go where?" she asked.

"Amsterdam. We'll make it there, somehow."

"If we do, we'll have to keep running."

"From Erich?"

She held fast to his hand. "From Hitler. Eventually Holland will be as unsafe as Germany."

"By then we—"

"No, Sol." She had a new firmness in her voice. "This time we are going to South America...together. I have my own contacts now, in the underground, and Juan Perón has become a good friend. I will go to him myself. When we're safe, hopefully in Buenos Aires, then I'm sure he'll help us send for your mother and Recha."

They sat side by side at the bottom of the staircase, bodies touching, but not embracing. "You seem so sure of this friend's help," he said. "Are you and he—"

"We stand with one foot in the grave, and you cast innuendoes!"

"I'm sorry. There has been so much pain...."

Tears glistened on her face. "You're right," she said more quietly, relaxing the stiff set of her shoulders. "I've worked very hard to wrap Perón around my little finger." She lowered her voice. "Berlin is a perilous city, and I have been playing a perilous game. If I weren't such a good player, I could not be here talking to you. As it is, I'll be holding my breath the whole week. One word to Erich that I know you are free, and it's all over. He would guess at once where you are, and that we are making plans. We would lose our safehouse—and each other."

"What would he do? Have me killed?"

"I don't know. He's rising in the Party, but the way he hates them—"

She stopped, cocked her head, and listened. Sol heard the soft echo of a whistle.

"That's Konnie!" She stood up. "I have to go upstairs. I'll come down again before I close the shop. After that, I can't return until next Sunday, by which time I should have been able to contact Perón." She was talking fast, her voice insistent. "If I don't come, it means there's something I have to do with Erich, or that—"

He cut her short. "What about food?" he asked.

"There are supplies down there—enough for a week, if you're careful."

"Fräulein Miriam!"

"You see how things have changed." She snuffed the candle. Her voice held a hint of laughter. "Konnie is part of us now, so he allows himself to be much less formal...he no longer calls me Fräulein *Rathenau!*"

Afraid he might never see her again once he returned to the stinking brick crypt, Sol stood too, and took her in his arms. How he wanted to keep her there, to make plans, laugh, make love.

"I *must* go," she said, her voice strained.

He released her and listened to her footsteps until they faded. Back in the sewer, he thought about all she had said. Her reasoning was sensible—but sensible was not what he had wanted. She could have agreed to stay with him, he told himself peevishly. There *was* the alternative of slipping out after dark to contact Perón while he waited here for her.

Fool! He berated himself for thinking like a child. For the next seven days, he would be alone with his memories and his doubts. Such thoughts would not help him find the strength to live through the hours she was gone. He must manage as he had in Amsterdam, by reliving their lovemaking, pretending they were together with all the time in the world. Sometimes he had tried to understand why a makeshift marriage ceremony in a deserted cabaret, with God as their only witness, made him feel so tied to her, so hopeful that life would ultimately reward him for being a good man.

Exhausted, he closed his eyes. Instead of sleep, the vision returned——

——*"What does your Hitler propose to do with the Jews of Europe?"* Emanuel asks.

The woman bristles. "He is not *my* anything," she says angrily. There is an awkward silence between them. "He proposes to rid the world of them," she adds in a quiet voice, having apparently calmed herself.

"How? By killing them all?"

"If necessary."

Emanuel turns his face to one side and spits into the sand. He rubs his arms, as if his flesh has suddenly become cold.

"There is a ray of hope," the woman says. "A physician named Schmidt, under a doctor named Mengele, has developed a theory concerning the genetic passing of cultural attributes from one generation to the next. Hitler has offered a reward for each piece of tangible new evidence that furthers her research."

"And what might that reward be?" Emanuel looks skeptical.

"He has sworn to create a homeland for the Jews—in Madagascar. Each addition to Schmidt's research means a shipload of our people is sent to the Jewish homeland."

"This Hitler is like the god Apepi, who tried to stop the progress of the solar barque. They who trust in him, trust a serpent." He rises from the blanket and towers over her. "You have come here to provide their Schmidt with subjects for research." He pronounces each syllable with knifelike clarity. "Perhaps you can get the serpent to agree to one shipload per body!"

"With subjects as unique as your tribe, I think Mengele could get Hitler to agree to one shipload per person."

"Per *body,*" he says.

"The researchers want to examine the bodies of your ancestors, Emanuel. From the living, they want only blood samples. Blood. Nothing more. Your tribal whereabouts will remain a secret. Our meeting places will remain discreet."

He looks down at her, his face a study in contempt. "For over two millennia no one knew or cared that we existed. We were better off." He takes the meat from his mouth and drops it onto the plate.

"I will relay your request to my people. The decision must be theirs."——

The vision faded. Sol covered himself with his coat and slept. He woke to the sound of Miriam's voice. Responding more quickly this time, he climbed from the sewer.

"We only have a little while," Miriam said. "The shop is closed. Konnie has some errands to run. He'll be back in an hour."

Without saying a word, Sol took her hand and led her to Kaverne. There, on the carpet, they made love. Concentrating, Sol experienced each place where they joined. He wanted to imprint the sensations on his consciousness so that he could savor them later. Instead, he flowed into her and they floated in a magical space and time where nothing existed except the rainbow of love that once had been two people.

Afterwards, when he touched her, his love and desire for her seemed contained in a sheath of pride and of wonder that God had seen fit to bless him with such good fortune. He held her closely, trying to understand why the fog of self-doubt that he had lived with since Walter Rathenau's death was gone. Later would be time enough to examine that, he decided, pretending to be asleep so that Miriam would continue to lie quietly in his arms.

"I love you, Solomon. I am *your* wife, and no one else's," she said at last, as if in answer to his earlier doubts.

The words reverberated inside him, then etched themselves onto the deepest part of his soul.

Your wife, they echoed.

Your wife...

Chapter 8

Erich opened the long velvet box and examined the diamond bracelet he had bought for Miriam more than a week before, for no particular reason except that he thought it belonged around her wrist. He had been carrying it around ever since, hoping for a moment when she would seem receptive.

For the last few days, she had been more distant, more preoccupied than ever. The longer he waited, the less benign he felt toward her—and the less inclined to give her something bought in a fit of tenderness and longing. He was sure she would find a way to denigrate his gift. Not crassly sarcastic, but subtly and, thus, more emotionally devastating. He had no way to fight her verbal choreographies, except to play the stoic soldier and swallow his rage.

Worse yet, like a mother offering strudel because one's blocks were picked up, she would invite him to his reward between her legs—reminding him all the while that her hatred of anything Nazi or even vaguely military was being fueled by his weakness for her.

What would happen then? Doubtless another erectile failure and the pretense that her satisfaction was all he wanted this night. Small wonder that the act which he had in the past anticipated with pleasure now revolted him, as it had done ever since the business with Hempel and that poor prostitute. What had her name been? *Toy*.

There was only one female with whom he could truly share his feelings, Erich thought. The one who had loved him unconditionally.

Taurus.

Slipping into his black silk robe, he poured himself a cognac against the November dawn, pocketed the bracelet, and went outside. By the time he reached the kennels, he had disposed of the brandy. He was about to set the glass under a tree, where he could find it later, when he saw that the duty officer was Krayller—a loner who would certainly not find the need for a cognac unbecoming of the conduct of his superior officer.

"You weren't scheduled for duty tonight," Erich said.

Though Erich's tone was conversational, Krayller reddened. "One of the other men." His reluctance to name the man stemmed, Erich knew, from an effort to avoid getting the other trainer in trouble. "I'm filling in."

Erich tried to rearrange his features to reflect a stern demeanor in the face of the trainers again changing the duty roster without permission, but secretly the *esprit de corps* and self-sufficiency the trainers exhibited pleased him. He took pride in the fact that his men were different from so many German soldiers, with their rigidity and blind insistences. While his men certainly knew the value of following orders, he encouraged them to question. To think for themselves, unlike some of the so-called finest units— who reminded him of the Communist insurgents of his childhood whose takeover had failed because they'd lacked proper tickets to board the train. One conductor, armed with nothing but a ticket punch, had stopped a coup.

As a member of the Abwehr, the military-security branch of the armed forces, he had visited many units and often been on assessment teams. What others applauded made him shudder. He had asked himself: what would become of those units if the officers were killed, or if the commander were a Judas goat? What would become of the country?

"I've no problem with changes. Just make sure the paperwork's proper," Erich said, nodding at Krayller. "Oberschütze Müller visiting his sister again?"

The man hesitated, then nodded. "Yes, Sir," he said. "And thank you, Sir." He adjusted his carbine on his shoulder.

Erich thought about Ursula Müller, remembering the time when, both of them barely into puberty, she had tried to goad him into probing her with his *damaged* fingers. She was ready for something new and different she had said. His fearful refusal had triggered her sarcastic laughter and made him so angry that he had lied to the other boys—Solomon among them—bragging about something he hadn't done.

Now where was she, with her weak IQ and strong libido? A depressive, institutionalized by the New Order and forced to service the officers under threat of involuntary sterilization.

"You're forever filling in," Erich said. "Volunteering in an emergency I can understand. But you seem to make a career of it."

The corporal scooped up the affenpinscher, his constant companion, and held the black monkey terrier against his huge chest, playing with the forelegs. "The other men have families, Sir. Me...I'm a loner, a sort of...clown."

"Clown?"

"Like Grog, Sir." Krayller puffed up his corpulent cheeks, as if expecting Erich to join him in *Sch-ö-ö-n*, the clown routine the real Grog had made famous. When Erich did not respond, Krayller said, somewhat awkwardly, "Always smiling—always alone." He quickly added, "Except for Grog Junior, here." He patted the terrier.

"Fine, but don't let your generosity interfere with your regular duties," Erich said, ambling down the ramp that led to the garage underneath the mansion. "I don't want anyone falling asleep during drills."

"No Sir. I'll sleep after I'm dead. Nothing to do then but lie around anyway," Krayller called after him. "Just so they bury me with my smile painted on—Sir."

Until he pulled the chain of the dangling bulb, Erich was unsure why he had entered the garage, with its two rows of army and civilian vehicles lined up like troops awaiting inspection. Then he noticed Hawk, his bicycle since childhood, and thanked the impulse that had brought him down here. Someone—Konnie, perhaps—had washed the bike and polished its considerable chrome to a high shine.

Sch-ö-ö-n, he thought. *Beautiful.*

Pulling off his robe, he exchanged it and his empty glass for the military blouse he kept in his garage locker. Without thinking, he transferred the bracelet from the pocket of his robe to the pocket of his shirt. Then he snapped off the light and walked Hawk clear of the garage and up into the breaking dawn, aware that the feeling of oppression was draining from him.

Some of the shepherds whined or whimpered pitifully when he unchained Taurus from her dog-run. Others performed a retinue of tricks or simply, shamelessly begged. To no avail. Tonight, he wanted no other companion than Taurus. He hooked up her leash and led dog and bike past Krayller's post.

Older than any of the other dogs by half a dozen years, Taurus lifted her head like a princess and pranced along, basking in her master's affections. The corporal saluted smartly, and Erich returned it left-handed, a bit of occasional military irreverence the men seemed to enjoy.

Then he was off, dawn flooding the streets, Taurus's claws clicking against pavement as she trotted alongside. He rode slowly, both to savor the moment and in respect for the dysplasia that had invaded Taurus' hips and likely would eventually cripple her. She moved easily this morning; her pain seemed far away, no more than a dark cloud on a horizon. He opened his mind to her, exulting in her sense of smell and purpose. Her happiness at roaming and being beside him beat against his consciousness as colorfully as the wings of a lunar moth against a window screen. He was a boy again. He wondered if he had ever, really, grown up. Everyone else seemed so much older, so much more mature. Did they feel like boys, too, or was he the only one who felt forever boy, his dog beside him, clothespinned-on playing cards fluttering against his spokes?

They went up the Kurfurstendamm and down Mauerstrasse. When they reached Ananas, to which he realized he had unconsciously been heading the whole time, he was inordinately thirsty—and hungry for human camaraderie. He chained the bike to a pole outside the nightclub and threaded the leash around the handlebars. Almost paradoxically, in contrast to its wilder, cabaret days, the place was now an officers' club and never closed.

He glanced up at the spread-winged Nazi eagle on the marquee, remembering with nostalgic regret how the nightclub had once flown on wings of creativity and artistic verve. Once, when Miriam was the star; once, when Werner Fink's deadly humor was applauded even by those who feared its edge, and the likes of Bertoldt Brecht drank nightly at their regular tables.

Once, when there was hope.

Guard the bike, he mentally told Taurus, almost in afterthought as his depression returned.

Inside, in the foyer, a stolidly bosomed hat-check girl wearing a severe suit took Erich's officer's cap, eyeing him appreciatively. He wished she were one of the chorines from the old days, dressed only in feathers and flesh, then hoped she wasn't. Some changes he could not abide.

The atmosphere in the cabaret proper was subdued and smoky, not the usual gaiety and toasting by men coming off duty. Soldiers of all ranks meandered among the tables, beer mugs in hand, but conversations were quiet. There was a tension in the air in counterpoint to the atmosphere of *gemütlichkeit* he had sought. Many men just sat and stared at the pineapples that served as table centerpieces. Someone had painted them green, so that they looked like grenades—hardly the exotic, erotic symbols that once could buy a man a night between almost any woman's legs if not a lifetime in her heart.

But that change was not new, not since his last visit. There was something else odd, something he could not determine much less name. He looked around, trying to figure out what had changed.

The stage was darkened except for a tiny light above a drum set and a tuba cradled on a stand. It seemed almost funereal, the antithesis of the delightful exhibitionism of just a half-dozen years ago. Gone were acts like kohl-eyed Mimi de Rue—Miriam's stage name; she had dropped "Rathenau" in the hope of obtaining work—the professionally trained dancer who sang like a seductress. Gone too, though who knew where—Erich had heard that, miraculously, Fink had not been arrested—were *conférenciers* like Werner Fink, whose outrageous comedy had been like a Hitler salute right up the nearest Nazi's ass. Now, when there was a revue, Nazi comics about as interesting as beer left in a mug for a week introduced the acts.

Abruptly, Erich realized what had changed since his last visit. Except for one woman near the bar, clad in expensive black nylons and what looked like a pink house-robe, all the waitresses were gone. He was about to ask the nearest soldier about the change, when he noticed one of the trainers, Corporal Hans Müller, sitting in the corner, smoking, the back of his head against the wall.

"I heard you had gone to the, um, hospital," Erich said, ambling over to him.

The corporal nodded for Erich to sit down but did not in any way acknowledge his rank. "I went to the *nuthouse,*" Hans said. "You can say it, Herr Major. It doesn't bother me."

Müller thumped out his cigarette against the ashtray, swirled the wrong end in his mouth to make sure it was dead, and replaced it in his pack. Habit, Erich knew, borne of the Depression days that Hitler's military regime had ended.

"They released her," Müller said. "She was gone by the time I got there. Left. On her own. No money. No family with her. The doctor told me they needed the bed for someone *useful.* Someone who might return to society and produce strong Nazi babies." He looked around as if to make sure that they were not being overheard. "Nazi *bastards,*" he added in a low voice. "There's no room left in the Reich for old-fashioned sentimentalism, for compassion."

"I'm sorry," Erich said, at a loss for words. "Where is she now?"

Müller shrugged. "Your guess is as good as mine. Probably at the bottom of the Elbe. I wouldn't know where to begin to look. Aren't we all siblings in the eyes of the State? I'll just find another sister."

Erich stared at the grain lines in the table top. Had he contributed to her downfall by refusing her, he wondered. *Getting as bad as Solomon,* he thought. *Shrouding myself in conscience. Only real difference between a goddamn Jew and a goddamn Catholic is the degree of guilt. Has little to do with Jesus.*

In an attempt to lift a corner of his gloom, he listened to the conversation of the soldiers at the next table, heads together like chuckling conspirators, and then wished he hadn't. They were describing their latest sojourn with a Jewish prostitute. "Big-nosed bronco busting," one called it, trying for an American cowboy inflection. "They can't get enough of it. Not when *we* start poking them."

The conversation sickened Erich, though he knew he should be used to it. The Jewesses who worked the alleys had no other choice. Those who did not do it for food, did it in a desperate attempt to help rescue loved ones from work camps—begging for something as simple as a letter forwarded to the right authority. *Like Miriam with me,* Erich thought, annoyed with himself for making the comparison. *Except Solomon really isn't incarcerated.*

"I left her tied up, back there," the soldier went on. "Ready for the next one." His laughter, ringing hollow in the otherwise quiet cabaret, chilled Erich. *Back there.* There were prostitutes in here now? Not that there hadn't always been a working girl or two among the tables, but this was different. These were...*Slaves.*

Back there, beat within his brain.

They had a Jewish woman, perhaps several, tied up in the back rooms. Maybe even in Miriam's former dressing room, the one with the tawdry, half-peeled star on the door. Is that what it had stood for all these years...a Star of David?

His throat felt parched, and his heart thudded. He rose, quivering with rage, turned to face the soldiers, and saw the ratty high heels sticking up from beneath the tablecloth as a woman serviced the service man.

A pressure burrowed up his spine and hit the base of his skull. His head jerked back. "I—I'm sorr-sorry about Urs-ula," he said over his shoulder. In some part of his mind, unaffected by the lightning seizure that held him, the illogic of it all pulsed like a heavy Latin beat. Sexual union between Germans and Jews was forbidden, but rape of Jewesses and Jewish boys was condoned if not encouraged.

He stood, everything off-kilter. He watched the grins of the soldiers drain and the glazed eyes of the one receiving fellatio change from glassy to fearful.

"W-what is an arm-army without hon...without honor," Erich stammered, knowing that they would think him drunk. "J-ust l-look at you. W-what have we be-become."

In a single movement, he approached the table, bent down, and tugged at the legs of the woman underneath. She allowed herself to be drawn forth, but made no attempt to stand.

"Get out of here," Erich said softly. "And don't ever come back."

On impulse, he dug into his shirt pocket, pulled out the diamond bracelet, and dropped it onto the woman. Then, trembling, unable to catch his breath, he stumbled backward toward the door, careful not to turn his back on the young soldiers.

He yanked his cap from the hat-check girl's extended hands, and shouldered his way outside into a gloomy, overcast winter morning. Taurus gained her feet awkwardly, wagging her tail despite the pain of her dysplasia. He wanted to sag to his knees and wrap his arms around her neck but felt unworthy of her affection. Against the pole, Hawk too seemed apart from him, as though leaning away from his attention, a prize he did not deserve.

The door opened behind him. When Müller put a tentative hand on his shoulder, he did not pull away or otherwise resist the familiarity, though the corporal clearly was over the limits of military protocol. "Are you all right, Herr Major? You went white as a ghost."

Erich took a deep breath to slow his pounding heart. "I-I'm fine. Thanks for asking, Oberschütze M-Müller."

"Do you need to go back inside?"

"I'll never g-go back inside."

"Nor I." Müller held the bike while Erich unchained it. "And to think," he said, face flushed with the knowledge that he was out of line, "that I used to be proud to call myself a soldier," he finished.

"I understand. Only too well," Erich said, grateful that he had stopped stammering. He looked up at the marquee. "We need a nightclub without...without women."

"Where we can be ourselves," Müller finished, a look of finality and defeat on his face. "I think I need to walk," he said. "A long walk. Somewhere beyond the sun." He stuck his hands in his pockets and, softly whistling "Mack the Knife," walked away.

Erich lit a cheroot and dragged deeply. He knew he had to do something to slough off his anger over Ananas and his anguish about Ursula, though what he was not sure. He mounted the bike and pedaled around the corner into the early morning traffic, Taurus close beside him. Drivers, perhaps seeing his uniform, cautiously veered around him.

He steered down a side street—his old neighborhood—and the answer stared right at him. Visiting the butcher shop had always been a favorite part of his times with Taurus—a simple enough pleasure, and one that would certainly cheer him up now.

He stopped before the butcher's, chained his bicycle to a pole, and mentally commanded Taurus to *"Stay."* Taurus lay on the stoop, her head on the doorway threshold, eyeing the meat hanging behind the crescent-shaped counter. Half a pig, complete with snout and tail, dangled from a hook in the corner in full view of the customers because Faussan, the butcher, liked to perform his artistry as much as possible in public. His meat was, he claimed, the best in Berlin, and the show was good for business.

Good for his ego, Erich thought, standing before the counter and studying the meat beneath the fingerprint-smeared glass. He had rescued his first dog, Bull, from the alley behind the shop—rescue being the operative word, since Bull had clearly been slated for someone's dinner table...not an unusual event in the lean times following the Great War. The rescue grew more noble, and his frustration greater, with each retelling.

That had been the dog his father drowned. For Erich, father and butcher had become one. He hated them equally, and suspected that he returned to this particular shop so often to torment the owner.

Their encounter was always the same:

"Something I can get for you, Herr Major?" A tired voice, for surely the butcher knew what the answer would be.

"No dogs or cats today, no human flesh?"

"That's not funny, Herr Major." Followed by a whack of the cleaver. The man's paunch—so evident twenty years before—was gone, but the inevitable cigarette still peeked out from behind one ear. It was balanced with a pencil behind the other, announcing him to be a man of revenue. "That's not funny at all."

No Berlin butcher liked being reminded that Carl Grossman, who specialized in picking up peasant girls from the train station, or Georg Haarmann, who specialized in picking up orphan boys wandering around the station, had both been city butchers—and in more than one sense of the word. Grossman maintained he had not killed and cannibalized over two dozen women, until detectives agreed to let him confess the murders to his pet bird, which seemed not at all ill at ease sitting on his shoulder. Haarmann was mild-mannered, soft-spoken; during rape, he would tear out his victim's throat with his teeth, then boil and neatly package the result. Both men did a brisk wholesale business: Grossman in several local shops, Haarmann on the black market. After their confessions, there was, according to the papers, furtive inspections of larders and meat jars, furtive vomiting.

Today, as usual, the shop smelled of blood—the sawdust that covered the floor was clumped where droplets had fallen—but Faussan was not present.

"Your papa visiting the abattoir?" Erich asked the butcher's daughter, a pigtailed blonde with rounded shoulders who emerged from the back rooms, wiping her hands on a rag. She wore a bloodied apron and, surprisingly, a perfectly white blouse cut low across the bodice and gathered at the shoulders. Seeing him, her whole demeanor changed. The worn-out, bedraggled shop girl look vanished as with her wrist pushed back a curl from her forehead.

"Papa's at his telephone. We finally got one. I think he's called most of Berlin." She leaned over to wipe off the fingerprints, her weight against the side of the counter so that her cleavage was better exposed. She smiled when she saw Erich looking. "I'd be happy to help you, Herr Major," she offered in a sing-song, admiring his uniform, "any way I can. He will probably be tied up—for hours."

"Sausage. Smoked." He had half a mind to run a hand down the blouse. Would she object, or merely thrust out that wonderful chest even further? "A dozen links," he added, pleased that he felt less revolted by the idea of sex than he had in a long time.

"These big ones?" she asked, pointing. "I *love* sausage."

What she loved, Erich knew, had little to do with him personally. What the Führer had called an honor and a duty had given young women the moral license to sleep with soldiers. Officers were, as in the butcher-shop parlance, prime. Married or not, a young blonde pregnant by an Aryan officer was lauded and pampered. Once the child surpassed infancy, the State institutions gradually relieved her of her maternal responsibilities and eased her out the door. He wondered if she were aware of that.

"I've seen you with your dog before," she said. "I've watched the little game you play with her. Looks like fun."

"It is," he said. How often had he sat on the shop stoop, letting Taurus take a sausage from his mouth, so delighted by his dog's trust in him that he had hardly noticed this enchanting creature?

He glanced toward Taurus, paternally sentimental, and felt a surge of dismay. She was slowly bellying across the sawdust, heading for the pig. *"Back,"* he mentally commanded.

Perhaps it was the pride in his mind, perhaps the absence of the shop's owner. Whatever the reason, Taurus did not obey. She put her head down and looked up at him dolefully. When he repeated the command to back up, she rose and reluctantly moved back half a meter, until her hips were within the doorway. Then she lay down, and no number of repeated commands made her move. He knew that if he mentally scolded her harshly enough, she would obey, but she was old and almost always in pain. He let her lie.

The shop girl put a hand on his forearm. When he did not resist, she slipped around the counter with a dancer's dexterity and slid her arm through his. "I've been thinking about closing up for a while, while Papa's on the phone. You think I should?"

She was—what? Fifteen? Sixteen? Was she right now calculating the days since her last period, considering her chances...? He let the back of his hand rest against her side, then shifted to cup a fleshy buttock. She murmured throatily.

"Do you have a place?" she asked. "Or do we need to sneak upstairs?"

Why couldn't Miriam be so unsophisticated, so loving and willing? He steered himself from answering, *Why not here on the sawdust* and was about to say, "I have an apartment overlooking the Landwehr," when he again saw Taurus sneaking forward.

This time when she gazed up at him, she growled. *Jealous.*

Erich let go of the sweet, rounded buttock.

"What's going on here!"

Erich glanced toward the back rooms, expecting her father, but the voice came from a figure, a boy, really, standing in the front door, just behind Taurus. He wore a Hitler Youth uniform with the sash indicating *Block Warden,* which made him responsible for political correctness in the neighborhood. A pistol was holstered at his side. Erich had never heard of the Hitler Youth carrying pistols, not officially anyway, but he was happy when he did not hear about that organization at all.

"Bertel!" the boy said, as if unsure he had been heard before.

"Oh, Gregor." She clucked in disappointment and went back around the counter, working again at the fingerprints in passing.

Eyes narrowed, a hand on the pistol grip, the youth maneuvered around Erich and leaned over the counter. She backed up; he clutched her by the wrist. "I thought you said there would never be a next time."

"We were just talking, Gregor. Besides, you hardly ever come around anymore." She was pouting.

"You think it's easy being a Block Warden? We cannot put the individual above the State."

Parroting, Erich knew. *Just like I used to...*

He lifted up the sack of sausage, wishing he'd had time to take her before her boyfriend arrived, so he might have handed her over, wet-sex and all.

Like Hempel using Goebbels' castoffs, he thought with a strange combination of delight and disgust. *Sharing the seed.*

The direction of his thoughts caused a disconnect from Taurus. Seizing the moment, she leapt for the pig. It was not the power-ballet leap of which she had been capable just a year ago. More a standing take-off from pain-filled legs. But it was accurate. She grabbed the pig by the forelegs and, though probably intending only to yank off a mouthful, brought it down with a twist of her powerful head.

"Stop that!" Forgetting her boyfriend, Bertel clutched at the pig's wired-together hind legs.

Taurus growled, backing away, refusing to release her grip.

For several moments, dog and shop-girl pulled in opposite directions, like the two women, it occurred to Erich, fighting over the baby in the Solomon legend. Then the Hitler Youth stepped away from the counter, legs spread and weight balanced, like a gunfighter in a cowboy film.

Erich took out a cheroot. "If you shoot, you'd better hit your girlfriend," he said calmly. "Because if you hurt the dog, I'll break both your arms. *Then* I'll break your legs."

The young gunman turned his attention toward Erich.

Erich lit the cheroot.

"Kill," he told Taurus matter-of-factly. "Kill the little bastard."

Taurus was scrambling across sawdust and in the air before Erich finished speaking. Her whole weight crashed into the youth, who cried out as he was knocked against the counter. Almost miraculously, the glass did not break.

The boy sat on the sawdust, mouth open, arms and legs splayed out like a rag doll, while Taurus licked his face.

"Kill him harder," Erich said, laughing with Taurus at their private joke and dragging on the cheroot.

The boy sputtered, but appeared to be afraid to move away. Taurus licked the youth's lips and all but stuck her tongue up his nose.

"Good girl." Erich bent beside her as she backed off. He could sense the fury that rippled beneath her fur at not being allowed to do real damage, feel it as she growled softly.

"Would you like her to *kill* you too?" he asked Bertel.

"No *thank* you." The words dropped like icicles from her lips, but the light in her eyes danced with amusement.

He paid for the sausages with a banknote and backed out of the door. That was twice in one morning that he had been loathe to expose his back, he thought. Suddenly he wished Hitler's war would come—almost a foregone conclusion these days. A battlefield where one could recognize the enemy might prove less dangerous than Berlin.

Chapter 9

Erich mounted Hawk and rode off, thinking about the girl, Bertel, about Miriam, about the woman beneath the table at Ananas. How different the world would be without women! Not better, but less...complicated.

Müller's comment came back to him. *We need a place without women. Where we can be ourselves.*

With that in mind, Erich abruptly steered across traffic and headed for Friedrich Ebert Strasse. He usually avoided his home-street, especially now that his parents had returned to the apartment they had abandoned, and taken over the tobacco shop again. That thieves such as his parents could be gifted the business they had previously ransacked was indicative of the moral penury of the times. It sickened him—but whether because of the immorality or because he hated his father, he wasn't sure.

Today was Sunday, and his father had not yet opened the shop. Probably gone to Mass, now that he was wealthy; celebrating not the bread and wine, but the roast duckling and vintage sherry he and Erich's mother would later enjoy.

The idea Corporal Müller had given him overpowered Erich's scorn for everything the tobacco shop represented. He passed the place, its shades halfway down, the tall windows looking sleepy-eyed, and parked his bike next door, against the gold-plated guardrail above what was once Kaverne, Grand dame Rathenau's cabaret for the upper-crust. He looped Taurus' leash through the rail and descended the stairs. Like regressing into a past life, he thought, letting the cool, moist shadows invade him.

Shaking, he removed his lock picks, a memento from childhood, from the small leather pouch at the end of his key chain. He willed the shaking to stop, and was thankful, regardless of the trembling, when he was able to open the door.

He slipped in quickly, like a boy afraid the bogey man was coming, and shut the door quietly and firmly behind him. The basement nightclub awaited him at the bottom of the metal spiral stairs, dust dancing in the light streaming through the green, sidewalk-level windows.

The place smelled old and musty. Disused. The chairs were upended on the tables, and everything was covered with dusty muslin. He assumed, for lack of specific knowledge, that the ownership of the place had reverted to the furriers, upstairs, from whom the Grand dame had purchased it, though perhaps it belonged to Miriam and she did not know it. Had Goebbels confiscated all her property, or just the Grünewald estate? It was worth looking into.

He went slowly down the steps, the metal ringing, his eyes on the empty dance floor. *There* he—and Solomon—had first seen *her*, a sylph in white tights, form-fitting tunic, swirl of pale pink niñon. Her singing once again hummed in his ears, her subsequent can-can—with his first look at her leotarded thighs—danced before his eyes. She had been fifteen or sixteen then, probably the same age as the girl today at the butcher shop, he thought with a slight shame; he and Sol two years younger. *"Wenn der weisse Flieder wieder blüht,"* she had sung, with the voice of an angel. "When the white lilac blooms again."

Someone had stacked two sets of two tables each close to the dance floor and canopied the creation with a shawl, as though to form an archway through which dancers might pass. Kids, he thought; probably partying. He wondered if they had gotten in as he and Sol used to, with lock picks. They could not have come up through the ancient sewer that ran beneath the cabaret and the tobacco shop, because his father had welded the grate shut at the shop, and he assumed the padlock had been replaced at this end. Not that he was about to go down into the cellar to find out. The place held too many bitter memories.

His fingers, injured when the grate came down, throbbed. As though needing something physical to alleviate the memory, he pulled down the shawl.

Remembering when he had last seen it, that night of the cabaret's pre-opening celebration, he buried his face in the cloth. The effect of its scent, of Miriam's perfume even after all these years, was immediate: he was instantly aroused.

Her thighs, her armpits, the line of her jaw—each place her colognes and perfumes touched—had their separate scent which lingered with him long after it should have dissipated. Of the senses, his sense of smell and hearing were the keenest.

He put the shawl over his shoulder like a beach towel and ascended the stairs, thinking about how the place would make a wonderful club for soldiers stationed in Berlin. Where officers and enlisted could mingle and drink without the distraction of women and with only minimal talk of the Party and the Führer. He would have to find out who owned the place and get permission for such an establishment without inviting suspicion that he was seeking to rescue Rathenau assets. But stopping now and again on the stairs and drinking in the smell of the shawl, he vowed not only to attempt the endeavor, but to succeed.

As he reached the top of the stairs, barking began, then a frenzied growling.

Seized with fear for Taurus' safety, he slammed through the door, locked it, and raced up to the sidewalk, almost in one motion.

Gregor stood in the street, both hands on the pistol, which was aimed at the dog. The youth's eyes were engorged, the veins in his neck corded from anger. "She's a danger to the Reich," he said, not taking his gaze off the animal.

Gall rose from within Erich as though Satan's hand had reached into his intestines and squeezed, bringing forth his bitterest, most terrifying memory: Hitler forcing him to shoot Achilles, Taurus' mother, for chasing a prized peacock.

"Put the gun down," he said, "and I will forget you were ever here."

He would acquiesce to anything, *anything*, but knew better than to attempt to bargain with the young crazies the Hitler Youth attracted.

"Do you know what this bitch took from me?" The boy's voice was shrill. "Do you think I'll be able to perform my duties, once word gets out? The whole neighborhood will laugh! Bertel will never stop laughing!"

Erich moved forward so stealthily and smoothly the boy probably did not realize he was advancing. Years learning woodsman's skills and two months with Otto Braun, the German martial arts' expert who had fought alongside Mao Tse Tung, had taught him well.

"The next time you fuck your Bertel, your face will be in the pillow and you'll think she's coming," he said, seeking to dull the youth's mental edge. "But she'll just be laughing at you. *Laughing.*"

The boy swung the pistol, and fired.

But he was too late. Erich had already launched feet-first into a baseball slide. The bullet zinged over his head, knocked a shard of glass from a window, and then his right foot snapped up, connecting with the youth's groin. Years of training and a lifetime of anger went into the kick. Air whooshed from the boy's mouth. He dropped the gun, doubled over, and collapsed to his knees as he fought for breath.

Erich lifted himself up, calmly brushed off his pants—his knee was scraped and bleeding, but he pretended not to notice—and picked up the pistol. He unloaded it and, after holding a cartridge between forefinger and thumb, dropped the bullets down the sidewalk drain. They clinked as they hit. Lovely as church chimes, he thought.

He knelt beside the boy, clenched the youth's chin in his hand, and jerked the face his way. "Which do you want me to break first, your arms or your legs?" he asked, carefully modulating his voice. "Or would you rather I let Taurus loose so she can chew off your balls?"

The face, already bedsheet-white with shock, whitened still more.

"Answer me," Erich said, "or both Taurus *and* I will go to work on you. We're a team, you know."

The boy's tongue worked spastically, but no sound emerged.

Erich threw the pistol down the street. It hit asphalt with a clatter.

"You tell your girlfriend that the next time I stop for sausages, she better be ready for me. I'm going to have her every way I can think of. Right there in the sawdust, if I feel like it, with her butt propped up on a flank roast." He pressed an index finger against the youth's nose as though pushing a button. "You don't tell her that, I'm coming after you and..." A phrase occurred to him, part of a hit song the Georg Haarmann scandal had inspired. *"Mach ich Pökelfleisch aus dir,"* he paraphrased to the boy. "I'll make smoked meat out of you."

Chapter 10

Sol extracted a brown egg from his pocket. He held it up to the moonlight filtering through the cigar shop's plate-glass window and turned it this way and that, wondering at God's artistry for having made something so simple, so perfect. "If I sat on you long enough, would God turn you into a chicken?" he asked aloud.

The egg was the last of a dozen he had found in the sewer—together with cheese and bratwurst, a box of chocolates, candles, a pencil and notebook, and a supply of books—*his*.

He patted his coat pocket. The biography of Isaac ben Solomon Luria, the mystic, was there, as always; he carried it around like a symbol of life, as if having it on his person ensured his survival.

Aside from the small supply of food, the sewer contained a canteen and two bottles filled with water, plus a bottle of cognac which, judging by the quality, had been lifted from the wine cellar of the estate. There was also a blanket, a pillow, and a box of first-aid items—including, to his initial amusement, a snake-bite kit. He had felt less amused when he realized the kit was probably meant to be used in the event of a bite by a sewer rat seeking food and warmth.

Cracking the egg, he lifted it to his mouth and sucked out the insides. It slid easily down his throat. He crunched the shell in the palm of his hand, looked around for somewhere to discard it, then put it in his pocket. "Bless you, Miriam Freund," he said, feeling a surge of energy.

One more night, Sol thought, looking around—one more long, damp night, and we will be out of here. For six days and nights he had lived a reverse existence. During the day, so as to make as little noise as possible, he slept. At night—like a vampire bat—he emerged from the sewer to wander around the basement and the deserted cabaret. Sometimes, like now, he came up to the shop, but mostly the memories here were too painful.

Once, a few hours before dawn, he actually had the temerity to go into the street. Hat pulled down low like that of an American film gangster, he wandered the streets. But he did not look enough like a derelict to fit in with the alleyway vagrants, and he was certainly not elegant enough to blend with the wealthy nightclub set; he was neither SS nor Wehrmacht, and the middle-class—scholars and merchants alike—were tucked safely in bed.

He pulled a pencil stub out of his pocket, licked the point, and crossed Saturday off his calendar. He had found the calendar that night, on the sidewalk, after watching the owners of the furrier shop above the cabaret throw what remained of their inventory into a beat-up lorry and leave as if the very devils of hell were chasing them. Doubtless they feared an SS witch-burning for their former Communist sympathies. The calendar had blown from the heap of litter they had left behind. From what he had seen in his brief wanderings, it was the same all over the city: piles of discarded belongings defied the image of flawless organization and a perfect society.

He stared at the picture of a leggy blonde in a white bathing suit. She stood on a balcony that overlooked Lake Geneva, leaning against the railing to support herself and displaying an ermine coat which hung casually from one of her tanned shoulders, its silk lining exposed. The Alps lay behind her.

Furs by Helvetia
Surround Her With Silver Linings

He imagined Miriam wearing the fur; imagined the two of them strolling together along the shore of the lake. He had found himself smiling. The sooner he could leave the claustrophobic atmosphere of the sewer forever, the better he would feel. He felt trapped down there, panicked, obsessed with ticking off the minutes, the seconds, till Sunday.

He ran a hand over his scraggly beard and grimaced at his image in the teak-framed mirror that had miraculously remained intact on the cigar-shop wall. His beard had grown in patches and was mottled underneath with scaly brown blemishes. He was gaunt and haggard. There was no heat during the night. Though he wore his coat all the time, he had developed a dry hacking cough which could well be symptomatic of TB or something equally deadly. Typhoid perhaps?

Angry at himself for being so morbid, he thrust the calendar and a fist into a pocket of his coat and surveyed the shop. The windows and door had been replaced or repaired, but the store still had a dark, oppressive quality that could not be explained away merely because the lights were off. The sewer held its terrors, but the shop depressed him—and in a large way that was worse, much worse, for in here he had known love and happiness and his father's bright eyes and bad jokes.

How much better, he thought, if *Die Zigarrenkiste* were still like the other Jewish shops he had passed on his night of wandering, the exterior walls grimed with swastikas and excrement. At least then it would still *belong*. To his people. And thus to him.

Standing with his forehead pressed against the wall, he cursed the whole Weisser family—and himself, for ever having believed in them. He found himself wishing that the goon who had started the fire in the cellar would return and finish the job. Only the memory of his father kept him from dousing the shop in gasoline and putting a match to it himself.

How secure he had once felt in his beliefs! Secure and...virtuous. That was it! As if being part of Walther Rathenau's dream of God and good government made him better than he would have been as just Solomon Freund, a Jew with a yen for scholarship.

The New Order had taken care of that, all right. Stripped him of his virtue. Now Hitler's followers were the ones who felt purposeful and fired with moral rectitude.

He envied them.

Even in a Berlin given way to penury and pain, he coveted their sense of conviction...those beautiful couples, glad to give up their strolls through the Tiergarten. They knew—*knew!*—that devil-may-care lives were evil and there was beauty only in Nazi law and order. Now, Hitler Youth used sawed-off boards to practice maneuvers between manicured shrubs where the wealthy had walked. Today felt good to them and they believed in an even better tomorrow. Trivia did not trouble them; it meant nothing to them that theirs was a world where the premium on good cigars had been replaced by so pressing a demand for weapons that Berlin's stores had run out of toy guns.

From the Zoo Station came the rumble of the night train from Frankfurt, as always exactly on time, running with Teutonic precision. Now *there* was true virtue.

The sound of running footsteps outside cut through his thoughts. Instinctively he stepped into the shadows.

"Herr Freund?"

A small pair of hands planted themselves on the outside of the lowest window pane.

"Herr Freund?"

A boy's cap and dirty face poked into view. Feeling silly for his fear, Sol saw it was a youth eight or nine years old.

He made his way across the shop; the gaslight outside revealed the child, standing in filthy tweed cap, ill-fitting coat, and woolen knickers, while snow lightly swirled around him. One sock was down around a skinny ankle.

"I bring word from Miriam Rathenau!" The boy's mouth was so close to the pane that his breath made a small ragged circle.

Fearing to open the door, Solomon tugged at the window, trying unsuccessfully to open it a crack. "Tell me!"

The boy glanced anxiously up and down the street, then reached inside his coat. "You are Solomon Freund?"

"I am."

The boy drew in his cheeks as if he were biting the inside of them to lend him courage.

"You need food?" Sol set caution aside and inched open the door. "Shelter? I'd be glad to share what I have."

The child shoved a thick envelope toward him. "I have to go."

Sol moved closer and took the letter. Word from Miriam! His emigration papers? *Their* papers? He stared down at the envelope.

By the time he looked up, the boy had dashed across the street.

"Wait!" Sol waved frantically. "Come back!"

The boy reached the alley beside the apartment building that had been Sol's former residence. Stopping in the shadow created by a cornice, he turned around.

Sol stepped into the swirling snowfall, concerned more for the child than his own safety. The beadle had told him of a boy he had tried to take out of Berlin, the son of a rabbi whose parents were transported. The youth, determined to remain in the city to search for his mama and papa, had slipped away in the confusion and crowds at the train station, too quick and too late for Beadle Cohen to find him. Could this be that boy?

Looking petulantly at the ground, the youth shuffled toward Solomon, pigeon-toed and tentative. A blast from the station stopped him. The ground shook. There was a *chug-whoosh* of the engine and of airbrakes releasing as the night train pulled away.

"Come quickly!" Solomon shouted above the din.

Suddenly the unmistakable wail of a police car shattered the night. A Mercedes squealed around a corner, fishtailing on the icy asphalt. Like a roach surprised by light, the boy scurried down the alley.

Run! Sol screamed at himself. Into the shop! Hide in the darkness and pray they aren't looking for you—-

What kind of man was he becoming, he thought as he reached the door, that he could hope they were after anyone but him...even a boy—a child?

Asking forgiveness from the boy and from God, he closed the door of the shop and pushed the letter into his coat pocket. Re-entering at this time of night could draw attention to himself, and running would be sheer stupidity. He must be like any merchant shutting up his place of business and strolling away—careful to hear and see nothing he was not supposed to.

Head down as though against the snow, he walked slowly but steadily toward the cabaret. When he could stand the tension no longer, he pretended to look at the watch he did not have, and tilted his head like any curious-but-respectful passer-by.

Overhead light flashing, siren blaring, the car had skidded to a halt in front of the apartment house. Two Gestapo agents in long black overcoats leapt out, pistols in hand. One of them, small and wizened—his hat had fallen off and Sol could see that he was bald—jumped the blue-spruce hedge and flattened himself against the wall of the apartment house like a combat soldier storming a pillbox.

"Halt where you are!"

The second agent, more youth than man, squatted at the alley entrance, pistol braced against his uplifted forearm as he aimed.

Paralyzed by the drama being played out before him, Sol stared through snowflakes gathering on his glasses.

The snap and whine of the bullet raged above the siren's scream. Sol tried to move, but his legs felt thick and heavy. His stomach heaved as he relived that moment he had witnessed Walther Rathenau's assassination...grenade spinning on the street...death shots hanging in the air.

Clutching his stomach, he forced himself toward the cabaret's stairs, gripped the handrail and swung himself down, slamming against the stairwell wall. Mustering what strength he still possessed, he peered over the edge of the sidewalk.

The men had disappeared down the alley.

He used his penknife to draw back the cabaret's jimmied deadbolt from its metal casing and eased himself inside. Standing on the wrought-iron landing, he rebolted the door. Sweating and shaking, he leaned against the wall.

Safe! Thank God!

He congratulated Miriam for having had the good sense to adjust the tumblers so the club would only *seem* to be locked. She had learned well from Erich and his lock-picks.

What am I thinking? A child's life was being threatened, perhaps for the very crime of having delivered him Miriam's message. He should be overcome with grief—and gratitude. But what if they captured the boy alive? Dragged him from the alley, what would he tell them? What *could* he tell them?

Slowly, as if the self-inflicted delay were punishment for his emotions, Sol took the letter from his coat's inner pocket. Using his penknife, he slit the edge of the envelope and, trembling, took out the single sheet of paper, folded many times. He recognized the handwriting at once as Miriam's:

Dearest, *They* move into *K* tomorrow—a perfect place to warm themselves, play cards, drink. Stay out of sight until I come—which may not be as planned. Look after the boy.
All my love.
MRF

Sol let the paper slip from his hands. It floated down among the tables, catching the dusty moonlight that slanted through the stained-glass windows.

K—*Kaverne*; MRF—Miriam Rathenau *Freund.*

If only he had insisted Miriam leave with him at once! Surely they could have bribed their way out of the country...but with what? *Erich's* money?

Outside, the siren stopped. On tiptoes, Sol peered through a hole made by a rock tossed at the window. The Gestapo emerged empty-handed from the alley. "Thank you, God," Sol whispered, with renewed shame and relief. "Now please send them away."

The men crossed the street and stood outside the cigar store. The bald one lit a cigarette, exhaled a mix of smoke and steaming breath. He said something to his companion, laughed loudly, and took hold of the door as if to check its security.

My God, I forgot to lock it! How could I have been so stupid!

Looking concerned, the man ground out his cigarette on the sidewalk and went inside, the other man surveying the street suspiciously. The lights went on. Sol cursed himself for his stupidity in dallying at the window; the cabaret was bound to be next. He must hurry, silently, to the sewer's comparative safety.

He started down into darkness. The first step squeaked and the metal spiral staircase echoed, amplifying the sound. He back stepped onto the landing and checked outside. Mopping sweat from his brow, he picked up the note from Miriam and descended the stairs with catlike caution. He crept across the dance floor and down into the sub-basement. Remembering the light, he felt around for the chain and pulled it on. The bulb popped and died.

He dropped to his knees, found and lifted the sewer grate.

After the night's crisp air, the sewer's stench billowed up like a tangible force. He held his breath, lowered himself onto the two-by-twelve and stretched upward to pull down the grate. It clanged shut. He groped for the boxes of provisions, wanting to touch them not so much for reassurance as for a focal point of existence. They were the immediate essentials of life, though how long a life was anyone's guess. He felt certain only that, for now, the sewer was the one refuge left to him in Berlin.

Chapter 11

Miriam had thought of Sol incarcerated in a camp for so long that it had become habit, like a bitter pill she'd had to swallow daily. Now that he was here, beneath her feet, she found herself tiptoeing around the shop. It was as if she were walking on his head and feared that she was causing him physical pain.

Every now and then she would forget for a moment and return to the images she had called forth over the years: Sol being beaten, starved, worked like a laborer. Then a board would creak beneath her soles, or the wind would whistle through the space between the shop door and the floor, and she would start guiltily, as if by forgetting she had somehow let him down. Again.

She had much to think about. She would have to be careful not to let Erich see a change in her. She would have to contact Perón. Most importantly, she would have to find a way to go down and see Sol—impossible unless both of the Weissers and not just Herr Weisser took the day off. She had been instructed to come in today because, he had said, a friend was unexpectedly coming into town and he wanted to be free to spend time with him. With any luck, his wife, Inge, would develop a headache, or remember a commitment to play cards, and Miriam would be left alone in the shop. By now, Sol would need food, water, possibly even medicines if the damp had made him ill.

Whatever it took, Miriam thought, she had to persuade him to go back to safety, to Amsterdam. And, if possible, she would send young Misha there with him. Though he might not agree with her at this moment, outside of finding his parents—a next-to-impossible task—reuniting the boy with the beadle would be the best thing she could do for him. She had been happy to find him a temporary haven with the underground group led by the furrier's son, but that was over now. She felt guilty about having been the person whose message had placed him in danger. On the other hand, they had already made Misha a message runner by then, and it had been only a matter of time before he would have taken it into his head to begin once more the futile search for his parents. All in all, he was better off where he was now, in Baden-Baden.

"Why are you staring into space? Is there no work to be done?"

The bell signaling her entry into the shop coincided with Inge Weisser's first criticism of the day. She had determined from the start to turn Miriam into *Aschenbrödel*, and Cinderella Miriam stayed. No matter what she did—not so much to please the woman but to keep the peace—Erich's mother felt obliged to spew venom whenever her husband was in earshot. Since he had entered behind her, this was one of those times.

She shed her fur, threw it at Miriam with a brusque instruction to handle it carefully and hang it up, and emplaced herself at the end of the counter. Her husband entered behind her, followed closely by none other than Deputy Commandant Otto Hempel.

"Sit, sit," Herr Weisser said, pulling out one of the chairs at the corner table. He pushed a box of cigars toward the man. "Help yourself. How about a schnapps to go with it? You are, after all, on holiday."

Hempel shrugged off his coat and smiled a feral smile. "A schnapps? In the morning? Why not. It's cold enough out there to freeze a nun's tits."

Weisser brought forth the bottle of cognac—his second best, Miriam noted. "How are things at the camp?"

"Tiring. Tiring. Those stinking Jews will never learn their place. I, for one, will be delighted when we have rid ourselves of all of them. And here? How is business?"

"Wonderful, Hauptsturmführer. We are most comfortable, Inge and I—thanks in great part to your...assistance. I have often wondered why God selected me for such good fortune."

"God? Perhaps." Hempel sipped at his cognac, put down his glass, lifted his cigar. "I suppose that makes me His instrument. Pity. I had hoped to take the credit. As I told you, I have great admiration for your son. When I came to you, it was because I wanted to ingratiate myself, shall we say, with his beloved family." He waved airily with the other hand. "I wish getting rid of the rest of them were as simple as that one. I regret not having kept the Iron Cross as a memento. You don't happen to have it, do you?"

Miriam froze. Though she knew that Sol could not possibly hear what these two disgusting excuses for human beings were saying, she almost expected him to intuit the scene and come flying up the stairs from the sewer, hands outstretched to grab Hempel by the throat—if she could restrain herself from doing it first.

Perhaps fortunately for her, the shop was invaded by a noisy group of officers. Stomping their feet to shake off the rain that had begun to fall, they entered the shop to buy supplies to take to Kaverne. The disarray, the noise and dust of refurbishing, did not seem to bother these officers of the Reich who gathered there at all times of the day or night—to play cards, drink, smoke cigars, and exchange stories about their conquests.

On the one hand, Miriam thought, their presence made Sol's hiding place a more dangerous choice; on the other, the combination of their noise, and that of sawing and hammering, served to cover whatever mishaps he might have in the darkness of the sewer.

Like everything in life, it was a toss-up.

She picked up the leather dice-cup from the end of the counter, shook it, and turned it over. Naturally, she thought, looking at her impossibly high score. When there are no stakes, I win.

Chapter 12

Someone, probably the beadle, had enriched the sewer with one of Sol's favorite treatises on the Kabbalah. The text was written in an ornate and frustrating style by an anonymous sixteenth-century physician accused of initiating impotence through sorcery. The man was found guilty of ligature, a necromancer's term that would later be incorporated into medicine.

The treatise appeared to touch upon such peripheral aspects of the Kabbalah that, at first reading, Solomon had thought the doctor lacked the acuity to dig deeper. Later, he had come to believe that the author had been afraid to go beyond the edges. Each rereading confirmed the clarity *behind* the words.

Our familiar, physical world, the author concluded, was only one part of a vast system of worlds, most of which were spiritual in their essence. That did not mean the spiritual realms existed somewhere else, but rather that they existed in different dimensions of being and that they interacted so much with physical reality that they could be considered counterparts of one another.

After six or seven rereadings by guttering candlelight, the physician's interpretation took on an increasing ring of truth.

"Spiritual realms exist in different dimensions of being," Sol summarized aloud. "They interact with physical reality. Thus, the spiritual and physical worlds must be counterparts of one another."

If gradation of *being* overlapped, he thought, could it not be possible that time did also?

By Wednesday he wished the visions *would* come—to offset the loneliness. If they came, he would try to place them within the context of his new theory. The visions did not come. To slow his bodily functions and to preserve his supplies, he ate and drank as little as possible. Thirst plagued him, but by the fourth or fifth day, he lost his appetite. What little he ate, he consumed out of boredom.

Boisterous commands erupted in the cabaret. Every now and then he heard hammering and the sound of furniture being scooted. Kaverne, he guessed with deepening fear, was being renovated. When the racket stopped, light laughter, men's voices, and military songs filtered down at all hours. He figured that meant that those who frequented the new club, SS or Gestapo, or Wehrmacht assigned to political roundups, pulled duty at odd times.

Even during the rare silences, he feared venturing up into the cabaret. Someone might come in unexpectedly, or he might leave evidence behind. An accidentally moved object might bring down Gestapo vultures.

Once, he stole up into the tobacco shop, amazed to find it empty after having heard people moving around up there at all hours. He had his hand on the door latch when he saw the sentry outside, patrolling the sidewalk between the shop and the cabaret. Keeping watch while those inside drank and sang. And, as likely, pretending to guard against Jewish assassins eager to murder good German soldiers.

Descending, Sol occupied himself with removing bricks at the sewer's east end, hoping to squirm into the major system, if need be. He succeeded only in substantially increasing the seepage.

On Sunday the tobacco shop, like the cabaret, was filled with rowdy laughter and the tromp of boots. Once, soft footfalls descended the tobacco-cellar stairs; Sol rose to his feet, certain it must be Miriam, only to have his hopes dashed when Frau Weisser curtly called her upstairs. Miriam did not come down again.

The night brought greater laughter above, greater depression below. By the next Tuesday, he cared only about the candles. Once they were gone and he was in darkness...what madness might set in?

He had read about experiments conducted in France's Chateau Caverns. Researchers discovered that subjects in dark isolation experienced metabolic changes. Biological time-clocks malfunctioned, approximating a forty-eight rather than twenty-four-hour cycle. People slept fourteen hours and stayed awake thirty-four, though their minds insisted their bodies underwent no changes.

Given the endless partying in the cabaret and the fact that the shop was staying open later and later to serve the new clientele, calculating time became impossible. The longer he was down in the sewer, the less he was able to tell how closely his mental time-count resembled reality. He grew more lethargic, less able to follow thoughts through to logical conclusions.

Have to keep moving, keep thinking., he told himself.

Chin against chest, he shambled back and forth, back and forth across the disassembled crates, through the sewer slosh that with maddening regularity raised or lowered around his shoes like part of an undercity tide—sixty steps there and sixty steps back, ducking under the boards below the grates at each end of the sewer, the distance seemingly preordained. Concentrating on parts he had memorized from the treatise, while his brain ticked off sixty steps...turn, duck...another sixty. A minute's slow walk...one and two and three—regular as a metronome in a sitting room where proper children performed Mozart and Mendelsohn and knew nothing of Nazis and the notion of world domination. Fifty-eight, fifty-nine, duck and, sixty, turn.

The seepage dripped as if playing counterpoint, forcing him to remember other music—most especially the Brahms Sonata he had heard Beadle Cohen play that first afternoon in the music room of the Judaica library on Behrenstrasse. The man was a violinist, a pianist, a wizard at setting Victrolas at precisely the right speed. "I am responsible for the upkeep of the temple," he had told Sol, "but I am equally responsible for the upkeep of my own wits and soul."

Aside from his duties at the temple, and his love of influencing the minds of children, only three things in his life mattered—books, music, and the study of the Kabbalah. Yet, except for sporadic gifts like *The Life of Luria*, the beadle had not spoken with Sol in any depth about Jewish mysticism until after the deaths of Rathenau and Grace and their discussion about dybbuks and lost souls and prophesies.

Searching for balance, Sol had gone to the library seeking something to help him overcome his sense of loss and inadequacy. Too short to reach a top bookshelf and too impatient to retrieve the library ladder, he had looked around for help—and there was the beadle.

Within that seemingly simple act of having discovered him in time of need, the beadle said, lay the first lesson of the ten *Sefirot:* the existence of fundamental forces of divine flow. The beadle's interpretation of the Jewish mystics, Solomon was later to realize, was tempered by his appreciation of the science of Einstein and Planck. Before God created light, and time therefore began, the beadle told him, the universe was random...but no longer; God did not roll dice. The aisles and avenues the free will can walk were divinely mapped, the journey preordained but not predestined. Beadle Cohen's being in the library was no accident, he argued, for God had known since before time began that he would be there.

The universe according to the beadle...as orderly as the number of steps in the sewer.

At their next meeting, the beadle talked of the Zohar, which he considered the foundation of the Kabbalah and the metaphysical basis of Judaism; he also gave Sol more books, dustier than usual.

Sensing his parents would disapprove, Sol had confined his reading to the old man's drafty garret above the library, with its two tiny windows shaped like a dove's wings. He had said little to his parents about his discussions with the beadle, even when his school marks dropped and Papa's questions and anger surfaced.

After a year's study, he had understood only that the Kabbalah encompassed a wealth of thinking one could not comprehend fully even in several lifetimes....

The last candle guttered and died.

He stretched out his arms as if to keep the walls from closing in, and stumbled onward. The muck again broke over his shoes. When he pulled off his shoes and wet socks, his flesh seemed puffy and slick. Something slimy was attached to his ankle. A leech.

He shuddered, and felt like hurling the treatise into the sewage. What use was it to him now! What use had his obsession with the printed page ever been! Erich had been right all along: in a world spinning out of control—a *dreidel* with blanks instead of letters—learning for which there was no immediate and practical application was effete snobbery.

The muck continued to rise.

He rolled up his trousers and paced on. Fifty-nine...duck...sixty...turn.

A rat, mewling, scuttled between his legs.

He threw crate parts atop one another, climbed on the makeshift island. How many days, he wondered, since he had seen Miriam? Made love to her? She knew the extent of his provisions and the health risk of staying in the sewer. She would get him out.

Something nuzzled his ankle.

He cried out, drew up his knees. The rat scurried off, but soon padded back through the slosh. Sol imagined it up on hind legs, nose twitching, sniffing the air, watching him for signs of weakness. He hoisted himself onto the two-by-twelve.

A canteen and a seaman's bag containing what little food was left hung near him. At least that was out of reach of the rodent! Digging into the bag, he found cheese stuck to the brandy bottle.

He peeled it off, ate most of it, threw the rest toward the other end of the tunnel, and immediately regretted the action. Knowing food was near would make the rat more aggressive.

The rat scampered, and he laughed. Like one of Erich's dogs gone to fetch! A wheezing seized him; he doubled over, coughing.

Trembling, he climbed down to the rickety island, trying to catch his breath. His lungs sounded as if they were filled with fluid. Sweat stung his eyes, and spectral motes of light danced before him in the darkness. In his desire to hear something living, he listened for the rat—imagining it fat and furry and asleep, dreaming of cheese and human flesh.

The coughing began again, pain piercing his lungs.

"Hear that, Doctor Rat? What do you think? Pneumonia?" He fought to keep his breathing steady, but the slightest inhalation sent a cartilaginous crackling through his ears and chest.

"This keeps up—you'll have a real meal to remember!"

For a long time he tried desperately to hold onto the vestiges of consciousness despite his feverish sweating and shivering. In the dark, only the rat and the sweat that ran in rivulets down his forehead and back seemed tangible.

The rodent stopped running when he fed it—bread, cheese, nearly a kilo of rancid corned beef that he found in the bottom of the seaman's bag, wrapped in a necktie.

A necktie, in a crypt! Sol chuckled—coughed—went on with the game. He sent the rat scurrying for food. He placed morsels in a circle around himself, as if he and the food were a ritualistic offering. He slept, sensing the rat running across his legs, sniffing his armpits and crotch, licking salt from his hands and hair. He began to welcome the possibility of being bitten. Pain was reality, was it not?

He shook the canteen. Precious little left. Seepage dripped onto his shoulders. He tried to stand, but his senses were awry. Which were the walls—what the floor? A paroxysm of coughing shook him. His head pounded. Tottering like an old man, he reached for the walls or the plank to steady himself, unsure they would be there, then sat back down, cradling the canteen like an infant.

"As the result of the liberation of Ethiopia by our Italian friends", a gravelly voice said in German, *"we have been given a unique opportunity."*

"Go to hell!" Sol waved his hands, pleased at being able to muster the strength to react. The canteen, its cap unscrewed, slipped from him. He lunged...clutched darkness, fell into the muck, struggled to right himself.

"Pardon me," he gasped as he crawled back onto the wood. "My mistake. *Welcome* to Hell!"

Chapter 13

"*Welcome to the world of the dead!*" the voice replied.

A stench like that of Limburger cheese. A burst of light. A round of soft applause.

Sol lost interest in the canteen and turned toward the sound, for a blue glow told him a vision had come to divert him——

——*A bulb in a metal collar hangs garishly from a slatted-board ceiling.* A tall man dressed in a surgical gown and gloves hits his head on the bulb and sets it in motion. The increased circle of light reveals Emanuel, legs spread, naked, strapped into a chair.

"Let us hope the world of death will place us on the path to immortality," the tall man says. He reaches up to stop the motion. Then he bows slightly, in deference to the applause of a semi-circle of SS officers wearing white gloves and dress swords, their faces made amorphous by the shadows.

"I apologize for the odor." He looks amused. "We doctors are immune to it, but some of you, those who are not physicians, may be less used to the smell of death than others. It is not always quite this putrid, gentlemen...*lady!*"

He emphasizes the last word and holds out a hand—a magician introducing his assistant. Judith Bielmann-O'Hearn, wearing an apron similar to the doctor's, emerges from the shadows. She is pushing a cart laden with surgical equipment. She does not look at him as she rolls a gurney from the corner, over beside Emanuel. The gurney is rigged with gutters on both sides, and at its foot is a large sink with a faucet, to which Judith attaches a long rubber hose.

The doctor adjusts the light so it shines down directly on the table and the mummified body that lies on it. "Take a look, gentlemen. A century of lying entombed, and the elder-of-elders you see here—disinterred by kind permission of that man in the chair—is more alive than many of my patients. Jews, you know, are forbidden to embalm their dead, a religious law the Elephantine Jews chose to ignore." He wrinkles up his nose. "If you think he smells bad now, you should have been around yesterday when he was exhumed!"

His humor is rewarded by uncomfortable chuckles. Though the body on the table is slippery with gravewax and the limbs look like sweet-potato tubers, the head is graced with a full head of hair.

"In a moment," the doctor goes on, "we will begin the autopsy. Keep in mind that embalming does not preserve the organs, so to examine *those* we must use our living specimen."

Emanuel strains against the straps that hold him down; Judith begins to cry audibly.

"Stop sniveling," the doctor tells her. "You got what you wanted. Your boatload of Jews is en route to the new homeland of Madagascar. However, the ship *can* be turned back. I suggest you co-operate."

"But, Herr Doktor Mengele, I did not know—"

"Nor, they say, did Judas. Did you think we carried the latest scientific equipment all the way here to Addis Ababa merely to see Ethiopia?" In an aside to the officers he says, "With the help of X-ray crystallography, we will be able to examine the unique, recently discovered subspecies of Jew, the Elephantines, and compare an ancient, though remarkably preserved, specimen to its modern counterpart—a living black prince!" He makes a sweeping gesture toward Emanuel as though introducing a trapeze artist.

"Please," Judith begs. "If this—this *demonstration*—must be performed, use me."

Mengele frowns. "Of what possible use could a flabby flat-chested Irish Jewess be to the cause of science? You have your boatloads. I suggest you adhere to your promise."

"But you said you would only need the Elephantines' *blood!*"

"And what good is blood if the vessel is not taken into account as a major variable? Be serious, woman! I'll vivisect every member of the tribe if need be! Now, silence! I will have silence!"

Judith steps back into the shadows, her face dark with pain.

"Herr Doktor Mengele." A voice from the crowd. "Why do you feel this subspecies of Black Jew is such a good candidate for your experiment?"

Mengele smiles. "Black Jews represent two races rather than one. We considered that alone to be worthy of study, which is why we turned our attention to the Cushitic Falashas. Now, thanks to the efforts of Frau O'Hearn here, we found the perfect subjects, the Elephantines, as they've come to be called."

Obviously conscious of his stage presence, he moves around the gurney to be closer to the audience. "Analysis reveals that even though they have been separated from the mainstream of the Jewish species for twenty-four hundred years, these Elephantines have a genetic anomaly corresponding to similar anomalies observed among various other relatively isolated Jew-subsects. After identifying that gene and placing it in mice, we found that, regardless of overcrowding in the cages, those mice carrying the gene appeared to experience *far* less distress when subjected to such living conditions, as compared to our control mice. In fact, some of the genetically altered mice appeared to *thrive* in such an atmosphere."

"Ghetto conditions?" the voice asks.

"Exactly." Mengele adjusts his monocle, thrusts out his hand.

Eyes filled with hate, Judith steps into the light, holding a scalpel. It looks as if she might stab the doctor, but instead she slaps the instrument into his glove.

"Any further questions before we begin?" he asks the audience.

"Yes, Herr Doktor," a squat SS colonel says. "Do you really believe it possible to isolate the enzyme—or gene, or whatever you call it—which contains this...this *collective unconscious* we've heard about? The *thing* that supposedly could enable you scientists to combine the natural cunning of the panther with the conniving of the Jew?"

"Anything the mind can conceive is possible, Standartenführer."

The doctor casually slices around the corpse's head and pulls the scalp down, opening it like a coconut shell. Judith turns her head and looks away.

"We have been working with dried blood serum for a decade," Mengele continues. "Now we are beginning to make rapid progress. Recently, for instance, Americans isolated the pituitary hormone. The real question is, how many ancient Elephantines will we have to exhume and compare with their living relatives before our results prove conclusive or the hypothesis proves false."

Straining slightly, he slices the body from the base of the throat down. Judith removes disintegrated grey matter from inside the corpse. A wavery vapor seems to arise, as if the spirit of the man has cried out against the violation. Emanuel moans softly but does not avert his eyes.

"These Elephantine Black Jews are remarkably resourceful and tenacious," Mengele says, "particularly when one considers the cowardice and physical ineptitude of other Jews. The specimen in the chair, for example, fought the Italians for years even after the liberation was formally declared. We could have used a few more like him when we marched on Cairo."

The testy murmuring his last comment provokes apparently pleases Mengele, for he smiles wryly before continuing.

"Enough conjecture. Let's begin at the beginning. Following the performance of the athlete Jesse Owens, the Führer personally instructed the scientific community to undertake a study of the musculature of African athletes. It seemed to the Führer that each subspecies might have physical characteristics which in some way could enhance the superior characteristics of our German youth."

The colonel again raises his hand. "We are here because your work, and that of Doktor Schmidt at Sachsenhausen, has enormous potential for bolstering performance on the *battlefield*, not the athletic field. I wish to know about morale. Would not surgically realigned soldiers, as you have called them, feel racially impure? Grafting musculature from Negroid subspecies onto our brave boys…I don't know, Herr Doktor." The colonel shakes his head uncertainly. "I doubt the men would stand for it…or if I could bring myself to lead troops that are not one-hundred percent…*German*. It would seem an affront to…"

"God?" Mengele gives the officer a patronizing smile. "To create the perfect Aryan, we are forced to contemplate the idea that perhaps we have been too narrow-minded. We might consider the possibility of creating, by combining natural selection and modern science, men and women of *inferior* mental, moral, and racial stock who nonetheless possess enhanced strength, speed, and endurance. These traits would enable them to serve the Fatherland equally well on the battlefield…or in the barnyard."

He lifts his hands palms out, silently begging forbearance. "I am the first to agree that this poses a moral question. Is it in our best interest to transform inferior humans into soldier-workers—non-Aryan *drones*—in order to reduce the loss of German blood on the battlefield and loss of time spent performing menial tasks?"

Mengele eyes the audience with a look of satisfaction, then turns to Emanuel and pushes aside the swatch of torn blanket that covers the naked man's groin.

"I remind you that I am a physician, not a philosopher. I leave moral choices to gods and dogs." A ripple of relieved laughter answers him. "Please, observe closely." He holds up the scalpel, glinting in the light. "The muscle fiber of most Negroes uses oxygen inefficiently. This results in explosive bursts of speed—witness Jesse Owens—but poor endurance. In other words, natural selection produced Africans that ran *away from* large animals, not ran them down." More chuckles. "In other parts of the world—Europe for instance, among some North American Indians, and in a few places here in Africa, such as among the Ethiopians," he lays the side of the scalpel on Emanuel's inner left thigh; the black man quivers and squeezes shut his eyes, "conditions were such that long-distance running was required."

Replacing the monocle, Mengele bends over his subject and cuts a careful incision from the groin to the knee. Sweat shines on Emanuel's blue-black skin and his body arches. Mengele cuts perpendicularly at each end of the incision and carefully peels back the epidermis, exposing tissue. Blood wells in the wound and streams down the leg. Emanuel twists his head from side to side and his features scream silently with pain, but he does not utter a sound. Judith stands immobilized. When Mengele orders her to sponge the area, her hand trembles convulsively.

"They say sprinters are born, not made. This is because sprinters' muscles, unlike those of distance runners, cannot be developed regardless of the amount of athletic training." Mengele draws the scalpel toward himself through the tissue as though exquisitely filleting a trout. The black man's mouth, turned toward the ceiling, opens. He still makes no sound. "However, we have found that a few select runners, a very select few," Mengele lifts an index finger for emphasis, "have a high proportion of muscle similar to those of sprinters...*but still maintain the efficient use of oxygen characteristic of the long-distance runner.* Put another way: they can run very fast—very far. Or vice versa." He breaks into a boyish grin.

Rising, he drops the monocle expertly into his free hand and, balancing the reddish-pink tissue across the scalpel, transfers it to the gurney. He skins off a tiny slice and, using tweezers, places it in a specimen jar.

"We have found evidence of all this in many Ethiopians—also in Kenyans, I might add, though subjects available for analysis have been harder to obtain in that nation. Here we can rely on our Italian friends. So! Many Ethiopians possess this rare combination of sprinters' muscle and oxygen efficiency. They are slender, from a high-altitude country, and raised in a culture where long-distance running for communication and hunting was necessitated. Mark my words, gentlemen—even without the benefit of modern training methods, an Ethiopian such as Prinz Zaehev Emanuel here could win," sarcasm surfaced in his voice, "an Olympic marathon."

With a showman's skill he gestures toward his star performer. Everyone laughs. Emanuel is unconscious, his head tipped against his left shoulder, blood meandering down his leg and pooling on the floor. Judith is on her knees, sponging the linoleum.

Mengele scrapes tissue from the mummified corpse into a second jar. "Imagine a future," he tells the officers, "in which human drones who thrive in extremely crowded conditions are capable of working at great speed and with tremendous endurance! Imagine how well we could use the assets and abilities of the lesser races, for the benefit of the Fatherland...and with minimal impact upon German *Lebensraum!*"

The officers look at one another. Heads nod; eyebrows raise in affirmation.

"Frau *Doktor.*" Mengele labels the specimen jars and places them in a box. "Take these to the laboratory. When the film has been developed, bring it back."

Judith gets up from her knees, takes the box with a distasteful look. She almost drops it, and makes a sound. What emerges is a gurgle——

Solomon awakened into the sound, but it was not Judith's; it was his own. He tried to shift an arm. A leg.

I'm just dreaming I'm awake, just dreaming! he told himself, but he knew his eyes were open. As was his mouth. *If I can just say something!*

No sound issued through his lips. He could not move even his tongue. Then, relieved, he felt movement, only to have his relief turn to horror. His tongue had not moved. Something else—

—a spider.

He felt its velvety pads claim purchase on his chin and cheek as it struggled to extricate itself—legs, head, thorax—from his mouth. He could see nothing in the pitch darkness, could not brush it away as it crept up his face and passed across his left eye, hairs twitching against his pupil.

Wake up! he screamed at himself. *Wake up!*

The spider climbed his upper eyelashes and tested his brow. Taking its time, it spun a web...crossing and recrossing the left side of his face...drawing sticky gossamer from his brow to his mouth. Still he could not move. Could not scream. Could feel only the spider—and tears spawned by fear rolling down his cheeks.

Time passed, how much he had no way of measuring save for the racing of his heartbeats, until the blue came, flickering, changing from hyacinth to cerulean and finally, to cobalt——

——*dusk. The sky is deeply blue and refractive, as if a bowl of colored crystal has been turned upside down.* Angry clouds skewer the horizon. Mengele, scalpel in hand as though it is a cigarette, leans against a waist-high semi-circular balcony wall of whitewashed masonry carved with arabesques. The SS officers stand beside him and in the portal of shadow created by the open balcony doors.

On the ground far below, black men, women, and children—most dressed in white muslin tunics or colorful sateen robes—raise their voices in a litany sung in a strange tongue. Their skin appears darkly chestnut in the light, a sea of bronze faces.

"They call this event 'Maskal,'" Mengele tells his audience. "It honors Queen Helena's supposedly finding Christ's Cross. To give thanks, she lit a bonfire in Palestine so big her son Constantine saw its glow back in Constantinople. Christians never have been known for choosing verisimilitude over hyperbole."

The officers chuckle. Below, the sea of spectators parts; a procession of priests carrying tasseled ceremonial umbrellas, and laymen and boys robed in embroidered satins and carrying incense and elaborately molded golden crosses, serpentine in stately rhythm toward the tallest of three towers of piled wood.

"Time to show our respect for the newest subjects of our Italian friends," Mengele says. He and the other officers snap to a Nazi salute as the procession winds below, followed by a parade of white-gowned men holding straw torches aloft. Next come brass bands and then floats, heavy with flowers, sporting flaming crosses.

The trailing celebrants, more than a thousand strong, carry wicker baskets filled with bread and daisies.

"Perhaps in another two thousand years the Ethiopians will celebrate a much more lasting and meaningful cross," Mengele says in a low, impassioned voice, "the swastika!"

"*Sieg heil!*" his listeners say quietly but earnestly.

Judith appears in the doorway behind them. She slips a scalpel and a piece of cut surgical tape into her lab coat, then clears her throat. "Herr *Doktor*," she says, "the X-ray films are ready."

The priests below begin to circle the towers, bowing, blessing what the flames will consume, swinging incense burners like pendulums and filling the air with the scent of jasmine and sandalwood. Mengele breathes deeply, appreciatively. "Let us go inside—committed with new purpose," he says.

The other officers stand aside respectfully as he enters the room. Brows furrowing, he pauses and covers his nose. "Our prince has emptied his bowels. He apparently has no respect for medical history or for our sensibilities."

Emanuel, apparently still bound to the chair, has fallen sideways onto the floor. When the doctor starts to nudge him with the toe of a shoe, the black man leaps up. Shrieking, babbling, he reaches for the doctor's neck. Pulls it close. Bites.

Mengele squeals. Gargles. Chokes. His thick flesh bulges against the black man's fury, and a bone snaps——

The scene dissolved. The voices stilled. Solomon felt warm blood on his hands and, in them, the movement of a furred thing.

Grimacing, he dropped the rat into the seepage. Without pity, he listened to it flop and cough in its death throes. If the Kabbalistic tradition of the transmigration of souls were truly part of the order of the universe, he reasoned, then transmogrification must also be possible: man becomes animal; and animal, man.

He forced himself to become calm. Had he not just now placated whatever spirit had pervaded the sewer, Berlin, and his life? The rat was Mengele. He—Solomon—was Emanuel...and free at last.

Chapter 14

No matter what he did, the sadness in Misha would not go away. It so enshrouded his thoughts that he was hardly aware of the passage of the days.

When he had literally bumped into Fräulein Miriam after the beadle's departure from Berlin, he'd still had hope. He had waved farewell to her from the limousine when Konrad dropped her off at the tobacco shop, believing her when she promised to do everything she could to get news of his parents.

"It could take time, Misha. And the news will probably be bad," she said, holding him close. "Do you understand what that means?"

He understood. But understanding and acceptance were not the same thing.

Konnie drove him to a block of flats at the dark end of Kantstrasse. There he was taken in by a rough-looking group of young people who, he quickly learned, were part of the underground. The flats, Konnie told him, had belonged to the furriers who had owned the shop next door to *Die Zigarrenkiste*—above the sewer where he and the beadle had taken refuge. This was confirmed when one of young men gave him a fur coat to use as a blanket and identified himself as the son of the owners of *Das Ostleute Haus*. He was given enough food to survive, a blanket on the floor, a few books, and instructions to stay out of the way.

He was not sure how long he had been there when he ran his first message, perhaps about a week. He was given a tweed cap, a coat of sorts, and a pair of warm knickers, and sent out into the snow. Two days and half-a-dozen deliveries later, he was handed a note from Miriam to Solomon Freund. What he knew he would never forget was creeping uncertainly across the street to the tobacco shop and seeing Herr Freund's gaunt, bearded face appear behind the plate-glass window. He had scaly brown stuff on his face, and was coughing as if he had pneumonia or something.

And suddenly there were sirens, and a Mercedes with Gestapo and guns and shots, and he was racing down an alleyway like a hunted animal.

The next morning, one of his companions awoke him before dawn.

"The Gestapo know what you look like," the youth said. "It is too dangerous for us—and for you—to stay here. Go to the corner of Kant and Niebuhrstrasse. Konnie will be waiting for you there. Don't say anything. Just get into the car."

Misha did what he was told. By the end of the day he was ensconced at the home of Fräulein Miriam's dressmaker in Baden-Baden, where Konnie had driven him on the pretext of taking her several bolts of fabric to make into dresses for Miriam for the upcoming holiday season. The trip across the country and south was a long one, but the car was comfortable and warm, and he slept most of the way. It was dark when they got there and he was hungry.

Madame Pérrault fed him at once. She was a pretty woman, bright, cheerful, and practical. He liked her.

The next morning, she put him to work at the button-covering machine to earn his keep. To his surprise, he enjoyed the work.

The machine looked something like the microscope at school, except that the top was hinged. There was an indentation on the ledge for a metal shell, and another in the lever.

Madame Pérrault would hand him scraps of fabric that matched the outfits she was sewing. He laid a scrap on the ledge, pressed in a shell, and covered it over with the fabric. Then he inserted a smaller shell into the lever and pressed down.

The top fitted into the bottom and became a covered button which she could trim and attach to the clothing of her wealthy customers.

He quickly developed a rhythm and produced, she said, more buttons each hour than she could make in a day.

He expected to be hidden away, in a place like the sewer. To his surprise, Madame Pérrault simply told him to be careful not to talk to strangers, bedded him down in a small attic room where she stored her supplies, and introduced him as her cousin's son, come to visit from the city. He was well fed and reasonably well clothed. She patched his trousers, kept his shirt clean, and treated him with kindness.

Still, she was not his mama.

When Fräulein Miriam returned with Konnie, she returned the bolts of cloth, had a brief discussion with the seamstress about patterns, and took him into the garden.

"I have no news for you," she said, kneeling before him. "You must be patient."

"I want to come back to Berlin with you."

"You are safe here, Mishele." She stroked his head. "Is Madame not treating you well?"

"That's not it at all," he said, staring her down. "I want to be there when you find my mama and papa."

She sighed heavily. "I thought you understood, Misha. The chances are we will not find them. Berlin is a dangerous place. You are better off right here."

"Then I will walk to Berlin. I will. Truly. I want to come…home."

"But I can't take care of you," Miriam said. "Herr Freund, the man to whom you delivered my message, is in the sewer."

"I can stay with him in the sewer. Please."

"I cannot get him out, let alone get you in," she said.

"Please."

She looked as if she were about to say something more, but remained silent. He took that to mean yes. Remembering his manners, he went indoors to say farewell and thank you to his hostess who looked shocked, kissed him, and said he could return any time he wished.

He went outside to the car. It was gone. Only his earlier resolve kept him from bursting into tears.

"Sometime around Christmas I will have to go to Berlin myself for fabrics and threads, and to visit family," Madame Pérrault said. "If you still want to return, I will take you with me."

Reassured, but still angry at what he saw as Miriam's betrayal, Misha settled back into the routine of the household. Days passed, then more than a week, not unpleasantly, and as it did, so did his anger. He remembered how Miriam signaled him away on the day the beadle left, and then rescued him. He remembered her explanation and her kindnesses. When the time came for Madame Pérrault to make her trip, he had almost forgotten his anger.

But he had not forgotten why he had to return to Berlin.

"I cannot take you to Fräulein Miriam," she said, when he reiterated his wish to go with her. "She has more than enough worries. I will have to take you back to the underground. They will take you in if you are willing to be a messenger for them again."

"But the Gestapo…?"

"By now, hopefully, they have forgotten you."

"Do the others know that I am coming back?" Misha asked.

"Perhaps yes, perhaps no. I sent word, but I have not had confirmation. You will have to take your chances."

"Will you tell *her* where I am?"

"Of course. She would want to know."

At the end of the day, with a quick kiss, a hug, and a wish for his safety, Madame Pérrault pressed a bag of food into his hands and deposited him on the sidewalk, two blocks from the flats on Kantstrasse. Behind him he heard her say quietly, "Merry Christmas, boy. Happy Hanukkah."

Suddenly afraid, remembering no-neck and the sound of jackboots and gunshots, Misha ran the two blocks in the darkness of what he now realized was Christmas Eve. Though he slunk into the building and tried to be quiet, his footsteps echoed hollowly in the deserted stairwell.

When he reached the flat, he found the door ajar. The place had been ransacked and there was no one there. Terrified, careless of his own safety, he charged down the stairs and away from the building. When he stopped running, he found himself at the fence of a small, concrete school playground on Niebuhrstrasse. At the back of the playground, he could see a large tree, beneath which stood a cluster of garbage cans. He scooted over the fence and headed straight for them.

Upending one of them, which happened to be empty because, he supposed, of school holidays, he crawled inside and, despite the freezing cold, fell into a sleep filled with nightmares of fat men with boots and guns and no neck. He awoke at dawn to the sound of Christmas church bells. Shivering and stiff with cold, and silently thanking Madame Pérrault, he opened the bag of food and ate a roll and a piece of sausage and tried to plan his next move.

All he could think of was Fräulein Miriam and the sewer safe-house. He waited as long as he was able, hoping some other idea would come to him. Finally, driven by the cold, he crawled from his hiding place, scaled the fence, and started toward the tobacco shop. When he got there, the lights were on and the door was ajar.

Thank God, he thought, bursting into the shop. "Fräulein Miriam," he said. "Help me. Please. You must hide me in the sewer with Herr Freu—"

Hands gripped him from behind and turned him around. He had not noticed the two men sitting at the table in the corner, a miniature Christmas tree and two brandy snifters between them on the table. The one leaning forward to hold him looked like an older version of the uniformed man with whom Fräulein Miriam had breakfasted that morning at the Kempinski Café; the other wore the uniform of the men who had chased him down the alley. Misha stared at his hair, which shone as brightly silver as the tinsel on the miniature tree.

"So that's where he is," the man who held him said. "I might have known."

"What a charming looking youth," the silver-haired man said, smiling. He motioned for the older man to release the boy and, taking hold of Misha's wrist with one hand, tussled Misha's hair. "And how fortuitous that he should bring us this information. I will leave you to take care of him for me, Friedrich, while we take care of our morning business."

Misha struggled against the grip of the man who held him.

"Don't be afraid," the silver-haired soldier said. "We're here to help."

"He is a handful," the other man said.

Misha craned his neck to look outside and prayed desperately that he would see Fräulein Miriam headed toward the shop. His view was blocked by the ugly, no-neck man, who was leaning casually against the plate-glass storefront, smoking a fat cigar.

He stopped struggling.

Chapter 15

Thirst. The faucet in the sub-basement beckoned like a mirage. He lay on the crating, lost in vertigo, suffocating in the stench, listening to his own panting. The darkness wheezed with each breath. His mouth worked spasmodically, like that of a sleeping infant searching for the breast. Sometimes he ran a hand along the slick wall so contact with physical reality outside himself would tell him he was still alive. His muscles, lacking water, ached; his scalp itched with lice or fleas. He had clawed, scratched, torn at his clothes, but the insects continued feasting.

Finally he crawled from the drain to the antique sinks in the sub-basement corner beneath the stairs. One of the tap handles had rusted off; the other, though loose, was intact. He used a packing-crate endboard for a pry bar. The handle turned, protesting and squealing. Belching, groaning, the tap dribbled—then gushed.

The water, rusty, burned his parched throat. He retched, spat, cursed the plumbing as he let the tap run, then cupped his hands and slurped. The metallic taste was still present. Though he knew what drinking rust might cause, he filled his canteen and tried shutting off the tap. The handle spun loosely in its collar.

Putting a thumbnail in the headscrew to secure it, he pressed down on the handle. A major victory—the only casualty one-half of a thumbnail. Now the tap fizzed like weak soda water.

For a moment he felt like sneaking up the stairs and peering under the cabaret door as he had as a child, when he had first seen Miriam-- the featured performer at a private party her grandmother had thrown in the cabaret—but common sense won out, and he lowered himself back into the drain.

He slept fitfully and awoke feverish, his guts gripped by a steel hand. He drew up his legs and pushed his fists against his stomach, praying that the cramps would leave him.

Warm wetness suddenly flowed between his thighs. Diarrhea. He might as well have filled the canteen with seawater.

He picked himself up, his movements jerky, uncoordinated, a marionette with an unskilled master. What transcendence, he wondered bitterly, did the Kabbalah prescribe for lifting body rather than soul? How fortunate the composer who'd spent his life creating music in honor of Judaism, only to be killed by a Torah scroll which fell from its cabinet and struck him on the head. That seemed fitting for a scholar; rotting and dying in a sewer did not.

He boosted himself onto the plank, lay dizzied and panting, then groped for the seabag. At the bottom were two crackers. He put one in his mouth, chewed, massaged his throat to get it down. Like force-feeding a reptile, he thought angrily.

Faces shimmered in the blackness. *His father, in the rocker, floating above Friedrich Ebert Strasse by holding himself up by the Iron Cross ribbon around his neck. Then appeared Mutti and Recha, waving good-bye as a train streamed beyond the end of its tracks and sank with a hiss into the North Sea. Miriam, eyes smiling as she fellated Erich, who leaned nonchalantly against a tree, a German shepherd beside him on a choke chain.

Rathenau. Shattered bone and flesh blackened by powder burns, a Reichsbanner handkerchief pinned to his cheek.

Stop! Sol reached to squeeze the apparition into nothingness. Pinwheels of light exploded inside his head. Above him, boot heels clattered on concrete. He seized Rathenau by the throat.

And lost his balance. Clutched the plank, upside-down like a sloth, he fell with a splash.

He tried to climb from the seepage, but his hands slid down the wet wall and he toppled backward. When he arose, sputtering, he heard a hinge squeal. Light lanced into the blackness. He raised his hands to shield his eyes, begging a vision to come erase the nightmare of whatever new reality had invaded his awful domain.

"You are right, Herr Weisser," someone said in a northern dialect. "There *is* a Jew in here—and he stinks like a pig!"

Sol pawed at the light.

"Merry Christmas, Jew," the man continued in *Plattdeutsch*. "Climb from your sty!"

Delirium followed. He felt himself crawl onto the board and was yanked by the arms through the drain, then sent hurtling up the stairs. He staggered into the cabaret and collapsed. Someone said, "Jew football!" and kicked him in the ribs. He lay weeping on the floor. Before him lay shards of a wineglass, like the one he had crushed underfoot at the end of his and Miriam's marriage ceremony. He took hold of a shard, gripping it so tightly that it dug into his palm. Through his fog of pain and humiliation, he saw blood rise between his fingers. The sight of it brought a peculiar sense of relief: the pain felt sharp and clear. *Clean.* Self-inflicted, and returning to him a bit of dignity he had thought gone forever.

The fog lifted from his eyes.

"What day is it?" he gasped. "What date?"

"Stinking Jew doesn't even know when Christmas is celebrated!"

Again he was kicked. He doubled over in agony. *So many days in the sewer. Weeks.* The darkness had worked its black magic on his senses all too well.

He looked up, saw Miriam's shawl draped around an autographed picture of Hitler.

"Herr Freund?"

A child in a ratty coat entered Sol's sight. Where had he seen the boy before? When?

Blood trickled from the boy's nose. He was crying quietly. "I'm sorry, Herr Freund," he whispered. "I didn't mean to— Those people in the tobacco shop...I thought they were your friends. I thought they would hide me down *there* again."

"Whatever happened, it's all right," Sol whispered back as he struggled to stand. A soldier shoved him with a rifle and he went pitching up the metal stairs, but he reached back and took the boy by the hand before he stepped out of Kaverne and into the street.

Chapter 16

If I don't get out of the car right now, I'll be sick.

Miriam tapped Konnie on the shoulder. "Let me off. *Here.* I'll walk the rest of the way to the shop."

By the set of his back, Miriam knew he disapproved. That made two disapproving males in the last hour; Erich had insisted she did not look well and should stay home.

Climbing from the car, she pulled her coat closed against the biting cold. Sick, all right; but not from the weather. Sick with worry. Sol—down there two weeks, with too little food and drink.

Not that she had good news for him. Perón was apparently not in Germany. Last Sunday, she had tried to get down to the cellar, but the shop was never emptied of its beer-happy customers popping in from Kaverne. With the shop that busy, the Weissers had not gone to Mass. They had watched her every move, calling her back if she were out of sight even for seconds.

Today would be equally busy, but it was Christmas. Surely the Weissers would go to Mass. It was only a matter of time until some soldier wandered down to the sub-basement, perhaps to sleep off a drunk, saw a candle within the sewer or heard a noise. Someone coughing. The shuffling of feet.

She quickened her pace.

"Merry Christmas!" a barrel-organ man called to her.

"Merry Christmas." She slowed down and dug for a coin to deposit in his hat. On impulse, she said, "Come to the shop later. I'll find you a good cigar."

He grinned and ground out the beginning notes of *"O Tannenbaum."* She walked on, head lowered against the wind.

From a block away a siren blasted, drowning out the carol.

She looked up.

Konrad, disobeying her instructions to go home to his family and spend Christmas Day with them, had parked the touring-car up against the curb in front of the shop. He seemed to be signaling her to stay back.

She stepped into the shelter of a doorway and waited as a car with SS insignia pulled up in front of Kaverne and three men got out. Two of them, rifles in hand, hurried down the cabaret steps. The third loitered at the sidewalk. She recognized him from the estate. She frowned, puzzled.

Hadn't Erich said that Otto Hempel was now deputy commandant of the Sachsenhausen detention center? Had he flown that little plane of his back to Berlin to personally oversee an arrest?

Oh my God, she thought. Sol. Flattening herself against the wall, she pressed her hand to her mouth to stifle a scream. Friedrich Weisser burst from the shop, dragging Misha by the hand. He and Hempel exchanged looks. He prodded Misha toward the steps, and the three of them disappeared.

Frozen with fear and cold and nausea, she watched as a silent column of men, women and children, flanked by guards with shepherds, rounded the far corner.

She had seen such lines before—emerging from side streets and alleys— guards and shepherds herding them along the avenue. Quiet Jews. Heads down. Men carrying satchels; women with babies bundled in lovingly crocheted shawls and patchwork blankets, as if El Greco, ordered to paint a tragedy in somber hues, had carelessly splashed his canvas with bright colors. They moved with the steady step of people headed for a train they knew would not leave without them. Some had children tagging along like exiles from a classroom. Others were murmuring thanks to God for giving them the foresight to have put their sons and daughters on the special trains to Amsterdam and Zurich.

When the column stopped in front of Kaverne, not a person moved. No one murmured, or looked toward the cabaret. *They know why they're stopping,* she thought desperately. *They've seen it too many times.* They were in a funeral march, mourning themselves.

Moments later Sol and Misha stumbled up the steps that led down to Kaverne and sprawled headlong into the street. Misha stood up first and stooped to help Sol. A guard shoved the boy aside and ordered the column to move on.

Miriam bit into her gloved hand as Sol staggered to his feet. The child looked terrified. Sol, painfully thin and apparently more humiliated than frightened, seemed to be concentrating on the physical act of walking.

Keeping a fair distance behind them, Miriam followed. Once in a while, a face appeared at a window, pulling aside a lace curtain to stare out. On every corner, Nazi flags snapped in the breeze. The snow had stopped and, as the procession passed the first corner of the Tiergarten, the sun filtered through the clouds. Passers-by standing among dried and dead shrubs stopped to stare.

The column reached the Zoo Station and paused beneath the huge clock, its horn-blowing cherubs decorated with holly.

At the far side of the station, a dirty steam engine stood in front of three boxcars and a caboose. The train had apparently been conscripted from a tourist run; wilted streamers and deflated balloons dangled from the cab.

The guards released the pins of the boxcar locks and pushed the doors open with a clang. "Get in!" One motioned with his carbine.

No one moved.

"In!"

A heavy-set woman with a baby in her arms approached a guard cradling a submachine gun. The shepherd heeled beside him rose. Growling. Hackles raised. The woman detoured around the dog, unknotted her scarf and shook out her curly hair, as though doing so would improve her looks and her bargaining power. "They have made a mistake. I have done nothing."

The man gave her a fatherly smile. "You're not a Jew, eh? Just born to the wrong parents?"

"I've done nothing," she repeated.

His smile broadened. "If you've done nothing, you're a non-contributor to the State and should be eliminated."

"I don't mean I've done *nothing*. I mean I've done nothing wrong." She uncovered the infant's head. "Nor has my little one."

"Are you Jews?"

"Yes."

"Then you are criminals."

"Don't you understand?" She grabbed his sleeve. "I am a German."

The man's smile froze. He issued a soft command, and the dog at his feet growled again and leapt. The woman fell beneath its attack, one arm raised in a feeble effort to ward off the animal, the other tightened around her child. The dog sank its teeth into her cheek, ripped out a hunk of flesh and bit down again. She shrieked. Her curls bounced obscenely as the dog shook her head side to side. Blood pooled on the asphalt.

Miriam saw that Sol was not watching the terror, but rather the guard. *Do nothing,* she silently begged him. *Nothing.*

The baby rolled from her arms and lay kicking, too young to know its danger as the animal backed off and shook itself as though after a swim. Blood from its jowls showered the street.

Lying on her side, the mother reached for the child. Her legs just moved anxiously while her upper body remained in place, like a live insect pinned through the head.

The dog padded over to the child, poked its nose beneath the blanket, and opened its huge jaws.

Miriam could not move. She felt cast in amber.

"Down, Prince," the soldier said softly. "Good boy."

The dog backed away from the baby and the guard knelt to feed it a treat. As he petted the dog, he leaned his submachine gun against his leg, calmly unholstered his pistol, and shot the woman between the eyes. The roar echoed inside Miriam's bones, turning marrow into flame. Blood and gray matter sprayed the street.

"Anyone else done nothing wrong?" The guard looked around. Several people were vomiting. Others cried softly and covered the eyes of their children.

"You two!" He pointed at two prisoners. "Remove that mess."

One man, trembling and white-faced, obeyed. The other paid for his hesitation with his life.

"All right, you!"

The third man obeyed at once. The first man had already scooped up the child in a massive arm and handed it to the nearest female prisoner. Now the two men carried the dead woman up the ridged plank and into the nearest car.

"Everyone in!" the guard commanded.

As if seeking shelter from a city gone mad—or sure that what awaited them could not be worse—the people crowded into the boxcars. A horn blasted, like the animate sound of Miriam's conscience. She too had done nothing. *Nothing!* Not one move to help the woman. Nor could she attempt to help Sol and Misha without endangering them and herself. If only she had fled with Sol either of the two times he had begged her to! *It's my fault. My fault,* she cried inwardly in despair.

"Come, Miriam." Konrad appeared behind her and took her arm.

Like a little girl—perhaps because he finally called her *Miriam*—she did as she was told.

"Oh, God, Konnie! Why?" she whispered as she slid onto the front seat and, needing his strength, clung to his arm and put her head against his shoulder. Her sobbing made her whole body heave. "I don't understand. They killed that woman and then the man—"

"I saw," he said quietly.

"It was cold-blooded murder! All she did was ask a question. She wasn't even resisting arrest. She had a baby in her arms.... How do they justify it?"

"The records will show that the man disobeyed orders and the woman resisted arrest...or tried to escape."

"Escape the SS, and rifles, and dogs? Risk retribution—to their families, their friends?" Would she, she wondered? "Where will they take them?" she asked, feeling stupid. They always said the same things: *A holding facility— a resettlement camp—until emigration or vocational relocation can be arranged.* Meanwhile, their houses, land, possessions were confiscated. They called *that* redistribution of wealth. *All Germans must share evenly,* the rhetoric explained.

Damn the rhetoric, she thought, and damn them all to Hell. What had happened, what was continuing to happen, was as fathomless as Solomon's concept of an infinite nothingness at the center of the universe. By ridding the society of its Jews, the Reich was creating a moral void; those who insisted on the laws of justice instead of the jungle were being driven out.

"Where do you want to go?" Konrad asked.

"Take me to Erich's flat."

She needed to be alone—and *not* at the estate. Alone to think, to plane, to examine her Jewishness. And she was Jewish, wasn't she? *Wasn't she?*

If Erich is behind this I will kill him, she thought feverishly. *Poison, I'll do it with poison and watch him die.*

After sending Konnie home to Christmas dinner, she let herself into the apartment, kicked off her shoes, and lay down on the bed without bothering to draw the curtain that separated it from the rest of the room.

There had to be something she could do to help Sol! Gripping the pillow, she fought to keep the panic dammed that brimmed along the edge of her consciousness. Perón was not around. There had to be someone influential who could find out where Sol and Misha had been taken. That would be the first step. *Find them.*

She brewed coffee and began to pace around the flat. She was on her third cup when she thought of Werner Fink, the outrageous *conférencier* with whom she had worked when she had been the star attraction at the Ananas cabaret.

He was certain to have connections; otherwise how would he have avoided arrest for so long, especially since, as he had told her, he had a twin brother incarcerated in Sachsenhausen? What hold might he have on the Nazis that had kept him free for so long? Photographs, perhaps, of orgies in after-hours cabarets, to be made available should he disappear? He was a survivor, that one.

Her own underground connections, with which she had helped save a dozen desperate lives, were of no use to her now that she needed them; the network had been compromised. Erich had told her that the furriers had been arrested.

What else did he know? There was no point in asking him. If Erich could tell her that Sol was in camp, knowing that he was safe in Amsterdam, he was capable of any lie. A better question was, how influential was he? The Gestapo knew about the safe-house. Did they know about her, too? Was Erich the reason she had not been arrested as well?

Had he found out about Sol's return, and was he responsible for—

No, she decided, forcing herself to calm down. Even Himmler could not have interceded had the Gestapo found out about her. Her cover remained intact because she had insisted that communications be double-blinded. No one knew the others' identities. The day after Erich had told her about the Lubovs, her last communiqué had arrived, telling her the network was dissolved until further notice.

Sol's arrest probably had nothing to do with the use of the hideout as a safe-house. Yes, he had been discovered hiding down there, but that did not link him to the underground. After all, he had been using the sewer as a refuge since childhood.

Perhaps, then, Erich knew nothing about today's happenings. Wait, she told herself. Reserve judgment.

Coffee cup in hand, she wandered around the small flat. Though she had a key and was often in the area, she hadn't been here since moving into the estate with Erich. Doubtless he had, she thought, noting the remains of a meal on the table.

The place had never been a typical bachelor refuge, barren except for beer and bratwurst and the hope of feminine conquests, but now there had been changes that stirred her to even deeper anger—a candelabra, probably "liberated" from Jews, a four-poster brass bed, exquisite Danish linens, the Dresden china. She opened the pantry. It was stocked with canned venison marinated in sour cream, Norwegian salt herring, assorted sausages, and fine French mustards. She wondered if the prostitutes Erich brought here were women who reminded him in some way of her, or if he specialized in officer's wives, whose pre-coital and post-coital whispers might serve him in the Party.

For all she knew, they had even furnished the place for him. She ran a hand along the small claw-footed bathtub that sat before the balcony doors and doubled as a base for Erich's desk. According to Erich, it had been the darling of Friedrich the Great's personal physician, and it had taken three strong men half a day to maneuver the tub up the stairs.

She lay back down on the bed, finally exhausted.

Had Erich forged Goebbels' cramped handwriting to waylay prize pieces of furniture from Jewish inventory? Had he lied to her about Sol because he loved her that much, or because what one did to a Jew didn't matter? Either way, maybe his guilt about the lies had caused him to leave her bed and spend most of his nights in the room that once had been her uncle's. Perhaps Erich's need to prove himself with other women was tied to her and, therefore, to Solomon.

Should she tell him about Sol—offer forgiveness for his lies in exchange for help—or would she simply get more lies?

No, she thought. Take vengeance. Use him. Match him lie for lie.

She buried her head in the pillow. "God, what am *I* becoming!"

She closed her eyes.

The sound of a key turning in the lock awakened her. The flat was dark. She could hear a woman's laughter—low, sensual—and Erich, fumbling with the door. She slid off the bed and stepped behind the corner of the wardrobe.

"Make yourself at home, Anneliese," Erich said. "Pour a bath, for both of us. I'll go down and arrange for dinner." He put a flame to two candles, set them on the table, and transferred the dirty dishes to the sink. "Be right back. Make yourself beautiful for me."

Erich sounded inebriated. Not drunk, but well on the way. The woman heated water, filled the tub, added bath oil, and stripped, flinging her clothes onto the carpet. By the time Miriam knew what she had to do, Anneliese had raised one leg to climb into the tub.

Miriam stepped into the room.

"A threesome!" The woman seemed unperturbed by Miriam's appearance. "Erich said I'm his birthday surprise—but this *is* pleasant! What fun!" She was pretty, in her late thirties, long dark hair, high cheekbones. They could almost have been sisters.

"Leave." Miriam handed the woman her clothes. "I'm his wife."

Anneliese shrugged. "All the same to me," she said. "He promised me two hundred marks. I'll leave, but I want my money."

Miriam rummaged in Erich's dresser. She found a stack of notes under his shirts and gave some to the woman. "Now dress," she said, "and get out."

Chapter 17

"Anneliese?"

Must be on the toilet, Erich thought, touching her tub water. It was warm and silky with oil. He heard the chain being pulled and the subsequent flush.

Undressing, he slipped into the tub, anticipating how relaxed she and the water would make him and thinking about the dinner he had selected. Trout *au bleu,* garnished with spring peas, pineapple, and wild mushrooms. Dilled potatoes sautéed in butter and surrounded by sweetmeats. A natural-state May wine from a Rhein-Hessen vineyard.

For dessert he had chosen one of his favorites, cream cheese tucked in a peach and flamed with kirsch, accompanied by a bottle of Rothschild he had tucked away in the Bierstube wine cellar for just such a special occasion as a birthday. Followed by Viennese coffee with whipped cream and a generous helping of sherry.

What on earth was she doing in there? "Anneliese!"

"In a minute," she said softly and sweetly from the bathroom.

He lay back in the tub. He was not so drunk yet that he could stop wondering why every whore he brought here looked like Miriam, spoke like her, walked with her particular grace.

Close to sleep, he allowed himself to drift, the tepid water seducing him. He dreamed that a sheath encapsulated him. On a white beach, a shepherd bayed, its howling a river of sound cutting into the furred, spiked foliage that lined the shore. With each howl the placenta around him breathed, but he could not cry out for help lest the film that clung to his lips suffocate him. He was an infant, helpless, drowning in amniotic fluid. What he could not understand was why he liked it, why it felt warm, comfortable, secure.

He awoke pleasantly to a line of warm red liquid curling down from his shoulder and across his chest, just visible in the candlelight. For a second he thought he had been knifed and, strangely, it hardly mattered.

"Wine massage?" The voice was soft and female.

Erich swiped at the red liquid, tasted it, and laughed. Without turning his head, he secured a cheroot from among his clothes on the chair, lit it, and lay back, still half asleep. In the flickering candlelight he saw her silhouette on the wall above the bed as, continuing to kneel behind him, she began working the warm wine into his shoulders and scalp.

At last, a woman who knew how to please. A satisfied murmur passed through his lips. No quick hump and head for the door, this one. He would invite her back.

"Sich verwöhnen lassen," she whispered huskily. "Let yourself be pampered."

Pampered? An understatement. He felt the beginning of an erection.

Her hands stopped moving and she shifted position. He could see her, but not well, at the edge of his peripheral vision. With one hand she unbuttoned and opened the robe she was wearing—his robe, revealing a silk slip. He was unsure if her slight smile reflected amusement or contempt. My God, he thought, this one really does look like Miriam. Yes, she would definitely be a rehire. For many nights.

Happy birthday, Erich, he told himself.

"Your hand has fed me well, but I can no longer accept your charity." She let the robe slide to the floor. "You really haven't had your money's worth, Erich Alois!"

"Miriam!" Was he still having a nightmare? He lurched upright in the tub, the bitterness in her voice instantly sobering him. "Where's—"

"I paid her the two hundred marks her and sent her home."

"I never said I was a monk." Annoyed at himself for sounding defensive, he shrugged and lay back in the tub, relaxing, as if to show her her being there did not upset him. "I have asked you for nothing. Why can't we forget—"

"Forget!"

He regretted having opened his mouth. When he was a boy, after a fight with Solomon about something insignificant, he had overheard Frau Freund say of Sol, "My son's words go from the lung to the tongue." The underpinnings of his self-anger took hold.

"I don't mean forget the larger picture," he said. "Nothing can right the wrongs done you years ago." He reached up and touched her hand. She pulled away.

"Life isn't real to you, Erich. Just one big hall of mirrors."

"You and your Jewish sense of the dramatic" He stared at her body in the soft candlelight. "I won't be taunted," he said suddenly. "Especially not by you."

"Is that your limit? When Uncle was alive I used to think the world was without limits because I was a Rathenau. I didn't realize that even he had me on a leash. The older I got, the more freedom I thought I had acquired, the more limits were secretly being imposed."

"What has that to do with us!"

"It has to do with me, and with what I wanted then."

"You still want what you want, when you want it."

"I'm still a Rathenau."

He wondered why her statement did not bother him. "What was your uncle really grooming you for? Not to be a dancer, I think. Marriage? To some foreign blueblood? An old-fashioned marriage of alliance?"

"Politics."

"Politics! I don't believe it!" He laughed derisively. "Did he hope to get you a seat in the Reichstag?"

"He found politics depressing and ugly. He had no intention of marrying, so *I* was to be politics' antithesis. His canvas."

"Purity on a pedestal, while he toiled in the mud of political trenches!" He motioned with thumb and index finger as if indicating a headline. "Miriam Madonna Rathenau, Virgin of the Grünewald."

"Not virginal, but at least not vile."

He blew cigar smoke toward the ceiling. "The man was an anachronism," he said, feeling suddenly small despite his lean muscularity. Turning abruptly, he pulled her down to him and kissed her hard, sliding his tongue into her mouth and along her palate, and then releasing her just as abruptly. "If only we had lived in another time," he said hoarsely, "maybe things would have worked out differently."

She raised her hand as if to slap him, then let it drop. "We did live in another time." Glaring at him, she stood up, put her hands beneath the slip's straps as if to slide them off her shoulders. "It's late and I'm tired. God forbid I should *upset* you, so either have me or have me leave."

Beneath the silk, her back and buttocks looked like tawny shadows. How could one so beautiful talk so cavalierly about sexual pleasure?

"Well, make up your mind," she said coldly.

"That's enough!"

She leaned down toward him. "And if I go on talking? What'll you do? Punish me? Take away my family estate?"

Furious, he stabbed out his cheroot in the water and, reaching up, gripped her by the throat. He tightened his grip on her neck and put his other hand on her breast, not caressing her so much as clutching it, clinging to her. But the pent-up rage of all his hatreds had not left him. Pulling her toward him, he again kissed her hard on the lips, put his arms around her waist and drew her awkwardly onto the rim of the tub.

She nuzzled her mouth down against his shoulder and, without warning, sank her teeth into his flesh.

Immediately, insistently aroused, he pulled her further onto the tub rim, forcing her knees apart, rising up in the water and pressing his hips against hers, unmindful of her angry squirming.

"You bastard!" Suspended unnaturally, she cried out in pain and anger. "I hate you."

Fighting as if for her life, she twisted from his grasp and climbed awkwardly off the rim of the tub. She picked up his jacket and began tearing off the Nazi insignia as if it were alive. Then she hurled it across the room and limped over to the bed.

"What's your game, Miriam?" He touched his cheek where she had hit him. "Tell me the rules so I can play too!"

"I want you not to be a Nazi. I want Solomon. I—"

"I can't change things no matter how much I'd like to turn back the calendar. I sit at my desk, intent on mapping out security, and instead find myself staring out the window for hours, thinking about the people out there I'd like to know, whose lives I would like to share. You're not the only one who *wants,* Miriam. I *want* too! Not possessions, not even power. Just to be part of others' lives." His emotion expended itself. So did his erection. "But I don't know how," he said quietly and bitterly.

He sat up and, elbows on his knees, put his head in his hands. On my birthday! he thought. Why is she torturing me like this on my goddamn birthday! Still, he could not stop himself from talking and—*telling her.* Maybe, he thought, he was rambling was *because* it was his birthday, the day he had hated for so long. "So much is happening out there, so much we can never know," he went on. "I feel locked inside myself...isolated from everything, everyone, that could have had real meaning for me."

He felt ashamed. He had never spoken like this to anyone before, not even Solomon. "I've no right to tell you my troubles," he said, staring at the rose-colored water. "Especially after the pain you've been through."

"Save the poetics for your Hitler Youth virgins." She lay down on the featherbed, face buried in the silver-tasseled pillow that homely Magda Goebbels had given him in remembrance of the time she had stayed the night with him.

He said nothing, waiting for her to do something. Anything. He felt too embarrassed and weak to fight any longer.

"I never credited you with the capacity for honesty," she said finally, in an emotionless voice. She lifted her head. "Everyone has the right to burden others with their despair, at least sometimes."

"Would things have been better between us if—"

"Had things been better, would you have lived differently?"

"You mean, would I have divorced myself from the Party? Would I hate Hitler more than I do? Probably not."

He rose from the tub and toweled himself. "Miriam? Miri? I'm sorry if I hurt you just now."

His mind in tumult, he knelt at the foot of the bed and massaged her feet. He had wronged her again, but was it, he wondered, really his fault? Was any of it? He could not have saved her estate, not even if she hadn't been off in her precious world of Parisian art and ballet. As for her taunting, she should know better than to treat him like some insentient being; he was a man, with a man's needs.

Yes, he had lied to her about Solomon. Intercepted the letters to her. Pretended regularly to be checking on Sol's condition, mostly to make certain that she would not take matters into her own hands and try to find him, but at least he had never truly planned the lie.

And the things he had done to keep her from learning the truth—things for which he had hated himself—he had done for her. Why else would he so degrade himself, except to hold onto her regardless of the price? Besides, he had lived that lie in the full knowledge that the man was safe in Amsterdam with his mother and sister. He had even broken a vow to never speak to his parents again. After they had ransacked the tobacco shop, he had phoned, reprimanding them. They swore they had stolen nothing; knowing they would be accused of a theft of which they were innocent, they had simply left town for a while—until, they had said, the real culprits were found.

Though he wanted to pretend that the lie was truth—the past could not changed, after all—the discussion had grown heated, and he had ended up slamming down the receiver, angry with himself for bothering with them again.

"I really am sorry I hurt you, Miriam," he said. "But God knows I've waited so long for you—"

"God? What do you know of God!" Hugging the pillow, she turned onto her back. She narrowed her eyes and glared at him, an expression of hatred. "Save your sorrow for the virgins with swastikas on their wings. That's what you're good at!"

"I'll show you what I'm good at."

Standing at the foot of the bed, he had the fleeting thought that perhaps the nickname Javelin Man had reached Miriam. Had she, not knowing his reasons for staying away from her bed, laughed at him on those many nights he had slept away from her? He looked at his penis. She wouldn't laugh at him after tonight.

Roughly, he pulled her forward until he was between her legs.

"Stop it, Erich! God*damn* you, let me go!"

Tightening his grasp, he entered her.

"You'll pay for this." She gasped. "I promise you'll pay!"

He concentrated, pushing deeply inside her. "I already did," he said. "You gave Anneliese two hundred marks. Now earn them."

Squirming and kicking, she tried to fend him off. Then, releasing the pillow, she gripped the rods of the brass headboard and let him slam into her with orderly, methodical strokes.

He gripped her hair. Turned her head to the side so that she faced the wall. "Count the money, as if I just gave it to you."

"You're crazy!"

"Now!"

"One...two...three..."

He reveled in the hatred in her voice. "Slower!"

"Four..."

"Again! From the beginning!"

"One..."

Hoping to delay orgasm, he closed his eyes and thought of his shepherds, seeing each with the clarity of a delirium dream. But he soon lost all control. Covered with sweat and unable to delay any longer, he came and crumpled on top of her, continuing to thrust—while she continued, tonelessly, to count—until sleep enfolded him.

He dreamed of a ship buffeted by the sea and of the beach where shepherds howled. When he awoke, the sun had broken through the clouds and he was alone, cold and uncovered yet strangely fulfilled. He climbed out of bed and padded across the carpet to the mirror. Contemplating his image, he decided he was better looking than ever.

Behind him, he saw the meal he had ordered the night before. It lay untouched, browning around the edges. They must have delivered it after he was asleep, after Miriam left, he thought. What a waste!

He walked over to the table, poured himself a glass of wine and nibbled at the dessert, a little astonished that he felt absolutely no contrition. If he owed Miriam an apology, she owed him one too for her lack of gratitude. He had taken her in. Kept her safe. As for Sol, he was safe in Amsterdam. *He* knew that, even if Miriam did not.

Chapter 18

April 1939

"Why don't you get up, get dressed and come with me, Miriam? An outing will do you good. You've hardly left the estate since...since Christmas."

Erich avoided looking into Miriam's eyes and allowed his gaze to rest on the slight swell of her belly. In the past he had avoided pregnant women. They had appeared clumsy to him, repulsive, their eyes filled with a secret awareness that excluded him and the rest of the male world. Yet the idea of this child—his child—conceived though it was in anger, continued to excite him.

"You really want me to get up before dawn and come with you to Abwehr headquarters?" Miriam's voice was laced with sarcasm. "To do what, pray tell—enlist in the military? Today's Easter, Erich. You should go to Mass. You and all your Nazi friends. I'm having lunch with Werner."

"Never mind," he said bitterly.

Annoyed with himself for having made the suggestion, Erich swung his legs out of the bed they again shared. Women were peculiar...Miriam no less than the rest. He had expected fury when he demanded to return to her bedroom, but she had simply shrugged, saying she did not care where he slept or with whom. She did not refuse him when he touched her, though he sensed that she knew he was sustaining his erection by reliving what he had come to think of as the Christmas Rape.

Not that she showed any real interest in him, or anyone else except Werner Fink. Erich indulged her need to spend time with that troublemaker because it got her out of the house—

He stopped himself.

The truth was that she had asked for little since Christmas, except to be left alone. Unnerved by her long silences, he had gone on his knees to ask her forgiveness. His apologies, profound and constant, were met with disinterest: a cold stare, a cold shoulder.

"Why do you stay with me, Miriam?" he asked quietly.

She answered simply, giving him the same reason she had always given him. "You are your brother's keeper."

He stood up and looked down at her. She was anything but a fool, this niece of Walther Rathenau: a permanent reminder to him of Solomon and of his own weakness. She knew what was best for her own well-being and that of the child.

"Miri, it's Easter," he said, determining to try one more time. "All I have to do is pick up some papers at headquarters and then slip out for the day. It's too late to get to Oberammergau, but we could drive into the country, perhaps to the Harz."

"I told you—" She doubled up suddenly, as if in severe pain.

Erich struggled to find the lamp chain. By the time he had the light on, she was lying with her back arched, pressing her fists into her silk-gowned belly.

"What's the matter? What is it!"

"How should I know! I've never been pregnant before."

"What does it feel like?"

"Like pain."

His rudimentary medical training in the military had not included childbirth. He felt helpless. Grappling for the telephone to call for help, he knocked her photograph off his nightstand. "I'll have the car brought around."

Her features contorted. Struggling, she rolled onto her side and pulled up her legs. "It's only the fourth month!" She was gasping. "I must be losing the baby!"

Grabbing a handful of crumpled silk, Erich pulled himself toward her. He thrust his lips close to her ear. "You can't lose the baby—our son! You hear? Please, Miriam!"

In his anxiety, he thought he heard Goebbels' laughter. He stopped to listen. Fool! Probably a radio broadcast coming from downstairs or, at worst, the Gauleiter with another hopeful starlet.

"I think I'm okay now," Miriam said after a time, her face to the wall.

"You *think* you're okay?"

She took a deep breath. "Lately I'm sure of nothing."

He dropped the telephone in its cradle as if it were a megaphone threatening to announce his incompetence to the world. "Can you sleep?" he asked as gently as he could. Hoping to soften her attitude, he reached over her and placed his hand on her belly. "Let me feel him, Miriam."

"Stop it!" She batted his hand away. "You're like an old horse trader gloating over his prize mare." After a moment she relented and took his hand in hers. She placed it on the slightly mounded flesh of what had once been a dancer's slender belly, to the right of center.

He had learned how to listen through his fingers to the tiny intermittent flutters.

His son!

She moved away and turned to stare at the velvet flocked wallpaper. It's normal for her to emotionally distance herself in preparation for motherhood, he told himself. Animals do it, so why not humans? She would redirect her attention to him after the birth. For now, the boy was rightly her main concern—

What nonsense! he thought. The truth was, she hated him, and for good reason. Given time, and the birth of their child, she would forgive him. He could not expect her to forget, but surely forgiveness was possible.

Meanwhile, given her physical changes and the larger ones to come, her attitude was actually something of a relief; it excused his occasional desire for other women—like Leni Riefenstahl, the film director. Trim body. So sure of herself. She was said to prefer women, but that only made her all the more exciting. Not that he intended to do anything about his desire for her—those days were over—just that it was natural to contemplate...

While Miriam dozed, he dressed. By first light he was outside. The day smelled of spring and he felt good despite Miriam's surliness; on impulse, he chose to ride his motorcycle to headquarters. There would be no going to Mass this day or any other in the new Germany. More and more people—like the *woman at the Passion Play in Oberammergau during his bivouac in the Black Forest—confused Hitler with God. He felt no such confusion, but he had long since lost his taste for the overt trappings of Catholicism. Besides, Mass was not exactly part of the Party platform; all officers made it a point to show up for duty—and punctually!—on this day, or face possible reprimand.

Still, policy and his own angers could not keep him from celebrating the Earth—God's creation. The breaking dawn was beautiful, and he thoroughly enjoyed the ride to Oranienburg, home of Abwehr headquarters and once home of his glory on the athletic field.

After reporting in and collecting the papers he needed, he wandered into the officers' club. He downed three large rolls with cheese and liverwurst, and half a pot of coffee.

Tomorrow, he thought, he would make sure Miriam and the child were all right. He would take them to see Doctor Morell. He congratulated himself for being important enough to have Miriam taken care of by Hitler's personal physician. Perhaps he would have a check-up himself; he had been getting far too little exercise of late.

With that in mind, he decided to leave the cycle in front of headquarters, where it would be seen, and enjoy an Easter stroll before sitting down to the paperwork that, as usual, he had allowed to pile up. A Sunday morning hike—just like in the Wandervögel days. Whistling softly, he headed down the main road and toward the mortuary, which lay about two kilometers out of town. He would turn around there.

However, he soon abandoned his plan and cut through the woods. Pines, beeches, and hemlock rose into an orange Easter dawn; mushrooms had proliferated from the spring rains, and their smell permeated the air. He stopped to examine one of them, wondering if he could still tell the difference between mushrooms and toadstools. He was crouching near the ground when voices claimed his attention. Curious, he followed them out to the road and found the good people of Oranienburg, released from work by the holy day, gathered along the Waldstrasse.

"An Easter Parade?" he asked one of them pleasantly.

"Might call it that." The man grinned and pointed at a column of men just coming into view.

"Who are they?" Erich asked.

"As if you don't know!" The man stared at Erich's uniform.

"Haven't been around this area for a long time."

The man shrugged. "Whatever you say. It's the labor detail from Sachsenhausen on their three-kilometer stroll to the quarry. Mostly political prisoners—but enough Jews to make it worthwhile!"

Erich's stomach clenched as the sorry group headed toward him, herded by rifle butts and billy clubs. They looked beaten and starved. As the head of the column passed him by, he saw those who appeared to be the oldest of the men—though it was hard to tell—squeeze to the center of the human cage without breaking rank. Their comrades supported them as best they could.

"Blüt für Blüt!—blood for blood!" shouted a townsman in a lederhosen and a green felt hat decorated with a red feather.

Next to him, a woman in a tight-bodiced dirndl took up the chant. She smiled companionably as she raised her Brownie to photograph the Easter entertainment

I didn't know, he wanted to shout at the ragged column. The prisoners looked half alive—skeletons staring out of skulls whose eyes had seen too much death.

God! I didn't know.

The woman with the camera hurled a stone into the ranks.

Soon everyone was claiming the right to kill a Jew for Jesus before sunrise Services. Blows were rendered with clubs and broomsticks, with fireplace pokers hurriedly gathered from neat little houses, with stones plucked from gardens seeded with berries and beans. Young children hurled eggs and insults, their obscenities drowned by the shrieks of the prisoners as their rifle-bearing masters beat and shot them into submission.

The men along the outside of the column peeled off like old paint, skeletons performing a ghastly dance; they fell and were trampled by others fighting inward in their battle to survive.

"No," Erich whispered. The rumors about the detention centers, the abuses, the humiliations—true. All of it. Holy Mother of God, they were true.

Could Hell be any worse?

An elderly man next to Erich spat in a laborer's face and shook his fist. "It was because of *you* that our Lord was crucified!"

The inmate straightened his shoulders and wiped off the spittle on the striped sleeve of his prison uniform. A rock bounced off the temple of the man next to him. He swayed. His friend held him up and they staggered on.

Erich looked around. At least Sol was not here, facing the good people of Oranienburg—so blind to all but hatred. Their tile and shoe factories loomed unmanned, the machinery silent—and why? To commemorate Easter in a Germany that had officially declared the Christian god a manifestation of the Jewish disease. Yet the claptrap continued about Jews killing and bleeding Aryan infants for Passover rituals...and they went on blaming the Jews for the death of Christ. Were they stupid, bloodthirsty, or simply naïve?

He did not know; all he was sure of was, when the truth of this surfaced, not one of them—neither man, woman, nor child—would admit to having been here this day.

Nor, he thought sadly, feeling sick, would he.

Chapter 19

At the rear of the column, Sol wiped the residue of an Easter egg off his face. The good people of Oranienburg must have run out of stones, he thought. How fortunate.

He bent and offered his fingers to Misha, who licked them clean. Sol smiled gently, but the boy did not smile back. He seemed to have forgotten how. And no small wonder. Yesterday it was Christmas, now it was Easter. From Chanukah to Passover, they had been living in a Panoptikum, a house of mirrors called Sachsenhausen.

Abruptly, the Oranienburg gauntlet was behind them—the morning "Running of the Bulls" his new friend Hans Hannes called it.

Turning his head, he glanced back toward the camp. It was a nightmare, a zoetrope filled with slides of the black and white pain of Dadaism and filled with savage, sinister people turned inside-out by despair. Caricatures George Grosz may have rendered—only the camp artist was not Grosz or Van Gogh. He was SS Captain Hempel.

His whip was the brush, the flesh of men his canvas. His favorite subject lay inherent in his introductory speech to new arrivals: "This is not a penitentiary or prison. It is a place of instruction. Order and discipline are its highest law. If you hope to see freedom again, you must submit to severe training. You must convince us that our methods of training have borne fruit. You must deny your old way of life. Our methods are thorough...."

Translated, that meant, "...you will not go hungry. Not if you will eat ruthlessness for dessert after your entree of cruelty."

Each step toward the quarry sent pains shooting through Sol's stomach and spine. Beside him, around him, fellow inmates with torn flesh and broken bones stumbled on through fields black from spring plowing. He remembered other days in these grain fields. Athletic festivals. Erich-the-Teuton practicing his javelin; or he, Erich, and Miriam walking through the woods, talking, listening to birds.

It troubled him when birds sang here now. Their freedom and the beauty of their songs mocked him.

The column reached the quarry. By now, for some, standing took too much effort. They collapsed onto the marly ground.

"Boy!"

Hempel dismounted from his stallion. His silver hair shone in the early morning light, and his eyes brightened with pleasure as Misha came running to him. Using the tip of the barrel of his pistol, Hempel caressed the boy's cheek. He moved the pistol to the other cheek, and repeated the gesture.

Misha whimpered but did not cry. Far too small to carry out the work of the hard labor detail, he had to march with them. The order had come directly from Hempel, whose penchant for boys—the younger the better—was no secret.

"Eyes front!" Hans whispered to Sol. "You won't help the child by getting yourself killed."

"You were out of step back there, you little bastard!" Hempel said.

"Ja, Hauptsturmführer!" Misha said. "Forgive me, Hauptsturmführer! I am a wretched Jew, unworthy to lick your boots."

Sol glanced quickly at Hempel. The captain was smiling.

"Fifteen on the stock might make you worthy," Hempel said conversationally. "What do you think?"

"Ja. Thank you, Hauptsturmführer."

Remounting, Hempel spurred his horse. His wolfhound, busy and bloodied from the roundup of straggling inmates, joined horse and rider.

"Be strong, Misha," Sol whispered to the boy when he returned to the ranks. The child was so terribly young! He did not deserve the ugly lessons he would learn from that master of the grotesque, Otto Hempel.

Misha stared as man, horse, and dog ran into and onto and over prisoners—who screamed as bones, brittle from dietary deficiencies, broke like twigs.

Dear God, let the boy stay conscious throughout the whipping, Sol prayed. As long as he counted the lashes aloud, he would get no more than those assigned. Would it be the cane whip or the horse whip? The length of flex-steel, perhaps? The immediate agony was all that differed. Whatever was used, his buttocks would become raw mincemeat. Later, Hempel would doubtlessly abuse him or, worse yet, hand him over to the guards who had a taste for gang rape. Camp gallows-humor insisted they raped because they believed that by doing so they spread the seed of National Socialism.

Sol shut his eyes.

A Kapo's stick pushed into the small of his back. "You! Filth! Into the pit with the rest of them!"

The column broke into rows and snaked downward into the cold shadows that filled the limestone quarry. Sol descended the steep steps that had been carved into the pitside, trying to imagine himself entering Persepolis or one of the Egyptian digs that had so seized the world's imagination a decade before.

"All right, you lazy Jew. Get those hods rolling." The slap of Pleshdimer's stick across his ribs reminded him that this was no archaeological dig. The Kapo raised his voice. "The rest of you—move yesterday's stones up the hill!" He shouted loudly enough to be heard by the guards who stood at the top of the pit, holding dogs and machine-pistols at the ready. "On with it, or tomorrow I'll be gone and someone who really knows how to teach you the value of industry will stand here in my place!"

Sol joined the rush to secure a stone that could be balanced on his back with one hand, leaving the other free in case he stumbled or fell. Stumble, and he would be forced to pitch himself sideways into a long and possibly fatal tumble down the jagged rubble that banked the steps. Fall, and he would receive an immediate beating and twenty-five lashes; fall backwards—knock down other prisoners and halt progress—and death would be the easiest punishment.

Prisoners were grouped by the color of the patches sewn onto their sleeves. Each group worked a different part of the pit.

The red-triangled politicals and green-triangled criminals usually got the best of it, breaking and shaping stones; the violet-triangled Jehovah's Witnesses and black-triangled work-dodgers and anti-socials were next in the caste system.

The prisoners the Nazis labeled the worst degenerates in the Reich, the Jews and homosexuals, were lumped together. The homosexuals wore pink triangles, the Jews yellow ones. Solomon's was crossed with a green one. His crime: defiling a German sewer.

Together, his two triangles formed a Star of David.

Like beasts of burden, the Jews and the homosexuals carried rocks to the top of the quarry, a double-dozen steps up an almost perpendicular incline. Denied medical attention during illness or following an accident, deliberate or provoked, and on half rations, the sick and the starving hauled the boulders. Up; and run down. Up; and run down—

Sol shouldered his first burden of the day. The best he could find was a shapeless rock that weighed at least forty kilos. He had become a connoisseur of weights, able to judge them with a kind of sick precision. There was a time he had weighed eighty kilos, a time his mother had bragged, "God should only make a bull's haunch so lean and tough as my Sol's." Now he guessed his weight was about fifty-five kilos. Driven by fear, he found he could carry rocks all day he would have had trouble lifting when he was in good health.

He pictured himself balanced on a scale being held not by Justice but by the Angel of Death. On the other side of the scale was a different kind of boulder, heavier and much more important: the burden every Jew had to carry.

"Move!"

The guard amused himself by hitting Sol across the shoulders with his gun—his "fat squirter," as the prisoners called the weapons—and waited impatiently, eagerly, for someone else to slow down.

Sol wavered, sucking air to replace the breath stolen from him by the unexpected blow. Only those guards circling the top of the pit around the limestone crusher occasionally missed an opportunity for cruelty, because they had the distraction of their shepherds straining against their leashes and slavering as they eyed the inmates they had been trained to hate.

Sol wondered if any of them had been bred in Erich's kennels.

Bent double by the rock, he staggered up the steps. His eardrums felt ready to burst from the interminable shouting, and his joints, not yet warmed to the task, felt cemented. Soon his bones would feel ready to crumble, and the pit's shadows would invade his lungs like a cold dark hand.

The hours passed in a blur of pain and fatigue.

"Sing!" Hempel ordered.

His comrades, grinning, took up the command for the camp song. "Sing, you scum!"

The column twisted, going down alongside itself like an indecisive caterpillar. The inmates running down the steps, mindful of the guards' demands, kept their knees lifted as though for a soccer drill.

"Dear old Moses, come again," they sang. *"Lead your Jewish fellowmen...once more to their promised land."*

Sol stopped singing and put down the rock. Eyes rigidly forward, he prepared himself for the dash down the hill.

"Sing!" A guard kicked him in the shin. He reeled—and sang:

"Split once more for them the sea..."

Beyond exhaustion, he fell onto his side. Arms and legs moving spastically, he murmured the rest of the song.

"When the Jews are all inside
On their pathway, long and wide,
Shut the trap, Lord, do your best!
Give us the world its lasting rest!"

Arms enfolded him. Like a dying spider, he continued to move. Finally his limbs slowed and he sagged in Hans' arms. His head lolled, his mouth opened, closed. Spittle drooled down his chin.

"It's over." Hans' voice. "We're dismissed to the barracks."

Sol realized he was no longer at the quarry. "Hot roll call"— exercising until the weak collapsed from exhaustion, and were shot—had just ended.

Later, wedged into his "Olympic" bunk, the top of five wooden tiers and so narrow that he could only slide in and remain in one position, he could not sleep. The barracks, designed for eighty and filled with three hundred, stank of the sweat and vomit of men too crammed together to rise and relieve themselves. The prisoners who had chosen to lie on the avenues of dirt floor below became receptacles for the urine and excrement that fell from above, but—too tired and weak to awaken—they did not know it until morning.

With only about forty centimeters between his bunk and the ceiling, Sol's bunk was too high up, too inaccessible to be subject to inspection like the one Misha shared with Hans Hannes—a "trap" bottom bunk. What he would give for half an hour of rest in a soft bed! Thirty minutes. The time it took to make love or put together a noodle pudding, or to kill—how many?

He thought about Misha.

The boy had not marched back with them; he had not yet come back to the barracks. Sleep, Sol told himself, knowing he would need strength when Misha returned...if he returned.

"I can't sleep either," Hans whispered, standing up.

Though not a Jew, he had requested and been granted quarters in the Jewish barracks. He wore the pink triangle of a homosexual; the guards loathed him perhaps even more than they hated the Jews and the Gypsies. He reminded the guards too much of many of their own.

Whispering so as not to disturb the others, Sol asked, "What happened to the Gypsies who arrived yesterday from Burgenland?"

"They had some kind of infectious eye disease. I heard they were taken to the hospital in Jena. You should tell them about your eyes, Solomon. It might be your way out of here."

"The politicals occasionally get emigration papers," Sol said. "The only way out for the rest of us is feet first." He thought about Carl von Ossetzky, released when he won the Nobel Prize for literature. What good had freedom done him? He had died anyway as the result of the torture and inhumanity he suffered here.

"At least ask them for spectacles," Hans insisted.

"I did. Before I knew what went on in the sick ward."

"Apply to the Chief Security Office in Berlin for a visitor. If they allow one, your visitor can bring you spectacles."

"Sometimes," Sol answered, "it is better not to see."

"Shush!" Hans silenced him. "They are bringing the boy back."

He disappeared. Sol scooted to the edge of his bunk. He had barely enough room to turn his head and look down.

"Did they not tell you, Misha Czisça, that death through sorrow is forbidden here?" Hans whispered. He lifted the boy in his arms and carried him to his bunk. The boy lay with his back to Hans, staring at the far wall. Now and again, despite Hans' whispered protests, he scraped his fingers along the filthy floor to take a handful of dirt and transfer it to his mouth.

Hans bent over him. He was weeping quietly. A tear, dripping from his chin, fell into Misha's hair.

"Son of a bitch!" He looked up at Solomon, his face white, his eyes red-rimmed but suddenly clear and intensely blue, as if hatred had lent them new life.

Staring at Hans, Solomon saw a fragile, empty vessel. The face of death lay beneath the mask of the man who had seemed always to possess greater stamina than any other person in the barracks.

Hans Hannes, with his humor and humanity, reminded him of Grog, the clown, for whom the world was no longer *"Schö-ö-ön."*

"He can have my daily ration of bread and soup," Sol whispered, his own eyes filling with tears. "I would give him my life, if it would stop him from blaming himself for my imprisonment."

"To stop him you must live, not die," Hans said. "He told me our beloved Hauptsturmführer found it too distasteful to do the beating himself. He handed Misha over to Pleshdimer. Then Hempel salted his wounds and licked them. Licked them! The man should be locked up in the kennels with the rest of Standartenführer Koch's dogs!"

The boy's dry-eyed sobs quieted. "Is he asleep?" Solomon asked.

The actor nodded and covered Misha's limp body with a threadbare blanket. The boy awakened and tried to sit up, but fell back in pain. "The leather strap. He soaked it in brine, Hans. There were holes in it."

Gently, Hans turned the boy over. Blisters were forming where the flesh had come through the holes in the leather strap.

After Misha fell back into an exhausted sleep, Sol descended from his bunk. Together, he and Hans walked over to one of the barracks's two tiny windows.

"Punishing someone that way—for being out of step, for God's sake!" Sol asked. *"Why!"*

"Why ask a fool's question, Solomon? Go to sleep. Tomorrow we go back to the quarry. You will need all your strength." He turned his back on Sol, leaned against the windowsill, and looked out.

Sol returned to his bunk and passed into a fitful sleep filled with dreams of the past months. He was on the train from Berlin, coughing and feverish from the fetid damp of the sewer. Tramping down Karacho Way into the "camp for protective custody." Stumbling through gates inscribed, "My Fatherland—right or wrong." He dreamed of a hospital bed, Dr. Schmidt bending over him, saying, "You will serve us yet for many years." And he heard laughter—not human—as the visions and the voices intruded, mocking him.

"I thought I'd be killing lice," he heard a voice say from one of his childhood visions.

Then another: *"Give me your axe!... You've hurt me enough, you've hurt me.*

He blinked. He was in the quarry. Such an indulgence, the voices and visions, compared to what he now must endure! The weight upon his back displaced them. There was only the next step to climb, the bent back of the wretch before him, the sweat runneling down his face...and the rock. Always the rock.

Up.

Deposit the rock.

Down, singing of Jewish destruction. Up, a skin-and-bone machine whose only reality was pain so great it congealed within the flesh like pus. Certain each trip up the quarry steps would be his last, that he would drop dead and slide down the rubble to stare through vacant eyes at those too foolish to embrace the long sweet sleep of eternity.

He put down his tenth rock—or was it his ten-thousandth?—and raised his head. The other prisoners were sitting or lying about. He lay down where he had stood, savoring the cold stony ground and the feathery clouds chasing each other across the sky.

They brought sleep, and he dreamed he was dreaming...a dream within a dream....

He was a bulldog. Stocky, large, jaw square, eyes red with anger. When he awoke within the dream, the anger was still in him. He growled up at the edge of the pit, at the circle of shepherds. They disappeared. A wall of blood rose to a crescent. Curled at the edges. Began to trickle, then to pour down the hillside, meandering among the rubble, branching again and again until it reddened the limestone talus.

At the top of the pit, the shepherds returned, lifted their heads, howled at an ice-white moon.

In the pit, the blood became a torrent. Engulfing him. Red-black and gelatinous, and as stinking as the pheasant he'd shot during his family's one vacation in the Black Forest and had left too long in the sun....

Streaming into the pit, the blood turned blue. Blue as the veins beneath the skin of living skeletons. He felt a vision coming, and could not keep it from engulfing him. He was too tired. The light was big, and blue as cobalt——

——a lamp pours light onto two women on cots set in an alcove of a crumbling brick wall, under an unframed picture of the Führer.

The older woman, wearing a pink slip, is sitting up, smoking, reading a letter, a dirty sheet draped over her legs. "Doktor Hahn must have written this in the lab. See how cramped the handwriting is?" She shows the letter to the younger woman. "He writes that way when he's excited, otherwise he has the most beautiful penmanship. And see this smear?" She taps the paper with a fingernail. "Graphite...and not from a pencil, that's for certain." She nods conclusively. "Definitely written in the lab."

Nightgowned in ragged flannel, the other woman looks dolefully into a shard of mirror she holds, and checks her hair. "I don't know how you can constantly read and reread those love letters. You even make notes in the margins, as though they were some kind of grammar exercise. How can you be so stoic? Your Otto wrote those two years ago! Don't you wonder where he is...*if* he is?"

Her eyes fill with remorse and she puts down the mirror. "I'm sorry, Lise...*Doktor* Meitner. You must think me morbid."

"Nonsense, Judith!" Lise mashes her cigarette in an ashtray on the cot. "You've husband and child. Your concern for their safety suffuses your every thought and breath, as well it should. But just because they incarcerated Otto Hahn doesn't mean he's come to harm. He isn't Jewish, after all. Besides, even Hitler would think twice about exterminating a Nobel Laureate, no matter how outspoken. How ironic! They detain him for practicing the Jewish science of Bohr and Einstein, then as punishment demand that he go on practicing."

She carefully folds the yellowed pages of the letter and places it among others in a tin, removes a brick from the wall, inserts the tin, and replaces the brick. "Otto Hahn is with me every moment. His love guides me in every experiment we perform."

"And if we achieve critical mass?"

"He'll be there too. Especially then."

"Even if it means giving the Nazis—"

"The power of the atom? In exchange for guaranteed freedom for our people? Yes, Doktor Hahn will be there should that happen, even if only in spirit."

The younger woman stretches out on her cot, her head upon her extended arm, and looks at Lise with loving admiration. "You never expect to see him again, and yet you go on...."

Lise chuckles sadly. "When the Nazis split us, they split our atom. If you and I and Professor Heisenberg split the real atom, Doktor Hahn and I will remain forever split. They'll see to that. A female, Jewish Nobel candidate working alongside a Gentile Nobel Laureate who preaches the Jewish science he practices? That smacks of miscegenation, even though I was raised Protestant. The Nazis wouldn't hear of our being together again. But while we're apart...well, there is always hope. So we continue working."

The younger woman sighs. Despite lines of worry and overwork that crease her forehead, she now seems at ease. "Will I ever be as wise as you? My Franz may only be a laborer, but he's more knowledgeable about life than I'll ever be. And you with your—"

"My hopes—dead hopes—for a Nobel?"

"Yes. Being your lab assistant is an honor, Doktor Meitner. Sometimes, though, I wish you'd been my mother."

Lise frowns petulantly. "So you could have begun studying radium as a toddler? I would have made a terrible parent. I can see you now, a two-year-old worrying about nuclear properties and chain reactions." She reaches for another cigarette.

"And about your chain smoking." Judith takes the cigarette and wags a finger of admonition at Lise, who snatches at the cigarette and laughs when she misses.

Her laughter dissipates as the resonant chords of a Bach fugue played on a pipe organ fills the room.

"He's at it again," Judith says, suddenly sullen. "They only give us four or five hours' rest, yet every night Heisenberg plays—"

"He's a very good musician. Sometimes I think he'd rather devote his life to Bach's theories than to Bohr's."

"I hate him," Judith says bitterly. "He sold out to the Nazis. He's worse than Göring. Werner Heisenberg has the capacity to take a moral stand. The world respects him. Instead he simply gave in. At least he could have emigrated! Einstein did, and Fermi and Slizard...who knows how many others. Now, with Bohr gone as well—"

"Heisenberg has no love for Hitler."

"He lectured in Switzerland and visited America." Judith says. "He didn't have to return."

"Should he have left his family behind?"

"Others did."

"Others did not have the weight of the scientific community on their shoulders."

"They bore the weight of the *Jewish* community," Judith says. "That's why they're helping the Allies."

Lise looks pained. "And who is helping European Jews while the United States chases the atom's Holy Grail? Has so much as a single conventional bomb been dropped on a death camp? The Allies surely know of the camps by now, yet nothing is done."

"Our people would die if the camps were bombed!"

"They'll die anyway, except those you and I manage to save." Lise's hand trembles as she lights a cigarette. "Why not destroy the slaughterhouses and slow down the killing?"

"*Everyone* will die, if we give Hitler what he wants," Judith says morosely. "I don't know why you agreed to this insanity! And me a part of it! A scientific breakthrough here...ten thousand saved." She moves her hand around on the cot as if picking up and setting down chessmen. "Another breakthrough there...ten thousand more. What happens when we run out of breakthroughs and must deliver the real thing? What good will have become of all this! Are you so naïve as to think Hitler will keep his promise to send all Jews to that homeland he's creating in Madagascar?"

Bending closely, Lise says in a low voice, "We pray to Jehovah that the war will end before the bomb is born."

"And in the meantime?"

"In the meantime...as long as the Nazis remain divided about Jewish science, they will continue to dole out to a dozen research facilities what little heavy water there is available, instead of concentrating efforts and supplies. The bomb could be delayed for a decade."

Lise's voice has risen earnestly. Judith puts a finger to her lips.

"The music drowns out our whispers," she says. "Why else do you think Heisenberg plays the pipes for half an hour every night, rather than immediately returning to his family in Hechingen? Even he isn't that much of a music enthusiast. He gives us time to talk—to assess—to plan."

"Doktor Heisenberg knows of our deal with Hitler?"

"Of course he knows," the older woman says impatiently. "Is he a part of it? I'm not sure. He's very complex, especially morally. He feels that if Germany doesn't have the bomb, we won't be able to stop the Allies from using theirs, should they create one. And yet...give the Luftwaffe the bomb? Who can say what Heisenberg thinks! You think he wasn't upset when the papers called him a White Jew?"

"The usual Nazi logic. Destroy the best."

"That's why there's hope! You bash in the brains of a wolf and it may go on snapping, but not for long."

Judith curls into a ball, to sleep; the cot has no blanket. Lise reaches to turn off the light, but the door opens and an obese man with a pink and white complexion enters. Judith jerks upright, crossing her arms protectively across her bosom.

"I have two lion cubs at my home in Berlin," the man says. "They remind me of you ladies. Cuddly but dangerous."

Lise stands and, with an air of arrogance, leans against the wall and drags on the cigarette. "Is this your idea of a surprise inspection, Feldmarschall Göring?" She blows smoke in his direction. "Play games with *this* physicist and you can bet your jackboots that her mind goes blank in the lab tomorrow!"

"Someday, Doktor," he says genially, "that mouth of yours is going to get your tongue torn out."

"Someday I will be eliminated like the troublesome burr that I am. Until then, you need me. I know it. You know it."

"That day might come sooner than you think." Göring licks a palm and smoothes back his hair. "In the meantime, let us not forget that uncooperative laboratory assistants arrive in Auschwitz by the boxcar load...as do their families."

Her face anguished, Judith puts her head against her fists.

"You promised—we work without provocation," Lise says.

He looks at her with disdain. "And you promised delivery. Until then, promises are just...promises."——

Sol awoke panting from the stuffiness of the room. He was not in the quarry, as he expected, but back in the barracks. Had he ever left? The sky was dark and the moon, framed in the window, filled the barracks with liquid silver. Hans was standing with one hand gripping the barracks's noose. He gazed toward the sentry tower.

Taking hold of the next bunk edge, Sol once again slid from the cramped space and crept among the sleepers to stand beside his friend. The camp's gate was open, and people were being herded inside. "Another pogrom," Sol said. "If only they knew how much easier it would be for them if they died now." He took the noose from Hans and tugged at it.

Hans laughed bitterly. "I've heard the dead are taken to the crematoria in Gotha and Eisenback. Also Weimar. That's where my father has his farm. The soil there is being spread with a new fertilizer. Gray-white. They sell human ashes to the farmers, Solomon. They are mad, all of them."

"Shush. You'll bring the Kapo down on us."

Hans turned back to the window. "Know why I was imprisoned? For watching a couple copulate in a city park outside of Stuttgart. *For watching!* The man was a Party official. I thought they would let me go...you know, like the man who goes to the Kaiserhof with his secretary and meets his brother-in-law having a night on the town. They are silenced by mutual guilt."

Solomon put an arm across Hans' shoulder and gave his friend's upper arm an affectionate squeeze. The boy moaned in his sleep.

"I love that boy, Solomon." Hans' eyes welled with tears. "He has dignity far beyond his years, but they're taking it from him."

"He is young and strong."

"Young enough to believe in God and good men of government?"

"He will survive. You and I will see to that."

"You will have to do it alone, Solomon." Hans gripped a bunk post, his face wracked with anguish. "Sooner or later, they will get me. Ten years ago some sociologist decided there were over a million homosexual men in Germany. Himmler rounded the number up to *two* million and swore to rid the Reich of them all. In the so-called Dark Ages, homosexuals were drowned in bogs or rolled in blankets for use as faggots during witch burnings."

"I heard talk that you pink-triangles are to be marched to the camp brothel. If you perform with a woman, you'll be released into the civilian labor force."

"Perform!" Hans grabbed his groin with such hatred, it seemed he wanted to tear off his genitals.

"If you refuse, they'll kill you," Sol said.

"They'll kill us anyway." Forehead against the post, Hans said quietly, "When I was making movies one after another, working literally night and day, UFA put me on anti-depressants. For my mental health, they said. They had me working seven days a week. I was so tired, and always afraid for my brother. Their damned anti-depressants gave me priapism. Know what that is, my friend?"

Solomon shook his head.

"An eternal erection." He looked at Sol through eyes filled with agony. "The pain—you cannot believe the pain, Solomon. The beatings we endure is nothing compared to it." He released a slow breath. "Priapism results in a form of gangrene," he said.

"Your name will become a part of medical history," the voice in the Ethiopian vision echoed. "The hospital's a death trap for both of us," Sol said.

A movement outside caught his eye. He watched Pleshdimer cross the yard, a thick-necked murderer who, as Hempel's human watchdog, had found his calling in Sachsenhausen. To him, passion and cruelty were synonymous, but the fear he inspired in all of the prisoners was multiplied tenfold for Misha, who had several times seen the man outside the camp.

"HEIL HITLER!" the loudspeakers boomed. "PRISONERS ARISE!"

Less than ten minutes till roll call. Sol had to hurry in order to have precious seconds in which to relieve himself in the holes in the floor of the room that adjoined the barracks.

"I'd sell my soul to see Hempel dead," Hans said. He lumbered over to the sleeping boy and shook him gently to arouse him.

"You'd sell your soul for a bowl of semolina soup," a voice from Sol's childhood whispered in his head.

As quickly as he could, he straightened his bunk, collected his bag with its dry piece of bread—remnant of the previous day's rations—and relieved himself. Still, he and Hans and Misha only just made it outside in time for roll call. Holding a roster on a clipboard, Pleshdimer made his morning announcements, his huge forehead furrowed in concentration.

"Three, sev-en, sev-en, ze-ro four. Hos-spit-tal." He used a forefinger as a pointer. Gap-toothed, he looked up and grinned. "Today you work in the quarry. When you get back they will examinate you, Jew."

Sol felt a sick, sinking feeling in his gut. *"Your name will become a part of medical history."*

"Nine, se-ven...." Pleshdimer stopped and pointed at Misha. "The Haupsturmführer wants you in his quarters when you get back."

Sol saw raw fear in the boy's eyes.

"Is this your season of sadness, Solomon Freund?" a voice in Sol's head asked.

"The *world's* season of sadness," he answered, joining the column headed for the gate and the quarry.

Chapter 20

Terrified of what the day would bring, Misha dawdled alongside Hans. He knew that eventually he would have to join the line of shuffling humans leaving for the quarry, but every minute he stayed behind seemed like a gift of time, delaying what lay at the day's end.

"I was watching. Listening," a man said, emerging from the closest building to address Misha. "Do whatever you must to survive. Someone has to tell them about this when it's over. You are young and strong. You can make it."

As quickly as the man had appeared, he was gone.

Hans held onto Misha's shoulder. "Bite off the bastard's cock if he tries anything," he whispered into the boy's ear.

"How can I do it, Uncle Hans?" Misha asked.

"You bite down, like this—"

"No. Don't make jokes." The boy shook his head impatiently. "I meant, how can I survive?"

"You can because you must," Hans said. He prodded Misha into the line before he continued talking, very softly, so as not to be overheard by the Kapo. "You must think of yourself as a soldier, defending yourself against the enemy."

"But I have no weapons."

"Yes, you do." Hans paused. "Listen carefully. You have weapons, but they are hidden. It is simply a question of finding them."

Pleshdimer was heading toward them down the line. Automatically, they stopped whispering.

"Let me give you some suggestions," Hans went on when the Kapo had passed. "The first thing you must learn to do is cry."

Misha shook his head, remembering his promise to himself.

"It washes out the eyes and is good for the soul!. If you think you have forgotten how, I can teach you. I am a great actor. I can cry on command."

"What else?"

"You must think about something you were going to do, something you were struggling for before all of this—"

"Like my bar mitzvah?"

"Precisely. Remember your lessons and repeat them to yourself as if you know with absolute certainty that your bar mitzvah will come to pass. I have been to a bar mitzvah. I know that it requires much work, much planning. You must plan every detail, down to the shine on your shoes. Debate the menu with yourself, day after day. Month after month if need be. Wake up with it in your mind. Go to sleep thinking about it."

None of that made sense to Misha, but he stored it away in his head so that he could think about it later.

"One more thing," Hans said. "I met a man once, from Poland. He told me something I will never forget. He said that life is nothing more or less than a huge ledger. On one side, there is a list of all of the good things that have happened to you, and all of the good things that you have done. On the other, a list of all of the bad things that have happened to you, and," he smiled gently down at Misha, "the bad things you have done—even if they were not done on purpose. If you have any luck at all, the good side will always be longer than the bad side. Only when that is not true is life no longer worth living."

"I don't understand."

"You must keep such a ledger, Misha. It will become one of your best weapons."

"But I have no paper, Uncle Hans. No pencil. Even if I did, they would take it away from me."

Hans chuckled. "And you told me not to joke," he said. "I had forgotten that children were so literal. You must keep the ledger in your mind, Misha. That way you will never run out of pages or lead."

He stopped talking and left Misha to his thoughts. What nonsense, Misha thought. Ledgers and bar mitzvahs and tears. Those were not weapons. Guns were weapons. Hateful things, like guns and whips and—

Pleshdimer returned down the line. "Good thing you stopped your chit-chat," he said, jabbing Misha in the thigh with his stick. "I was about to stop it myself by stuffing this in your mouth." He waved the stick in front of Misha's face.

Misha shrunk from it. *I hate you*, he thought. *Hate you, hate you, hate you.*

That was it, he knew suddenly. There was an event he could plan down to the last detail, and he did have a weapon after all. In fact if hatred was, as he suspected, the most powerful weapon he owned, he had just discovered within himself an entire arsenal.

Misha picked up his feet and squared his shoulders. As soon as he could, he would tell Sol about this, he thought, watching the line snake around a bend in the road. Uncle Hans, too. Then the three of them could become warriors together against the enemy.

With that in mind, he opened a page in his thought-ledger and began to make his first list: enemies on one side, friends on the other.

Without knowing why, he included amongst his friends the man in the corpsman's uniform, the one who had stepped out of the shadows to tell him that he had to survive.

Chapter 21

How long was it since he and Misha and Hans had been reassigned from the quarry? Sol wondered. He was beginning to lose track of time again, the way he had done in the sewer. Here, it felt worse. In the sewer there had been hope...and darkness to keep him from seeing his own physical degeneration.

Here, he not only saw his own, he saw others'.

Misha worked in the morgue next door to the *Pathologie,* where prisoners were experimented upon—vivisection and dissection on a stainless steel table with sloped troughs for collecting blood. The boy's job was to pry out gold teeth and search for gemstones in the rectums of corpses awaiting transport in Oranienburg garbage trucks to the city's crematorium. He said he did not mind it too much because of his new friend, Franz, a corpsman who had apparently dared question the huge casualty list at the camp and earned himself an assignment as *Pathologie* guard. He was the same man who, Misha said, had spoken to the boy kindly on the last morning of his quarry duty; a German of apparent compassion who, upon occasion, sneaked Misha a chocolate bar, which Misha shared with Sol and Hans.

The choice, he insisted, was his.

Hans had been reassigned to the brickworks, then to the Klinker factory's ships in the Oranienburg Kanal, to the holds and the heat and the dust. His job was to shovel coal and rubble up onto sloped platforms. More often than not, he said, it fell back on him.

His multiple injuries had been compounded by a hacking cough. Judging by the color and particles in his sputum, he was already a victim of the early stages of black lung disease. His skin was becoming permanently discolored; any attempt at a smile caused his lips to crack into ridges of blood and dust. He was also forced to perform in the brothel twice a day and often several times on Sundays, when the Klinker factory closed to give management a rest.

Instead of effecting his release, his priapism had brought him under Schmidt's scrutiny. He was made to move from woman to woman while Kapos whipped him, used electro-shock, or shoved numbing suppositories up his rectum...all in the name of science.

"Sooner or later they'll neuter me," he told Solomon. "Then I will kill Schmidt and myself."

The choice, he insisted, was his.

They were given a choice, all right, Sol thought bitterly. Cooperate and survive; fight and die...if you're lucky.

He thought back to the first day of his own reassignment, the day he became Doctor Schmidt's prime guinea pig in her eye experiments...an attempt to reduce the problem of night blindness in pilots. She had injected dye at the outer edge of each of his eyes. When it took effect, there was an hour of photographing and peering and examination through various lenses. He had to lie still and keep his blinking to a minimum, or suffer Schmidt's syringe in his stomach.

The choice, she insisted, was his.

The process was repeated once or twice a week. Each time she repeated the same questions. Was your father sensitive to light? As a child, did you prefer dark places?

After the sessions in the laboratory, he was free until roll call—not out of compassion, but because Schmidt wanted him nearby in case she wished to repeat some part of her experiment. He was to have no food or water until dinner—why, he did not know. His was not to question, but to accept and survive.

That was his mandate.

Meanwhile, he could not ignore the fact that Schmidt's dyes were accelerating the deterioration of his eyesight; he was beginning to perceive colors differently, like the gray pebbles beneath his feet, which were beginning to look purple. But as his peripheral vision deteriorated, the clarity of his central vision improved. He wanted to see less, not more. Blindness would spare him the sight of all the horrors; with luck, it might even induce the SS to bless him with a bullet in the neck.

Until then, life would continue to be made up of eye days and, when Schmidt did not send for him, foot days.

Today was a foot day.

He looked down at his shoes. Inside, his feet were slimed with blood and dirt, and crammed so tightly into the too-small shoes that he made macabre jokes to himself about being a Chinese princess.

At the request of local shoe manufacturers looking for "a true test of durability," a walkway was built along the edge of the roll call area. The walkway's *raison d'être* was the provision of superior footwear for Germans to more comfortably carry the banners of truth and racial purity to the ends of the earth.

Sol picked up a sandbag and began to walk. As he did at the beginning of each foot day, he read the signs along the edge of the walkway, hand-lettered, blooming like large white flowers: Give Sacrifice and Glory to the Fatherland! Obedience. Industry. Honesty. Cleanliness.

For the rest of the day, the track would define his universe. Each path-length averaged six thousand steps. He was required to walk it—back and forth—seven times. Even wearing good, firm shoes, negotiating forty kilometers of stretches of cement, cinders, crushed stones, and broken glass embedded in tar, gravel, and sand would have been difficult and painful; in shoes a full size too small, carrying increasingly heavy sandbags, the foot days added a new color to the fresco that was Sol's life: the color of blood.

He smelled it everywhere, tasted it. Saw it in the wake left by the line of feet walking the shoe track. Up and down—

Familiar with every hazard on the track, his only defense against the deadly combination of pain and boredom was to resort to the same tactic he had used in the sewer: counting his steps.

Seven hundred twenty-six...seven hundred twenty-seven....

He continued walking and counting until he reached the far end of the walkway, the one nearest *Pathologie*. A scream interrupted his counting.

In the brief silence between screams, Sol turned and started back toward the beginning of the crescent-shaped walkway.

...six thousand and one...

Like a flagellant, he had learned to relish the pain. Dragging his feet, feeling the blood ooze, he gritted his teeth in a kind of pleasure as a matching pain pulsed behind his eyes. There was a flash of light, and then another. A blue glow grew out of the walkway and enveloped him.

Grateful that the universe defined by the track was about to be expanded, he did not try to shut out the vision——

——*Lise Meitner and her assistant sit on the edges of their cots, staring hopelessly at the floor.* Göring stands over them.

"Our lab...shut down!" Lise utters in disbelief. Now she peers up, her face strained. "But we were making such progress."

Göring chuckles haughtily. "We have no need of parasites like you, now that we'll soon have," he pauses for effect, "the bomb."

"Impossible!"

"The Copenhagen plant made certain breakthroughs—"

"So Bohr did give you heavy water before he escaped."

"Before he was kidnapped!" Göring snaps.

"But the partisans—they blew up the Norsk-Hydro power plant!"

"Those inept traitors?" The Feldmarschall tilts his face toward the ceiling and laughs so hard that he takes out a handkerchief and wipes tears from his eyes. "We let the British jellyfish *think* they had succeeded. We hadn't counted on the Americans having Bohr as well as Einstein, so we circulated the sabotage story so people would think we were still using heavy water as a neutron moderator instead of...graphite."

"You're lying." Suddenly pale, she speaks without conviction.

"We no longer need your cooperation *or* your brilliance, Doktor Meitner. We have everything we need in the notes that *Doktor* Hahn coded into your love letters. We've had your material for months."

Lise goes white.

"That's right, Doktor. Critical mass. We've had your notes, Copenhagen's success, and now we're tooling up at the Mauthausen camp at Ebensee. The bomb's to be built in a cavern carved out of granite by Jewish half-wits and whores just like you two."

"My letters. My notes. How!" Lise asks desperately, of no one.

"Oh my God." Sobbing, Judith reaches for her. "You said the letters were just reminiscences, and I believed you. I thought I was tricking them...protecting you...."

"Perhaps we'll keep you alive, Doktor, until the weapon is finished and field tested. You will love the site we've picked. A second-rate military target, but ideologically perfect." Bending with difficulty, he lifts Lise's head by the chin, as if to kiss her. "The heart of the land of milk and honey. Jerusalem."

"My soul is dirty," Lise whimpers. "Let me die."——

"Get on with it!"

The crack of a whip, Captain Hempel's personal gift to Kapo Pleshdimer, punctuated the order and dissipated the vision. Sol stooped to pick up a heavier sandbag. He squeezed his feet into a pair of shoes yet another size too small and began, again, to walk—and to count—

Five thousand, six hundred twelve...five thousand six hundred thirteen....

The usual screams filled his imaginings as he tottered toward his milestone. *Pathologie,* directly in his line of vision, expanded and contracted like a creature alive, its brick belly filled with shrieking death. How he longed to suck at that breast. Sol slowed down. Leaned his body toward her.

"Walk, Professor!"

The Kapo's stick cracked against Sol's ribs. He doubled over, straightened up, counted, turned, pushed himself forward. Five thousand and.... Had it been days since he had seen Hans? Weeks?... Five thousand and...

"Walk!"

Let me die, Lord! Sol's thoughts echoed the voice from the vision. It contained all of the elements of the others. Again it showed the abuse of Jewish talents; again it talked of a Jewish homeland in Madagascar. If only he understood what it all meant—not that it mattered anymore. Still, he would rather go to his death knowing than unknowing. He was almost happy when he saw a blue glow——

——*gossamer veils of blue, dust-moted light filter through a stained-glass window onto a man seated at a pipe organ.* He is blond and broad shouldered, and looks as athletic as he is musically talented. The Bach concerto he plays reverberates throughout the tall reaches of a rococo church that was obviously once a castle.

Göring enters the nave, pushing a stumbling Lise before him.

The man at the organ continues to play feverishly, his arched fingers pounding the huge, tiered, ivory-inlaid keys. His head is lifted as though he sees something reverent in the tall brass pipes.

Göring opens the door. The organist does not turn around. Outside there is a bell tower and a flagstone landing. A long, very steep flight of stone stairs serpentines down the thumb-shaped limestone ledge on which the *Schlosskirche* perches. Beyond the castle-church lies farming country and half-timbered houses with gingerbread roofs.

"At least let Judith go," Lise pleads.

"As soon as my bodyguards finish with her, we'll let her go—to Auschwitz." Göring grabs her by the hair and drags her down the steps.

"I didn't deceive you about the graphite, Herr Feldmarschall! I swear I didn't."

He hits her—twice. She staggers back, then rocks forward and...pushes. He fights to keep his balance, but is too heavy. Fat arms flailing, screaming, he tumbles down the stone steps——

——The vision faded. Sol twisted uneasily on his bunk. Dawn filtered through the barracks window. There was movement in the barracks as others who had not slept prepared for a new day.

Chapter 22

Lately, the Rathenau rose garden had become Miriam's place for private and often dangerous thoughts. No one interfered with her inside the house, but that did not diminish her feeling that somehow her mental plotting and scheming could be overheard.

It was, she knew, a monumental foolishness. The only person who could possibly know what she was thinking was the baby, if, in fact, fetuses, embryos—whatever it was at this stage—could *know* anything.

Sitting in the rose garden at sundown on the day of summer solstice, she contemplated her future. She could see herself, with Erich; in her more optimistic moments she could see herself with Sol. But she found it almost impossible to place a child, her child, in the picture.

If by now, almost six months into her pregnancy, she was supposed to be feeling maternal, something had gone wrong. If she were master of the universe, she decided, the first thing she would do would be to make men's bodies capable of childbearing.

Even feeling the way she did, she could not help but smile at the very idea. Husband, home, children—weren't those what *women* were supposed to want? When this was over, this black period in German history, there would surely be those who would tell her that she should have been satisfied with what she had. It was, after all, so much more than most.

Maybe so, but she wanted more.

Had she fought against the flow, and failed, she might have been content. Or maybe she was just being optimistic and naïve, the inveterate performer thinking that life was going to work out with the form and balance of a play. Poverty did not appeal to her, but it had never frightened her either. At least, having tried and failed, her failure would have been of her own volition. But the Nazis had come, and taken away her will. They tore her mansion from her womb, and tore her from her mansion. Her birthright. She was back again, but it was not the same, for it was no longer hers. Its walls did not enclose and protect her, they were her cage—as her body was the child's.

One thing she did know: men would surely be more careful about making babies if there were no way to know before the fact who had to go through nine months of physical changes and emotional instability.

"What you're feeling is perfectly normal," the doctor kept saying. "Your body chemistry is not the same as it was, why would you expect to feel like yourself? Get out more, Frau Alois. Walk in the rose garden. Occupy yourself. Knit baby clothes."

Frau Alois.

There was never a time that she could hear herself called that without cringing. She kept telling herself that a rose was rose was a rose, but it didn't work.

Knit baby clothes! She should sit and knit when her world was falling— had long since—fallen apart.

Well, at least one thing had gone right. Erich had managed to remove the threat of the blood transfusion. Never in her life would she forget that conversation between the two men, walking ahead of her on the night of Hitler's birthday party. A beautiful spring evening, the air still, allowing snatches of their discussion to be easily overheard as she walked behind them. *"In my opinion, your wife's reformation needs something more. A doctor at Sachsenhausen…conducting experiments…. Total blood transfusions…. If Miriam were to be transfused with Aryan blood, no one would dispute her place beside you in the New Order."*

She stared at the blood-red profusion of roses around her and, lulled by the warmth of the day, fell into a state between sleeping and waking. She felt her head nod and saw a figure with a watering can, spraying roses with water that ran the color of blood. The roses fell to the ground, but on the bushes, here and there a petal remained, dangling between thorns like pieces of torn flesh.

She jerked herself fully awake. She could not allow herself to become morbid. It was not healthy for her or for the baby. She had asked the doctor about that. Whether her thoughts could transfer themselves to the child she was carrying.

"We're not sure how much transfer there is between mother and embryo," he'd said. "Or, for that matter, the other way around."

She hadn't really thought about that until now. Perhaps she was being influenced by whatever was growing inside her. Was it a boy or girl, normal or shaped by her past and its father's. Bonded to her, and yet a stranger. Stretching her, she feeding it, blood and food intermingled, one with the other.

"I thought I might find you out here, Señora."

Miriam jerked herself fully awake. "Domingo," she said happily.

"You sound pleased to see me. How pleasant," the South American said, bowing with mock formality. He plucked a rose from the closest bush. "Why do all beautiful things have thorns," he said, sucking a drop of blood from his finger where a thorn had scraped it. He breathed in the scent of the rose. "It smells almost as lovely as you," he said, presenting it to her. "I had no time to purchase flowers for you before coming here, though why I would continue to do that when you are surrounded by the best I do not know."

Miriam smiled. "Don't ever change," she said. "I would be lost without your flattery. I *am* happy to see you."

"I just returned to Berlin and was told that you had been trying to get in touch with me. And I have news for you besides."

"Of Solomon?" She started to rise from the small bench upon which she had been resting.

"Mostly of Erich."

She sat back down. "Tell me," she said listlessly, as if the conversation no longer held her interest.

"May I sit down? I have not slept in many hours and I am more weary than usual."

She felt immediately apologetic. "I'm sorry, Domingo. I am not always polite of late."

He sat down next to her and took her hand. "You must not speak to anyone of what I am going to tell you. It is the reason I returned to Berlin sooner than expected, but for now it must remain a private matter between us. Soon, very soon, the Herr Major will be called in to headquarters. He is to be given a double promotion—"

"A *double* promotion?"

"It is not quite what it sounds. There are strings attached. I am not sure how to phrase this. The words sound so ridiculous."

He looked at her, as if to be sure he had her full attention. Apparently satisfied that he did, he continued. "I won't go into the history of all of this," he said. "You may even be aware of some of it. Certainly you must have heard that there has been much debate about what the Führer calls 'the Jewish question.' Part of that debate has included suggestions for the deportation of all Jews to a homeland far away from Germany. It appears that a location has been settled upon. Madagascar."

"Madagascar?" Miriam said the word slowly, but her mind was racing, remembering. There were two people who had spoken to her of Madagascar. One of them was Sol. Over and over, he had told her about his visions, and about the single link between them: the creation of a Jewish homeland in Madagascar. The other was her Uncle Walther.

"He told my Uncle that all Jews should be penned like animals in Madagascar."

"He?"

"The Führer. I remember Uncle Walther telling me about it. And Sol...." She stopped. She would think about that connection later. "No matter," she said. "What does this have to do with Erich and his promotion?"

"I suppose the only way to say this is to say it. Erich—and his canine unit—are to lead the first resettlement effort."

Miriam frowned. "Erich and his dogs? I don't understand."

"Before the end of the summer, a ship will leave for Africa. He and his dogs and trainers will be on it. There are military reasons that I cannot discuss which require my presence on board, and—"

"—Am I to stay here," Miriam asked slowly.

Perón shook his head.

Miriam stood up and began to pace agitatedly. Perón simply watched her. "There's more to this than you're telling me," she said, stopping to stare down at him. "Who else is to go? Which Jews?" She sat back down heavily beside him. "Which Jews?" she repeated.

"I am not sure, Miriam. Rumor has it that they will be—perhaps have already been—handpicked from one of the camps. They will be artisans, mostly. Builders, carpenters. Farmers, too. People logically suited to be part of such an advance party. Fewer than two hundred in all, but enough to use for a major international propaganda effort."

Miriam started to shake. "Solomon," she said. She gripped Perón's arm. "You must do it for me. You must arrange for Solomon to be on that ship."

"Erich would never allow it," Perón said.

"Then," Miriam said quietly, "he must not know until it is too late."

"You cannot get your hopes up, Miriam," Perón said. "This may not be possible. Besides, from what you have told me your Solomon is hardly an artisan. Did you not say that he is a scholar by avocation and a bookkeeper by trade?"

"He has the heart and mind of a professor. He is also a linguist. There will surely be a need for someone able to speak...what is the native language?"

"Sad to say, my education is lacking. I admit, I do not know the answer." He thought for a moment. "How good is his French? I do know that the French influence is enormous in that part of the world."

"He speaks excellent French," Miriam said, "As do I."

"I am not sure how much I can influence the choice of settlers," Perón said. "This much I promise you. I will do what I can."

"And I," Miriam said, "will do what I must."

Part II

"Never shall I forget these things, even if I am condemned to live as long as God Himself."
— Elie Wiesel

Chapter 23

June 1939

The dying sun cast an orange glow across a sky feathered by clouds and painted a web of intricate shadows on the concrete at Solomon's feet. He laughed bitterly at God's sense of the absurd.

Why provide such beauty to watch over a concentration camp?

Sol stood at the hub of Sachsenhausen, one of Germany's monuments to Hell. Within the pyramid of the outer fences, the camp's eighty-six barracks, hospital, and guards' quarters spread out behind him in an enormous semicircle. As he looked at the barbed, electrified wire and at the sentry towers placed at one hundred and eighty meter intervals, a seductive thought occurred to him: one false move—a single motion toward freedom—would set the whole barbaric machine into motion. For a split-second...before they mowed him down...he would be in control.

A surge of power infused him. His heartbeat increased. Contemplating death, he pulsed with new life. It was a heady sensation, meaningless to anyone not in his position, probably beyond their comprehension. With a single, casual pace beyond the boundaries set for him and his fellow prisoners, he could impel a small army into action, disrupt its mealtime, create disorder. Best of all, he could add to the mound of paperwork with which the ever-so-meticulous Nazis documented their days and nights.

Then the crack of the Kapo's whip announced evening roll. As Sol turned to stare at the barracks guard, his sense of hopelessness returned to ask, "And so?" He discarded the urge for martyrdom and began to search the faces of the gathering inmates for his friends, Hans Hannes and nine-year-old Misha Czisça, who had been missing for two days—they and that damned pederast, Captain Hempel.

Instinctively Sol glanced in the direction of *Pathologie*. The hospital's windows winked obscenely at him in the sunset, like the ten diamond-fruits of the Kabbalah's Tree of Life. Inside lay the face of death, eyes shiny and open and eager...promising, finally, a surfeit of terror.

Roll call began and ended, and still he stared at the building, certain that it held the answers to his friends' disappearance. Yet he hoped. Always hoped...and prayed.

Two screams came from *Pathologie*.

The Kapo, a convicted murderer elevated to the status of barracks guard, turned toward the building and smiled. He intoned the daily litany: "You must make ever greater efforts to honor the Reich and throw off the burden of the Jewish yoke—dismissed!"

The prisoners moved toward the barracks, all but Sol who set out grimly in the direction of *Pathologie*. Before he reached it, the clopping of a horse's hooves rang through the yard, and Captain Otto Hempel emerged from between the hospital and another barracks. He rode easily atop his mount and, as always, his black-muzzled wolfhound loped alongside. The boy, Misha Czisça, staggered in the lead, his movements impaired by a lidded, army-green watering can attached to a strap across his shoulder. The can hung awkwardly beneath his armpit.

The horse snorted and shook its head, as if bothered by the presence of youth.

Sol whipped off his cap and snapped to attention. "Good evening, Hauptsturmführer Hempel!" Give the required greeting. Do not look at the deputy commandant. "May the Teutonic gods and the spirit of our Messiah Adolf Hitler go with you this night!" Sol added, trusting in Hempel to misread the sarcasm.

"A beautiful evening."

His tone benign, Hempel reined up beside Solomon. Leather creaking, he rose in the saddle like a handsome lord-overseer—lean, without appearing hard-muscled, silver-haired without appearing elderly. Except for a red and black scarf around his neck, his uniform was without decoration: the quintessential captain. "Some day the Reich will be so far-reaching, there will always be such a sky beaming over it." The captain gestured upward with his bone-handled riding crop. His other hand rested lightly on his pistol. "Such weather makes a man feel truly alive—eh, prisoner?"

"Ja, Hauptsturmführer!"

"Good! We are in agreement." He relaxed into the saddle and thrust out his boots in wordless command.

It is our duty to survive and tell the world, Sol reminded himself. Do whatever the captain wants. Lick his boots. Shine them with your cap. Pay special attention to the instep. Say, "Ja, Hauptsturmführer."

The horse urinated, splashing Solomon. He kept at his job.

"You are the one they call Professor, not so?"

"Ja, Hauptsturmführer."

"Your name?"

Sol held up his arm. Prisoner number 37704.

"And they call you Professor! You have the mind of a sparrow." The riding crop rose. "Your *name!*"

"Freund, Hauptsturmführer. Solomon Freund."

"I thought so." Hempel smiled as if at some private joke. "Long-time friend of Major Erich Alois."

He touched Sol between the eyes with the butt of the crop. "You will keep yourself alive. You will remain healthy in mind and body. One day you will have the privilege of testifying in a court of law about your *friend!*" Using his whip, he pointed at the puddle the horse had left. "Clean that up, then follow us."

He spurred the mount. Misha, who had not once met Solomon's gaze, hurried to stay ahead of the animal as they headed in the direction of the *Gärtnerei,* site of the commandant's hothouses, huge flower and vegetable gardens, and—source of his greatest pride—his hog farm. Sol quickly joined them. It was dusk, and sentry spotlights swept the area. There is a world, Sol thought, where dusk is the time for drama and love.

"Take care of the roses," Hempel told the child.

Misha nodded. Dazed, he lifted the lid of his watering can, then raised on tiptoes to kiss the tip of Hempel's riding crop.

Turning to Solomon, the captain said amiably, one gentleman addressing another, "Those are the Kommandant's prize hybrids. His 'Centurions,' he calls them. They've won several awards at the Reichsblume Konkurenz in Hamburg." He drooled his expensive Indian chewing tobacco into the can. "Go with the boy. Help him tamp the soil—get a little German earth under your nails."

Misha moved to the rose beds, weeping softly. Sol backed down the row and crouched beside him. The blooms smelled almost obscenely sweet after the sour odors of the camp. He glanced in Hempel's direction, wondering what lay behind his being allowed to linger here.

Hempel waved pleasantly.

Sol buried his face in a cluster of roses. Assailed by a memory he could not quite touch, he closed his eyes and placed the petals, warm and velvety, against his skin. His mother's nightgown had smelled like this, fresh out of the dresser drawer with its sachets of dried rose petals, but it was Miriam's spirit that suffused him. Miriam, the love who once...still...embodied for him all that was beautiful.

He opened his eyes and reveled in the rose's color, red as a sailor's sunset.

"Miriam," he murmured, caressing the blossom gently with his lips, as if its petals were her womanhood and he a free man making love to her for the first time, drinking in her softness.

A drop of warm liquid touched his skin. Thinking it to be one of Misha's tears and pleased that the boy had at last been able to allow himself the solace of tears, Sol looked up at him.

"I'm sorry," Misha said.

"It's nothing. " Sol smiled. "If a drop of water on my arm is the worst crime you ever commit against me—"

"I'm sorry, Uncle Hans." Sobbing, the boy tilted the watering can. Talking to it and not to Solomon, he said, "I'm sorry. I'm sorry."

The searchlight moved and returned, capturing the child like a player on a stage. Sol stared at the fine spray of burgundy liquid. He felt another droplet on his skin. When the spotlight returned, he stared at it lying on his flesh like a perfect garnet.

"The Kommandant insists there is no better fertilizer," Hempel called out.

Sol looked from the watering can toward the captain, who nodded and laughed. A sudden urgency started Sol's heart pounding like a jack hammer. "Misha? What have you been saying!"

"They d-drained him," the boy stammered. "Like all the others." His tears came more freely now as he began to water, his back rising and falling with each exhalation as though he were an ancient pump. "Mama!" he called out. "Mama!"

"Put the can down, Misha. God of our Fathers! Put it down!" Sol took the boy by the shoulders. "Listen to me! That's not our friend in there. He's here with us. His spirit is in us both."

The boy's face tightened into a bud of hatred. He flailed his arms, hitting Solomon's chest, scratching his cheeks as he tried to break free, and spilling the remainder of the blood from the watering can as it flew from his grasp.

"One day I'll kill him." He looked up at the captain, who had dismounted and was ambling toward them. "I'll kill all of them!"

"Misha, listen to me—"

Sol stopped. The wolfhound, gliding like a phantom between the rosebushes and gardenias, had joined his master. They were now within a meter of the boy.

"Kiss it!" Hempel held out his riding crop.

Misha leaned forward and Hempel instantly twisted the handle hard against the boy's lips. "The Professor and I have business to attend to," he said. "Remain here at attention until I return."

He looked at the dog and snapped his fingers. "Guard!" Hackles raised and teeth bared, the dog moved in front of the boy, watching him with shiny eyes. Hempel shifted his gaze to Solomon. "If the boy moves so much as an eyelid, the dog will kill him. You come with me!"

They went along the west wall and cut in at *Pathologie*. Sol wanted to run from the place. Beneath the harsh lights of the outer room were rows of neatly labeled jars filled with formaldehyde and human organs. Eyeballs floating in fluid watched his fear.

The captain knocked at the slightly open door of the examining room.

Doctor Schmidt looked up. "I see you found him. Well, don't just stand there. Come in, come in, both of you."

Sol blinked against the fluorescent desk lamp that turned the doctor's face into a serene blend of light and shadow. She had removed her surgical cap. Her dark well-brushed hair cascaded across her shoulders and her eyes were soft, expressive, brows and lids set off with just the right touch of make-up.

"I didn't have to go far to find him, *Medizinalrat*."

"Today we had a fruitful session with a friend of yours," the physician told Solomon. "His name was..." She ran a slim finger down a long list. "Ah, yes. Here it is. Hans Hannes. Original name Hans Fink." Smiling sweetly, she added, "He called out your name several times."

"What do you want with me, *Medizinalrat?*"

"All in good time," the woman said. "We try to observe the niceties around here whenever possible, don't we, Otto?" She looked up at the captain. They exchanged a confidential nod.

Hempel picked up a folder from the desk. Opening it, he drew out a paper rimmed with a logo of golden wreathwork. "Why we have to go through these formalities is beyond my understanding."

"It is the law," Schmidt said.

Fighting to keep calm, Solomon squinted at the tiny print. He could read the line in bold and the signature beneath it:

In order to rid myself of my perverse sexual instincts, I hereby apply for castration.

Hans Hannes Fink

A wave of helplessness weakened Sol's knees and he sagged against the wall. Some twisted logic dictated that castration needed the written permission of the victim. Mere sterilization—a privilege generally reserved for the handicapped, the retarded, and Jews who'd had intercourse with Aryans—could be carried out without consent. In truth, homosexuals were rarely castrated, but Hannes had suffered fiercely from priapism—muscular deterioration that left him with a perpetual, excruciatingly painful erection. That made him different...just as Sol's eye disease set him apart. He knew Schmidt must be longing to scoop out his eyeballs and add them to her collection.

"I won't sign anything," he said. "Not now. Not ever."

Hempel raised a fist and took a step forward.

"Now, Otto, you told me you needed him alive and, besides, you know how easily your blood vessels tend to break at the knuckles." Schmidt picked up what looked like a list of names printed beneath an official letterhead. "We have another reason to keep him reasonably fit, which is why I asked you to find him for me. My old friend Eichmann is taking another stab at immortality. This prisoner is on the list of those selected. See for yourself."

She handed Hempel the sheet of paper, and turned to Sol.

"In a few days you will be issued new spectacles," she said. "Meanwhile, take care of your eyes." She looked up at Hempel. "Pity. This case interested me. Freak diseases always do."

She lifted a canning jar from atop a black filing cabinet that stood behind her. Within floated testicles and a purplish, uncircumcised penis. Holding the jar before her face, she studied the contents. The jar magnified her face like a mirror at the Panoptikum. "Did I tell you, Otto, I have you to thank for this wonderful specimen? You were the one who first talked to me of tabun. Though your interest in it has, of course, a different base than mine, your enthusiasm led me to acquire a small supply of it in liquid form."

She set the jar at the desk edge nearest Hempel and went on speaking as if she had forgotten Sol's presence.

"Have you any idea how effective tabun is?" she asked.

"I just know the nerve gas works," he said.

"How it works, that's the wonder!...inhibits the action of the enzyme cholinesterase...causes uncontrolled muscular contractions, followed by paralysis...and, finally, death." Her eyes were bright. "I placed a few drops on Hannes' spine during coitus, while he was performing in our brothel. You should've seen how it affected him—even with his special, shall we say, equipment." She put her hand on the jar and leaned forward confidentially. "When I was young, I read how Darwin cut off the legs of a frog engaged in coitus, and the frog continued to perform." She tapped the jar lid with a fingernail. *"This* rivals...no, *eclipses* Darwin's experiment." She gave Hempel a warm smile, then turned to Solomon. "Otto has arranged for this specimen to be shipped to Berlin via his mother in Strassbourg. She is fascinated with our work here."

"How can you, a doctor, do this?" Sol asked. Despite feeling weak with fear, he wanted to take hold of her neck and wring it like a chicken from his uncle's barnyard.

Schmidt patted the jar. "You think me a monster? You are wrong. I admire you Jews. You gave the world its first judicial system, its first efficient society, its first schools, some of its first doctors. The list of your achievements is endless."

She leaned closer. Perhaps realizing that the tops of her breasts were showing, she spread a hand across her lapels. Sol pulled back, as if she were diseased. He looked around for Otto Hempel. The captain had gone.

Relieved, Sol told himself that he had imagined it all. Misha and Hans were safely back at the barracks. He must take care to reconnect with reality.

"Listen to me," Schmidt said. Her voice held a lover's caress. Sol's gaze rested on the jar at the edge of her desk, the momentary flare of hope extinguished. "Though science and medicine interest me above all else," she said, "you would be hard pressed to find a better humanitarian."

Chapter 24

Crouched against the barracks' wall opposite Hans' empty bunk, Solomon watched those fellow inmates who were awake mill about the area. They were skeletal. Stuporous. Compliant. Gray, amorphous figures in striped pajamas.

May their souls find rest, he thought, trying one more time to pray for Hans. One more time, he could not find the words. No matter how deeply inside he reached, all he found was pain. He could not even pray for the living anymore; the prayers stuck in his throat. He just kept seeing that jar in *Pathologie* and hearing Schmidt's last words: *"You'd be hard pressed to find a better humanitarian."* And something else...he could not quite remember what...about Eichmann, and spectacles, and some absurdity about taking care of himself!

Not that anything Schmidt had said mattered. He did not care what diabolical scheme she and her colleagues were cooking up. He did not need new glasses. He needed to be left alone, to do nothing. Think nothing. To reach the state of *ayin ha'gamur,* that complete nothingness which the Kabbalah described as the last obstacle facing rational thought when it has reached the limits of its capacity.

He had imagined that when he reached that limit, that place where human understanding would be insufficient to make sense of the world, his consciousness would explode into nothingness.

But *ayin* was still denied him.

"Oh God, let me die," a woman pleaded, her voice filling the void inside his head. *"Let me die."* An infant mewled and something laughed, something at best partly human.

Cradling himself with bony arms, Solomon began to rock. Back and forth, back and forth.

Remembering.

...He saw himself as a boy Misha's age, being battered by disembodied voices and sounds that only he could hear. Painfully, he recalled the day that brought shape and form to those voices and sounds, bringing him a series of visions that terrified him beyond measure. He heard the squeal of brakes and the explosions that shattered the sun and gentle silence of a Sabbath afternoon. He saw his friend's car careen to the side of the road and looked at the face of death through cobalt-blue eyes filled with tears. He swam inside them, defenseless and drawn into the dying; he felt again the thing take residence in his body....

The thing—that was how he had thought of it then, before he learned about dybbuks and ghosts, before his secret voices gave way to visions. A *thing*—bringing black moods, long silences, the easy tears and dark circles that came from sleepless nights spent agonizing over what sin he might unknowingly have committed to warrant such punishment.

He still did not know the source of the visions, but he had come to understand that the dybbuk inside him had given substance to the voices. It was the key to the visions. Strange, he thought, how repetition brought mundanity in its wake, no matter how fearsome or bizarre the experience. He had long since moved away from his childhood fear, through acceptance and curiosity, and on to a hunger for interpretation and understanding.

Some visions came to him in their entirety, but came only once; others began slowly, building over years like serial stories. And there were fragments, too, that came and went so quickly they might have been dreams had they not contained the common strains that appeared in each one: each had its hero, its victim, its dybbuk; each spoke of a Jewish homeland in, of all places, Madagascar.

Sitting there, he catalogued the visions: Jews forced to work for National Socialism, building bombs, fighting on the Russian Front, helping with medical experiments. Jews assassinating politicians, gathering huge sums of money for the Nazi cause, operating a death squad from a unique type of airplane they called a helicopter. There was even a Jew who taught others to counterfeit foreign currency, thereby ruining enemy economies.

Ultimately, each had a single, overriding theme: Nazi abuse of Jewish assets and abilities.

He would distract Schmidt by telling her some of the stories, he decided. She could study his flawed second-sight to find out why he could not apply his powers to something as simple as knowing what was going to happen to his friends. Better yet, to preventing it from happening. That would surely be more entertaining than diseased eyeballs.

The flashes of light that inevitably heralded a vision interrupted what was becoming a bitter discourse with himself. *"Dayenu*—enough!" he said out loud. "Oh Lord of the Universe, grant me *ayin.*"

But the flashes of light came again, followed this time by the cobalt-blue glow that also presaged every vision. God is apparently not listening, he thought wryly, or perhaps the patent on the concept of nothingness applied only to realms of theosophy—to His universe and not the devil's. Even for God, it must be difficult to distinguish a single voice in an outcry from Hell.

Since there was no escape, Sol gave himself up to a potpourri of scenes from a past and future as familiar to him now as a series of old films many times revisited.

———*a full moon shines down on the domed keep of a ruined castle and on a dozen beehives rising up like ancient columns behind a black man.* He is lanky and rawboned, bald except for a bowl of hair at the crown of his skull. His left shoulder is draped with a white cloak. He sits on his haunches, forearms across knees—hands turned palms up, fingers crabbed. "I want to be considered a *whole* Jew!" His face is etched with anguish, his voice strained with emotion. "Can't they understand that?"———

———The scene faded. Another replaced it. Sol repositioned his body and watched———

———*a bulb in a blue metal collar hangs garishly from a slatted-board ceiling.* The bulb swings to and fro, to and fro, over the head of the tall, aproned doctor who has bumped into it and set it in motion. The room is awash in the cobalt reflection of the bulb's collar. The stench that fills the air is like that of aged Limburger cheese.

"Welcome to the world of the dead!"———

A hand shook Sol's shoulder. "Herr Freund," Misha whispered. "They are taking some of us somewhere tomorrow. I heard them talking about an experiment, and I saw trucks."

Sol saw an image of an Opel Blitz, its canvas back open like a carnival crier's mouth. "I prefer to die right here."

"Come to bed. Please!" The boy shook him harder. "You need to be rested."

Sol's unresisting head snapped back and forth against the boards. His lids were heavy, his eyes listless, his energy so sapped he had not enough left to curse the guards. He could see the boy, eyes swollen from weeping, but the child's face had a gauzy, pointillist quality. He thought of Hans. He is drinking honey wine with Emanuel, he told himself, deliberately confusing reality with the vision of Ethiopia.

"Don't you know what's happening to you!" the boy screamed. "You're willing yourself to die."

Yes, Sol thought. He was becoming *Schmuckstück*—costume jewelry—an ornament bejeweled by sores.

"Please be Herr Freund again," Misha begged. "Please don't die! I don't want the ghost inside you to jump into me!"

With slowly mounting resolve, Sol pulled himself away from the opiate of introspection. "What could you know of ghosts?" he asked Misha.

"Everything."

Misha's gesture took in the world. Solomon smiled. Even here, now, lost among the forgotten souls of Sachsenhausen, childhood encompassed enviable absolutes. "Why would my...*ghost* choose to go to you?"

"If I were right next to you and you were dying," the boy said, "it would come to me. I know about dybbuks. They're evil dead people, ones whose dreams we live in."

"If you believe in such things, Misha, you must stay away from me."

Though clearly terrified, the boy shook his head.

Even in his state of apathy, Solomon knew the urgency of the boy's fear of dybbuks—those souls unable to transmigrate to a higher world because of the enormity of their sins; souls that sought refuge in the bodies of living persons, causing instability, speaking foreign words through their mouths. He remembered begging his mentor, Beadle Cohen, to help him exorcise the dybbuk. The beadle had led him, instead, to the Kabbalah.

"You are strong, Solomon," the beadle insisted. *"The dybbuk has opened doors for you to see what other men cannot. Continue to be strong and it will leave as it came. Meanwhile, try to understand its message."*

Why had that alien and separate personality cloven to him! If he were guilty of some secret sin that had created an opening for the unquiet soul to enter his own, it was one committed without knowledge or malice. Now, at nearly thirty, he believed that goodness rested in a single tenet of life—in treating your fellow man as you would be treated. Had that been his sin? Had he, at not quite thirteen, neglected to live by that creed?

Taking pity on the child, Sol let himself be led to Hans' bunk. They lay down together. Misha put his head on Sol's shoulder. A tear pressed out of his right eye and trickled down his cheek. He swiped at it angrily, as if it had no right to be there and prove him human.

Sol wanted to cry with him, but who was he to allow himself that luxury? He was nothing special, nor was his suffering. He closed his eyes and held them shut. He wanted nothing more of this world. "Tell me exactly what you meant just now," he whispered.

"My papa is...was a rabbi. One time a man came to the house so Papa could get rid of the ghost-thing inside him. Papa called it a dybbuk."

"What makes you think I have a dybbuk inside *me?*"

"Your eyes are strange, like his," the child said. "Papa said the man saw things we could not see. Heard them too. You know. Inside his head. Things from the past and from the future."

Sol thought again about the recurring figures in his visions: the Ethiopian Jew, his black head bald but for the crown of hair that looked like a *yarmulke;* an old man and a woman, robed in tattered blankets and bent over a steaming tea pot; an infant held up to a horned totem by a disembodied brown hand. He knew of no such men, no such baby, no such realities. And the other visions, like Göring talking about something called critical mass, or experiments on the mummified corpse of an ancient Hebrew.

How tired he was of it all—of visions of people in a past and future that made no sense.

"Do you know what legends are, Misha? Myths?" he asked.

The boy nodded. "Papa called them stories based on a grain of truth."

"Did your papa rid the man of his dybbuk?"

Misha disentangled himself and turned on his side. "When the ghost came out of the man, I thought it went into me," he said in a whisper. "Papa laughed and said he had made sure the closest thing to the man was a big black cat. That was right before..."

"Before what?" Sol asked.

"Before they took Mama and Papa away. Papa put me outside on the fire-landing. He said, 'Mishele, now *you* must be quiet as a ghost.' I heard noise. Shouting. I stayed out there all night. When I went back in, the front door had been knocked down. Mama and Papa were gone. Sometimes..."

The boy hesitated. "Sometimes," he went on, "I think I turned into a ghost and that's why the Nazis punished Mama and Papa." He was trembling—weak with memories. "Maybe the Hauptsturmführer is my real papa, as he says...."

"Stop that!" Sol insisted. The child must have an aunt, an uncle, someone who could attempt his release. Such miracles did happen. Money. Someone knew someone willing to...

Sol stopped himself. There were dreams and there were dreams. Better to be *Schmuckstück* than to hope falsely, for that could just bring deeper despair. Especially to Misha. Hempel would never let the child go. Not alive.

"Listen to me, Misha. I cannot, will not, return to that hospital alive."

He lay on Hans' bunk, listening to the echo of his own words inside his head. Hempel had recently ordered the windows and doors kept closed for "security." Sweat, breath, and body effluvia mingled in a heat as oppressive as a steam bath. With less than a foot of sleeping space per person, the inmates slept spoon-style, arms thrown about each other like caricatures of connubial bliss. He could not so much as lift an arm. In his own bunk, no more than a hand's width separated his face from the roof joist. Searching for air in the stifling barracks, he had worked free a composition tile. By lifting a bit of the roofing, he could breathe in the night.

Whatever this was, it was not living.

When sleep had claimed the boy, Sol made himself a promise. He would have no more of this. Head twisted toward the moonlight, he planned his own execution. He would carry no more stones, hobble no more with bleeding feet along the shoe-track designed to test footwear for good German soldiers. Above all, he would not lie alive beneath Schmidt's instrument.

If they wanted his eyes or his testicles, they could remove them from a corpse.

Gripping the edge of the bunk, he wriggled out of it. Below and beside him were the sweat-slicked faces of over three hundred wretches hacking and choking in their sleep...swaddled in striped bunting, asleep in the Führer's arms.

Sol moved among them, careful to awaken no one. Oddly calm, he made his way toward the far corner of the barracks, where the inmates had hung a tattered blanket to provide suicides with a triangle of privacy. As he reached out to pull aside the blanket, it occurred to him that he might not find the noose empty. There were not too many days or nights that it went unused.

The noose dangled empty and alluring.

As if wanting a witness to his act, he shuffled to the window and wiped away the accumulation of breath with his sleeve. The sentry tower was silhouetted by a new moon, and he could see a helmeted guard bending his head to light a cigarette. A good German soldier, smoking on duty? Shame!

He turned to face the noose and bumped into Misha.

"Herr Freund, you mustn't." The boy tugged at Sol.

"You should not be here," Sol said sternly.

The boy let go and took a step backward. "I *am* here," he said, "and I will stay. You're in this camp because of me. The Nazis would never have found you if I hadn't led them to you. Only I didn't know it was going to happen. It will be your fault if your dybbuk finds me—but you will *know*...."

The sentry light swept across the window, highlighting the expression of raw fear—and courage—on the young face. The child was right, Sol thought, relinquishing the moment. He must alleviate Misha's fear.

Then he would be free to do this for himself.

Chapter 25

Under cover of night, the religious among the almost-dead gathered outside Barracks 18 to pray for themselves. Sometimes they were led by a rabbi. More often than not, the task of leading the prayers fell to the physically strongest among them. The bodies of those who died during prayers simply lay there until the morning detail carried them away, along with the others who had died in their bunks during the night. For the time being, the Nazis found this piling of corpses convenient and chose not to interfere.

Tonight was *Shabbat*—Sabbath. Rumor had it that a rabbi known for the depth and breadth of his studies had recently been brought into the camp. If the reb, whose name Sol had not been able to ascertain, remained among the living, Sol thought, he would be conducting the Service. When he had first come to the camp, Sol had tried, for Misha's sake, to find out whether the boy's parents had ended up here. Often, people were sent to Oranienburg first from Berlin, so he had asked everyone who had been there if they had met Rabbi Czisça and his wife. He discovered only, from someone who had shared the journey with them, that they had indeed been transported to Oranienburg. Whether or not one or both of them were still there, alive, was a question that remained unanswered. Since men and women were separated upon arrival, here at Sachsenhausen and at the holding camp in Oranienburg, he was unlikely to learn more about Misha's mama. As for the rabbi, Misha's papa, he would ask that again tonight. Perhaps this new rabbi would turn out to be Rabbi Czisça himself; such coincidences abounded in the strange sub-culture of the camp.

"Go back to sleep, Misha," Sol whispered, saying nothing of this to the boy for fear of raising his hopes in vain. "I will find the rabbi and he will get rid of the dybbuk so that you need not be afraid."

He led the boy to the bunk and made it out to Barracks 18 without incident. In the quadrangle separating the barracks from Nazi quarters, thirty men hung from a crossbar. Each time the searchlights swept the area, he could see them jerking and convulsing. Earlier that evening, they had been hooked onto the crossbar by the same rope that cuffed their wrists together behind their backs. Though they would be dead by morning, in their present pain they begged for death now. Huddled against the wall, in the blackness of the night, Sol listened to their wails and to the chanting of the congregation of the dying.

Almost at once, as if their lament had drawn it to him, the strains of a Bach concerto began inside Sol's head——

——*gossamer veils of blue dust-moted light filter through a stained-glass window and onto a man seated at a pipe organ.* Blond and broad-shouldered, he is obviously as athletic as he is musically talented. His outward appearance is that of the idealized German farm boy.

The Bach concerto he is playing reverberates throughout the tall reaches of a rococo church that looks as if it were once a castle. Pale blue Grecian designs and rectangular moldings trimmed with gilt separate the walls from the ceilings. Everywhere there are frescoes with Biblical themes——

"Who is there?"

The words, heavy with Spanish accent, dissipated the vision and the music and the blue light. Sol turned toward the voice. A searchlight swept the area and he caught a glimpse of dark skin.

"Solomon Freund."

"Welcome. I'm Reb Nathanson."

Sol felt a deep sense of disappointment and realized how much he had been hoping to be able to bring the boy good news. "I need help, Reb," he said without further preamble.

"Who among us does not?"

Despite himself, Sol chuckled softly at the hint of humor in the rabbi's voice. "I have long believed there is a dybbuk in me," he said, feeling more at ease. "The time has come to have it removed so that I can—"

"I understand," the rabbi said. "I have dealt with such matters before. If you are right, God willing I can make it disappear. At worst, I will persuade it to leave you for one of those wretches on the crossbar. It can cause no harm in that labyrinth of the dying."

"Can that be done?"

"Anything is possible. Now be quiet. It is enough to risk our lives for a purpose. For idle chatter it is stupidity."

"Is there.. ?" Sol restrained himself from laughing aloud. He had been about to ask if there were danger in the ritual. What could be more dangerous than being out here after roll call, shrouded only by the night and threatened by the constant sweep of the searchlights. If the Nazis so much as suspected the performance of a Kabbalistic ritual inside Sachsenhausen...

"I'm ready," he whispered, though for what he could not imagine. "What do you want me to do?"

"Lie flat on your belly. That way, if you must cry out, the ground will muffle the noise. I will put my hands on your head and keep them there until I have removed the demon."

If there is one, Sol thought, lying down.

The searchlights passed again and he waited for the rabbi to begin...what? An exorcism in a charnel house! The incongruity of it was absurd. "Aren't you afraid it will enter *you?*" he asked.

"It wouldn't dare." Moving soundlessly, the rabbi straddled Solomon's back. "I'm sorry there is no time for niceties." His face was so close that his warm breath raised the hairs on Solomon's neck.

"You are named after Solomon, the wise king and arch magician of the Hebrews." The rabbi was panting, bearing down hard. "He created the incantation I am about to use. When you are ready, repeat it with me until I tell you to stop: *Lofaham, Solomon, Iyouel, Iyisebaiyu*—Leave this man and give yourself to..."

"*Lofaham, Solomon, Iyouel, Iyisebaiyu...*"

"Don't stop! When I feel the dybbuk coming, I am going to use an ancient Hebraic incantation. Take no notice. You keep repeating those four words...."

The taste of bile filled Sol's mouth and a wave of nausea engulfed him. He saw, again, some of the people in his visions—a woman, eyes anguished, begging to die. A blanket-robed old man, lashes and brows furred with frost, kneeling in the snow beside the frozen body of a young soldier. The Ethiopian, staring unmoving at the disemboweled body of his ancestor.

"Prepare yourself," the rabbi said softly. "If it is in you, it will fight to stay there."

More than anything else in the world, Sol wanted to put an end to this. Then he thought of Hans Hannes Fink lying mutilated on a stainless steel table, and he chanted the words of that other Solomon over and over, until he could hear only the ragged sound of his own voice, feel nothing but the throbbing in his head, see nothing but the sweep of the searchlight.

"*Shabriri*—Diminish!" the rabbi commanded.

Silence. The soft pad of a prisoner's bare feet.

"Are you in pain?" the rabbi whispered, his voice gentle. Sol felt the dirt beneath his cheek...and nothing else.

The searchlights swept by, catching the crossbar where the hanging men had ceased their movements. He stared at their bodies.

"Say the words again."

"Lofaham, Solomon—"

"Stop." The rabbi removed his hands. "All I can do for you, Solomon Freund, is ask for God's blessing. You had a dybbuk in you once. It is no longer there, but I believe it remains flesh of your flesh and blood of your blood. Whatever is in you *now* was always yours—and always will be." Very softly he said, "Let us pray together."

Replacing his hands lightly on Solomon's head, he began the traditional blessing: *"Boruch Ato Adonoy, Elohaynoo Melech Hoolom.* Blessed art Thou, O Lord our God, King of the Universe..."

Flooded with memories, Sol heard little more until the final words of the prayer. *May the Lord make His countenance to shine upon you and bring you peace. Amen.*

More at peace with himself than he had been in a long time, Sol returned to his barracks. He went straight to the corner that held the noose and unhooked it from its nail. Holding it firmly, he mounted the stool. With his head touching the rafter, he looked out across the camp. The other barracks lay like a series of crypts in a moonlit cemetery. Would God forgive him this act?—and what, he wondered, lay beyond the moon's gray-gold shroud? Some other reality? Or would he at last attain that state of complete nothingness that called to him like a teat to a baby lamb.

Certainly the act of dying no longer held any great mystery. A body was a body—nothing more. He would be stacked in the morgue, and Misha and the other boys who were put to work there would search his orifices for valuables. The Nazis allowed a noose per barracks out of expedience, not mercy. Each dead Jew made the Führer's task easier. Nevertheless, suicide was not popular on camp reports; Schmidt would certify "death due to accidental strangulation" or "suffocation as the result of pneumonia."

He closed the curtain and tested the rope. It held firm. Pulse racing, he put the noose over his head. The knot cuddled against the back of his neck. He fondled it. Where best to place it? he wondered. Where it lay now, it might cause him to twist and struggle several more seconds than necessary.

Cupping the knot in his palm, he turned it to the left and drew the rope tight. Gazing at the moonlight ribbed among the rafters, he took a deliberate, calming breath and shut his eyes. The stench of the blankets wafted into his sinuses. Around him the sound of snoring rose in crescendo. His pulse pounded behind his eardrums and the muscles along his calves tensed. He wondered if the Nazis would take his teeth; those of hanged men were supposed to be important in sorcery. Far away, he heard the mocking laughter of Erich Alois Weisser. He thought he heard the old man of his visions speak longingly of the taste of ginger tea.

"Yiskadal.. ," he began. But mourning for himself seemed blasphemous. Perhaps Miriam would...

Miriam.

"I'm so tired, Miri," he whispered. "So very tired."

Stepping from the stool, he kicked it gratefully aside. The noose around his neck held tight. His legs dangled. His body turned beneath the rope.

"You must live, Solomon. Live!" said Emanuel, the Ethiopian Jew. *"You have not yet fulfilled your destiny."*

Could the voices not leave him in peace even now, at the moment of dying?

"*Survival, Solomon! Therein lies your duty!*" said Margabrook, the old man wrapped in the blanket. "*There are things to be done that only you can do.*"

"*How dare you, Solomon!*" said Lise Meitner, raising her voice to be heard above the organ strains of the Bach Concerto he had heard earlier. "*Only God has the right to order the Universe.*"

Sol tried to respond. He could not. His own voice was no more his than his body, and the dark that surrounded him was an emollient, amniotic and safe.

"Don't you dare die, Herr Freund!"

Misha's voice reached out from the other side of death and Solomon opened his eyes. Moon-bathed rafters wavered and wheeled above him, and the sounds of his own gasping and choking roared in his ears. Shadows exploded before his eyes. A dry fire seared his throat. He clawed at the rope around his neck, tearing at flesh he knew to be his own.

"I've got your legs! Grab the joist!"

Through retinas that threatened to burst, Sol saw a hand groping at the air in slow motion, as if its fingers had a separate existence. He was a puppet, dangling, his strings intact, watching his hand—the puppeteer—relearn the art of manipulating its toy.

Grab the joist, he tried to tell the hand.

His fingers clutched the wood. His vision cleared. It became intense, precise. He saw his fingers grip the wood, watched the splinters peel off and pierce his flesh. The pain was sweet. He leaned into it, accepting it with gratitude as, suddenly, he knew he was not ready to die.

With God-given strength, the child bolstered Sol's weight, suspending him like an upended log. For an instant, a window in time, gravity abandoned its grip upon Sol. It was time enough for him to loosen and open the noose.

Collapsing to the floor on top of Misha, he clutched his throat and struggled for breath. Stale barracks air passed in and out of his throat, cool and sweet as late-blooming lilac. The voices of the other prisoners demanding quiet greeted him like a symphony. He wanted to embrace them all. Then their voices stilled, and he was faced with the certain knowledge that he would never again have the passing courage to put an end to his life.

Cradling his face in the crook of his arm, he wept for himself and for all of the others without choices.

"You're...squishing...me!"

An elbow poked Solomon's ribs. Still weeping, he rolled aside.

"Why did you do it, Misha?" he asked, his voice hoarse from its recent battle with the rope.

"I owed you your life."

"So we are even," Sol said seriously. "Now go to your bunk. There is little enough time left for rest."

"You, too, Freund," someone said. "Hang yourself or go to sleep!"

Shaking, Sol arose and climbed up into his own bunk. Death had been denied him; as for sleep, there was little chance of that tonight. Some things, he thought, were a matter of choice, while others...

Just how much of life, he wondered, was truly a matter of choice? How much inevitable, given the impact of the collective unconscious of the past on man's actions?

A new idea came to him.

What if there were another collective unconscious, a storehouse that contained *future* knowledge? Imagine how *that* would impact man's present behavior!

The concept exhilarated him. Was *this* what he was meant to learn from the voices and visions that had plagued him through life and tried to keep him from dying? Nothing happened without reason, of that he was convinced. Yet was not what had happened to him and to his people insane?

Willing, for the first time, to try to induce the second sight with which he had been blessed—or damned—he lifted his secret place of roofing and closed his eyes. Perhaps the answers to his questions lay somewhere in his past. He would journey there through his own memories and through those of the two people with whom his life had been inextricably bound.

For what was left of the night, he journeyed through his own past...and Erich's...and Miriam's, but the answers to his questions still eluded him. All that was clear was that yesterday he and Misha had watered the commandant's roses with Hans' blood. That yesterday, he had tried to take his own life. And that the moment had passed. He could not give in now. He had to survive, if not for his own sake then for Misha's. For all of the Mishas, and for his mother and Recha, if they were alive.

For Miriam, if she still cared.

She had no place here, so he must not think of her except in the small dark hours when he could not help himself. Then, listening to the weeping and hacking, smelling the odor of death in the barracks, he would balance his love for her with his hatred of Erich, and wonder which was stronger.

Chapter 26

As Misha had predicted, a line of trucks stood outside the camp. Their tailgates were down, and the back ends yawned open. Without being told, Sol knew that he and Misha were about to be swallowed up. Further than that, he refused to speculate, even when he, the boy, and over a hundred inmates, selected for whatever the Nazis had dreamed up, stepped through the gates of Hell and into the waiting trucks.

Always in the past, the selections had meant a new work detail, at one of the Krupp factories perhaps, or a transfer to another camp. A worse camp, though it was hard to believe that such places existed. Still, he refused to theorize. He accepted the clothes that were flung at him, *real* clothes, held his arm out to be vaccinated, watched to see if anyone dropped dead from whatever was introduced into their veins, and climbed into the truck. With Misha's hand in his, he listened to tailgates slam shut, and jerked forward as the vehicle set out down the road.

No one spoke on the journey. They sat on the trucks' wooden seats, backs bent, forearms on thighs, and retreated into their own worlds, jouncing without complaint and staring at the metal floor's landscape of scraped paint. When the trucks halted, they spilled out. Prodded by guards, they clumped along a dusty unpaved track toward a farmhouse that stood alone on a hill just beyond. Few of them looked up. Those who did, Sol among them, saw no Oranienburg lines of Jew-haters, no quarry, no shoe track. No one was bludgeoned or shot for faltering.

Around the fields, around the farmhouse, was the greatest miracle of all. There was no wire.

No electrified, barbed, garroting wire, ready to be slipped for sport around the neck.

At the end of the dusty track they entered the huge farmhouse.

Holding firmly onto Misha's hand, Sol looked around him—at crumbling plaster walls and a floor which had been torn up in numerous places, revealing dirt below. The air within the house seemed preternaturally still and reeked of mildew. Clearly the place had been closed up for a long time.

Men coming in behind him forced him forward, away from the apparent safety of the first room into what looked more like a great hall than a farmer's quarters. His mind took in the impossible reality of a dozen crates marked with Red Cross stencils, knowing the guards had played such tricks before, replacing the precious cargo with body parts or human excrement.

A small murmuring began, but neither Sol nor Misha spoke. Then, with a suddenness that smacked of careful staging, an exceptionally tall, café-au-lait-colored man stepped into the room. He appeared from behind a mocha and cream colored curtain which hid an alcove that reminded Sol of the one at *Die Zigarrenkiste*. The shock of his appearance was as much due to the fact that he matched the curtain, as it was to its unexpectedness Sol might have thought he had plunged into a vision, had it not been for the tugging he felt from the small hand that clutched his.

The man who stepped into the room was a marvelous sight. His color and stature gave him the bearing of a character out of the pages of *The Arabian Nights*. He was white-haired, and swathed in a white cotton shift. A mouse-like creature crawled from his collar. It glanced around with huge eyes before retreating inside the shift.

The man smiled, a smile of reassurance and security that reached his eyes.

"I am wearing a *lamba*," he said. "My shy little friend is a lemur." He paused and smiled again. "And now you have had your first lesson about Madagascar. Welcome to your first stop on the road to my island."

"*Welcome*," the man called Mengele, the one in his vision, had said, Sol remembered. "*Welcome to the world of the dead.*"

And there was another, older memory, but no less haunting: "*Send all the Jews to Madagascar. Pen them like wild dogs, tame them, and use what assets and abilities they possess for the good of humanity.*"

Walther Rathenau had told him that, Sol thought, but they were not the statesman's own words. The Foreign Minister had simply been repeating what Hitler and the National Socialists espoused, even then, in the days before the Führer was empowered. Sol had been a boy, the Great War less than four years past. Rathenau died, killed by an assassin's bomb, but the ugly idea—apparently born long before Hitler—had not.

The brown man stopped smiling. "Have you listened to your dreams, little sparrow?" he asked, looking directly at Solomon. "Have you learned from them?"

A chill tiptoed down Sol's spine. A gypsy woman had said almost the same thing to him once, long ago. And how did this man, apparently an African, know his childhood nickname? Was Erich behind this new madness?

"I am Bruqah," the African said, "a member of the first tribe to inhabit the island to which you are bound."

As he pulled the curtain fully aside, Solomon almost expected to see his father hanging by the neck. Instead, he saw two sagging shelves, filled with dozens of books. "Some I brought with me from my island," the man said, "others I find...found...in second-hand bookstores in Berlin." He lifted a rolled-up paper from the corner, glanced around as if assuring himself they were out of Nazi earshot, and said, "Maps, too. The Nazis have not yet burned all books. I wonder why they bother to burn books of the world when they wish to burn the world itself?"

He stepped forward and put a hand on Misha's head. "You are safe here, little one," he said to the boy. He looked at Sol, as if imploring him not to counter the lie. "Within the hour, the Nazis will order the Red Cross boxes opened."

Before Sol could say anything, the man stepped back into the alcove and was gone—doubtless, Sol thought, past some panel and into another room or into a passageway that led out of the building. Like going down into the cellar beneath the tobacco shop, where lay the sewer, and the rats, and Sol's memories.

Within the hour, the Red Cross boxes were opened. The inmates were instructed to eat their fill. They fell upon the food, but having been so long deprived, they could not eat much. Even the little they did consume made many of them retch.

Later, Bruqah returned.

Then began the first of many lectures, the African speaking to Sol in French—apparently more comfortable for him, despite his perfectly reasonable command of German—and listening intently as Sol sifted and interpreted for the others. Sol did not always fully understand what he heard, and had to ask Bruqah for explications. Occasionally, he was able to embellish with what he remembered from his own books, read so many years ago.

Madagascar lay, Bruquah and then Solomon related, in the Indian Ocean, off Africa's southeast coast. The world's fourth largest island, it was an enigma beside which many of Africa's darkest secrets paled. Having broken away from the mainland a hundred million years ago, it developed a unique flora and fauna. Its northern rain forests, the world's densest, teemed with orchids and lemurs; the spiny deserts of the south were home to latex trees, whose sap caused blindness, and to harpoon burrs which tore flesh to ribbons. Until they were hunted to extinction about a thousand years ago, pygmy hippos roamed the land. There, too, stalked the giant, flightless Aepyornis— the elephant bird known as the *roc* in the Sinbad story—whose rare, semi-fossilized eggs, still found on occasion, were worth a fortune.

Perhaps even more startling than its plants and animals was the fact that the island, only two hundred and fifty miles from the mainland, had remained uninhabited until five hundred BC Even then, the settlers arrived not from Africa but from Java, three thousand miles to the east. Only later came the people of what were now Mozambique and Somalia, followed by Arabs and, finally—the last to add people on the island—waves of pirates, mostly British.

"Why Madagascar, Herr Professor?" a man asked on the third day.

The remark was a miracle, Sol thought, for the silence of the past days had been that of men who had lost the will to question. He hoped that the one question would trigger a barrage of others, but his hope was in vain. The hush that followed made him wonder if the others remained quiet because they had lost the will to question *anything*. Were they disinterested, or simply more interested in the question than the questioning?

"We Jews are to be given a homeland," Sol said, choosing not to argue about the man's means of address.

"He who gave us Sachsenhausen has had a change of heart?" the man said.

With a brisk movement of his fingers, Sol motioned everyone closer. As they scooted forward, it occurred to him how natural it felt for him to be before them in this manner. He had always been shy, but he felt no shyness now. Satisfaction warmed him.

"I think Hitler, our Führer," he raised his voice to make it easier for eavesdroppers or in the likely event that there was an informer among them, "wishes to exercise control," he had to restrain himself from saying *seize control*, "of the Indian Ocean's shipping lands...not to mention helping the Italians maintain their presence in Ethiopia, the southern entrance to the Red Sea. Couple that with the larger picture. Would not world opinion side with a beneficent Führer more readily, a Führer who gave bedraggled Jews a place of their own? Who, truly, could object? The French control the island, but I have learned from Bruqah that the idea of sending Jews there *began* with them. The British have already blockaded us from emigrating to Palestine. The Arabs would surely think our presence in Madagascar less a burr than if we returned to Jerusalem. And the South Africans, our nearest powerful neighbors, have welcomed Jewish settlement."

He watched the quiet faces.

"Then only the Malagasy might object," someone said, more wistfully than sarcastically.

"Yes." Solomon fought to keep the emotion from his voice as he looked at Bruqah. "Only the Malagasy."

Chapter 27

"I'll be waiting to hear every detail," Miriam told Erich.

He could not possibly know how profoundly she meant those words, she thought. Nor should he.

She modulated her voice carefully, making sure it contained no urgency. "Enjoy your moment. You deserve it."

"Shall I send your regards to Perón?"

"Do that." Pleased that his tone lacked any hint of the sardonic, she added, "You might even think about asking him to the estate for dinner. It wouldn't do you any harm to humor him."

A frown darkened Erich's features, but his annoyance was directed at the tie he had knotted and unknotted several times. "Do this for me, would you? I can't seem to get it right."

Relieved, she retied the knot. "Good luck," she said again, kissing him lightly. "Now go."

He put on his jacket. "I may even come to like that Perón of yours," he said. "Last time I saw him, I asked how he felt about the church. He said, 'The priest who serves best, serves dinner.'"

She laughed. He looked surprised and happy, as if he could not quite believe she might let him go without so much as a single invective about the Party. Her tongue never would be as sharp around Solomon, she thought as Erich left the room. Or would it?

Maybe Erich was right about marriage being purely a female-endorsed institution designed to annoy men. He had once asked her why women packed away romance with the wedding pictures, to be peeked at when they deigned—and then only for an instant.

As if romance had anything to do with *their* being together!

There had been moments, transient as the dream of a better tomorrow, when she had tried to believe the lie of love between them. But then the longing for Solomon returned, or her fears for him, or her guilt at living like this. There was nothing she wanted she could not have...except Solomon, and the freedom to be a Jew.

She stood at the window and watched the lights of Erich's car disappear as he drove off the estate. When she was reasonably certain he was not coming back for something he had forgotten, she finished dressing and went to the garage.

Konrad was already behind the wheel. When they got to the Zoo Station, Werner Fink was pacing impatiently beneath the clock.

"Werner!" She kissed him hurriedly on the cheek. "Sorry I'm late. We only have a few minutes. I had to wait for Erich to leave." She looked at him more closely. His eyes spoke more than ever of hatred, and of a need for vengeance. She took hold of his arm. "What's wrong? Is it Sol?"

"I got word that my brother is dead. They said he signed a paper requesting castration. *Requesting!* My brother? They showed me the death certificate. It said, *'Adverse reaction to anesthesia during voluntary surgery. Cause of death: Heart Failure.'*"

Miriam glanced at the station's clock. Eight. Thirty minutes from now Perón was due at the Reichschancellery. Time enough to hear about Solomon and about the underground, and to be a friend. She reached for Fink's hand.

"If I could blow up this whole country, I would!" he said.

To add one word was an exercise in redundancy, Miriam thought. Of the people in her life, only Erich did not fully comprehend the extent of her hatred for Germany.

"Come, I'll walk you to the car." Fink moved her through the people thronging the Zoo Station. "About Solomon—"

An iciness enveloped Miriam. What good was her planning and scheming if something had happened to Sol? She placed her free hand on her belly as if to reassure the unborn child.

Fink watched her and smiled sadly. "A new generation," he said. "Why do we do it, Miri? In a world like this, why does the human race keep propagating?"

They exited the station. She could see Konrad waiting for her across the street. "I am so terribly sorry about Hans," she said simply. "I wish there were something more I could say, or do—"

"There isn't, darling." He paused. "Look, forgive me for being so wrapped up in myself today. It's not your fault that those bastards—." He stopped. "You have been very patient with me, Miri. Let me tell you about Sol. I would not have kept you waiting had the news been anything but encouraging."

"Thank God!" Miriam let out her breath.

"When I heard about Hans, I went storming into the Bureau...in fact, the way I carried on, I can't really understand why they didn't arrest me at once. I suppose it's because I'm a public figure...one of their token gestures to the free world, at least for the moment." His tone was heavy with bitterness. "Anyway, while I was there, I asked about Solomon and they told me."

"That simple?" Miriam laughed. "I can't believe it! Erich insists he has tried everything. Poor man. Occasionally, on my better days and when he is attempting so pitifully hard to please me, I even succeed in feeling a little sorry for him. He appears to truly believe that I am deluded and that Sol is in Amsterdam."

"Maybe so." Fink sounded unconvinced. "The ways of the German bureaucracy are not to be questioned. Nevertheless, I tell you, that's exactly how it happened. I asked—and I received. Sol and a contingent of other prisoners, excuse me—*free laborers!*—have been moved from Sachsenhausen to a holding area—"

So Perón had succeeded! Miriam felt a stab of guilt at having doubted him, tempered by annoyance that he hadn't managed to let her know. "Where? I want to see him!"

"Hold on, young lady. Not so fast. They haven't released him. They have the prisoners under heavy guard at an old, abandoned farm on the outskirts of Oranienburg. It would be far too dangerous for either one of us to go there, but I did send one of our people—a local farmer—to snoop around. The prisoners are being fed, bathed, and rested. He said it almost looks as if they're conducting some kind of school in the farmhouse. He saw Solomon—at least, the man thought it was Sol."

"How did he look?"

"How should he look? If I were you, I would prepare myself for a very different man than you knew." Fink glanced around. He appeared to see something that made him uneasy. "We don't have much longer," he said.

"Have our people found a new safe-house?" Miriam asked. Since Sol's arrest and the loss of the sewer as a safe-house, she had entered a new network. Bigger. More dangerous. Without the double-blinds which, though safer, were more cumbersome. However, her role was smaller than before. She delivered messages from Werner to Konrad, who passed them on somewhere, to someone...

"Safe-houses have become as difficult to find as a Nazi who can laugh at himself." Fink's grin held a little of his old wry humor.

"We must go," Konrad said, approaching them.

"Go, and God bless." Fink kissed her cheek. "I've told you everything I know. If I learn anything new, I'll be in touch."

Before she could say anything more, he was gone.

"Where are you meeting with Colonel Perón?" Konrad asked, opening the car door for Miriam.

"We are to pick him up at the Hotel Adlon and drop him off near the Reichschancellery."

"And then?"

"The estate. Tonight is Erich's big night—and mine. I have to be rested when he gets home. My head needs to be clear."

"Aren't you pushing yourself a little too hard under the circumstances, Lady Miriam?"

"I'm not pushing myself hard enough!" She looked down at her belly. "Our lives are at stake!"

Juan Perón was waiting for them outside the Adlon. He was talking to a tall, café-au-lait man wearing a white caftan. In one hand the stranger held a polished, carved walking stick; in the other, a roll of ivory-colored paper.

Miriam opened the window.

The brown man stared at her and bowed as if to acknowledge that he knew her. He walked toward the car, his movements graceful and rhythmic, like a dancer moving to secret music in his head.

Both men slid onto the back seat, Perón first. She moved over to the far side, fighting a combination of anger that her friend had allowed her to suffer for longer than was necessary and irritation at a stranger's presence. What she and Perón had to discuss was private, and not a little dangerous. Nor could the discussion be left for another time. What was he thinking of!

"This is Bruqah," the colonel said. "Bruqah...Miriam Rathenau Alois."

The man called Bruqah smiled and put out a brown hand. "So you are Miriam," he said. His voice was soft and husky, with that same trace of music she had sensed in his movements.

Despite her resentment of his being there, Miriam smiled at him. She turned to Perón. "Getting a little paunchy around the middle, aren't you, Domingo? Too many dumplings, I think."

"Domingo?" Bruqah sounded puzzled.

"My middle name." Perón eased himself into a more comfortable position.

"Where I come from, we do not have what you call middle names. We have given names and earned names, which are something like your nicknames."

"Where is that you come from?" Miriam was fascinated by his ability to speak German without the guttural quality which most foreigners, and so many natives, imposed upon it.

"Bruqah is from Madagascar," Perón said, answering for him.

"I suppose the missionaries taught him German?"

"Missionaries taught that to save a soul, one loses life. Not so good an arrangement, I think." As if he now saw the humor in what he had said seriously, he chuckled. "I learn your language at Lüderitz, in German South West Africa. Now I study at your university...where your colonel found me."

"You're studying German?" she asked.

"Souls of plants. What you call 'botany.'" He grinned, showing his teeth.

It was Perón's turn to chuckle. "I've never heard you voluntarily loquacious before, my friend." He looked at Miriam. "Nor have I forgotten your comment about my corporation. Are you not, perhaps, calling the kettle black?" He patted her stomach, then lifted her hand and kissed it. "Only joking, of course. You are as beautiful as ever."

"And you, Domingo, are a beautiful liar. You remember me thin and beautiful, and I try my best to preserve the illusion. The truth is, I'm fat and I'm clumsy—"

"And beautiful!" He lifted her hand and kissed it again.

"I feel fat and ugly. And tired." She fought to keep her rising panic out of her voice. Perón was studiously avoiding talk of Sol, perhaps because of Bruqah's presence, but more likely because she had been right about him in the first place. He enjoyed her company, which could have been reason enough for his agreement to try to help her and for the secret meeting and rendezvous. Sol's transfer to the farmhouse was probably a coincidence.

"Relax," Perón said. "I have not forgotten the reason for this rendezvous, though I would prefer it were a romantic tryst."

"Can you tell me...?" She glanced at Bruqah.

Perón did not miss the implication. "He is part of the plan. Like Konrad, he is that rare creature—a trustworthy ally. Must be the Christian influence."

"I am Malagasy," Bruqah said, bristling. "We know of honor."

"The plan?" Miriam urged, determining that she would not let him know quite yet that she had already been informed about Sol's transfer to the farmhouse. "Tell me you have arranged everything, that Sol and the child and I are going to live happily ever after."

"Now you are asking me to play God," Perón said. "I have power, yes, but it is not absolute." He looked at her and smiled. "All right, my lovely and persistent Miriam. Let me tell you what I *have* been able to achieve. I spoke to Hitler and his cronies and planted my ideas...our ideas. They listened, closely if I may say so."

"And?"

"And, sweet Miriam—" He laughed at her impatience. "And my words have taken root. Solomon has been moved to a holding area—"

"I know. Werner told me."

He looked disappointed, like a child whose surprise had been spoiled.

"What else?" she asked insistently.

"I will tell you that my destination is Lüderitz. Yours is Nosy Mangabéy, a tiny island at the mouth of a bay on Madagascar's northeast coast. The roll of paper Bruqah is holding is a series of topographical maps. I used your rationale to manipulate Solomon into the advance party. In fact, the others call him the Professor. Bruqah has been going to the farmhouse to teach him about Madagascar, and Solomon, in turn, teaches the others—"

"You saw Solomon?" They were approaching the area of the Reichschancellery, and there were so many questions she wanted to ask.

"There is no time left for conversation," Perón said. "I have not seen Solomon yet. I must not seem to be too enthusiastic. However, Bruqah tells me Solomon, like all of the others, is thin, sad, but alive and functioning. Tonight Bruqah and I will show the maps to everyone concerned with this plan, including Erich and the Führer. Your Erich will be bringing home the details to you tonight—that is, provided the great German bureaucracy has not already changed its mind."

"But Juan—"

"Enough! You will have to wait for the rest...unless you wish to go to your other sources."

His voice reflected mild annoyance with her for having spoiled his dénouement, and much irritation with Hitler, whom he found to be a distasteful, officious little man invested with too much power. In Miriam's judgment, the Argentinean appreciated the Nazi Party but was not enamored with it; he did what he felt was right for Argentina and for himself. Clearly, he had political aspirations. Clearly, too, she would hear no more today until she heard it from Erich later tonight.

Not by any means for the first time in her life, she wondered why she attracted men with such volatile personalities. Javelin Men, as Erich called them, whose need for prowess outweighed their sensitivities no matter how hard they tried. Erich and Perón had that in common. They were the Magellans, the Vasco De Gamas and Columbuses, explorers because of a need to prove themselves to the world rather than simply because they were internally driven.

Sol's explorations were metaphysical and philosophical, though in their own way just as demanding. With him, however, *she* could be the volatile one, the balance between other-worldliness and pragmatism. She could hardly wait, she thought, to be that for him again, and for herself. Playing a part on the stage was one thing; playing it day and night, around the clock, was another.

Chapter 28

Moonlight drenched the renovated Reichschancellery's marble steps. Ascending them, Erich felt blessed by the light and wonderfully dwarfed by the building, its Doric columns lifting into shadows like sentries. He was Alexander, claiming his territory.

When he entered, a corporal took his hat, cloak, and gloves, bowed stiffly, and escorted him through huge doors into a hall tiled in aquamarine mosaic. In the next room, round and domed, stood other officers, clustered in groups. Most were SS, with whom he had little in common, among them Otto Hempel—who had dallied briefly at the Oranienburg labor camp in preparation for his present assignment at Sachsenhausen.

A demotion would have been more satisfying, he thought, acknowledging Hempel's greeting with a cursory nod. The man inevitably threatened his good spirits. But not tonight. Not when he expected to be the only one being honored with a double-promotion. He must create an impression of strength and imperturbability.

The other officers were smoking nervously or sipping cognac brought by a woman whose hourglass shape drew many second glances. One golden cordial, in a thin-stemmed, tulip-shaped liqueur glass, remained on her tray. Erich took it. In the doorway of the great gallery, said to be twice the length of Versailles' Hall of Mirrors, after which it was modeled, he toasted himself.

The corporal opened the gallery doors to Adolf Hitler and a phalanx of functionaries. The Führer stood with Goebbels, Bormann, Hess and Eichmann, the four framed in moonlight muted by the windows' deep niches. Standing slightly apart was Colonel Perón.

The assembly snapped to attention with an echoing clack of boot heels. Arms sprang to salutes. Feet squarely planted, eyes keened as though he were reviewing a parade, Erich joined them.

"Heil Hitler!"

At once he felt uncomfortable, as if he did not quite fit into his own skin. Just words, he reassured himself.

The Führer and his entourage returned the salute. His soldiers waited for a signal that would indicate his mood of the moment.

Eyes gleaming, cheeks puffed, Hitler gave them their cue.

"Glory to the Fatherland! We must promise obedience, industry, honesty, order, truthfulness...sacrifice!" Jerking his arm to his side, he clenched his hand into a tight fist and opened it, slowly, reluctantly, as though by doing so he relinquished some of his power over the gathering. "Gentlemen, let us dine."

He wheeled and walked up the hall; the order of functionaries reversed, the rest of the assembly following like migratory birds. Erich could detect a communal nervousness as they entered Hitler's living quarters which, to Erich's surprise, proved warm and inviting. The architect obviously had respected the apartment's Bismarkian past; he had kept the beamed ceiling and wainscoting. In contrast to the cold ostentation of the receiving areas, a fire burned in a fireplace graced with a Florentine Renaissance coat-of-arms, and leather-upholstered chairs the color of bittersweet chocolate completed a look of male domesticity.

Entering the dining room, Erich thought fleetingly, and not without regret, of his bachelor quarters above the Landswehr. He had given them up as a gesture to Miriam, though not at her request.

Civil servants and soldiers mingled without regard to rank, a violation of protocol Erich found distasteful. He watched the surge toward the food, laid out on a sideboard of palisander wood against the far wall. Oxtail soup—rich, brown, and gelatinous. Silesian Heaven casserole of dried fruit, pickled pork, and dumplings. A peach tart accompanied by Pilsner, and a Rhenish wine.

Past three glass doors that formed the opposite wall lay a garden with a startling profusion of roses.

"Beautiful roses, mein Führer," he heard someone say. "The new hybrid from Sachsenhausen?"

"Centurions," Hitler said. "Remarkable species."

As was his custom, Hitler waited until the company had almost finished the meal before he ate—his fear of being poisoned was well-known. After picking at his meal, vegetables garnished with minced white radishes, he remonstrated about the decadent French infatuation with hors d'oeuvres, sauces, and pastries, and boasted how fasting, combined with a vegetarian diet, gave him strength.

Now he rose from his chair, glass lifted. "Power for the Fatherland! We must be rid of the flab that cost us the Great War."

"The flab and the Jews!" Bormann shouted as everyone rose.

"They are one and the same!" Hitler said. "The Jews are a people of excess, whose ideal is to gorge their bellies and wallets at the expense of good

Germans." He tapped his glass of mineral water. *"This* represents what I seek for Germany. Purity!"

"Prosit!"

The doubt and horror that had lingered with him since his visit to Oranienburg settled on Erich's shoulders. Hitler demanded absolute commitment. Absolute purity. If he and his cronies decided the baby was, after all, half-Jewish...the order to kill Achilles might be repeated—with a child. *His* child.

Erich refilled his glass, keeping his hand steady. The Führer was the essence of the nation; he could have Erich assigned to guard Sachsenhausen convoys. After what he saw in Oranienburg, all else—even losing his dogs—would be a benediction in comparison. He had to believe the worst of what he'd heard about the camp, that it was a pesthole of disease, a place where human suffering was considered necessary for the larger scheme of the Reich.

The larger scheme! That was why he loved his dogs so much. They lacked understanding of man-made complexities—understood only generalized goodness and suffering.

Whatever his double promotion entailed, he vowed, fiddling with his linen serviette, he would refuse to be involved with hurting the Jews. He would not do anything that resembled his father's treachery toward Jacob Freund. Perhaps the past was not sacred; perhaps, as Hitler claimed, only the present counted. Nevertheless, he was not going to repeat his and his father's mistakes.

The small-talk became less reserved than before dinner, but he spoke only when spoken to. When Leni arrived to film the official events, he felt relieved that the evening was almost over.

Hitler clinked a knife against a glass. "Our army, the one the imperialist powers did not allow," he waited for the muffled laughter to cease, "continues to strengthen into the world's finest peace-keeping force. I have personally encouraged many promotions due to excellence. Some of those who have been promoted were invited tonight to sup at the table they serve." He paused again for polite applause. "Would those being honored step forward."

The promotees formed a line, Erich among them. He felt as impatient and self-conscious as a boy awaiting Eucharist during Mass. When his turn came, Hitler shook his hand, took hold of his shoulders, and turned him toward the audience.

"The imperialists," Hitler said, "are afraid of shadows and of Germany's clear vision. They fear we wish to renew hostilities with France over Alsace-Lorraine, as if we would shed a single drop of German blood to gain control of the Alsatians who have switched sides so often they no longer know where their loyalties lie!"

Laughter followed. Glasses were lifted. "The only Alsatians the Fatherland wants are the shepherds raised by this young genius with canines. His army of dogs lives up to the heart and wisdom of our highest Aryan aspirations.

For that, and for future services—the details of which not even he, as yet, knows—Alois has been accorded the rare honor of a double promotion, to full colonel."

The Führer applauded as the assembly rose to its feet. Swept up by the Hitler's impassioned speaking, Erich felt excited. Yes! He could have it all! Miriam, his dogs, the glory that was due him!

As the applause died, however, a shroud fell into place. His doubts about the Party had been eroded too easily by the Führer's speech. His weakness embarrassed him.

After dinner, while officers formed amiable groups or stepped into the garden for a smoke, Erich sat where he was, watching Hitler with Bormann, Hess, and Eichmann. Bormann was speaking earnestly, as if to counter the rumor that he took just a little too much pleasure in "arranging" the Führer's finances.

Perón joined them for a moment, then walked over toward Erich as Hitler and the other notables filed through a side door.

"The Führer wishes you to remain after the others leave," Perón said. "There's to be a meeting. You, Eichmann, Hempel, Riefenstahl." He ticked them off on his fingers.

"What is it all about, Juan—if I may call you Juan?"

Perón smiled. "You may call me anything you like." He left as abruptly as he had approached.

Trying not to dwell on the possibilities, Erich watched the diners disperse. Some congratulated him, offering platitudes about how a man's worth eventually surfaced and was recognized. Ultimately he found himself alone except for the steward's helpers clearing the tables. He ordered coffee from a waiter he knew to be a member of the SS and, forced to wait, allowed himself to dream.

Since his rank now equaled Perón's, the South American had to be part of Hitler's plan for Colonel Erich Weisser Alois. That could only mean one thing: Erich and his canine corps would help lead the Fascist revolution in South America. That would explain the double promotion. Any rank below Perón's would diminish the Germanic presence; any above would hint of imperialism, like Bismarck's error when, during the Great War, his envoys had tried to persuade Mexico to attack the United States.

Alois and Perón.

Everything fit, as if his life were part of a grand design shaped for this moment; his role in military intelligence, his guerilla training under Otto Braun, his knowledge of Catholicism...all were essential for a German-Argentinean thrust through South America. He tried to recall which cities were where, and what strategy the South American generals, San Martín and Bolívar, had used. If only he'd studied harder at the *Gymnasium!* Too late to worry about that. He would act informed and responsive toward Hitler's and Perón's proposals tonight, then plunder the university's library in the morning and seek out the best Spanish tutor in Berlin. With the right incentive, he could learn—and face—anything.

Like the matter of Miriam.

Ironically, everywhere except in Germany she was a Jew. How would the South Americans react to her?

Cross that bridge later, he thought, imagining a Fascist conflagration with Hitler, Mussolini, Franco, and Degrelle in Europe; Hirohito in Japan; Chiang Kai-shek with his Blueshirts in China; the German-American Bund Party in the United States; the recently disenfranchised Integralistas in Brazil. And the Argentineans.

Together they would burn the world clean of the Communist threat and the decadence of democracy. Leading the troops, he would be the swordtip of a revolution, its fiery wedge!

The stewards exited, and he allowed himself a congratulatory smile.

"You look pleased with yourself, Herr Oberst," Colonel Perón said, re-entering. "The Führer will be ready to see you," Perón glanced at his watch, "in fifteen minutes. The meeting will be brief. He is most weary."

"Be so kind as to give me an indication of the subject of this meeting," Erich said, forcing himself to keep his smile.

Clasping his hands behind his back, Perón looked thoughtful. "At my instigation, the Führer has arranged to give you and your dogs an opportunity to prove your worth. I am told you consider them the equal of any good German soldier."

Erich's smile broadened. "How is it we are to prove ourselves?"

"As part of a two-part operation." Perón sat down and lit a cigarette. "In brief, I wish to view a particular naval operation in the South Atlantic. You are to accompany me."

"And that operation is?"

"A military secret, even from you, Herr Oberst. Outside of the highest officials, only the captain of the *Altmark*, whom you shall meet in due time, knows those details. I can tell you that I will be with you as far as Lüderitz, a port on the west coast of Africa."

"I see," Erich said, but he felt a mounting confusion. He struggled to maintain his professional reserve.

"I told you that this is to be a two-part operation," Perón said. "The first, the one I am to view, is top secret."

"And the second?"

"You and your men and dogs, together with a contingent of SS and free laborers, will proceed to Madagascar. Yours will be the advance party for troops that will secure the island for the Reich."

Madagascar! Erich thought. A stroke of genius! The Italians had invaded and defeated Ethiopia, and now Germany would have Madagascar. With the Italian hot-heads in control of the southern entrance to the Red Sea, Hitler had to make a similar move. Whoever held the island controlled the Indian Ocean. That meant control of oil.

The top secret operation Perón was to observe, Erich figured, must be an invasion, to help galvanize Perón's belief in the German cause by demonstrating how, with Germany's help, he could acquire not just his country but his continent!

"What is the timetable for the primary invasion?" Erich asked.

"If the invasion comes, it will come in good time."

"*If?*" Erich's excitement halted. "There are no immediate plans?"

Perón shook his head.

"Then why am I being sent to Madagascar?"

"As you're no doubt aware, Poland has become increasingly aggressive. Should the Poles be foolish enough to spill German blood, your Führer intends, as he says, to crush them like roaches. He knows, however, that the problems he will have to contend with after peace is restored will be staggering. Over three million Jews in Poland alone!" Perón paused, as if to allow the information to take hold. "The Führer is convinced that a foothold in Madagascar will give him a solution to the Jewish question. He wishes to transport all Jews there to form a country of their own."

"I'm being sent to some *remote* African island where I am to wait out the war with the *remote* possibility that *perhaps* Germany will use the objective?" Erich felt his temper rising.

"Calm down, Herr Oberst." Perón's eyes flashed a warning. "Let me attempt to explain. As you know, your Führer is determined that he must rid himself of the Jews. You may not, however, be aware that your government has been trying to work with the Zionists to arrange for secret convoys to Palestine. Those talks have broken down. The British have cancelled all immigration approvals to Palestine and pressured Greece and Turkey not to accept Jews. They have sealed off the coast of Palestine with a flotilla of destroyers and intensive air reconnaissance. An alternative must be found."

The words peppered Erich's mind like shotgun pellets. Absurd!

"Hauptmann Eichmann favors resettling the Jews in a farming area near the Polish town of Nisko," Perón went on, "but Madagascar is not out of the question. If not Poland, then the island. The Poles apparently think the same thing, because two years ago they sent researchers there to see if Jews could be relocated in the island's Ankaizina region."

A nightmare. It could not be happening. Not to him.

"The idea's not new," Perón said. "Napoleon had such a plan, and Bonnet, the French Foreign Minister, recently made a similar suggestion. Here, Eichmann is the one who thought the thing through— in concert, naturally, with your Führer."

"Will we make war on Madagascar?" Erich asked wearily.

Goebbels joined them. "The Führer hopes to persuade France to cede us the island. After the indigenous population has been moved to the mainland, the Sicherheitspolizei will orchestrate the Jewish resettlement in non-German ships."

"Another camp," Erich muttered.

"A homeland," Perón said.

Erich looked up, amazed at the conviction in Perón's voice.

"You will have six months to get this program on its feet," Perón said. "Do that, and the Führer will scrap plans for resettlement in Poland and institute resettlement to Madagascar. You will insure that the Jews *work*. Once the colony is established, production and trade will be managed by German-run organizations. There will ultimately be purely German and purely Jewish businesses. The merchant bank plus the issue and transfer bank will be German. The trading bank and production organization will be Jewish."

"I'm to stay in *Madagascar*, while Germany glorifies herself in Europe," Erich said in disbelief.

"The Führer will let Miriam accompany you, assuming you both approve. Leni Riefenstahl—I believe you know her—will film all this for the Reich. She would like to include a sense of domesticity. I believe she is also planning to do a documentary on the Bushmen, and at least one other African film, so you will see a lot of her, as you will Otto Hempel."

"Hempel! Going too?"

Perón ignored the outburst. "The war with Poland, if it comes, is unlikely to last. France is too worried about Mussolini and Franco to risk a war with Germany. You will return here soon enough."

"What if the war drags on?"

"Then, Herr Oberst," Goebbels said, walking toward the door, "you wait— and enjoy the tropics."

Erich stood up and shoved his chair hard against the table. "So you have found a way to rid yourself of me and my dogs."

Goebbels did not turn around.

Breathing hard, Erich looked at Perón.

"This has nothing to do with Goebbels," Perón said, his smile not wavering, "though it is true that you do not exactly inspire his love. I myself have heard him say that your dogs stink like Jews."

Chapter 29

Looking into Miriam's bedroom and watching her sleep, Erich decided he would never understand the female psyche. The last thing he had expected from her was enthusiasm about Madagascar. Anger, yes. Neutrality, perhaps. But open enthusiasm? Just when he had begun to accept Solomon as a permanent specter between them?

In the two weeks since the Reichschancellery, she had been almost excited—sorting, packing, asking questions about what she should or should not take in the single steamer trunk allotted her. Maybe they would have a real marriage someday after all, he thought. One that included lovemaking. Not just sex. Certainly not rape. Perhaps one day she would let go of the pain of her thighs digging into the rim of a metal bathtub—

He reached for the book Leni had sent him after the meeting at the Reichschancellery. *The Memoirs of Mauritius Augustus, Count de Benyowsky.* Her accompanying note explained that, after her current projects were finished, she wanted to do a feature-length about the Count. She and her crew would film Erich's trip as far as Lüderitz, divert to do her Bushman shoot, and rejoin him to continue filming the Jews after their base camp was in place. Then—the project dearest to her heart, the Benyowsky movie. The Count, she wrote, bore startling similarities to a good friend of hers, recently promoted to colonel.

In the autobiography, Benyowsky liberally mixed fiction with fact, but the lies were so outrageously inventive that Erich found them amusing. He felt drawn to the Hungarian, an eighteenth-century aristocratic adventurer captured by the Russians during the Seven Years' War.

Escaping from a Siberian penal camp, Benyowsky and his fellow exiles had stolen two ships and eventually ended up in northeastern Madagascar. There they had encountered malaria, native unrest brought on by the jealousy of European traders competing for economic rights to the huge island, and humidity that could wilt even the strongest of men. Undaunted, he had borrowed an idea from the Americans, and with supplies and moral support from Benjamin Franklin had founded a colony and written the island's first Constitution, guaranteeing equal rights for all. The result was peace between the tribes.

As drums beat and nearly naked women danced beneath an African moon, thirty thousand warriors laid down their *assegais*— spears—and prostrated themselves at his feet. In gratitude, they proclaimed Benyowsky *Ampandzaka-bé,* Chief of Chiefs.

The memoirs had given Erich insights he could never have found in Goebbels' military documents. Madagascar began to fascinate him, especially after his five or six meetings with an island native named Bruqah, who was to be his guide and translator. The man was a fascinating dichotomy—knowledgeable, an excellent teacher, outwardly Westernized—yet in many ways that combination of mystic and pragmatist he had only seen before in Solomon.

Maybe Madagascar would give him a way to design for himself a place in history *and* to spit in the Führer's eye. What if he created a homeland for the Jews, not founded on ghetto or camp conditions, but on equal rights? A true homeland. He, Erich Alois Nobody, recipient of an empty double promotion and false promises. *That* would earn him Miriam's forgiveness...and maybe even God's.

Were it not for Otto Hempel going to Madagascar too—

He forced himself away from thoughts of that pig and indulged instead in a fantasy of dancing women and beating drums and thousands of grateful warriors laying down their dogwood spears to prostrate themselves at *his* feet—all the while chanting *Ampandzaka-bé.*

Like his flirtation with Leni, this too was a pleasant and harmless fabrication, he told himself, staring at Miriam, who turned awkwardly in her sleep.

"Bruqah!" she cried out.

He tried to remember when he had mentioned that name to her. Not that there had been any reason to avoid doing so; she would be meeting the Malagasy herself soon enough.

Miriam was again breathing regularly, sleeping more easily. Their bedroom's French doors were open, and a lightly humid breeze carried with it the intermittent barking of the dogs reacting to the full moon. Tonight, he thought, the grand house encapsulated him. For once it was an extension of himself...its stone his cells, its heritage *his* heart, and not only Miriam ex-Rathenau's. Tonight he could believe that the events of that cabaret night when he had first seen her—the night he had met Rathenau, and Miriam had danced upon his boyish desire—had been no accident of fate, but rather destiny, preparing him to claim the important things that had been Rathenau's.

He was finally master of this castle.

Rising quietly, he slipped into his smoking jacket and went downstairs, intent on quieting the dogs. When he opened the front door, he discovered a messenger about to knock.

"Heil Hitler!" The messenger clicked his heels together and saluted.

Erich returned the greeting, though without enthusiasm. "Must you come in the middle of the night? Can nothing in this country wait until morning?"

He glanced past the young man and, surprised to see a bicycle instead of a motorcycle in the driveway, realized this was not one of the usual messengers from headquarters. They were all beginning to look alike, these young Nazis, he told himself cynically. So blond and fervid.

"My apologies, Herr Oberst. I was told to deliver this package immediately." The messenger swung his knapsack off his back and pulled out a receipt book, pen, and a small box wrapped in butcher paper.

Erich signed and dated the proffered page. The messenger noted the time after checking his watch, stepped back, and again saluted. It irritated Erich, having to comply.

The young man lowered his arm he looked at Erich expectantly.

"Well?" Erich asked. "What are you waiting for?"

"Are you—are you going to open it, sir?"

"Is it any of your business?"

The messenger suddenly looked flushed. "I'm sorry, sir. It's just that everyone at headquarters is talking about," he glanced around and lowered his voice, "the *project*, sir. It's damn exciting!"

"And you thought you could carry back another piece of gossip to fuel the fire," Erich said, looking at him sternly. "I'm afraid you will have to return empty-handed."

"Yes sir. Forgive me, sir."

The young man turned and hurried toward his bike. Erich waited until Krayller had let him out the gate before he examined the box. He did not open it immediately but rather held back, checking its heft, as though it were a birthday or Christmas gift.

The butcher paper had no return name or address. He ripped if off and tossed it aside. The box proved to be likewise unmarked. As he opened it and pulled out a jar with a metallic-gold lid, a premonition of fear mixed with an urge to kill someone gripped him with such force that he almost dropped the jar. Then, gingerly, he held it up to the light.

Bile filled his throat. He placed a hand on his chest and sucked a short breath to keep from retching. There was no mistaking the contents—a set of purplish genitalia. Shaking, cursing his weak stomach, he set the jar down on the stoop.

An envelope the size of an invitation and embossed with fleur-de-lis lay in the bottom of the box. He tore it open.

Inside, neatly folded, he found a death certificate.

Solomon Isaac Freund, prisoner 37704. Adverse reaction to anesthesia during voluntary surgery. Cause of death: heart failure. 10 June 1939. Detained 1 January 1938, Stuttgart. Entry into camp system 3 January 1938, Marienbad. Relocated Sachsenhausen, 14 August 1938.

He refolded the paper slowly, stupefied by the enormity of the irony. For over a year the lies he had been telling Miriam had been the truth. Solomon, in Sachsenhausen...Hempel's camp! But how! When had he returned to Germany? And why Stuttgart!... Something to do with Miriam's past? Had he contacted her? Did she know the truth?

He sat down and ransacked his mind, trying to recall if Miriam had acted strangely about the time Solomon returned, but it was too long ago, and her moods were so volatile anyway! Perhaps, he thought hopefully, Solomon had been on his way *to* Berlin and was arrested before he ever contacted...

My God, what was he thinking! Solomon dead, that bastard Hempel surely somehow responsible, and he was hoping that...! To his horror, he found that he had unconsciously put a hand on the jar. He lurched away, then swiveled so his back was to the thing, and shuddered. Jesus, Mary, and Joseph!

His mind sprang back to the paper. He shook as he fought to unfold it. There! He jabbed at the information as thought to point it out to someone.

Designation: pink.

Pink! Solomon, arrested not as a Jew but as a queer! Surely there was some mistake!

His mind raced through memories as if through the narrow, chaotic streets of some medieval city, reason and feverish logic opening doors long battened down as though against a plague. For the first time in his life the past made sense to him.

That was why Solomon would wince whenever anyone made derogatory remarks about queers! Why he had to be goaded into buying that hot little whore with the banana-shaped tits, only to emerge afterward so repulsed with himself that he looked sick. *That* was why Miriam...

So that was her obsession with Solomon! Not because he was having her every night after they closed up shop, *but because he wouldn't.* Or—he had to cool down hysterical laughter bubbling up at the back of his brain—*or because Solomon couldn't.*

He thought about Miriam, that Christmas in the apartment. Wanting him, not wanting him, seducing and denying, until he had no other choice but to take her by force. She probably had not spread her legs for someone since returning to Berlin, since touring out of...Stuttgart.

Stuttgart!

Could it be possible that Solomon had returned to Germany not for Miriam, but for something buried in her past that he thought might resurrect the manhood he had never had?

Solomon Freund, a fucking queer! Erich looked at the jar with angry disgust. All that time Solomon had squired Miriam, claimed to be in love with her, when in reality he had desired...The thought made him ill.

Desired me.

That was why Solomon had not abandoned their friendship when Erich joined the Party...why Miriam seemed happy about Madagascar. It was not Erich Alois she hated, he decided, for though he had raped her—well, sort of raped—that union had given her what she wanted most. A child. And now...a chance to raise that child outside Nazi Germany. It all made sense.

He stood up. He would give her more than that chance, he vowed to himself. Once he had the colony established and in running order, then if she wanted to raise the boy as a Jew, he would consider it.

Ready to head back to the shepherds, he strode around to the kitchen, opened the lid of one of the garbage cans, and let the jar slip from between his fingers. Good-bye, *friend,* he thought, and slammed the lid down.

The dogs yelped and strained at their chains upon his approach. *Those* were real friends. You know who feeds you, he thought affectionately.

Taurus fought to lick his face when he squatted beside her. He hugged her neck so tightly that she had to lower her back and pull her head down to keep from choking. Her body rippled with power beneath the gold and black coat. She was more vicious since she had tasted blood, but that did not make him love her less. Nor did her dysplasia, especially since her performances requiring intelligence and not just physical prowess equaled or exceeded those of the other dogs—as if she had been created to remind him that a disability cannot defeat a true champion.

He stroked her head gently. Did he really have the right to subject her, or any of the dogs, to the long voyage and the tropics? Was he placing personal gain before the health of his troops? Madagascar's dampness was bound to affect Taurus' hip joint. Filled with fluid, it was edging from its socket. And what about brain fever? Dogs unaccustomed to tropical sun and humidity were highly susceptible.

Lantern glow interrupted his solitude. He squared his shoulders and stood up.

"Redwing," Krayller said. His affenpinscher bared its teeth, as if grinning in recognition of Erich who was its feeder, as he was of all the dogs.

"Comfort," Erich replied, completing the password exchange.

Krayller stooped to pat his terrier. "Sir?"

"Yes?"

"Will you be taking Grog with you?" The huge man's voice was heavy with emotion. "Rumor has it that I will not be going to Madagascar. Is Grog slated for a new trainer?"

"Rumors don't run an army. Brains and oil do." Erich looked down at the black monkey terrier. "I'm not positive who is going."

The trainer drew a distraught breath. Hitler himself had presented the little dog to the corps, a gesture Eva Braun had apparently inspired. At first Krayller had been insulted when Erich put the animal in his charge, but the dog proved quick and intelligent, with a sense of comedy that provided relief from the seriousness of the work with the shepherds.

"I will leave you now, sir." Krayller swept the light along the line of tethered dogs and began to walk off.

"Just a moment." Letting go of Taurus, Erich walked toward the far wall.

"Sir?"

"When I reach the back fence, let the dogs loose. Pull the pin and let them run with their chains attached."

"*What?*"

"You heard me."

"But, sir, the other trainers are asleep or in the city—sir!"

"Do as I say!"

Nearing the iron gate, Erich looked up at the sky, studded with stars. Along the horizon of chestnut trees, long feathery clouds shone silver and bright, and he thought of the dogsled that had taken Benyowsky across Siberia. *Master of this castle. But who is really master of these grand, graceful animals?*

"I can't do this, sir." Krayller sounded plaintive as a child. "Unless the dogs are muzzled, without their trainers here they will tear each other apart, even if they don't wrap their chains around something and choke to death."

"You will do as I tell you."

"If you insist on doing this, sir, I must wash my hands of all responsibility for the consequences."

"That goes without saying. You are not my keeper."

On impulse Erich closed his eyes and lifted his arms, as if seeking affirmation from the clouds. Did his destiny, he wondered, like the Count's, lie in Madagascar? He could hear Krayller tinkering with the main pin designed to disconnect all the animals from their runs in case of fire or other emergency.

That's it, he thought. He would let his real friends decide his destiny. His only friends. Should they obey orders and attack him, he would refuse to take them to the tropics—assuming he lived through the attack—but if they disobeyed an immoral command and bound to their feeder like children to a loving parent, he would set aside his fears for them. For then they would not be Nazi puppets but true German soldiers, capable of thinking for themselves.

Yes. He willed forth his resolve. Let the dogs decide.

They came bounding, barking and snarling, tongues and tail wagging with excitement. When they were near enough so that he could see their dark-velvet eyes in the moonlight, he issued an unspoken command:

Kill me!

For a moment the dogs kept charging. Then those in front slowed and parted, whining, their ears uplifted, some now looking backward as though listening to a secret signal.

Kill me! he commanded again as Taurus stormed past the others, no longer fast but her determination undiminished, eyes gleaming with fury. With a primeval rasping deep in her throat, she leaped.

And, even as he fell beneath her weight, she began to lick him.

Chapter 30

He rolled with the dogs, feeling their panting and excitement as his own. When he and they were spent, he lay in the grass and looked at the clouds, physically and emotionally exhausted but happy. He thought about inventing lies for the clouds, images that he could not see but felt a more imaginative man might, then settled for reveling in their ordinariness. Clouds were clouds were clouds. He let his mind roam among them, inventing realities that fit the lies of his life and talking to himself as he so increasingly did. He played out the dialogue in his head, divorcing himself from his own responses as if he were an eavesdropper listening to two people speaking about him.

He remembered a conversation he had not had with Solomon, but should have. In his head, his friend asked about his relationship with the Party. Solomon had always seemed frightened to mention it, except as vituperative aside, as though sarcasm could safely shield him from his friend Erich Alois' potential enmity. From his quaint little lies, like the Amsterdam fairytale? Quaint little lies in extenuating circumstances, such as Hitler's increasingly obvious intention to rule the world if not the universe, that might make an officer in the Reich abandon a friend who was also a rival?

So Solomon was careful about asking Erich about the Nazis.

"My feelings toward Hitler?" Erich imagined himself answering. "They parallel my feelings about my father, who rants when there's an audience, but when it's just the two of us is afraid to lift his voice or his hand. Like the time at Pfaueninsel. There was a crowd around us when Achilles attacked the Reich's precious peacock, but when Hitler whispered to me to shoot her I heard fear in his voice behind that assurance and command. He was afraid of how he would look if I refused. So now I fight him my way, with every step and with every breath. I do it not only because of what he made me do, but also because he is a fool and a coward. A *hamster* who sells lies instead of other men's half-rotted produce. He has no honor. That's the one thing I cannot abide."

And so I fight him, but without his knowing. It's dishonorable, I know that, Solomon, but what other avenue...*alley*, I should say, is open to me, given that kind of opponent?"

"You're not exactly the rebel type, Erich. Perhaps as a child, but you are fooling no one now, except maybe yourself."

"I'm a rebel against rebelliousness."

"And that's how you define Adolf Hitler—as a rebel?"

"As far as I am concerned, he has rebelled against all that is sacred."

"So now you claim to fight him. By wearing the uniform. That's hardly what one would call sabotage, or even espionage."

"When I was taking my Abwehr training at Tegel," Erich said, "there was a retarded boy—a man—whose only job was to clean the blackboards. Every day after classes he arrived with his bucket and rag. Always grinning.

"One day our instructor was using a projector, and because the classroom was small, he shone the projector against the board instead of a screen. The retarded man arrived early, who knows why. Oblivious to the lesson, he began erasing and washing the board. The instructor was livid, but just stood and watched.

"The retard reached the place where the picture was projected. A graph regarding troop movements, if I remember correctly. He kept erasing and washing, but naturally nothing came off. I was the first to stop laughing. That's how it is with Herr Hitler and myself. He's going to keep thinking he has all the answers, and I'm going to keep trying to erase the board."

He realized he was actually talking aloud, as though Solomon were among the clouds. *Fitting*, he thought. Solomon with his head in the clouds, and me with my mind on theoretical physics, the only subject other than Imperial German history that I enjoyed at the *Gymnasium*. Well, those times are over now. School's out. For the whole country, it's out.

Thinking about school, about training, he experienced a pang of anxiety as he realized the dogs were no longer muffed against him. Then, relieved, he saw that they were sitting in a circle half a dozen meters away, perfectly equidistant from him and each other, each in its respective place. A zodiac, with Aquarius at twelve o'clock. He smiled at Taurus seated at five o'clock, her head regally lifted, ears back. He could sense her joy in the pride he felt for the dog team, but for the moment she was too ensconced in her role to acknowledge him as friend. In the affenpinscher's absence, he had become, for her, the center of the pack, the hub of the wheel of the zodiac.

That was the way they had been trained: the affenpinscher presided; the other dogs obeyed and guarded that central position.

Unlike with most guard dogs, trained to follow their handler's lead and to move against an enemy in a typical flanking pattern, he had built his corps to respond to one another, and to attack outward from the hub. That would best assure that headquarters remain inviolate, especially, as he hoped, if his main base were behind enemy lines.

In Madagascar, it occurred to him, he would always be behind enemy lines. All he need do was assume that the Malagasy were the enemy.

The whole damn island was in France's back pocket, wasn't it? What a prize the island would make if—when—war broke out in Europe, a median in the midst of Indian Ocean shipping lanes! Not that he would give Herr Hitler anything other than a bullet in his heart, but were he, Erich, to control Madagascar, what a hole card he would have.

He looked at the dogs, sitting like guards before a castle keep, barely blinking, seemingly so patient but, he knew, waiting with high anxiety for an order to begin whatever game he required.

He mentally reached out to Taurus and felt the effort it took her merely to maintain an uplifted head. Her pain made his eyes water. How could he subject her to the rigors of the rain forest? She and the others were mentally ready—but was she physically capable? Were any of them?

"*Come*," he silently commanded Taurus. She glanced around at the other dogs as though confused at being singled out to break the formation, and at last left her post. "*Come all*," he ordered, and the rest followed, beginning with Cancer and continuing around the clock.

Taurus lifted her head once more. How she loved leading, Erich thought, feeling her happiness.

At the edge of the cobbled, crescent-shaped driveway the men had set up a dog pull. That Erich had not yet scheduled the event was due less to the dogs' condition than to indecision about how it should occur. Most of the trainers wanted a competition, dog against dog to see which could pull the most weight, while Erich found that motivation misdirected—more appropriate to humans than to animals. Teamwork was difficult enough to perfect among the dogs. Like prima ballerinas forced to become chorines, they held onto their individuality. His focus was on the finer details of unit cooperation. Still, the trainers had a point. If all of the dogs literally pulled together, how, they asked, might they assess the teams' weakest and strongest links?

The blocks of concrete sat on the sled like a pyramid awaiting ruin beneath wind and rain. It was time to move the thousand-kilo mountain.

Erich called to Aquarius. He could never feel the other dogs in the team as strongly as he could Taurus. Largest and most powerful of the Zodiac team, Aquarius was slow to respond, eyeing Taurus as if for confirmation or approval. That Taurus was clearly the leader among the shepherds despite her age and infirmities brought a slight smile to Erich's lips, though he tried his best to block the emotion lest Aquarius feel slighted and under or over-perform as a result.

He hooked Aquarius into the traces and mentally issued the command. Taurus and the other dogs looked on as Aquarius strained. The dog lurched, straining, sliding back against its own efforts, claws scraping on the tarspayed cobbles. On the second try, the mountain of concrete broke loose and began to move. The shepherd kept low, seeming to dig its claws into the tar as the mountain slid forward.

"*Go!* Erich commanded. "*All the way across the drive. You can!*"

The sled slid more easily as Aquarius' powerful shoulders hunched into the trial.

"*Yes!*" Erich cheered.

Aquarius reached the far side of the drive and entered the grass, digging up divots, belly almost touching the ground. Behind him, the sled touched the lawn.

"*Enough,*" Erich said. He patted the dog while the others looked on jealously, wanting his affection.

"Now you," he said aloud to Taurus, though even before he spoke she was moving in an excited circle. He pointed to the traces. She ambled over, the hitch in her hips almost imperceptible. "Good girl," he said. Her tail wagged in answer, and her happiness and determination beat against his mind like a frothy surf.

He unhitched Aquarius, still catching his breath, his chest heaving. Taurus waited patiently, almost seeming to distance herself from the insult of any form of leash, while Erich hooked her up. Aquarius shook himself and trotted back to take his post in the circle.

Erich knelt and held Taurus' head in his hands. Touching her that way gave him an odd sense of déjà vu: *lifting Miriam's chin and kissing her at the wedding.* The wedding was simple: Konnie, the trainers, a few Nazi functionaries as a matter of form. Hitler had been unable to attend but sent his good wishes. No family members or friends. She had none left who were not Jewish, and they in Switzerland; as far as he was concerned, he had none—period.

Now that Sol was gone.

Had I known about his perversion, he would have been dead to me long before the goddamn jar arrived.

He gave Taurus a final pat, and stepped back. A breeze had come up, and for a moment the scent of roses and freshly mown lawns from the surrounding gardens assailed him. It felt good to be alive. He put the horror of the jar behind him.

"*I love you,*" he told his dog.

As if sublimating her happiness into determination, rather than wag her tail she leaned into the task of pulling the pyramid back across the drive. Unlike Aquarius' surges to jump-start the weight, she strained forward without moving, her shoulders level with her hips, the forelegs taking the bulk of the load. It was, Erich knew, poor form, especially given the size of what she was expected to carry, but she seemed loathe to engage in tricks which, while effective, would render her less than regal.

Her entire body took on the look of a freeze-frame: jowl set, eyes bulging, shoulder muscles bunched beneath the skin. He could feel the dysplasia raging as he opened his mind to her misery, hoping the combined psyches would will her onward.

Pain sliced from one of his hips to the other with such force that it sent him staggering. His mind reeled with agony. It shot up his spine and clutched the base of his skull. Breath issued loudly through his lips. He tried to cry out her name but only gasped as the pain triggered a series of lightening seizures, shaking his body like minor aftershocks of an earthquake.

In the split-seconds between its beginning and its end, there came an intense awareness of greenery around him. He was no longer at the estate that once had belonged to Miriam Rathenau and now was the property of the Nazi Party, as she herself was—officially. He was amid thigh-high grass beneath a white moon crimped into an otherwise ink-black sky like a notary punch. The night was hot, oppressive; oppressive, too, was the dark tangle that, surrounding him, seemed to press toward him as if to listen to another of his dialogues carried on in solitude. At the top of a gentle slope above him, a dozen dressed stones and totem sticks, all the height of a man, stood beneath the moon which backlit half a dozen dogs which walked upright, like men.

As instantly as it had come, the image vanished. Once again Taurus was before him, pulling with all her might but unable to move the mountain. Aquarius joined her, followed by Pisces, Virgo, Sagittarius with her clipped tail, Libra. Then all of them. Before Erich could object, they clamped their mouths upon the traces and, tugging backward as Taurus continued to pull, brought the pyramid scraping along the drive.

The satisfaction that flooded Erich washed the pain away, his and Taurus'. For the first time in months, he felt free of anxiety and dread, utterly at peace, without concerns or plans for what the dogs' teamwork would mean in the greater picture called Madagascar. This is the satisfaction, he decided, I would have known after lovemaking with Miriam, had not the Party turned her away from me. He assessed the loss without remorse or self-pity, no more emotionally involving than the clouds that were clouds.

Chapter 31

A sound invaded Erich's consciousness, unmistakable and too-familiar, coming from the direction of the west gate.

Few sounds in the universe approximate that of a round being chambered. There is about it a certainty of its own importance, like the hiss of a highly venomous snake. Someone or something *else* holds the power of life and death, and the myth of immortality is briefly, however briefly, dispelled.

Erich's attention leapt toward the sound. What he saw commanded his full attention: Heinrich Wilhelm Krayller, who had dreamed of being a circus clown but whom fate and Hitler had conspired to make a clown in the Nazi circus, stood with his Karbiner 90 beneath the chin of Sachsenhausen's Deputy Commandant, finger on the trigger, face rigid with wrath.

Hempel's head was tilted back from the pressure of the muzzle. Though he clearly was attempting to maintain his military bearing, his eyes registered fear.

On the other side of the men, two other soldiers also faced off: Krayller's affenpinscher stood before and below the larger wolfhound, neither dog moving, both tight with fury, tails set like sticks.

"I'm going to kill you, you son of a bitch," Krayller said, his finger tightening on the trigger. Krayller, who would not harm so much as a fly unless the defense of his country or its women or children necessitated it, had murder in his eyes and held the power of God in his hands.

For a moment.

As suddenly, the power shifted. He dropped the carbine to the ground and clutched his throat, staggering backwards into the affenpinscher whose neck was being jostled between the wolfhound's jaws.

The terrier kicked ineffectually as it lay on its side, fighting with no more sound than a wind wafting through the linden trees that lined the Grünewald's streets. Then its rump flopped twice upon the driveway and the little dog lay paralyzed, chest rising and falling, eyes staring…and the shepherds charged.

Everything happened almost without sound, like a silent movie where only the tick, tick, tick of the turning metal wheel indicated that there was a mechanical helper that balanced the magic of film. Perhaps, Erich thought, the dogs sensed that there was no need for sound, that nothing but death would deter one like Sturmbannführer Otto Hempel who bent effortlessly and lifted up the corporal's weapon. Without looking at Erich he said, "If your dogs so much as rub against me I'll kill your friend here." He moved the carbine toward the terrier. "I'll kill them both."

My friend? Erich reacted with surprise. Was that what he and the trainers had become. No. He would not countenance that, not after what had become of the only real *friend* he had ever known.

Solomon *Freund.*

He called off the dogs.

They halted but refused to sit, as he commanded. Instead they moved nervously along an imaginary boundary drawn across the drive, anxious to finish what they had begun.

Corporal Krayller picked himself up, blood seeping through his fingers which still rested against his neck. He looked up at Hempel with terror and, Erich realized incredulously, a certain measure of awe.

"You sick bastard," Erich said to the Deputy Commandant.

"That I am, Herr Oberst," Hempel replied, casually checking the button of his sleeve. "Not only emotionally but actually. Points of fact, I might add, of which I am intensely proud."

Erich bent over Krayller and, despite the soldier's attempt to keep his hand over his throat, examined the wound.

"Not deep," Erich concluded. "He didn't cut the jugular."

"I am a surgeon in that regard," Hempel said. "Keep that in mind, Herr Oberst."

Relegating his anger to the back of his mind, Erich lifted Krayller by the arm, the corporal cradling the affenpinscher. Krayller pointed toward Hempel, trying to tell Erich something, but the wound or perhaps his fear had momentarily taken away his ability to speak. Erich patted him on the shoulder and sent him trundling toward the first aid locker in the garage, the shepherds parting before him and the terrier, the guard of the hub of their team, with the respect one might accord royalty.

"You don't belong here," Erich told Hempel. "Neither you nor Goebbels, with his starlets and whores. But especially not you."

"I never liked this place anyway. I *rejoiced* when I was given Sachsenhausen. There, we know how to eradicate the stench of Jews." Hempel stooped to pat the wolfhound, who accepted the affection without returning it. "But where either of us live, or with whom we work or socialize, is not our decision to make. We are soldiers, are we not?"

"Only *you* would call yourself that."

"It seems, Herr Oberst, that others do not share your opinion, so it is best that you keep silent concerning your feelings about me." A slight, wry, almost seductive smile creased his lips. "As you already know, we will be working together, *closely* together, at least for the foreseeable future. Herr Reichsführer Himmler himself has placed me in charge of security on the Madagascar expedition. What you may not yet know is that my Boris," again he patted the wolfhound, "will be replacing that insult the bleeding corporal over there calls a dog."

The wolfhound, at the hub of the shepherds, Erich thought. My God. My God. It took every effort of his being not to protest. Hempel was awaiting that protest, would revel in it. And it would be futile. For an instant, he saw the jungle of Madagascar with startling clarity. In the distance, a dog howled. The moon, pale and heartless, felt like a cold hand upon his bare shoulder.

"Do you hate me because my friends are Jews?" Erich asked abruptly, unable to contain himself. "Or because I stayed away from you when I was in the Freikorps Youth."

"You would have enjoyed my...company."

"Did the other boys?" Erich asked angrily.

"Those who did not at first—learned to."

"You are...despicable."

"And you, Herr Oberst, are too close to our Führer."

Then Erich understood. The realization startled him, made his mouth dry. What had brought him such despair, such hatred of himself and of Hitler—the Führer's order to shoot Achilles—had caused others to assume a closeness they found threatening.

"We will never allow your dog into the Zodiac," he said.

The captain was stroking the wolfhound's head. In the two years Hempel had lived at the estate, Erich had never seen him show affection toward any animal. The transparent turnabout sickened him.

"I don't know whose boots you licked, but you can unlick them," Erich continued. "You have no place in my corps."

"Reichsführer Himmler might think otherwise," Hempel said.

"The Reichsführer might like to know about your little episodes with Goebbels' whores," Erich said. "You think Toy didn't tell me how you ordered her not to wash after Goebbels humped her? Out of his bed, down to your room...." He stuck his hands in his pockets and started away. "As you can tell, Herr Sturmbannführer," he said over his shoulder, "Toy gave me more than a smoking jacket before you relegated her to the docks."

He was past the garage before Hempel's voice, surprisingly articulate, buffeted him. "And I have the transfusion papers, Herr Oberst. They have sat on my desk for a year," he said. "Strange how I keep forgetting to send them to *Medizinalrat* Schmidt so your dear wife can be scheduled."

Erich continued walking, afraid that if he stopped and turned around his horror would be visible. All the favors he had called in to stop the transfusions...all for naught. Fool that he was, he had thought his own best efforts had halted the insanity."

"I will leave Boris chained here at the gate," Hempel called out after him. "Treat her well."

Erich walked around to the dog-runs behind the mansion. The shepherds followed him, moving with a heaviness that told him that his mood of despair had transferred itself to them.

"Herr Oberst?" a sad voice called out to him from the bushes.

Krayller stepped into his line of sight. There was bloodied gauze wrapped around his throat and he held Grog in his arms. "It will happen, won't it?" he said without preamble.

"I'm afraid so. We will find you...another place."

"I have no other place," the corporal said. "We both know that. It's back to the Wehrmacht for me...unless Hempel sees fit to have me court-martialed and shot." He appeared on the verge of tears as, with a hamhock-sized hand, he stroked the terrier's head. The affenpinscher tried to lick his wrist. "What stupidity, pointing my carbine at an officer!"

"You should have shot him," Erich said.

The corporal's gaze leapt up—surprised and hopeful.

"I would have helped you dispose of the body."

Krayller looked toward the west end of the estate. "But not now," he said. "It's too late."

Erich nodded. Yes, it was too late, he thought. Hempel would waste no time making arrangements for the implementation of the papers, should he not return to Sachsenhausen.

The corporal pulled up his massive chest and slowly released a breath. His shoulders sagged. Sorrow seemed to pervade his very being. His eyes were moist. "I can't leave Grog," he said. "And I won't fight in the trenches. Not for Hitler. Certainly not for the likes of Hempel." He eyed Erich's holstered pistol. "You might as well shoot me now."

"Such talk is foolishness, if not insanity," Erich said. "You can have my motorcycle," he told the corporal.

Krayller narrowed his eyes, not comprehending.

"It's yours," Erich said, "if you will do what I should do. Take your dog and my cycle," he reached to pet the affenpinscher, who appeared to enjoy the attention and was, amazingly, none the worse for wear after the incident with the wolfhound, "and ride to Switzerland. Don't even think about looking back."

Chapter 32

Misha and Sol were looking out of the window when the staff car pulled up to the end of the road. Pleshdimer, who was driving, stayed behind the wheel while the Sturmbannführer walked to the farmhouse.

"Bruqah said I would be safe here," Misha said.

"And so you have been," Solomon said. "But not even he could guarantee that it would last forever. Besides, you don't know that he has come for you."

"Yes, I do," Misha said, looking around desperately as if for a hiding place. "The alcove," he said. "The one Bruqah uses. It must lead to the outside. I could run away."

"We are due to leave the farmhouse within twenty-four hours. Why risk being shot by one of the guards? That would not be wise."

As if staying here and waiting for *him* is *wise*, Misha thought, but he stayed where he was.

The hours that followed were, at best, a blur. He was instructed to pack what clothing he had been given since his arrival at the farmhouse in a small sea-bag. Then he was escorted by the Sturmbannführer to the car. Pleshdimer was asleep and snoring in the back seat, a bottle of alcohol loosely in his hand.

Hempel placed Misha in the passenger seat and took the wheel. Misha was within easy reach of the man's groping fingers. In desperation, he thought about the list, going over and over it in his mind as the fingers pushed and pulled—

The next thing he actively remembered was spreading his legs as he lay on a bunk bed in a small cabin on board a ship. Hempel had apparently told Pleshdimer to wait outside.

The Sturmbannführer leaned against the wall and waited. Knowing what he had to do, Misha took off his clothing, folded everything, and piled them neatly on a small dresser that was built into the corner of the cabin. Then he lay down on the bunk.

Hempel drew two pairs of nylons from his pocket. He wrapped them around Misha's wrists and ankles and tied each one tightly to one of the metal posts that anchored the top bunk to his. At once Misha's hands and feet began to swell.

"A half hitch followed by a clove hitch," Hempel said, standing back to admire his handiwork. Having done that, he did *The thing* to Misha.

"I have a present for you," Hempel said, when, for the moment, he'd had his fill of pleasure.

Misha stared up at his own reflection, distorted in the sea-green metal of the upper bunk, and tried to obey Bruqah's instructions. "Think of yourself as a dolphin," the Malagasy had said. "Let his words and his acts wash over you like sea water." It had seemed like a wonderful idea at the time, but it didn't work now.

Not that Misha was surprised.

How could anyone be a dolphin if, as Bruqah claimed, they stood on their tails and chittered, and played tag around ships, and led lost sailors to safety through dangerous waters and sharks and everything. Besides, he didn't have a tail or fins, nor could he hold his breath for very long at all.

But he wished he could.

He wished he could hold his breath until he died.

"Get dressed," Hempel ordered, untying Misha's bonds.

Misha did as he was told. When he was fully dressed, Hempel held a package out to him. The boy looked down at the blue wrapping paper and the bow that littered the package like a tangle of curls.

"You must earn it, of course," Hempel said, pulling the package away. He was already breathing heavily again.

Misha lay back down. His gaze returned to the top bunk. Mechanically, he began to unbutton his trousers. "Skip that part," Hempel ordered, putting a restraining hand over the boy's.

Misha shut his eyes.

"Don't close your eyes," Hempel said. "I would hate to have to order *him*," he nodded his head toward the closed door, "to slit your eyelids so that you will be forced to watch." He unsnapped his stiletto from the wrist attachment within his sleeve. "Have you ever seen someone with his eyelids cut off, Misha darling? Have you ever seen eyelids fried in a pan? They jump around like squid. It's quite fascinating to watch."

Misha said nothing, not even when, using the stiletto, Hempel flicked the buttons from Misha's shirt. He lowered his face and licked each nipple before cutting the shirt the rest of the way off and starting on Misha's trousers.

I am a dolphin, Misha thought. I am free as a dolphin.

Except he was not a dolphin.

He lay looking at his distorted face in the sea-green metal.

"Do you like what I do to you?" Hempel asked huskily. "Does it make you feel warm inside?" He laid the package down on the bed and pressed both hands against the insides of Misha's groin, making the genitals mound up. "How do you want it tonight? How would you like me to do it to you."

God help me, Misha thought, saying nothing.

If there is a God.

If there are dolphins.

"Tell me," Hempel insisted, "or must I cut you? I once sliced off a boy's penis for less insolence than this. Is that what you want?"

Misha searched for words, but thought itself stopped as Hempel slid a finger inside him. He heard Hempel sigh. Even hating him as he did, he knew that the Sturmbannführer was somewhere else, on a ship and a sea of which Misha had no part.

"How could any man want a woman, or even another man, when there is such tightness available," Hempel said. "Except you must talk to me..." his voice turned even huskier, "my love."

He rested the tip of the stiletto against Misha's testicles, and sat back. Fear and pain raced through the boy's every muscle, up his every nerve.

Hempel reached for the package, tipped it onto its side, and pulled the ribbon. The lid fell off, revealing white tissue paper. He reached inside and pulled out a black chocolate-brown turtle-neck sweater and a flat, smaller box, such as might hold a woman's bangle.

He shook out the sweater, held it in over the boy as if to see if it was the right size, and laid it aside. "Open it," he said, handing Misha the smaller box.

Diffidently, Misha did as he was told.

Inside the box, curled into a bed of cotton, lay a heavily jeweled dog collar.

"Beautiful, is it not?" Hempel removed it from the box and leaned down to kiss Misha. "Lift your head."

Again, Misha obeyed. Hempel fastened the collar around the boy's neck. "Fits perfectly," he said with satisfaction. He stood up. "Regretfully, I must leave you now, but I shall return in a matter of hours." He bent to stroke Misha's hair. "Rest. You will be a good boy while I'm gone, won't you?" He patted Misha's side. "We will talk when I return." He retied Misha's hands and put the stiletto, which had fallen onto the sheet, back against Misha's testicles. Then he adjusted his uniform, and opened the cabin door.

Pleshdimer entered as he left.

"If the knife falls, you know what to do," Hempel said.

The door had barely closed behind the Sturmbannführer before a new round of terror began for Misha. While Hempel was the sexual aggressor of the perverted two-man team, and as such caused physical pain, that was not his primary intent.

For Pleshdimer, however, the thrill lay in the causing of pain itself.

Now, dropping to the floor, surprisingly agile despite his heft, he knelt at the side of the bunk. With a flick of his finger, he knocked away the knife.

"Look at what you've done," he said, leaning over Misha. He stank horribly of cheap liquor and body odor. It was a point of honor with him never to bathe, lest, he said, the water wash away his man-smell. Women liked that, he said, and his daughters had liked it even better.

"It's not fair," he said seriously. His eyes, set like globules of white fat amid the oily corpulence of his cheeks, appeared to shine with genuine sorrow. "The Sturmbannführer won't let me touch you the way I wish to. The way you would like. The way I did with my own children, my daughters." He opened his arms, eyes closed in serenity.

Misha had heard the stories. Everyone had. He pictured the Kapo's daughters, strung up in the barn like sausages.

Pleshdimer untied the nylons from Misha's ankles. "You dropped the knife. You know what that means." Tucking an arm around Misha's calves, he drew up the boy's legs to his forehead, bending him nearly in half.

Misha closed his eyes again as the belt came down, buckle first. "How can you, a Jew, do this?" he cried out.

The belt slashed down harder. "I'm no more Jewish than God!"

Blood ran down Misha's buttocks and he could feel the stranglehold of the collar around his neck. The small cabin closed in on him, and he wondered if this was what it felt like to be a dog in a kennel.

"You hear me, you little son-of-a-bitch?" Hempel shouted. "Just because I had some ancestor who humped some Jew cow once or twice—don't mean a thing!"

When he finished, Misha knew, the Kapo would hurry to find Hempel and report that the boy had needed disciplining. And when the Kapo was angry, he often forgot things.

Things like nylons. Like stilettos.

Maybe he will forget to retie my legs, he thought. Maybe he will forget about the knife.

Maybe when the knife is mine I will learn how to be a dolphin.

Chapter 33

Fog hung like used cheesecloth around Kiel's Hochwaldt Wharf, and smelled as bad. Erich frowned with disgust as he stuck his head out of the window of his touring car and peered up at the grey ship. *Altmark,* she proclaimed in meter-high letters.

Her construction, the proud captain, Heinrich Dau, had told him, was a masterpiece of deceit. To the unwary, she seemed just another old steamer. In reality she was well built and less than a year old. Every centimeter of her 178-meter length and 22-meter beam was designed to maximize space while minimizing bulk. Her 11,000 ton gross had a loading capacity of 14,000 tons, and her four nine-cylinder M.A.N. diesel engines were capable of 21 knots.

Most impressive, or so Dau would have him believe. With his lack of naval experience, what Erich heard meant little to him. She looked about as interesting to him as a used-up whore.

Stevedores, their knitted caps pulled low against the dampness, moved silently around the wharf, their carts piled with boxes to be loaded onto the ship. Light from the large triangular docklamps reflected off puddles and off the harbor's rainbowed oil slicks, but none of it looked inviting.

A panel truck drew up. Cameramen piled out, complaining of the chill and the odor of rotting fish, and clowning as if preparing to film a comedy and not the loading of camp Jews onto a military transport. They quickly turned the dreary dock into a complex of lights and tripods.

Fools! Erich thought. Or were they?

They worshipped Movietone News, others bowed before Hitler. Both were dictators invading the privacy of their idolaters. Soon he would be rid of all propagandists. He would feel whole again. He and Miriam and the baby—especially the baby—deserved more than the Führer's empty assurances that manhood and statehood went hand in hand with the Fatherland.

"Stay!" he commanded Taurus, and stepped from the car.

A cameraman, pulling equipment along on a cart, followed him to the ship. As they started up the gangway, the ship's stack blasted as if in greeting. Erich pulled back his shoulders, not for the cameras or the petty officer piping him aboard, but for himself.

Captain Dau, small and wiry, and apparently nonplussed by the camera, rambled forward to meet him. A graying beard poorly hid a weak chin, but his face, wrinkled and weathered, was not a stupid face, and his eyes were cold and shrewd.

Erich returned the greeting respectfully. He would spend a long time confined with the old man; it would not do to antagonize him, a Nazi hard-liner. Dau's military exploits had been legendary for a quarter of a century. It was said he would flee a fight only if the Seekriegsführung—the Naval High Command in Berlin—would allow him to re-engage the enemy as soon as possible.

"You two ready for us up there?" Leni Riefenstahl called out from below. "I want you shaking hands."

"Ready for our 'historic first meeting?'" Erich asked Dau.

The old man reluctantly put out his hand. "In my day such foolishness would have been rewarded with a trip to the Front."

"Miriam will be here shortly," Leni yelled.

Erich waved in acknowledgement.

"A few more takes, with the boy in the picture," Leni shouted.

"Boy? What boy?"

Leni pointed to Erich's left, to a pale young boy in a black, turtle-neck pullover.

"Come on over here," Erich said, wondering whose idea it had been to include a child on the journey. Judging by the look on Dau's face, the boy was certainly no relative of his. "What is your name, son?" he asked, lifting the boy onto the rail, and balancing him with one arm.

"I am Misha," the boy said.

"And to whom do you belong?"

"Haupt...the Jews...myself—"

"Never mind. We'll figure it out later. For now, put your arm around my neck and hold on tight."

Leni smiled and gave him the high sign.

After two takes of what was actually their fourth meeting, they were spared further attention by the arrival of twelve army trucks. Erich released the boy, leaned his forearms on a rail and watched a squad of soldiers emerge from the first. Placing themselves well out of camera range, they raised their rifles to their shoulders, and waited.

One at a time, bucking like unbroken steeds, the trucks' engines were killed. Now their lights winked out. Escort guards, weaponless in deference to the audiences who would view the film, climbed from passenger seats and strode around the trucks to pull the pins on the tailgates, which came clanging down.

The cameras whirred.

A dog and trainer jumped from each of the remaining trucks. Only Krayller was missing, reassigned—along with the affenpinscher—to a military pool.

"Escorts," Leni explained into her microphone. "We must make sure the one hundred and forty-four boarding Jews are safe from Jewish traitors who might seek to sabotage our Führer's grand experiment."

Erich looked over at Hempel, who stood near two trucks that had arrived earlier, carrying the forty guards he had selected for the mission. If anyone is likely to sabotage this experiment, it's that son of a bitch, Erich thought. And that damned orderly of his, Wasj Pleshdimer. What a beauty! The man was rancid as a month-old fish.

Pleshdimer. Hempel. He repeated their names angrily under his breath. Sometimes he agreed with the worst of Hitler's methods. The *Altmark* was scheduled to reach Madagascar in forty-two days. If either of them so much as spoke harshly to his dogs or his men, he would plant their severed heads on the landing beach.

"Let the Jews out before we run out of film!" Leni shouted at Hempel. "Idiots!" she said to her chief cameraman, without worrying about being overheard. "The whole trip better not be so disorganized."

Pleshdimer started toward her, but Hempel put a restraining hand on his arm. "Let them out," Hempel ordered.

The inmates, wearing clogs, spotless trousers, light jackets and caps, climbed from the trucks. In accordance with Goebbels' instructions, nothing about the boarding was to appear involuntary; it was to look like an orderly emigration, not a chaotic exile. Each man carried a satchel, one side inscribed with a swastika, the other with the Star of David. They looked like determined workers undertaking an important mission for the good of all European Jewry.

"Thanks to the generosity of our great leader, these Jewish volunteers are being resettled on the African island of Madagascar," Leni said, playing the dual role of overvoice and director. "It is our Führer's desire that they live there in peace and that others of their kind follow to make their homes along the island's balmy shores—a paradise of curious lemurs and colorful orchids. These men will work the very soil which scholars believe may have been the original site of ancient Lemuria, the remnant of a sunken continent known as Gondwanaland."

Pushing away the memory of Sachsenhausen's walking cadavers, Erich surveyed the living cargo. They looked passably healthy after a month's sequestering and proper meals, but even at this distance he sensed their anxiety.

"Keep in mind," Captain Dau said, "that if one Jew causes trouble at sea, the lot of them go overboard." He thumped his Meerschaum pipe against the rail. "Into the water, all of them."

"You are in command—at sea."

A wistful smile played around Dau's mouth, softening its hard edges. "The sea has her own criteria concerning necessity. I remember when..."

Erich blocked out Dau's words. For all the captain's military mien, he was like most old men; he sought an audience for his stories.

As Dau rambled on, Erich watched the line of Jews thread on board. Most, he had been told, possessed specialized skills that would be useful in Madagascar. One, for example, was supposed to be a scholar who spoke fluent French and had been schooled for the past two weeks on Madagascar's customs and culture. He might prove invaluable if Bruqah, who was black, after all, and thus prone to laziness, took off when they reached the island.

Invaluable...or would the scholar remind him of Solomon? Erich gritted his teeth. He had no business feeling guilty about Solomon's death. He had, after all, helped him get to Amsterdam. If the stupid queer was so brainless as to come back, why should *he* give a damn?

"...is that not so?"

"Is what not so!" Erich said abruptly, momentarily forgetting his resolution to treat the old man with respect.

"I suggest that in the future you listen when I speak, Herr Oberst. You might learn something."

"I might, indeed." Erich had not intended the words to sound sarcastic.

"Do not underestimate me, Herr Oberst." Dau sucked at his empty pipe, shook it once, and placed it in his vest pocket. "I saw more action in the Great War than you could dream of. Now I have brought this ship back from helping Franco against the Republicans. I know my purpose in life, and how to wield the power the Seekriegsführung places in my hands." Erich could see a burning, icy patriotism in the man's eyes. "Your little vacation southeast of Africa is not my primary mission. Interfere with the real reason the *Altmark* sails, and I will shoot you for treason as easily as I'd squash a Jew or a June bug."

Clearing his throat, Dau excused himself and stalked toward his cabin, leaving Erich to swear under his breath as he lit a cheroot.

"Notice the man about to board the *Altmark,*" the overvoice said. "He is bearing a jeweled scroll, known to the Jews as the Torah, a word which, strangely enough, also means 'an African antelope.' This Torah is alive in a different way, for it contains the entire body of Jewish religious literature. It is a gift from our Führer to the new Jews of Madagascar."

Curious, Erich leaned over the rail. He had seen a Torah only once, at Sol's bar mitzvah—covered in white satin and encrusted with jewels and gold braiding.

Head bent, the man carrying the scroll made his way slowly up the gangway. The skin on the hands that held the scroll was dried and wrinkled. Short hair emerged from his scalp like bristles on an old porcupine, and blackened, misshapen toes stuck out of the end of his clogs.

Suddenly, as if sensing Erich's gaze upon him, the man stopped walking and looked up. The other Jews, on their way to the open steel hatch that led to the holds, flowed around him like a stream around a rock, but still the man did not move.

"Hello, old friend," the prisoner said quietly.

Erich stared into a face so shrunken the eyes looked like big shooter's marbles.

"Do you truly not know me? ...or do you not wish to?"

"Solomon?" The word emerged as a whispered plea. As the man continued walking toward him, Erich gaped in disbelief. A rush of anger and anxiety make his skin tingle. "But I thought you were..."

"In Amsterdam?" Now abreast of Erich, Solomon stopped and looked at Erich's uniform. "You know what the English say about the best laid plans, Herr Oberst. I'm one of the chosen, I'm told, despite my appearance." There was a hint of the old Solomon, with his wry acknowledgment of the inappropriateness of things. "They even offered me the option of sharing quarters with Bruqah."

"Take the offer."

Alive! Erich thought. Alive! Hempel had faked the death certificate! He reached out a shaking hand as if to take Solomon's, then pulled back. What if he were diseased! What if Hempel had not faked *all* the information? Erich glanced at Solomon's clothing, searching for a pink triangle. The clothing was without special identification.

"Angst and hatred are contagious," Solomon said quietly. "Suffering is not. I prefer to be in the hold with the others." He adjusted the weight of the Torah and placed a hand on Erich's shoulder. "We have lived in sewers before, you and I."

A hefty sailor, sensing trouble, stepped from the rail and raised a fist. Grateful for the chance to reassert authority, Erich held up a hand to warn the sailor away. "The free laborer lost his balance, is all." He glanced down at the camera crew, hoping the filming had stopped. He had to be careful not to cross the fine line between acceptable behavior and favoritism.

"I thought you were being threatened, sir," the sailor said.

"Thank you, but there really is no problem." Erich could feel Solomon staring at him. "This man and I are old...knew each other as children. When he came on board and saw me at the rail, he became emotional and lost his footing."

He turned to face Solomon, wanting to say something more, but all he could see was Solomon's back as his friend followed the other Jews down through the hatch.

Chapter 34

The Rathenau limo pulled up at the end of the tarmac. Barely able to think or feel after seeing Sol, Erich returned to the rail. Bruqah climbed from the car and watched Perón help Miriam out.

A cameraman closed in.

"No!" Erich raced down the gangway, stuck a hand over the lens.

The cameraman blanched and backed away.

"Be reasonable, Erich," Leni said. "The story of Miriam Alois, stalwart German wife accompanying her husband on so arduous a journey despite her pregnancy, will make them cry with happiness out there. We can't bypass such an opportunity. Bruqah is much too colorful a character to pass up, and Perón would not forgive me if I did not get him on camera!"

"Then wait!" Erich replied brusquely. He ran toward Miriam. "How are you feeling?" he asked, still too affected by his encounter with a live Solomon to think clearly.

"Are the...free laborers on board yet?" She was making an effort to keep her voice light, but her unmistakable earnestness set him further on edge. "You saw them?"

"Yes. I, I saw." He was no better at sounding casual than she.

Miriam placed a hand on her belly as if troubled by its weight. "Get me on board, Erich. You know how I hate these films!"

He straightened up. *"Mach schnell,* Leni—or turn the cameras off!"

"Camera one!" Leni shouted.

"Ready."

"Camera two!"

"Ready."

"Sound!" There was a slight pause while a microphone attached to a long beam was rolled over to the limousine. "Sound!" she repeated, when it was in place.

"Testing," the sound man said. "Say something please, Frau—"

"What would you like—"

"That's enough. Ready with the sound."

"Most of you watching this film have seen Frau Alois before," Leni began, loudly enough to compensate for the whirring of the cameras and the clacking of the metal reels. "You know she is bearing the child of Oberst Erich Alois."

Erich watched Miriam compose her features. He knew what an effort of will this was taking, and he could not but admire her fortitude. This was the girl who'd won his heart that night in Kaverne. The inveterate performer. Not the other Miriam, the one whose attachment to Solomon made him doubt himself. Here were the traits he wanted passed on to his son. How could he bring himself to tell her that Solomon was aboard, and spoil everything?

She had taken the news of Solomon's death very hard. The death certificate must be a mistake, she had insisted. Knowing what he did about Solomon's perversion, he had found himself genuinely pitying of Miriam rather than being jealous of Solomon. He did not tell her about the jar, though he did send a corporal to check the camp's files—he could not bring himself to face the place in person. Besides, the risk was not worth it. He was likely to attack Hempel. Kill him, even. Ridding the world of that slime would probably mean a firing squad for him, and incarceration for Miriam.

The corporal reported back that prisoner 37704's papers were in order, and eventually Miriam had stopped grieving, at least openly. Perón had been a big help with her, though it irritated Erich to have him sniffing around so much, and that strange Malagasy, Bruqah, had also seemed a calming influence.

And now what to tell her! If she found out about his Amsterdam lie, she would keep on equating him with the rest of the Nazis, regardless of what miracle he might perform building the Madagascar colony...or what love he might show her and their child. So, what if she did not find out...what if Solomon died en route to the island? The world would be better off without another cock-sucking queer, wouldn't it?

Erich shuddered at the idea that he was capable of such thoughts—and yet—

"Cut!"

He had missed the rest of Leni's spiel. No matter. The only important thing was to get Miriam to the cabin so she could rest. He did not want to take risks with the child.

"Bruqah! Herr *Oberst* Perón! Please be good enough to escort Miriam on board."

He trotted to his car to get Taurus. By the time he went up the gangway, through several hatchways, and into the cabin that was to be home for the voyage, Miriam's escorts had left. She lay on the cramped lower bunk, looking around the tiny room which, Erich knew, was no match for the one she'd had on her return trip from America with her uncle. They had traveled in luxury aboard the *Titanic*'s sister ship, the RMS *Olympic*. This was a metal cell smelling of diesel and thrumming from the engines.

He sat down on a metal pull-down seat opposite her, Taurus at his feet. "You must rest."

"Yes, sir." She saluted. "Herr Oberst!"

Telling himself she was teasing him, he rose and opened the cabin hatchway. Later, he decided. He would tell her the truth later, when she was rested. In fact, there was really no reason the whole thing could not wait until they reached Madagascar. Miriam would be spending most of the voyage in the cabin; Solomon would be in the hold. She would not see the Jews until they debarked, and the chances of her finding out that he'd known from the start that Sol was alive and among them—

Yes, he thought. That would be best for everyone. He clanged the cabin door shut behind him, exited the cabin area, and led Taurus across the deck. His heart was beating rapidly, and he was having difficulty concentrating. Just how much did Solomon know, and how much Miriam? Should he interrogate Solomon? He could hardly ask him about his sexual preferences; killing him would be easier than that. Besides, it made too much sense not to be true.

He would not question Solomon yet, he decided. Whether he had gone specifically to Stuttgart or had been arrested on his way to Berlin was irrelevant. He had never made it back to Miriam, that was clear. She was a fine performer, but not *that* good. She might delude an audience, but not the man she lived with...not over the long term.

Lifting Taurus into his arms, he climbed down through a hatch and into the windlass house, where the other dogs were kenneled. Ten of the other eleven shepherds, seeing their feeder, began to whimper and whine and pace. Hempel's wolfhound ignored him; Aquarius, apparently disturbed by being penned inside a room, lay listlessly in his cage.

Holding Taurus by her leash, Erich stood in the middle of the room and looked at the cages with wonder and satisfaction. A master could be deformed or diseased, yet you would still love him, he thought, feeling closer to the dogs than usual. What he had once felt for his parents, even what he felt for Miriam, paled by comparison. All else was superficial. Ephemeral. Surely no other friendship could rival this loyalty and devotion.

He took down an army folding-stool from a nail near the huge green refrigerator which stretched across the other end of the windlass house. Sitting down before Taurus' cage, he released the dog and opened the door. He patted her squarish head.

She wagged her tail, eyes keen and dark and mirroring the light as she pressed her muzzle against Erich's thighs. He scratched behind her ears; she nuzzled closer, murmuring deep in her throat.

He ran his hand down her back, reveling in the stiff, silky coat. As he rubbed her hindquarters, her foot thumped the floor spasmodically. She looked dismayed, as if she had no idea where the sound came from.

From the corner of his eye Erich saw movement among the other dogs, but when he stopped stroking Taurus and looked around, the dogs seemed still—almost docile. Grinning, he bent and hugged his favorite. He glanced uneasily at the others, expecting the usual jealousy when a feeder paid attention to one and not the others.

The dogs appeared strangely quieted by the scene; they lay chewing their cage wire, a look of insensate ease in their eyes.

He went to give Taurus a final scratch—and then he saw the movement again. He scratched Taurus vigorously. Her leg began to thump, and all but Hempel's elegant wolfhound took up the movement, thumping their legs like a line of chorines.

Erich stopped scratching Taurus. The feet stopped moving.

He tried it a third time, a fourth. Each time was the same. At first it was merely amusing. He lifted Taurus' head and stroked the animal's throat, and again watched the others. They ceased to chew the cage wire and raised their heads, eyes brightening as though in enjoyment.

So that's how Zodiac works, he thought. I communicate my instructions to Taurus, and she passes them on to the other dogs.

The other trainers were simply that: trainers; Taurus did the rest. She was the hub of the emotional wheel, the leader of the pack. No matter if the response were purely imitative, or if a true empathy existed among the twelve shepherds—she was the catalyst for the unit. The leader. Without her, his dogs were rabble, as a crowd without a leader was a mob.

He gripped the animal's head and held it close, thanking her for the lesson he had just been taught. Shutting his eyes, he saw a beach studded with Nazi skulls, like the icons of Easter Island, and beyond it, a homeland. He would be the catalyst that made the seemingly impossible happen; he would leave a legacy for Miriam and Solomon and the other Jews, one that would earn him forgiveness.

And admiration.

Chapter 35

For Sol, the close, dark confines of the *Altmark*'s hold was like a sewer inhabited by a giant, sweating, sentient amoeba made up of men's bodies. Each time a body crawled to the open 55-gallon drum that passed as a toilet, the amoeba changed shape. When the hatchway's circular handle spun and the door creaked open on its huge hinges, it tensed with fear. When the opened door meant only that it was time for those nearest the door to transport the sacks of drum slops up the ladder or bring down jerry cans of soup, water, and bread, the mass breathed a sigh of relief.

As with the other sewer, the darkness destroyed any accurate sense of time. Try by whatever ingenious methods they invented, the inmates could not gauge how much time elapsed between each opening of the hatch, nor was there any pattern to when the jerry cans could be acquired.

Not knowing, the inmates invented fictions and served them up in the darkness like succulent dinners. Those who had gone up to dump the slops overboard or to pick up the cans from the kitchen reported sighting cliffs through the fog or the sun setting starboard. This led to speculation and story-telling, both of which helped pass the time. Once, a man returned to report that the ladder had thirty-nine steps, as in the American spy film. Even those who had seen the film listened like eager children to its retelling.

To all this Solomon made no contribution, not because he was miserable but because he preferred to spend the time in introspection. Avoiding thoughts of the present or future for fear of sinking into despair, he re-examined the fragments of his past, with the thought that nothing happened without purpose. First he concentrated on language: Jacob Freund's homespun philosophy, Beadle Cohen's scholarship, Walther Rathenau's eloquence.

Then, knees drawn up and eyes closed, he let himself drift into happy familial memories. His father behind the cigar counter. *Mutti* and Recha after a recital, taking down the Passover dishes. Miriam waltzing with him, holding him, kissing his eyelids.

When he slept, his unconscious extrapolated from his memories. His dreams were, for the most part, such as all men dreamed. He took pleasure in their substance, finding even the occasional nightmare tolerable because it was based in a reality he could track down and understand. He began to experiment, deliberately turning his thoughts to events in his past and challenging his mind to make of them whatever interesting dream-fiction it could.

To a small degree, he succeeded.

Once, having dredged up what facts and memories he recalled about the Berlin zoo, he dreamed of taking Miriam there. His muse created pastel images worthy of Watteau or Renoir. She in ruffles and lace on a warm, hazy day; he in flannel trousers, his straw hat set at a carefully careless angle. Arm-in-arm, they strolled between the cages. Lilacs were in bloom. He plucked a white sprig and tucked it in her chignon.

"*Wenn der weisse Flieder, wieder blüht,*" she whispered.

Hoping to repeat the dream, the next time he was ready to sleep he again dipped into his memories of the zoo. This time his muse placed her next to the monkey section. She wore a drab brown raincoat. The sky was slate-gray. A lemur similar to the one he had seen at the zoo as a boy pushed its long ebony arm through its cage bars and, screeching "*Indri! Indri!*, Behold!" dug its nails into the side of Miriam's neck.

Sol awakened to a pounding headache and to cobalt-blue light. Trying to ward off a vision so close after a nightmare, he pressed his palms against his temples, but succeeded only in increasing the ferocity of the pain in his head——

——*a girl of about eight fights against thin ropes that bind her, naked, to a carved wooden post almost twice her height.* She runs her fingers along its chipped designs.

Perhaps thirty other intricately carved posts are grouped behind her, each topped with the skull of an ox. In the background, beyond a flickering fire, stand monoliths and menhirs that evoke Stonehenge.

"This is no dream." The voice comes from the girl, but her lips do not move. "Your father is gone and you stand in *aloala*, the shadow of death. This *valavato* was built by the Antakarana as a dwelling for restless souls whom they sought to honor and console with sacrifices."

"*Human* sacrifices, Jehuda?" This time the girl's lips move, the voice frightened, girlish...hers. "Are you to be my *alo* when the Nazis sacrifice me to their god? Are you to mediate between my family and my ancestors?"

"You have no family left and they have no god but Hitler." Tough, older, masculine, the voice comes from somewhere inside her.

"Father said the Antakarana believe in Zanahary, the Creator, and in Andiamanitra, the Fragrant One," she tells the voice.

"The Antakarana are gone; dog-men now own the *valavato*."

"Does that mean that I am not to be sacrificed?"

"It means I believe you will be given a choice between torture or staying alive in the dog-men's service. You will need all the strength and hope you can gather, Deborah."

"*You* chose life!" the girl shouts. "*You* chose to survive no matter what the cost to your soul—or to mine!"

"To choose survival was a sin only because I did so out of fear," the inner voice answers.

"Will you help me overcome my fear, Jehuda?"

Laughter floats among the stones. "I cannot help you," the voice answers. "This is the time for your gift to me."

The girl strains at the ropes. "Help me!" she calls. "I'm over here!"

Here, her voice echoes against the stones. *Here*——

Solomon awoke to tumbling sensations. He did not know the girl or understand the vision, but from Bruqah's lessons he recognized the totems, fashioned to celebrate the death of an island nobleman, someone whose social standing also warranted the water buffalo horns that guarded the burial area.

"Madagascar." He let the word roll from his mouth. It echoed behind his residual headache like the obscure music of a calliope. *Mad-a-gas-car.* He said it again, louder; it seemed to hang in the darkness like a banner.

"Why a homeland there?" someone asked.

"Why not?"

True to tradition, Solomon answered the question with a question. There was laughter in recognition of the rhetoric.

As silence resettled, Solomon could sense each man mull the word, allowing it to absorb strength and texture, like moist terra cotta under the touch of a blind child.

"Madagascar," someone said.

Leaning against the hold's metal wall, Sol relaxed into the familiarity of his old haunting-ground, darkness, and took comfort in it. Like the Jews after their Babylonian exile, like Moses' followers, the prisoners must come to terms with another Diaspora, he thought. Like those other times, the end was in God's hands, but daily survival was in their own. Meanwhile, he was ready, at last, to think of the present—about Erich; and Misha, now Otto Hempel's cabin boy; and Miriam. At the farmhouse, Colonel Perón had told him she was well. And pregnant.

Whose child! he had wanted to ask. Mine or Erich's? Instead he chided himself. *Why should it matter?* "At Sachsenhausen there are more learned men than I," he had said to Perón. "Ones far more deserving of being given a second chance at life."

"Thank Miriam's obsession with getting you out. She talked me into engineering this. You may not be able to thank her in person until you arrive in Madagascar—"

"Miriam is going?"

"Miriam and Erich. But how could you have known? Your old friend is in charge of the expedition."

Later, Bruqah also brought word of her; they had even managed to exchange a few notes, cryptic and hopeful—

A man across the hold shouted in his sleep. What kinds of nightmares, Sol wondered, haunted him? Did he dream of people he would never see again, and times he would never relive? Did Miriam? How he longed to hold her—

Patience, he told himself. You are alive, she is alive, and you are headed in the same direction. The rest is up to God, *mazel,* and our inventiveness.

To calm himself he let his mind roam over his lessons in the Kabbalah. How happy the times had been when he and Beadle Cohen explored the cosmos and the eternal!

"*Nothing* is random," the beadle had told him. "Before the beginning of time, when light had not erupted from its shell and our universe was miniscule, then—*then!*—chance ruled the cosmos. And God was that universe. *Everything,* opposite of nothing, is not random, and *everything* is now the universe. Therefore, the cosmos as we know it is no longer miniscule—and this cosmos is also God."

The discussion had ended there, only to be taken up again a week later, when Sol had had a chance to try to understand what the beadle was saying:

"We are the mind of God or, more exactly, a single thought in the mind of God. The universe will continue to expand while this thought continues, and when the thought dwindles and dies, the universe will again contract to that tiny *nothingness,* and randomness will again prevail. The process of the beginning, expansion, and death of the cosmos may take a hundred billion years, yet all that time is but one thought in the mind of God."

"So *everything* is God," Sol remembered saying. "Everything, and nothing."

Many Gentiles, the beadle explained, limited God through their belief that man existed in His image. Jews conceded only that the soul of man might exist in God's image. Still, he said, there was a time when man was one with God, and true ecstasy lay in knowing that we contained in our hearts a microscopic memory of that unity.

Sol thought about that now, as he had then. It led, as always, to a re-examination of *ayin.*

According to the beadle, God directed *everything,* while *nothing* by definition could not be directed—there was nothing to direct. Humankind was the mind of God or, more exactly, an anomaly in the mind of God. God was the universe, which meant the universe was itself sentient. When He ceased to think that thought, the universe would contract and, at least as we knew it, cease to exist.

The correlation excited Sol as much now as it had the first time he had come to that conclusion. He felt a need to talk. Since he could not expect the others to be interested in the complexities of chaos versus order, he spoke to them of his meeting with Walther Rathenau and of how he had walked with pride in the Foreign Minister's shadow. He spoke of the Adlon, and of the assassination. Later, urged on by the others, he warmed to other tales: lunch in Luna Park, the morning Recha tried a cigar, the smell of potato pancakes, evenings on an astrakhan rug strewn with tinsel and pine needles. At first, he spoke only of Berlin and of his own experiences, but increasingly he found himself digressing into the Talmud and the Kabbalah. The more he talked, the more his voice, whose timbre had so embarrassed him in his teens, took on a power that enthralled his listeners, and the more he found he could comfort the others with his rich images.

"What does it really mean, this Madagascar business?" a voice asked, after Sol had finished repeating a Talmudic parable about a wanderer who had to learn to obey the unfamiliar laws of a strange land into which he had stumbled.

"I don't know. Perhaps a chance at freedom?"

"How will we break free of our Nazi captors?" another asked.

"Only God and fear are masters of men," Sol said with as much conviction as he could muster.

"We have no chance against their guns or their dogs."

"Chance is random, as at some points in time the universe is," Sol said, hoping his listeners would at least recognize the concept. "Unity must be our weapon. Only therein lies hope."

When no one responded, he felt lonely, set apart, as if his academic skills were somehow less valuable or manly than their physical ones. Few of the others were educated men, as if Hempel or Erich Alois, or whoever had done the selecting, had deliberately ignored other men of scholarship. He alone among them had attended a university. Each possessed specialized training of some sort, but their thoughts and responses were couched within the confines of job skills and religion rather than academe. They could all read and write, Sol thought proudly—surely no other culture could boast of such universal literacy—but the Nazis had obviously decided they had little need for men of gown and mortarboard. Or perhaps the Nazis were as afraid of scholarship, and other Jewish assets and abilities, as they were respectful and fearful of the mantic arts.

If Hitler were not a maniac, Sol reasoned, he was either stupid or possessed by his own dybbuk, in whom was vested the conscience of past German guilt...a guilt deepened by the terror and shame of the Great War. The Führer could own the world if he chose to ransom those Jewish assets and abilities, use them to his own ends, use such men and women as those who inhabited visions.

"Please, *Reb,*" the man next to Sol whispered insistently. "Give me your blessing."

"I am not a rabbi," Sol said.

"You speak like a rabbi, and you have chosen to be our teacher. Are not all rabbis teachers?"

"Yes. But not all teachers are rabbis," Sol answered.

"Bless me, Reb," the man repeated.

Sol placed his hands over the man's head, and in his heart he felt the sadness of the man's soul. Though he told himself that such intimate knowledge came out of comradeship, he knew better. In some part of his being, he had always known better.

"I am Goldman," the man said. "Pray for me. Teach me. Teach all of us."

During the voyage, Solomon had resisted names and identities; he had wanted no more attachments like Hans Hannes and Misha Czisça—one dead, the other...

"I will tell you all what the beadle taught me." He lifted his voice. "More than that, I cannot do."

The lessons began in earnest. Mostly they dealt with emotional and spiritual survival. The voice and confidence of the teacher in him surfaced; passages and parables filtered through and began to flow. The world of action, the world of human existence, had two parts, he explained: the physical, where natural law and material things prevailed; and the spiritual world of ideas and ideals.

In language reduced to its simplest form, he described the existence of the world of angels, the world of formation or feeling according to the Zohar. The human soul, living as it did in the world of action, was multi-sided, capable of distinguishing between good and evil and equally capable of failure and backsliding. In contrast, the angel was unchanging, its existence fixed within the qualitative limits it had been granted upon its creation.

"Then an angel has no chance at self-betterment," someone said.

"That's right," Sol answered, pleased with his student. "On the other hand, humankind can better the angels."

Sensing that he was on the verge of passing on the beginnings of understanding, he continued with growing fervor. "We are the fathers and mothers, and midwives of the angels. Each sacred act we perform, each spiritual transformation we create, is part of an angelic essence." He let that settle in. "The angels we create must live in our world, the world of action, but they can influence the higher worlds, especially that of formation. In that manner, we can reach out for the Divine and, in a sense, direct it."

He paused to feel the effect of his words.

"I have heard that angels sometimes come down from the higher realms," a pleasant voice said from across the hold. "Also that a prophet or seer or holy man, sometimes even an ordinary person, can be visited by angels from the higher worlds."

"So it is said," Sol replied.

"Then I think you must have received such a visitor."

Whispered assent became clearly voiced approval and, finally, applause. Sol received the accolades in shocked silence. Was it possible? Had the visions from which he had tried so hard to divorce himself not been ones of evil, but rather keys to a higher kingdom beyond his understanding or interpretation?

"I—" he began, knowing a response was expected.

From far to his left came the clanking of metal. Light leapt into the room as the hatchway was thrown open by two guards with carbines at ready arms.

Lifting his hands to shield himself from the glare, Sol waited for his eyes to make the adjustment. At the bottom of the ladder well, crammed into the small space, were forms he assumed to be other guards.

"If they try to harm us, we must fight—with bare hands, if necessary," someone whispered.

"No more hells like Sachsenhausen," another answered.

A tall figure shouldered its way between the guards and blocked the opening. The amoeba tensed.

"Topside!" Otto Hempel bellowed. "Everyone!"

Wondering what new torture had been devised for them, Solomon followed the others up the ladder. The shock of emerging into the brilliance of a red-orange sun sent him reeling. His body felt weaker after disuse than it ever had during the arduousness of camp life, and the sun, glaring at him like the eye of flame at the end of a black tunnel, blinded him completely. Panicked, he shut his eyes and tried breathing deeply of the salty air. He choked on the humidity and opened his eyes.

His peripheral vision offered nothing.

By looking straight ahead, he was able to distinguish shapes. At first they were surrounded by bright haloes that dulled any detail he might otherwise have made out. As the auras dissipated, he grew more frightened. Those objects and colors he could see were etched almost too clearly. The gray of the ship, the whites and browns of the Nazis' uniforms, the compressed emotion glowering in the officers' eyes. They took on the clarity of a still-life seen through a keyhole.

His eyes had become a camera lens, able to see only the point of immediate focus; his vision was confined to a small circle. Beyond that, everything was black.

Just because I have eye problems is no reason to assume my eyesight has deteriorated permanently, Sol told himself, trying to arrest his panic. *More* than likely, all the others confined to the hold were having similar problems adjusting to the bright light.

Holding onto the shoulders of the man in front of him, he raised himself onto the balls of his feet and squinted at the horizon. The freighter was outside a small bay. He could make out land of some sort, a gently sloping brown breast spotted with greenery and with shapes that were either buildings or huge rocks. He tried to visualize the map of Africa he had studied briefly at school and again at the farmhouse. There were two fairly major ports of call for ships en route to the Cape of Good Hope: Walvis Bay, a British enclave, and Lüderitz, a German port of call. Both were in South West Africa.

He concentrated on the gathering assemblage of Nazi guards and sailors. The sailors stood to his right; the guards, some with dogs heeled at their sides, stood at attention at the rail in front of the contingent of Jews.

"Heil Hitler!"

Hempel's voice. As everyone responded, Sol turned his head to place the scene more in the center of the tube of his vision. The pederast stood on the bridge, to Erich's right. Ascending the flight of steps that led to the bridge was a spry, bearded naval captain. Once on the bridge, he began to speak.

"Two days ago we received a wireless message from the Seekriegsführung." He held up a sheaf of papers. "It seems the Führer has given orders to the Wehrmacht to repel the Polish aggressors. As a result, we have changed course to avoid official shipping lanes and to prepare for a call to duty."

He cleared his throat and stood with stiff military bearing, eyeing his crew. After a theatrical pause, he went on speaking slowly and deliberately, hammering home each word.

"This morning, September 2, 1939, will be remembered in history as the day England and France declared war on the German Reich—a decision they shall come to regret."

Again he paused. "Now, let me acquaint you with the primary task the Führer has allocated to the *Altmark*."

So this was it, Sol thought. War—and a homeland for the Jews in Madagascar. Now all that was left to confirm the accuracy of his visions was for the Führer to hold a place in the homeland hostage against the use of Jewish assets and abilities to help him win the war.

Chapter 36

"Though we shall not have the privilege of entering actively into the fight," the captain continued, "the task the Führer has selected for us is indispensable, and we should feel honored. We are to act as the floating supply base for a German battleship destined to turn these seas into a graveyard for the enemy."

Standing rigidly, Erich felt rather than saw Hempel move up behind him. "The crates Fräulein Riefenstahl filmed for the witless Red Cross?" Hempel whispered sarcastically, "Did you really believe they contained farming equipment? The Führer would never waste cargo space on Jews! The supplies are for the battleship *Graf Spee.* Hear me? The *Spee!*" Then he added, "Except for my Storch, Herr Oberst. The plane's in the hold, all right, disassembled and waiting, but only *for me.*"

In angry panic Erich clenched his fists at his sides but did not turn around. Hempel, the subordinate officer, made privy to top secret information, while he, in charge of the land operation, was told almost nothing! He had been biding his time, waiting for an opportunity to confront Hempel about the "death certificate." He would have to wait a little longer.

"And as for you scum!" Glaring, Dau pointed down at the Jews. "I would love an excuse to throw you all overboard!"

"The Führer might not like that!" one of the Jews called out.

Hands dexterously sliding along the rail to support his weight, Hempel flew down the stairs and bounded across the deck. Even without the added momentum he was a force to be reckoned with; his fist connected with the closest Jewish jaw, and the man crumpled.

Grinning, Pleshdimer separated himself from the other guards. Hempel nodded; the Kapo lifted the inmate and pitched him overboard.

The cold water of the Atlantic brought the man around, and he screaming for help.

"For God's sake, have someone throw him a line!" Perón said huskily, beside Erich.

Erich fought the urge to give the order. Pleshdimer stood between the men and the rail, a serene smile on his lips, and Erich was sure the Kapo would kill anyone who obeyed, regardless of the consequences. Life had no meaning for him. Murdered his whole family, someone had said, and hung them up like sausages.

Are you any better, standing here, Herr Oberst? he asked himself.

When we reach Mangabéy, he thought, I will be in charge. Then I will do something about the guards' sadism...and about Otto Hempel. There would be no punishment without a trial in *his* homeland. No more deceit.

He searched for Solomon, but was unable to distinguish him in the press of inmates huddled together in shock. His gaze swept Bruqah's and the sailors' faces, some of which were white as their starched uniforms. Not murderers either, yet they too did nothing. He was thankful that he had confined Miriam to their cabin, telling her that Dau did not want her on deck during muster, but in reality not wanting to risk her seeing Solomon. At least she was not witness to everyone's moral inertia.

The Kapo grinned, showing his teeth, then spat into his hands, wiped them on his pants, and returned to the ranks.

In the water, the prisoner was still screaming.

Leni Riefenstahl signaled for her crew to stop filming, and stepped toward the bridge. "Someone do something," she said. "Your little melodrama bores me."

Otto Hempel walked casually to the rail, drew his revolver, and fired two shots into the sea. The man in the water went silent.

Dau turned toward Perón. "I apologize for this disturbance, but as military attaché in the embassy of our Italian friends, you must surely understand the value of discipline."

Lifting the megaphone, the captain again addressed the men. "We are outside the port of Lüderitz. We will wait here for the *Graf Spee* to arrive. Captain Langdorff and the rest of the *Spee* officers may wish to inspect our ship. Should that occur, Fräulein Riefenstahl will film the event. It is therefore imperative that the *Altmark* be clean."

His glance sought out Hempel's. "Proceed."

The major snapped heels together and saluted. "Shower detail!"

Erich noticed Leni gesture to her crew to stop filming as four barefoot sailors in rolled-up pants and striped undershirts stepped from the shadows beneath the bridge. Each held a fire-hose nozzle.

"Jews strip! Everyone else out of the way!" Dau commanded.

Once the Jews were isolated, valve wheels squealed, and water roared at them from the twisting hoses. Arms flailing, they fell before the onslaught; water tore at skin, splashing off it into the sunlight and creating a rainbow water-dance that lasted until they all lay on the deck in a tangled heap of arms and legs.

"Shut off the water! Free laborers, on your feet!"

Soon, very soon, Erich promised himself, he would teach Dau and Hempel that "free laborer" did not describe slaves but rather men who labored in freedom for their own good and that of their community.

"Jews—to the windlass room for shaving! Head and groin!" Dau boomed through the megaphone. "There will be no lice aboard my ship. You will return with buckets, brooms, and rags. Every centimeter of this ship will shine…and if so much as a rivet is ruined, the sharks will feed on that saboteur's hands. Heil Hitler!"

"SIEG HEIL! SIEG HEIL! SIEG HEIL!"

Chapter 37

Erich looked tanned, vigorous...young, Solomon thought, looking down as his own nakedness as he stood in line waiting to be shaved. The surge of hope that touched him in the hold was gone, a delusion of the darkness. Being thrown overboard seemed suddenly not so terrible a fate.

"Next!"

Sol stepped forward and stood at attention. The ship's doctor had selected three Jews with barbering experience to do the shaving. Sol stared straight ahead and tried not to think about the man on the stool who lathered Sol's groin, turned the penis to the left and right, scraped the razor along the skin.

The doctor looked up from his clipboard and extended a hand toward Sol. "Tyrolt," the doctor said, introducing himself. "You must be the linguist I've heard about."

Shocked, unused to courtesy unless it preceded a beating, Sol hesitated. Dare he respond? Dare he *not* respond? "Freund. Solomon Freund," he said finally, purposely not saying his camp number and trying to forget the man working at his groin as he shook the doctor's hand.

"Relax. And—don't worry. They cannot force me to cut off your family jewels." Tyrolt put a gentle hand on the barber's shoulder, and smiled at Solomon. "Freund? *Friend.* Perhaps we will be. Friends, I mean."

"I am a Jew," Sol said simply.

"And I am a doctor." Tyrolt checked his list again. "Says here you are to go back to the hold while the rest of your friends swab the ship." He looked at Solomon carefully. "Is there a reason for such preferential treatment?"

"I was not aware I had been singled out, *Medizinalrat.*"

"Tyrolt will do nicely, thank you. Is that clear?" The doctor's warm smile belied the arch to his voice.

"Yes, Herr...Tyrolt."

"Others may command this ship and its cargo but I am in charge of the health of those aboard. You need exercise and sunshine and air. Is that understood?" Before Solomon could open his mouth to reply, the doctor added, "You will report to the galley. Tell one of the cooks that I said you are to be given duty outside."

He patted Solomon on the shoulder, then moved down along the line of Jews, talking quietly, offering encouragement and checking eyes, ears, and teeth, and leaving Solomon to wonder if the doctor truly possessed compassion or was merely deranged.

An hour later, about to hoist the last of five huge garbage cans onto his shoulder to dump it aft, he was still considering Tyrolt's response. The doctor should be warned that his aberration was dangerous, Sol thought, scooping congealed grease from the bottom of the fourth can. Removing the thick elastic cord that secured the lid, he sloughed off the grease into the fifth can, the last one he would have to dump, after which he must shine all five with steel wool. Not that he minded; the labor was satisfying after the confines of the hold.

Potato peelings lay atop sodden newspaper. Sol watched a seagull hovering overhead; gourmet dining really was in the eye, or stomach, of the beholder. Then a sound like the whimpering of a puppy drew him to his knees. He squinted into a small metal alcove behind the cans, where oily rags and other flammables were kept until disposal, and made out a small figure pressed into a foetal ball.

"Herr Freund."

"Misha! What on earth!"

"Help me, Herr Freund! Throw me overboard! I tried to jump, but I got scared. The sea looks so deep. But I can't go back in there. To him. I...*can't!*"

He began to sob, dangerously loudly.

"Hush, Mishele. Let me think."

Heart aching for the child, Sol stared across the sea, to the coastline. *Could it be possible?* A can containing the boy might drift that far, or maybe Misha could float part way, then climb out and swim. Sol lifted the lid of the can and, filled with desperate hope, buried his arms elbow-deep into peelings and newspapers and grease. There was enough cushion there to protect the boy—

He stopped dreaming. The sea was deceptive. What looked like a couple of kilometers was likely to be twenty or more. Even if he could figure out the tide, the currents might carry the boy further out to sea instead of toward shore.

"Action Stations!" a voice crackled from loudspeakers.

Sol shoved Misha back into the darkness. "Stay down!"

Activity aboard the *Altmark* turned feverish. Naval officers ran to and from the bridge, ordering seamen to carry or collect various items. Two sailors climbed aboard from their painter's platform against the hull, where they had been busy changing *Altmark* to *Sogne*.

"Ship ahoy!" said the loudspeaker. "Smoke north-northwest!"

Solomon clung to his garbage can, using his body to shield Misha from sight, as seamen rushed to the rail, bumping past him. Officers sprinted to the bridge.

The engines thrummed and shuddered; exhaust from flues filled the air with diesel stench as the *Sogne* retreated, charging and lifting, blinding sparklers of sunlight dancing across the waves.

"If it's a British cruiser those Beefeaters will sink us sure if they find out what's in our holds," one sailor told another as he loaded his carbine and checked the safety.

"We should be arming the Jews," his companion said. "It's their goddamn war, after all."

"They would turn against us in a minute."

The flag of Norway was run up. Solomon peered toward the horizon in the hope of seeing the pursuing vessel. He could make out a column of smoke. A warship, silhouetted by the sun.

If the ship following them were British, would the English rescue them? Beneath their airs and dress of tolerance, were they or any other race less prejudiced than the Germans?

How long could he and Misha hang onto the can and tread water if the captain threw the prisoners into the sea?

A light from the silhouetted ship blinked rhythmically.

"Morse code," a sailor said. "Gustav...Sophie."

"Gustav Sophie!" the loudspeaker screeched.

The officers on the bridge began to applaud, and understanding dawned on the enlisted men. Jumping up and down, cheering, they watched their signalman blink back confirmation. Some of them rushed inside the ship's superstructure and emerged with cameras.

Gustav Sophie. The *Graf Spee!*

The pocket battleship approached with amazing speed. Sol could see it clearly in the center of his tunnel vision. Slashes of gray and green camouflaged its upperworks and turrets and false bow wave; its gun tower was massive and, above the bridge, the war mast stood bulked like an automaton. Beyond the powerful superstructure stood a crane, and above the funnel a catapult. Doubtless beneath the tarps lay a reconnaissance seaplane, which the crane could pluck from the water after a mission.

The *Sogne*'s boats were lowered in a series of splashes. Metal clattered, and sailors swung down with the agility of gymnasts to wait as cargo cable and the head of a six-inch oil line were snaked down. The first boat, carrying Erich, took off toward the *Spee*.

Feeling relatively safe from scrutiny, Sol moved the cans aside and stooped to see Misha. "I can't do it, Mishele. I...just can't." He struggled to keep his voice from cracking with hurt. "It's too dangerous. Right around the corner is a door that leads inside. I'll tell you when it's safe to go back."

Misha looked up at him, eyes brimming with tears. "Kill me, Herr Freund. Kill me and *then* throw me overboard."

"Hush now," Sol whispered, thankful that he had heard voices directly above him and had to stop talking. He looked up. Dau stood on the bridge, watching Perón and Bruqah, Miriam between them, walk toward Solomon. She had one arm resting on the sleeve of Perón's green uniform, the other holding the Malagasy's cloth-draped arm as he moved along using his constant companion, his carved lily-wood walking stick. She wore a crisp white seersucker dress and a floppy matching sunhat, and was chatting as amiably as a Tiergarten stroller.

How beautiful she was, despite the swollen belly that had transformed her balls-of-the-feet dancer's walk into the slightly awkward one typical of pregnancy, Sol thought. His heart did a schoolboy somersault.

As if she had heard it, Miriam stopped walking. Tilting her head at a coquettish angle, she laughed sweetly, lifted the edge of her hat, and observed the man dumping slops.

Chapter 38

Calling upon every last reserve of inner strength she could garner, Miriam avoided Sol's gaze. If she looked into his eyes, she would have to embrace him, and she dared not do that. Not now, not here...no matter how long she had waited.

"Oh, Domingo, Bruqah, look," she said. They would surely know that her performance was directed at Dau, she thought, glancing quickly up at the silver-haired man on the bridge. "A Jew doing an honest day's work! How amusing! I'm going to talk to him."

She moved forward and touched Sol's shoulder. He jerked away and slammed the can-lid shut.

"Tsk! Testy aren't we," she said, giving a bravura performance.

"Let the man be." Perón distanced himself from her as if to show his disapproval, and raised his voice. "Have you not punished him enough?" Bruqah looked at her, nodded as if to tell her he understood, and left.

"You are so rigid sometimes, Domingo." She pouted, holding onto the rail. "Do I know you, Jew? Tell me your number!"

"My camp number, Frau—?"

"I would hardly be asking for your telephone number!"

"Come along, please. This is foolishness," Perón said.

She glowered at him darkly and, ignoring his admonition, opened and raised the camera that hung by a cord from her gloved wrist. "Let me get his picture. His head reminds me of a doll I played barbershop with as a child." Finger on the camera's button, she looked straight at Solomon. "Say your number!"

"Three seven seven zero four."

Midway through the number, she snapped the picture, then looked down at his forearm. 37704. "Looks like *Hölle*—Hell—upside-down." She laughed delightedly. "Someone must have singled you out for special treatment! I must inform my husband that there is a Jew named 'Hell' on board. It will amuse him. Tell me, did you request that number?"

"Request?" He laughed bitterly. "The number belonged to the last prisoner who—who passed away before I entered the camp."

"A special number," she said. "You must be a special person."

"I am a Jew."

"Nothing else?"

"Nothing important."

Perón tugged gently at Miriam's elbow. "They are waiting for me on the *Spee*. Allow me to escort you to your cabin."

"I am quite able to find my own way back," she said arrogantly. "I may look like an elephant, but I do not need a trainer. I have been cooped up there long enough."

He opened his mouth as if to protest, but she cut him short. "I can assure you, I'll not fall overboard," she said, her voice rising, "though perhaps I'll amuse myself by having this *special* prisoner thrown to the fishes."

After trying a final time to convince her, Perón gave in. She rewarded him with a smile and a "Heil Hitler!" He looked up at Hempel. "Ready to escort me, Captain?" he called out.

"Right away," Dau answered, and disappeared off the bridge.

Perón went on his way, stopping only once to look back.

"Forgive me. It was necessary," Miriam said under her breath. "Are you well, Solomon? You look terrible. Oh God, I've waited so long for this moment, and now I don't know what to say except that you must trust me and you must live. You must!"

"That sounds like one of Erich's ultimatums." His voice sounded flat. "I too have waited, Miriam. And for what? This?"

"I have kept you alive, Solomon. It wasn't easy for me, either. You're aboard this ship because of me."

"I know."

"I have not betrayed you, Solomon," she said quietly.

"The child—"

She clutched his wrist. "We have very little time. The charade Perón and I played out is worth a few minutes, no more. Once we reach Madagascar, we'll find a way—"

"We?" Solomon looked at her belly. "You, me, and the child? And Erich? Whose child is it, Miri?"

Her eyes held his for a long time before she looked down. When she finally spoke, the words sounded empty—rehearsed—even to her. "You were the one who told me to go to Erich. I am his, at least for now." She gripped his wrist more tightly. "I have to go."

She glanced around anxiously, then kissed her fingertips and touched them to his lips. "I thought I heard Hempel's voice." She looked terrified. "The man's an animal. The way he treats Misha..." Her tears broke and flowed freely. "The boy is being brutalized, Solomon. When he wakes up, when he lies down, in the shower, with the dog sometimes." She tried not to sob, but could not help herself. She pulled a handkerchief from her sleeve. "He begged me to throw him into the sea, and let it swallow him."

Solomon straightened up and took a deep breath. "Hempel's been abusing him a long time."

"What can I do to help him!"

"Probably nothing."

The sound of a motor broke the stillness. Miriam looked down to see a boat crossing from the *Spee*. It was carrying Erich and several other officers. "I must go before Erich sees me," she said. "He claims you're dead. Maybe he even thinks so himself. It's all so terribly complicated! That day they took you away, I thought my world had ended." She stopped. "A few days before we sailed, Erich showed me a death certificate. God knows where he got it, but his grief seemed genuine, Sol, it truly did. If it hadn't been for Domingo to set me straight..."

"He knows," Sol said quietly. "He knows I'm alive. The day we sailed, he saw me coming on board, carrying the Torah. We spoke."

And he never said a word to me, Miriam thought. Erich's lies suddenly took on a new dimension that made her head swim. He thought she believed that Solomon was dead, and he was going to leave it that way. What did he intend to do, she wondered, throw Sol overboard before they reached Madagascar? Have him quietly murdered? Or had he simply not been able to face me with the news?

"I don't understand. Why hasn't he told you! What difference would it make?" Sol asked.

"None, I suppose," she said softly. "Or maybe it would. Maybe it would make all the difference in the world."

Chapter 39

Much as Erich had longed for the feel of solid ground beneath his feet, his return to terra firma was less than satisfying. It had taken him several days to find his sea legs; now, to everyone's amusement except his own, he swayed like an old sea dog.

More disappointing still was the fact that Lüderitz was little more than a village. The town, whose sands he had imagined littered with diamonds, was cloudy with copper dust that turned the faces around him into golden-red masks and lined his scalp with grit.

It did, however, have a bar. There, surrounded by bullflies and curious Negroes in rags and peppercorn hair, he, Perón, and Leni listened to Bruqah talk about Lüderitz—and about Africans.

"Is it always so hot?" Erich batted at an insect on his neck.

"This the cool season, Herr Oberst." Bruqah downed a warm beer shandy in three gulps and raised his walking stick for another. "You think it is bad here? Wait for Madagascar!" He grinned. "The rain pour, you pray for sun. Humidity she come, you pray for rain." He laughed and gulped the beer.

Not only was the heat oppressive, Erich thought, but there were such a *lot* of Blacks! They made him uneasy. Compared to them, Bruqah looked brown, almost bronze. He was glad he was packing his Walther, gladder yet he had not allowed Miriam to come along.

In contrast to Perón and himself, Leni looked annoyingly fresh, as young as she had more than ten years ago in her mountaineering-movie phase. He had seen her in *The White Hell of Pitz Palu,* among others, and had found her far more attractive than the mountains, the real subjects of the film. When the mountaineers had conquered peaks, he had imagined himself conquering Leni...just as he had promised himself he would do with Miriam Rathenau.

So far he had not done too well on either count.

"When I live here, natives they call me Tsama-Melon." Bruqah cupped a hand on each side of his mouth. "'Hey Tsama, hey you come help me plant!' they call. In Madagascar I plant travelers' trees. They always have water for thirsty people. Because of that, they call me Tsama. These people here are Herrero, mostly. The Bushmen, they live beyond the sandveld. Nine maybe ten month they go without water." His lips were chapped from the days out at sea. When he grinned, blood showed in the cracks. "Only tsama melon juice, is all." He indicated with forefinger and thumb. "So life, she is precious to Bushmen. Precious, like *this*." He poured a drop of beer onto his hand, and held it out.

A tall, sinewy-muscled Black who had been staring at Erich put a hand on Bruqah's shoulder. Bending, he whispered in the Malagasy's ear. Bruqah nodded, and the man stepped back.

Erich feigned disinterest.

"What did *he* want?" Perón asked irritably, but quietly.

Bruqah leaned across the table toward Erich. "I tell you, Herr Oberst, if you promise you don't go fly off the stove." Apparently not expecting Erich to answer, Bruqah said, "This man and the others...they want to see your hand."

"It's none of their goddamn business." Erich spoke without emotion. As was his habit, he held his right hand over his left.

"They think your hand is magic."

Erich moved both hands off the table without revealing his dead fingers and unsnapped the holster strap of his pistol. Fear and anger displaced curiosity in the faces around him.

Leni touched his forearm. "They mean no harm." She flashed him a look that said, *Stay calm. For me.*

He slid his left hand beneath his leg and snapped his right fingers for another beer. Another infantile female contradiction, he thought. She would be more impressed if he controlled himself than if he sent the bunch of them hurrying outside so there could be some peace and privacy inside. Women relied on men for protection, then condemned them for taking a stand against a possible threat.

The Blacks drew together. Some were murmuring. Suddenly, everyone was quiet. Erich followed the tallest one's gaze outside.

A bare-breasted woman with enormous buttocks came padding down the dirt street. A crowd of followers seemed to be encouraging her to do something.

Leni stood up and trained her camera on the woman, who raised her arms, heavy with bracelets, over her head.

Fingers interlocked, the woman began a slow, shuffling dance, weaving in and out of the lacy shadows of an acacia tree. A gray-haired Black threw a smoldering stick onto the ground; others added twigs and small branches...the beginnings of a fire.

Without looking away from her camera, Leni felt for her camera bag, opened it, and handed Erich various pieces of equipment. He wiped off the table with his sleeve before setting them down.

"Herreros and Bushmen don't usually dance together," Leni said with excitement.

"Here in Lüderitz, oh yes," Bruqah said. "When German people take this country, the Herreros flee into the Kalahari. Many died—no water. Five and fifty thousand out of seventy thousand. Bushmen helped many survivors. So they be friends here, now."

The crowd around the woman began to clap and sway. The woman, her head uptilted and only the whites of her eyes visible, stamped her feet against the dust. She was chanting softly. Her huge buttocks jiggled beneath her loincloth, and dust puffed around her.

"Janha Janha Jan-ha!" the crowd chanted. She snaked her hands over her breasts, neck, face. Her fingers gripped her peppercorn hair, released it, started again; breasts, neck, face, hair...

Linking arms, the crowd started moving in a circle, clockwise first, counterclockwise, clockwise...

Leni crouched as if on a battlefield, and scurried close, jabbing and feinting with the camera as she tried to snap pictures between legs.

"What's happening?" Erich attempted to follow her as she wormed her way through the growing crowd, but she was too agile. The press of spectators quickly filled up the empty space she had created. He tried to peer over everyone but couldn't see a thing. Wrinkling his nose at the Negroid stench, he pushed his way after her, his hands together like a wedge.

One Black looked down at Erich's hand and anxiously leaned away to let him by. Soon the others were nudging each other, intent on letting him through without their touching the mangled hand. About time it came in useful for something, he thought, easing his way through the crowd.

The tall, very black Herreros gave way to an inner group—tiny brown Bushmen with thick, flattened noses and small perforated gourd-rattles around their calves.

Four Bushmen, imitating young gazelles by holding *gemsbok* horns against their foreheads, jumped through the inner ring and into the center of the circle. Gyrating, they approached the woman and retreated, approached and retreated. Pelvises pulsing and shoulders rolling, they yowled and grunted and gesticulated to the moaning of the other Bushmen and the pounding hands and feet of the Herreros, who rushed from the outer edges of the crowd to the inner circle to throw imaginary spears at the dancers.

"Watubai na! Ha! Watubai na!"

Her breasts bouncing as she rolled her head, the woman in the center patted herself as if she were cooling flames breaking through her flesh. She made a nasal sound and clicked her tongue.

Leni repeated the sounds. Without taking her eyes off the woman, she motioned Erich to hurry forward.

"What is it!" Erich shouted above the noise of the dancers as he pushed his way toward her. The Bushmen were more difficult to get through despite their smaller size. His hand did not seem to trouble them.

Leni drew a word in the dust: *n/um*. "I think that's what she's saying!... The slash represents the tongue click." Her eyes shining with excitement, Leni pronounced the term, clicking her tongue in the middle of the word. "It's a fire-hot power they claim boils up from their bellies," she said as she stood up, nearly having to shout for him to hear her. "Fills their heads like steam. Helps them talk with the gods and perform healings. *Kai*-healing, it's called."

"Crazy," Perón said, having reached them.

"To you, perhaps, but not to them! Try to watch with an open mind and then tell me how crazy it is."

From the direction of the sand spit that formed Lüderitz's western end, there emerged two men carrying a ratty stretcher. On it lay a small naked boy. The crowd parted and the bearers passed between the Herreros and the inner ring of Bushmen, who threw dried crushed leaves mixed with dust onto the prostrate figure. While the Herreros continued their spear-throwing motions, the Bushmen in the middle of the circle leapt high into the air and fell on their knees, twitching and trembling and rolling their eyes upward, their chanting more rhythmic now except for the occasional wail that rose into the branches of the acacia tree like the cry of an exotic bird.

Erich edged forward to look more closely at the patient. The boy was a classic case of malnutrition: his belly distended, arms and legs thin as sticks, face so gaunt it seemed all eyes.

"*Kai!*" the woman screamed, toppling to her knees. "*Kai!*"

"*KAI* MEANS...," Leni started to yell in Erich's ear. Abruptly everyone was quiet. "...pain. Now watch."

"You appear to know a lot about them," Perón commented.

"A director can't film unless she knows *what* to film."

The woman wrapped her arms around herself and tilted toward the flames, beside which the stretcher bearers had laid down the boy. Her nose and forehead were among the embers. When she lifted her head, smoke plumed from her hair. Her face was unscathed.

"It's not possible," Erich said weakly as the woman crawled toward the boy and laid her hands gently on his cheeks. "Some kind of trick."

The stretcher was withdrawn. The woman lay beside the boy, her arms around his shoulders and his head cradled against her chest; she began groaning and wailing. Her limbs jerked uncontrollably. Four squatting male dancers surrounded her. One massaged her with dust. The second rubbed sweat from his armpits onto her body, while the third dipped into a small tortoise shell held by the fourth and rubbed herbs into her scalp.

When they stepped away, a hush came over the crowd. The circle tightened.

"She's near death," Leni whispered. "The others are trying to bring her back from the spirit world."

All of this time there had been no sign of life in the boy. Now Erich could see tears emerging from the outside corners of the child's eyes and rolling down the sides of his face.

The woman opened her eyes and raised her head. Leaning over the boy, she scraped his cheeks with her fingernails—a cat sharpening its nails against a piece of bark. She was purring softly, her trembling less violent, like a woman after lovemaking.

The boy's head moved slowly side to side. When it was stilled, his mouth opened and Erich saw something twitch inside. One of the male dancers seized it and, with a milking motion, drew it slowly from between the boy's lips.

Erich's stomach turned over as he watched a two-meter-long worm emerge from the boy's mouth.

"Tapeworm." Leni kept snapping the shutter.

"Sleight of hand!" Erich insisted.

"Believe what you want."

The four males drew knives from sheaths attached to their legs and hacked at the worm, cutting it into a hundred pieces. The crowd began to depart. Two women, one elderly and one in her late teens, lifted the boy to his feet. With their help, he walked away.

The male dancers collected the pieces of tapeworm and, crossing the street, pitched them into the harbor. One of the men returned to kick apart the small fire. Lifting a stick on which a flame continued to burn, he glanced at the woman. Her hips bucked once and she lay still, one arm crooked beneath her cheek, the other stretched out above her head. She appeared at first to be asleep; but apparently sensing the man's presence, she opened her eyes and looked up at him.

"*Hamba Gashle,*" she said.

"*Salamba Gashle,*" he answered, and wandered off, leaving her where she lay.

"What did they say to each other?" Erich asked Leni.

"*Hamba Gashle,*" Bruqah said, coming between them. "Go softly." He gave Erich a tolerant smile. "*Salamba Gashle.*" He took a swig of beer. "Return softly."

"What about the woman?" Erich asked. "Are they just going to leave her there?"

"She might as well rest there as anywhere."

Erich checked his watch. "I'd better get back to the ship pretty soon."

"Then it is time to begin our farewells. You take care of that young Frau of yours," Perón said amiably, lifting his beer bottle as though in a toast. "If you two need to get off that island, *ever*, you know what to do."

Erich settled back in the chair. The ship, and Miriam, could wait. He glanced at the line of dirt along the nape of Leni's neck and wondered why it added to her attractiveness. He wished she were going on to Madagascar now, instead of weeks, maybe months, from now. And Perón. Erich hated to see him depart, too, though he was uncertain if he genuinely liked the Argentinean or whether it was a matter of Perón being an ally in a ship filled with enemies.

Perón would accompany Leni as far as Windhoek, help her and her crew hire the native guides and rent the trucks they would need for the Kalahari, then board the train for Walvis Bay, where a Spanish freighter waited to take him to Buenos Aires.

One last beer, Erich decided, and he would call for the tender to take him back to the ship. He tipped his chair back slightly against the stucco wall. Evening was coming on quickly. The acacia's shadows lengthened, ribbing the street like the scarifications he had seen on some of the Negro faces. Cicadas began to shrill.

"The Bushmen believe the moon is hollow, and that's where their souls go when they die," Leni said, her camera pointed toward the darkening sky. "What a wonderful sense of eternity, to feel that on desert nights you can reach up and touch Heaven."

Erich glanced up. "If what I saw today was an indication of Heaven, I'd rather live in Hell." He sucked at the beer and looked at Perón. "That spectacle reminded me of Luna Park."

"What we witnessed was hardly what I would call an amusement," Leni said. She turned to Perón. "What would you call it?"

A heated discussion ensued, about Left and Right wing politics, as it inevitably did when those two got together. Not wishing to get involved, Erich shut his eyes. The cooler temperature relaxed him, and he found the sounds of the insects strangely satisfying. He thought about a girl he had kissed at Berlin's Luna Park. That same girl, a woman now and waiting in his cabin aboard ship, had grown all too quiet of late. He had almost welcomed her outburst this morning, when he told her that he would not allow her ashore.

A warm hand touched his cheek, moved down his neck, and returned to caress his forehead and massage his closed eyes.

"I'll miss you, Leni," he said softly, and kissed her palm.

She ran her fingertips over his nose and up and over his left ear. The gesture was more playful and exploring than erotic, filling him with a drowsy comfort rather than with urgency. He felt no need to open his eyes or lift his arms to embrace her. His mind slid with the ease of an otter through a wealth of memories and pleasant imaginings. He saw a white moon, large as he remembered his first wafer at Eucharist to have been, and beneath its brilliance a heavily mustached man in parka and mittens, standing with outstretched arms on a bald mountaintop. Below, as far as the eye could see, was jungle.

Benyowsky, he heard his subconscious say. He opened his eyes.

The Negress healer was huddled before him. She reached up to his chin, wiped away his sweat, licked her fingers. *"Kamadwa."*

He lurched off the chair and grabbed it to fend her off as he might a circus tiger. A camera flash flared, and for an instant he experienced red blindness. When the color cleared, he saw Leni who was frantically changing bulbs.

"Kamadwa!" The woman inched toward Erich and made a crabbing motion with her outstretched hand. *"Kamadwa mastna ha!"*

"Get away from me!"

"Calm yourself, Herr Oberst Germantownman," Bruqah said. "She wants to drink your sweat only. She says she has seen your soul." Now he looked at Erich meaningfully. "A jackal's soul, she says."

Chapter 40

The *Sogne* bellowed her position, plowing through the Cape's gray night and storming sea. A foghorn sounded as if in answer.

Jackal, Erich thought, clinging to a handle on the wall of the darkened bridge. *You're goddamn right.*

He had been drinking heavily since Lüderitz, but he had always been a heavy drinker. However, unlike his papa, the sullen-drunk, *he* could handle it. When he got tight, he became...he tried to think for a moment. *Logical.* That was it. He would sit straight as an arrow on a stool and be Goddamn Logical. He might reel when he attempted to walk, but as long as he stayed in one place he was Goddamn Logical. Some of his best thinking had come at such times.

Javelin Man, Jungle Man, Jackal Man...Goddamn Logical Man The foghorn seemed to sound it out. Fuck Hitler and Hempel and Papa and Dau. He was Goddamn Logical.

"She's closing, Sir," a seaman said as he shut the bridge's sliding door, muffling only slightly the bellowing of the foghorn and the shrieking of the wind. "Bearing south-southwest at twenty knots, as nearly as I can tell." The seaman shook the water off his listening-horn and set it down in the corner. It looked more like a megaphone than a listening device. One more thing to announce Jackal Man to the world, Erich thought.

"As nearly as you can tell?" Dau removed his pipe from his mouth and lifted a brow.

"Bearing south-southwest and twenty knots, Sir."

Dau smiled wryly, replaced the pipe, and flicked on a tiny light above the maps, which were covered with plastic and fastened down with gold screws. Sweat gleamed on his forehead. "Hold steady," he told the seaman at the helm. "We must appear to be just another freighter fighting a storm."

"Yes, Sir."

Clinging to the rail that bordered the instrument panel inside the darkened bridge, Erich looked over Dau's shoulder. The nautical maps meant little to him, but the oncoming ship, its horn increasingly loud despite the closed door, was an obvious danger. Almost certainly British. A destroyer of the *Hipper* class, the seaman had guessed.

Erich turned to stare again through the spray-washed windows at the windswept seas. I am not afraid, he assured himself. I am not drunk. I am Javelin Man. I am Jackal Man. I am Jungle Man. I am Goddamn Logical. Just seasick, is all. And...tense. It is logical to be tense in such a situation. Goddamn logical. How effective was a soldier, after all, without a little tension?

The scene outside was mesmerizing. Froth spilled across the decks with the ferocity of boarding pirates as the bow disappeared beneath the ocean. As the ship reared again, water cascaded off her sides to the dancing accompaniment of St. Elmo's Fire—balls of static electricity that glowed inside the fog and along the edges of the sea. Despite the transfer of supplies at Lüderitz, the *Sogne* remained heavy with oil and provisions for the *Graf Spee* and for the landing at Nosy Mangabéy. The weight slowed them down, yet did nothing to stabilize the ship against the storm that had the *Sogne* pitching like a canoe.

The seaman again opened the door and stuck the listening-horn outside.

"It's the Jews in the hold," Dau told Erich, having to nearly shout to be heard. "I *knew* they'd bring us ill luck. You must ready your guards to lighten the ship."

"*The Jews caused the storm?*" Erich struggled to keep from laughing. "Aren't you according them too much power?"

"Every major power that's tolerated them since the Diaspora has been destroyed."

"Coincidence."

Dau shook his head. "History's no more random than the sea."

"I understand that storms like this are common off the Cape."

"So is calm. I've stood at Agulhas..." Dau sucked thoughtfully on his unlit pipe. "The southern tip of Africa isn't the Cape of Good Hope, you know. It's Cape Agulhas." He tapped his forefinger against the map. "That's where the Indian meets the Atlantic. I have been there on calm days when there is a perfectly straight line of foam between the two oceans, all the way to the horizon. Uncanny. Makes a man believe in God."

He put his hand on the map. "Care to see where God held the world while He shaped it? Here is the imprint of His thumb." With his pipe stem Dau pointed toward where his own left thumb was, in the gap separating Java and western Australia. "Here, between Burma and India, see the index finger? And here," he indicated the Arabian Sea and the coast of Somalia, "is the impression of His other fingers." He poked Erich gently in the chest with the pipe stem, and smiled. "An old sea dog's musings."

"Instructions, Sir," the seaman asked, shutting the door.

"Maintain course." Dau turned to Erich, his face hardened. "Have the Jews shackled and brought topside, Herr Oberst."

They go overboard over my dead body, Erich thought, but instead of arguing—Goddamn Illogical to argue with an asshole like that—he went below, staggering toward the stairs that led to the maze of corridors and the hold. Slamming against the walls, he lurched up the hall and down the steps, until he found his way to the windlass room.

The trainers were there, seated cross-legged on the floor like a bunch of Indians from an American cowboy film, holding or grooming their charges. The dogs lifted their heads when Erich entered, but other than cursory glances the trainers paid him little heed.

To keep from falling down in front of them, he held onto the handrail, which ran around the room like a ballet barre, but pretended to hold it nonchalantly, as if he did not need its assistance, even in the storm. At his feet, Müller vomited into his puke bucket and went back to ministering to Aquarius, apparently not giving his own seasickness a second thought.

The atmosphere was sullen, sullen as Papa at his sherry. At first Erich could not understand why, or why they continued to ignore him. Then it came to him: all of the trainers had been there during the worst of the storm, tending to their animals. All except Krayller, of course. And him. The only dogs' cages not open were Taurus' and the wolfhound's. Maybe he *had* been drinking a little too much, thanks to that goddamn Dau, always beckoning him to the bridge. Except Dau had not called him up there this time. Or had he?

Erich couldn't quite remember.

He unlatched Taurus' door. She slowly padded out, and lay down again. He sat beside her and maneuvered her head across his lap. Borrowing a rag from Fermi, the little wire-haired trainer he had nicknamed after the Italian physicist, he removed the lid from the water bucket, dipped the rag, and began washing her. Her coat was stiff with vomit.

His own stomach clenched. He wanted desperately to throw up, and, with equal desperation, wanted not to do so in front of the men. It was the usual problem: if he opened his mind to the dog, he would feel her joy...and pain; if the dog were in pain, he had difficulty keeping his mind closed.

"The wolfhound's trainer hasn't been here?" he asked, as usual avoiding using either the man's or the dog's name. He had been forced to allow them into the unit, but he refused to *absorb* them into it. They would remain outsiders until he could rid himself of them.

"Franz comes down fairly often," one of the trainers mumbled.

"Franz? I thought the trainer was—"

"It is the corpsman," another said. "He's the only one of those bastards you can trust. Sturmbannführer Hempel's *man*," the trainer seemed to choke on the word, "hardly ever shows his face around here."

Erich looked at the wolfhound, so sick its muzzle lay in a puddle of bile, and felt like shuddering. Keep your mind closed, he told himself, remembering suddenly what had brought him down here.

He patted Taurus, who responded to the affection by attempting to lick his hand, then he stood up, this time unashamedly holding onto the rail. "Zodiac," he said.

The men continued their grooming.

"Zodiac," he repeated, with greater emphasis. One by one they looked up at him, their faces registering shock that he was serious about the command.

"*Now?*" Holten-Pflug asked, his face so white that even seasickness could not account for the pallor.

"Impossible...Sir," Fermi said. "The dogs are too sick."

Perhaps, Erich thought, he had trained his trainers too well. The need to question orders, if the dogs' welfare were at stake, had been a top priority with him, though such preaching had gone against everything he had been taught—if not everything upon which the entire German army and the very character of the country was built.

Dau's earlier words, though, overrode all other considerations: *You must ready your guards to lighten the ship. Have the Jews shackled and brought topside.*

The order, not meant to be questioned, was insanity. They were *his* goddamn Jews, and no goddamn sea captain with barnacles for brains was going to tell him what to do with them.

"Not a complete Zodiac," he told the men, backing off his original intention. "You go outside the door. I'll see if the dogs take their respective positions."

Reluctantly, the trainers patted their charges, rose to their feet, and filed out.

He would not, Erich decided, use Zodiac unless Dau pushed him to the wall regarding the Jews-overboard issue. He had no intention of obeying that order; it was merely a matter of how far he would go in disobeying it. Zodiac protected, insured him against Dau. The strategy divided a field of battle into a clock, with each of the twelve shepherds securing the position respective to its name. The wolfhound, occupying what had been Grog the affenpinscher's position was the hub, the center of the wheel.

If he thought of the ship as that wheel, the dogs could attack its various parts should Dau insist on carrying out his insane order regarding the Jews. Or, Erich decided, he could call only the bridge the wheel—appropriate, after all—and have the shepherds attach there. *If* they were not too sick to respond at all.

There was only one way he could balance the illness. He must open his mind to them. Not just to Taurus, whose lead they would follow. To all of them. Given the situation, they would need the emotional wherewithal he could provide.

He was Jackal Man. He was one of them.

He gripped the rail and opened his mind, sending out what strength he had left. The dogs resisted. Pathetic, he thought. Pathetic. Like even the best of soldiers under the best of conditions, they needed kick-starting; a kick in the butt.

The dogs stood and shook themselves, as if determined to throw off the seasickness. Erich's stomach roiled. His mind pitched harder than the ship.

Rather than moving to their positions on the imaginary clock, the dogs remained in the middle of the room, close to one another as if for comfort, and looking back at the cages.

Erich concentrated harder, so hard that it was all he could do to maintain his grip on the rail.

The dogs, Taurus among them, turned their heads and looked at the cages as if for guidance.

No, not cage*s*, Erich realized. *Cage*.

They were watching the wolfhound, which had gained its feet.

Erich recognized his error. The dogs were waiting for a signal. They followed Taurus' lead—absorbed Erich's commands through her. But the unit operated as a unit first, single-minded in its purpose, and the hub was its center, its headquarters. A spoken command went to the unit's center; a mental command went to Taurus—and likewise to the unit's center. Grog, by far the smallest of the dogs, had had final approval of all human commands, but had been loyal almost to a fault, forever happy to please.

The wolfhound had loyalty to none but itself.

The realization, combined with the dogs' seasickness, so wrenched Erich that he lost his grip and collapsed against the wall. Pain shot through his shoulder socket.

The door opened.

"You're not to!—" Erich started to say to whichever trainer dared enter before the exercise was over, but it was Otto Hempel who stepped inside.

"Captain Dau sent me down to see how you're progressing with the Jews," he said. "I had some of my men start bringing the cargo out into the ladder well, for easier shackling." He smiled slyly. "Not that you wouldn't have done it yourself."

Erich crowded by Hempel and, shoving past the trainers who were waiting to return to the dogs, went hand-over-hand along the corridor rail. The light from the nearest ladder revealed Jews huddled in the well, looking up as if both wanting to climb, and being petrified to do so. He squinted down against the dimness, but could not see Solomon.

He's watching me, Erich thought. Wishing me dead.

"At your call, my boys will come down and get started," Hempel said. "But you must give the order. Technically, they're still your Jews."

Throw them into the sea? Throw Solomon into the sea? If Dau gave the command, would he have any choice but to carry it out? Without the dogs' help, any resistance on his part could mean his own execution.

The intercom crackled.

"We have passed muster as a Norwegian vessel headed for Mozambique to exchange lumber for sisal and bauxite. Due to the storm, there will be no boarding. That is all."

"We shouldn't need an excuse to kill Jews," Hempel muttered as the trainers entered the windlass room.

Hempel shut the door and spun the handle, then turned and seized Erich by the lapels, shoving him against the wall. "When the *Spee* was here I saw your wife above decks, trafficking with your Jew friend. A *man* would throw him overboard."

Erich's mind was racing so fast that he had to fight to keep his anger directed wholly toward Hempel. *Miriam...and Solomon. And she had said...nothing.* "You're asking for a court martial," he blurted out.

"Am I? I don't think so. Save your threats for someone you can scare. I've nothing to fear from the likes of you...*Oberst.*" He almost spat the word. "But don't worry. I won't report you—yet. Not until I have what *I* want." With another shove, he let go of Erich. "I intend to run my own show, with *my* boys, once we reach the island. Get used to the idea, or I'll have Dau notify the Seekriegsführung about you."

Erich tightened his left hand. His dead, stiffened fingers, shoved through an eye, would be as lethal as a dagger.

"*A man would throw him overboard...*"

Hempel's words echoed Erich's basest thoughts.

Laughing caustically, Hempel turned on his heel and walked toward the bridge. Filled with guilt, Erich followed him. Sailors and officers stood shoulder to shoulder before the starboard window, hands cupped against breath-frosted glass as they watched the British destroyer pass. Even with its outline broken by the fog, it loomed large, a gray behemoth closing on him with the relentlessness of a predator.

Chuckling, some of the seamen told him how the destroyer had signaled them to be careful of the *Spee,* adding that, being from a neutral country, the *Sogne* would probably not be a target.

Their joviality made him feel all the more isolated. They were together, and he on the outside, set apart because of Miriam and Solomon, and his own stinking conscience. The thought of his weaknesses made him feel as if he were suffocating. What power did he have over anyone as long as he was on Dau's ship! Hempel was Dau's kind of man. *He* was not. Never would be.

He looked up again at the oncoming destroyer and was filled with dread as though she were a premonition from God, for suddenly he was certain of the depth of Miriam's deceit. No proof except the weakness in his gut. Their...child. *His boy.* He felt sick to his stomach.

On impulse he shouldered open the door to the flying bridge. The storm whipped his head and shoulders.

"Close that!" Dau bellowed.

Salt spray beat against Erich's cheeks and clothes. Slipping and sliding, he stepped out and lunged toward the rail. Around him, balls of St. Elmo's fire jittered and danced like phantoms.

Dau opened the door. "Get in here, God damn you!"

Erich shook his head. The gesture was enough to send him off-balance. He fell to his knees and slid toward the rail, conscious of the ship's creakings and clankings and the howl of the wind. One arm looped through the rail, he fought against the waves that sluiced up from below bridge and washed over him.

Dau shut the door.

The destroyer was now directly opposite the *Sogne*. The thought of its power roared in Erich's blood and head. She sounded her stacks in mournful greeting. He shivered with cold and fearful delight as a sliver of moon broke through the clouds and played across her camouflage, revealing her war mast and guns.

And her name. *Glowworm.*

That goddamn music box! No wonder she listened to it so much. Because all this time...she *knew!*...

The ship began to fade behind the fog. Trying to see, Erich batted at the spheres of St. Elmo's fire, now less than a meter from his face. A fiery edge of the sphere brushed the rail, and an electrical shock surged through him. Surf and froth slammed against the bridge. His feet went out from under him and he slid helplessly toward the stairs that led to the main deck.

His head smashed against metal. He heard a crack but felt nothing. His head was pounding, and his hold on consciousness as tenuous as his grip on the slippery deck. He tried to stand up, reeled, felt something seize his brain with a force he had not known since his two grande mal episodes during childhood. Teeth chattering, he tumbled onto his knees and into blackness....

The lights in the cabin were bright, Dr. Tyrolt's stethoscope cold against Erich's naked chest. Erich pushed the instrument away and shielded his eyes. He had dreamed that he was centered in the bright lights of Leni's cameras.

And what strange images had haunted him, he thought, closing his eyes. He could remember crawling from Caligari's cabinet and into a jungle twisted with lianas and tendriled with mists reeking of fishflies. Tree frogs croaked, and parrots and magpies cawed. A flush of orchids bloomed beneath the dense green canopy; their beauty mocked him, and something seemed to wish his death—a black form that came toward him, leaping from tree to tree, closing quickly. Trumpeting. Wailing. Sending him fighting for purchase on the mud and moss. He dropped to all fours and crawled wildly, not caring which way the tangle turned him as long as it was away from the black manform's caterwauling. Then he was crouching, naked and on all fours, on a cone-shaped hill blackened by fire. Heeled near him on the blackened breast were his dogs. Night had fallen, and the jungle below was a green and silver sea. In the light of a melting moon, chameleons and frilled geckos skittered across his flesh, their rust-red eyes ogling him, their tongues darting out to taste the sweat that meandered down the sides of his nose....

He blinked several times, arched his back against the tremendous fatigue that suffused him, and looked around Tyrolt's cabin. The door was open. In the corner, Bruqah strummed his *valiha*. He plucked one of the twenty-two strings and a soft sound, amplified by the *valiha*'s resonating bamboo tube, floated through the room.

"Doctor Tyrolt!"

"I am here," Tyrolt answered from the passageway. "We have all been very worried about you."

"My head is killing me. Is there any reason why he must play his goddamn music at this particular moment?" Erich pointed at Bruqah.

"We thought it might soothe you," Tyrolt said, entering the cabin.

Bruqah pointed an elegant finger at his own forehead and smiled. His wrinkles deepened. "You bruised your bejesus pretty bad, Herr Oberst!"

Moaning, Erich felt the lump on his head. He lay back down and stared at the upper bunk.

"Take it easy." Tyrolt placed a weather-hardened hand on Erich's chest.

"I'm fine. Just a little dizzy."

"You took quite a beating. Whatever possessed you to go out there, anyway?"

Erich blinked but did not answer. He looked toward the porthole. It was still dark outside. Black and dark.

Chapter 41

Miriam glanced out of her cabin porthole, the binoculars Juan had given her within easy reach. In the background, the last slowed-down notes of Paul Lincke tinkled on her music box, working its magic. To her disappointment, the storm was abating. She had enjoyed the increased motion of the ship and the sense of danger—a change from the boredom that had set in since Leni and Juan disembarked. The HMS *Glowworm* had long since vanished. The coincidence neither escaped nor surprised her, not that she wanted to interpret its meaning. Life had a way of proving to her that coincidence was a synonym for serendipity.

The cabin door opened; she snapped shut the music box.

"Brought you a patient, Miriam," Dr. Tyrolt said as he helped Erich to her bunk. "Went out on the bridge without permission, and took a nasty fall. Should be fine, though. Call if you need help."

"A little childish to go out there, wasn't it?" she asked in a tight, controlled voice. "You might have drowned."

"My devoted little wife. Would you have shed a tear if I had drowned?"

I wish you had, Miriam thought, watching him stretch out his foot and kick the door shut as Tyrolt exited.

Erich ducked his head to clear the upper bunk and rose unsteadily to his feet. He put his hands on her shoulders and turned her to face him. "I believe we have some talking to do."

His touch was gentle, but something in his eyes warned her that she was in trouble. Whatever had driven him out onto the deck in the storm had not been pleasant; instinct told her that it had something to do with her.

"You should rest." She forced herself not to back away.

"You should rest," he mimicked. "Sweet mother-to-be Miriam Alois, epitome of caring and virtue! But we know that's not the real Miriam, don't we! We know the *real* Miriam Alois is all subterfuge and lies! How long have you been lying to me, Miriam?"

She tried to pull away. "You're hurting me, Erich! Let go!"

"How long have you been lying to me, Miriam?" He tightened his grip. "How goddamn long! Lying about that queer!"

"*You're* talking to *me* about lying? You must be joking!" she yelled, letting go of her carefully maintained controls. She visualized Erich dead, killed by her pity and loathing. She should have killed him with the wine bottle when she had the chance, that day at the flat, instead of thinking better of it. How stupid to believe that he might help her—help Solomon—unless he could profit by it.

"You want me to tell you that Sol is a homosexual? You really want to believe that, don't you? And that I stayed with you out of love and never loved Solomon. Well, I won't. I won't!"

Damn him. He could convince himself of almost anything, like that night...believing that, under the circumstances, she had wanted to give him a wine massage!

Before she could speak, Erich's face went white, then flamed to red. "You and Hempel!" he shouted. "Toying with me! Lying to me!"

And Juan, she thought, as Erich raised his hand. With a deliberate motion, he hit her across the face. She was unprepared for the force of the blow.

"Erich—" She sank to the floor and leaned against the cabin wall.

"Get up!" He raised his hand as if to hit her again. Instead, he walked over to the porthole and stood with his back to her, absent-mindedly cracking his knuckles, but otherwise silent.

With effort, she rolled onto her hip, too hurt to speak.

"Tell me the truth about us," he said without turning around.

"You want me to make it easy for you?" she said at last, sure now that he would not hit her again. "You want me to admit that I've lied to you? About Solomon? About the baby?"

"Your guilt is your affair," he said quietly. He sighed, and let his shoulders slump. "I'm only interested in my own guilt in this. That's why I'm going to do things *my* way once we reach Madagascar. Hempel may try to sabotage the project. Every success will be his, each failure mine. I must confound him." He made a fist. "Beat him at this game. Confound them all."

"And Solomon? What of him?"

"The only hope you have for your safety, and that of the child, is to stay with me."

Pain seized her and she clutched her belly as the ship rolled. "My God! See what your brutality's done? The baby's coming!" She clawed at the smock as though tearing it off might relieve the pain. "God, please. Not here. Not now!"

"I'll get the doctor."

"Promise you won't harm Solomon!"

He looked at her with a scorn he had in the past reserved only for the likes of Hempel. "I won't kill him, if that's what you mean. I wouldn't think of it. I'm going to let him get as close to you as he can, and then," his eyes brightened, "and then I'm going to take you away from him. Forever. I can live with the fact that you don't love me. I can live with a marriage of convenience. The only thing I can't live with is being made a fool of!"

"If you don't keep your word, I'll tell them—"

He leaned down, grabbed her wrist, and twisted. "Tell them what!"

"That I was..." She stopped to allow another wave of pain to pass. "That I was already married to a fellow Jew when you...when you...'saved' me!"

He swung at her again, the back of his hand coming toward her cheek, and abruptly withdrew. "I'll find Tyrolt," he said coldly.

Almost as suddenly as they had started, the pains were gone. In a few days, four or five at most, they would be anchored in Antongil Bay. The baby would not be born on board, after all. She put a hand on her belly; the child kicked, harder than usual—as if it were trying to voice its objections to what had just happened. She felt a surge of love. Funny, she thought, the myriad shapes and forms love can take. She would give her life for Sol, yet if he ever laid a hand on her the way Erich had done, she would leave without a backward glance. And there would be no forgiveness. Yet she knew she would, eventually, forgive Erich, who had raped her, lied to her, beaten her.

Why?

Because, it occurred to her, she did not love him—but pitied him for his weakness. Because he did not have her, and never would.

And the child's father?

Thanks to the Christmas rape, she did not know which man that was, and she was tired of wondering about it. Better to think of something else, like the fact that, in a few days, it would be the start of the Jewish New Year. *Rosh Hashanah*. Normally a time of forgiveness, of celebration, hope, prayer, thanksgiving.

Normally.

Nothing about her life was normal. She had never felt more abandoned. The burden of pretense had been a heavy one; its removal should have been sufficient compensation for her loneliness. It wasn't. There was too much was still unresolved.

She returned to the porthole, her watching post, and stared into the fog. The storm was diminishing. She could no longer hear the wind. The next few days would be long, and even lonelier than before. She had read everything on board, including all of Erich's books about Madagascar, except the one he kept locked in the brass-hinged sea trunk. She missed Perón's company, especially since she respected him so completely. How very much he had done for her...for *them*—she, Solomon, Erich, the baby. She even missed

Leni, Nazi or not, for her dry sense of humor and interest in the world of dance.

But Juan and Leni were gone, and she was left with her own company and Bruqah's. During the next few days he brought in her meals, massaged her aching back, and spoke of all manner of things in a fascinating mix of innocence and wisdom, as if infant and sage had conspired to occupy the same body. Erich continued sleeping in the cabin, but their uneasy truce did not include conversation. He crept into his bunk late at night, when he was sure she would be asleep, and was gone before daylight. On the few occasions she had awakened before he left, she turned awkwardly to face the wall—and remained silent.

Today, convinced they must be closing in on their destination, she had spoken to him—pleasant words, despite her need to scream; words that eased their truce a little.

The cabin door opened. She turned, smiling; she expected to see Bruqah.

It was Erich. He avoided her eyes. "We've dropped anchor. Get ready to leave ship. Bruqah will help you."

He left the cabin and she returned to the porthole. The usual fog had shrouded the sea since dawn. As she stood there, it began to lift. An orange sun shone through a halo of clouds, highlighting a green saddle of hills, thick with vegetation and laced with mist, as if a trillion caterpillars had woven a webbed shawl to protect the slopes from the morning. Along the shoreline, she could make out wavelets shuddering against a mangrove-flat whose red, scalloped edge was overhung with interlocking roots and veils of moss.

A light knock at the cabin door claimed her attention. "Come in, Bruqah," she called, knowing Erich would not have returned. "Is that Nosy Mangabéy?" she asked, without turning around. "That small island at the mouth of the bay?"

"Yes, Lady Miri...." He sounded as if there were more he wanted to say, but his voice trailed off. His hands, normally so relaxed, were clenched into fists at his sides.

"What's wrong, Bruqah?" Miriam asked.

After several moments, he mumbled, "They're back, Lady Miri."

"Who's back?" She was growing impatient with his reticence. When he shook his head, obviously reluctant to answer, she took hold of his wrists and looked at him insistently. "Who? Tell me why you're suddenly afraid. Who has come back to that little island?"

With a finger that was quivering slightly, Bruqah pointed to the island. "There is smoke rising from the first hill, Lady Miri."

Another interval of quiet.

"The ghosts," he said finally. "They have returned. They have come back to the island where the dead dream."

Chapter 42

Misha started the day with a sense of purpose. He was going to search for a gun. He had no idea how to shoot one, but he could learn. He had seen Sachsenhausen guards shoot them—shoot *people* with them—often enough. If they could do it, he could, too. He had to, that was all there was to it, because if he could kill some of the bad people on his thought-list, everything would come into balance, or even be weighted to the good.

He pictured the ledger sheet. At the top of the bad side of the list were Pleshdimer and Hempel who appeared over and over, once for every time they did something bad. He had done the same thing on the good side, like putting in each birthday separately and not just lumping them under 'birthdays.'

Fair was fair, so there was also one Hempel entry on the good side. Hempel had been nicer to Misha since the escape from the stateroom at Lüderitz. In his relief that the boy had not fallen overboard, the Sturmbannführer had given him the run of the ship.

He took full advantage of the concession, exploring the ship from one end to the other, but staying out of trouble and out of everyone's way, especially Hempel's, because nicer did not mean nice. He had not stopped doing *the thing*, just decreased its frequency.

Come nightfall, Misha had to go back to more of the same.

As the sun sank lower, each pitch of the ship became a clock, ticking him closer to confinement and pain; each toss made him remember the mental tally sheet.

On the one side were the good people of his life: Papa, Hans Hannes, Solomon Freund, Fräulein Miriam. The other side was filled with hunger and pain, with the Nazi men breaking into the apartment, and, over and over again, Pleshdimer and the strap, and Hempel doing *the thing*.

Free for the day, Misha found his way into the cargo hold where the military equipment was stored. He sensed that guns were in the metal and wooden boxes that were stacked within the hold, but his attempts to open them proved futile.

Behind the stacked boxes, as if mocking him by the show of strength he could not use, was an airplane. Its wings had been removed and wired to its sides. There was also a tank, not much larger than one of the armored cars that sometimes roamed the streets of Berlin. Tarps only partially covered them. He climbed on both, wishing, exploring. The tank had a machine-gun mount, but the guns was packed elsewhere.

"Rat-a-tat-tat," he yelled, imagining himself sighting down the weapon and firing bursts as Hempel, Pleshdimer, and the other Nazis charged toward him, falling like the dominoes Papa had taught him how to stack in long rows.

When he tired of his solitary game, Misha made his way on deck. To his surprise, the ship had anchored and, in the distance, he could see land. Could it be Madagascar, he wondered?

He stood at the rail and looked down. He could see movement in the water, dark shadows which he took to be sharks.

Setting aside all thought of swimming to shore, he wandered to the windlass room. He hid in the shadows, watching the soldiers come and go. He recognized some of them as dog trainers, yet he could tell by their uniforms that they were real soldiers. What a wonder that would be, he thought, carrying a gun and commanding a powerful animal! Would anyone dare hurt him again? Would he even need a tally list? He liked the trainers, and had thought about putting them on the good side of his ledger, especially after the one Colonel Alois called Fermi let him into the hold to pet the dogs. Once he even fed them, under the trainers' watchful eyes.

He leaned out of the shadows and tugged at Fermi, who was the last to pass by him. "Could I visit the dogs?" he asked.

"Sorry, Misha. I don't have time to take you down right now," Fermi said.

"I could go in by myself."

"Never, ever go near the animals alone," Fermi warned. "They might chomp you in half."

The dogs were better now, he said, except for Aquarius who was still terribly seasick, and Taurus, who had a fire in her hip.

"Why don't you put out the fire," Misha asked, imagining smoke and flame.

Fermi laughed, and tousled his hair. As the trainer walked away down the corridor, Misha thought about putting him separately on the good-side of the tally sheet, and the dogs, too.

Noticing that Fermi had failed to rotate the door handle behind him, Misha crept from his hiding place by the ladder well that led to the hold. He put a shoulder against the door and shoved. It clanged open against the wall.

All but three dogs—the two sick ones and Boris, the wolfhound—came to the front of their cages, trying to thrust their noses through the wire. He went to the front of the cages, pretending he was passing in review, much as he and the other inmates had done back in Sachsenhausen whenever Hempel had wanted, the other men said, to be admired. He kept his hands carefully at his sides.

Several dogs wagged their tales. "Don't be fooled by the tails," Fermi had told him. "Means nothing, with these dogs. We taught them that trick. Wag and bite, wag and bite."

The wolfhound perked up its ears, but did not look at him. It stood and shook itself, gazing toward the left wall. Misha had lain awake often enough at night, listening to the creaks and groans of the ship, and to the scurrying of rats and roaches in the hollow walls. He supposed that to be what the dog was doing.

The dog whined and pranced as much as the cage would allow, increasingly nervous and animated. Maybe it's the island that's making him nervous, Misha thought, remembering what Bruqah had told them at the farmhouse about dead spirits on the island, and how animals could hear them. Maybe that *was* Madagascar he had seen out there.

As if they had been triggered by the wolfhound's nervousness, the other dogs—all but Aquarius and Taurus—followed Boris' example. Their nervousness transferred itself to Misha, who began to think that he, too, was sensing something very strange and mysterious outside the ship

"Good boy," he told the wolfhound, and released the latch. The dog instantly pushed open the cage door and, ignoring him, dashed toward the eastern wall where he stood whimpering.

Is that how Major Hempel feels about me when I ignore him, Misha wondered. He fell to his knees and, heart pounding from the sense of danger, put his arms around the dog's thick, warm neck. The animal did not resist, so intent was it on the wall. Did the dog not realize there was a door, at the opposite side of the room?

As if it had heard him, the wolfhound shook itself free and went to the door.

"No," Misha said softly, crawling after him. "You can't go. Whatever it is you want, you have to stay here with me."

He stood up, took hold of the dog's collar, and walked the animal back and forth. The wolfhound appeared to relish the pacing, as if it partially relieved his anxiety. The other dogs watched, whimpering. "Good boy," Misha kept saying. "Good, good boy. Just like me."

We are friends now, Misha decided. He scratched the dog behind the ear. The wolfhound pressed its head forward in pleasure.

Then Misha heard footsteps in the corridor. The dog looked toward the east wall, whined deep in its throat, and let itself be maneuvered into the cage without resistance.

After relatching the cage, Misha secreted himself behind some crates of dog food. He would watch the trainers carefully from now on, he decided. He would learn how they handled the dogs. These dogs were special, Fermi had told him. Smart, tough, trained to kill.

With your help, Misha thought, eyeing the silver-blue tag that said "Boris" on the cage door and fingering the collar around his own neck, the bad side of the list will grow shorter.

Chapter 43

"We have stopped moving forward," Solomon said. "They will be coming for us."

He sensed Goldman turn toward him in the dark of the hold.

"Moving. Not moving. What difference does it make?" Goldman said. "No one has been down here for days. They have probably decided to let us die in our own filth."

No one had been allowed above decks since Lüderitz. The storm had turned the hold into a hell-hole, and the question of whether or not they would die of disease before they reached Madagascar was never far from anybody's mind. Guards had brought food of sorts and drinking water, but the prisoners had none to spare for cleaning themselves or the floor, which was slick with a sour combination of vomit and the swill that had sloshed from the latrine-drum during the ship's relentless pitching and tossing.

In this last part of the journey, he made no attempt to stop himself from thinking about Miriam and the child she carried. He thought about their lovemaking in the cabaret and convinced himself that out of that had come the child. No matter what, he knew he would love the child, as he would always love Miriam.

And Erich.

Though with Erich, the love was tainted. Veiled in the confusion of wanting to hate him.

Finally, on this day when the ship's movement stopped, he thought about this so-called homeland. Berlin, the only home he knew, would never be his home again; now Jerusalem was the only homeland he wanted, not this ersatz place called Nose Mangabéy which Hitler and Hempel and, more than likely Erich, would turn into another camp or, at best, a ghetto.

What, he asked himself, had he really learned, on this long journey from boyhood to manhood? That he could see into the lives of strangers, and not into his own, and that the only constant in life was change?

If that was all, was it enough? Would he ever understand why the German people needed to suck at the breast of the beast of riot, the beast that was the manifestation of their guilt?

Nothing, he told himself again, happens for no reason. In some lifetime, if not this one, then another, he would learn the meaning of all that had passed...of the dybbuk, and the voices, the cruelties and the joys.

"Put your hands on my head," Lucius Goldman said to him, in a voice filled with fear. "Bless me before I die. Speak my name among the angels."

"I'll be sure to do that," Sol replied, though he wanted to suggest that no self-respecting angel would enter the *Sogne's* hold.

As Sol reached for Goldman, the door was flung open. Sturmbannführer Otto Hempel, standing in the doorway, smacked his billy club against his palm. "Deckside! On the double! Move, you swine!"

Sol watched his fellow prisoners squeeze toward the door, all but the one next to him.

"Bless me by name, *shakkid,*" his friend said urgently.

Shakkid? I am no teacher, Sol thought, let alone a great one. I have too much learning yet to do.

Goldman gripped Sol's arm. "Tell the angels the farmer from Juterbourg planted well, even though this is what he reaped!"

"The Nazis did not bring us all this way to kill us."

"Ha! Isn't that what life is all about? The child learning to walk so he can reach the grave? You go along. I will stay here."

"You will not!" Sol said under his breath, taking Goldman's arm and pulling him to his feet.

Unresisting as a child, Lucius Goldman allowed himself to be led up the ladder's thirty-nine steps. Together they emerged, tottering, from the ladder well and joined the Jews who were struggling to form ranks on the steaming deck, Misha among them. Seeing him, alive if not well, Sol said a quick prayer of thanks and dispelled the image of the boy jumping overboard.

"You're all going into the boats!" Hempel shouted. "You would be rowing if we thought you wouldn't row in circles."

Shading his eyes, Sol squinted toward an orange sunrise broken by low clouds. Looking down at the glassy aquamarine sea, he watched a sea-cow bob a welcome to the newest Jewish exodus. After the dark of the hold, he was surprised and pleased at how clearly he could see the mammal. It played in the corridor of his vision, cavorting around as if the *Sogne* were its bathtub toy.

He saw hills beyond, lush with greenery, seated beneath a plume of smoke. But something felt wrong.

Pushing away encroaching panic, he focussed on the shore. Gnarled roots lay curled like giant sleeping snakes. He could see them clearly. Too clearly. As if centered in a telescope lens.

He could see nothing else. What little had been left of his peripheral vision the last time he was in the light was gone.

"Move!" Hempel pushed him. "Think we have all day? You're to get in the lead boat with that Rathenau bitch." Raising his voice, he said, "Eight Jews in the lead boat. You other swine into the dinghies, and count yourselves lucky you don't have to swim with the sharks. Welcome to your home sweet home!"

Hempel kicked Solomon in the small of the back. Sol stumbled and went down, fighting to suck air into his lungs. He was vaguely aware of Hempel nudging him with a boot toe and of hands helping him to his feet.

"I'm all right." Sol shoved away the hands that reached to help him. "Look after yourselves."

He found his way onto the Jacob's ladder, took two hurried steps down the ropes, and stopped. Dangling, unable to move up and afraid to look down, he thought of Erich hanging in the sewer.

"Have a problem, Jew?" Kapo Pleshdimer's voice floated up from below. "Afraid of heights? Jump and I'll catch you."

Clutching the rope-ladder with both hands, Sol lowered himself.

"Do you hold your seasons dear, Solomon Freund? Is this your season of madness?"

He missed his footing, sprawled headlong into the lifeboat assigned as a tender to carry them ashore...

And looked up he see Miriam's face, ghastly pale in the center of his tunnel vision. He crawled painfully toward her.

"So much as breathe hard, Jew, and I'll see to it the dogs tear out your throat." Pleshdimer grinned amiably and, stepping over Solomon, settled himself on the seat. Leaning down until he was close enough for Sol to smell his rancid breath, the Kapo opened his mouth and clicked a fingernail against his upper and lower front teeth. "What flesh the dogs don't rip away, I will."

Sol brought his feet up beneath himself and lay still. Miriam turned toward the sea, her back toward Bruqah, who was massaging the back of her neck with long brown fingers. "I don't know what I would do without you," she said to him. "Thank you, my friend."

He rose and, stepping across, lifted Sol's elbow. "Lady Miri says—come."

"I want him right where he is." Pleshdimer pushed the man away and spat in Miriam's direction, then jabbed Sol with a foot.

Bruqah steadied himself. "Herr Oberst Germantownman say—"

The Kapo drew himself aside and allowed Solomon to be helped to his feet and led forward. "Go to hell!"

"No—go to Hell-*ville!*" Bruqah laughed heartily and slapped his thigh as if at a private joke. Leaning close to Sol, he whispered, "Hell-ville Britishman town—northwest side of Ma'gascar, on Nosy Bé!"

"Wherever it is, I wish you'd go there and stop babbling," one of the sailors said. He picked up his oar and patted Sol on the butt as if the Jew were a recalcitrant child.

Pleshdimer and the other sailors roared with laughter. "Come on, come on, let's go!" The Kapo motioned like an orchestra leader.

The boat pulled through the water. Swaying, Bruqah helped Sol onto the seat next to Miriam and placed himself at their feet.

"*Shana Tova*, Solomon," Miriam said. "Happy New Year." She looked down at the brown man. "Again I have reason to thank you, Bruqah."

"Help me, Bruqah! I don't want to die!"

That phrase again! Involuntarily, as when he had been a child in the sewer, Sol clamped his hands over his ears. "Help me, Bruqah," he whispered. Tentatively, as if touching her would restore his sense of reality, he placed his hand on Miriam's blanket-wrapped shoulder.

"*Shana Tova?* Is it really--"

"A few more days."

"Are you well?" He avoided the traditional, hopeful response of *Next year in Jerusalem*. Trembling, he wiped a trickle of sweat from her temple.

She put her hand to her face where Solomon had touched it. "If it weren't for the baby, I'd be dead. We'd both be dead."

"What?"

"There is hope for us," she said. "Erich is determined to turn Nose Mangabéy into a settlement...a homeland." She lowered her head. "No matter what happens, we must stay alive. For the sake of our child."

"*Our* child?"

"Biologically? God knows. But you are my husband in His sight. This is our child."

Solomon sat in silence as the boat moved shoreward. He watched the saddle of hills loom larger and higher, and was almost grateful that his head ached with so many questions; it relieved his physical pain. Could the child really be his? What was his connection with this man Bruqah? And what of the island ahead? Was survival possible there? For him, Miriam, the child, the other Jews?

"Antongil Bay," Bruqah said, letting a hand dangle in the water. "More fish here than rays in the sun! Good shark, too."

He stared thoughtfully across the water. When at last he looked at Sol, his eyes were glazed, their expression hard. "Nosy Mangabéy not a good place, I think. Full of the dead."

Solomon looked up at the approaching jungle. The strengthening sun was burning off the mists; they rose from the interior like smoke from the nostrils of dragons, curling from roots and branches and tall, pale, skeletal tree trunks. The closer the boat drew to the wall of greenery, the louder came screeching and cawing from the jungle. Fruit bats hung from branches like dark linen, as undisturbed by the gulls and paradise flycatchers that wheeled in and out of the mists as they were by the approaching humans.

The boat scraped to a halt against the rocky shore. Miriam put her head briefly on Sol's shoulder, and Bruqah leaned forward, shielding them both with his body.

"During the storm, after Erich found out that I knew you were alive, he...he beat me." She was crying softly, her arms around Sol's neck in open defiance of what Pleshdimer or anyone else might do. "We came so close to a life together, you and I."

"We will find it yet." Sol turned to the Malagasy. "Help her, Bruqah," he said, paraphrasing the words from his vision.

"Yes. And you," Bruqah said. "I will help you, too."

Children

of the

Dusk

Part I

"Everything that is really great and inspiring is created by the individual who can labor in freedom."
— Albert Einstein

Prologue

Grasshoppers blackened the moon.

The Malagasy laughed delightedly and pointed what was left of his fist at the predawn sky. Abandoning his guardianship of the limestone crypt, he shrugged off his ragged, clay-colored loincloth. By the fading light of the stars, of glowworms, and of the last embers of the coconut husk fire, he began a sinuous dance of triumph. He moved around the moss- and ivy-covered totems that dotted the area, carelessly swatting at the mosquitoes and the rain flies that heralded a tropical downpour. When he tired of the dance, he removed a liana from one of the totems, wove it into a garland, and placed it on top of his grisly red and salt-and-pepper head like a crown.

He ran his misshapen fingers down the totem. Miniature zebu horns topped an arabesque of curling leaves. Carved lemurs balanced on one another's backs, looking outward with huge, whorled eyes.

The grasshoppers moved away from the huge egg-yolk moon, away from the Zana-Malata who grinned a toothless grin. *"Minihana!"* he shrieked. "Eat!" He opened the gaping pink hole where his nose and mouth should have been, pushed his tongue outward in the manner of an iguana, and drew a stream of glowworms into his throat.

He exhaled a burst of fire and chuckled at his own cleverness. Soon, he thought, it would be time for *lambda*, the dressing of the dead, and only he knew who waited inside the crypt. He and the tree frogs and the glowworms. Meanwhile, he could wait. Here, in isolation, time meant nothing to him— any more than it did to those who were buried in the *valavato*.

He moved around the totems that dotted the area. At his feet, a *dô* snake slithered away, carrying with it the soul of one of the dead who haunted the burial ground. Behind him, five short, black men, eyes painted with white and black tar circles, bodies pulsating with a luminous white mud, appeared out of the rim of trees, cavorted a moment, and disappeared.

As if it, too, knew that changes were imminent, the rainforest chorus stopped. When only the bats sang *a cappella* in the damp tropical air, the fox-lynxes raised their long faces to watch him. The aye-ayes and the larger lemurs fled; the zebu sauntered down the hill, bells clanking hollowly and dewlaps swaying beneath their chins.

The Zana-Malata stayed where he was, listening to the voices of the dead. Chief of all he surveyed, he stared down at the crescent coral reef three hundred feet below the burial ground. On the horizon, his keen eyes discerned the lights of a ship moving toward him. He glanced at the moon hanging over the horizon.

It was beginning. The ghosts were returning to Nosy Mangabéy, his island where the dead dreamed.

Chapter 1

Nosy Mangabéy
10 September, 1939

Sitting on the damp sand, Solomon Freund watched as lifeboats and launches traveled back and forth from the *Altmark* to shore. Some brought only men; others carried equipment and supplies loaded by the freighter's cranes and his fellow Jews. A large, awkward-looking raft, made of wood strapped onto empty fuel drums, was being readied to carry the small tank from the ship to shore. Knowing the German military, there was doubtless some order about the landing, but to Sol it seemed chaotic. He wondered cynically if Abwehr manuals contained explicit instructions for hacking a path through a rain forest.

Limited by his tunnel-vision, Sol tracked the boat which brought Major Otto Hempel. The SS officer strode from the water, his wolfhound and nine-year-old Misha Czisça in tow. Reaching the beach, he looked out over the water with ill-disguised disgust. Sol turned back toward the ship and saw Erich Weisser Alois, Abwehr colonel, riding in the last boat. Erich. Despite his hatred, Sol could not avoid thinking of his childhood friend in the familiar. Head uplifted, eyes surveying the surrounding jungle as if he half expected natives to come rushing out and throw themselves at his feet with offerings of gold, Colonel Alois stepped from the launch. Behind him, two Jews carried his beloved German shepherd, Taurus, strapped to a hospital stretcher.

"We're going to have to cut a path to the top of the hill," Erich said. He turned to Hempel. "Give the Malagasy a machete." He nodded toward Bruqah, their coffee-colored guide. "After you've supplied all of your men with machetes, give the Jews the rest."

"The Jews?" Hempel asked. "Is that wise?"

"Are you questioning my orders?" Erich's voice was dangerously quiet. "Take one squad and lead the way. Use Bruqah to guide you. I am sure you will at least agree with that, since it is his primary function here," he went on, having apparently decided to downplay the matter of

Hempel's insubordination. "Freund, stay with them and take care of Mir...the woman. Pleshdimer, you and Taurus bring up the rear." He raised his voice. "We are going up that hill." He pointed toward the jungle. "There will be no relaxation of discipline. For the sake of every Jewish life here, I will say this once, and once only. You are to use the machetes for creating a path. Look as if you see them as weapons, make one movement that smells of an attempt to escape, and we will shoot half of you Jews and let the dogs finish the rest. Now move it!"

Without so much as a glance at his heavily pregnant wife Miriam or at Solomon, he turned his back to them and waited to be obeyed. Hempel, obviously furious, strode toward the ridge of trees, his omnipresent companions trotting behind.

Bruqah, ever the Malagasy aristocrat though he was for the moment a guide, watched without comment or movement.

"Do you not fear them?" Sol asked him.

"Pah!" Bruqah spat onto the wet earth.

"Does anything frighten you?"

Bruqah threw his head back and laughed uproariously. "You ask questions like a small child." He helped Miriam to her feet. "What Bruqah fears you cannot understand. Not yet."

"Tell me."

"Bruqah only fears things of man and not of man," he said softly, all trace of laughter gone.

"You are right, I do not understand." Sol was reminded of the days in the farmhouse outside Oranienburg where he had first met Bruqah. The Malagasy had been assigned to prepare them for their journey and sojourn here. He was apparently studying botany at the university in Berlin when he was offered the job in exchange for transportation home. The more he had come to know Bruqah, the more convinced he was that the events were less coincidental than they appeared.

"We of Africa accept she mystery," Bruqah went on. "It is for Europeans to need understanding. Belief be truth here." Bruqah pointed his walking stick at a twig. "What be this, Lady Miri?"

"A twig," Miriam said wearily.

He tapped the twig lightly with his cane. A chameleon skittered into the underbrush. Bruqah smiled. "Come, Lady Miri. Come, we go, Solly."

Sol caught himself grinning. No one had called him that since he left his mother in Amsterdam. Seeing his smile, Miriam returned it with one of her own. He saw a glimpse of the young girl he had once known and felt a transient stab of hope as they entered the jungle. All his life he learned through riddles. His father had said it was part of the Judaic tradition. Perhaps by solving the riddles of this new land, he would find answers to his old problems, as well.

Sunlight gave way to the dark and dankness of the rain forest. Sol's physical discomfort was increased tenfold by his inability to see more than a couple of meters ahead. A high-pitched chittering spoke of living creatures disturbed by the human intruders, and around him, pinpoints of light flickered on and off, as if the forest were peopled by a million glowworms. Were it not for the moisture that hung in the air and covered him with a film of sweat, and the mold and moss that enveloped everything like a possessive lover, he might have been in the Black Forest.

Abruptly, the chittering stopped. A raucous sawing began, followed by a series of deafening squeals which rose to a crescendo and shook the bamboo and ferns into responding. Leaves rustled and dripped and snapped back, ignoring his swinging machete. When he looked behind him, the forest seemed to have regenerated. He could hear the others, Jews and soldiers alike, fighting their way through the heavy undergrowth.

Ha-haai! Ha-haai!

Soft and shrill and mournful, the cry echoed through the forest, its sound so chilling it made Solomon's teeth ache.

He lifted his machete. Behind him, he heard the unnerving, metallic snaps of safeties being flicked off as, again and again, the sound came, piercing through the branches overhead.

A guard, panicked by the unfamiliar sound, opened fire.

Ha-haai! Ha-haai!

"Eeee-vil!" Arms raised, Bruqah followed the sounds with a shaking finger.

"Probably a harmless monkey," Hempel said contemptuously. "Stop acting like a bunch of children."

"There are no monkeys in Nosy Mangabéy," Bruqah said in a low voice, the veins pulsating in his neck as he strained to see up into the jungle canopy. "Not in all Madagascar."

"What was it?" Solomon asked.

"H'aye-aye," Bruqah said, imitating the sound. He turned away from them and moved through the tangle of ferns and vines, parting the foliage with his walking stick and his machete. In an instant he had disappeared.

"Come back here!" Hempel shouted.

Bruqah returned, clutching his head, wailing and spinning as if he were performing a ritual dance. Gripping his face, ogling the newcomers to the forest, was a red-and-gold striped iguana the length of his arm.

"Do something, one of you!" Grabbing Sol's machete, Miriam chopped wildly at the bush ahead of her. She collapsed, crying, as Bruqah reeled toward her.

"For Christ's sake!" Hempel shouldered past Solomon. He tore the giant lizard from Bruqah and, holding it upside-down and squirming, cracked its back and threw it to his wolfhound, Boris. Pleshdimer, the Kapo who served as Hempel's man-servant, crouched at the dog's side and grinned as it tore the reptile to pieces.

"Whatever's amusing you," Hempel said, "you might remember that one of these days you'll be glad to dine on that same meat."

"Are you all right, Bruqah?" Miriam asked in a small voice.

"I'm all right, Lady Miri." Bruqah signaled Solomon to come closer. "That thing." He stepped aside for a moment to allow Hempel and his machete crew to work past them. *"Liguaan*, like you," he told Sol. "She eye the future while she eye the past."

"How do you know...?" Sol stopped. He would examine the meaning of Bruqah's words later. Right now Miriam needed his attention. He helped her to her feet. She looked exhausted. He wanted to pick her up and carry her, but he was too debilitated; even with Bruqah's help it was all he could do to half-drag her along.

The climb grew steeper, the forest more dense. Layers of branches crisscrossed overhead. The leaves underfoot were slick from the humidity and lack of sunlight. Millipedes and beetles ran over their legs, stickers jabbed their arms, wet ferns, rough as a cat's tongue, stuck to the sides of their faces. Looking for ballast, they found themselves grabbing onto the yellow pitcher plants that seemed to flourish in the forest despite the weak light. When they did, a sticky syrupy substance erupted, bringing armies of flies and ants and mosquitoes against which there was no defense.

"Be careful," Bruqah said, when he saw them touching the pitcher plants. "For some people, pitcher plants dangerous. Make them breathe bad. Die, even."

Sol slapped at his neck and looked at his hand. On it lay a mosquito the size of an average fly. "Look at this thing," he said. "It's big enough to roast for dinner. We'll probably all need quinine, which doubtless our Nazi friends have brought along." If we don't die first from malaria, he told himself. "For the time being, we had better do what they say."

They resumed their climb. Eventually they found themselves in a boggy meadow. Only the lack of incline, the larger expanse of clear flat ground between trees, and the fact that those who had gone ahead of them were gathered together at the far end of the clearing, gave them any sense that they had crested the hill and exited the forest. Near them, leaning against a tree, was Hempel. "Wait here," he told Pleshdimer. "Shoot anyone who gives you trouble. I'm going to see what's beyond those trees."

After Hempel walked away, Sol helped Miriam to sit down, her back against a log. "Nothing happens without a reason."

He said the words out loud. He had to. For one thing, nothing short of his favorite rationale, which generally worked for him even under the most arduous circumstances, would stand a chance of reaffirming his faith. For another, the steady deterioration of his eyesight brought on by *retinitis pigmentosa* required—demanded—the reassurance of the sound of his own voice. As if knowing his hearing was unimpaired would somehow make the fact of his loss of vision bearable.

Now if I could only discover what those reasons were, he thought, life would begin to make sense.

Maybe.

Gasping after the hike up through the rain forest, he wiped his glasses and looked around as best his tunnel vision would allow. He watched the guards and his fellow prisoners...free laborers...file onto the relative flatness of the boggy hilltop meadow.

Dusk was descending, the sun setting behind the western edge of the dark overstory of foliage that surrounded the meadow. Night, he had been told, would come quickly in the tropics, almost like a curtain being rapidly drawn, but for the moment the side of the meadow in which Sol stood was cast in brilliant light. The air was so moisture-laden that the sunlight seemed to refract, lending the meadow an ethereal quality which was quite unnerving after the brooding darkness of the rain forest. He wondered how much of the odd light was due to the sunlight and humidity and how much to his own weak eyes. The disease had stolen all of his sight except for a circle of clarity, nearly devoid of color.

He wasn't going to be much use to himself, let alone anyone else, once blindness set in. When that would happen was anybody's guess; *that* it would happen was inevitable.

He moved his head from side to side to examine his new environment. Wreathing him in green, slender white-barked trees rose two hundred feet, where they spread their dense leafy canopy, blotting out the sky and perpetually dripping water. Curtains of gray moss, and creepers and lianas, hung down in a tangle from the trees; parasitic orchids sprouted from the trunks. At ground level, huge ferns, gleaming with moisture, grew higher than a man's chest.

Here and there, Sol intuited rather than saw a spot of color: the red acanthema blossoms, which Bruqah had warned them were deadly poison; the blue dicindra vine which opened in the early morning, closed up as the sun reached its height, and reopened briefly at dusk. His basic impression was that of a vast, oversized, gray-green world, an alien place, inhospitable to man.

By contrast, the hilltop meadow seemed almost congenial. Judging by the charred snags partially sunken in the marsh and by the singularly large count of dead trees, there were times of the year when there was relief from the wetness that hovered around them like a living entity.

At the far side of the meadow stood what Sol took to be a tanghin tree, at least judging from what he remembered seeing in Bruqah's crude drawings. Beneath the tree, a lopsided, thatched shack, constructed of mud and wattle and pandanus palm fronds, stood on uneven stumps that elevated it a meter off the ground.

"Man who lives there carries storm in she heart," Bruqah said, misusing the personal pronoun as he almost habitually did. He sauntered closer to Sol, walking stick in hand, long, bronze-colored legs moving him with fluid ease through the meadow grass.

"Is he one of your people?" Sol asked, hunkering down next to Miriam, who was resting at his feet, her head against a log and one hand on her nine-month pregnant belly.

Bruqah shook his head vehemently. "Zana-Malata can live only within she own self. Same as me. My people, Vazimba, no longer a tribe. We are like traveler's tree. We nourish Malagasy who need us."

Miriam opened her eyes and looked down the west side of the hill through a break in the foliage. She pointed toward another, smaller hill. "This island can't be more than five kilometers square," she said to Sol. "One of Erich's books called it two hills and an apron of rain forest."

Bruqah spread his arms as if to encompass the sun. "Once before, this island drowned in blood. Bruqah died, then."

"You mean your ancestors died," Sol said.

"I mean Bruqah," the Malagasy said quietly. "You know little, Solly. But you will learn...next time island drowns in blood."

Sol watched what looked like a ground squirrel poke a berry into its mouth, masticating with absolute concentration. The human intruders were of no concern, the food its universe. A deep envy overwhelmed Sol. How dare it be wiser than he, to know such single-mindedness of purpose? He must learn survival from such animals.

He looked around, assessing his friends and adversaries, who sat or stood milling in four groups. The largest group were his fellow Jews, one hundred and forty-two men who, against his better judgment, called him rabbi and leader. They had been plucked, like himself, from the degradation of Sachsenhausen, to be in the lead party for the Nazi's planned forced exodus.

Next in number were forty Nazi guards, also products of the camp, hand-picked for the expedition by Hempel, who had returned and stood with a hand on the shoulder of Wasj Pleshdimer, the murderer who in Sachsenhausen had been elevated to barracks guard. Both men appeared to be looking at something down slope of the shack. At Hempel's feet, his wolfhound whined. Also at Hempel's feet, leashed like the dog, was young Misha. A great sadness took hold of Sol, and he promised himself that he would find a way soon to communicate with the boy.

He looked at Erich, the man whom he had once called blood brother and, at Erich's insistence—inventing a ceremony to match —a brother-in-blood. Why, Sol chided himself, had he never before considered the implications of that syntactic twist? For him, *blood* had meant kinship. For Erich it had meant...what? He claimed he had no family. His mother and father, though still living, were dead as far as he was concerned. Miriam was his by right of marriage but not love, and the child only possibly his, and that perhaps by virtue of rape. He loved his dogs and communed with them, or so he asserted, but they were hardly blood relatives. Still he did love them, all twelve of them but most especially Taurus, and he certainly felt affection for the eleven other trainers who made up his zodiac team. The Abwehr canine command had been selected by Himmler himself for the expedition, probably because Erich and his men had proven too powerful, and possibly too non-Nazi, for Reichsführer Himmler to allow them to remain in Germany any longer.

As for the Nazi Party, which so many officers loved as family, Erich Alois hated it.

Lounging in smaller groups among the others were sailors from the *Altmark*, the supply ship for Germany's indomitable raider, the *Graf Spee*. They would leave soon, Solomon was sure, and with them Tyrolt, the ship's doctor. Miriam was doubtless dreading that, for she would soon need medical attention. And Sol too needed Doctor Tyrolt. Not for his physical needs but for his psyche. Tyrolt alone among all the Nazis he had met was a man Sol felt he could trust.

Several dogs jumped up, growling, as two ox-like animals, humped and sporting enormous dewlaps, huge ears, and curved horns, wandered from beyond the shack and into the clearing. Their appearance broke Sol's reverie.

"Zebu," Bruqah said, brightening.

Sol knew that the animals, while not sacred to the Malagasy, were the main measure of wealth among the islanders.

"*Zebulun*," he said to Bruqah. "Jacob's tenth son. Father of the tribe of Israel. What might he have thought of this place?"

Bruqah wasn't listening. He stood, hands on hips and head thrust forward. The mouselemur perched on his left shoulder also leaned forward. It was as if both man and animal were appraising the zebus' worth.

Pleshdimer raised his rifle and Bruqah's face went vapid with horror.

"No!" Bruqah ran toward the Kapo. "Please, no, do not shoot!"

Pleshdimer hesitated. Hempel squeezed his shoulder and the Kapo swung the rifle across his back and took off in a waddling run toward the animals. Waving his arms and yelling, he chased the zebu from the clearing.

Sol looked down at Miriam. He was about to tell her he would find her some water to drink when Erich came striding across the meadow and stopped beside them. Sol ignored him, effecting a studied nonchalance. Erich steered his gaze clear of all of them. "Will whoever lives there come back, Bruqah?" he asked, pointing at the lopsided shack.

"Of course." The mouselemur, which seemed to be perpetually on Bruqah's shoulder, shifted position away from Erich. It clung to Bruqah's hair, its sad, dark eyes too large for so tiny a head. "All Malagash come back. Living or dead, they come. As Bruqah come back."

"Bruqah is Vazimba. His ancestors came from Indonesia," Miriam said, to Sol's surprise. He wondered how she could talk to Erich, after all he had done to her. "He told me that his people were Madagascar's first inhabitants."

Sol started to say something to Miriam, then stopped as it dawned on him that she was not speaking to Erich at all, not looking at him but through him. As though he did not exist. What had Bruqah called Nosy Mangabéy, back on the ship? *Island where the dead dream.*

He shuddered, wondering where the ghost that had inhabited him for seventeen years had gone.

"Vazimba, first race," Bruqah said. "Zana-Malata, last race." His teeth were bared in what could have been mistaken for a smile, but a hard look had risen into his eyes. "We are beginning and end, he and me."

"You know the man who lives there?" Erich asked.

"For too long." As if to end the discussion, Bruqah reached up to one side, plucked a fig from a tree, and handed it to Miriam along with a piece of wild ginger.

"*Ha-haai! Ha-haai!*"

Like spectators at a stadium, heads turned in unison to look in the direction of the sound, Erich's among them.

The cry came again from the northern edge of the surrounding forest, this time followed by the body of a creature that looked like a cross between the flying squirrel and the lemurs Sol had seen illustrated in the books about Madagascar. With the grace of a trapeze artist, the animal leapt from the overstory and landed on a beech branch entwined with liana the size of a man's arm. Slowly, almost insolently, the creature raised its plumed tail.

"*Ha-haai! Ha-haai!*"

Sol stared at the coppery ball of fur. Its two enormous, sad-looking eyes seemed to stare back at him with human intelligence. Its tail was wrapped around the liana and its fingers gripped the branch.

As if carefully timing his action for maximum dramatic effect, Hempel unsnapped his holster, and lifted and aimed his Mann. Misha seized the opportunity and scuttled toward the closest group of Jews, two of whom put their arms around him protectively. The wolfhound hunkered down in the grass and waited.

"*Ha-haai! Ha-haai!*"

The major smiled a tight-lipped smile and clicked off his safety catch.

"Don't shoot," Erich ordered, apparently fascinated by the creature.

Hempel did not immediately lower the Mann. The aye-aye, with almost human understanding, lifted its left hand and pointed at Hempel. It had a thumb and three fingers, the middle one of which extended far beyond the other two—fleshless as the finger of a corpse long dead.

"H'aye-aye have finger of death," Bruqah said.

The mouselemur on his shoulder squeaked and burrowed down, but the Malagasy did not appear to notice. He stood perfectly still, his usually placid features rigid with fear.

Commanding his wolfhound to stay, Hempel strode toward Bruqah. "Shut your mouth, or I'll kill you where you stand."

Something made Sol look back at the aye-aye. Its hand was still raised, its long bony finger extended toward the wolfhound, which had risen to its feet in defiance of Hempel's orders.

Back arched, snarling, Boris turned to face the trees.

Into the silence came a muffled roar, like the distant thunder of an approaching storm, followed by another. Clearer this time. Closer. Accompanied by the pounding of hooves through the underbrush and a blur of movement, a massive boar, head lowered, burst from the brush. In a lightning movement that defied the creature's lumbering bulk, it lifted the wolfhound high into the air and held it up there, a bloody trophy impaled upon one curved horn. Lowering its head once more, it shook off the dog's body, and raised its foot. A shot rang out. The boar looked up, snorted, shook itself, and trotted back into the forest.

Hempel walked over to his dog and nudged it with his boot. Like statuary imbued with life, the rest of the stunned watchers returned to movement. The shepherds, growling, tugged at their leashes, and the aye-aye, its business apparently finished, leapt back into the overstory.

"Dead?" Erich strode over to where Hempel stood, gun in hand, and looked down at the wolfhound. Even at a distance, Sol could see that it was a bloody heap of fur and flesh.

"Might as well be," Hempel said. "Fat lot of good he will be to me now."

"Shoot him."

Erich issued the order without raising his voice, yet loudly and firmly enough to be heard over the shepherds.

Hempel turned to face him. "Who the hell are you to order me to shoot my dog?"

"I am the commanding officer of this operation."

Hempel paused, raised his gun, and aimed down at the dog. "For now," he said.

If he could shoot Erich instead, he would, Sol thought, watching the unfolding tableau. Miriam had told him about Killi, the dog Hitler had ordered Erich to shoot during the Olympics party at Pfaueninsel—Berlin's Peacock Island. Sol wondered if Pfaueninsel torchlights flickered, now, within Erich's brain.

But Erich was not looking at the wolfhound, or at Hempel. He was staring at a bare-chested, sinewy black man who had stepped from the shack and into the clearing. He was clothed in a ragged clay-colored loincloth that matched the red that peppered his curly white hair. As he stood surveying the newcomers to his domain, two animals with red fur and feline faces joined him, muzzles twitching.

There's more lunacy here than *The Cabinet of Dr. Caligari*, Sol thought, as the shepherds again started up their insane barking.

"The dogs they care not for the fossas," Bruqah remarked.

Hempel swiveled and pointed the Mann at the newcomer. Judging from the look on his face, it would not take much to make him use it. Small wonder, Sol thought. Simply looking at the wiry black man was a challenge. There was a gaping pink hole where his nose and mouth should have been. The hand he held up to Erich in mock greeting was eaten away like the flesh of a leper. Dangling from his fingers like an offering was a large gray wriggling worm.

Seeing that he had Erich's attention, the man tilted his head. With some innate sense of drama, he waited just long enough to allow the horror around him to peak. Then his tongue emerged to envelope the worm and draw it down into his throat.

"Pisces, no!"

Pulling free from his trainer, who was apparently too caught up in the spectacle to hold firmly to the choke chain, one of the dogs bounded at the black man.

The fossas whirled around and darted into the underbrush. Reacting almost as fast, the black man leapt toward the hut and scrambled beneath it. The dog leapt after him, frenziedly digging his way under the structure.

Sol waited for the screams of pain which must come when a trained killer tears into the flesh of man. He turned his head to look at Erich, then at the faces of the other watchers. Their expressions held varying degrees of expectation and horror.

From underneath the hut, came a mewling conciliatory cry, and the faceless creature crawled out on his elbows. Swiveling on his stomach, the muscles on his lean back glistening with his sweat, he reached underneath the hut and drew out the dog by its chain.

The dog lay passively where he left it, inert, defeated, head hanging limply.

Sol turned his attention back to Erich. A series of emotions played across his features: puzzlement; admiration; jealousy; and finally anger. Either the creature's empathic abilities with dogs far exceeded Erich's own or this was another demonstration of African magic at work.

The stranger stood up. The hole that had once been his mouth turned upward in a ghoulish imitation of a smile. Placing his hands on his hips, he bowed slightly as if acknowledging his victory. Sol heard Erich's dog, Taurus, whimpering softly from her stretcher; dysplasia—inflammation of the hip joint—had rendered her almost incapable of walking. Beside her, likewise bound to a stretcher, lay Aquarius, ill nearly to the point of death from the long journey.

One dog crippled, one near death from seasickness, one gored to death, one turned into a rag doll by some crazy Malagasy...and we've just arrived, Sol thought. Perhaps there is hope for escape after all.

"Bruqah!" Erich turned and shouted. "What the hell! Who—*what*—is that *thing*?"

"Zana-Malata."

"Leper?"

"Syphilitic." Bruqah gripped his crotch for emphasis.

"By the looks of him, that thing turns twigs into something less benign than chameleons," Miriam told Sol with an edge of fear.

Sol started to reassure her but stopped when he realized that he felt much the same way. Apparently sorcery was endemic to Africa. He was sure they would find out soon enough what that meant to them. For now they both had watch and learn.

"Let the dogs go!" Erich commanded. "Stop that bastard!"

Snarling, nine healthy shepherds leapt forward. From the encircling forest, varicolored birds lifted into startled flight. The screams of lemurs joined with the softly insistent shrill of an aye-aye hidden in the trees.

The dogs never reached their victim.

When they were close enough so he could surely feel their heated breath, the Zana-Malata crouched and patted the earth.

Sol watched in disbelief as the animals that comprised what was probably Germany's finest canine contingent stopped in their tracks and, in unison and panting heavily, crawled on their bellies to huddle like house pets around the man's feet.

Again, Sol witnessed Erich's struggle to understand the Zana-Malata's control over the dogs.

"How the devil—?" Erich asked Bruqah.

The Malagasy tapped his temple. "He like you with the dogs, Mister Germantownman."

Sol turned his attention back to the Zana-Malata. Ignoring the ruckus, the syphilitic made his way across the clearing toward Hempel. Either because he recognized the Zana-Malata as a potentially powerful ally, or perhaps because he, like the dogs, was an animal being controlled, the major moved toward him. Misha left what little protection and comfort the prisoners could offer and, knowing he would be beaten if he failed to stay close to the major, trailed behind, head down.

Motioning for Hempel to follow him, the Zana-Malata bent down and gathered the wolfhound in his arms. Seemingly without effort, he lifted the animal and carried it into the shack, leaving Sol to wonder if the heat had already affected his brain and caused him to imagine the whole thing.

Pistol in hand, Erich burst past the dogs. They rose to their feet and shook themselves, disoriented. He leapt the shack's steps and slapped past the zebuhide door, only to re-emerge moments later. For a split second he went rigid. His hand shot out as if seeking support, and his head snapped up.

"M-must have g-gone out a b-back way."

He waved the gun, but it seemed to be a motion without purpose. Sol waited for him to order dogs and trainers, perhaps the guards as well, into the surrounding rain forest to search for the man. Instead, he stumbled down the steps. "F-forget him, f-for now," he stammered.

Sol had not heard Erich stammer in fifteen years. Had the lightning, petite mal seizure—finished almost the moment it occurred—had a greater effect on him than usual?

"W-we'll deal with him later," Erich told his troops. Confidence was returning to his face and voice, and his stammering was already less pronounced. "We have a military compound to build. W-we must always—*always*—keep our primary mission in mind."

Moving with an easy kind of grace despite the heat, the soggy earth, and the momentary physical lapse, he turned to look at the inhabitants of his new empire.

"Though I...I'm a man of action rather than words," he began, "I feel I should inform you of why you are here and what our plans are for you." He started a slow pacing in front of the men, who gathered together despite the animosity between the guards, sailors, and dog trainers. The prisoners likewise clustered, though apart from the Nazis.

"Four hundred years ago," Erich continued, "this tiny island, here in the middle of Antongil Bay, was the site of the hospital of a colony began by one Augustus de Benyowsky, a Hungarian-Polish Count who attempted to civilize the local tribes...and wrote Madagascar's first constitution. Two hundred years after that, the island served as a base for British pirates. Later, it belonged to the French. Now"—he made a fist, showing his resolve—"it is the F-Fatherland's turn. What we create here on Mangabéy is only a beginning. Eventually, we will also p-penetrate the mainland." He turned his attention toward the prisoners. "Shiploads of Jews will follow you here. This is your new homeland." He looked at Sol. "Your Jerusalem—"

Sol stopped listening. Erich's desire for a benign dictatorship was pathetic. Even if he meant what he said, Hempel would never allow it. The Jews' hope for survival lay in Sol's recovering his wits and strength. He recalled the voices of his mentors, voices from visions he had experienced for seventeen years as the result of the dybbuk, the wandering soul, that had possessed him since that terrible day when he had witnessed the assassination of Germany's Foreign Minister, Walther Rathenau, a Jew, and Miriam's uncle.

Eyes closed, Solomon recalled the words of Beadle Cohen, his mentor: *sometimes souls seek refuge in the bodies of living persons, causing instability, speaking foreign words through their mouths.* Such lost souls, the beadle had maintained, were unable to transmigrate to a higher world because they had sinned against humanity.

You must live his dybbuk's voices had told him. *You have not yet fulfilled your destiny.*

Survival, Solomon! Therein lies your duty! There are things to be done that only you can do. Only God has the right to order the universe.

God and not Hitler! he told himself bitterly. That madman and his insane designs on Madagascar had to be stopped. Hitler did not intend to make the island a homeland for Jews, a haven safe from a Europe that would like to obliterate them. It would not be a sanctuary but the world's largest prison camp. A place where Hitler could pen up Jewish assets and abilities and use them for his own evil ends. He remembered a joke Bruqah told him on the *Altmark*, which was no more funny now. Referring to a British pirate village that had once existed on the far side of Madagascar, he'd said, "This be the other side of Hell-ville."

How, Sol wondered desperately, are we to stop this insanity and escape at the same time?

"That awful man...the Zana-Malata!" Miriam whispered, slipping a hand up into Sol's and clutching her belly with the other as she rocked back and forth. "This place! I can't make it, Sol. I hurt. I...I hurt, Sol."

Stooping beside her, Bruqah put his hand on her stomach and tilted his head as if he were listening to something or someone. "Your baby will come soon, Lady Miri," he said. "You must rest."

Sol sat down on the grass, and placed his hands atop Miriam's, on her belly. How many days before the baby arrived? "We will escape this somehow," he said. "But we need to learn the terrain first, and gain strength."

"You speak wisely," Bruqah said, standing up. "When time comes, I help."

"What will you call the...our...child?" Sol asked Miriam, seeking more than anything to distract her.

She looked into his eyes, and he could see her love for him through her pain. "Erich, if it's a boy," she answered. "I must. I am his wife, by Hitler's law. If it's a girl? Erich doesn't want a girl—"

"What name would you choose for our daughter?"

"She will be...Deborah."

The three syllables seemed to tumble from her lips and hang in the hot, wet air.

"Deborah," Solomon repeated dreamily. Then his body tensed and a cobalt-blue light engulfed the space around him.

A girl of about eight fights against thin ropes that bind her, naked, to a carved wooden post almost twice her height. She runs her fingers along its chipped designs. Perhaps thirty other intricately carved posts are grouped behind her, each topped with the skull of an ox. In the background, beyond a flickering fire, stand monoliths and menhirs that evoke Stonehenge. Then, as though a sound machine were turned on, her voice breaks through into Sol's consciousness as she twists in terror against the ropes. "Help me, Papa. Help me!" she cries out. "I am Deborah. Why do you not know me!"

The light faded and his body went slack as he emerged from the psychic flash, one he had experienced several times since the dybbuk had left him.

The prophetic dreams of a visionary and psychic, according to Beadle Cohen. "Deborah, the prophetess and judge. The fighter who was instrumental in freeing the ancient Israelites from the Canaanites," Sol said.

Hope from a well Solomon had long since thought dry flooded his being. "Perhaps, after all," he said, "there will be a next year in Jerusalem."

Chapter 2

"Deborah means 'bee' in Old Hebrew," Miriam said. It took her a moment to remember how she knew that. The information came from the mouth of Judith, whom she did not know—who probably did not even exist—yet whose presence had been haunting her in these last days of pregnancy.

"As there are no monkeys, so there are no common bees in all Madagascar," Bruqah said. "It is fitting name for first woman—"

He seemed to be talking to himself, Miriam thought, assuming him to mean the first Jewish girl-child born in this place.

"How would you know that meaning," Sol said, frowning at her. "You have not studied such things."

"Judith told Emanuel—"

"Miriam!" Sol shook her reasonably gently. "What could you know of what Judith said? She was the woman in one of the visions the dybbuk brought *me*."

"Perhaps the dybbuk got bored with you and decided to vacation with me for a while." She made no effort to hide her weariness or to disguise the edge of impatience that took hold whenever Sol spoke of the dybbuk. His belief in its existence inside of him and, now, in its disappearance from him, was immutable. It was also his business. On the other hand, it had caused more than enough trouble for both of them over the years.

Seeing the hurt and confused expression in his eyes, Miriam immediately regretted her lack of self-control. The truth was, she *had* heard what she had heard where she said she had heard it, still she knew that Sol hated her propensity for making caustic remarks in the midst of travail. It was the ex-performer in her, she supposed. The defense mechanism of the singer-dancer that had inured her from the lust and insults of Berlin cabaret audiences who had known she was Jewish, and therefore legally available for rape...if only alcohol could help them overcome cowardice long enough to climb onstage. Sol surely understood that veneer. He had one himself, only he called it *philosophy*.

Distracted by introspection, she at first ignored an unfamiliar buzzing that was attempting to penetrate her consciousness. When it became so intense it was almost a thrumming, she looked upward to find its source. All that she could see against the canopy of tree and sky was Bruqah, staring with fearful eyes toward the outer fringes of the rain forest.

She made a lethargic attempt to push herself to her feet.

"Get down!" the Malagasy yelled.

Even as the words left his mouth, a dark cloud emerged from the surrounding forest and spread across what little sun remained. The shadow touched Miriam and she squinted upward. Panic set her heart racing like waves against the shoreline as the darkness deepened. All human sound stopped in the clearing as heads and eyes turned upward.

A quiet whirring began high in the air. Starting *pianissimo*, it grew rapidly into a crescendo that drowned out the incessant calling of the lemurs and chittering of the birds. Mesmerized, prisoners, guards and dogs watched the dark cloud move toward them. When it looked as if it would envelop them, the guards came to life, pointing their carbines this way and that.

"The hand of God," said quietly.

As if in answer, the sun went black, and Miriam realized the cloud was alive.

Grasshoppers swarmed in from all sides, the cloud so thick that guards and prisoners alike danced and batted and cursed the deluge of whirring, maddening, gray-green wings. Sol threw himself across Miriam, who could not stop herself from whimpering with fear as the insects, some as long as fifteen or eighteen centimeters, alighted in her hair and on her face.

"Get them off me, Sol, get them off!" she yelled, batting at them to no avail.

He fought them, but it was a losing battle. They invaded his clothes, and then his nostrils and ears. He tore at his shirt and hair. Around him, Nazis jerked like marionettes. The dogs howled and leaped and snapped, or ran in terrified circles.

Sol brushed the insects from Miriam's face but he was unable to stop the horde. He hugged her, covered his head, and squeezed shut his eyes. Miriam did the same, aware of grasshoppers on the bridge of her nose, exploring her nostrils, and fluttering against her eyelids.

Suddenly she felt Sol go rigid. His arms felt like iron around her body.

"Not here! Not now!" she thought, knowing immediately that the trauma of the swarming had triggered a psychic episode, and that the darkness behind his lids had exploded with cobalt-blue light. When she felt his body go slack, she knew that the vision held him in thrall. For as long as it did, he would be useless to everyone, especially to himself. Dybbuk or no dybbuk, he would always be a visionary, able to glance into the future.

Not that it did anyone any good, Miriam thought. The visions always seemed out of context until the event was upon them.

She felt Sol thrashing on top of her and pushed him off her belly. The vision had apparently ended, she thought, curious despite her skepticism and her fear of what was happening around—and on—them.

"Solomon?"

The word emerged as a whisper. Sol rolled fully off her and looked around. He appeared to be dazed by fear and by the spectacle of the meadow, seemingly so benign when they had emerged from the track that ran up the rain forested hill, acrawl with myriad insects. Most of the grasshoppers had settled, and were eating. Now and again a few whirred into the air, only to alight again on the closest solid object. The Nazis and prisoners were brushing themselves off, the insects suddenly listless after the fury with which they had arrived. The guards wore sheepish expressions, a result, apparently, of their cowardice before something as innocuous as grasshoppers, disturbing though they were in a swarm. The prisoners picked off the insects gingerly, unafraid, unhurried. After all, what was an insect, after what they had endured in the camps and during the long, dark voyage in the *Altmark's* hold?

The dogs shook themselves and pranced about like pups, sniffing the intruders. Except we are the intruders here, Miriam thought.

"Solomon?" she asked again. "What did you see?"

"A blue fog broken by sentry towers," he said. "Within the fog, people moved amorphous as ghosts. I felt ringed by darkness, by the fog, and by the moving bodies that stayed at the center of my sight, like players on a stage. Then bats winged past, hundreds of them, smelling of oranges—"

"Bats?" Miriam shuddered.

"I was holding a machine gun. I could feel the vibration of it. I squeezed the trigger, once, twice, three times, unable to stop, and laughed as spent cartridges flew from the weapon. Below, people shrieked and swore, and always there were the bats, soaring into the line of fire, bursting like balloons—"

He stopped, and she realized he was not looking at her. She followed his gaze and stared upward, transfixed, past the foliage.

Sweeping in arcs across the waning light were fruit bats. She had seen them in the half light of predawn, when the *Altmark* weighed anchor in the lagoon. They had hung like black lingerie from the trees just inside the forest perimeter, and Bruqah had regaled her with tales of what delicious stew they made, pungent with the odor of the fruit on which they gorged.

But they had not come to gorge on fruit.

They had come for the grasshoppers.

Grateful for his protection, Miriam allowed Sol to cover her head with his arm as the bats wheeled down to feast. Though she knew they had not come to hurt her, this was hardly her idea of a day at the Tiergarten.

She closed her eyes.

When she opened them, her fear having given way to curiosity, she saw that the grasshoppers were still feeding on the grasses, oblivious or uncaring that they in turn were being eaten.

"I'm all right now, Sol," she said.

He removed his arm from her head and started to rise. As if on signal, the insects took flight. The flurry, followed by the bats again taking wing, nearly bowled him over. He sat down hard on the ground.

Miriam chuckled. "I don't mean to laugh at you, Sol," she said, "but this is all too crazy for words. What else can one do but laugh?"

When the last of the bats had flitted away into the shadows, she turned over and sat up. She felt amazingly calm as Bruqah helped her to her feet.

"I suppose you're going to tell me those were the spirits of the dead on this island where the dead dream," Miriam said, her voice almost jocular.

"Perhaps," he replied, "they be *messengers* from the dead."

She shook her head in exasperation and brushed herself off. Bruqah took hold of her wrists.

"You are bonded to the child you carry, Lady Miri," he said seriously. "Bruqah is bonded to this land." His eyes searched hers. "Maybe you chase away ghosts, you and Solly and the baby. But do not think the grasshoppers they come by—how do you call it—by coincident. Nothing happen by accident here."

Sol nodded, and Miriam felt the echo of her own earlier musings. Maybe Solomon was right. Perhaps there *was* a reason for everything, and if so, perhaps this insanity *would* eventually make sense.

But all of that notwithstanding, right now it was not reason that she sought. What she really wanted was a hot bath, a loofah to scrub away some of her weariness, and a real bed with a real mattress.

All of which, she thought, labeled her—and not Solomon—as the ultimate dreamer.

Chapter 3

Erich stood in the middle of the compound, watching the Jews use block and tackle to hoist logs for the three sentry towers. Other Jews were building the tall crib that would serve as a water tower. The camp would never survive on the meager spring at the bottom of the knoll.

He was oddly proud of the efficiency of the Jews, managing to complete so much work in two days.

The Jews!

Next he'd be calling Hitler the Savior. Had he allowed the Party, with its insidious and constant propaganda, to infect his mind like those idiots had at the Passion Play at Oberammergau? He had gone there for solace and, he had told himself, spiritual healing after those sleepless nights in the Black Forest, where he had taken his advanced Abwehr training. Someone in the audience had whispered "Berlin" when *Bethlehem* was mentioned, and suddenly the program had taken on new meaning. By the time Christ was raised upon the Cross, people's eyes had become bright with anger and resolve. It hadn't taken genius to read their faces. The Jews had killed Him, of course. It was always the Jews. The audience, though, would not let that happen again. *They* would not crucify the new Messiah, for if the audience had its way, there would be no more Jews.

No, he thought. He might have been gullible then, but not now, when he knew the *real* Hitler. Not the public man who stood on the Reichschancellery balcony and fluttered his hands like small birds, as Solomon's papa used to say. The one who thought nothing of insisting that a young Abwehr officer—who may not have loved the Party, but certainly his country and his Führer—put a bullet in the brain of his favorite dog, the only unwavering friend he had ever known. All because Achilles had bitten one of their screeching Pfaueninsel peacocks. What had the Führer expected, when the damn thing was strutting around like a long-lashed transvestite whore?

As for Taurus, Killi's daughter, he had begun to live with the morbid feeling that she was nearing the end of her capacity to survive in this unrelenting heat and humidity. The dampness aggravated the existing inflammation in her hips; an open invitation to disaster. Her disability had increased markedly since they'd arrived—though perhaps the defect simply was more noticeable now that the animal was free of the ship's confines.

With only minor satisfaction, he watched the log floor of the headquarters tent being emplaced. Next to it stood the medical tent, the first structure to be finished. He wanted to visit Taurus, to comfort her, but to go to the medical tent could mean seeing Miriam, and he didn't want a confrontation. Instead, he reached out, as he had done so many times, and touched Taurus's mind with his own. A dull throbbing grew in his hip, as he took some of her pain onto himself, trying to ease her burden for a short time. How he detested his inability to help her more!

Angered, his thoughts returned to the people who had sent him here. He would show them all, Adolph Hitler included, he reassured himself. He would oversee the building of the base camp here on Mangabéy, and the creation of the docks at the mouth of the Antabalana River, over on the mainland. He would stand with his zodiac team of trainers and shepherds and watch the first voyagers of the greatest exodus in history disembark from the ships from Europe. But Madagascar would not be another concentration camp. As far as he was concerned, his charges were colonists—not slaves or prisoners. If every one of them happened to be of the Jewish faith and that satisfied the Reich's larger plan, so much the better.

Come what may, he would spit in the Führer's eye. Whatever Hitler wanted he would get, but not the way he wanted it. He, Colonel Erich Alois, would see to that. At the top of the list was presenting the head of Major Otto Hempel on a stick. On the beach on a stick, turned toward the East, so the son-of-a-bitch could watch the sun rise each morning while the flesh rotted off his face. He would crush them all. All. Whatever it took.

Erich lit a cheroot and watched the match burn down. Deliberately, he let it singe the unfeeling flesh of his damaged left hand. He stared at the skin, fishbelly white ever since his fingers were caught in a falling sewer grate during childhood. Despite the lack of full use of his hand and by virtue of his unwavering regard for what it meant to be a soldier, he had risen in the world of perfect Aryan men; by unfaltering compassion for the animals that were his charges, he had ventured close to the heart and soul of Germany. Had it not been for that night on Peacock Island, he might have become Hitler's personal security. As it was, he had come so close that Himmler, fearing the heat of an encroaching new power, had named him head of the Madagascar Plan and shipped him off to Africa, hopefully to be forgotten.

Well, they would find out that he wasn't to be discarded that easily, but first he had to cure this weakness of his for compromise.

Thinking of the Jews, *his* Jews, as colonists, was fine in the long term, but perhaps not immediately expedient. Hempel must not know his larger design, or the major would be on the radio to Himmler. Then it would be Erich's head on the stick.

Along with those of all the colonists.

He and his trainers were all that stood between Hempel and the colonists' slaughter. The major had no more wanted an African assignment than he himself had. Why Hempel had not turned it down was a mystery.

Because he wanted to kill the Jews?

Ridiculous, Erich thought. Hempel could have done that much more conveniently in Sachsenhausen.

Erich came to the same conclusion he had come to each time he'd posed the question: Hempel was in Africa because of him. That and some other agenda which had not yet come clear. Meanwhile, Hempel would try to kill the colonists—for himself, for Hitler, for the Reich. For whatever sick reasons he gave himself. Like the good people of Oranienburg; Erich had watched them last April, spending Easter sunrise stoning Jews for Jesus.

With Hempel in charge, the killing here would surely include Solomon Freund. Include Miriam...and the child.

My child, Erich thought.

Mine!

Regardless of what Miriam claimed. What did it really matter if she said she was emotionally and spiritually married to Solomon Freund. She was legally *his* wife.

The child is mine, as is Miriam. As they all are.

Mine to save.

Mine to use.

Feeling a great deal better, he noticed Solomon coming toward him, threading past colonists carrying fence posts across their shoulders. Till then, he had tuned out the noise around him, a skill he had developed with some deliberation. He prided himself on his concentration. The lesson had been easily learned once he'd understood that it was merely a matter of priorities. Like a frog after a fly, or a dog sleeping while cabaret music blared from the Victrola, he tuned in only what was necessary.

Pity Solomon had never developed that trait, Erich thought, looking at the man whom, during his younger and impressionable years, he had considered his brother. Lanky nearly to the point of emaciation, despite Erich's having come to loggerheads with Hempel to assure the colonists had sufficient rest and food and fresh water. Large hands incapable of real work, only of holding books or of stocking shelves in the tobacco shop their fathers had co-owned. The mind of a philosopher or a fool, if those were not the same thing. Erich snorted, appreciating his own humor.

Solomon looked around the compound as if he were searching for the comedy. "You find something funny in all of this...Colonel Alois?" He tagged on the title as if it were an after-thought, yet quietly enough that it was clear that he remained fully cognizant of his place as a Jew in the Nazi hierarchy.

"You don't?"

"What could possibly be humorous about building an advance camp for what we both know to be a sham?"

"That's precisely what makes it so funny. All this effort for what Himmler will almost certainly never allow. Not unless we can convince Hitler himself of the wisdom of going through with the plan. It's like the old question: if six men can dig a hole in sixteen hours, how long does it take three men to dig half a hole?"

"There's no such thing as half a hole."

"I think that's why I liked you. You were always able to figure out my riddles. What a pity you seem unable to use that mind of yours for anything *important*. You're an enigma, Solomon. An enigma. This operation reminds me of when I was beginning my military training, back at Berlin *Akademie*. We'd dig a hole, the officer in charge would toss in a cigarette, we'd fill up the hole and have to dig up the cigarette. No shovels the second time, only our bare hands. Then we'd fill the hole again. Most of the other cadets took the exercise as hazing, but when I'd finished filling the hole I realized what an important lesson I'd learned: I'd arrived back where I had begun, but now I knew where I'd been...and who I was." He gazed off toward the rain forest, where a parrot was cawing. He had kept one of the cigarette butts. Kept it for a long time afterwards. Whatever had happened to it, he wondered.

He rubbed his chin and, feeling the stubble, realized he had forgotten to shave. "Did you want to talk to me about something in particular," he said, "or is this just a social visit?" Again he chuckled at his own cleverness.

"I've come to you with a..." Solomon lowered his voice, "a request from my people."

"What is it you want, vichyssoise and a fine Rhine wine for dinner? An evening at the Paris Follies?"

"This is a request for something that is likely to increase the men's productivity."

"Appeal to my Germanic sense of order and efficiency, is that it?"

"I too am German...Herr *Oberst*." An even lower voice.

Whatever was left of Erich's benign mood dissipated. Sol's arrogance in calling himself a German angered him. "You are a Jew, Solomon Freund. A shopkeeper's son and a Jew."

"Yes, Herr Oberst. I am subhuman. I am feces. Offal that should be washed from the earth."

"Don't give me that Sachsenhausen crap, Solomon! This is *not* a concentration camp!"

"I'm trying to find the route to your heart, Erich, assuming you still have one," Solomon said in a quiet undertone. "You hold all the cards, and we both know it."

"That's how life is, Solomon," Erich responded. "Complicated, and not often fair. If you are expecting anyone to care—"

"*You* care, Herr Oberst. You care whether or not this operation succeeds. And you care about us. Us *Jews*. Deep down, you care."

"If that's your assumption, by all means continue to delude yourself. It's your right as a Jew." Erich had begun to tire of the game. "Just tell me what you want, and I'll consider it."

"Thank you."

"I said *consider* it," Erich said sharply. "Now what is it?"

"Sundown tomorrow begins Rosh Hashanah, the Jewish New Year. We wish to hold a short Service at sundown, at the start of our High Holy Day, and an even briefer one at sundown the following day. We would need the Torah—"

"You're asking for permission to hold a religious Service, a *Jewish* religious Service, during a German military operation?" Erich started to correct himself to *Nazi* military operation, but decided he did not want to give Solomon the benefit of knowing that he made the distinction. "This joke of yours is less than funny, Solomon. First you fuck my wife, and now you want to fuck up my colony. *With* my permission, no less."

He watched with pleasure as the blood drained from Sol's cheeks, his face suddenly as white as when he'd emerged from the hold of the *Altmark* and into the tropical sun.

"This is not about you and me," Sol said at last. "It is not about Miriam or the child. This is about the men. This is about finishing the building of the compound exactly the way you want it. And on time. My people will work better if they are shown some humanity."

Erich tried to stem his rising fury. Almost unconsciously he found himself unsnapping his holster and folding his fingers around the clean, hard feel of the Walther's walnut grips. It took considerable will to let loose of the pistol and resnap the holster. "You ever touch Miriam again, I'll kill you." His gaze burrowed into Sol's with an intensity he could not control. "The child is mine, Solomon. Do you understand that?"

Sol looked at the ground, not replying.

"Do you understand that!"

"Yes. Oberst."

"Now get back to work. I don't care how you do it, you and your Jews, but get my compound built!"

With an expression of defeat and exasperation, Sol executed an about-face and strode off. Like it or not, you will learn who is king here, Solomon, Erich thought. You will have to acknowledge that, as you will finally have to acknowledge the true parentage of the child.

In an effort to set the incident aside, at least for the time being, Erich reassessed the state of the encampment. He told Pleshdimer, who was overseeing the completion of the headquarters tent, to make sure that the Jews bladed the deck evenly; he didn't want everything lopsided—his bed and operations table, especially—in what would be his command post and his home for God only knew how long. Pleshdimer saluted but Erich didn't return the gesture. He would not waste the recognition on someone not truly a soldier, particularly one whom Hempel had illegally made a corporal because the fat Kapo had a knack for finding succulent boys for the major to bugger. As far as Erich was concerned, Pleshdimer should have a machine gun shoved up his ass and the trigger pulled.

The man gave him the creeps. Slit the throats of his two young daughters, people said. Hung them from a rafter so that they would bleed into pans, which blood Pleshdimer fed to his prized sow. For that he had been sentenced to Sachsenhausen and placed in charge of honest, hard-working men whose only crime was that they had been born Jewish. Come to think of it, he saw why Hempel appreciated the Kapo. They were two of a kind.

Where was Hempel, anyway? He should be supervising all of this. "Kapo! Where is the major?" Erich called out at the fat man's receding back.

Pleshdimer glanced furtively at the Zana-Malata's hut, just beyond the perimeter of the camp. "I don't know, Herr Oberst."

Idiot, Erich thought and headed toward the hermit's shack. Halfway there it occurred to him that perhaps he had not been entirely wise in instructing the Kapo to tell the prisoners to do *anything*. Who knew *how* he would go about enforcing the command.

By now, Erich was no more than a dozen meters from the hut. He could see Hempel's boots, resting against the outside wall. Suddenly he did not wish to venture closer. He hadn't seen the Zana-Malata since their arrival, and didn't want to. The syphilitic had made a fool of him and the dogs, no denying that.

"Major Hempel!"

After several moments the major emerged, pushing through the zebu-hide door and descending the three shallow steps. He did not bother to salute, or to excuse his lack of boots. He was chewing vigorously.

"I am giving the Jews permission to hold a religious Service," Erich said. "It will boost their productivity." He felt instantly annoyed at himself for rationalizing his actions. "Tell your men not to interfere with the proceedings."

To Erich's surprise, the major offered no objections. Not even a look of disdain. His face remained bland, as unruffled as his silver hair. Erich found himself glancing from the major's forehead to the armpits of his army blouse. The man never seemed to sweat, despite the withering humidity.

"My men have been without fresh meat for weeks," Hempel said. He pulled a piece of cartilage from his mouth, examined it, and tossed it away.

"There was plenty of meat aboard the *Altmark*—"

"I said *fresh* meat," Hempel interrupted. "Aboard ship, everything was canned."

To emphasize his remark he lifted a brow and gazed over Erich's shoulder—he was more than a head taller—toward the edge of the rain forest, where one of the zebu was tied to a stake. The animals had drifted in and out of the meadow, but Erich could not recall having seen one tethered.

He weighed the request. "Am I to take it that the beast belongs to your syphilitic friend?"

Hempel shrugged, as if he either did not know or did not care.

"Go ahead," Erich said, "but any ownership problems are your responsibility. If you know who owns the animal, arrange for some kind of payment."

Not that he really cared, Erich thought. The Zana-Malata had embarrassed him; taking the man's cow—or whatever—would be just punishment.

With two fingers, Hempel signaled to a guard who was lounging, a rifle in hand and a straw in his mouth, beside three prisoners installing metal bands on poles. The soldier pulled the weed from between his lips and started running.

Pandemonium ensued. Within seconds half-a-dozen guards were galloping, yelling, toward the zebu. Befuddled, it simply stood and watched them come on, swinging jouncing carbines off their shoulders. Behind them trundled Pleshdimer, belly flopping, eyes glistening like huge fat globules.

He and the guards formed a semi-circle around the animal, which stood without moving, apparently torn between attack and an attempt to break her tether and make a run for it. When none of the men moved closer, she returned to cropping the nearly barren ground on which she was hobbled.

Hempel checked the action on his Mann, glanced at Misha, who had thrust his head out of the door of the hut, and holstered the weapon. He looked as if he was about to stalk toward the zebu, but instead he went back to the steps and called the boy to come to him, using the same tuneless whistle with which he had commanded his wolfhound.

Chapter 4

Misha heard Hempel's whistle, but he did not move. Despite having watched the Zana-Malata and Hempel dine on the wolfhound the night before, and again today, he had not come to terms with the fact that he was expected to act as Boris' replacement.

"A mongrel like you should consider this an honor," Hempel had said, placing the dog's collar around the boy's neck. "Boris was every bit a thoroughbred, presented to me by Himmler himself. He would consider you a poor replacement."

Misha tugged at the collar. His fingers came away with several dog hairs stuck in the cracks of his broken nails. He pulled the hairs out and blew them away.

Coughing the dry, hacking cough that had started almost from the moment Hempel put the band around his neck, though the collar didn't feel all that tight, Misha wiped his hands on the sides of his raggedy pants. From his crouched position, he could see through the gap between the zebu hide and the door frame. He had heard the conversation between Hempel and Erich, and knew what was to come. He could only guess at what the major's mood would be afterwards.

Though the hut was dark and stank of food, the fact that he was alone provided a few moments of relief from the constant expectation of bad happenings. The only other time he could think was at night, when Hempel slept and Misha lay awake, going over the list of good things and bad things that had happened to him in his life, making sure the balance was still all right. Some nights he went over his plans for killing Pleshdimer; others, he mapped out in exquisite detail several alternative plans for killing Hempel. And he had added the Zana-Malata: alive, on the bad side; dead, on the good side. Not that the Zana-Malata had done anything bad to him. Yet. He must be waiting, like Pleshdimer had done. When Misha was at the camp, Pleshdimer had treated him like the other prisoners. Better, maybe, once

Hempel *adopted* him. That hadn't changed until they were out of the camp. Then the major started to reward Pleshdimer by allowing him to hurt Misha.

Pleshdimer wasn't allowed to do the *thing*, but that didn't mean much because it wasn't what the Kapo wanted. Tying Misha down and hurting him with the edge of his knife, that was what he wanted. Being mean. Threatening him. Making him scared.

How he hated all of them, Misha thought, edging outside because he had no other option. He couldn't pretend to be asleep, because Hempel had seen him glancing through the doorway. If he tried to stay inside, Hempel would come to drag him out, or worse yet send Pleshdimer to get him. Besides, the Zana-Malata would be back soon, and just looking at the syphilitic made Misha want to vomit. He sensed that the black man was evil, not just ugly.

There was hating and hating, Misha decided. The one kind was for a reason, like the way he felt about the people who had taken away his parents. And Pleshdimer and Hempel. Anything about them was automatically on the bad side of the list.

Then there was hating like the way he felt about Boris, which had little to do with the wolfhound and almost everything to do with its owner. True, he had never especially liked Boris, but he knew that was from how he felt about Hempel and not from any particular dislike of the dog. Perhaps, had the animal been properly trained like Taurus and the other shepherds, it might have been more receptive to children; it might even have communicated with him, or he with it. He had certainly felt sorry for the dog when the boar gored it. To hear Boris' roar of pain followed by a cry of helplessness and then silence had chilled him.

And to end up being cooked and eaten!

He couldn't really hate Boris after that, Misha decided, as he pushed through the zebu hide and blinked in the light.

"I was calling you, Misha," Hempel said. "Come. I want you to be present for the first flowing of island blood."

Chapter 5

The entire series of events was staged and un-military, Erich thought as he watched Misha come out of the hut in a half-crouch. Hempel motioned for the boy to follow as he strode toward the zebu and its would-be killers.

Erich started after the major but was stopped in his tracks by the trainer he had nicknamed Fermi. The man approached him, holding a closely choke-chained Pisces at heel at his side. The dog kept glancing toward the zebu and the guards but made no attempt to pull his trainer in that direction. His obedience pleased Erich, after the display of insubordination with the Zana-Malata when they had arrived.

Fermi looked down at the red dust on his boots. "The guards have been talking all morning about killing the zebu," he said in a quiet tone of respect. "Fresh meat would be fine, especially after the weeks on the ship. I would like to make certain there will be portions for us and for the dogs."

"What makes you think I would neglect my animals or my trainers?"

"You have a lot on your mind, sir."

Erich was flabbergasted at the intimation that he could overlook his primary responsibility. His primary love. "You and the dogs will be taken care of," he said, somewhat more angrily than he had intended.

Fermi glanced up. "Thank you, sir." He saluted and made his way toward the kennel area.

Removing his cap, Erich wiped his forehead with the back of his hand. In this heat it was no wonder the dogs were suffering, he thought. But suffering was one thing, brain fever another. Though they didn't have that, the danger of its happening was real. Already they were irritable and uncoordinated, not at all the fine corps of healthy animals he had loaded onto the ship. He could only pray that they would make the adjustment soon, or he would find himself in charge of a ghost unit.

"Does it really take that many men to kill a tethered animal?"

Erich turned, startled to find Miriam behind him and annoyed that he had not heard her approach. He prided himself on being aware of what was going on, not only around him, but anywhere nearby. Of thinking like a dog, he had told people when he was young. "Don't you start in on me as well," he said.

"Oh yes, by all means, let the boys play. Maybe you should dust off your javelin and join them."

My javelin, Erich thought, wondering what had become of that. He'd been so proud of his skills with it as a youth, had even fantasized about participating in the Olympics, and he'd come close, too. Miriam walked toward the doomed animal. He wondered if she expected him to follow. He did so. He would not join in the sport, as she called it. He had never killed for sport. In fact, he had never actually killed anything. Except Grace, Taurus' grandmother, who was nine-tenths dead by the time he'd used his javelin to put her out of her misery. And Achilles, of course. Taurus' mother. He had killed her. But that wasn't by choice, either. Not his choice. That was Hitler's doing. Erich was merely following orders, as any good soldier must.

If only Miriam could understand that. Solomon, also, but Miriam most of all.

He watched her move toward the zebu. The cow about to be killed seemed to draw her irresistibly, as if it needed her presence to dignify its slaughter. She stood slightly apart from the guards, who had lined up in front of it like a firing squad.

The animal kept feeding, pulling up her head every now and again to stare at her executioners, as if she defied them to look her in the eye.

"Let's not ruin the meat," Hempel said, striding up. "Just one of you will do. Johann?"

"Sir?" the blond radio operator asked.

"You're the youngest. Put a bullet through her brain."

"Yes, sir!" The youth raised and sighted his Mauser. Erich felt a brief though undefined satisfaction when Miriam turned away, momentarily shutting her eyes.

The shot sent birds twittering from the forest.

The cow bellowed and staggered in a circle, head turned around nearly to her back as though she were troubled by insects along her spine. Her protest rolled through the morning and set the dogs howling. Then she toppled sideways, as if she had been pushed over by some enormous force. Her legs stiffened even as she dropped and her head nodded twice against the ground; her tail slapped once, and she lay still.

Johann grinned and lowered the gun. A hush fell upon the pasture and the surrounding ring of forest. Erich could see the animal clearly: ribs prominent, rheumy eyed, covered with flies.

Shouting, the guards pulled out daggers and threw themselves upon the beast, laughing as they slashed the belly and gutted her. Pleshdimer squirmed among the others like the largest member of a litter, squealing as he tore out the upper intestines. They gleamed like sausages. He drew them toward his mouth, as if he could not wait for the cookpot before he gorged himself, then changed his mind and wrapped them around his neck like a boa.

Chapter 6

"A pretty killing, you think?"

Bruqah knew that to the foreigners' ears—all but Miriam who understood him intuitively, and Solomon, who was learning to do so—his words, spoken in his melodic voice, often acted contrapuntally to his meaning. Eventually they would all understand, even Colonel Erich Germantownman. Understand and remember.

"You walk with the grace of a man who hears secret music in his head," Miriam said, as if the dancer in her had suddenly become acutely conscious of her clumsiness.

Bruqah smiled, acknowledging the compliment. As always, he carried his polished, carved, lily-wood walking stick, and the mouselemur sat at the nape of his neck, clinging to his hair. He was shawled from shoulders to waist in his white *lamba*. Already taller than everyone else, it created the illusion he wanted—that he towered above them. They were so easy to trick, these foreigners, he thought. They drew fast and faulty conclusions because doing so was less tedious to them than thinking. By creating the assumption of magic for themselves, they rendered his skills as a master illusionist superfluous. He had appeared with the mouselemur no more than twice before they took to whispering of it as his familiar. The same was true of his appearances and disappearances...as if from nowhere, to nowhere. They never quite felt his absence and always anticipated his presence, which was just the way he wanted it.

"I tell myself this Rosh Hashanah of Solomon's must be of great concern to you. Must be, or you would not encourage this sacrifice," he told Miriam.

"Killing the zebu has nothing to do with what the Jews want," Erich butted in. "The guards know nothing about the Holy Day."

Bruqah smiled again, condescendingly this time, and brought the mouselemur around against his chest. He stroked its fur and ran his fingers along the thick tail that tapered abruptly at the end like the nib of a fountain pen. The creature made stuttery, appreciative sounds.

"I think they know. I think they know more than you think, Mister Erich Germantownman. You are full of death, you Germans. Yes, I think they know." He pointed toward the Nazi flag, which dangled—as though wilted by the humidity—from the first pole the Jews had erected, one near where the gate was being built. "Even your flag is the color of death. We Malagash wear red and black as shrouds."

"So do we, since the Nazis came to power," Miriam said.

Bruqah shifted his gaze back toward the zebu. The animal's master had allowed it to overgraze. He pointed toward the cow's barren patch of ground. "All over Madagascar...the same." He allowed his anger to enter his husky voice. It was simple, yet no one seemed capable of understanding: they burned the forests for the *savoka* to grow, then grazed the zebu until even that grass was gone. He shook his head sadly. "I was once the worst offender."

"You?" Miriam asked.

Until the trees taught me, Bruqah thought, and I learned from the lemurs. All of which took lifetimes. "There is a saying. *Omby milela-bato, matin'ny tany mah-zotra*—the zebu will lick bare stone, and die in the earth it loves." He ran his hand from the mouselemur's head to its tail, causing the tiny animal to shudder with apparent joy. "We Malagash measure our worth by our cows, but we allow them to kill the land that is our mother...and theirs."

"We Germans measure our worth by—what, Erich?" Miriam said in an ugly tone, looking at the butchered zebu with undisguised disgust. An apparent wave of pain, reflected in her face, passed over her. "By our...our scientific accomplishments?" Her breaths began to saw. "Or our industrial efficiency?" She shot Erich an angry glance. "Or by our capacity for killing?"

"You weren't always this harsh, Miriam." Erich's voice trailed off. He stared past them, as though something held him motionless. Neither was it a sight that gave Bruqah pleasure.

At the edge of the rain forest stood the Zana-Malata, holding up the head of Hempel's huge wolfhound. Bruqah watched Erich carefully. He saw him glance from the dog to Hempel and back. Rather than revulsion, the colonel's face held an expression of anticipation and something tantamount to envy. He wants the major's head on a stick, and the sooner the better, Bruqah thought.

"I wasn't always hard and you weren't always a Nazi," Miriam said.

The words were barely out of her mouth when her eyes rolled backward and her knees buckled. Bruqah stepped forward, but Erich was closer to her. He caught her as she collapsed. She winced and, clutching her belly, doubled over in pain.

"I am ashamed to be part of the human race," she said in a whisper. She looked at Bruqah, and the animal wrapped around his neck. "Small wonder you hold lemurs in higher esteem than man." Glaring at Erich, she straightened up and pulled free of him.

"Concerning some men," Bruqah said, "I could not agree more."

Chapter 7

"The guards do delight in death," Erich said.

"Don't all Nazis?" Miriam asked.

With what he felt was great self-control, Erich refrained from making an angry retort in the face of her insolence. He watched a zebu foreleg being drawn down like a lever while the meat was sliced near the socket. Someone produced an axe, and a hacking against bone began. Why don't they just quarter the cow and be done with it, he thought.

"I need to sit," Miriam said.

She stared at the grass for a moment as if examining it for crawling things, then, holding onto Bruqah's arm, sat down. He stood over her like a bodyguard—the two of them apart and yet together in a way that Erich envied. Away from the compound, he felt closer to her, less restricted. He experienced a territorial need to defend her, as if Bruqah represented a threat. He was worried about her, in much the same way that he was worried about Taurus. They were his; they belonged to him. He had brought few enough possessions with him to the island, so it made sense to him that he would want to ensure that the ones he had brought were not endangered.

He started to say something to Miriam, but saw by the set of her mouth that anything he said would only trigger more harsh words. Turning on his heel, he walked toward the hill that he had been wanting to explore. It lay at the other side of the pasture, a fair enough distance away from the encampment that he thought it might afford him a place to be alone when he needed to think things through without constant interruptions.

In no mood to encounter anyone, he skirted the meadow and the Zana-Malata's hut by taking a trail through the jungle on the steeper, northwest side of the saddle formed by the island's two hills. En route, he distracted himself by trying to identify some of the flora and fauna he had read about in the books he'd passed on to Miriam. According to those, the rain forest abounded with life, yet he had seen comparatively little of it. He could only conclude that his eyes were not yet trained to see through Madagascar's disguises—the way his stomach was not yet trained to digest the figs and wild ginger he had eaten, forcing him to drink half a bottle of schnapps during the night to quiet his stomach cramps.

Erich began to climb. At first he found himself fascinated by the series of tall, carved, wooden posts which, judging by the curved zebu horns at the top of each one, were the burial totems he had seen pictured in his books about Madagascar. A few were taller than his head, but most were chest-high and about the size of his biceps in diameter, stuck like ornate needles in a green pincushion. He found them beautiful and odd and could not but wonder who might be buried beneath them.

Slowly his interest gave way to fatigue. As his calves and thighs started to feel the strain of the climb, he regretted his lack of a machete and thanked whoever it was who had forged the existing narrow path to the top. If this was to become his hill, his refuge from the problems of Hempel and Miriam and the Jews, there would have to be a wider path. And, he thought wryly, he had better rid himself of the thirty-one-year-old city-boy weakness that had developed in his muscles since the demands of rank and family had curtailed his daily workouts. He would take Miriam's advice, he decided, ignoring the spirit in which it had been given. He would fashion himself a javelin and use that and daily walks up this hill to get into shape.

He put his arm back, took several long strides which carried him through the last of the trees and onto the top of the hill, and threw an imaginary javelin. The action felt good.

Very good indeed.

He leaned against a heavily sculpted totem and saw that there were more than two dozen of them, each bearing the skull of an ox. At the crest of the hill stood a stone menhir—what looked like a three-sided rock house dug into the hillside. The roof was a huge stone slab overgrown with moss. At the northwest corner stood a larger totem. It, too, bore the skull of an ox, this time crowned with a woven liana garland.

He examined it up close. He could make out miniature zebu horns, curling leaves, carved lemurs standing on top of one another's backs and looking outward with enormous eyes.

He put out his hand to touch the totem, and quickly withdrew it as the thought occurred to him that the syphilitic had probably forged the path and woven the garland. Automatically, he turned full circle to make sure that the hideous black man wasn't standing somewhere watching him. Assured that he was alone, he forced himself to relax.

He resolved to order Hempel and his men to open and examine the crypt, for who knew what buried treasure might lie inside. It could even contain some key to the true story of his hero, Count Augustus Benyowsky.

Standing on the crest of the hill, Erich watched the tropical evening prepare to swallow the *Altmark*. By morning, the ship would be gone, on its way to rendezvous with the *Spee*, which needed "mother" to feed her oil and pick up prisoners, British seamen from the *Africa Shell*—her third victim sunk south of Madagascar. He felt little regret that they were leaving so soon. He had only been on the island for two days, yet he felt oddly at home.

If only....

He looked down at the area he had chosen for the base camp. The encampment was roughly the size of a soccer field. The far corner had been set aside for the Jews, some of whom were still at work emplacing the tall posts of an eastern sentry tower. Others, barehanded, strung barbed concertina wire across the fences they had just completed. As for electrifying the fences— which Hempel was trying to insist upon—there were other, more urgent uses for the generator when they got it up and running. First and foremost, it had to be used for lighting the compound at night and for pumping water into the water tank if the rain could not keep it full.

He turned his attention from the compound to its second flanking hill, a second knoll. The hill itself was starker and narrower than this one and looked almost like a natural chimney. It was shielded by a canopy of trees alongside the sheer limestone cliff that formed its western edge. The natural camouflage made it a perfect southeast sentry post for the encampment. He'd have the Jews cut a road up the back and build a breastworks, an easy job, once that Jew, Goldman, finished welding the armor plate to the front of the small tank as a blade. The *kleiner Panzerbefehlswagen*, with its machine gun and armor plating, would serve as bulldozer and, later, as a deterrent to any would-be attackers from the main island. So it had proved to be a good idea after all, bringing the tank instead of the obvious equipment. Proved that no one, not even Otto Hempel, could be wrong about everything. Of course, Hempel had wanted to waste precious cargo space on a large raft-barge to bring the tank ashore. Erich had found the much simpler solution of using the emptied fuel drums from their resupply of the *Spee* to make a raft much like the floating bridges they'd built in his Wandervögel days.

Which left only the plane, in terms of large equipment. There was certainly no place on this little island for a landing strip, so the Storch had been retrofitted with floats. It would take off from the lagoon. That was Hempel's domain, as were the reconnaissance flights which had to be made over the mainland.

Yes, Erich thought, he could be happy here, if only Taurus were not taking the climate so hard, and if only he could avoid conflict between his trainers and Hempel's men, and the major's syphilitic friend, and....

Putting the question of Miriam and Solomon aside to examine later, along with his assessment of Hempel's true motives in accepting this assignment, he looked across the meadow at the trainers, exercising their animals while

Taurus lay helpless in the medical tent. Picturing her haunches swaying like the butt of an overweight old woman, he cursed the responsibilities that separated him from the dog. Yet, guiltily, he admitted he was also thankful for the whirlwind of duties. Achilles' execution was merciful compared to what he was watching her daughter endure.

The pampas of Argentina yearned for the likes of his shepherds! Maybe he should use the seaplane for escape. Take the dogs and the baby, and let the rest rot. From what Perón had told him, Buenos Aires seethed with women beside whom Miriam was a dishrag.

Yet despite his desire to leave, Mangabéy island seemed to speak to him in tongues he understood. It was his, in a way the Rathenau estate could never have been.

Gazing at the horizon, he tried to imagine with what newborn hope Benyowsky must have stood on this same hill and peered over the aquamarine bay that was to become his kingdom—the site of his *heldentod*—his hero's death. After the white suffocation of Siberia, the Hungarian must have been enraptured by the green lace shawl of rain forest and swamp. It was here, on Mangabéy, that he had built a block-and-bamboo hospital to quarantine those of his men who suffered from smallpox. Here, he found rest from the rigors inland...until he was forced to open the veins of his beautiful French wife, to bleed her of malaria.

Or maybe the other version was true, the one that had been as much in his dreams as in Benyowsky's diary. Erich had dreamt about the ships *Peter* and *Paul*—which the Count and his fellow prisoners had stolen in Vladivostok with the aid of Aphanasia, the warden's daughter. Barred by France from founding a colony on Formosa but given a go-ahead for Madagascar, he had sold the leaky vessels in Canton, where Aphanasia had expired of a fever. Then Benyowsky sailed to Paris, to fetch his French wife. In the dream she had become a ballerina with the Stuttgart and was on tour in Paris. He had seen them sailing into Mangabéy.

Erich struggled to recall the rest, but the memory eluded him. He lifted his hand and with an index finger surveyed the shoreline, until he located the mouth of the Antabalana River. There, in 1776, Benyowsky declared the island independent and, inspired by his friend Benjamin Franklin, wrote its first Constitution. He could feel the Count's presence, flickering pure and transcendent in the gathering evening, like the light of the fireflies that sparkled along the meadow's edge. Even the bats, wheeling and diving and soaring, seemed like black, winged offerings in the Hungarian's honor, and the very frogs seemed to chorus his name: *Ben-yow-sky, Ben-yow-sky, Ben-yow-sky.*

Erich shut his eyes, the better to recall one of his favorite scenes in the Count's diary. He could see it clearly: three thousand Sakalava warriors, in a circle according to region and rank, prostrate at the Hungarian's feet. He could hear the drums pounding as dancers swayed in the moonlight, see the Count and the King of the North slicing open their left breasts with an *assegai*, throwing the spear aside, sucking each other's blood and swearing fealty while the warriors rose to toast Benyowsky with clay chalices brimming with the blood of freshly killed zebu.

Ampanandza-be! they cried.

"Chief-of-chiefs!"

Ampanandza-be!

"We have returned," Erich said in a low, strained voice as the warriors' yowling echoed through his skull.

Learning about the Count and knowing that he, Erich, was coming here, had been more than enough inducement for Erich to do his homework.

So what *had* he learned, outside of the obvious, he wondered.

That the rain forest of northeastern Madagascar—the world's densest— was home to the Betsileo, and scattered groups of Antandroy and Tstimileo also lived there, as did the Tanal, the warriors legendary for their ferocity. That together, the tribes could prove a formidable force, and with the probable exception of the Tanal were known to unite against a common enemy. Hadn't Benyowsky said in his diary that thirty thousand northeastern Malagasy had gathered to pay him homage? The Count was given to hyperbole, but the point was not lost on the colony's European financiers: the tribes could come together, and quickly, in support of a new venture. Or against it.

What was most frequently said of him was no exaggeration— that his greatest talent lay in turning enemies into friends.

Erich sensed rather than heard a soft whimpering. He cocked his head and listened. Convinced that it was Taurus calling out to him for help, and angry at himself for wasting time better spent, he rushed down the hill and across the marshy ground toward the compound.

Chapter 8

Miriam awoke in a stupor and gazed blankly around the medical tent, her eyes bleary and puffy. She remembered heat shimmering on the meadow; guards, with knives drawn, descending on a fallen zebu; sudden light-headedness. Right at this moment, she had no active memory of how she had made it back after watching the nauseating display of bloodlust in the meadow.

She lay there concentrating and bits and pieces returned to her. Like fragments of a dream, they did not fully add up, yet she had confidence that ultimately they would. She saw herself sitting on the grass; Bruqah's singsong voice and kindly hands held her safe and she did not pull away.

"What do you wish to say to me, Bruqah?" she'd asked, looking up into his eyes.

"We believe the dead speak softly through the voices of the unborn, but only some can hear them."

The rain forest had seemed close, as if the pasture and compound had shrunk. She felt protected by it. Sunlight had seeped into the verdant growth. Where before she had seen only darkness, she saw slim unbranched trunks, speckled with light and latticed with tree-fern, and lace-fans of lichen and moss.

There is a way through the forest, Bruqah's eyes told her. Hempel's men dragged the zebu carcass toward camp, leaving a wet, fly-ridden trail. Pleshdimer pranced along, a clown in a parade, the intestines around his neck like a boa, and she'd felt ashamed to be part of their human race...

With effort she sat up. Her flesh felt clammy. A medical gown, damp with sweat, clung to her skin. Someone had undressed her, probably Franz, the corpsman. Certainly not Erich, whom she vaguely recalled having seen striding toward one of the hills.

He was doubtless angry at her for something, and if not at her directly, then at himself for loving her.

She put up her hand to her face as if it still stung—as if the handprint were even now upon her cheek where the bastard had slapped her while they were aboard ship.

And why had he hit her?

That one was easy to answer, she thought. Because she'd lost patience with the whole lie and admitted her love for Sol. As if Erich hadn't known that all along. The question that was far less simple to answer was why his hitting her had been unexpected; she had long known of his uncontrollable temper, his violence, his subsequent remorse...so seemingly heartfelt, so ultimately shallow.

Not only had he hit her, he'd hit so hard that she had immediately begun what proved to be false labor. In the midst of contractions, she had begged Erich not to hurt Solomon.

"I won't kill him, if that's what you mean," Erich had said, looking at her with a scorn he had in the past reserved only for the likes of Otto Hempel. "I'm going to let him get as close to you as he can before I take you away from him. Forever." His look of contempt had darkened. "I can live with a marriage of convenience, but not with being made a fool of!"

Since then, with each passing hour, she had grown increasingly sick with apprehension. It wasn't just the pregnancy or the mind-numbing heat that was making her ill; it was waiting for Erich's anger to resurface. Someday, she knew, he would drop his pretense about wanting to help the exiled Jews, however much he might currently believe in the façade, and act out his hatred of Sol. If that meant killing everyone to rationalize his revenge, so be it. He had the capacity for such a thing, though he swore that violence repelled him. In reality, it was violence in others that he loathed, not his own.

In an effort to stop the replay in her mind, she pushed aside the mosquito netting, grabbed her hairbrush from the bed stand, and began to brush with firm and practiced strokes. How Erich had loved to look at her, she thought, loved to stroke her legs and hair. Especially her hair. How she hated that hair, right now!...lank and sticky against her skin. She hacked at it with the brush but, quickly enervated, let her hand drop to the sheet. She sat staring down at the brush, too emotionally drained even to cry.

From beyond the screen separating her cot from the rest of the tent she heard the dogs' whimpering. Scissors, she thought. Corpsman's kit.

She swung her legs over the side of the cot and struggled to stand. The action, though minimal, made her head swim. The tamped-earth floor felt cool against her bare, swollen feet, but only momentarily relieved her stupor. She took off her gown and put on a cotton slip-dress. Giving up, she grabbed the hand mirror from the bed stand and stumbled forward.

The two sick dogs who were her tent companions lifted their heads as she neared. For now, they were the only patients in the tent other than herself.

Two other patients, showing the onset of malaria, had been quarantined in their tents. Several prisoners were also suffering from illnesses and accidents, but Erich had given in to Hempel's demand that they be treated in the wired-off, Jewish sleeping area the guards had named "the ghetto."

Miriam gave Taurus, craning up the furthest, a scratch on the ear, and looked around. Except for the mess tent, the medical tent was the largest in the compound. One screened-off corner, with pallets for flooring, served as a scrub area and held the trestle table that would be her delivery table. Though she was frightened about delivering in such a remote area, she felt confident with Tyrolt. The ship's doctor was gentle, caring, and obviously skilled from his years of mending men at sea, despite his lacking all the academic training a city physician might possess.

She found the corpsman's bag beside the microscope and rummaged among tubes and tools and gauze until she located the scissors. A mosquito droned near her ear; she batted at it hard enough to kill a horsefly. Damn things! Despite her request that the flaps be left open in the hope of a breeze, the tent was a bug-filled hothouse. Petroleum jelly smeared on the cot braces helped keep crawling insects out of her bed, but the flying bugs ate unremittingly. No matter how she arranged the cot's mosquito netting, insects found a way inside, especially the vicious gnats the soldiers called no-see-ums.

She leaned on a pallet that had been left propped against a tent pole, positioned what passed as a mirror between the slats, and gripped a clump of hair. Taurus whimpered and put her head down, looking up with woeful eyes. Miriam stared into the mirror, at a blotchy, puffy face she barely recognized. Had pregnancy changed her so much, or was it the awful voyage and this heat, this terrible heat?

Or just being married to Erich Alois?

She snipped—hard. Hair dropped into her lap. She cut again, and the second clump seemed to fall in slow motion. She felt faint and sick to her stomach at the same time.

Taurus nuzzled her head against Miriam's hand. "Poor thing," she said, dropping the scissors. She glanced over at Aquarius, who was making a feeble attempt to get into the act. "And you," she said gently. "You aren't going to make it, are you?" Erich's dog was in horrible pain from dysplasia, but it was Aquarius, unable to recover from seasickness, that was dying. Miriam listened to the breathing. Hers, theirs. Taurus', raspy but regular; Aquarius', a rattle. She felt sorry for Ernst Müller, Aquarius' trainer. The man was so upset by his animal's condition that he'd become hysterical the last time he had visited and been ordered from the tent. She had seen the hurt in Erich's eyes when he had had to do that, and wondered anew how any one man could love so much and hate so much at the same time.

If only it weren't for the child, she'd even now be with Sol.

Or maybe she wouldn't be on this island at all. Maybe none of them would. With Juan Perón's help, and without Erich's knowledge, she had finagled Sol's release from Sachsenhausen and onto the ship bound for Madagascar. Getting herself on board was no problem as long as Erich believed the child she carried was his.

As to which of the two men was the natural father, she had no idea. She and Sol had been secretly married, not by civil decree but in the sight of God, before Sol left for Amsterdam. Her civil marriage to Erich had come later, when he told her that Sol had been captured and sent to one of the camps. She'd believed she needed someone with influence in the Party to keep Sol alive.

New fury filled her. She retrieved the scissors and chopped at her hair again. If this would relieve the heat and Erich's ardor, she would crop herself bald.

She stopped and shut her eyes. Block out the world, she thought. Let me faint——

——She is lying on stone, her ankles fastened by straps, Shallow depressions in the stone fit her form perfectly. As though made for her. She turns her head, and beyond the open door she sees tiny gyrating men, dancing jerkily as marionettes. Sweat streams off her forehead as contractions roll through her with a pain she swears aloud she cannot endure. Not one more——

The baby kicked hard, drawing Miriam out of her dream. If indeed it had been a dream. In a state of semi-awareness, she tuned in to several conversations that seemed to be taking place around her. She had heard a few of the voices before, at other such moments, though where she could not at once recall. Emotionally, she had a sensation of *déjà vu*, that sinking sense of eavesdropping on the past, and yet it did not seem truly to be her past. She was bathed in sweat and filled with a new fear. Judith, Emanuel, Lise—the names were linked by only one thing: Solomon's dybbuk-inspired visions.

As a lover and a friend, as a wife and a *Jew*, Miriam knew she should, *must*, consider Sol's visions real—both the ones inspired by the dybbuk, which appeared to be happenstances in some kind of universe that paralleled their own, and the psychic flashes, the glimpses into their own futures, to which he had become so much more prone since the dybbuk had left him.

Had not Beadle Cohen called him a visionary? Had not Rabbi Nathan, internationally recognized for his writings about the Kabbalah, confirmed this?

Had they not both said that he had been possessed by a dybbuk—a wandering soul seeking atonement for sins it had unintentionally committed while alive? But when Nathan tried to exorcise it, the dybbuk was already gone. Only the visions remained. Haunting Sol.

And now me, Miriam told herself in terror. And now me.

She shook her head. She could not fall apart, not with the baby to consider. Besides, her trials were nothing compared to what Solomon and the other prisoners had endured.

One way or another, she would figure this out. "Right, Taurus?" She scratched the dog's head again.

Taurus looked at her with dark, velvety, pain-dulled eyes and responded with a whimper. She tried, and failed, to wiggle from the box. Miriam stood up and, clinging to a tent pole for balance, looked out through the green netting at the encampment. A light rain had begun, more mist than drizzle and completely unlike the previous quick tropical downpours that had struck with the swiftness of a passing cloud and ended as quickly. She stepped outside and lifted her face to the mist, as if she were welcoming a lover. The slightly cooler air enfolded her like a huge sweaty hand. The grass will like this, too, she thought, noticing that a considerable amount of grass was gone already, tramped down to spongy, red laterite soil as the men worked. During the time she had been in the tent, an hour or so, she guessed, looking toward the dusky, sunset sky, its clouds the color of dirty gauze, the prisoners had finished putting up the northern fence. Taut barbed wire twisted between rolls of concertina wire. It was beginning to look like Sachsenhausen.

Then she heard the quiet cadence of Hebrew coming from near the spring, and she felt her spirits lift.

"Dog food would taste better than what they've been feeding us!" A voice called from the direction of the mess canopy.

"Couldn't taste worse! I can hardly wait for that zebu to be ready."

She jumped as a guard pounded his mess kit against the garbage bucket for emphasis and metal clanged against metal.

"Dog food? Those goddamn shepherds eat better than us," one of the men said, loudly enough for everyone to hear.

Several others with Mausers over their shoulders formed a knot around him, dangling their kits by the handles like a group of armed beggars.

As usual, it occurred to her with a kind of perverse pleasure, she did the opposite of what Erich would have wanted. She pushed through the men and, conscious of the hard lust in their eyes, entered the mess tent. What sexual innovations, she wondered, could they think up for a woman nine months pregnant!

The smell in the tent added to her nausea.

The cook strode forward and joined in the complaints. "It's that damn canned meat! How do they expect me to cook decent *Klopsen* with canned meat? Tonight, at the party, when we eat the cow, you'll taste cooking." He pressed together the tips of his fingers, kissed them noisily, and waved them in the air. "Once the generator's hooked up for refrigeration, all the food will be fine. Just like the Sturmbannführer says."

He walked away and stood, spoon in hand and arm against the tent pole, watching the Jews.

"He used bad meat on purpose. I'm sure he did," one of the men said under his breath.

Surely there's something in there that they like to eat, Miriam thought. She looked across at the supply tent which held enough food to keep the nearly two hundred men fed for three months, until they learned to live off the land and on what the prisoners cultivated. It occurred to her that food was not the issue. *Boasting* was. These idiots were actually *boasting* about the hardships they were enduring. Good German soldiers, priding themselves on hardship. On hardship and on victory, no matter what the price.

Uncomfortable beneath the lurid stares from the guards, she crossed her arms beneath her breasts and looked apprehensively toward the knoll. While she was inside the mess tent, darkness had fallen with the rapidity of a stage curtain. She could just make out Erich half-striding, half-running toward the encampment. Over to one side, she noticed the ship's doctor and the unit corpsman, in earnest conversation, walk slowly in her direction.

"Don't worry about the delivery, Franz," she heard Tyrolt tell the corpsman in a hushed voice. "You'll do fine. I feel terrible having to leave her like this, but orders are orders. The *Altmark* must be gone by morning. Not that I'll be sorry to be away from this heat."

Leave? Miriam felt rising panic. The corpsman was pleasant enough, but he was no physician. She had thought—been told—that Tyrolt and the *Altmark* would still be around when she gave birth.

"She's more *blutarm* than I would have expected," the doctor went on, "but anemia is common under these circumstances. Make sure she eats red meat, and get rid of that man Pleshdimer. I know he's been helping out, but he has no business in a medical tent."

So the blood workups *were* more than mere precaution!

"I won't be able to bother the Herr Oberst unless it's an emergency. Even then one must be very careful unless it is a problem regarding the dogs."

Tyrolt looked around, and then replied quietly, "A fourth of this company treat dogs like humans, the rest treat humans like dogs. It makes me damn glad I'm navy. Your job, Franz, if you're half the humanitarian I think you are, is to bring what sanity you can to this craziness by giving the woman your utmost. She needs rest, proper food, and loving attention. Keep the Rottenführer and that goddamn syphilitic away from her. I saw them peering around the screen at her while she slept. Imagine waking to those two!"

He spotted her in the semi-darkness.

"How are you feeling, Miriam, and why aren't you resting?" he asked, in his gravelly voice. He smiled at her, and she returned his smile. She liked this tall, skinny man, with his Kaiser Wilhelm mustache and ever-present five o'clock shadow. He had made the long sea-voyage bearable for her, and along with Bruqah had helped her keep body and mind together following Erich's blow-up. Maybe Tyrolt did lack some of the experience and fancy academic training of a city physician, but he was gentle, caring, and obviously skilled. If only the *Altmark* were not sailing so soon, or if at least she had some guarantee that he would be on it when it returned with fresh supplies and, according to the plan, a new load of Jews.

"How do I feel? Hot, scared, irritable, and not a little terrified. What about you?"

"I feel...apolitical." He put an arm affectionately across her shoulders. "And more than a little philosophical. But then I usually do...which is doubtless why they've kept me so long at sea. I'd bore my patients to death if they didn't have to listen."

Releasing her, he stood back and looked at her carefully. "Your hair," he said. "What did you—"

"I cut it. It's *my* hair!"

Tyrolt chuckled. "Seems reasonable to me," he said. "I trust the Herr Oberst will not be too upset."

Miriam shrugged. She had bigger things to think about, like what it was going to be like giving birth here, with only Franz, an inexperienced corpsman, to help. The guards' stares drilling into her back made her feel all the less secure. Whom did they hate more, she wondered, the Jewish prisoners, or the Jewish wife of the colonel in charge of operations?

Not that she was Jewish anymore, according to the Reich. Hitler had decided that she had been "orphaned at birth and *stolen* by the Jews." She was a Rathenau, he said, only by name, not blood.

An unlikely charade, but not all that uncommon. One of Hitler's top generals had been Jewish, she was aware; his heritage had likewise been changed by official decree. Political and military need overruled prejudice when the situation warranted. She had consented to the decree, even to the making of a propaganda film in which she renounced Judaism "and all its evils," not only to save her own life and possibly Sol's, but also to put herself in a position where she might help other, less fortunate Jews.

Many of the prisoners did not consider her Jewish. "Better death than denial," she had heard whispered. And the guards, she was sure, considered her just some "Jew whore masquerading as a German."

As for Hempel's opinion of her, she thought, seeing the major walk into view, that could doubtless fill a book. He was flanked by Captain Dau from the *Altmark* on one side and by Misha on the other. Slapping his billy club against his palm, he ambled across the compound. Immediately, some of the guards formed behind him. They were Totenkopfverbände—members of the Death's Head Unit—and the ugly looks on their faces showed they wished to live up to their name.

"Disgraceful," Hempel said. "I have never seen such behavior in an officer. Babying *Jews*. Pandering to their every demand. A religious service! What next?"

"Alois told me, 'A holy Jew is a happy Jew,' whatever that's supposed to mean," the ship's captain replied. "Well, I've washed my hands of it. I've no authority here over how he trains his animals, two or four-legged, but it won't go unnoticed in my report, I can assure you of that. I tell you, it borders on treason!"

"He crossed that line a long time ago," Hempel said stiffly.

Almost involuntarily, Miriam linked her arm through Tyrolt's and put her head against his shoulder. She needed someone strong to keep her from lashing out at Hempel. Yet she could not help but continue to wonder what motive really lay behind Erich's orders that the Jews be treated humanely—as long as the work progressed on or ahead of schedule. She wanted to credit him with compassion, but she could not quite convince herself that he hadn't long since shed whatever modicum of it he might once have had. Could he think it possible that she would give her heart to him if he demonstrated some newfound ability to love?...or had he transcended that particular need and replaced it with some new conceit?

Maybe it was much simpler than that. Perhaps he had become afraid enough of the wrath of *his* God that he was willing to go to any lengths to obtain forgiveness, even if it meant infuriating Hempel into killing them all. Or could *that* be his purpose? To make *certain* that Hempel killed all of them?

"I can't stand this a minute longer," Miriam said. "I want to join Sol and the others."

"You can't, my dear, and you know it," Tyrolt whispered to her, looking down at her seriously. "No matter how much you'd like to." Casting a furtive glance in Dau's direction, he added, "Forgive me for saying so, but of late your feelings have become transparent."

He was right of course. She could no more join the other Jews than Erich could renounce the Party. For Sol's safety, the child's, her own, she must remain in Erich's custody for...how many more months—or years?

Hempel and Dau strode past them. Tyrolt left Miriam's side and faced the two officers, causing them to pause.

"You should not judge Herr Oberst Alois too harshly." Tyrolt lifted a brow, as if to indicate to the two officers that he wished his words to be given careful consideration. "People with the hope of freedom outwork slaves at a ratio of something like five to one."

Dau looked at him blankly. "Is this a medical opinion? If not, keep your heretical ideas to yourself, Herr Doktor." He turned to Hempel. "I shall take my farewells, Herr Sturmbannführer. I look forward to hearing that you have the encampment running and a good water supply secured. No doubt I will be one of the first to know, since once you have fulfilled the initial part of the plan I'll be ordered back here with new supplies and," he laughed, "old Jews. Funny, isn't it, how they all look old to me."

Hempel flipped his half-smoked cigarette toward Tyrolt's shoe and, advancing, glared as he ground it out with the toe of his boot.

"Rottenführer Pleshdimer!" he yelled.

The Kapo hurried from the kennel area. "Heil Hitler!"

"The Oberst said the Jews would be allowed their filthy rites provided each day's work is completed up to then, is that not correct?"

The Kapo smirked. "Ja, Sturmbannführer!"

"The area was not properly policed." With the toe of his jackboot Hempel pointed toward the cigarette butt.

The Kapo saluted and lumbered off toward the Jews. The men took no notice, but from the gloom of the rain forest, a dozen eyes reflected the waning light. Probably lemurs, Miriam thought, her heart pounding with anger at Hempel. If the forest creatures weren't careful, their curiosity would earn them the stewpot.

Absently she scratched a mosquito bite on her arm. When she stopped, there was blood under her nail. "These damn bugs," she said. "No matter how I arrange the netting, they find a way inside. If you are still worried about my iron count.... And they'd better keep that fat Latvian Pleshdimer away from me," she said irritably. "I can't stand the sight of him. Last night I heard him outside the tent, mumbling about *Kalanaro* coming. God knows how long he stood there, staring at me. He and that hideous Zana-Malata."

She wanted to add, but did not, that Pleshdimer reminded her of Hitler's personal physician, that revolting Doctor Morrel who had performed the conception-date tests. Even Eva Braun, who doted on the Führer's every word about who and what were excellent, had told Miriam she found Morrel dirty and disgusting.

"Let's go over to the medical tent," Tyrolt said. "I want to give you a thorough examination. Tomorrow...." He paused. "I have duties that will keep me aboard the *Altmark* for a while."

"I overheard you," Miriam told him. She took a deep breath to quell her rage and the threat of tears, and wondered why God could not keep Tyrolt on the island for a few more days.

Chapter 9

"I examined Miriam as thoroughly as I could under the circumstances," Tyrolt said, speaking quietly to Erich as they headed toward the compound gate. "She should be able to manage. Physically. Just keep Pleshdimer and that syphilitic away from her, or she's likely to have a nervous breakdown." He hesitated. "And be sensitive to her condition when you see what she's done to her hair."

"Her hair?"

"She chopped it off. I can't say that I blame her, in this heat."

"What about Taurus?" Erich asked, almost as if he hadn't been listening. He had sat with his dog during Tyrolt's examination of Miriam.

"I am not a veterinarian, Herr Oberst. I have told you that before. You know the animal has dysplasia. You also know that there's little help in such cases. I could try a shot of morphine, but the results would be temporary, at best...."

They had reached the compound gate. Tyrolt put out his hand. "I almost forgot," he said. "Captain Dau sends his greetings."

"And I mine." Erich shook the man's hand. "Heil Hitler!"

"*Zieg* Heil!" The doctor smiled wryly.

Erich watched the physician head down the broad path that wended to the beach. Not a veterinarian. Then what good was he?

He caught sight of Pleshdimer strolling toward the mess tent. "Rottenführer!" he called out.

The corporal glanced anxiously toward the medical tent, and Erich saw the Zana-Malata scuttle like a beetle toward the concertina-wire fence. Maybe Tyrolt was right. He'd have to keep a closer eye on those two, and on Hempel as well. Worried about Taurus, he'd neglected a primary rule: In the chess game of life, stay at least six steps ahead of an adversary. He had already allowed Hempel too many moves since the wolfhound's death.

He increased his pace to catch up with Pleshdimer. "I could use a cup of good German coffee," he said as pleasantly as he could, falling into step with the corporal.

"Shall I bring you one—sir?" Pleshdimer avoided his eyes.

They reached the opening to the mess tent. Erich watched the men toss tin plates and army-issue cutlery into a large cast-aluminum tub. The clang of metal against metal was the only sound in the mess; gone was the usual raucous laughter of camaraderie between guards and crewmen. The guards stood in line on one side of the tent, the trainers at the other, each group glaring. "I'm sorry to have missed the farewell dinner for the *Altmark*," Erich said in a slightly too-loud voice, trying to relieve the tension. Pretending to ignore the men's antagonism toward one another, he used a hot-pad glove to lift the lid of the largest pot. "So that's how zebu smells. Gamier than a cow, but still beef."

"Shall I dish some up for you, sir?" the cook asked.

"I'm not hungry," Erich answered. "Whatever is left is to be split between the dogs and the Jews."

Hempel's men stiffened and a few of the trainers smiled.

"Do you have a problem with that?" he asked the guard closest to him. The man stared stonily ahead. "Good. And while you're about it, make sure the Jews' netting is in place. We have no need to deal with a mass outbreak of malaria."

"The Sturmbannführer will object, sir," Fermi said.

"To what, the food or the netting? I will inform him of my orders myself. I suppose I will find him with his new friend—"

"Eating the leftovers of the wolfhound, which he seems to prefer to this," the cook said.

He obviously bore no fondness for Hempel, Erich thought, before the meaning of the words took shape.

"He *ate* Boris? Are you saying the man *ate* his dog? If this is a joke—" He remembered Hempel emerging from the Zana-Malata's hut chewing, recalled the cartilage he had pulled from his mouth. Erich had assumed it was lemur, or some other local animal.

"As you say, it was *his* dog...*sir*," one of the guards said.

Without a further word, Erich strode out of the tent toward the Zana-Malata's hut. He found Hempel seated alone at an open fire. Probably the same spot where he roasted his wolfhound on a spit, Erich thought, with a feeling of sick disbelief. He wondered at which point in his grief the major had conceived of the idea to consume the animal.

Grief?

Erich thought about Taurus and the sympathetic pain that seized him whenever he visited her.

The campfire sputtered, sending sparks among the stars, then another figure appeared. At first he thought it was Misha or Pleshdimer, but with a sense of nervous anger, he realized it was the Zana-Malata. The major continued sitting with his head down.

Staying out of sight, Erich observed the black man. Tertiary stage syphilis, he guessed. Bruqah as usual had been enigmatic when mined for information, with that infuriating habit of speaking in riddles and losing his syntax as it pleased him. However, a picture had emerged of the Zana-Malata tribe, if one could call it that. Mulatto outcasts, ostracized because of the congenital syphilis nearly all of them carried. The disease was a legacy from their European-pirate forefathers, William Kidd among them, who had made Northern Madagascar a base of operations.

The gnawed mouth with its pink, frilly flesh; the rheumy eyes; the black skin taut over cheekbones or so loose it hung like fruit-bat flesh from toothpick arms...the effect made Erich's skin crawl. How could lovemaking lead to such horror?

Hempel's knife glinted and he handed the Malagasy a strip of meat.

Erich felt his breath catch in his throat. He knew that something more than a dining scrap was being passed between the two silhouettes, something that demanded more than courtesy or congeniality. Given to a subhuman, no less...Erich fought the urge to wrench a Mauser from one of the guards and put a bullet in each of the figures before the fire.

Time enough for that, he decided. When and if matters were set right, or perhaps went very wrong, he would not hesitate to kill. Especially someone like Hempel.

"Herr Sturmbannführer," he called out.

Hempel looked up.

"The following is not a request. It is an order. I have instructed your men to give the Jews mosquito netting at once. I have also ordered the cook to split the leftover zebu meat between the Jews and the dogs—"

"You ordered *my* men—" Hempel rose to his feet. "How dare you. *I* control them. *I*—"

Erich turned and stalked back to the HQ tent. He chased the young fool Johann away from the radio for the night, pulled a bottle of schnapps from the crate in the corner, and sat down.

Drunks like his father disgusted Erich. He himself could handle alcohol, and at that moment he needed a drink. Just a shot, to settle his nerves. Maybe two.

Chapter 10

"Heave!" Pleshdimer bellowed.

Sol drove his shoulder into the narrow, green-barked log he was using as a lever. Just a few more centimeters, he thought, as the generator moved, almost into place.

Helping to maneuver it up the road from the ocean had been like toting his own prison up the hill. Everyone sweating and swearing—insects bombarding them in the barely breathable air beneath the forest canopy. The tank had done the pulling at that point, Sol and the other men on the detail scurrying to keep thin logs under the generator as it moved. Pleshdimer, like a minor god Hempel had deified, was up on the back of the tank cajoling, complaining, threatening.

Now that they were so close to finishing, the tank had been removed and they had only the strong backs of himself and his fellow Jews to emplace the machine.

"Again!" Pleshdimer bellowed. "Push, you scum!"

Half a dozen men grunted and metal groaned, and at last the generator stood square. The Kapo came forward, brushing dirt from his hands. He was grinning. "We hook her up tonight!"

Electricity was essential, Sol thought. Erich had said so.

Of course, he had no plans to electrify the fence around the Jewish sleeping area. He had assured Miriam of that, and she in turn had told Sol.

He eyed the fences with angry resignation. It was as though reality had been born with the rise of the moon, and the barbed wire coils on the fence seemed thick and formidable.

There were too many other uses for the power. In the morning, the *Altmark* would sail, and communications would need to be established with German operatives in Italian-held Ethiopia, who would relay messages to and from Berlin. Water had to be pumped from the spring into the encampment's water tank. The camp would need lights—particularly searchlights. But the fences would only be electrified if it became necessary to keep out intruders.

"Or to keep us in," Sol said under his breath.

"What'd you say?" Pleshdimer growled.

"Not a thing, mein Kapo."

Sol stepped from beneath the tarp and waited in the shadows cast by the tent for one of the guards to escort him to the supply tent for a toolbox. He found the ritual of getting needed supplies to be one of the compound's more interesting ironies. The guards rarely retrieved things themselves, even if they were the ones who intended to use them. Since no Jew could be trusted with tools, getting something as simple as a screwdriver required at least two men—one with a finger on a trigger.

"Can't you work without making a racket!" Erich slapped the inside corner of the tent.

Pleshdimer saluted the canvas. "Heil Hitler!"

"The hell with that! Just keep it quiet!"

"But we're..." the confused Kapo looked at the guards, who were smirking, and lowered his arm, "providing power, Herr Oberst."

"What you're providing me with is one hell of a headache. Who's out there, anyway?"

"Pleshdimer, mein Oberst." He added, a pride-filled smile breaking across his face, "Rottenführer Pleshdimer!"

Solomon noted with surly amusement how the Kapo had adopted the rank Hempel had given him even though no pay or uniform or induction had been effected. A corporal in the SS menagerie? Hah!

"You take your garble, Rottenführer, and drown it."

"Ja, mein Oberst," the Kapo quietly replied.

"*Now!*"

With a morose flip of his hand, Pleshdimer dismissed the men. Solomon walked to the sleeping area with a triumphant jounce to his step. After saluting the guard at the gate and being frisked, he sprawled across the matted grass and listened to the birds and lemurs, his face washed with sun. He did not even mind when a cobalt-blue haze enveloped him——

——As if in a fog, he sees Miriam lying naked and in labor, legs spread and knees up, on what appears to be a stone slab with carefully hollowed depressions for shoulders, buttocks, heels.

Candlelight reveals cobwebs above her. Beyond her feet, a skeleton in an army officer's uniform slumps in an oval wicker chair suspended from a chain.

The candles gutter. A breeze from beyond a rough-hewn doorway swirls the fog within the stone chamber. She squints against the candlelight, trying to raise up off the stone and prevented from doing so by the straps at her ankles and wrists.

He can see through the doorway, now. Beyond lies a gentle, grassy slope bordered by thicket. At its top, tall stones seem to be reaching for the moon. There are posts among them, carved totems topped with what look like buffalo horns.

Papa? Help me, Papa!

A girl is tied, naked and struggling, to one of the totems. He can see the face clearly, etched with anguish, her hair hanging in tangles down past her nose. She blows at the hair and renews her struggle with her bonds.

Three figures, man-shaped but hunched, wearing animal skins, stalk laterally across the slope, knives at the ready, moving toward the girl.

Papa!——

As swiftly as it had come, the cobalt-blue haze dissipated. Refusing to dwell on the prophetic meanings of the vision, Sol closed his eyes and strove to keep his mind blank but for the trill of the rain forest. With Bruqah's help, he had learned to distinguish the calls of the white-headed *Tretreky*—a vanga—from the warbling *Poretika* and the omnipresent starlings, but there was no way to pin down the birds' German names without begging Erich for books, something he was loathe to do. Bruqah's facility with German did not extend to winged creatures.

Except for *Spatz*.

In Berlin, the Malagasy had seen people feed the sparrows and had been amused that food would be wasted on an animal that people did not eat. His amusement was compounded by learning that Sol had fed them so regularly that Erich had—much to Sol's dismay—nicknamed him *Spatz*.

As if awakened by birdsong, a nocturnal lemur, not yet settled after its night of roaming, took up the melody of the rain forest. Its voice sounded shrill and lonely—though Sol was sure his perception was colored by Bruqah's explanation that nocturnal lemurs tended to be solitary animals, while those that prowled by daylight were social and sounded quite different from their night brothers.

Far to the left, another lemur answered, its caw piercing the drone of the cicadas. There followed the tinkle of a music box playing "Glowworm."

"*Glühwürmchen, Glühwürmchen, Glimmre, Glimmre,*" Sol sang quietly. No matter what else happened in his life, he would never be able to hear that music without replaying the first time he had seen Miriam. The first time Erich had seen her. The night they had both fallen in love with the beautiful and charming fifteen-year-old niece of Walther Rathenau as she performed at KAVERNE, the nightclub her wealthy, socialite grandmother opened next door to the Freund-Weisser tobacco shop.

How extraordinarily beautiful she had been, Sol thought. Not that she was any less beautiful now, just older, wearier.

He blinked open his eyes and sat up to find the canvas-covered area around him filled with activity. He realized his reverie had been deeper and longer than he'd supposed. Squinting in the direction of the music, he saw Bruqah, *valiha* in hand, seated cross-legged in the path that ran between the Jewish sleeping area and the main fence.

The Malagasy listened intently to the music box, then plucked out a reasonable rendition.

"Must you?" someone asked.

"Maybe some of us enjoy the music," a different voice said. "Close your ears if you do not wish to hear it."

The *valiha* and music box lifted Sol on a wave of sentiment and set him down, like a castaway, in a Berlin separated from the real world. He lay for a moment beneath his eiderdown, in the bedroom whose ceiling with its three cedar beams hovered in the haze of life without his glasses. He'd been young, then. At least he saw himself that way. He tried to manipulate the memory— to cast himself a dozen years later, Miriam beside him, but to no avail. Dread and doubt ticked loudly in his mind, and he found himself eyeing the Malagasy suspiciously.

What motive, he wondered, lay behind Bruqah's apparent devotion to Miriam and, to a somewhat lesser extent, to Sol? The voyage—a free ticket home—that much was understandable. But Miriam had said that the Malagasy had refused all offers of money, and not only from Erich, but from her as well. So what did he want? After all, the instant Erich stepped on Nosy Mangabéy, he was invading Bruqah's country, unless Bruqah was truly a collaborator intent on some future, greater reward.

In which case, befriending Jews made no sense at all.

Sol scrutinized the *valiha* player. Bruqah was so engrossed in his attempt to imitate the music that he scarcely looked up from the strings except to stare disconcertedly at the box and try another chord. After a dozen measures, he frowned and shut the box lid. He reached beneath his *lamba*, removed a small ring-tailed lemur from next to his stomach, and tucked the box in its place. Squinting toward the dogs, who were pacing and yapping nervously, he patted the lemur on its rump to shoo it toward the fence. It went hesitantly, constantly looking back, like a raccoon loathe to give up food found at a campsite. At the fence it lifted its tail and, as if aware that the shepherds were chained, sauntered with a diffident air between the wires.

"I awoke him too early. He is social, that one."

"Like you?" Solomon asked.

Bruqah laughed lightly as he placed the *valiha* across his knees. "*This* Bruqah neither alone nor part of a pack. I be traveler's tree."

"You refresh whoever needs help," Solomon said rhetorically. He knew the traveler's tree legend. Symbol of all Madagascar, it provided water and sustenance to those who might otherwise perish.

Bruqah shook his head. "Not willingly."

When he looked at Solomon, the Malagasy's eyes were so deep with meaning that Sol felt fear ripple up his back, as though he were arching like a cat.

"He who thinks Zanahary, the Prince of Creation, made land solely to serve man will awaken to find himself buried beneath it," Bruqah said.

"Then why are you here?" Solomon asked in a hush. "Why do you stay with us now that you're..." To his chagrin he found it difficult to say the word. "Now that you're home," he managed.

Bruqah leaned forward, thumb and forefinger of his right hand outstretched as though he meant to reach between the wires and snare Solomon's nose—a child's game. Instead he carefully took hold of a barb and turned it to and fro, as though in scrutiny.

"Fence is *fady*," he said.

Fady. Taboo. There was no longer music in his voice, and the glimmer in his eyes had gone from flat to fierce. Solomon realized the *fady* that Bruqah now referred to was not the *fady* of which he so often spoke. *Fady* to eat white on Wednesdays, *fady* to sit with the feet extended toward the east, *fady* for a woman not to wear a skirt. This *fady* was of a different, deeper quality. More basic, Sol sensed. And not just to Bruqah.

"Why is it *fady*?" Solomon probed. "Because Nazis strung it?"

Confusion showed in the Malagasy's face. "Your people strung it, Rabbi. Are you also Nazis?"

"You know what I mean. Don't play coy, Bruqah." Sol cautiously put a hand atop Bruqah's fingers, on the wire. "Why is the fence *fady*?"

"Lines turn the forest back—and black," Bruqah said.

"You talk in riddles." Seeing that the remark appeared to trouble the Malagasy, Sol added, "...my friend."

"I am supposed to. I am *mpanandro*—an astrologer."

Sol tightened his hold on the Malagasy's hand. "Tell me, *mpanandro*, what the stars say about why a Vazimba named Bruqah befriends *Vazaha*—we Europeans."

"If I told you, would you believe? Sometimes, stars lie." Bruqah's thin lips twisted into a wry smile.

"More often, astrologers are charlatans."

"There is that."

Out of the corner of his eye Solomon saw Pleshdimer approach with his enormous bucket on his shoulder, as if bound toward the kennel area to feed the dogs.

"Tell me!" Sol whispered.

Bruqah's eyes flicked in anger toward the Kapo, then turned in earnest toward Solomon. "You have dwelled in dreams too long not to know the answer, Rabbi. Why does a traveler's tree grow beside a path? Why are some men *fato-dra*, bound by blood, or the spirit of the newborn dead restless until it is exalted through the feast of *tokombato*?... *Fa fomba vao*, because it is custom. I know not how else to answer you, Rabbi." Leaning closer to the fence, he said, "Would your temper be untroubled if I told you I seek the child?"

"My child? Mine and Miriam's?"

"Yes, if it be your child."

"But why would you want the baby? I don't understand."

"And you call yourself 'Rabbi'!"

"I am not a rabbi. Nor have I ever claimed to be. It's just an honorary title that the others—"

"In that case, you are a fool."

Glaring, Bruqah drew back as Pleshdimer came to stand between them. "Buggering each other through the wire?" he asked Sol. He lifted a shoulder-high strand. "When she's hot, we'll let you Jews close as you want to the fence."

"The Oberst"—Sol had started to say 'Erich'—"won't stoop to that. He knows we are men of our word."

"Not a Jew born that can be trusted," Pleshdimer said soberly and a little sadly as he set down the galvanized bucket. On top of a pile of what looked like skinned rats lay an undercooked, reddish-gray haunch, days old and crawling with maggots. Sol's stomach wrenched.

Bruqah looked at the animals in the pail in horror. "Lemurs!" he said.

The Kapo picked up a stringy hunk of meat. Drooling as he chewed, he lowered himself to a sitting position and wiped his mouth with the back of his hand. "I would offer you some, Rabbi, but it isn't koshered." He laughed uproariously at his own cleverness, pulled an uncooked lemur breast from the bucket, and offered the meat to Bruqah. "Want some of your own kind, monkey man?"

"Zanahary did not create His creatures so you could fill buckets," Bruqah said.

"It's not for *me, Neger*." Pleshdimer patted his ample belly. "Sturmbannführer Hempel *personally* sees to it that I get the best meat. Nothing is better eating than dog, except..." He winked and snorted. "...except woman." Nodding toward the kennel area, he used his teeth to twist off another enormous bite, and dropped what remained into the bucket. "The shepherds dine fancy tonight!"

He stood, lifted a leg to fart loudly, and sauntered along the fence. Sol stayed inside the sleeping area and moved laterally to keep up with him. "Does the Oberst know about this?" he asked. "Do the trainers know you're feeding the dogs lemur?"

Pleshdimer picked meat from between his rotted teeth, and worked his jaws as if to exercise them.

"Why should they care what goes in those dogs' mouths and comes out their butts?" he said finally. Belching, he ambled across the grass, leaving Solomon to clutch the fence.

Well, let the dogs eat the lemurs and each other! Sol thought. The shepherds weren't any concern of his and, besides, the meat was probably good for them. Why should Erich care? Why should he, Sol, care even if Pleshdimer did give them something that wasn't proper or—he mentally grimaced--or kosher. As far as he knew, the only thing that differentiated those dogs from the ones at Sachsenhausen was the hand controlling the choke chain.

He gripped the fence so tightly that the wire cut into his palm.

...*the hand controlling the choke chain.*

Erich's hand.

His was the hand that controlled the wireless key, with its connection to Berlin and the *Sicherheitspolizei*; held the lifeline of the hundred and forty some Jews, including the one in the womb...if indeed the child was the progeny of Jewish parents.

His papa's voice came to him from the past: "*There is no such thing as being half Jewish.*"

He thought for a moment about what he had just seen and about the uses to which he could put the information. If Erich did not know what the dogs were being fed, reporting it could possibly put him in Sol's debt. Even if he did know, telling him could do no harm. Either way it was a sign of good faith that might ultimately stand the Jews in good stead.

"Jew wishing to exit on an errand!" he called out as he ran toward the guard at the gate. "Jew begging permission of his betters!"

Erich had made certain concessions to keep the guards happy.

After Sol explained that he had important information meant for Erich's ears only, he was allowed to walk alone toward the HQ tent, the guard's glare drilling into the back of his neck. Of the Jews, only Sol had the freedom to move about the camp with relative ease. The soldiers—even the trainers—resented it, and in a way Sol couldn't blame them. He *was* an enemy, after all. When not pulling guard duty, the soldiers stacked their rifles tripod-style in front of their tents. And the supply tents, crowded with boxes of ammunition and weapons, were within reach if a man bent on destruction were not carefully watched. Once the generator was in full operation, the radio could transmit messages to French forces at Diego Suarez or to the capital, Antananarive, if HQ could be accessed for a few minutes. Even Erich's gun—

"A gift for you, Rabbi." Bruqah's voice was low and emotional as he emerged from the latticework shadows cast by the sleeping area fence.

Sol glanced furtively to see if the guard was watching. He was. The man shifted nervously from one foot to the other.

"If it is not important, may *dô* snakes slide from my ancestors' eyes!" Bruqah said, passing his hand across Sol's and leaving something metallic in Sol's palm. The shape was familiar, but he dared not look down, for fear the guard would come running.

"It was in the box of music," Bruqah whispered. "Lady Miriam say it yours. Germantownman would love to possess it, I think."

Suddenly the shape made sense. Sol passed his thumb across the object, his mind immediately atumble with painful memories.

Papa's medal.

"That's an Iron Cross," he whispered. He wiped the mud from both sides and ran a fingertip down it. He could feel the inscription, etched into the back so lightly that the casual observer would miss it.

He remembered how Jacob Freund had gone over the original engraving, cutting deep into the metal for fear someone might attempt to delete it.

Solomon seized Bruqah's wrist and wrenched the Malagasy closer. "Where did you get this!"

"Germantownman take it from music box drawer. He say, 'This was my father's.' Lady Miri say he lie."

"Erich told you this was his?" The depth of Erich's self-deceit made Solomon feel weak. Suddenly, the world of Erich Alois made sense. By taking the Iron Cross Sol had left with Miriam, Erich had rid himself of one father and given birth to another. He no longer had to think of himself as the son of a guttersnipe raised to entrepreneur by a Jew. He was reborn out of his own Imperial-German imagination, his patriotic heritage fashioned as easily as he had forged a new surname. Born Erich Weisser; reborn Erich Alois to ingratiate himself with Adolph *Alois* Hitler.

"This belongs to me," Sol said quietly. He gripped the Iron Cross and squinted toward the headquarters tent.

He heard an undercurrent of sound beneath the noise of the generator and the jungle. It seemed to emanate from along the fence. He looked in alarm toward Bruqah, who put a finger to his lips.

"Look!" Bruqah whispered.

Along the perimeter of the fence stood a gathering of lemurs, too numerous for a single group. Sol had seen them move through the forest when he and other workers had cut the jungle's slender trunks to build the compound, but he had never seen them like this, prancing around with eyes as huge as eternal questions.

"My friends," Bruqah said, smiling. He scanned the forest. "Me and lemurs share a past. We the same, me and these," motioning back and forth with a hand. Lifting his eyes, he looked intently at Sol, "Dreams be mirrors, and mirrors dreams, Mister Rabbi. You must dance there...among your dreams."

A whirlwind of images swirled out of Sol's memory. "I know you, Solomon Freund," a Gypsy said. "I am a dancer in the dwelling place of dreams." An old blind man with a lemur called an indri asked him, "Are you a dog-headed boy, Solomon? Is that what your dreams say?"

Solomon looked at the Iron Cross. "Who are you, really, Bruqah?" he asked. "Can you help us...help me?"

"Only man who help himself win battle, Sollyman," Bruqah answered, turning toward the last rays of sunlight. "Child will come soon," he said. "The Kalanaro have been waiting."

Solomon spotted the natives in the fringes of the jungle. As black as the Zana-Malata, they were pushing forward through the foliage, coup-coup machetes and *assegais* in hand. They looked like small warriors, bodies pulsating with smeared mud in the sudden darkness of dusk.

For a moment Bruqah stared earnestly toward Solomon. "Luck to all, Rabbi. Danger find you, you find island's hill," Bruqah whispered in a hurried staccato. "Burial place. Sacred with lemur soul. Even Germantownman would not disturb."

The Malagasy turned away. In seconds he had disappeared into the blackness of Solomon's peripheral vision.

"Come back!" Sol rasped, turning to follow the other, but he could not find him. He noticed, instead, that a guard had left the gate and was starting toward him. Being caught with the medallion could mean death. Who would believe that he had acquired it by means other than theft?

The HQ tent. His only chance: hide the cross, let Erich discover it. Sol hurried on, pretending to be oblivious to the guard's presence.

As he neared headquarters he heard a voice slur from the medical tent beyond.

"Can you ever forgive me?" Erich asked.

Sol approached the HQ tent with the elaborately played respect one would expect from an underling...from a Jew. Cap clutched in armpit, head bowed, shambling steps. He raised his knuckles to knock quietly against the tent post holding up the front canopy. And all the while, his ears were tuned to the voices in the medical tent.

"It's not my forgiveness you really want, Erich," Miriam said.

"Solomon's?"

"Your own."

"Would Solomon follow your lead—if you could find it in your heart to forgive me?"

The cold muzzle of a rifle touched the nape of Solomon's neck. "Move, or I'll kill you."

"Would you want him to forgive? Would you debase yourself so much, Erich Alois?" Miriam said. "It would surely be debasement in your view, would it not?"

Solomon stood with hands lifted, the medallion clenched in his palm, as the guard walked in a semi-circle, faced Sol, and peered into the HQ tent.

"The Herr Oberst isn't here," the guard announced, eyes narrowing with suspicion. "Not the radio operator, either. *No one.*" He moved around Sol with the cautious wrath of a cur sniffing a rival. "Just what did you think you could get away with here, Jew?"

He jammed the barrel into Sol's gut. Sol doubled over in pain but managed to keep the medal concealed.

"Get back to your sty! Sturmbannführer Hempel will hear about this!"

"The Oberst is next—"

"Silence!" The guard swung the rifle butt-first, missing Sol's forehead by a centimeter.

Sol staggered toward the sleeping area. He hesitated as he entered the gate, allowing the guard time to kick him because a boot was better than a bullet, and crumpled, groaning, onto the matted grass. As he lay with his face in the sod, trying to wheeze air into his lungs and drive out the fear and humiliation, he wondered if he should get word to Erich about the incident. The colonel's orders had been explicit: no beating or berating of prisoners unless they deserved it. The problem was that Sol could not say anything without revealing that he'd overheard the conversation in the medical tent, and Erich was not beyond killing him for being privy to his weakness.

The pain subsided and the guard drifted into shadows to smoke a cigarette. Sol crawled over to the edge of the fence. He felt the paralytic fear instilled in him in Sachsenhausen. The only difference was that here the unfinished construction made in-compound movement relatively easy.

Then a knee bore down against Sol's back and a guard gripped his hair, forcing up his head. Grinning, the guard slapped the flat of his bayonet against Sol's cheek.

"Did you summon them, *Rabbi*?" the man said, directing Sol's vision to the lemurs. "You and your Jewish sorcery?"

"Stick him!" another voice said.

The guard lifted the weapon. "What, and spoil the fun? The Sturmbahnführer has plans for him."

Chapter 11

Erich thought he remembered Taurus calling him sometime during the night. Remembered staggering to the medical tent, collapsing to his knees before the dog and wrapping his arms around her warm neck, mentally begging her to forgive him for bringing her to this terrible place. He remembered standing over Miriam, she lying beneath netting as hazy as a wedding veil.

"Can you ever see it in your heart?" he thought he had said.

After a long silence, she had answered, "Someday, perhaps. If you think my forgiveness would help."

"And Solomon?"

"What about Solomon?"

"Would he follow your lead?"

"Do you believe he could? Would you really want him to?"

He awakened to a false dawn heavy with humidity. It made his sinuses swell and brought on a headache behind his eyes. When he dragged himself out of the chair he'd slept in and looked outside the tent, there seemed to him to be a sheen to the air, as though the sky had fractured and fallen. He winced and closed his eyes, wanting nothing more than to shut himself in for the day—alone with his military books and maps, the smell of dusty canvas, and what was left at the bottom of the bottle.

"Bastards," he said, with the triumvirate of Hempel, Pleshdimer, and the syphilitic clearly in mind. "We'll see about you after the dogs and I get through with you."

He had no intention of using his dogs for guarding the Jews. That was the job of Hempel's...*boys*, as Miriam was fond of calling the guards. Erich had never seen the dogs as guard dogs but as sentry dogs and combat troops. With Taurus and Aquarius out of action, he was loathe to do much training; the dogs needed to acclimate to the heat. Much to the anger of the guards, he had placed the dogs and the trainers on light duty.

A hand touched his shoulder "It's the animals, sir! Come quickly!" Fermi's voice sounded like a megaphone.

Suddenly fully awake, Erich followed the trainer. He felt himself running as though through glue to the kennel area, a feeling of renewed despair sticking like sweat against his skin. The trainers were each struggling to bring a raging shepherd under control. Pisces had wrapped his chain around his run-pole and was up on hind legs, straining against his bonds, jaws snapping and eyes filled with frenzy. Snarling, Gemini was sprinting the length of her run with such force that each time she reached the end she was thrown off her feet and lay squirming and growling, tugging her head against her collar.

"They're fevered, sir. I think this damn humidity's got to them." After great difficulty Fermi managed to snap a choke chain onto Pisces' collar and lift him to the dog's full height, temporarily controlling the animal while Erich, squinting against the urge to sleep, clamped Pisces' jaws together and slipped on a muzzle. "Feel his nose, sir! Hotter than a nipple on a French whore. All the dogs' are."

Shivering and gnashing his teeth against the leather restraint, Pisces abruptly twisted from Erich's grasp and insanely pawed the air as Fermi fought to control him.

"It's not distemper, is it?" Fermi was clearly worried.

"They wouldn't all have it." Erich's voice sounded outside himself. He realized he was watching himself as if from a distance. "You see?" He knelt and lifted the upper gum, revealing the canines. "No pink froth." He anxiously searched the forest. "Something outside the compound has them riled. The Kalanaro, maybe?"

"Kalanaro, sir?" asked Holten-Pflug, Sagittarius' trainer, a chubby staff sergeant with a boyish face.

"Those pygmies with the glowing face paint." Erich silently cursed himself for having spent the night with the bottle. He tried to think about the Kalanaro as he rose to his feet and peered around the jungle perimeter. He thought he recalled digging through books from his footlocker earlier in the night. He had found no mention of the Kalanaro in the military literature or the supplemental guides. He had counted eighteen tribes—plus the Vazimba and Zana-Malata, who functioned as individuals rather than in groups. In his mind's eye he remembered demographic maps; he had even found the location of the Mikea, a tribe so small and mysterious that they had been considered mythical until a decade ago.

The Kalanaro were not among the eighteen.

They were not listed among the sub-groups: the clans and moieties. Nor among the lists of non-Malagasy peoples inhabiting the country.

Bruqah had proved no more enlightening. "Kalanaro," was his only answer. "They not hurt you. They be spirit-guardians of Madagascar."

"Spirits, my ass," Erich had said, but the Malagasy had refused to say more.

Returning to the moment, he said, "No, I don't think this has anything to do with the Kalanaro. The dogs all seem to be straining toward the main gate."

"What, then?" Fermi asked, going to help Virgo's trainer.

"I'm not sure," Erich said over his shoulder.

Virgo struggled in the trainer's arms and gnashed her teeth. Her eyes bulged, but at last, within his loving arms, she briefly settled, whining and quivering. Erich followed the dog's gaze. She was glaring past the ghetto and the compound gate—glaring toward the hut.

Emerging from the doorway, the Zana-Malata stepped aside as several guards filed out and, in a mob, headed toward the compound. Hempel was in the lead, with Misha trotting alongside, leashed by a choke chain. The syphilitic followed. The two guards at the gate snapped to ready arms and saluted when Hempel entered.

Nostrils flaring and eyes so intense they seemed about to pop from her skull, Virgo renewed her frenzied, deep-throated growl. From the medical tent, he heard Taurus. Trying to tell him something.

That's it, isn't it, girl! When I was at the crypt, you sensed trouble and wanted to warn me.

More guards had emerged from their tents and were joining Hempel, several smacking truncheons against their palms as, a mob now, they marched toward the Jews.

"Let the dogs go," Erich said.

Totenkopfverbände: Death's Head Unit. He'd show Hempel what death was all about!

"Sir?" Fermi questioned.

"Do as I say!"

Fermi looked from his commander to the oncoming mob, and then suddenly, like the precision squad that they were, the trainers sensed their predicament at the same time. They were weaponless but for the dogs. Between themselves and their rifles, stacked outside their tents, were Hempel and his men on the one side and, on the other, over a hundred and forty Jews who would tear any German soldier apart if they had the chance.

The guards began to chant. "Kill the Jews! Kill the Jews!"

With perverse pleasure Erich saw the faces of his men harden. He had trained them well—though they were untried in battle, he was sure they could be as savage as the dogs. Fermi's face shone with fierce delight as he unmuzzled Pisces.

The Jews, seeing two packs of jackals doing battle over hunks of meat—them—started running around within the sleeping area and yelling to one another, searching for anything with which to defend themselves.

"Release...now!" Erich commanded. Then, mentally, he ordered the dogs to restrain the guards.

Slavering and crazed, ten of the twelve dogs of the zodiac raced indiscriminately toward anything that moved.

"Get the guards!" Erich screamed.

"Kill Jews!" the guards intoned.

Instead of responding like Erich's trained killing machine, the dogs behaved like sharks in a feeding frenzy.

"Herr Oberst!" Holten-Pflug shouted above the din. "The dogs' water dishes! It looks like someone's dribbled blood—!"

No wonder the shepherds were going crazy. Having tasted blood, they wanted more. Now controlling them would be a thousand times more difficult.

"Who fed my dogs blood!" he called out when he was near enough for Hempel to hear.

Hempel's men stopped their approach and grew silent, all except Pleshdimer, who shouted, "I did!"

Erich felt heat rise into his cheeks. "Shoot that man," he said to the guard closest to him.

The guard did not move.

"Rottenführer Pleshdimer is SS, and thus not subject to your orders." Hempel withdrew a cigar from his pocket and moistened it by drawing an end over moist lips. "None of the guards are. You are Abwehr, we are Totenkopfverbände." After lighting the cigar with a match, he held the red end before the mouth of the Zana-Malata.

The syphilitic encompassed it with gnarled flesh that once had been lips, and inhaled deeply, a look of pleasure entering his eyes.

"You may do as you wish with your shepherds and Abwehr chimps," Hempel said, "but my unit is *mine*."

"Then command your unit to conduct the execution. Or do it yourself. You are still subject to my orders."

With his holster strap unsnapped and one hand on the grip of the Walther, Erich glared at the Zana-Malata, who must somehow be responsible for this insurrection. Hempel was crazy, but he was not stupid, certainly not stupid enough to pull this kind of maneuver so early in the game. Play the professional, he reminded himself. If they see chinks in the armor, they may crumble the castle.

He drew his pistol and kept the weapon steady as he pointed it at Hempel. "Or do you intend to disobey your commander, Sturmbahnführer?"

Hempel smiled a reassuring smile, as though he intended to gather Erich in and grace him with his confidence.

"So you are, officially," Erich said in a tight, hard voice, "disobeying a direct order?"

"That is correct."

Erich's finger tightened on the trigger.

Puuuh.

The Zana-Malata had craned his neck so that his head was level with the gun when he blew the smoke ring. Tinged with blue fire and writhing with worms, it floated around the barrel and fastened onto Erich's flesh. His skin burst into flames. He screamed, fired, and dropped the pistol.

The bullet went wildly astray.

Slapping at his good hand with his dead fingers, he tried a roundhouse kick at the Zana-Malata. Off balance, he missed.

"We each have our units to command," Hempel said.

"We'll see about that! Guards, arrest those three!" he shouted, trying to be heard above the barking and growling. When no one moved to obey, he added, "They're to be shot for treason against our Führer!"

The men did nothing. It was as if they did not even know that he was there. Disregarding the pain in his hand, he grabbed a tall man by the shirt. "You heard me! Arrest them!"

The guard stared past him, making no effort to respond.

With the back of his dead hand Erich struck the guard across the face. Blood burst from the man's nose. Erich looked at his hand in horror. *Oh my God, I've struck an enlisted man.*

The man appeared hardly to notice. From somewhere close by, Erich heard again the sound of rubber against flesh. He swore to himself, pushed past the guard, and headed for his tent—and his MP-38 submachine gun. He would take all of them on himself, he thought irrationally. Behind him, he heard Hempel issuing orders and speaking to the Zana-Malata.

"Our revered Herr Oberst has struck an enlisted man," he said. "Calm the dogs, my friend. You men are dismissed. We have won."

You have won nothing yet, Erich thought. What he needed was more manpower. A guerrilla force. The Kalanaro, perhaps, who were forever popping up with that bird-shit on their faces like targets in a shooting gallery. But he wanted mercenaries who would act like soldiers, he thought, not like a bunch of gibbering monkeys.

The "sit and wait" military order, he figured, was not a Führerbefehl—a direct order from Hitler, not to be questioned—but had come from Goebbels. As a field commander, he had a certain latitude. The guards were young and, in their demented way, idealistic; they wanted to do battle, not oversee Jews creating a matriculation center in the middle of nowhere. Promise them that they could march on Antanarivo, the capital nestled in the country's cool, central highlands, and they would abandon Hempel like fleas from a dead dog. The take-over of Madagascar with a handful of untested German troops and support from local tribes, that would appeal to them.

He burst into his headquarters tent and grabbed the submachine pistol.

A few of his trainers and their dogs—all of whom were to be trusted since they were Abwehr—could stay behind to maintain the island base camp, with its superior radio and secure position. They would also provide protection for the corpsman and Miriam and the child. Erich would take Taurus and the rest of the trainers and shepherds.

As he turned to leave he spotted the bottle of schnapps, not quite empty from the previous night.

One drink, to settle his nerves. As he poured the amber liquid, it occurred to him that playing the hothead was what Hempel wanted of him. Well, he wouldn't fall into that trap. Otto Braun had taught him to disappoint his enemies. The secret of guerrilla warfare, Braun had said, was to out-think your adversary.

He sat down and put his feet up on the desk. Drinking the alcohol he had poured, he reached out, drew aside the tent flap, and saw that the compound was clear. The Jews had settled down again, the dogs were back in the kennel area, the guards had dispersed. Hempel was surely stewing in his own juices right now, upset that the young colonel had proven too cool-headed to rise to the major's bait.

He settled back again, chuckling at his wisdom, and closed his eyes, imagining his troops marching into Antanarivo, the windows of the city's whitewashed buildings open, women waving flowers and men cheering.

Chapter 12

Misha pretended he was somewhere else, not on a log beside a fire pit outside the Zana-Malata's hut, but on his father's knee in an easy chair in the tiny apartment off the Ku'damm.

In his imaginings, his father, a rabbi, was reading to him again about how Abraham did not hurt his son but prayed to God, and about how Abraham knew Sarah and also knew things about Hagar who had a son named Ishmael and slept by a well. He told himself that when the story ended it would be bedtime, and his father would shut the book with a dramatic snap and kiss him goodnight. Misha would be ushered off to bed by his mother, happy that life was good.

The boy could only sustain the illusion for a short while before reality intruded. He shifted position, straddling the log and using his hand to tug at the leash so that he would have more room. With his other hand he pulled bark from the log, wondering what he could do to cause something bad to happen to Hempel, like a fire to consume the hut while the major slept.

When they were in the hut together, the Zana-Malata dawdled at similar things, using roots and sticks and powders and impressing Hempel with the uses he found for them. Surely *something* could happen if he, Misha, kept working at it.

The Zana-Malata was only the second black man he had ever known. He didn't like him, but not just because he was ugly. His papa had taught him that no man was ugly unless his heart was evil. Ugliness, like beauty, papa had said, was something that lay beneath what was visible.

How unlike Bruqah the Zana-Malata was, the boy thought. Hempel said the Vazimba was just another nigger African, no more trustworthy than a hyena, but he was wrong. Bruqah was wonderful.

The Zana-Malata eased from his sitting place and, leaning forward, seemed to pull a thimble from midair. He passed it three times around the perimeter of the smoke, eyes closed serenely, appearing to savor the smell. He put his face into the smoke and slowly slurped from the thimble, then offered it to Hempel, who had squat-crawled forward, his hand on the black man's back. The thimble was still full. Hempel took it and looked at the Zana-Malata with solemn eyes before he drank, tipping his head back and tossing the liquid toward the rear of his throat, like Misha had seen his real father do sometimes with schnapps.

Hempel handed back the thimble to the Zana-Malata, sat on the ground, and laid his head against the log. He looked up at the stars and sighed contentedly. "Do you know," he said to no one in particular, "that I once stood in a sleet storm all night at parade-rest, without a coat, just because I knew that Reichsführer Himmler would sometimes look down from his window? There must have been a hundred of us, men of all ages, and we kept up the vigil without ever planning it among ourselves or debating whether we should continue once we'd started. It was during a winter solstice celebration, at Wewelsburg Castle. After a book burning. God what a night that was!"

He stretched out his arms, seemingly lost in thought. Misha watched him. He didn't know what to think about Hempel anymore. He remembered hating him, but lately he didn't feel anything at all except shame. He had learned to separate himself from the pain and hatred that had at first overwhelmed him when the major did the *thing*.

"Bring me some wine, boy," Hempel said, letting go of the leash attached to Misha's collar. "On second thought," he picked up Erich's Walther from where it had been lying in the grass, emptied out the bullets, and placed the gun between Misha's teeth, "the Oberst is certainly asleep in a drunken stupor by now. Sneak this into his hut and bring back whatever's left of that good schnapps he's been drinking."

Misha dropped the gun, which was far too heavy for him to carry in that manner. "Pick it up and carry it," Hempel conceded. "If he wakes up while you're in there, don't speak to him. And be quick about it."

Obediently, Misha set off through the tall grass that bordered the hut site. "I said be quick," the major called out, and threw a rock at him.

He wouldn't go any faster, Misha thought. If it meant more rocks and worse, which it surely would, that was the way it was. He knew it was a small rebellion, but it was enough to lend him the courage to stop en route to the compound and dig up the zebu horn the guards had left after they hacked up the animal. It had looked so much like the Shofar that the cantor had used at his father's High Holy Day Services that he had buried it at the base of the tanghin tree, hoping to get it to Solomon in time. That way, though he couldn't be there himself, he'd be there in a kind of way.

He tucked the Walther into his waistband, and holding the Shofar in his hand headed around two prisoners who stood between him and the HQ tent.

"That damn leash and collar. We should take it off," one of the prisoners said, reaching for Misha.

The other man grabbed his friend by the wrist. "Don't be a fool!" he said. "You think it would make things better for any of us? You think it would make things better for the boy?"

Misha held up the horn. "A Shofar," he said, coughing, his voice hoarse from disuse. "For Herr Freund."

The first man took it from him. "I'll make sure it gets to the rabbi," he said.

Misha saw tears glisten in the man's eyes. He made a weak attempt at a smile and went on his way, guided by the quarter moon which hung in the sky like a grin and shone down on the Panzerbefehlswagen which Goldman and Bruqah were working on. He remembered Hempel saying that it should be used to blow the hell out of the devils they would encounter on the mainland, and Colonel Erich saying...he could not remember what the colonel had said.

"Halt or I'll shoot!"

The boy patted his waistband to make sure the pistol was there and lifted his hands. The guard who had called out to him lowered his rifle and Misha went into headquarters, which he knew doubled as the colonel's sleeping area and the radio center. It was much smaller than he had expected, and very messy.

Colonel Erich, seemingly fast asleep, lolled over a bottle.

"So what'd ya come for," he said, opening unfocussed eyes. "Hempel send you to beat me with the dog leash?"

He chuckled, and his head flopped around as though he could not control it. Then he lay down, stretched out, dropped the bottle, and began to snore.

Standing there in the moonlight, Misha felt truly separate from Hempel for the first time in months. He felt a part of himself return, the way he had felt when, after his parents were taken, he had worked for Miriam in the underground. A message runner whose world was Berlin's alleys and sewers. He tried to remember how he had felt during those headlong flights through the city, threading through crowds, hearing his footsteps echo down deserted alleyways, his socks constantly down around his ankles. If only it hadn't been his mistake that had gotten Herr Freund arrested!

Don't dwell on it, he told himself. Don't even think about it. He's not here, now.

But the fear and the memory of pain caught in Misha's throat and stayed there. Hurrying, he placed the pistol beside Erich and picked up the bottle. It was almost empty. For a moment, he felt again as he had while working for Miriam and the underground, strong and invincible.

Until Erich sat up, put both hands on his own forehead and, turning his face toward the ceiling, began to laugh. Loudly, with such drunken force that the sound sent Misha rushing from the tent.

Chapter 13

"This," Hempel said with a calm that Erich knew belied his seething, "is an outrage."

Erich placed himself between the major and the Panzer, jockeying slightly whenever Hempel tried to step around him and get to the tank.

The major did not frighten him, Erich assured himself. Maybe years ago in Berlin, around those campfires on Lake Wannsee, when he had feared that the Freikorps-Youth leader might not like him; but no more. Fears of the likes of Otto Hempel had died when his boyhood died...whenever that was.

Behind him, Goldman again fired up the arc welder, adding a shower of sparks to the brilliance of the morning. Erich did not turn to look. He smiled inwardly as Hempel flinched. Only from the welding light? Erich wondered. Or because Goldman—a Jew, no less—was cutting and welding on the major's toy.

Putting on a blade. Turning a tank into a bulldozer.

He thought of cutting off the tank's barrel, just to spite the major—like a proud soldier with his dick sawed off—but he dared not push the changes too far, too fast. There were the volatile guards to consider. The previous day had shown him how tenuous was his position with them—if indeed he had not dreamed the whole thing.

Besides, who knew what Malagasy might attack Nosy Mangabéy once word spread of the German invasion, however small? Madagascar was French, and even those tribesmen who held no love for the Frogs—which, he assumed, would be most Malagasy—might not take well to any more foreigners on their beloved red-clay soil.

"Next time you have some question about my orders, you will come to me, your superior officer, for your directive." Erich looked up into Hempel's cold gray eyes. "Is that understood?"

Not a flicker of emotion showed in the eyes. The blankness unnerved Erich.

"I will do my duty...Herr Oberst."

"I will see that you do, Herr Sturmbannführer." Erich spoke slowly, articulately. "There is a stone gravesite atop the western hill, where the Jews are working. A crypt of some sort. Have one of the Jew...Jew*ish* details open it up. I wish to determine the hill's potential as a pillbox to guard that flank. If the crypt seems appropriate, begin the fortifications. Send ten men. I shall join you later for the opening of the tomb."

"Ten *men*? Or ten Jews?"

"Ten total."

"Then two men and eight Jews."

"Whatever. Dismissed, Herr Sturmbannführer."

Hempel saluted stiffly. Without emotion he stepped back and did a smart about-face. As he walked toward the Jews' sleeping area, he lifted an arm and snapped his fingers. Three guards, carbines in hand, came running from near their tents, at the other side of the compound.

Erich marveled at their loyalty, but wondered how effective they would be as real soldiers. Herding and clubbing Jews at Sachsenhausen was hardly equal to fighting the French and British in the trenches. Not that he himself had done any real soldiering, or that fighting for the Nazi Reich could ever be an honor. *The height of my life was my time in the trenches*, Adolph Hitler had written. Erich would fight, and well, he assured himself; and willingly. But not for Hitler. He would fight in the hope that the past would return, that a new Kaiser would be proclaimed.

He remembered Solomon's pewter Hessian soldiers and a sense of nostalgia filled him. How courageous each had seemed, lined up on his bedcovers around the hills of his knees. When he'd played with them with Solomon, he would lift a cuirassier or foot soldier and peer at it so intently that the uniform would appear to take on color and the face, expression. How could the farm boys and city toughs who followed Otto Hempel possibly compare? How far Germany had descended!

"Herr Oberst Alois? Ready for your inspection, sir!"

Goldman stood at attention, his welding mask crooked in his arm, the look in his eyes—or so Erich thought—one of respect. Or was he deceiving himself, he wondered. One could never tell with Jews.

Now I'm sounding like Hempel.

He moved around the machine, pretending to inspect the welds but unsure what he should look for. Who but a master welder or engineer could determine without testing if the blade arms, made from two of the tank's side plates, would not buckle at the first full load? He would need a whole motor pool of machinery to create a full-fledged landing facility on the mainland, once base camp was well-established here on Mangabéy, but for now the converted Panzerbefehlswagen would do. It would have to.

He stepped back as more men gathered. Jews on in-compound duty, mostly, and a couple of trainers with their dogs, which sat panting against the morning heat, watching curiously. The guards avoided the converted tank, walking out of their way to keep from crossing too close.

Erich caught himself on the verge of praising the Jew, and sliced short the near compliment by declaring, "See to it that it's perfectly maintained. I'm holding you personally responsible!"

"Yes...sir!" Goldman all but smiled.

Erich relented. "Good job," he said. "Is there some small favor I can grant you to show my...the Reich's...gratitude."

"The Torah, sir," the man said without hesitation. "We need it for the Service tonight."

"I will see to it," Erich said, remembering that Sol had asked for it when he'd requested the Service, but without the vaguest idea where it had been placed.

As if Goldman had read Erich's mind, he said, "I believe it is in the black man's hut...sir."

"*Where?!*"

"You kick the bejesus out of jungle with this, Mister Germantownman!" Bruqah said, popping his head out of the turret. He grinned and slapped the machine.

As I would like to kick the bejesus out of you for perturbing my land, Erich thought he saw the Malagasy's eyes say. He wondered if Bruqah had been inside the tank the entire time Goldman was welding, but that too became secondary as the Panzerbefehlswagen rumbled into life, spitting blue exhaust.

"I drive you!" Bruqah shouted.

Erich leapt onto the machine, ready to tear the Malagasy's head off, but no sooner was he close than Bruqah clutched his wrist. The African had amazing strength for one so thin, Erich realized. The grip was near to cracking his bones.

"I good driver," Bruqah said in a voice just loud enough for Erich to hear. He gave the guards, emerging from beneath the mess canopy, a broad, theatrical grin.

Erich pried the Malagasy's fingers from his wrist. "Where on Earth did you learn...?"

Bruqah continued to grin at the guards. "German Southwest Africa, where I learn to speak German. War with South Africa. Many, many battles."

Erich knew about Bruqah's having lived in the German protectorate where he had earned or was given a trip to Berlin. Botanical study at the university, or some such thing; until now, Erich assumed it had been political, an excuse to train another African operative. How and why Bruqah had left Madagascar, Erich was uncertain. He made a mental note to try and find out. Perhaps Miriam would know. She and the Malagasy had been close aboard ship. Too close, in Erich's estimation.

"I take you...how the North Americans say? Around the blockhead. We take Lady Miri, too, maybe? Or does Mister Germantownman plan to lazy around here all day like a pet lemur?"

Erich stood on unsure legs as Bruqah dropped back into the turret and drove the machine toward the gate, the soldiers parting like a sea. "Pretty good ride, eh Germantownman?" the Malagasy shouted from inside.

The tank lumbered around the compound, kicking up dust and grass.

"We go back for Lady Miri, like I say?" Bruqah asked. "Ride she and baby?"

"No," Erich said. But an image of Miriam as a young girl, riding with him on the Ferris wheel at Berlin's Luna Park, induced him to change his mind. Soon Miriam was propped as comfortably as possible on the Panzer.

Standing in the turret, Erich directed the driving. It was a heady feeling, as though he were leading an armored charge. His headache, lately a regular morning event, became a tolerable throb, and he did not let the sight of Solomon being marched off with a detail of woodcutters spoil his festive mood. Everyone merely had to be patient, himself most of all, he decided. Things would work out for the best, if the Panzer was any indication. Who but a Jew could see a plowshare in a sword? *That*, if for no other reason, was why the Madagascar Experiment would succeed!...because he, unlike blind fools such as Hempel and Hitler, understood the value and purpose of the Jewish people.

They had three months to secure Mangabéy as a base of operations and build a dock and receiving station on the mainland, at the mouth of the Antabalana River. If they failed, Goebbels would send no more Jews.

Well, he'd meet the deadline with weeks to spare.

He leaned nonchalantly against the turret as Bruqah drove the machine across the compound yard, and signaled for the gate to be opened. Then they were in the meadow proper, spewing chaff and dirt as Bruqah ran in the *savoka* stubble alongside the forest.

Erich motioned straight ahead, feeling like the commander of an armored division going into battle.

They neared the Zana-Malata's hut.

In an inspiration born of hate, Erich banged his fist against the turret to get Bruqah's attention. "There!" He pointed toward the hut. "Go there! Knock it down!"

The tank stopped. Bruqah ground the gears, but the machine only wheezed and sat still.

"What's the meaning of this!" Erich yelled.

"Zana-Malata protect his home." Bruqah cranked up the engine again and jammed the tank into gear. Within meters it stopped again.

Erich grabbed the Malagasy by the edge of his *lamba* and, surprised by his own strength, fairly yanked him from the driver's seat. Bruqah arose choking, flailing his arms ineffectually against his assailant. Erich jumped into the driver's seat and positioned himself. How to begin? he wondered. It angered him that, despite his years in the military, he had no working knowledge of armor. As a member of the Abwehr, the intelligence sector, he'd had less opportunity for combat training than did a line officer, and even most of them lacked specialized skills regarding most weapons, but it infuriated him that he knew so little. He hit the accelerator. The tank ran in reverse. He braked, left the machine in idle, and climbed from the turret.

"Take us home," he said to the Malagasy, who was reclined across the top plating.

The words were scarcely out of Erich's mouth when, from inside the hut, there came a piteous screech of terror so penetrating that it rose even above the noise of the tank. At first he thought it was a dog, or one of those fox-lynxes that intermittently emerged from the rain forest. Fossas, it had said in one of the books he'd brought. He had a footlocker full of books. Madagascar, tactics, *The German Shepherd Dog in Word and Picture* by Rittmeister Max von Stephanitz. The one book he'd had since boyhood.

A moment later Misha's small form hurtled from the hut, rose to all fours, and crawled toward the smoking ashes of the fire pit. A simmering anger displaced Erich's sense of bravado.

Jumping down from the tank, he stalked over toward the boy. The child swiveled and backed up, bare feet stepping through the fire pit, face distorted with such terror that one might have thought the tank was chasing him. The taste of bile swilled into Erich's mouth—residue of last night's drinking, he assured himself; as a soldier he could stomach *anything*.

Except for a dog collar and a pair of ragged, cut-off pants, the boy was naked. Furious, Erich flashed back to his own youth and his years in the Freikorps, with Otto Hempel as the youth group's leader. He remembered the night he ran away from home and came across Hempel and two boys who were no more than children. He remembered the man's grunts, and the snap of a whip against one boy's fleshy pink buttocks in that Ku'damm alleyway.

"Come here, Misha," Erich said, his hatred of Hempel rising to new heights.

So terror-filled a moment before, the boy's face became suddenly, inexplicably blank. He ceased backing and bowed, mechanical as a tiny wooden monkey held between two sticks. "I am a filthy Jew not fit to kiss your feet," he said. The dog paws danced against his chest. Tears brimmed and began trailing down his cheeks. "Filthy and not fit!" he said again. Coughing, he lowered his face, striking the top of his head with angry fists, as if attempting to beat his own brains in.

"Stop it!"

"...to kiss your...feet!"

"Stop it, I say!" Erich seized the boy by the shoulders and shook him.

"...to kiss your feet...*sir*!"

The boy's eyes rolled up and he slumped sideways. Erich caught him by the waist, and the child doubled over like a sandbag. Lifting him up, Erich started for the hut, then changed his mind and carried the boy to the tank. Hempel's property or no, the child was *not* going to endure again whatever had just transpired in that shack. The hell with Hempel: a man who did not own his own soul had no right to own anything else.

Then he remembered the Torah.

He handed the boy to Bruqah and strode quickly toward the hut. As he drew near, a pungent odor of overripe oranges hung in the air. He saw one of the Kalanaro creep up to peer beneath the doorway's tanhide and watched him retreat, whispering and pointing, as another joined him, nodding excitedly. Seeing Erich, they skittered away behind the tanghin tree—pygmies with heads like hairy coconuts and mouselemur eyes too big for their faces, shining black as boot polish. Their lurking and scuttling along the edge of the *savoka* gave him the creeps, but he renewed his intention to find out if they were trainable.

Wrenching aside the zebu hide, he entered the hut, squinting against the smoke rising from the brazier. As his vision cleared, he saw the major seated on a mat and bent over the Torah that had been carried aboard ship and used in the documentary being made by Leni Riefenstahl, Hitler's favorite propaganda-film producer. The silver scroll-caps had been pried off. Hempel held one; the Zana-Malata, the other. The syphilitic was wearing a breast-covering of crocodile skin trimmed with tufts of bright feathers. He sat in a crude raffia chair, legs apart, his breechcloth lumped in his crotch.

He cackled as if in response to something Hempel had done, and bent to slurp a mouthful of sea urchin that overflowed his other palm, gumming the soft meat like a toothless crone. After licking his fingers, he raised the scroll-cap and chortled.

"*Prosit!*" Hempel toasted, lifting the second silver cap. With his other hand, he picked up a stick and stirred the contents of a large cast-iron pot that sat among the brazier's coals. Steam and an aroma reminiscent of Grand Marnier drifted from the pot.

Hempel inhaled deeply. "Flavored with fruit bat. At first I found the idea revolting, like something out of the Middle Ages, but it's delicious."

Smiling, he looked up at Erich through bleary eyes that reflected the brazier's glow, and lifted the liquid-filled scroll cap. "*Rano vola,*" he said. "The national drink. They add water to the leftover rice that sticks to the bottom of the cooking pot, and boil it."

He sipped, then with forefinger and thumb lifted out a sauce-covered wing. Popping it into his mouth, he crunched down on the tiny bones, smacking his lips. "Just what we should do to your Jew friends. Use them as flavoring. Do you know how sweet human fat smells?"

He laughed and, closing his eyes, flared his nostrils in mock anticipation. "But pardon my manners, Herr Oberst." He gestured for Erich to sit down. "Pull up a mat. Luncheon in Madagascar is a delightful event."

Finishing the drink, Hempel put down the scroll cap and, ducking his head to the Zana-Malata's lap, used the edge of the breechcloth to dab his lips, which sent the syphilitic into renewed gales of laughter.

Straightening, Hempel held up a hand as if to halt an accusation before the senior officer had a chance to speak. "No, Herr Oberst. Not drunk. *I have never in my life been drunk, nor shall I ever be. I am merely* contented."

He stretched up an arm and ran his fingertips along the Zana-Malata's dark, chaffed cheekbones, like a photographer sensing the spirit in his model before a session. "He's shown me my dreams."

Erich's stomach turned, and he fought to contain his anger. The major needed a straight jacket, he thought. Insubordination was no longer the issue; evidence for a firing squad lay at his feet. Taking the Torah could be construed as theft, a capital offense on a combat mission.

Looking from the Torah's de-jeweled sheath to the tiny pyramids of sapphires and pearls that gleamed in the sockets of the water buffalo skull in the corner, Erich asked, "By whose authority have you stolen and desecrated Party property?"

Hempel laughed sarcastically. "By yours and God's, or do you consider those to be one and the same?"

"You disgrace the uniform of the Reich."

"And you, Herr Oberst? I assume you have come to reclaim the Torah in order to loan it to the Jew vermin so they can practice their unholy rites—within a German military installation, no less!" Hempel was grinning, but his eyes narrowed as he spoke. "For your information, you gave permission for the killing of the zebu, and insisted that righteous payment be made to the owner." He pointed at the Zana-Malata and then at the Torah. "Owner, payment. It was what he wanted. I merely delivered it to him. Now if you have nothing more pleasant to say, I suggest you leave."

"Not without the Torah," Erich said. "And you might as well know that I am taking the boy, Misha, with me, too. You have buggered him for the last time."

His right hand settled on his pistol grip and unsnapped the holster, expecting and hoping that Hempel would try to hit him with whatever it was he was holding. He tensed his forearm for a block and used his peripheral vision to locate Hempel's forward knee. That was where the bullet should go. It would drop him nicely, but would not greatly delay the court martial. A good lesson for the troops.

To his astonishment, Hempel merely shrugged.

The devious bastard was doubtless playing with him, Erich thought, wanting him to believe that he had won so that he would be caught offguard by his attack...when it came, and whatever it turned out to be. He had a feeling it would pay him well to watch his back.

Without a further word, Erich picked up the Torah and the scroll caps, and left the hut.

He found Bruqah gazing toward the shack. "Zana-Malata gather magic like bee gather honey." He straightened his *lamba* and slid back down into the turret, eyes flashing toward the colonel. "Mister Erich-Germantownman be wise to hold she temperament from now on."

He clanked down the hatch and started the engine.

Erich looked at Miriam, who was holding Misha. The boy was skinny enough that despite her bulk she could cradle him on her lap. Erich hoisted himself up and, sitting down on the slitted plates above the engine, stroked the boy's head.

"Misha," he said softly.

Looking over his shoulder, Erich told Bruqah, "Drive up the hill." It would be good for Miriam and the boy to be up there away from the compound. Besides, he wanted to be present when they opened the crypt, which should be any time now.

The Panzer growled and snorted and turned on its treads without forward motion. The child's eyes opened suddenly and fearfully, and his body stiffened. Thinking that boy might fall from Miriam's lap, Erich put out a hand to steady him. Miriam pushed it away with a strange motion. Though her eyes were open, he got the disquieting sense that she was asleep; smiling serenely, she placed forefinger and thumb under the boy's brows and lowered the eyelids as one might those of the dead.

Chapter 14

"Into the cage, *Hundescheiss*."

Clutching at tufts of grass, Solomon crawled toward the tiny prison. He found the cage and jerked open the door with a clattering of chain.

He pulled himself inside and sat as he had done so many times at Sachsenhausen, head scrunched down against drawn-up knees. Hempel kicked him to make him move further in, then slammed and chained the door.

Do what you must to me, but stay away from Miriam, Sol prayed, wondering why he imagined that his words could have any meaning for the God who seemed to have deserted him all over again. At that moment, it seemed to be as unlikely a possibility as that of appealing to Hempel having any effect.

Any *positive* effect, he amended his thoughts.

"See how much good your precious Torah will do you sitting out here in the sun," Hempel said, adding, "and I remind you again that you can thank your friend, the good Herr Oberst, for this little holiday." The guards who had hastily built the cage laughed.

Sol heard a familiar metallic grating as Hempel checked the magazine of his pistol. He fought the dread that threatened to overcome him. Again it's come to this, he thought. So much of my life dependent on Erich's actions.

His heart beat wildly, pounding against his chest. Don't let the hate crowd out hope, he told himself. Surely Erich will save me, as a matter of pride, if nothing else.

He heard Hempel and his men walk away, still laughing.

Sol's tension abruptly uncoiled, and his body sagged with helplessness. Slipping from around his legs, his arms fell to his sides. He thought he heard himself mumbling a prayer, but he hadn't the energy to listen or stop. His mind seemed incapable even of subvocalizing the words, yet his lips kept moving. Insects buzzed and bit him and ran up his arms and legs, seeking his sweat.

Deborah, the blazing sun beat out on his head. *Deborah.*

The name came to him on the humid wind, rustling the grass and touching him so tenderly that he felt compelled to repeat it. "De-bor-ah." Tongue against frontal palette, a brief compression of lips, a tiny outrush of breath.

The whispered syllables gave him such reassurance that he opened his eyes despite the pain and disorientation, but instead of the compound and the hut, he saw cobalt-blue light pinwheel before him——

——*Amorphous figures move about him in a pulsing blue haze.* Unfamiliar hands grip him. He squalls for the woman who lies nearby, wanting her love.

Mama, he wants to say, but can only wail.

White, ragged, fearful heads leer down from the edges of the fog. He sees zebu skulls. In the corner of a hut.

A thousand needles stab his eyes, but Solomon squints harder, concentrating his focus, his face thrust as much as possible between the bars.

In a glimpse immediately overwhelmed with blue pain, the haze lifts——

Zebu skulls! In the corners of the hut!

Was he seeing into the future again?

The breeze wafted against his face, cooling him enough to allow the pain from the beating he had received at Pleshdimer's hands—and Hempel's instructions—to penetrate. Intruding into the pain came a renewed maelstrom of blue——

——*Fingernails as long as talons tie a length of wire around a blanket of cypress palm.*——

——*Through the door of the Storch, he sees Hempel raise his Mann.*——

——*The Zana-Malata rushes toward a baby wrapped in cloth.*——

"Leave her alone!" Sol screamed, shaking the bamboo bars.

For a moment the talking in the compound, the tinking of hammers against metal, the sawing in the jungle, all ceased. The only sound in the universe seemed to be the thunder of his anguish.

"Deborah! My God! Miriam!"

Tears of fury burst from him and he ground his knuckles against his eyes, hating all the agonies they'd witnessed. "Do something, Erich!" he ranted. "Prove to the world that you've got some courage."

His body slackened against the bars and he cried, his breaths an angry rasping. When his anger was spent, his normal vision—poor though it was—had returned. He saw bamboo and grass and wire, and an orange sun, and he could hear the dogs yapping and yowling, pacing back and forth on their runs like expectant fathers.

"Erich," he whispered. "Take care of Miriam and the child."

You must dwell among your dreams, the wind whispered back.

It was Bruqah's voice, but it reminded him of something deeper in his past. He smelled ginger cakes and apple-peel tea, and he thought he heard the crunch of autumn leaves underfoot. When he squinted upward, the sunlight seemed to have coalesced into a tunneled steep of stairs with a red-orange orb at their end, and he felt as if he could hike through the sky and unlock the sun, a vault containing the power of his meditations and memories, if only he were willing to confront the moon and his nightmares as well.

"Miriam," he heard his lips tell him, as his muscles tightened and his body convulsed, a single spasm. His self stepped away and he fell into a state that was neither vision nor delirium, but something at the same time newer than the infant Miriam was carrying and more ancient than the universe itself...

He labored up the stairs and into the heavens, following a Gypsy's call, holding onto bamboo rails that were the scrolls of the Torah and Zorah so that he would not stumble or turn back. The compound and the island and the Earth fell away behind him, while around him the ten stars of the Kabbalah shone in a night sky. As he neared the moon, he heard voices, increasingly distinct, greeting and gently admonishing him for not having traveled skyward sooner. His father was there, and Hans Hannes, his friend from the camp. Rabbi Czisça was there, too, an older version of Misha. Their souls—all of them—danced joyously within a Bushman's moon.

He hesitated, fearing that if he stayed here for even a minute he might never return to the world that he knew. Unready yet to leave it, he stretched out a trembling hand and touched reality—and a halo of cobalt blue——

——"*I don't think Wilhelm worked for the SD for the money*," a woman's voice says. "And I never accepted his explanation about his becoming a spy simply because he was German. I'm sure he lived in Tehran because the morphine content of Iranian opium was thirteen percent, five percent higher than that in Beijing, where he'd formerly been living."

Solomon looks around. He is in a large cell with a small window which is higher than his head. Five other people are in the cell: a muscular black man in raggedy shorts, withdrawn into a corner and staring listlessly at his scarred left calf; a gray-haired woman leaning against a wall and smoking a cigarette; a man in a fez, standing behind a hurdy gurdy; a young woman in a Siit pilgrim robe, kneeling beside an old man who wears a tattered woolen coat and has an ancient carbine across his thighs.

"Then the war broke out," the young woman continues telling the old man, "and Wilhelm found himself in what was probably the most isolated capital in the world. He so wanted to be part of the conflict!"

The old man tilts up the carbine and starts cleaning it with a rag. "Sounds like he was addicted to being addicted."

The elderly woman flips her cigarette onto the straw floor and grinds it out with the toe of her shoe. "Talk! All you two do is talk!"

The younger woman grabs the carbine and shakes it. "What would you have me do? Talking stills the pain! I was raped—God only knows how many times." Her voice abruptly lowers, and her face becomes a mask, eyes pale and distant. "But that pain is nothing compared to what I feel about having—"

"I harbor more than a little guilt myself," the elderly woman says in a shaky voice.

Holding his back as though he has bursitis, the old man rises. "Let's face it, we were fools."

"Except him." The elderly woman nods toward the black man, who is silently crying. "He alone among us is truly innocent."

The hurdy gurdy man, head lowered in a look of shame, sluggishly turns the handle of his machine. The metal fingers, hitting at a wrong speed, play "Glowworm" out of tune, flat and funereal.

Solomon gropes through the blue light as though the air can be parted like a curtain. "Wanda," he hears himself say to the younger woman. He gazes at her thin, almost childish body and eyes made vapid with woe. "Wanda Pollock."

He steps forward and puts a palm on the older woman's shoulder. "I'm dreaming," he says.

"A wiser Solomon would know otherwise," she quietly replies.

"For over twenty years I've heard a woman crying. 'My soul is dirty, let me die,' she'd say. That was you?"

The elderly woman nods.

"And you, begging for borscht and ginger tea?" he asks the man in the ragtag coat whom his dreams called Schutze Margabrook.

The old man turns and gazes blankly toward the moonlight streaming between bars of the window as Solomon moves past the hurdy gurdy and stands, hands clasped, over the black man, as though he were beside a grave. "I dreamed that from you the evil ones took the sinew that had made you a human gazelle."

Eyes brimming, the man does not lift his head. The hurdy gurdy man stops playing.

"Dreaming," Solomon says again.

"Dreams are mirrors, and mirrors, dreams," the old woman says softly. "Perhaps you're still asleep in your bed on Friedrich Ebert Strasse."

"We've waited all these years for you to face your Self and touch the truth," Wanda interjects.

"And what is that truth?" Solomon asks.

She gives him a slight, condescending smile as her attention appears to drift. "German troops raped me after they took Warsaw. I escaped to Pinsk, where Russian troops raped me and shipped me to Siberia. Later I was sent to Iran. When the KGB discovered I was living with Wilhelm, they let forty soldiers gang-rape me, hoping to learn things about him that I didn't know. For four days, until he was able to rescue me."

"The truth," the elderly woman says in a voice filled with regret, "is that a child is about to be born whose soul is a dybbuk's. A dybbuk who is collaboration made manifest."

"A dybbuk you must vow to kill."——

——"Oh my God, they've killed you."

Solomon blinked and saw someone crawling rapidly toward him through the grass. As he neared, Sol could see that it was Max, a man in his early twenties. He looked over his shoulder to assure he was not seen.

"I'm alive," Sol whispered hoarsely. He thrust a hand between the cage bars to wave Max away. "Get back to the others. The Nazis'll shoot you if they catch you roaming about."

Max drew near and stopped, panting fiercely. "No one's paying attention to us. Even the sentries aren't watching." He stabbed an index finger toward the nearest tower. "The rest are all down at the east end, with their rifles ready. Look! See them?" He pointed toward the far edge of the perimeter, beyond which stood the Zana-Malata's hut. "And there, just outside the jungle. Do you see them?"

"The Kalanaro?" Sol asked.

Max nodded.

At the east end, someone fired a shot in the air, and Sol watched in disgust as the Nazis hooted and jumped about in triumph when the Kalanaro disappeared into the bush.

"It's this place." Max looked around timidly at the jungle. "This Africa. It isn't real."

"I think there are probably some pretty strange things in Africa," Sol said. "Things no Whites will ever understand. But this...." He too looked around, though more in anger than fear. "This isn't Africa. This is Europe—transplanted."

Yet his mind wasn't on his words. He was mulling over what Max had said. Where among the camp shadows, he wondered, did reality end and illusion begin? And was that the demarcation—if one existed—between his dreams and his wakefulness?

"Why do the Nazis hate Jews?" Max asked abruptly. He turned onto his side and watched the spectacle at the far end of the camp as though he were lazing on a village green, listening to a summer ensemble. "I've been thinking about that a lot, lately. They can't all think we were responsible for the death of their Christ. They've officially renounced Christianity anyway. They know we fought alongside them in the Great War, and surely they all can't be so blind as really to believe that 'subhuman' business. Look at what we've done, Rabbi! The schools we've founded, the Nobel Prizes we've won, the courts...." The ease left him, and his face squinched with incomprehension.

He stared at the sky, apparently too saddened to express himself in words any longer.

"They don't hate the Jews," Sol said.

"*What?*" Max eyed him with suspicion. "And to think I called you 'rabbi'!"

"This time the persecution's no purge or pogrom. Those days died out with the Christian kings, who wanted to kill us only if they couldn't convert us. In their minds, our religion posed a threat to the world's salvation. What Beadle Treichzat termed a 'rational' hate. Like hating an enemy."

Squinting, Sol could see the white-splotched faces of the Kalanaro slowly emerge from the foliage. "With the birth of modern dictators, we've become the focus of an *irrational* hatred. Like being afraid of the dark. The Nazis don't hate us—they fear us. They don't want to convert us to National Socialism, they want to exterminate us. We represent reason and scholarship and justice, the very things the Fascists and Communists must burn from the globe if their ideologies are to survive. We're the finger-pointers...those who remind the world's conscience that 'Thou Shalt Not.'"

"Moral law," Max said, eyes brightening with admiration as he picked up the thread of Sol's logic, "versus the law of the jungle." He squeezed Sol's hand and smiled. "I shall find the Oberst and request your release," he said. "If they want someone in there, let them take me. You are needed here."

He smiled one more time and, turning, crawled away on his belly like a guerrilla.

Chapter 15

Bruqah maneuvered the growling tank along the track that now pierced the rain forest and ran up to the gravesite. Erich looked out over the foliage into a sun that appeared to have been dipped in Miriam's rouge and hung in a sky colored by her blue eye shadow. Directly above him, cirrus clouds the color of beaten copper feathered the sky. Watching as the glow dulled and the deep, aquamarine bay took on a crinkled sheen, he asked himself why he had never noticed such things until Miriam came to live with him.

Came to live with him?

Hardly the right words—but he had put his bitterness behind him, he was sure of that. The days when he worried about her emotional outlook toward him—and did demeaning things to win her approval—were part of a world gone mad. Love took many forms, myriad faces; what she felt toward him would change when he showed her how high he was capable of rising above the Nazi miasma.

The tank reached the bottom of the saddle between the two hills and angled up the second slope, the forest once again enclosing the machine as though in a tunnel. Sunlight filtered between fronds, dappling the machine and making the leaves spangle. Branches scraped along the sides or swooped low as if to decapitate him. The tank growled and jolted as its blade shoved aside felled trees and brush. He supposed he should exult in how rapidly and efficiently the Jews were opening up the forest, but he found himself surprisingly saddened by the neat roadways and new clearings the axes and blast cord created. The rain forest gave him the boyish delight of secret places, secret things, mysteries begging to remain unsolved. Perhaps his decision to have the Jews broaden the larger of the two paths that led from the hut to the *valavato* had been unwise, even if it had made military sense. He would have preferred to keep the hill more remote. His place except when it was needed to defend against attack.

Abruptly, the tank stopped.

"Look there, Mister Germantownman."

Bruqah's voice sounded icy. Ducking a branch, Erich looked down to see the Malagasy, eyes rigid with fury, pointing into the thick of the forest. Ahead, behind layers of greenery bursting with orchids and snaked through with lianas, Erich could discern the shapes of the Jews, working amid the undergrowth. The *thuk thuk thuk* of machetes and axes rose above the idling of the engine. Though he could make out a guard standing with his gun across an arm, he could hear no voices, no shouted commands or other harassment. He felt gladdened that the guards seemed to be obeying his orders regarding the Jews. *You do not train a dog by beating it,* he had reminded Hempel's men.

"Looks fine to me," Erich said.

Bruqah lowered his hand, but his angry mien did not change.

Startled—the Malagasy usually was so easy-going—Erich followed Bruqah's gaze into the brush. His eyes were directed toward something much more immediate than men clearing the jungle. He tried to figure out what it was, but flowers and ferns kept drawing his attention, softening his resolve as if their colors were infusing him with their beauty. "Tell me!" he ordered at last, exasperated.

The Malagasy shook his head as though in disbelief, climbed from the driver's seat, and dropped to the ground. He walked into the foliage, moving with the grace of a lemur.

Erich swore under his breath and went after him, pulling apart brush the Malagasy had passed through seemingly without effort. Veils of moss brushed against his face with the mockery of a woman's hand. A liana's large inflorescences scraped like grotesque fingers across his shoulders.

In a grotto of undergrowth swarming with mosquitoes and so suffocatingly hot that sweat burst from beneath his hairline in itchy rivulets, Erich caught up to Bruqah, huddled, head down, before a totem no thicker than a woman's wrist. It was broken off at an angle about a meter above the ground. The Malagasy had his eyes pinched shut and his face was drawn with emotion.

"You promised, Germantownman," he said in a sad voice. "You said island's past would be persevered."

"Pre*served*," Erich corrected testily, rummaging among the shattered branches and forest duff for the rest of the totem. To Bruqah, each mention of the past seemed inviolate. No sense arguing with the Malagasy over the loss of an artifact; he *had* made the statement, which was meant to be taken in a broader context. The hill abounded with hidden markers radiating in an indecipherable pattern from the taller ones surrounding the limestone crypt site at the hilltop. Destroying a few was unavoidable as the necessary paths and clearings were cut.

"Here it is." Erich held up the length of totem he had found. The broken end had sheered off strangely. The lily-wood totem was cleanly broken, as though it were shale. It looked as if percussion, instead of the blast itself, had severed the stick. He guessed that the forest—capable of intensifying blast waves as well as blocking them—had caused the break: an effect similar to that of an opera singer shattering crystal.

The totem otherwise was not damaged. Its arabesque of curling leaves reminded Erich of the intricate, petal-like candles so popular at Easter. A more representational series of carvings—lemurs balanced atop one another's backs and looking at him with huge, whorled eyes—formed the middle. A set of miniature zebu horns, common on other totems he'd seen, adorned the top.

"You want me to have it put back together?" Erich asked. "Some of the Jews are excellent craftsmen."

"The damage is done."

Best to let the matter drop, Erich decided. If Bruqah did not want the totem repaired, it would make a good walking stick. Erich tried it out for size as he pushed back toward the tank. Just the right height and heft. It gave him a feeling of balance and power. No wonder, it occurred to him, the members of Germany's Old Order had relished such things.

From behind him came a screech and Bruqah emerged onto the track, a ring-tailed lemur riding merrily on his back, its arms around his neck. He was climbing back onto the tank when Pleshdimer came waddling toward them, waving his arms as he stumbled over cut-but-uncleared brush and tree trunks. "Herr Oberst, come quickly. Time for the uncovering!" the Kapo said breathlessly.

"Surely all the surrounding brush hasn't been pushed aside already!" With an irritable gesture toward the downed trees among which they were standing, Erich added, "Look at this!"

Pleshdimer hunkered down his head, like a turtle retreating into its shell, and gazed greedily from the tops of his eyes. "Good enough, the others say, mein Oberst. Plenty of time for clearing after the uncovering's done."

The protuberant eyes, the oily lips, the neck's rolls of fat filled Erich with disgust. He followed slowly.

Increasingly narrow and confined, the path enclosed them. Soft, spiky stamen of crimson browneas dusted Erich with pollen as he ducked through the last of the foliage and into the sunlit gravesite.

He had expected to see the two guards sitting and smoking on the crypt's grass-covered mound while around them the Jews carried away the brush and saplings they had delimbed. With its towering, delicate totems of mahogany and lily wood, this was no place that the tank could plow through after the initial clearing was done. Work here had to be slow and methodical—no blast cord, no mistakes.

Instead, the guards were digging as madly as the Jews, looking not in the least resentful.

A great scallop had been dug out along the front of the grave, exposing the stone entrance. Erich intended the crypt to be a pillbox—his west-end protection. It would have a good view of the bay and an excellent field of fire toward the crescent-shaped lagoon below, where the Storch was parked.

Pleshdimer waved a finger toward the digging. "The jungle told me we'll find gold and treasures inside," he said.

"The jungle," Erich repeated. "What next—voices from a burning bush?"

"He thinks he heard the wind whisper," Bruqah said softly, coming up behind Erich. The Malagasy's eyes glittered impishly. "Ravalona's resting place has been so long forgotten, my patience grew weak-willed."

Erich grinned. Seeing the guards shoveling frantically gave him perverse pleasure. According to Bruqah, the grave was empty—of bones, not just gold—a fact Erich had emphasized before any of this had begun.

"This only crypt on Mangabéy," Bruqah said. "Many more over there." He pointed toward the mainland. "Fancy. One has big airplane," he stretched his arms wide, "like dead man ride in life."

The crypt they were about to open was unadorned except for the surrounding totems and a shroud of mossy grass that did not seem indigenous to Mangabéy. It was built, Bruqah had said, as Ravalona would have wanted it; she was said to have appreciated simplicity above all else. Perhaps that much was myth, Erich thought, an outgrowth of the sadder part of real history: a native princess captured, along with her maidservant, during the slave trade and shipped to the island of Mauritius. What had perhaps begun as a kidnap-and-ransom attempt had ended in tragedy, for the young woman had died of a fever and never returned home. Her body had gone unclaimed, despite Benyowsky's efforts to rescue her alive and, that having failed, to retrieve the corpse.

The guards had apparently not heard Erich's words regarding the tomb; or, at least, were not heeding them—a small slight, but one of many. Whispered innuendoes, eyes that went blank during salutes, personnel switches on his posted duty rosters because *Hempel* had approved the change, or claimed to.

Let them dig, he thought. Maybe it'll teach them to listen.

Shovels scraped limestone. The chiseled, discolored blocks emitted a fine yellow dust that sprinkled across the upturned red soil each time a guard brought a blade down the side of the crypt to dislodge dirt. The guards spoke in rapid whispers, their eyes avoiding Erich's; they swore and shooed away Goldman when he asked if the white rocks at the bases of the totems were to be kept or cleared. With a small smile and a nod Erich indicated that the rocks were to remain, and Goldman resumed his work.

That was the difference between the guards and the Jews, he decided. The former were paid not to think; the latter never stopped, as they had proven in the camps by staying alive.

Aristida bunch grass had grown in the long, unbroken vertical line of rock that indicated a door in the crypt; the tomb had not been opened for a very long time. It occurred to Erich that that was a good thing, though he was uncertain why. Perhaps because he too liked his history inviolate, he thought.

The grumble of the Panzer interrupted his reverie. The tank came crashing through the underbrush, bending and then snapping saplings. Resolutely Erich stalked toward the machine and signaled for a halt. The tank stopped. Bruqah poked up his head.

"Were you not told to leave this machine where it was?" Erich demanded. "You complained about the ruination of the hillside artifacts, yet you endanger the tall ones here."

Bruqah shrugged. "Damage already done," he said. "I forgive you." He climbed down and put a hand on Erich's shoulder.

Erich shrugged it off. "Where did you leave Miriam and the boy?"

"Misha awoke. They walk a bit to here." Bruqah disappeared down the turret and shut off the tank, which stopped idling with an angry huff. The Malagasy walked over to where the entrance was being uncovered.

Bruqah pulled up a lump of grass and, holding it by its knot of dirt and roots, ran his fingers through the coarse strands as if through a head of hair. "The dead inside tomb dream of daylight," he said.

"Are you attempting to provoke me?" Erich asked in a low voice. "You said the tomb was empty."

"Except for longing." The Malagasy placed his hand upon the stones, a wistful look creeping his eyes. "To be buried away from home is to be lost. When body cannot come to family burial grounds, stone is raised beside highway or main path so soul can find way home." He stopped and scratched his head, as though searching for words to match complex thoughts. "For common man is enough," he went on, "but for Vazimba...." He stopped again. "People given untruth after Ravalona die. Servant said Princess soul enter Count. People bow at him. French soldiers come—"

"I know the rest," Erich said. Benyowsky was by then without power. Learning the truth, the people fled from him and he was killed by his friends the French—and did not rise from the dead three days later as he'd promised.

"Crypt was built in hope that queen come home," Bruqah said. "She come soon."

"She died a hundred and fifty years ago," Erich said.

"As you measure time."

The guards, fingers crammed into crevices and backs bent in effort, were attempting to open the stone entrance. Waving his arms for work to cease, Bruqah approached them. The guards moved aside tensely and suspiciously.

"He'll claim you have to know magic words," one of them mocked.

Bruqah gave him a patronizing smile. From somewhere beneath the *lamba*—a pocket, Erich supposed—he pulled out a piece of gristle. "Witness, *Zanahary*," he said to the sky, "this offering from a tender and well-raised zebu killed only yesterday."

Closing his eyes, he tossed the meat high into the air. It came down among a group of Jews, who dodged it. The guards broke into nervous laughter.

Bruqah took out a second piece of meat and held it up in his palm. He swung his hand to and fro, as if toward the corners of the earth, saying, "Witness, O Ancestors. Though we cannot mention you all by name, yet all are included in this prayer! Do not make yourselves spirits without homes. Save your children from witchcraft! Bless we all!"

He cast the meat at the feet of the nearest guard, who backed up apprehensively.

"Witness, O Earth. We give to you because you give to we."

The calling of the birds and insects and the breathing of the other men pulsed in Erich's ears, and in that instant he was transported home. Father Dahns genuflected before the altar, bronze figures of Mary and Joseph looked down from their niches at a little boy standing wide-eyed between his parents while they likewise genuflected, he gripping their hands and wondering about the Holy Mother and her carpenter husband.

"Damn you," Erich said under his breath as the Vazimba sat down on his haunches, head bowed, arms limply hanging.

"What? No more mumbo jumbo?" a guard asked, leaning against the stone work. A boa constrictor slithered out between his legs, its back reticulated with red and orange, and the young soldier cried out, dancing aside as though trying to stamp out a fire. He shivered as he watched the animal sidewind into the taller grass.

"*Dô* snake," Bruqah said. Crossing quickly through the grass, he cut off the snake's departure. Finding feet in front of itself, the serpent lifted its head, burrowed forward, and coiled once around an ankle. The Malagasy looked at Erich and, teeth clamped together, grinned widely as he lifted the leg, the snake dangling. "They vessels of the souls of the dead," he announced.

"I thought you said this crypt was empty," Erich said again, and immediately felt the guards' angry glares.

"I am not *always* right, Mister Germantownman." Bruqah pulled the snake off his leg and, after holding it out at arms' length to appraise it, shucked it, curling, off his arm and dropped it unceremoniously amid the weeds. "Open it, we find out."

The guards quickly jumped to and pried at the door with all their strength. The stone moved easily, surprising the men and throwing them off balance.

He's nothing more than a poor man's magician, Erich thought, less able than the syphilitic but probably also less evil. He stared down the guards and strode toward the tomb. They looked away to avoid his eyes.

Moving sideways through the narrow door, he entered the crypt. Cool darkness swathed him, bringing a sense of relief after so much humidity. For a moment he stayed still, drinking in the calm and feeling wonderfully separated from the world outside, with all its heat and tempers.

"Bring me a flashlight," he ordered finally, half-expecting that, when he flicked it on, he would see Solomon peering up from the musty blackness, arms cradling a terrier in the sewer hideout of their youth.

Instead, the light revealed a molding corpse in a soldier's uniform, reclining in a raffia and mahogany chair suspended by frazzled ropes from the ceiling. Erich could see that the body was rotted. Gray flesh mottled with age had given way to brown bone along the cheeks and nose. The eye sockets were empty except for dark pulp at the bottom of the round. The lips were gone, the teeth uneven.

Erich accidentally nudged the chair as he moved closer to examine the body. The head nodded forward, chin against chest, what was left of the wig nearly slipping from the skull. Over a shirt of heavy muslin the corpse wore an embroidered dress coat, threadbare with age, wrist-length sleeves ending in cambric ruffle showing their tatter, the coat's once-gleaming metal buttons glinting dully in the light. Tiny buckles at the kneecaps embellished the black-velvet breeches. The bottoms of the legs, tucked beneath the rest of the body rather than dangling, were outfitted in close-fitting high boots and gaiters decorated with white, woven cloth.

"Benyowsky," Erich guessed in a low breath. His heart pounded with such excitement that his usual fear of the dead seemed to vanish.

The dank low-ceilinged room proved to be empty save for the near-skeleton and three small ceramic bowls, scrimshawed with blue ships upon a blue floral sea. The bowls sat upon a stone pallet which protruded from a side wall and was perhaps meant as a resting place for a body. The floor was also stone, though furred with a fine, wet moss. When he touched it, Erich made a face and brushed his hands clean against his trouser leg.

Bruqah entered.

"You know who that is," Erich said, sensing the Malagasy's lack of surprise.

Bruqah picked up a wrist as if checking for a pulse, and set the arm down again.

"I thought you said Benyowsky had been buried at the *far* end of the bay, near the mouth of the Antabalana River," Erich accused.

"*Entombed*," Bruqah corrected. "Not *buried*. And please to remember my people remove and re-shroud the dead whenever the *lambamena* needs replacing—or when living spirits feel the need."

"For Malagasy dead, yes, but for Europeans?"

Bruqah moved slowly around the corpse, scrutinizing it. "Was Count never Malagasy? Had he no roots in this our land?" He looked at Erich. "Was he never *Ampandzaka-be*?"

The words chilled Erich. Just the dankness of the tomb, he told himself. He drew his shoulders closer together, crossing his arms. "Someone brought the body here. Who would go to such trouble?"

"Zana-Malata awaits return of soul of Princess."

"And you?" Erich asked, as the guards peered in the doorway. Erich lanced his light toward them. "Out!"

Muttering, they withdrew.

"I, too," Bruqah said softly. "I, too." More loudly, he added, "Body faces east, where spirits of our ancestors rest. Legs are tucked. Forbidden to extend feet to east. Carefully done, all right."

"Someone went to a lot of trouble," Erich said, hesitant to divulge his suspect for fear Bruqah might disagree—and whatever small sense Erich had made of the matter would unravel.

"Count has waited long years for his woman to return. He yearns for her, I think. He knows she near, I think."

"You know too much," Erich said sternly. "Or at least you think you do."

Using the flashlight as if it were a lance or staff, he ushered Bruqah from the tomb. Glancing back, as the lamp passed the bowls, he thought he glimpsed rice and what looked like chicken fat within two of them, but subsequent sweeps revealed only that the bowls were empty. He emerged, squinting, into the light and heat of the day.

"We want to look," a guard said. "See for *ourselves*."

Erich gave him the light, and the two guards crowded toward the crack. "If I find you've touched him or searched his pockets, I'll court-martial both of you," he warned.

He sent the Jews packing, shovels over shoulders. When the guards exited the grave, he dismissed them as well, and told Bruqah to go and find Miriam and the boy. Alone at the site, the world, even this new world, seemed very far away.

Everything was going to work out fine, he thought. And if all else failed, there was always Plan B: the Storch that waited at the lagoon below. The problem there was that Hempel was the only person on hand who knew how to fly. Plus, the Storch was only built for three; he didn't know if a fourth passenger would be possible. Who would be the other passenger?

Miriam?

Could she ever be happy knowing they had left Sol behind?

Taurus?

From far below, an engine coughed and purred into life, as if responding to his thoughts. Erich stood up and looked down into the lagoon, where Hempel was conducting his daily check of the plane's engine. Sunlight sparkled off the Storch's fuselage. At this distance, the plane looked like a toy.

Erich wished he'd had the time and foresight to learn to fly. In Berlin, he had thought escape would mean boarding one of the rubber boats that, hooked together, would form the pontoon raft they would build to ship the Panzer and other heavy equipment to the mainland.

That was then.

He realized now that losing oneself among the jungles of northern Madagascar or among the human jungle at Antananarivo, the capital, would be insufficient. He would have to abandon his former existence altogether, which meant putting distance between himself and Mangabéy as quickly as possible. Ergo, an airplane.

This airplane.

He strode up the dirt mound and sat down on the crypt's grassy top. Obeying the admonition about not extending his feet, he kept his legs tucked. The hair of graves, he thought, recalling a poem he'd once read. He broke off a handful of blades, bent one in half and tried to make a whistle. Managing to squeak out a spluttery sound he looked around guiltily, fearing he'd been seen or heard, and tossed away the grass.

Chapter 16

Misha lay on the grass at Miss Miriam's feet, feeling outside of himself, seeing himself, happy that for a while there had been no pain except the heaviness in his chest that made him want to cough all of the time. He thought about what he would want to be when he grew up, that is if wishes were horses and he still lived in Berlin and still lived with his parents. It was a game he played when he wasn't thinking about how he could kill Hempel and Pleshdimer.

Today the answer was easy.

He'd be a magician, like Jean-Jacques Beguin. Papa had taken him to see Beguin, and afterward he, Misha, and Papa had talked about if Beguin could really read people's minds. His papa said there were only two kinds of magic, the real magic of God and the false magic of men. Misha wondered if his papa was right. Maybe there was also a third type: God's magic given to men.

"Mishele, what are you thinking?" Miriam asked.

He started to answer, but his words were cut short by renewed coughing.

"That's a nasty cough," Miriam said. "When we get back to the medical tent, Franz must give you medicine—"

"No," Misha said quickly, remembering the burning stuff that the Zana-Malata had given him. "To cure your cough," Hempel had said. Only it hadn't cured a thing, and it had given him terrible nightmares. He remembered the Zana-Malata, face streaked with glowing white slashes, tilting Misha's head sideways and up and pouring a thimble full of fiery red liquid between his lips. When some had dribbled from the corner of his mouth, the Zana-Malata caught it up with his index finger and forced it back inside his mouth. He choked, and the syphilitic's watery eyes mocked him. The man had pinched Misha's lips shut to keep him from spitting up. He'd gagged, but could not pull away.

The fire had filled his veins, making his skin burn as though from the inside and yet giving his body an easy, drowsy feeling at the same time. It was as if he could take a razor blade, slice open his flesh, and step out of it, like a clown passing through a papered hoop and into the ring of the Berlin circus. His mind had sped up the more his body slowed. He had seen images: two fossas watching him from the hut's corner; the skull of a water buffalo, stubby candles burning in its eye sockets.

  He remembered lying on the floor of stripped saplings, a breeze fluttering the edge of the zebu-hide door, and then the hut dissolved. The walls shimmered, wavered, undulated into air. He'd felt himself floating above the meadow. The forest canopy blended into a crenelated green cap covering each of the island's two hills, and around Mangabéy white wavelets shuddered against black and tan shores. The bay was aquamarine, shiny as satin and underlain with the dark irregular shapes of reefs and ledges. Further beyond, the broad crescent of rain-forested land rose felt-green up steep slopes, to lap at pinnacles that jutted above the jungle canopy like peaks of a ragged crown. He was free. He remembered closing his eyes, feeling the sun against his cheeks and the wind in his hair, and thanking the Zana-Malata and the fiery drink.

  Then he was back in the hut. The good, warm feeling was gone and the Zana-Malata stood over him. He wore a rattan hat, brimless, its fringes dancing darkly in the shaft of sunlight that penetrated the hut's dark interior. Misha had felt like crying. But he would not cry, he never cried. On the morning after he left the fire escape, where Papa had secreted him and climbed back into the shambles that had been his home before the Gestapo broke in, he had promised himself he would never cry until he and Papa were united once more. Still, he'd heard the whimpering in his own throat and felt the trembling as the Zana-Malata squatted before him, seized his wrist, and brought forth a short dagger he had been holding hidden against his side.

  The Zana-Malata had pulled him slowly forward. He'd allowed himself to be drawn like an object at the end of a rope. The black man's eyes had flickered and he'd brought the dagger tip against Misha's neck and cut into his flesh.

  Laughing all of the time.

  Laughing...

  They were sitting in the shade, but the combination of heat and inactivity was making Misha drowsy. In a few minutes, he was fast asleep and dreaming—of Hempel, and Pleshdimer, and the Zana-Malata. In his dream, he lay on Miriam's lap on the jouncing tank, watching the clouds and wondering if he were not in fact up there, watching some other boy lying on the machine as it plowed across the meadow.

  "We should go, Misha," Miriam said, shaking him gently.

  He looked around. He was seated amid daisies and tall grasses. Through a break in the surrounding foliage he could see down to the shore. Shadows and sun flicked across his face, and he felt himself sliding into sleep again.

  "Lady Miri, Misha, Germantownman say it time to go."

  Bruqah's voice filtered through the bushes. Misha stirred lazily.

"Go, Misha. Tell Bruqah I could use his arm to lean on."

Misha stood up and offered Miriam his arm. She smiled and thanked him, and they moved in the direction of Bruqah's voice. They found him easily, and he took over the role of escort, motioning to the boy to go ahead.

Misha could see the tank through the foliage and ran toward it, but he was seized by a fit of coughing and tripped over a rotted log overgrown with passion-flower vines and covered with thornbugs and zebra butterflies. Picking himself up, he saw that he had stumbled into a grove of pitcher plants, as whitish-yellow and velvety as a midsummer moon. The remains of beetles and ants floated in translucent syrup.

Looks like honey, he thought, poking his finger into the stickiness above the plant's curled lip. He licked it off.

His pleasure at its sweetness lasted only a moment. He began staggering in a circle, gargling and gasping for breath. He could see Erich racing toward him from one side, and Bruqah from the other.

"What is it?" Erich demanded. "What!"

Misha could not answer. He pointed toward his mouth; the gagging grew more pronounced, and he fell to the ground.

Erich gripped Bruqah by the wrist. "What the hell!"

"Faking," Misha heard a guard say. "I've seen similar tricks."

"They pulled stunts like this back at camp, we'd pee on their faces," another guard said. "*That* brought 'em around."

Misha wheezed so heavily that it sounded to him as if he had an entire string orchestra locked inside his chest. He could see Pleshdimer waddling toward him.

"Stay away from him," Miriam said, placing herself between Misha and Pleshdimer. She knelt awkwardly and took Misha's head in her lap. He looked up at her fearfully.

"Oh God, what's that on his face? Some kind of a rash."

"You're going to be all right," Erich said softly.

Terrified, Misha quivered and lay still. He could hardly move, but he was fully aware of what was going on around him.

Bruqah squatted and pressed his fingers against the boy's throat, testing for a pulse.

"Is he...?" Miriam asked.

"Dead?" Bruqah shook his head. "Sometime easier, that. Dead forget pain." Looking up at Erich, he said, "Get water."

"Give him your canteen," Erich ordered over his shoulder.

No one moved.

"Water!"

"Here." The guard held out a canteen begrudgingly. Erich tore it from the man and started back toward Misha.

Bruqah put a hand on Erich's, halting him. "Water good?"

"How the hell do I know! Of course it is!"

"It not *rano vola*, but it do, if Erich Germantownman say it be pure," Bruqah said.

"You heard me say it is," Erich replied angrily.

Bruqah lifted the canteen from Erich's grasp.

"Now what are you doing!" Erich burst out.

"What I must," Bruqah said. "Am I not *mpanandro*-Vazimba...an astrologer? I warn Sollyman, pitcher plants most bad for some people."

Standing before the pitcher plants, he bowed his head. Then he extended his hand and, mumbling words Misha could not comprehend, sprinkled water into each of the elongated cups.

Erich grabbed Bruqah by the hair. "What the hell do you think that's going to do to help—"

Miriam put a hand on his wrist and he let loose of the Malagasy who ministered to the last of the section of pitcher plants, letting the water dribble across his tilted palm and into the cup. The mumbling never ceased.

"What happened?" Misha sat up and inhaled noisily.

Bruqah stood, grinning, and lifted the canteen as if in a toast. "Spirits happy now," he said. He drank deeply and smacked his lips. "Incantations make Bruqah thirsty."

He handed Misha the canteen. The boy drank deeply.

"Even the rash is gone," Miriam said. She hugged Misha to her.

"I feel fine, now," he said.

Taking him at his word, Erich led the way to the tank. They settled themselves, Misha again on Miriam's lap at her insistence.

He was sitting awkwardly upright when they passed the hut and, looking the other way, he saw Herr Freund, in a cage like an animal at the zoo.

"Stop," he said, jumping up and stepping right on Miriam's foot. "Please. Stop."

Erich looked in the direction of Misha's finger. "Stop the tank," he shouted.

He jumped off the machine at a run. Misha followed close behind, leaving Miriam sobbing and clutching at Bruqah who had emerged to find out what was going on.

"Not to worry. I bring Torah," Bruqah yelled.

Then they were at the cage and the Herr Oberst was issuing orders, and there was arguing, and finally Herr Freund was released. His skin was bright red and blistering.

"Who did this?" Colonel Alois asked in that loud whisper Misha had heard his own papa use when he had gone beyond anger.

The question was at first met by silence. Then Herr Freund looked right at the Herr Oberst.

"Who do you think did this? He thought he was punishing both of us," Herr Freund said.

"Come with us," Erich commanded.

Then Misha was in Bruqah's arms, the colonel in front, pushing back the flaps of the medical tent to admit Sol and the rest of them. The corpsman was inside with the sick dogs. He was the man called Franz, who used to sneak him chocolate and bread during his Sachsenhausen days.

Through half-closed eyes Misha saw Miriam, Franz, and Bruqah move toward the supplies, gathering things. Bruqah left, saying he was going to gather petitboom and Christmas-bush leaves so that they could boil them up and make tea for the boy's cough.

Erich hovered close, and there was angry pain in his eyes. He glanced toward the others, as if to assure himself that they were not watching, and with his fingers combed back Misha's hair.

"Otto Hempel won't hurt you again," he whispered. "I'll see to it."

Misha shook his head. "I have to go back, Herr Oberst," he said.

"No!" Miriam took hold of him and held him so tightly he could barely breathe. "I won't let you return to those...those monsters!"

"I must," Misha said, when she loosened her hold.

He wanted to tell her why, but somehow he knew that if he did his resolve would weaken. No matter what they did to him, Hempel and Pleshdimer and the Zana-Malata, being near them would make it easier for him to do what he had to do.

In his mind's eye, he conjured up his list.

Kill, it read next to each of their names.

Kill.

Chapter 17

Miriam looked at the sleeping boy. He blinked and twitched, but the soporific was working; in all probability, he would not wake for hours. Sleep would not dispatch the trauma he had endured, nor would it change his mind about returning to those animals, but at least he would be away from it for a little while.

She closed the mosquito netting around him and, after nodding thoughtfully toward Franz, went outside the tent to join Erich. He stood smoking a cheroot, looking off toward the west.

"Hempel has got to be stopped," he said. "Somehow I've got to break him."

"The whole operation has to be stopped," Miriam said. "This entire Madagascar insanity."

"What alternative would you suggest? Leave all of Europe's Jews in Hitler's hands, and let him annihilate them?"

"Things will be different here? Everyone will be penned on the island, with no way to escape. At least in Europe there's the chance that they can flee *somewhere*."

"Once the bulk of the Jews have left Europe, Hitler will have fulfilled his promise to the German people, to cleanse the continent of them. And he'll have what he really wants—the property they leave behind."

"You Nazis are all alike...simplistic answers for everything."

He tilted his head and blew a long stream of smoke. "You haven't been yourself, lately. The voyage, the pregnancy, getting settled here. I'll treat your remarks accordingly." He looked at Miriam and narrowed his eyes. "But don't overstep too often, Miriam Alois. You may find yourself on the wrong side altogether."

"When have we ever been on the same side?"

He lifted an insolent brow as if condescendingly letting her rant, and returned to smoking his cheroot.

A runner stopped at the gate, raised his arms, and let the guards frisk him. Panting, he marched toward Erich. It was Max, youngest of the prisoners, other than Misha. During one of several brief conversations, he had told Miriam that they had arrested him when he'd gone to get help for his wife, about to deliver. He had never learned the fate of his wife or unborn child, for he had refused, despite torture, to reveal their whereabouts. Due to her own condition—and perhaps, Miriam had to admit, to his exceptional good looks—he had a special place in her heart. She found herself smiling at him as, gasping, he saluted and delivered his message.

"I got permission to look for you at the crypt, but you had already left, Herr Oberst, sir!"

"And? Why did you wish to speak to me so urgently?"

"To tell you what they had done to Solomon Freund, sir."

"Rest easy, young man," Erich said. "Your *rabbi* has been released. Tell me, did you see Sturmbannführer Hempel on your travels up and down the hill? Has he assessed the hill as a forward post?"

"I would not be privy to such information, sir. The last time I saw Sturmbannführer Hempel he was headed down the other side of the hill, toward the lagoon. He left Kapo Pleshdimer—Rottenführer Pleshdimer," Max did not try to mask his disgust, "in charge."

Miriam could see that the young man held a certain amount of real respect for the colonel, despite the Nazi uniform. There was no denying that conditions here on Mangabéy were infinitely better than in Sachsenhausen, and much of that was Erich's doing.

And mine, she thought. If he only knew how much.

An explosion went *whump* from the far hill. They must be back clearing the last of the forest around the crypt, Miriam thought.

Erich listened intently, as if expecting to see part of the forest fall, even from this distance. Those birds that had not taken flight earlier rose into the air. As if satisfied that the explosion was part of the clearing and not some insurgency, he relaxed and stuck his head inside the tent. "Bruqah! Outside! I need you to drive the tank!" he said.

The Malagasy almost instantly appeared. "You need Bruqah? Who fail make machine go forward?"

"Just get in the goddamn tank."

"Erich?" Miriam said. "I wish to go back with you."

Erich scowled at her. "Forget it. Not in your condition. This isn't the Autobahn, you know."

"You are going to the crypt. I need to see inside it."

She had realized by now that somehow she had lost the memory of a part of the day and replaced it with another of the bizarre waking dreams—visions as Sol called them—that had come to her with increasing frequency since their arrival on the island. Something told her that the roots of this one were to be found inside the tomb. Had it not been for Misha's unfortunate run-in with the pitcher plant, she'd have asked to be taken inside the crypt when they were up there earlier in the day.

Without much effort, she reconstructed what she had seen in her mind's eye...

She lay on stone, her ankles fastened by straps, shallow depressions in the stone fitting her form perfectly. As though made for her. Sweat streamed off her forehead as the contractions rolled through her with a pain she swore she could not endure. Not one more. Then she turned her head, and beyond the open door she saw tiny gyrating men, dancing jerkily as marionettes....

"Please, Erich," she said. "Franz can stay with the boy."

"Very well, then," Erich said. "But you are not to blame me if this overtires you. *You*, whatever your name is, ride in the tank with us. Make sure my wife rides safely."

"Yes...sir, Herr Oberst!"

Miriam wondered if the young man's enthusiasm were the result of helping her or of riding rather than walking. There *were* some things best left unknown, she decided.

Bruqah drove slowly, the tank barely bucking on the deepest ruts. This time, being on the machine gave her a particular excitement she had not experienced since girlhood, the kind of pleasure she had known when one day she, Sol, and Erich rode bicycles to the *Siegessäule*—the Victory Monument—and later that afternoon, drenched from a sudden rain, had broken into the abandoned Belford mansion and within five acres of underground wine cellar had pretended to be knights-and-lady. Erich had been Tannhaüser and she Lady Venus; she could not recall what role Sol had elected, except that he had surprised them all by winning. That was the first time she had seen him when the ghosts came....

It was all too long ago to belabor.

She forced her attention upon the moment and caught a glimpse of what it was like to play toy soldier. Perhaps, she thought, the attraction of the military *wasn't* just killing.

"This is absolute foolishness," Erich said suddenly, when they were halfway up the hill. "Stop the tank, Bruqah, we're going back. I don't have time to waste. I've already inspected the crypt and I've the building of the dock to oversee. Max, help Miriam off this thing. Then Bruqah and I will head down the hill."

Bruqah did as he was told.

"Erich...," Miriam said, her anger rising.

"I've made my decision."

She could see by his expression that he would brook no argument. When they arrived back at the gate she allowed Bruqah and Max to help her to the ground.

"Tell me what you found in the crypt, Bruqah," she said, keeping hold of his hands as he leaned over the edge of the tank.

Quickly, almost in a whisper, Bruqah filled her in. "Some say Count never try to bring her here. Even he never know her, some say. But one thing every man know for damn sure: she die of fever, and never return. Not even for *lambamena* ceremony."

"The dressing of the dead."

He looked at her with a pain-filled expression. "We wait rebury her, one day."

Miriam sensed Erich's growing impatience, but did not want to cut Bruqah short. "I'm sure that will happen."

"Anything possible. Everything have reason. Mister Sollyman specially know that." He shrugged as if to relieve himself of an emotional burden. "I run same risk when I not in Madagascar. There is place for my bones in crypt at kidney lake where alligators carry ancestor's souls. I am woman and man, both. My people need my soul, else blood run thick again. Aye-aye say—"

He shuddered, clearly afraid. He was always so proud and strong that Miriam was loathe to let go of his hand.

"Bruqah! Let's go!" Erich said.

Miriam chuckled at the great army commander needing a Malagasy to operate his modern machinery.

The tank pulled away, leaving Max to escort her to the medical tent. Feeling the need to walk after Erich's brusque treatment of her, she sent him on alone into the compound and meandered down a path that led toward a copse of slender trees.

She found herself in a tiny clearing, almost a grotto. There was a well-worn bench and the grass was tramped down, as though the place were often used. She sat down, thankful to take the load off her feet. Letting her head tip back, she breathed in the humid air and looked up toward the bowl of deeply blue sky. She felt strangely at peace, despite the heat. And despite the larger, terrible questions: birth, survival.

She thought of the maze of events that had brought her here, and of her own manipulations of those events. She'd relied on her friendship with Juan Perón, who had so adored her when he had first danced with her, when she was young and beautiful and optimistic. She wondered fleetingly what he would think of her now, with her chopped off hair and ungainliness. It was still a mystery to her why Erich had never said anything about her bout with the scissors. Even Sol had said little except, "It will grow back."

Which was probably what her Uncle Walther and Perón—or Domingo as she had called him, using his middle name—would have said. They had indulged her, the two of them. In those days, he was a young attaché to the Italian embassy, and she was being groomed by her uncle to enter the political arena. "Half Jewish and, soon, all woman—now *that* will set the Reichstag on its ear," Uncle Walther had told her. Not that she'd ever wanted to be anything but a performer.

Perón, still wanting to please her many years later, had requested that Erich Alois be placed in charge of the Madagascar Experiment. Or at least in charge of initial operations. Himmler had surprisingly acquiesced. He had approved, as well, her accompanying her husband, and signed without hesitation an order releasing one Solomon Isaac Freund, Jew, fluent in French and experienced in accounting, to be interpreter and supply clerk with the advance party.

She had deluded herself into thinking that Himmler's decision was based on Erich's qualifications. After all, Erich and his trainers were in charge of security for Goebbels' headquarters, and there was word that his expertise in security and his genius for dog training might land his zodiac team the coveted job of guarding Hitler himself.

Only weeks later did she learn that Himmler had approved Perón's request out of political, not military, expediency. Regardless of Hitler's having declared her "without Jewish blood," she remained Jewish in Himmler's eyes. And she was the perfect ploy. Goebbels, with Himmler's blessing, had hired Leni Riefenstahl to make a propaganda film, with Miriam in a title role. *Pregnant wife of Colonel Erich Alois—stolen from the cradle by Jews and raised by the traitor Walther Rathenau, once Germany's foreign minister—is now bound for the African island of Madagascar. The island is the remnant of the sunken continent of Lemuria, home of the great winged Roc that attacked Sinbad.* There she would serve husband and Fatherland, as in his compassion the Führer created a homeland for the Jews.

The documentary would play to teary-eyed audiences in the Reich's theaters—more likely in theaters all over the world. Like her first film, when *the young and beautiful Frau Alois*—who no longer felt young or beautiful— renounced Judaism and all its evils and placed a wreath on the graves of the young anarchists who had assassinated her uncle.

To save Sol.

To keep her love alive.

She sighed and closed her eyes, wishing she could forget. The baby kicked. She smiled and placed a hand on her belly. The Nazis had taken her mansion and her money, and severed her career. They would not have the child. Or Solomon, if she could help it.

"Deborah," she whispered, repeating the name again and again. Feeling the child move as had happened each time she'd spoken the name aloud. The child was a girl, she was sure of it, a girl-child aware of the mother who bore her.

Images began to bombard her. She gave in to them——

——*Again, she lies on the stone hearth, the shallow depressions fitting her form perfectly, as though carved for her.* Her belly rolls like the sea. She stares at it in horror. The baby is coming, the pain jerks her head back, and still the unnatural rolling of her belly continues. Through the doorway she sees pygmy dancers, whitely glowing, undulating. An eternity passes before the pain lets up enough for her to move. A hand with nails like claws touches the outside of her thigh. In horror she looks down her body, but the hand darts away. Behind the rows of guttering candles there is a blanket-draped figure.

An elderly white woman wearing bifocals, her safari hat wrapped and tied under her chin with a bright yellow chiffon sash, enters the stone room. She reaches out for Miriam but does not touch her. Her hand, the same hue as her khaki jacket and pants, remains suspended in air, as if she fears to touch the woman on the dais.

"You have choices, Miriam," she whispers. "Your child is bringing you one reality. You do not have to accept it."

"Who are you," Miriam asks, struggling to rise above the pain.

"I am Judith," the woman says. "Dr. Judith Bielman-O'Hearn."

"Thank God," Miriam gasps. "A real physician."

"Not a medical doctor," Judith says. "An anthropologist. I work with the Falasha—the Black Jews of Ethiopia. Hitler has plans for them...uproot them from their ancestral home and send them here to Madagascar. Mussolini has approved the idea. As has Stalin, with the Ukrainian Jews."

The pain is excruciating. Miriam screams, wishing the woman would help her or go away.

"I have come to warn you of the Malagasy. He wishes to control the child."

"The Zana-Malata? I wouldn't let that...that creature—"

"Yes, he is evil and power-mad. He confuses the dybbuk in your child with the soul of Ravalona—"

"The *what?*"

"The dybbuk that was in Solomon was in his seed...."

Before Miriam can fully comprehend what she has heard, Judith says, "But it is the other one, the one called Bruqah of whom I speak. He knows the child is not a vessel for Ravalona, but fears what the false belief that it is will do to his people. It is he whom you should fear."——

——*Tekiah*.

The first note of the Shofar sounded—long and melancholy. In ancient times, it had summoned Jews to battle.

So the Juterbourg farmer had succeeded in fashioning a Shofar out of the zebu horn Misha had found, Miriam thought, glad that the trumpeting had broken the spell of the vision. For a moment all other sounds ceased. The guards' talking and clatter, the dogs' barking and baying, the lemurs' and insects' chittering in the jungle that surrounded the hilltop pasture on which the encampment sat—all stopped, as if man and beast recognized, for whatever reason, the traditional call to worship on this Rosh Hashanah, the first day of the Jewish new year.

Sundown had surprised Miriam again. Already it was almost dark and the cooler, evening air pressed against her skin like a soft hand. She half-ran toward the encampment, hampered by her bulk. In the southeastern corner, beneath the limestone knoll that served as the fourth sentry tower, she could see the prisoners gathered around Solomon, heads bowed but bodies upright in defiance of the four machine guns that were trained in their direction.

Miriam felt her heart sink as Pleshdimer grinned at her in passing and lumbered toward the Jews. The bowed heads did not seem to notice him coming, but from the rain forest, a dozen eyes reflected the dying sun. Lemurs, probably. If they weren't careful, their curiosity would earn them the stewpot.

Shevarim. The second note. Broken. Mournful.

If only she could attend the Service, but having "officially" renounced Judaism, anything contradicting that would bring down Hempel's wrath, much less Erich's.

Or maybe it wouldn't.

Their beloved Führer Himself had defined her as Aryan. Even on a remote Madagascar island they could not obviate His orders and live without fear. She was safe, surely.

"When, Solomon, will we find a way to live together in some semblance of normal life?" she whispered.

Perhaps, she thought hopefully, she could watch the Service from a distance, yet close enough to put herself among the prisoners should Hempel and his ilk decide to interfere. Were she in danger, Erich would be more likely to intercede on behalf of the Jews.

She shook her head, chiding herself for her assumptions and angry with her self-centered attitude. She had the baby to consider, she reminded herself.

Besides, what right had she to think herself welcome in the company of a congregation of men who had survived Sachsenhausen!

Chapter 18

Teruah.

The third note of the Shofar sounded—sharp, staccato, expressing the pride and the pain and the hope of Solomon's people. This time, the forest animals replied as if in counterpoint.

Looking over the bowed heads of the huddled Jews, Solomon remembered the last important time he had stood at the *bimah*. His bar mitzvah.

What an event that had been for him and for his family.

Now, he stood before the others near the narrow spring that ran over the cliff from the embankment. Standing to one side were the few men who no longer believed that their God listened when they prayed. Above him, pointing down at the piece of cloth he was using as a *yarmulke*, was a machine gun. Beyond the prisoners, two of Erich's dog trainers held Krupp machine pistols, while half-a-dozen others stood beside their dogs, fingering the choke chains nervously.

In obedience to Erich's orders, Hempel's men kept their distance.

"*Baruch Ato Adonoy, Elohaynoo Melech Ha'olom,*" he intoned after Goldman, serving as cantor, lowered the Shofar. *May the Lord make His countenance to shine upon you and bring you peace. Amen.*

Sol kept his voice hushed. No sense waking the dead—or at least those who, priding themselves on spreading death, were morally so.

"For obvious reasons, I'm going to keep this brief," he began. "We are here today to honor a beginning. For us, this Rosh Hashanah is more than a New Year and a time of remembrance and judgment. As Jews we must examine our past wrongs, where in deed and thought we have failed our Father...*land,*" he added, glancing uneasily toward the men with the dogs. "We stand here beneath the eyes of He who created us; our actions and conduct must serve not only as an example for those who follow us, but also as the springboard— the base camp—for the fact that they *will* follow...*if* we not only obey"—*our consciences,* he wanted to say—"but work as men possessed."

He continued with the sermon, keeping it short yet striving to ensure that his fellow prisoners understood his message, both explicitly and implicitly. On this Holy Day, his people prayed to be included in the book of the righteous who would live one year more. Even the dead, it was written, prayed for the living. This holy day was when the Jew reviewed his history and prayed that he would find contentment and hope in Jerusalem. Such was the dream of all Jews since the Diaspora. So this wasn't Jerusalem, but it also wasn't Sachsenhausen. How bittersweet that they had reason to give praise to Adolph Hitler.

Sol had carefully thought out the sermon. He wanted to be certain that a subtle but clear message underlay his words, one conveyed by inflection and nuance. The fact was that ultimately each of them would have to decide in his own heart whether he should work with the Nazis—compromise with evil—to build a sanctuary here for European Jewry. He, Solomon, knew of Hitler's plans to transform Madagascar not into a homeland for Jews but a ghetto where he might pen up Jewish assets and abilities for his own ends. The Führer wanted to rid the world of Jews, but keep at hand what they could give him. The list of Jewish achievements, especially in industry and science, was endless; even a madman such as he would not be so foolish as to give that up. A Nazi-dominated Jewish island off the east coast of Africa would guarantee ongoing use of the ideas and human energy the Jewish people possessed; it would also protect Fascist oil interests in the Gulf states, ensure Italian imperialism in Ethiopia, and break up British shipping lanes between India and South Africa.

The notion of a Jewish homeland on Madagascar had not originated with Hitler. Napoleon had considered it; Bonnet, France's Foreign Minister, had supported such a plan; the Poles had sent a contingent to Madagascar to study the matter. But Hitler clearly had a greater design, if he intended to go through with the project at all. Hadn't he said as much to Rathenau way back in '18?...*pen the Jews on Madagascar, and use them like dogs.*

Right now, on tiny Mangabéy island—an area of land almost as small as the infamous Alcatraz, in the United States—the plan was but a seed. Solomon and the other prisoners could help assure the survival of European Jews, in a world grown insane with hate; but in building what Hitler wanted, they would run the risk of supporting what he might do on Madagascar. Should they attempt to create a sanctuary—or sacrifice themselves and sabotage the mission?

His personal history drove him toward the latter course, which was not surprising after his many years of studying the texts of the great Kabbalist, Isaac Luria. Luria had believed that *galut*, the exile of the Jewish people, was a reflection of the self-imposed exile of God Himself, who withdrew to make room for the world.

How much simpler it would be, Solomon thought, to believe as many Kabbalists did that *galut* was a condition of a universe in need of redemption, rather than a circumstance imposed by man. So firm were they in that belief, that many of them went into exile by choice, both seeking expiation and in order to participate in what was thought of as the divine exile.

He spoke of that in his sermon. With enemy ears trained upon his words, he could not talk much about their present reality. Had he been able to do so, he would have said that if Hitler lacked a destination to which to send European Jewry, he would be forced into compromise, however self-serving. For how else might he deal with the millions of Jews with which he must contend now that he had invaded Poland and annexed Austria and Czechoslovakia? And he would not stop there. It hardly seemed possible that even he could hope simply to kill them all.

The prisoners kept their heads down as Solomon spoke. Not only in reverence and to avoid arousing suspicion, but also because each mulled the questions, considered the ramifications—and remembered home and loved ones. Dare they throw away whatever chance they had to see those loved ones again, in exchange for the pitifully small reward of *possibly* keeping Madagascar out of Nazi hands? Even if the project failed, should Germany attack France it was likely that Madagascar, though nominally French, would side with Hitler. There was considerable Nazi sympathy here, as there was in South Africa. Solomon knew there was another variable, one each man could not avoid considering, though none would ever admit having thought about it: Solomon Freund, whom they had chosen to act as rabbi, was or had been involved with Miriam Rathenau Alois. Misha, who had worked for her before his capture, had told them that. She was *here*. The women they loved were...where?

If they were even alive.

Nearing the end of the Service, Sol signaled Goldman to take over the reading from the Torah. That night they would share in the eating of the head of a fish, so that they would all be heads and not tails in the year to come; tomorrow, singly because they had not dared to ask permission to gather again as a group, each man who still believed would cast away his sins against God beside the stream.

For now, he must ready the bread they had saved and the honey they had gathered—symbolic of their joy and gladness in the Lord.

Deep in thought, he did not immediately see Miriam standing near the outer fence. Seconds later, panic rose in him, though not at the sight of her there, or of the half-a-dozen Kalanaro armed with spears who danced, and glowed, in the dusk.

What caused his pulse to quicken was the sight of Dr. Judith Bielman-O'Hearn, standing large as life at Miriam's side. He could see her clearly in the sentry tower's spotlight.

Sol blinked and tried to focus with weak eyes, wondering if this could be another of the visions that had plagued him since childhood, the visions that had become so much more terrifying after he had witnessed the assassination of Miriam's uncle.

But there had been no cobalt-blue light to presage this vision, as there had always been before; and, despite the shadows and his eyesight, the woman's figure had a clarity to it that had never been true of his amorphous ghosts.

The Kalanaro leaped and cavorted and spun in silence, brandishing their weapons, their heads like hairy coconuts, their eyes charcoal-rimmed and too big for their faces. Mouselemur eyes.

Forcing his focus, it became apparent that the Kalanaro were covered with a white substance that appeared to pulse and wink—

"You all right, *Reb* Solomon?" the man next to him asked, placing a light hand on Sol's arm.

"May you be written down for a good year," Solomon said, choosing to use the traditional Rosh Hashanah greeting in the hope that it would lend him strength.

"Prisoner three-seven-seven-zero-four!"

Hearing his Sachsenhausen number, Sol jerked his attention to the left, moving his whole head rather than his eyes to compensate for his lack of peripheral vision. Pleshdimer, his fat carp mouth downturned in a sneer, stood beside the spring.

"I'm talking to you, Jew!"

Solomon shoved the bowl and bread into the nearest man's hands, raced toward Pleshdimer, and snapped to attention. Erich had ordered the Kapo not to speak to the prisoners in a derogatory manner, but Sol knew that beneath Pleshdimer's fat was a strength that could break a man's neck like a twig. Erich's orders or no, it was life-threatening to treat the Kapo with anything but the greatest show of respect.

Sol saluted. "Yes, Herr Kapo Pleshdimer!"

"Herr Kapo Rottenführer Pleshdimer!" the man bellowed into Solomon's face. "I'm army now, you know."

"Yes Herr Kapo Rottenführer Pleshdimer!" Were the pygmies still there? Sol wondered. Were they watching? Was Judith?

He glanced from the corner of his eye; as usual he saw only dark gray where his eyesight failed him. He turned his head, slightly. The dancers were gone.

Judith was gone.

Pleshdimer hit him.

The punch came from the side. Sol heard a cartilaginous crackling in his left ear even before he felt the pain. Then something roared through his head and he slumped sideways to his knees, struggling to hold himself up with his right hand.

Pleshdimer kicked him beneath the chin, snapping Sol's head backward and catapulting him onto his shoulder blades. He lay there, schooled by the terrible lessons of Sachsenhausen into knowing he had to arise immediately or face further punishment.

"You will look at me when I speak to you, scum!" Pleshdimer boomed from above.

He squatted and stuck a cigarette butt between Sol's lips, then scooped up red mud from beside the spring and mashed it against Sol's mouth, rubbing hard with the heel of his hand.

Solomon managed to rise to his knees and struggled to stand, careful not to spit out the cigarette nor wipe off the mud. Let no man refuse what gifts Wasj Pleshdimer gave; Solomon had learned that the hard way, too.

"Yes...Herr Kapo...Rottenführer...Pleshdimer, sir," Sol forced himself to say. He felt blood coming from his left ear, trickling down beneath his collar.

"What's going on here!"

He looked up through eyes half-shut in pain to see Erich striding toward him, pistol in hand. He's going to shoot me, Sol thought. So be it. He would not again endure what he had been through in Sachsenhausen. He would not.

"This Jew scum...disrespectful! Disobedient!" Pleshdimer lowered his voice toward the end, as if suddenly less sure of himself. "I found this!" He pointed, shaking with anger, at the cigarette butt hanging from Sol's lip.

Erich took the butt and flipped it away in disgust. He cocked the pistol, glared at Sol—and abruptly swung the barrel toward Pleshdimer. "I don't care what you found! You ever touch one of my Jews again without my consent, I'll tear your eyes out and stuff them down your throat."

"Rottenführer Pleshdimer did not find the offensive item." Major Hempel ambled into Sol's tunnel vision. "I did. Captain Dau and I discovered it days ago near the mess tent—obviously, and probably purposely, overlooked by your *colonists*." The major said the last word as though it made him want to spit.

"Are you saying that the Jews improperly policed the area?" Erich asked.

"I have yet to see them maintain *any* part of this camp to *my* satisfaction," Hempel replied.

"We both know what your standards are, Herr Sturmbannführer." Erich spoke with equal animosity. "Jew blood to fertilize the flowers. Jew flesh as fodder for pigs. Except this isn't Sachsenhausen. We have no prize hogs here on Mangabéy." Erich barely came up to the major's lapels. Without tilting up his head, he looked into Hempel's eyes with a withering glare that made the major look small. "A Jewish child to warm your bed," Erich continued. "*That* you have had here, and at the boy's insistence will have again." Erich holstered his gun. "That is my one concession to you," he said. "Watch yourself, Herr Sturmbannführer, or you'll be left without any concessions."

"Don't threaten me, Herr Oberst."

"No threat, Herr Sturmbannführer. A promise. Your proximity to Himmler means nothing to me here. My orders to create this camp came directly from the Führer himself."

"Through Reichsführer Himmler," Hempel reminded him.

"It matters little which postman delivers an envelope," Erich said. "Only who signed the letter."

As if fighting to save face, Hempel switched subjects back to the original point of contention. "What about the cigarette, Herr Oberst."

"What about it."

"I believe you will find many more butts by the mess," the major said in a raised voice. "Ones your precious *Jews* failed to police."

Solomon glanced toward the mess and saw two or three of Hempel's men, watching the proceedings, flip cigarettes to the ground. Before looking back at the confrontation, he caught a glance from Miriam. Her stance reflected raw fear, though whether for him or herself he could not tell. He did know that if Erich lost this or any other fight with Hempel, it would be the beginning of the end. Erich held the better hand, but he was running out of cards. Hempel was not one to be cowed, and if Erich failed to have the prisoners police the area again at once, he would in effect be countermanding his own orders regarding the Jews keeping the camp spotless.

"Herr Oberst! Herr Sturmbannführer!"

Johann, the radio operator, burst from the HQ tent, waving a piece of paper. Solomon knew the type well: young, Aryan, eager to please and to rise in the ranks of the Party. He was blond and boyish, with that youthful enthusiasm Solomon had in the past decade too often seen translated into Nazi fervor.

"Our troops have laid siege to Warsaw!" the boy called out.

The fact that Hempel took the note and did not give it to Erich, the senior officer, did not escape Sol's attention. He was sure that Erich noticed the slight, but the colonel remained aloof, almost implacable, as if fully expecting the major to pursue the matter and report to him in turn.

Hempel visibly brightened as he read. "Seems the prayers of your Jews are in vain." He handed Erich the message. "The Reich is unstoppable."

"Your implication concerning the Jews is obscure, Sturmbannführer." Erich scanned the message. "As always."

"Then perhaps you are not aware that your Jew dogs are committing sacrilege," Hempel said evenly.

"Sacrilege?"

Hempel touched the top edge of the paper with an index finger. "Subhumans bowing before a dead god on the eve of the Reich's triumph!"

Drawn by the announcement, Hempel's men began gathering. They watched Erich as hungrily as they had the zebu. Solomon knew Erich's dilemma had suddenly worsened. If he allowed the Service to continue, he would appear to be elevating the status of the Jews above that of the Reich; stop the prayers, and Hempel had won an easy round.

Erich stepped back and lifted his head in what was clearly a poised, staged effect, like that of a great orator. He seemed to be calm, but Sol knew Erich Alois was steaming.

The colonel looked from man to man.

"You've no answer?" Hempel asked.

Erich put his hands in his pockets and rocked back on his heels. He was not the relaxed, intuitive thinker that Solomon himself was, but one who either arrived at a conclusion from a logical base—or spun off into anger. Sol knew from long experience that Erich's control at this moment was a fragile thing.

"I do not believe I was asked a question, Sturmbannführer," Erich said, his contempt evident.

A nonplused Hempel opened his mouth to reply, but Erich shrugged and stepped toward Solomon, who straightened as rigidly as a statue. "Free laborer Freund," Erich said, "you are to close your service tonight by praising the Fatherland and praying to the fiction you call God that this latest German endeavor will bring its rightful due. Is that understood?"

"Ja, mein Oberst!" Sol knew he must do everything within his power to keep Erich in control. If that meant vowing eternal allegiance to the Reich and to Erich Alois in particular, he would acquiesce without a second's thought. Had he not, after all, once licked horse manure from Hempel's boots back in Germany, to keep himself alive? Humiliation meant little. Once endured, he merely locked it up in some small part of his psyche he never re-examined unless forced to do so. It was the physical humiliation he could no longer abide...and not just his own. Watching the torture and slow, painful dying of friends was so much more horrific.

"When you are through, you will personally lead a detail to scour this compound for cigarette butts."

"Ja, mein Oberst!"

"Dismissed."

Solomon did an about-face, stepped up before the other Jews, formally summoned them to arise, and standing at attention guided their voices in prayer. Learning to weed substance from irrelevancies, he thought. A light rain, more mist than drizzle, had begun. It made Miriam's clothing cling to her skin.

"That was a trick," Hempel was saying behind him.

"Any fool knows that Jews are too devious to be duped," Sol heard Erich say, his voice receding.

Solomon smiled at Otto Hempel's minor defeat. That's one for you Erich, he thought—and one for the rest of us.

Part II

"Those who profess to favor freedom, and yet deprecate agitation, are men who want rain without thunder and lightning. They want the ocean without the roar of its many waters."

— Frederick Douglass

Chapter 19

Erich grew increasingly edgy throughout the next days. Hempel had not made any move to avenge himself for having lost out to him about the Rosh Hashanah Service. Except for the detail roster, followed by minor complaints—the kind of thing all commanders had to endure—the days following the Rosh Hashanah Service had been uneventful. That Hempel would take his revenge was a certainty; what form that revenge would take was anybody's guess. This business of making Erich wait for the other shoe to drop had become part of a pattern.

The two of them had faced off twice. Erich had emerged one morning to find the Jews digging a trench around their quarters. The major had apparently come up with some unbelievably stupid idea of having them actually move into and sleep in the trench. Not only were there vocal objections to the idea of preparing the ground for what looked like a mass grave, but there was the question of standing water in a tropical environment—a perfect breeding ground for mosquitoes and all manner of disease-bearing insects and fungi.

He had put a stop to that immediately, with surprisingly little resistance from the major.

There was also the matter of electrifying the fences around the Jewish quarter. He had consistently told Hempel that he would not countenance this, yet perhaps doing so would allow vigilance to be relaxed a little, giving him more free time, or at least relieving some of the mental pressure. The generator could certainly handle the extra load: he was glad, for the first time, that he had agreed to take the behemoth, despite the difficulty they'd had—even with the tank for assistance—dragging it up the hill.

For now, what was weighing most heavily upon him was his concern for the dogs, the two sick ones, particularly Taurus, but also the others. Despite his best efforts, they were not responding properly to him or to the trainers. He knew they missed the leadership of Taurus, but that was not enough to account for their constant vacillation between restlessness and sluggishness.

He, too, felt restless and sluggish. Mostly, Erich decided, he was bored. By the time he went to bed and fell asleep, cradling a bottle, he had filled his day with what seemed like a thousand things—none of them relevant to him. Miriam provided no companionship. She acted drugged half of the time and disinterested or angry the rest. Although as their officer he felt close to the trainers, he had no real friends among them, and drinking alone was hardly a substitute for camaraderie.

"I wish to speak to you about the fence, Oberst."

Erich had arisen at dawn despite a hangover and was standing in the center of the camp, watching the Jews ascend the water tower to continue filling the tank. He braced himself as the major approached, but Hempel appeared surprisingly at ease.

"The matter of the fence has already been discussed," Erich said.

"Insurrection will come from the inside!" Hempel said. He pointed toward Solomon, who was emerging from the medical tent and heading toward the Jewish sleeping quarters. "Just look at how lax your security is. That Jew...number three-seven-seven-zero-four...coming and going as he pleases. Like he's at some kind of social event."

That Solomon might have spent part of the night ministering to Miriam renewed Erich's anger, but he struggled not to show it. "How is it you recall his number so easily, Herr Sturmbannführer?" Erich asked. "Have you an *interest* in him? His name is Freund. Solomon Freund. And no, we will *not* electrify the sleeping area." Erich made a final decision. "What danger exists comes from with*out*. Did you not see those two Kalanaro, dancing and taunting us from the edge of the forest last night? Not that you spend enough time in the compound to worry about security! You don't give a hog's damn about security, Sturmbannführer. All you care about is Jews. And that goddamn Zana-Malata."

"Do not use his name in vain, Herr Oberst. Don't you...dare!"

Hempel abandoned all pretense of congeniality. Giving Erich a hard smile, he turned on his heel and was gone.

Wishing he had forbidden Misha to return to Hempel, Erich strode to the medical tent. He greeted Miriam indifferently and went over to the dogs. Taurus' condition remained unchanged, but Aquarius lay with his head hanging over the edge of the grass-filled box Müller had fashioned. The dog's ragged panting boomed in Erich's ears.

"Misha," Miriam muttered.

"Sir, my dog is dying and no one is doing anything to help," Ernst Müller said, entering the tent. "There must be something...."

Erich defined Ernst in simple terms: dog trainer; brother to Ursula Müller, the school girl who had taunted half the boys at *Goethe*

Gymnasium, Erich among them. Her conduct had caused her brother much pain.

Maybe that was why Ernst loved his dog so much. Why Erich and all trainers loved their charges. Because the love was simple, without pain. Without reproach.

Aquarius' breathing grew louder and more ragged, as if the dog were trying to suck the tent sides in and out, struggling to draw the dusk into weakening lungs. Then he gasped—a bellowy exhale that ended in choppy breaths. And stopped breathing.

Memories from the training center in Berlin assailed Erich. Aquarius, the most respectful and obedient of all the dogs, approaching his food dish with doe-eyed gratitude. First to conquer the horizontal training ladders at the estate; everyone so happy that Ernst yelped with joy and threw his hat high in the air. The dog leaping from the apparatus to grab the cap in his mouth, leaping into the sun....

Ernst stooped before his dog, arms around the animal, crying.

"Stop it," Erich said softly. "Get a hold on yourself."

Müller shook his head.

"You think I don't know what you're going through?" Erich's voice rose in pitch. "You don't think I've lost a dog before?"

"I don't care...what you think." Ernst spoke in cobbled, sawing breaths. "You're not...me. You're not...any of us, no matter what...you say." The corporal raised his head and added quietly but sincerely, "You bastard. You brought us here. You'd like everyone to *think* it was Himmler's and Goebbels' idea to bring us to this hellhole," he said after a moment. "Maybe even you believe that. But you wanted it. You wanted to prove yourself. Prove *us*. The *team*. But we're not a team anymore, are we, Herr Oberst! Hempel's wolfhound...dead. And now Aquarius...dead."

Erich turned away to stare outside.

"Perhaps you're the one who should get hold of yourself, Herr Oberst," Müller said.

"Under the circumstances I will overlook your words," Erich said. "Have the body of your canine soldier ready for a memorial service in exactly," Erich checked his watch and turned to face the corporal, "one hour. Is that understood?"

Apparently in no mood for military etiquette, Müller simply nodded.

"Heil Hitler," Erich said.

"Heil...," Müller lifted himself to his feet and returned the salute even less enthusiastically than it had been given. "Hitler."

Erich ducked through the tent flaps and was almost bowled over by the syphilitic, who pushed past him and went straight to the dog's side.

"*Chien...chien...beau.*"

Müller made a fist and lifted it menacingly in front of the Zana-Malata's deformed face. "Go. Away." His fist shot out. The Zana-Malata caught it in his claw. Gaining superior leverage, he wrenched Ernst's arm to the right, forcing the trainer to his knees. Then he pushed Müller back and, stepping over him, went outside.

Rubbing his arm, Müller returned to Aquarius, gently stroking the dog's ratty coat, mumbling to himself.

Embarrassed by the man's grief, yet understanding it only too well, Erich went outside and watched the trainers move about the kennel, feeding and brushing their charges. He saw the Zana-Malata depart the compound and head toward his hut. Hempel's habit of spending every off-duty moment with that revolting syphilitic, listening to his babblings with the deference due a fellow officer—that would cease, Erich decided. The chain of command structure on Nosy Mangabéy would be strong, even if it meant cutting away certain links.

Ernst exited the tent, returned with two more trainers, and exited again. Erich's hip was hurting him after being near Taurus so, satisfied that preparations were being made, he went to his tent for a breakfast pick-me-up. He told himself that he would review his maps, review in detail the logistics of moving to the mainland once Nosy Mangabéy was secured, but instead he sat with bottle in hand, staring into a corner.

An hour later, as per his orders, rifle shots rang out—three trainers firing volleys atop the limestone knoll, at the back of the camp. The guard at that post leaned in undisguised rancor across his machine gun, as if to avoid the dog handlers who had invaded his territory.

Erich barely made it there in time. He could see Miriam in the distance, picking orchids from the overhang of jungle against the fence. "For Aquarius," she had said, "I'll put them on his grave." He had not argued. The flowers befit a dog of such strength. After all, was not *orchid* Latin for testicle?

Dogs and masters formed a gauntlet. Erich stood at the one end, reading a passage from Von Stephanitz that praised the breed's loyalty and intelligence. Müller, tears rolling down his cheeks, stood erect beside the dead dog. Nearer the spring, Pleshdimer stood at attention, holding a leash; from the corner of his eye, Erich could see Misha at the end of it. While part of him wished that he had ordered the boy to stay in the Jewish quarters, another part hoped that Misha would successfully rid all of them of the triumvirate.

When the memorial service was over, Müller requested that he be allowed to bury his dog in private. Erich readily agreed. He had been thinking about what he could do to help assuage the grief of both the dogs and their trainers. The answer he had come up with would work better without Müller around, acting like a spare part.

"Holten-Pflug!" he called out. The trainer ran forward. "It's been far too long since we properly exercised the dogs," Erich said. He was about to suggest that they practice the Zodiac, when his attention was drawn to a group of Kalanaro. They were moving around in the last shadows of the morning, which lay near the track leading to the beach.

He pointed at the natives. "What do you say we bring in some of those black monkeys?"

"*Yes! Sir!*"

Holten-Pflug scurried to gather the other trainers and the dogs. Erich lit a cheroot, one of his last. He would have to ask Bruqah to provide him with whatever the island could supply in the way of a smoke. Liquor, too. Realizing that he had moved from sipping to solid drinking, he had counted bottles. There was no way that he had enough to last until Nosy Mangabéy was secured, the dock built at the Antabalana River, and the next major shipment of Jews arrived. At the rate at which he was emptying bottles, he would have to speed up the timetable—or build a still.

"That a kill order, Sir?" one of the trainers asked, when they had all gathered together.

"Not this time, I think," Erich said. He contemplated the request, remembering the night that Taurus drew blood from a whore's wrist on the streets of Berlin. He found the memory satisfying and that frightened him. "Search and seizure will do it," he said, looking toward the jungle. "I really just want to try to talk to one of them." Not that he had the slightest idea what language the little buggers understood. If the team succeeded, he would have to enlist Solomon's help. Or Bruqah's.

He watched the nine dogs and trainers fan out. Then, on impulse, he raised his voice. "If you meet with resistance," he said, "you have my full permission to kill."

Chapter 20

"Do not do this, Mister Germantownman," Bruqah said, stepping more hastily than usual out of the jungle.

The trainers looked at him, then at Erich. There was a sadness in them and in the dogs, Bruqah thought, but like good and proper soldiers, they had put aside their grief and looked ready to begin whatever maneuver their commander ordered.

"Search and seizure," Erich repeated confidently.

Dogs and men moved toward the Kalanaro, who disappeared at once into the rain forest.

Erich glared at Bruqah. "Don't you ever do that again," he said, his voice tense with anger.

"Do what, Germantownman? I did not do anything. I merely advised. Is that not my job?"

"Your job is to give advice when asked, not to interfere with my orders. Besides, I don't see the big problem. There seems to be an endless supply of the little bastards."

"They be like rain forest. You cut, it come back more and stronger." Bruqah did not allow his voice to reveal how appalled he was by Erich's callousness. The full truth was that the chase itself would antagonize the Kalanaro, but they would not be captured. The dogs and men would thread their way down the hillside. Reaching the mangroves and the tiny strip of beach, they would erroneously conclude that their quarry had paddled to the mainland, and return here frustrated with the insects and the fruitlessness of the search. "Jungle sometime like alligator. She like to swallow men and dogs." He grinned, deliberately showing his teeth. "Swallow Kalanaro too, maybe."

"We'll find them," Erich said.

"Maybe. They be glowworms. Here, yet not here. Sometime you no-see-um. Other time they full of light." Bruqah remained placid, his smile in place. The Kalanaro were perfectly able to take care of themselves, and the thought of agitating the Germans charmed him. The trainers were a different matter. He thought of them as apart from the others, and could not revel in their frustration. He had seen too much futility for that: burning off the central highlands for planting, then watching the thin red soil wash to the sea; warning his people not to hunt the giant flightless birds and pygmy hippos, gone now from the face of the land; pain piercing his heart each time a Malagash slaughtered an aye-aye because he feared its power.

"So you're telling me that we can't find them?" Erich's temper had cooled. He looked more amused than angry.

"I saying you do not wish to find them, maybe."

"Obviously what you are not telling me is more important than what you have said."

"Ob—viously." Bruqah had trouble pronouncing the word.

"I think that in future I should only ask you what I do not want to know." There was a hint of a smile in the colonel's eyes, as if the verbal sparring pleased him. "You will be surprised to hear that I believe you," he said. "But this time it does not matter if they find nothing. Sometimes it's the looking that's important. Sometimes, that is more than enough."

With a wave of his hand, the colonel turned his back on Bruqah and walked toward the road that led to the beach. Watching him, the Malagash admitted to himself, albeit reluctantly, that there were things he liked, even admired, about the Germantownman. It was just a pity how rarely those things surfaced, for had they done so more often, Erich might have been worthy of saving.

Chapter 21

"Herr Oberst."

Erich awoke as Fermi entered the tent. The trainer looked worried.

"Forgive me for disturbing your rest, sir, but we have seen no sign of Ernst since the burial. Some of us are worried about him, sir."

"He is undoubtedly somewhere mourning the loss of his friend." Erich made no effort to hide the bottle that lay on his cot. "Give him until tomorrow. If he hasn't returned, we'll search for him. Dismissed."

Fermi did not move.

"I said, dismissed."

"Pardon me, sir, but we have already searched for him."

"Did you look around the syphilitic's hut?"

For the first time, Fermi hesitated. "The major and the black man seem to be celebrating something in there," he said.

"I still say give him until morning." Erich sounded less convinced. "This is a small island, but there are any number of hiding places."

Fermi saluted and left. Erich uncapped the bottle and took a swig. He tossed and turned for a while, but an uneasy sense of foreboding kept him awake and, finally, drove him outside and in the direction of the Zana-Malata's hut. If those sons-of-bitches were celebrating the dog's death....

He was working himself up into a new round of hatred. He knew the fury that burned in him was not the cold bright anger that so often helped to clarify his thinking. Lately, he felt that clarity only sporadically. It came and went like the racing clouds that alternately obscured and exposed the orange tropical moon. The anger he was experiencing was reckless and dangerous, but he didn't care.

Behind him, the dogs' baying became more insistent, as if the animals' display of grief had reached a new plateau. It unnerved him until he decided the sound symbolized what military life was all about. What his dogs possessed and some human soldiers too easily forgot.

Devotion.

Discipline.

He gave a perfunctory salute as he went through the compound gate. The Kapo passed him with a gruff "Heil Hitler." Erich did not bother returning the salute, but watched in distaste as Pleshdimer headed toward the dog yard, head cocked to make room on his shoulder for his load. Probably more lemur meat, Erich guessed. The syphilitic seemed to take special delight in providing the dogs with the dietary change—as if there were a rivalry between him and that lemur-loving Bruqah.

To hell with them both. Just so the dogs got fed and stayed healthy. He didn't want to go through another memorial for one of his shepherds. Ever.

The sound of raucous laughter greeted him as he pulled aside the zebu-hide and entered the foul-smelling hut.

"Why, Herr Oberst," Hempel said, as if he were addressing an honored guest. "Do join us. Come. Sit down."

"I am here on official business," Erich said. "It has come to my attention that...what in God's name is that?"

"This, Herr Oberst, despite its crust of dirt, is the egg of the elephant bird, the *æpyornis*, which dwarfed the ostrich. Didn't they teach you *anything* in your precious Reichsakademie? Think of it—the largest bird known to mankind, and the Malagasy hunted it to extinction without giving the matter a second thought." He paused as if for effect.

Then he said, "We, the strong, must do the same to every Jew."

He placed the egg lovingly on a plank next to three porcelain bowls whose sides depicted a blue ship sailing into a floral sea.

"If we hold true to our *vision*," Hempel made a fist for emphasis, "there won't be a Jew left in the world. And, unlike with the bird, it won't be a shame."

Hempel's eyes shone and his voice rose, all trace of inebriation gone. "We are the strong. It is our birthright that we use the weak to our advantage." He waited for a moment, as if expecting Erich to agree.

When Erich did not react, Hempel gave a condescending smile and, with an usher's gesture, bade Erich to move closer. "Let us put aside our small differences, Herr Oberst, and break bread together." He drew open a palisade of strung bamboo Erich had thought was the left wall, but which he now realized was a curtain. "My mentor says we cannot partake of the truth of this great green land until we dine—in its depths, shall we say."

The Zana-Malata laughed, kicking his legs and slapping his chest, as the curtain was swung open its final meter.

Erich blanched.

Misha was huddled in the corner, next to a shovel. He was stroking Aquarius' huge, furry head, its melancholy eyes open and staring. Part of the animal had been skinned, and one hind leg had been cut off.

"If you dislike stew, I'll cut you a fillet," Hempel said. "Or some ribs, perhaps?" He drew a knife from a sheath on the wall. "Anything but the heart. The master says to eat the heart only at dawn, though for an honored guest such as yourself...." He eyed Erich with a mix of alarm and amusement and replaced the knife in its sheath. "You all right, Alois? The cooked meat has been bled and koshered. We wouldn't want to upset your Jewish playmates."

Erich pushed the child aside and sank to his knees beside the mutilated animal.

"Müller buried this dog." He looked at Hempel with unadulterated loathing. "You dug up the animal."

"Perhaps the boy did, Herr Oberst. Have you considered that?"

"And upon whose orders!"

"Why feed worms if you can feed the human spirit?"

"Take that shovel," Erich pointed toward the wall, "and re-bury the dog. Then burn this hut to the ground and report to my tent for summary court martial."

As he enunciated the words, Erich glanced over at the soil-encrusted shovel. Bending, he examined the dead animal's fur. Except for splatterings of blood, the hide was clean.

"This dog was never buried."

Hempel chuckled. "I said *perhaps* the boy dug it up. I never said he actually did so."

Standing, Erich drew his pistol. It felt extremely heavy, and he wondered, absurdly, if Hempel saw that he was shaking. "Where's Ernst Müller? I haven't seen him since...."

Hempel took a cigar and a wooden match from his breast pocket and lit the match by scratching it across the pistol grip of his holstered Mann. Biting off the cigar end, he spat it between Erich's boots.

"Where's Ernst!" Erich screamed.

"He had...objections...to our decision." Lighting the cigar, Hempel inserted the lit end into the mouth of the Zana-Malata, who encompassed it and inhaled deeply, a look of pleasure entering his eyes.

"*You murdered Müller because he wouldn't let you eat his dog?*"

"Don't have a tantrum, Herr Oberst." Hempel smiled reassuringly. "The worms are dining well. The balance has been maintained."

Erich aimed his Walther between Hempel's eyes and, leaning forward carefully, removed the major's weapon from its holster and tossed it toward the door. It hit the zebu hide with a *thoop* and fell outside. "I will give the free laborers an hour of prayer at sunset tonight and again tomorrow." A surge of power mixed with Erich's rage. "They'll thank God for delivering you into my hands."

He released the safety.

Hempel lifted an arm casually, as if to ease the pistol aside. "It is you who loves the Jews, Erich Weisser," he said sincerely, as if wondering why his commander could possibly be upset. "Unless you want your coming newborn similarly infected with Jewish contagion, I suggest that as soon as he is born you move mother and child here to the hut, where they can be safe." He opened his hands with the charismatic innocence of a salesman. "Once we obtain the power of the Kalanaro, we'll burn out the Jewish corruption. Until then...."

A bullet's too clean a death for this monster, Erich thought, his finger tightening on the trigger.

Puuh.

The Zana-Malata made a short puffing sound, and Erich swung around to face him, pistol raised. A halo of lavender flame rose from the syphilitic's gaping mouth-hole. The smoke ring fastened around the barrel of the Mann and tightened around Erich's hand, burning into the flesh as it had done the last time with the cold heat of dry ice.

Screaming, Erich got off one shot before he dropped the pistol. The bullet tore through the raffia a few centimeters from the Zana-Malata, who threw back his head and guffawed as Hempel stomped a jackboot down on the Walther.

"Don't you ever learn? Forget it, *Weisser.*" Hempel picked up the pistol, fastened the safety, and tucked the gun in his belt. Placing the lit tip of his cigar in his mouth, he inhaled as deeply as had his mentor. With a triumphant *puuh*, he released a similar circle of lavender fire toward the ceiling. "We each have our units to command." He smiled obsequiously. "There's no reason we can't work together."

"We'll see about that!" Erich staggered through the doorway and, tripping on the steps, fell to his knees in the grass. Starting to rise, he reached for the Mann that lay at arms reach.

A black foot stepped onto the pistol; a speartip touched his jugular.

Above him stood two Kalanaro, eyes charcoal-rimmed, wiry bodies covered with mud dimly glowing an eerie white, hair streamed back and waxed and gleaming. He stared at the *assegai*, aware of a sickness starting up from his stomach.

The Kalanaro laughed, then one picked up the pistol, and both went into the hut.

Erich watched the whitewashed buttocks disappear behind the tanhide, his hatred and anger mingled with a fear that set his heart pounding. He felt as unsure of himself as an adolescent—unable to consciously steel himself against the world around him.

But he knew he must.

He pulled himself to his feet and, furiously brushing off his uniform, glared toward the door and fought to still his shaking. A *Hamster*...a man who pedaled his bicycle out into the countryside to buy produce from farmers, and pedaled back to Berlin to resell it. The boot and buttlickers of the earth. That's what his father had been, that was what Pleshdimer and the Kalanaro were.

The parlor magic he had witnessed in the hut might earn the loyalty of an idiot like Pleshdimer, but all it would earn the syphilitic was a place beside the major, before a firing squad. And the Kalanaro? They would make it five executions.

When Erich reached the compound gate, the guard was slow to salute. Erich grabbed him by the lapels. "When I so much as look at this gate, you get that arm up stiff as a cock in a whorehouse! Understand?"

With a look of dark timidity, the soldier raised his arm.

Erich knocked down the arm. "Don't waste the effort *now*, soldier! Just bolt the gate. No one is to come or go unless *I* say. That includes the Sturmbannführer. Got that? Anyone tries to force his way in, shoot to kill."

The soldier nodded fearfully as he hurried to shut and lock the gate.

"Consider that a command directly from the Führer!" Erich said over his shoulder as he stalked toward his tent.

The man snapped his heels together and his arm shot up.

That was the way to treat the Totenkopfverbände, Erich told himself: ferocity plus patriotism. Hadn't Hitler similarly summoned the devotion of millions? Now, *before* Hempel's arrest, was the time to re-establish command dominance.

For that, he had some magic of his own: eleven dark dogs and the barrel of his gun.

Johann yanked off his headphones and, looking confused, jumped to attention. He was trembling: eyes sunken, forehead wet with sweat. *Malaria?* Erich wondered.

"We just received a transmission, sir," Johann said. "The Russians have joined the Reich in freeing Poland. May I have the honor of informing the Sturmbannführer and the men of this glorious news?"

Fighting to control his own trembling, Erich poured brandy into his canteen cup and, gulping it down, slammed down the metal cup against the table. "First I have a message for Berlin." The sweet, burning liquor almost took his breath away. "To Gauleiter Josef Goebbels."

It was the camp's first outgoing transmission—radio silence was to be maintained until the Antongil region was secured. The ill, excited youth virtually panted as he transcribed the heading.

Erich downed another brandy. The alcohol settled him enough so that his mind burned with a clean, cunning wrath; the words flowed effortlessly as he paced. "Your worst fears confirmed. Stop. Officer in question indeed involved—make that intimately involved—with racial inferiors and guilty of murdering a soldier of the Reich. Stop. Treason no longer matter of conjecture. Stop. Possible sabotage attempt imminent. Stop. Will proceed per former instructions."

After several moments the youth set down his pencil, his sallow complexion dark with anxiety. "Is that all, sir?" he asked in a quivery voice.

"Isn't that enough?" Erich replied contemptuously.

His trembling now even more evident, the youth thumbed through *The German Dog in Word and Picture* for the page that corresponded with the date—figuring the numbers of the days of the year in reverse. He laboriously matched up the dictated words with those in the innocuous book Erich had chosen as his code book, each word having an in-text counterpart in a complex system based on the date and page, and tapped the coded message over the wireless to German contacts in Italian-held Ethiopia.

Laughing inwardly, Erich signed off with "Sachsenhausen" rather than with his own code name, *Hawk*. If the relayed transmission got through British jamming at Malta, Goebbels would hopefully believe the message had come from the major.

Meanwhile, the guards were sure to assume Hempel was the officer in question. Any loyalty to the major would be severely strained if not severed. For once, Erich was glad the man liked being surrounded by the young and the stupid—and had recruited accordingly.

"See the corpsman about those chills." Erich sat down at the table. "Take the rest of the night off and get some sleep. I'll tend the wireless."

"Yes...*sir*!"

After Johann exited, Erich took a cheroot from the humidor Miriam had given him. He had to grasp one hand with the other to steady the match, but at last got the cigar lit and leaned back, sucking in the smoke deeply to calm himself. Well, he thought, the thing was done; the military shoring-up he would need to justify shooting a major would soon be firmly emplaced. HQ activities were top secret unless stipulated otherwise, but secrecy was the prerogative of old men and misers, not boys pretending to be soldiers. In an hour everyone in camp would know of the message. With luck, he would have little difficulty bringing the guards' always-simmering prejudices to a boil—against Hempel.

He reached into his foot locker for his MP 38 submachine gun and placed it across his lap. The metal with its light coating of oil felt comforting as he ran his hand from the barrel to the metal brace that served as a stock. He pictured himself squeezing off a round into Hempel's forehead. A powder-darkened hole between the eyes, the back of the skull burst open, a roar of approval from the men as he signaled for them to riddle the others. He would smile as the Zana-Malata screeched and Pleshdimer twitched and jerked, corpulent pig that he was. Blood would redden that eerily pulsing, whitish mud those shithole Kalanaro had smeared....

Glowing mud?

Something about that triggered a memory and sent him scavenging among his manuals. There *had* to be something about the Kalanaro in the military literature or the supplemental guides that he had missed before.

Glowing.

A memory tormented him, but he couldn't seem to recall it exactly. His mind felt fogged, and he kept seeing white buttocks and porcelain bowls. What was it? Something from physics, the only class he had liked at Goethe besides military history and biology—cutting up that calico cat. But what! He *knew* physics, and this was schoolboy stuff!

He remembered, and he uttered a triumphant chuckle as he leaned back and put his boots up on the locker.

Pitchblende.

Reports of Congolese crazies who smeared themselves with luminous tar in order to look like ferocious ghosts during battle had led to the discovery of the world's largest uranium deposit and, indirectly, to the physics of Einstein and Bohr. Now uranium was bound up in the incredible energy and wartime potential of Heisenberg's attempt to achieve critical mass. But there was a hitch: only three mining areas existed. The Czechoslovakian uranium mine was nearly exhausted; Canadian uranium was unavailable; and—for fear of aiding Hitler or angering him by selling to the Allies—the Belgians had shut down their huge mine at Shinkolobwe in the Congo to *all* buyers.

Was that what Hempel had meant by the power of the Kalanaro? Was that why he had allied himself with the syphilitic?

Eliminate Hempel, Erich thought as he poured more alcohol, and play Gestapo with the monkeys. He had learned persuasion from the masters, hadn't he? That conniving Goebbels may have paper-shuffled him off to Madagascar, but Daniel was about to emerge from the den.

Find the pitchblende deposit, and he would be a force to be reckoned with. A man of means. Perhaps, given the war, a national hero. Like Foreign Minister Walther Rathenau had been, he told himself bitterly, and blew a stream of smoke.

Chapter 22

"Drink."

Miriam lay in the nearly airless medical tent, so torporous that her limbs seemed without life. It was all she could do to open her eyes.

Above her, grinning down with rotted teeth, hovered a fat, oily face.

"Time for medicine," the Kapo said. Drool bubbled from his mouth and clung to his teeth like sea scum.

"Get away from me." She thought she had screamed, but the words emerged as a whisper.

"Drink," the Kapo said again. "Make the baby dream."

With a dirty finger, he pressed what looked like a liquid-filled thimble against her lips. She did not resist, because she could not.

Then he was gone, and she was staring at the knot where the netting gathered above her and thinking of Luna Park, where Solomon had won a music box for her. In the distance she could hear "Glowworm" playing, broken by the howling of dogs.

The shadows began to spangle. *Franz*, her mind said. *Franz*.

Slow fire suffused her veins as the liquid took effect. Perhaps though I die the baby will live, she thought as her body heated up. Her breathing was shallow, yet the sound roared in her ears. Each blink of her eyes required enormous effort until, with absolute clarity, she saw herself at the age of eleven. She was huddled on the back seat of a speeding convertible, the head of her sheepdog in her lap. "She'll be all right," Mama was saying from the front seat as Papa raced the car along the tree-lined road toward Zurich. "Don't worry, darling, she'll be fine, the vet's not far now." Miriam could not stop sobbing. What did Mama or Papa know, what did anyone except a vet or Heidi herself know about having puppies! Tires screeched. The car slid on the icy road and flipped upside down. She flew against a hillside and, landing amid rocks but without pain, watched the convertible flip again and land right-side up. As if she were seeing spinning pictures on a zoetrope, she saw a man, a woman, and a dog tossed from side to side like rag dolls inside the vehicle. The stench of gasoline permeated the air; even on the hillside Miriam could smell it. Then flames burst throughout the car like a flower suddenly in bloom, bright as a sun shining on...

...a sea, calm and sparkling with light. A porpoise surfaced as if through a mirror of liquid gold, flapping its fins and chittering at the *Altmark*. From the ship's rail, she saw people descend the rope rungs of the Jacob's ladder to dinghies manned by German seamen in white uniforms.

It was all familiar to her. Then it changed and no longer grew from her experience——

——*She sees Jews in black-striped pajamas, oars lifted, and other Jews, helping men, women, and children into the crafts.*

"Isn't it wonderful, Lise?" says a woman wearing a cloche. She is staring across the sun-burnished sea to the shore. "A homeland of our own. Just as the Führer promised."

"But we had to give so much," says a woman in a white lab coat.

"Our property, certainly," the first woman says. "But consider the alternative."

The woman in the lab coat looks at her with expressionless eyes. "I not only considered the alternative, I gave it to him. That's why you're here."

"I don't understand," says the woman in the hat.

"You don't want to understand," the other woman says. "Believe me, you don't want to understand anything."

The people on deck continue to press forward, and Miriam finds herself being pushed along with the crowd. She tries to extricate herself, but is so tightly wedged that she cannot move her arms. Immigrants keep moving relentlessly toward the rail and the Jacob's ladder. Their murmuring and quickened breathing rise in crescendo, and there is about them a smell that assails her senses. At first she thinks it the odor of people cramped in the hold during the long voyage. But it goes deeper than that.

The smell of fear. The smell of death.

"They have come to the island of lost souls to witness the birth of Deborah," Bruqah's voice says.

Someone places fingers on Miriam's bare arm, a sensation that chills her to the bone. The people press forward, eyes bulging, cheeks sunken, lips tight with determination.

"He kept his promise," someone says.

They are entering the rain forest. Despite the sun, mists curl up from among the foliage. Fruit bats by the thousands hang upside down, undisturbed by the gulls and paradise flycatchers that wheel in and out of the tendriled mists. The sea has turned the color of rust. The color of dried blood——

——"Your shepherd *bit* you?" Franz' voice. "That looks like more than a mere bite. Sagi tried to take your elbow off."

"Just bandage it."

Miriam recognized the voice as that of Holten-Pflug, the trainer who was always showing people pictures of his wife and daughter, back home in Wiesbaden, sometimes showing the same people the same pictures over and over again.

"You tell the Oberst about this, and there'll be more than an elbow that'll need attention."

"Don't worry." The corpsman chuckled. "We'll get you fixed up—and the Oberst none the wiser."

"It was an accident! Sagi didn't mean to hurt me."

"I understand that. Just hold still, won't you?"

"He's a good dog. Wouldn't hurt a fly except on command."

"You trainers and your animals," the corpsman said in a light scoff that indicated affectionate respect. "Sometimes I think you believe the war was invented just so you could show off your pets. Like some others I know," he added, his voice low and irate, "who treat Jews the same way. Hold still, now. This is going to sting."

A grunt, followed by the rip of adhesive tape.

"There. That's it."

Canvas slapped. A third figure emerged into the haze of Miriam's vision, breathing heavily.

"Johann," the corpsman said. "Sounds as if you need some quinine."

"It's not malaria, I tell you," a youthful voice panted. "I won't be quarantined." His gasping grew louder. "Nothing's keeping *me* from doing my duty. Especially not tonight. You hear me, corpsman? You confine *me*, and I'll..."

"You'll do what?" Holten-Pflug taunted.

"Leave him alone. He's delirious."

"The hell I am!"

The sounds of scuffling ensued. Something hit the tent wall and she could see murky figures move with the same jerky chaos as the shadows she had once witnessed on that experimental gadget called television, installed under the stands during the Berlin Games.

From outside came a frenzied yapping and growling—a clamor that shook her as if Erich had seized her during one of his tantrums.

Holten-Pflug uttered "Holy God!" and the showcased figures of the three men ceased moving.

The barking that echoed in Miriam's ears made the hair along the back of her neck stand up. Groaning, she managed to roll onto her side, facing away from the tent opening. Something landed on her cheek. A grasshopper.

"I have she, Lady Miri," Bruqah said.

She had not heard him enter. She turned her head and watched him walk the grasshopper outside.

"...*it is the other one, the one called Bruqah of whom I speak.*"

The voice echoed in Miriam's memory. *I refuse to believe that he is anything but what he has shown himself to be,* she thought.

"Tell me again about Princess Ravalona," she said when he returned to her bedside like a child begging for a story. "What did she...does she have to do with you."

"This my island. What affect island affect me." Bruqah perched at the edge of her cot. "My people await return of soul of Ravalona. Bruqah first man on island. They believe Ravalona first woman. My people believe soul wanders unless bones brought to proper homeland burial place. Ravalona die on Mauritius and not brought home."

He stood up and seemed to be deliberating whether or not he should continue.

"Bruqah male soul of Madagascar. Bruqah's wife female soul. So long she wanders, Bruqah incomplete. Count named vessel of woman, but because he false vessel, blood ran. Many people they die here."

"What does that have to do with me and with my child?" Miriam asked.

Bruqah looked surprised, though whether it was at her knowledge or her honesty, she did not know.

"If Zana-Malata wins—"

He stopped.

Miriam sat up with difficulty. "Are you saying that if your people mistake my child as the vessel that holds the soul of Ravalona, your island will run red with blood?"

"Even Bruqah cannot change history," he said, and as silently as he had appeared, he was gone.

Chapter 23

The howling of the dogs made Solomon shiver despite the heat. Wrapped in his blanket to ward off the mosquitoes, he lay on the sleeping area's matted grass, experiencing a strange sense of compassion over the death of Aquarius.

Plaintive as a bird grieving for a mate, the sound of Bruqah's *valiha* rose from the foliage. As usual of late, he played "Glowworm."

Gradually the dogs quieted; a hush settled through the forest, as if the plinks of Bruqah's instrument had brought them a sense of calm. Sol found himself remembering and longing for the romance of Chopin, the sweet genius of Mozart, the order of Bach.

Droning, a mosquito landed on Solomon's neck. He slapped at the insect. At least, he thought wryly, putting his head down and pulling up the coarse blanket, the insects weren't racists. They fed as happily on Nazi as they did on Jew. Still, when the malaria hit—Bruqah had intimated that northeastern Madagascar was the worst place for the disease in all Africa—it would be the Jews who would die first. The quinine was certain to be distributed unequally.

He looked across the sleeping bodies, and cursed his pessimism. Hadn't they climbed out of Sachsenhausen and the *Altmark's* hold? Didn't they have a canvas canopy that afforded some protection from the elements? Minimal though sufficient food? Fresh water from the water tank and from the spring at the bottom of the sentry-post hill that formed part of the compound?

Yet the mainland beckoned beyond the compound's barbed wire perimeter, beyond the shark-infested bay.

"You awake, *Rabbi?*" Goldman asked.

Sol groaned and rolled over. Lucius was a good man, but—

"I know this isn't a rest farm, but might I ask when you last slept?" Sol propped himself up on an elbow.

"Haven't been sleeping much...but I shouldn't trouble you."

Sol touched the back of the man's hand. "Tell me."

"It will soon be Yom Kippur."

"We're all aware of that," Sol said quietly.

"I've spoken to some of the others. They want you to lead another Service."

"They all want that?"

Goldman hesitated. "Not all. Some say it would be too dangerous..."

"They are right, my friend. I believe that the Oberst's self-control—and his control of this compound—are near the breaking point. To push the matter would be...most unwise."

"If you won't help, I will lead a Service myself."

Sol shook his head. "Perhaps next year it will be possible. This year we must ask God to hear the silent prayers in our hearts."

"We will pray together *this* year. My father and mother are still alive. Our prayers must reach God's ears *together*."

"God will understand, Lucius."

A tear rolled down Goldman's left cheek. Sol held the bristly head, comforting Goldman as he might a child. He felt a longing for his own family. Were his mother and sister safe in Amsterdam? "I need to think," he said. "Meantime, try to get some sleep."

Standing, Sol made his way across bodies lying tangled as lianas and, stepping out from beneath the canvas, walked over near the fence. He stared at the moon, wishing it could provide him with answers.

That Major Hempel and Colonel Alois hated one another was obvious. The prisoners had engaged in many intense, whispered debates about whether they could—and should—try to deepen that hatred and broaden the division between the Abwehr trainers and Hempel's Totenkopfverbände. Solomon had begged a halt to the discussions, for fear Jewish unity was itself being divided.

Regardless of what the others thought, to him the matter was clear. Should Otto Hempel seize control of the camp, all was lost. Helping Erich solidify his command, despite its making escape more difficult, was in the prisoners' best interest.

If Erich proved worthy of trust.

If.

Odd, he thought, that he should know Otto Hempel so well, while his former friend remained an enigma.

He heard footsteps behind him. "I told you that I need time to think," he said, expecting Goldman.

"I need your help, Solomon," Erich said.

"And I yours...Erich," Sol said, making his decision and risking the use of the familiar. "May I," he asked, thinking he might bring hope to Goldman and the others while simultaneously helping Erich put Hempel in his place, "make a request on behalf of the free laborers?"

"Give you a finger and you ask for a hand. Is that it?"

Solomon ignored the bait. "We would like permission to conduct a Kol Nidre Service, and to complete the Yizkor Service at sundown the following day."

"You had your prayers. There's been the devil to pay ever since." Looking toward Hempel's tent, Erich's eyes filled with a look of sly anger. "I'll consider it."

"We..."

"I said I'll consider it. Right now I have more urgent matters to attend to."

"You mentioned needing my help."

Erich hesitated. "Later," he said and strode off without mention of what had brought him to the Jewish quarters. Some advice to do with Miriam, perhaps?

"We heard everything," Goldman said, creeping into the moonlight. "Thank you. Perhaps even a Nazi heart can be opened."

"With a wooden stake," Solomon replied. What really lay within that heart, he wondered, watching the naked pygmies who had attached themselves to the camp during the past week leaping and cavorting among the shadows as they moved in a wild dance toward the Zana-Malata's hut. Glowworms?

Knowing he would find no rest that night, Solomon exercised the privilege that had, to his continued astonishment, not been removed, and made his way over to the medical tent. He found Miriam asleep, veiled by netting. Her eyes were squeezed shut; worry lines creased her forehead. She seemed oblivious to Taurus whimpering behind her, chest rising with each breath, fur rippling as if the muscle beneath were in constant spasm.

After a moment's hesitation—for fear of waking Miriam from the rest she so desperately needed, no matter how troubled it might be—Sol whispered *I love you.* For an instant she appeared to hover between sleep and waking. The worry lines deepened. Her hands tightened into fists.

Then she sighed and her shoulders sagged; her throat moved as she swallowed. In reflex action, her tongue touched her lips, like a small animal seeking moisture in the hot, oppressive tent. She turned on her side and put a hand protectively against her belly.

Solomon wondered if he had ever loved her as intensely as he did at this moment. Having been separated from her for so long, he had not fully internalized the changes her pregnancy had wrought. Until now, he had continued to think of her as his lithe dancer.

All this time, he realized, she had possessed what despite his scholar's aptitude—or perhaps because of it—he had never learned. The ability to be practical. The ability not to question life but to live it. He felt ashamed of how little he knew compared to what she'd had to teach.

Some day, he vowed, we will be a family. With Misha as our eldest.

The boy, too, confounded him. Misha had had a chance to escape Berlin, had been almost aboard the train with Beadle Cohen. He had chosen to run from that, from someone who cared, back to danger and Miriam, whom he hardly knew. An eight-year-old, determined to find the parents who had been taken from him. Now he had run again, from Miriam who cared, to people and things too dreadful to contemplate.

Strangely, Taurus also fit in the picture of the household developing in his mind. Yet Erich's she was, and his she would remain.

He could never forgive Erich. Of that he was certain, though in fact he had learned that it was not Erich who had been directly responsible for his arrest. What Erich had done to earn Sol's contempt had happened long before that, while Solomon was safe in Amsterdam. It was then that the man he had once called friend had lied to Miriam, telling her that Solomon had been incarcerated. Lying again, this time about his own status in the Party, he had promised to keep Solomon alive, perhaps even have him released. Her part of the bargain was to live with Erich and prove that she loved him; prove that Solomon was but a friend by renouncing her religion, marrying Erich, and making Goebbels' precious propaganda film.

Now that he was free from Sachsenhausen but not from the Nazi threat, did the future hold any promise for Miriam and himself? He had traveled so far since attempting suicide in the camp, yet in some ways he had not moved a centimeter.

"Don't take the baby, Judith!" Miriam cried out in her sleep. "She's mine! She's mine! Bruqah, don't take her!" Her mouth looked pinched and narrow with terror. Her hair hung damp and lank, her forehead so pearled with sweat that her skin glistened in the lantern light.

Sol did not know if he should wake her. Even what to do with his hands baffled him; they felt too large and ungainly for the spare body the months in Sachsenhausen had bequeathed him.

Miriam opened her eyes. "Sol?" She blinked, glanced around, turned her gaze toward him again.

"I miss you so much!" he said.

"I miss you, too." She shut her eyes, and he thought she would nod off again. "I keep seeing...images. Erich says your dreams have infected me." She tried, unsuccessfully, to sit up. "I told him I was going to join you and the others."

So that was what Erich had intended to talk to him about, Sol thought. "I want you with me, you know that, but you need to be here." His words did not come easily. After a moment, he added, "I heard you calling out the name 'Judith.' Is she the same Judith who...." He did not know how to phrase it. "Whom I've seen?"

"Elderly...khaki clothes. She spoke of Ethiopia."

How many times had Judith visited him in dybbuk-borne visions—she, and half-a-dozen others? "Judith *told* you she was from Ethiopia. *She spoke to you?*"

"She warned me..."

She fell asleep again. He had to consciously stop himself from rousing her. How was it possible that Miriam was seeing his ghosts? Beadle Cohen, interpreting the mystic language of the Kabbalah, had said that the dybbuk opened doors to others' lives being lived in this and in other realities. In his, Sol's, case, the visions were complicated by his own power as a visionary. His ability to see randomly into what he supposed was the future, or a possible future, came in the form of psychic flashes, brought to him—as they were to Isaac Luria and others like him—in a halo of cobalt-blue light.

Their past had been brought to him by the dybbuk, which was no longer a part of him: Judith, speaking of the exodus of the Black Jews from Ethiopia, which gave Mussolini control of the southwestern edge of the Red Sea; Peta, the Ukrainian Jew whose people fought for Hitler against Stalin, in exchange for emigration; Lise, the physicist who cried about having sold the secret of something called critical mass. All so that German Jews might be released. And others, who had come to him repeatedly, showing him lives that, real or not, told of their hopes for a Jewish homeland in Madagascar, free from the evil of the Führer. If they gave Hitler what he wanted.

Was their present and future to be shown to him, too, by his own psychic force?

He had seen Judith so clearly on Rosh Hashanah. Was it possible that she was here, in the flesh, on Mangabéy? Had Miriam seen a real woman or a ghost? Perhaps both? And if so, by what possible means could Miriam be tied to her, perhaps even to the others?

Sol remembered the terrible night he had tried to have the dybbuk—and the dreams—exorcised. Under cover of night, the religious among Sachsenhausen's almost-dead had gathered outside Barracks 18 to pray for themselves. Sometimes they were led by a rabbi, though more often the task of leading the prayers fell to the physically strongest among them.

That night, he had found a rabbi, one schooled in such Kabbalistic rituals as exorcism.

The incongruity of an exorcism in a charnel house had been absurd.

Over and over, under the press of the rabbi's hands, he'd chanted the incantation born of King Solomon: *Lofaham, Solomon, Iyouel, Iyisebaiyu*...Leave this man..." Even now, he could taste the bile that had filled his mouth, feel the wave of nausea that engulfed him. Ultimately, he could hear only the ragged sound of his own voice, feel nothing but the throbbing in his head, see nothing but the sweep of the searchlight. Until, finally, the rabbi said, "All I can do for you, Solomon Freund, is ask for God's blessing. You had a dybbuk in you once. It is no longer there, but I believe it remains flesh of your flesh and blood of your blood. Whatever is in you *now* was always yours—and always will be."

"...*flesh of your flesh and blood of your blood....*"

The child.

Was the child the new vessel for the dybbuk, removed there through his seed and linked to Miriam through her unity with the infant?

If so, the child was his, in fact as well as in spirit.

Taurus' renewed whimpering commanded Sol's attention. Consciously drawing himself into the moment, he listened to the shepherd's faulty respiration.

What might Erich do to someone ministering—or failing to minister—to his prize pet? What might he, Solomon, feel if he did not try to help the so obviously failing animal?

He loosened her collar, but it didn't help. She lay on her side, eyes vacant, a deep *huuking* sounding in her throat, her chest heaving and her rear legs kicking spastically. He felt as useless as he had when Erich had begged him to help Grace, Achilles' mother. The dog had been dying after giving birth. Neither he nor Erich had been able to save her.

"Touching a *German* dog, Jew?"

A hand gripped his hair, and his head was wrenched back as Pleshdimer and the Zana-Malata materialized out of his peripheral blindness. He suddenly realized how very much the loss of his peripheral vision had increased his physical danger.

"Something's wrong with her breathing," he sputtered, pulling away and losing a handful of hair in the process. "You had better find the Oberst."

"Giving orders?" Pleshdimer's voice was heavy with menace. "A Jew giving orders!" He grinned at the Zana-Malata...then slapped Sol so hard across the temple that his head snapped sideways.

"What the hell's going on here?" Erich pushed aside the Kapo and Zana-Malata and knelt beside Taurus. "What happened?" He lifted her head in his arms. He had been drinking again, Sol noticed—heavily, from the smell of him.

Taurus' tail flicked once, but otherwise she gave no sign of recognizing her master. Her weight went slack, and she slumped from Erich's hold.

"What can we do?" he asked Solomon.

We? Solomon's brows lifted. Suddenly it was "we"; everything had changed since their boyhood together, yet nothing had changed.

"Her breathing's labored," Sol said. "Why not talk to Bruqah? He has an amazing store of knowledge about..."

Erich put his head down on Taurus' chest. Apparently unable to hear a heartbeat, he kneaded the sternum with the heel of a hand, fingers interlocked, one hand behind the other. "Help me, Sol!"

Sol. Not *Solomon.* Nor, as he half expected, *Jew.*

In no position to refuse, Sol stooped beside Taurus, his hands awkward appendages disconnected from his desires. Ineffectually, he stroked the dog's coat. "Good girl." His voice sounded less than optimistic.

"Go back to your *books*," Erich said in disgust. "You always were useless in an emergency."

Sol's arms fell to his sides. A great stone upon his shoulders bore his head down.

"I suppose you're praying," Erich said. "You and your goddamned hocus-pocus, I swear you're as bad as..." He lifted his head, his gaze drilling the Zana-Malata. "What's that *filth* doing inside my compound!" He unsnapped his holster and brought his pistol up, leveling it at Pleshdimer's groin.

A shudder raced through Taurus. The *huuking* renewed. Fear clouded Erich's features; he thrust the gun back in the holster. "Get help!" he cried. "Get Bruqah...anyone!"

Sol turned to leave, but the Zana-Malata gripped his biceps.

"*Chi...en!*" the syphilitic hissed. He stooped and, shrugging off Sol's attempt to grab him, clenched shut the dog's frothing jaws. Erich frowned anxiously toward Sol, but kept massaging the heart as the Zana-Malata placed his mouth-hole over Taurus' nostrils and breathed into her, repeatedly raising up and sucking in air, only to utter "*Chi...en!*" and again lower his mouth over her nose.

Taurus gagged.

The syphilitic released his hold on the muzzle. The dog shook, opened her mouth—and began breathing.

"Her pulse feels stronger." Sol stooped to check the carotid artery. His eyes met Erich's, and the sense that the two men were remembering another dog, so many years ago, slammed into Sol like a fist. "The pain must have brought on a seizure. She'll be...fine," he tried to assure Erich.

"She'd better be." His head drooped, and he did not resist when Sol put a consoling hand on his shoulder. "Lose her, I lose everything."

The Zana-Malata straightened and touched the back of Erich's neck. "*Chi...en.*"

Erich batted away the man's hand.

Solomon clutched Erich's arm. "For heaven's sake! He saved Taurus. I think he's saying *chien*—French for dog! Maybe he's trying to tell you he can do something more for her."

"Don't be a fool!" Erich looked in disgust at the burbly, drooling hole. "Just because he grunted something you think is French doesn't mean I should put Taurus in his hands!"

Sol took hold of the black man's wrists. "*Vous parlez Francais?*"

The syphilitic nodded rapidly. "*Chi...en.*" He pointed toward Taurus.

"You studied a little French," Sol reminded Erich. Cocking an ear like a conductor listening for nuances from the violin section, he asked the syphilitic, "What *about* the dog?"

"*Chi...en. Beau.*"

"He says the dog is beautiful."

"So he knows two words. Madagascar is French territory."

"Maybe he can help Taurus. What harm could there be in trying?" Sol put a gentle hand on the shepherd, which was panting softly and gazing up in bewilderment.

"Harm? Taurus could die."

"Looks like she could die anyway," Sol said.

After a moment, Erich said in a tone of resignation, "Ask him what he wants in return for his help."

"In return?"

"If you think that's the Good Samaritan, you'd better look again. The older you get, Solomon, the more ignorant you act."

Solomon spoke to the man, who responded with vowels and drool and vigorous head shaking.

"He doesn't want anything," Sol translated.

"He wants what we all want." Erich gave him a hard look. "Control."

Rising, the Zana-Malata pointed at Taurus and outside, in the direction of his shack. He repeated the gesture, then took off at a lope toward the gate, waving for them to follow. The gate guard jerked his Mauser to his shoulder and eyed the syphilitic through his rifle sight, but the Malagasy paid him no heed. Looking back over his shoulder, he continued to wave them onward.

Erich's gaze again met Sol's, and Sol felt the weight of what Erich demanded. He hadn't changed. Should something go wrong, it would be Solomon's fault.

"Get the stretcher," Erich instructed Pleshdimer. "We'll do whatever must be done to see her through this."

Together, Sol and the Kapo loaded the dog onto the stretcher and followed Erich across the compound. A small crowd of guards pressed forward to see what was being carried.

Hempel joined them. "Seems your brightest star has fallen from the zodiac, Herr Oberst." Lighting a cigarette, he nodded toward Taurus. "But don't worry, she'll be fine as long as *he* cares for her."

With his cigarette he pointed toward the hut. A sparking curl spiraled from the hole in the thatch. "Don't go blaming yourself for your dog's condition, Herr Oberst. Don't blame yourself for anything that goes wrong. It's just that caring and *caring for* are different entities."

"As are the ranks of Oberst and Sturmbannführer," Erich said. "Keep that in mind the next time you think about going near that boy."

Hempel touched his cap as if to acknowledge Erich's transient victory. "My men and I find the little animal—*entertaining*." His eyes gleamed. "So versatile. It's a rare pet, after all, that can spit-shine boots. But," he lifted his palm in compliance, "I shall procure a mascot more to your liking. You may have that one put to sleep."

"This isn't Sachsenhausen," Erich replied.

"Nor is it some Berlin suburb. Manicured lawns and delicate sensibilities have no place in the wild, Herr Oberst."

He saluted, did an about-face, and strode toward the mess, leaving Erich to glower, a hand on the grip of his pistol.

"Let's go," Erich said darkly, under his breath.

At the gate, the guard saluted listlessly. With Erich in the lead, they hurried toward the hut. Grasshoppers sprayed out before them and crunched beneath their feet, and Sol could hear the rattle of Pleshdimer's breath as the fat man struggled to keep up. They moved along jerkily, Sol pulling at the front end of the stretcher and the Kapo yanking back, as if to slow their progress.

A searchlight illuminated the hut, and Sol witnessed a black arm reach around the tanhide door, urging them onward.

Taurus' breathing began to saw. "Faster!" Erich panted.

"No, Mister Germantownman."

The voice seem to hang disembodied in air. Erich crouched, pistol ready. In the glare of the searchlight his face took on a look of irritated relief as Bruqah stepped from the shadows of the tanghin tree next to the hut.

"Help them with the stretcher," Erich ordered.

Bruqah shook his head. "This hut," with a knuckle he tapped the mud-and-wattle exterior, "no place for white men now human air has touched Benyowsky." He seemed to be struggling to translate his thoughts into words. "Kalanaro in there sometime do bad magic. They what you call cap...cap—"

"Capricious," Sol guessed, helping him out.

Bruqah nodded his thanks. "They happy to help Zana-Malata."

"Help him do what?" Sol asked.

"Control what you call spiritual realm, Sollyman. Zana-Malata want child to live and major to succeed. He believe they help him kill those who ostra...ostra—"

"Ostracized," Sol said.

Again Bruqah nodded. "He believe child vessel for soul of Ravalona."

The man is afraid, Sol thought, disquieted. But of what exactly? Or perhaps it was more simple, a question of competition from someone who sought equal power.

Erich seized Bruqah by his *lamba*. "If anyone, or any*thing*, attempts to interfere with me, I'll consider it sabotage...an act of war. Understand one thing: Sturmbannführer Hempel and I are not all that different. Except I do not torture my enemies. I execute them."

He released Bruqah roughly. With a look of disgust, the Malagasy stepped back into the shadows of the tanghin.

"Just how many people *have* you killed, Herr Oberst?" Sol asked as he watched the Malagasy disappear into darkness.

Erich swiveled and jammed the barrel of the gun against Sol's cheek. Sol readjusted his hold on the stretcher, but otherwise did not move.

"Two," Erich said at last. "Both of them boys. The sons of fools who ran a cigar shop on Friedrich Ebert Strasse."

Chapter 24

The hut was sweltering. Eucalyptus branches glowed in a brazier, crackling and pouring off an oily smoke so thick it shellacked Erich's skin and smothered his forehead and cheeks with sweat. This is insanity, he thought, waiting for his burning eyes to adjust to the darkness.

He was almost sorry when they did. Chin against chest, shoulders sagged and arms hanging limply, the Zana-Malata sat behind the fire. He was staring lifelessly at the flames. Smoke seemed to curl from his peppercorn hair. He looked for all the world like a corpse that had died sitting upright. The two fossas crouched fearfully beside him, mewling and worming their noses against his shriveled legs.

He did not move.

Behind him a crudely woven raffia chair, hanging from the ceiling by a plaited rope, swung slowly back and forth. Firelight glinted off three blackened cooking pans and several zebu halters along the back wall. The flames of small, fat candles guttered in the empty sockets of a water buffalo skull that adorned an upper corner, its forehead painted with a swastika.

The fossas lifted their heads to survey the intruders. The fire popped, sparks cascading across the syphilitic's shoulders. Still he remained slumped. Filled with disgust and reluctance, Erich motioned with his pistol for Solomon and Pleshdimer to place the dog near the brazier and then go outside and wait. The fossas backed up, hackles raised; then, appearing to adopt a wait-and-see attitude, they hunkered down, watching suspiciously.

"What do you plan to do about the dysplasia?" Erich said, unable to control the ire in his voice as he crossed to the Zana-Malata.

Through glassy eyes the syphilitic continued peering into the flames.

Anguished that anyone could sit so mesmerized while Taurus lay so feebly, Erich put the gun close to the man's head. "Acknowledge me!" Erich fought to control his trembling. As if through someone else's eyes he watched the gun pull toward the syphilitic's head, like metal to a magnet.

"I said acknowledge me!"

When there was no response, a pressure that had been building inside him for a very long time erupted.

His finger squeezed.

Click.

The Zana-Malata sat impassive and unharmed. My God, Erich thought, ashamed at having actually pulled the trigger. He tried to holster the gun, but instinctively jerked the trigger again. This time, the gun was pointed at the floor.

Click.

Stupefied, Erich stared at the pistol.

The Zana-Malata toppled onto his side and lay with his head near a shelf constructed of a mahogany plank placed across two rocks. On the plank sat three empty white bowls, cracked and stained and obviously very old, each painted with the scene of a clipper ship sailing through an Eden of leaves. Where, Erich wondered, had he seen those bowls before? He couldn't concentrate. All he could focus on was the syphilitic's arm, outstretched on the lashed-sapling floor, the biceps baggy with diseased skin, the fist without fingernails.

Blood drooled from the Zana-Malata's mouth.

"The gun didn't fire." Erich backed up. Filled with turmoil, he felt like retching. "I didn't shoot you." He turned toward Solomon, whose face, obscured by the haze, looked expressionless. "I didn't shoot any—."

Except it was not Solomon. He had ordered Solomon to stay outside. Hadn't he?

The fire snapped, and a curl of smoke rose from the brazier. The heat forced Erich to shield his eyes. When his vision returned, Pleshdimer was licking the blood from the saplings.

Erich grabbed the corporal by the hair. "He has syphilis, you imbecile!"

Pleshdimer grinned with reddened lips.

Erich shoved the man aside. The Kapo fell against Taurus and settled down with his head across her back. "If the dog dies, we feast," he said.

"Get up and out! You have five seconds!"

Pleshdimer folded his hands across his paunch.

"One!" Erich screamed.

A memory of Miriam seized him, making his head pound. "*Count!*" he had commanded that night he had lost his temper and taken her by force. "*Count!*"

"*One...two...three...*"

"*Slower!*"

"*Four...*"

"*Again! From the beginning!*"

"Five!" For an instant the face before him was Miriam's. He squeezed the trigger just as Sol's hand gripped his wrist.

"Erich!"

The explosion roared in his ears. A centimeter from Pleshdimer's jugular a black hole appeared in the floor, and a blue puff of smoke leapt up from the brazier.

"You could have killed Taurus!" Solomon shouted.

Erich blinked. *Taurus*? He twisted his hand from Sol's hold and watched the corporal lurch his bulk forward and cower in the corner. Too drained and displaced to aim again, he knelt beside the dog. He made no attempt to control his fierce trembling. "Mein *schatz*," he murmured. "My love."

With a *plook* the Zana-Malata uncorked a crudely fashioned clay jug. The smell of chloroform pervaded the hut, and Solomon moved back toward the door and fresh air. Though the anesthetic made him dizzy and giddy, Erich remained near Taurus.

Pouring chloroform onto a ragged cloth and handing the cloth to Erich, the Zana-Malata indicated for him to hold it against the dog's nose. Erich signaled for the black man to recork the jug, the contents of which were making him dizzy. The syphilitic shook his head vehemently, lifted his gnarled, grotesque fist close to Erich's chin and opened the fingers. An ember burned on the palm. Erich pulled back from its heat. The fingers shut around the ember, the hideous mask that was the syphilitic's face registered no pain.

The hand reopened. In the palm lay what looked like a fruit pit. Propelled as if by a force not his own, Erich holstered the pistol and, taking the pit, stared at it stuporously, careful to keep his injured hand like a leaf-shaped paten below the other one, in case he dropped the thing.

"It's a tanghin pit," Solomon whispered, reappearing and squatting beside him, blending with the smoke as if he had lost all physical definition. "Bruqah says eating it induces a trance state."

The pit, fuzzed and creased, strangely fascinated Erich. "Tell him to get on with it."

Solomon gently took hold of the Zana-Malata's shoulders and spoke to him in French.

The Zana-Malata nodded, then crawled behind the dog and lifted her head. A small spasm rippled through the animal, and Erich shivered empathetically. He felt a vague sense of gratitude when the Zana-Malata directed him to cover Taurus' nose with the cloth. Trying to keep his head as far away from it as possible changed the angle of his vision and he saw Pleshdimer in the corner, face chalk-white and arms slack. The thought drifted away from him as he watched a fossa pad forward to lick Pleshdimer's palm.

The smoke was no longer going up through the roof-hole. It had broken into blue crescents shaped like ferns and curled down around him. He blinked and looked toward Solomon for help, but the hut was wreathed in thick tendrils of smoke and he could not see beyond his hand.

Which still held the fruit pit.

He set it down near the brazier.

The pit was an eye, staring up at him. His lids felt weighted.

The Zana-Malata chanted something unintelligible. He held a knife that spangled like a sword in sunlight. Erich knew he should disarm the man, but he was in too much of a torpor to move or even care. He raised his hand, but his arm fell—slowly. Everything seemed to move through glue.

The syphilitic maneuvered the anesthetized dog onto her back, parted her hind legs, smeared something black and tarry onto the fur and shaved her thighs. After each stroke he ran the blade between his fingers to clean off the hair. Then he cleansed the skin with a rag that smelled of antiseptic and poised the knife above the left thigh.

Must be going to sever the pectineus muscle, Erich groggily understood. It was potentially a lethal or crippling operation, but what other course had Fate accorded them? Where could a hermit on a remote island the size of a pfennig have acquired the necessary knowledge and surgical skills?

In the smoky vertigo in which Erich floated, anything seemed possible.

The Zana-Malata sliced open and peeled back the skin. Erich averted his eyes. The sight of Taurus' tissue, red as uncooked biergarten meat, made his heart thud with fear. He would give the black man anything—*anything!*— he promised himself, were the operation successful. Regardless of the outcome, he would assuage her agony, for her pain was his pain.

Holding the chloroform-soaked rag, he searched the haze for some point of reference to help him keep his eyes open without having to watch the cutting. His gaze fastened on the bowls, and he remembered having associated them with Benyowsky.

From...the...*valavato*, he told himself.

The bowls were no longer empty. One contained dry-cooked rice; one, greasy morsels of what looked like uncooked chicken skin; one, a tiny, neat pile of brown-and-white gratings. The fourth, a calabash, held water. Solomon emerged from the smoke, picked up the third bowl, and said softly, "The grating's from two of the tanghin pits."

Puzzled, Erich wiped a bead of sweat from the end of his nose and stared dully into the fire. "How do you know?"

"Bruqah told me."

"Oh. I see."

Except he did not see. Smoke choked his mind; Solomon's voice sounded as distant and disjointed as an echo in an abandoned sewer. The world around Erich seemed as wrong as a hailstorm in Paradise, wrong as a zebu stretching its black-and-white neck to feast on the weeping willow beside which he had carried out Hitler's order to shoot Achilles.

Solomon was bent over the mahogany plank, putting pinches from the first three bowls into the calabash. Turning, he offered Erich the concoction. "You must drink this."

"What is it?" Erich drew back.

"Justice," Hempel said as he pushed past the tanhide and entered the hut. "The tanghin tree's spirit will either kill you or protect you from the witchcraft the Zana-Malata must use to save Taurus." Apparently sensing Erich's confusion, he added, "The Malagasy assured me it's necessary. He tells me everything."

Malagasy? Erich wondered. Which Malagasy! The Zana-Malata spoke no German, Hempel no French; and he doubted that Bruqah would speak to Hempel at all. Was there some other language that Hempel and the hermit understood?

Placing the bowl in Erich's hands, Sol cupped Erich's fingers around it to make sure he would not spill the contents. "The Malagasy call the tanghin the 'ordeal tree.'" Solomon said.

"I suppose the Malagasy told you that," Erich muttered, fighting for his bearings, unable even to stand.

Solomon did not reply.

"Swallow it if you want to save the dog," Hempel insisted.

Shaking, Erich peered down at the bowl, stepping backwards with a cry of surprise as Solomon thrust one of the blackened cooking pans at him. Within it was what looked like gruel.

"Flour paste." Solomon scooped up some with a finger and held it, dripping and steaming, in front of Erich's nose. "Try to concentrate," he whispered. "I'm going to stuff this down your throat after the poison takes effect. Don't resist me. If you vomit, chances are you'll survive."

"You would save...me?" Try as he might, Erich was unable to speak without mumbling. A fog enveloped his will. He wondered why Solomon and Hempel, both of whom had reason to want him dead, would poison him and immediately administer an antidote. Then logic slipped away from him; he found himself mirrored in the ceramic bowl, and grinning.

"Bruqah says to tell you that to save an animal, you must be willing to sacrifice your humanness," Solomon explained.

Erich looked at Taurus. Beneath the Zana-Malata's knife the dog looked pitiful and hideous. Thighs parted and bloodied; a syphilitic surgeon; an operating room suffused with oil of eucalyptus. Erich wanted to howl at the absurdity.

Instead he took a deep breath to steel his resolve and brought the bowl to his lips. He gagged on the hot, thick mixture, but managed to swallow.

For a moment there was no sensation. He expected to feel pain or to be gripped by a seizure, but there was nothing. He seemed to be apart from himself in a world without feeling or sound, save for the booming of his own heartbeat in his ears. Then, clutching his belly, he sagged to his knees as his brain exploded in a shower of sparks. He was trembling so violently that he seemed to set the buffalo skull spinning, its swastika pinwheeling like fireworks above Berlin's Luna Park. The hut's pans rattled and the thatch riffled. Fire pierced his belly and bowels and arrowed through his limbs, his skull a burning coal.

"Help me!" he begged. "Feed me the gruel!"

He clamped one arm around Solomon's ankles and with his free hand gripped Hempel's boot, but when he peered up to implore, their faces were lost behind a smokescreen that pulsed with laughter. He was going to die; Solomon and Hempel had, after all, conspired to kill him. Taurus' so-called operation was a ruse for Jew and jailer to trick him into taking poison.

Air. He needed air. If only he could crawl to the door, all would be well, but he could not get his knees under himself. The hut pitched and yawed, and Solomon's and Hempel's legs blocked the way. Bamboo legs.

He reached between the bars.

"*Miriam!*"

Taurus, not Miriam, emerged through the fog to face him. She poked an enormous head between the bars, dark eyes drinking him in. Thankfully he reached for her, knowing her warmth and compassion would quiet the pain....

She backed away.

Taurus?

Rolling onto her back and lifting her forepaws, she panted happily as the syphilitic sliced between her thighs.

"All those dog shows, Erich," he heard Solomon say. "All the Strongheart films. Rin Tin Tin a dozen times. Why do you spend so much time at the Marmorhaus?"

And echoing around the hut:

"*Chi...en...beau. Chi...en...beau.*"

Erich covered his ears and put his forehead against the floor, but the words kept thrumming inside his skull. Sensing a presence before him, he looked up to find himself staring at the syphilitic's gleaming eyes. Smoke poured from the face-hole, smothering him in the stink of eucalyptus.

Stop! Erich shouted, but no sound came. He was a mute pleading for help in a world of the blind and the deaf. Only the fossas heard. They ambled forward curiously, garnet eyes shining in the firelight. Next to them, Achilles, dead three years, lay watching him while Taurus opened her jaws.

With the apathy of one about to be executed, Erich lowered his head and waited for her teeth to fasten around his neck.

I'm sorry, he wanted to say. *Forgive me.*

The blackened pan of gruel was shoved before him. He did not resist when hands forced down his head. As if the bitter paste were a last meal, he slurped and lapped. Taurus snarled and turned her muzzle sideways to bite, and darkness engulfed him....

"How do you feel?" Solomon asked.

Leaning against an outside wall of the shack, Erich retched. When the vomiting was over and he had stopped shaking, he watched the splay of searchlights sweeping across the camp and tried to remember what had happened inside the hut. The only thing he could clearly recall was holding a chloroform-soaked cloth over Taurus' nose. The rest was blurred and dim, as if *he*—instead of Taurus—had been anesthetized.

"She's all right?" he asked anxiously, trying to wave away a spotlight that zeroed in on them. In a low breath he swore at the effort it took to push himself from the shack's support.

"Seems to be fine," Solomon answered. "He was suturing her when I went in and brought you out here."

"You shouldn't have left her!" Erich started to move through grass, but winced as pain pierced his hip. Limping, he re-entered the shack.

And stopped.

The fossas were gone. Lounging on the far side of the smoldering brazier were two puny, bald Kalanaro, asleep with their heads pillowed against the Zana-Malata's legs.

Taurus, too, was sleeping peacefully.

The syphilitic's eyes smiled. He rubbed each man's head as if for luck. They continued to snore softly as he shifted out from beneath them and checked Taurus' hind legs. They were bandaged with palm fronds covered with mud and smelled of overripe bananas.

Erich clung to the door frame for support as a wave of intense pain attacked his hip and ran down the length of his legs, tearing at his nerves and muscles.

The syphilitic's eyes brightened. "*Chien...beau*," he said, this time pointing at Erich.

"Bruqah says to tell you that to save an animal, you must be willing to sacrifice your humanness."

The words came back to Erich on a renewed wave of pain. He gritted his teeth, waited for it to pass, and limped toward the outdoors.

In the morning, after a bottle of brandy, he would examine the price he had paid for Taurus' life.

Chapter 25

Most of the time, Miriam was grateful for the mosquito netting that was draped around her cot. At this moment, it felt like a shroud. If this is spring, she thought, just how bad is the full heat of summer going to be. She could tell by the movement of the netting that there was a breeze, but the same fabric that kept out small bugs also kept most of what little breeze there was from getting to her. This was compounded by the fact that there was little, if any, ventilation. Light shone through the tent opening, enhancing the contrast between the milky netting and the grasshoppers, moths, and crickets that perched on the outside of the gauzy fabric. There was even a stray butterfly, black with brilliant gold striations and four times as big as any she had seen in Berlin.

She remembered once, when she was a little girl, saying that she wished she had been born a butterfly. Now she wished for simpler things. Like a bath, or a good cup of coffee.

Or even just knowing if it was day or night.

Almost in self-defense, she drifted back into a drugged sleep. She dreamed of the Kalanaro, fourteen or fifteen of them, gyrating outside the ghetto fence. One man squatted and, cupping his hands, grinned with red-ochered lips and darkly painted eyes, his body whitewashed and glowing. The others ran at him one at a time and placed a foot in his hands. He lifted them, tossing them into a somersault. The landings were bone-jarring, onto buttocks or backs, but the Kalanaro squealed with delight and staggered to their feet again, to run full tilt toward the tosser.

A troop of ring-tailed lemurs wandered, tails lifted, into the frame of her dream. They padded along the fence's perimeter and sat down between the Kalanaro and the fence, watching the pygmies with benign curiosity. The Kalanaro drew away into a tighter semi-circle, the smiles gone from their eyes. One or two, without taking their angry gazes from the lemurs, knelt and took hold of their spears.

The dream changed.

In Miriam's womb, hairless puppies writhed, then burst squirming in agony from the rumble seat of the burning convertible that held the charred bodies of her parents, her uncle, her dog who gave birth as it burned to a profusion of flaming, twisted creatures.

She twisted from side to side in her dream torment, awake enough to know that she was dreaming, asleep enough to experience the nightmare. Hands pressed against her belly mound, her mind roared with the names of men whose faces eluded her. *Help me, Solomon,* she cried out. *Come to me.* She heard a glass break, crunching as if underfoot. She saw a parade of faceless lovers—a pale mask named Solomon, a rumpled uniform with an Abwehr insignia, the Grecian features of a dancer with the Stuttgart who had loved her first, often and well, only to slap her and call her Jew when she said good-bye. She saw a loose-skinned black man stinking of eucalyptus, who took her only in her nightmares, mouth-hole pressing down over her lips so that she could struggle but not scream.

Miriam awoke again.

The haze created by the mosquito netting was clear compared with the murkiness in her mind. How many times, she wondered, had Pleshdimer been beside her in the past several days, forcing upon her the liquid that filled her throat with fire and brought the chaos of nightmare? She lay in a tent; of that she was reasonably certain. That, at least, was an improvement. Sometimes she awoke thinking that she was in her Swiss home, or at her uncle's estate in the Grünewald, or in a chittering jungle, or swathed in cloud.

There was one thing of which she was completely sure: she was within days, if not hours, of giving birth. She put her hand on her stomach, willing the child to kick and let her know that it was still alive, for in her stupor she could not recall recently having felt any movement.

"God help me," she said out loud.

"He will."

"Franz!" Miriam tried to sit up. "I thought I was alone. Very alone."

"Easy, Frau Alois." She saw a movement in the netting and felt the corpsman's warm, comforting hands on her shoulders. "Concentrate on keeping yourself mentally and physically prepared for the delivery."

"Maybe the child is dead. I can't feel it kicking."

"Don't you remember, Dr. Tyrolt said it would be quiet before the birth? Preparing itself for life, he said."

Miriam nodded, though she did not remember. She shook herself free of his grasp, reluctant to lie down again in the damp indentation in the cot. "It's so hot," she said, pushing her hair away from her face. "Always so hot." She parted the netting and angled her face in the direction of the breeze. "You cannot know how I long for the ice and snow of a Berlin winter." Come to me Solomon, she thought. I need you here with me. Erich's orders had been explicit on that point. Sol was free to see her, until the birth.

"Where is my...my *husband*!"

"He'll be here soon enough, Frau Alois. Please, you must relax—"

"Don't patronize me!" She picked a grasshopper from her nightdress and tried to deposit it onto the floor. It headed for the entrance in a loud whirring of wings. She was annoyed, at Franz that he would naturally enough assume that she had been referring to Erich, and at herself for not having made her meaning clear. In fact, she thought, she was just plain irritated by everything.

"Patronize?" Franz shook his head. "I assure you, I'm just trying to—"

"And what's that God-awful stench!"

Franz walked around to face her. He tried to smile, but the effect was more like a grimace. "The smell of the tropics before the rain." He drifted to the entrance of the tent and stood leaning against the tent pole, looking out into the night, his body blocking her view. "Why would anyone want to bring a child into a world like..."

He looked at her, with embarrassment. "I didn't mean that, Frau Alois." Coming toward her, he took her hand as though he meant to kiss it. "Forgive me. I've tried to maintain a brave front in the face of things, but I guarantee you, you're not alone in being frightened. Like you, I wish I Dr. Tyrolt were here."

"I have placed myself and my child in your care," Miriam said.

"I'm sorry, I...." He lifted his head and she could see that he was actively attempting to arrange his features into a mien of competence. He gave her a distant, detached look that was less than reassuring. "Things will work out," he said softly. "Everything will be fine. You'll see."

Miriam's head had begun to pound. Her breathing was shallow and irregular. She returned her hands to her belly. "We've an important curtain call to make," she said, trying to lighten things up.

"I will stay with you," Franz said. "Or do you wish me to find the Oberst?" He paused. "Or Solomon Freund?"

Miriam closed her eyes. She felt distanced from everyone, even Sol. She loved him now, more than ever, but that love seemed to draw strength from her that she needed to survive. That she and the baby needed. To survive. Maybe, she thought, it was as Erich had so often insisted—that pregnant women drew into themselves, shutting out the men they loved.

"I want to go to Solomon," she said suddenly. "I want to have the baby in there. With the Jews. Where I belong."

"I cannot let you do that, Frau Alois. My instructions—"

"Damn your instructions."

She swung heavily off the cot. Dusk had come and gone, and night was descending. She could sense the shadows creeping across the tent top, the sky darkening to ink. Would the stars be out tonight? Would it hold any meaning for her, for any of them, if they were?

She listened to the work-noise of the prisoners, to the talk of the guards, to the occasional laughter.

The baby kicked. For a time Miriam was very still, her mind at rest, then a wave of pain washed through her. She took several deep breaths, and moved toward the tent opening. Franz did not try to stop her. Cobalt-blue light spread like paint over her mind.

"Sol," she cried out, pushing away the vision that was trying to intrude upon her efforts. "Sol!"

Her gaze searched the Jewish quarters and she thought she saw him in the glare of the searchlight. Then it illuminated Hempel, who flicked a finger toward Solomon, indicating for him to come. Solomon did so, at a sprint. As he reached the major, he whipped off his cap, stuck it in his left armpit and stood at attention.

Together, they walked toward her, and she toward them, with Franz at her side. When they faced each other, Hempel directed Sol to stand shoulder-to-shoulder with her.

Do what he says, Sol's body language said to Miriam. For the baby. Lick Hempel's boots if you must. I did so at Sachsenhausen, and you must do so, too, if it is necessary for survival.

Hempel paced in front of the three of them. There was about him a particular arrogance that Miriam had not seen since meeting him on her uncle's estate, before the major's departure for Sachsenhausen. He was the supreme lord-overseer—lean without appearing hard-muscled, silver-haired without appearing elderly: the quintessential commander.

Abruptly he stopped pacing and looked directly into Solomon's eyes. Sol showed no fear. His life, Miriam was sure, depended on his being able to show self-respect and false respect for Hempel at the same time.

"Did you have sexual relations with this woman...the wife of Erich Alois?"

Fear seized Miriam. If Solomon told the truth, would Hempel kill him—and her? If he denied the charge, would he be killed for lying? She wanted to cry out that she had never really been Erich's wife except by right of paper, but she remained silent.

Sol remained frozen at attention, apparently afraid that Miriam would be killed if he admitted what Hempel probably already knew to be the truth.

"Answer me, Jew!"

"Yes," Miriam said. "Yes, we made love."

Hempel grabbed Solomon by the Adam's apple as though to tear it from his throat. "Jews do not know the meaning of love. Everyone knows that. You rut like animals. We proved that beyond dispute at Sachsenhausen!"

He released Solomon, who rocked back on his heels, eyes watering as he tried to catch his breath without choking. Miriam started to reach for him, but as Hempel turned her way Solomon shook his head.

Hempel looked at her and cocked a brow. "You let a Jew have you? You let a *Jew* inside you?"

She crossed her arms, mostly to stop the shaking of her body. She could feel none of the pain which she had earlier thought must be the start of labor. "I, too, am a Jew," she said.

"The Führer says otherwise. He proclaimed you not only Gentile, but German. Gauleiter Goebbels himself offered to assure your status by arranging for a complete blood transfusion for you."

"I am sorry that I could not accept the Gauleiter's generous offer. And I am sorry," she lowered her eyes, "that I have not lived up to the Führer's trust."

Hempel's eyes flashed.

This is it, Miriam thought. The day of our deaths. Without changing her line of sight, she made herself aware of the sky. It was a rarified blue-black, velvet and studded with diamonds.

Hempel unholstered his Mann and placed its barrel against Sol's temple. With the index finger of his other hand, he lifted Miriam's chin as though to assess her beauty. "You will be kept from harm," he said. "Until the child is born. After that," he looked back at Sol, "you can live wherever you please, with whomever you please. If you live at all."

"You are not in charge of me, Otto," Miriam said, her voice contemptuous. "What makes you think—"

A shadow stopped her. Shielding her eyes from the searchlight's glare, she looked upward at the darkening moon.

A sense of awe settled about the compound as even Hempel peered upward. The shepherds began to whine.

As if sensing that the guards' attention was no longer riveted upon their weapons, a group of Jews moved in unison toward the area of the gate.

"Activate the ghetto fence!" Hempel yelled.

Miriam, too, had seen the movement, but unlike Hempel it had not occurred to her that the Jews might try to make a spontaneous break for freedom. Sol would surely have told her if such a thing were imminent.

Still, anything was possible, she thought, as grasshoppers swarmed in from all sides, filling the air, sizzling into sparks on the fence around the Jewish quarters. Guards and prisoners alike danced and batted and cursed at the deluge. The insects covered Miriam's clothes and head, eyed her from the bridge of her nose before droning away, sought to invade her nostrils and ears. Through the whirring, maddening wings, she looked around at the Germans' maniacal antics, at the dogs leaping and snapping, at the Kalanaro who had dropped their spears to scoop up and devour the crisped insects near the fence.

"What the hell is going on?" Erich asked, staggering from his quarters.

Hempel moved in front of Erich, looked at him momentarily, without speaking, and stepped back formally, as though about to issue an edict. "Why don't you take a cold shower and sober up, Herr Oberst," he said. "I'll take care of things here."

Erich swayed. "I dis-distinctly told you that fence was not to be electrified," he said, pronouncing the words with difficulty.

"Nor was it," Hempel said. "Until now."

"You had no business...I promised the prisoners...."

"I did what I had to do, Herr Oberst. I would have consulted you, but you were...indisposed."

Erich started to argue, then apparently thought better of it. He turned around and began to limp toward the Jews who were clustered behind the wire. Halfway there, as if he had just realized that she was there, he turned around and stared at Miriam. "Get her to shelter," he called out.

He looked, Miriam thought, like anything but a commander. Head hanging. Pressing at his hip joint as if to grab hold of an all but unbearable pain as he walked out of sight. Despite everything, her heart wrenched with pity at Erich's plight, that part which had nothing to do with Solomon, or with her, but rather with his humiliation by Hempel. And with a hatred between Erich and Hempel that went back seventeen years, to when Erich had been a member of Hempel's Freikorps-Youth unit.

"I am going into the Jewish quarters," Miriam said to Franz. "That is where I wish to give birth."

"This is not possible, Frau Alois. Surely you can see that for yourself."

"I can see nothing," Miriam said quietly. "Are you saying that you will not assist me in there?" She held her hands palms upward, as if in supplication, and they were quickly covered by grasshoppers.

"I am saying that I cannot," Franz said. He sounded at the point of tears. "To help bring the Herr Oberst's child into the world is one thing. To bring a...a—"

"Say it, you coward! To bring the child of a Jew into the world would be, what? A sin against the Fatherland?"

Miriam felt herself sway. Her fingers closed around the insects, crunching them to a pulp. Battered by renewed pain, she collapsed onto the ground. In a state of semi-consciousness, she thought herself beneath the canopy of her bed in the villa. She thought she could see Erich Weisser peering in through the chiffoned French doors that led onto the balcony, while behind him the night was ablaze with Berlin burning. An acrid stench permeated everything, as though the villa itself were part of the conflagration, and for an instant she expected to see smoke roil beneath her bedroom door. "Papa," she tried to call out. "Papa?" But Erich had never been part of her life when Papa had been, and nothing made sense. Where was Papa! Down having one of those predawn breakfasts he and Uncle Walther so enjoyed, three-minute eggs and the *Tageblatt* spread out across the table, each complaining and commiserating about the state of the Fatherland what with the war reparations, while her dog lay between their feet, fitfully snoring?

Returning to full consciousness, Miriam fought to get a grip on reality. She dug her hands into her hair and pulled off squirming grasshoppers in each fist. Shuddering, she flipped the insects aside. They whirred away and sat twitching on the ground.

A cry followed by a crescendoing ululation of African voices rose to greet her. She heard footsteps crunch across the grass, followed by a series of excited yells and more laughter.

"What *is* it!" She clutched the neckline of her dress as if to cover herself more thoroughly and looked around for Sol.

"Hempel take Solly back to Jewish quarters. I watch. I come. Noise you hear is lemurs, Lady Miri." Bruqah leaned over her. "At the gate." He smiled as if to reassure her. "They all over out there, beyond the fence. Running around like little children, teasing the guards." He took a few steps in their direction, and she heard the crunching again. He looked up at the moon. "Kalanaro have full bellies tonight, all right, after eating they."

His face clouded as Miriam doubled up in pain. "Baby not come yet, but soon. This what you call pretend labor."

For the first time Miriam smiled. "*False* labor, Bruqah."

"Trouble coming. I feel it." He bent down and lowered his voice so that only she could hear him. Pointing up the hill toward the crypt, he said, "I take you there for birth of child."

Miriam started to argue. He placed his hand gently over her mouth. "Do not battle with me, Lady Miri. I carry you if need be."

The Malagasy's mouselemur crawled out of his *lamba*, peered at Miriam from behind Bruqah's head, and scuttled back within the cloth.

"You're not wanted here," Franz said, without conviction. "Herr Oberst Alois has said that you're troubling Frau Alois." The corpsman glanced with a certain sheepishness toward Miriam, "and the Sturmbannführer has told us privately that you're a threat to the entire operation."

"Has told *us*?" Bruqah asked, chin rising with the aristocratic arrogance of one severely slighted.

"Well, some of us," the corpsman said hesitantly. "Most of the guards, anyway. I wasn't there when he said that, but I heard. They still confide in me. Some of the others, I mean." Franz looked at Miriam, and nodded. "They do." His former look of confidence had dissipated.

Bruqah eyed Miriam anxiously. "We must leave here," he said.

"And go where?"

She realized that her hand was on her abdomen, and that there was an undertone of hysteria in her voice.

"Away."

"The hell she is," Franz stated, stepping between them and glaring up at the taller man.

"The Sturmbannführer is in power," Bruqah said to neither of them in particular.

"Does the Herr Oberst know that?" Miriam asked.

"If he does not yet, he will soon," Franz said. He made a sweeping gesture around the compound. "It's rather obvious, isn't it?"

"We really must go, Lady Miri," Bruqah said with greater need in his voice.

Franz seized Bruqah's arm. "Everything will be fine now!"

With apparent effortlessness Bruqah turned his wrist toward himself and disentangled himself from Franz' hold. "You not believe that," he said.

For a moment Franz said nothing, staring at some point beyond Bruqah. Then he shook his head. "No," he muttered.

"Erich would never stand aside and see his command usurped," Miriam said. "He'd die before that happened."

But she knew her assurance was a lie. In the sleeping area, the prisoners huddled in woeful-looking groupings. Even from a distance she could see that no one was speaking. They watched with forlorn expressions as the Kalanaro piled through the partly opened compound gate and, spears raised, ran through the kikuyu grass after the lemurs while the Nazis laughed and shouted catcalls as if they were at a wrestling match. In the distance, she could see Erich silhouetted in the moonlight. He sat slump-shouldered in the dirt near the sleeping-area gate, staring up at the water tower. His body spoke the language of a man who had lost everything, a man for whom the loss of power *was* everything.

She stood up with difficulty.

"We go now, Lady Miri," Bruqah put his hands on her shoulders and she was glad for the touch, glad there was someone to hold her up, "while there are lemurs still left to dance—and distract."

The blackness lifted from the face of the moon and Miriam saw a hint of a sad smile in Bruqah's eyes. With equal sadness, she nodded. She was being forced away from Solomon once again, this time for the sake of the child. Sol would understand.

He had always understood, she told herself. That was his greatest asset, and his greatest fault.

"I'll go with you," Franz whispered urgently. He eyed Bruqah with temerity. "Let me stop at the medical tent for cotton bandages and some other supplies—"

"No," Miriam said. "We will manage without you, Bruqah and I. If you are right and there is mutiny to come, you may be needed here."

Half carrying her, Bruqah led Miriam away from the compound toward the *valavato*, though she couldn't say exactly how they had passed the fence without going through the gate. The walking seemed to diminish her physical pain, and she attempted to alleviate the rest by thinking about Franz. She remembered what he had told her once while folding linens:

"I arrived at Sachsenhausen, unfortunately, only days before Hempel chose me for this assignment."

"Unfortunately?" she'd asked.

"I didn't have time to harden myself to the suffering, as the others did."

She glanced back at the compound. From the rear, shaded by the ragged collar of darkness beneath the limestone knoll, the night was crisscrossed with the searchlights beamed from the three sentry towers and from the knoll's crest. A large ruffled lemur darted into the light and went tumbling as a rifle shot rang out; the Kalanaro descended upon the victim, laughter shrilling and spears pinioning it to the earth as, caught within the spotlight, the animal squirmed and spasmed in its death throes.

Her gaze met Bruqah's.

His face was a mask, devoid of emotion. She tried to whisper a condolence but he put a finger to his lips, his eyes so expressionless that she wondered if he were capable of feeling grief or fear at all.

Then she realized that the mask of his face *was* his grief; the pain of knowing the lemurs were being killed had frozen his features. He tried to hide his feelings because that was his nature—or perhaps because he wished to protect her, in much the same way that she often tried to cover her fear with humor.

"Bruqah..."

A trickle of perspiration meandered down from her brow and into an eye. Though her mind, absorbed by the drama she was enacting, had not allowed the emotion to sink into her consciousness, her body responded to the fear.

She started to moan, not so much from pain but from exhaustion, and the fear she could no longer fight. Above her she could hear the low, excited voices of the two guards on duty atop a tower. A match was struck, and for a moment an oval of harshly yellow light glared against the night sky. She held her breath when the match went out.

Bruqah poked down the head of the mouselemur come up to inspect the world. The gesture reminded her of a young Solomon, pushing his glasses higher up the bridge of his nose in order to improve his clarity of vision. They moved up the hill under the moon-dappled overhang until they neared where the track connected to the two new roads. Bruqah looked left and right, shoulders raised and head swiveling stiffly as if he were a proper policeman in someone's colony, and then, arm also stiff, motioned her onto the path.

"You be all right?" he asked her.

"For a sack of potatoes that's fallen off the cart once too many times," she replied and hobbled onward.

"I carry you now," Bruqah said.

"I'll transport myself on my own legs, thank you, and if I fall down, you'll help me up again."

"Woman foolish creature," Bruqah said. "Pretty soon I pick you up anyhow."

Slowly they began the ascent up the road that led to the *valavato*. The further they drew from the meadow, the thicker and higher was the forest canopy. All they could see of the sky was a narrow blue-black avenue pebbled with stars, its northern edge tinged chartreuse by the moon.

Chapter 26

"Herr Oberst!" Fermi shouted above the din. "It's the shepherds again!"

Erich blinked against his alcoholic daze and stared out at the compound. He swore, shouldered his MP38 and, pain slicing up through his bad leg with each step, hurried as best he could toward the dog-runs, insects crunching beneath his feet. He could hear the animals barking and snapping. For the most part, the grasshoppers had stopped their descent, but they had apparently made the dogs crazy. In the moonlight, he could see the dogs tearing around, only to be yanked from their feet when they reached the end of the wires to which they were chained. Then in circles, then again the length of the wire, only to be pulled off their feet once more.

"I don't know what's gotten into the dogs!" Fermi said.

Other trainers were sprinting toward the yard, alternately cursing their shepherds and begging them for quiet. A knot of guards had formed at the gate. They were engaged in animated conversation, pointing toward the yard. Clusters of Jews peered around like drivers viewing an accident in the streets.

"Get them under control!" Erich screamed as he entered the yard, but he was uncertain if his men could obey. The animals were raging. Pisces had once again wrapped his chain around his run pole. Despite her bandages, Taurus lunged with full fury toward the gate, was jerked off her feet and rolled in the dust, only to charge again, oblivious to Erich's presence. Sagittarius was desperately tugging backward against the chain, trying to rid herself of her collar.

The others were similarly out of control but, to Erich's relief, none tried to attack the trainers. Rather, they acted as if their masters did not exist: struggling against confinement, glaring toward the gate, whining as if injured when the men snapped on choke chains. Aries' trainer had managed to muzzle his animal.

"He's feverish, sir," Fermi said. "What's wrong with them?"

"Who the hell knows!" Erich yelled over his shoulder as he hobbled toward Taurus, who was growling and straining at her bonds.

"Look!" Fermi pointed toward the Zana-Malata and the Kalanaro who were, in turn, watching Otto Hempel walk toward them. Misha trotted alongside him on a leash, the wolfhound's collar around his forehead like a flapper's headdress.

Hempel stopped and shook his fist toward the moon. A group of Kalanaro joined him. Carrying spears, they moved with feline grace across the *savoka*. Within the compound, guards scrambled from tents and, fumbling with web gear and grabbing Mausers, rushed to the fence and brought their rifles to their shoulders. Not a word was said. Like a pig shoot, Erich thought with a delight that surprised him. No more need to convince the guards that Hempel had overstepped. They might hesitate to shoot a fellow German, but they'd love to mow down Africans.

Except, Erich couldn't allow it. He didn't believe Bruqah's talk about bad luck, but he could not afford to upset the Malagasy. Besides, once the shooting began there would be no stopping it, and first he had to learn where the pitchblende came from. And he would need miners. The Jews could hardly build the landing facility and mine the pitchblende at the same time, so he had to save the goddamn pygmies.

For now.

Involuntarily, he held his hand where the Zana-Malata had burned it with his African magic. Given what had happened the last time, he was loathe to let the little black men into the compound. Then again, what the hell, he thought. A man with uranium in his pocket could afford to be magnanimous.

"Let them in, but watch them!" he yelled to the men at the gate. He wanted to tell them not to let the major in, but would they obey him? Or would he be setting himself up for another defeat?

He petted Taurus, who strained but did not twist against his hold. A calculating growl sounded in her throat, yet she no longer seemed out of control. Erich suppressed a smile. Now she was a predator awaiting prey. When it came to stopping the Kalanaro, the dogs would turn the trick with greater spectacle than bullets—and in their wake leave survivors who might, out of fear, prove quite amenable not only to revealing the pitchblende's location but to digging it from the ground.

With a creaking of hinges, two guards opened the entrance. Hempel entered first, followed by the Kalanaro, spears pointed outward.

The searchlights centered on Hempel, who snapped his heels together, arm springing into the air, chin lifted, eyes like obsidian. "*Seig Heil!*"

"*Sieg heil!*" Pleshdimer cried, stepping from behind the medical tent.

Hempel bellowed the greeting for a third time, and the men answered, visible excitement in their mien.

The Zana-Malata dramatically stretched out his hands. Small flames burned in his cupped palms. The men began to murmur, now and again looking toward the dog-runs. A couple patted the syphilitic on the shoulders.

Comrades all.

Squealing with joy and brandishing their spears, the Kalanaro darted toward the Jews, who backed abruptly from the fence.

"*Vahilo minihana! Vahilo minihana!*" Hempel shouted. "Attack and eat! Attack and eat!"

The guard at the ghetto entrance tugged up his heavy gloves and swung open the gate, only to be bowled over by an outrush of Jews. Erich saw the guard's gun fall.

The machine gunner in the northwestern tower laid down a peppery line of fire at the prisoners' feet, and the forward surge of captives halted. The guards stepped forward, Mausers raised. For a moment Jew and German looked at each other anxiously, and then the prisoners withdrew into the ghetto, leaving the fallen gun.

"*Vahilo minihana!*" Pleshdimer yelled, raising a fist.

The guards laughed at the Jews who were racing to get under their canopy, seeking the false safety of the shadows.

The Kalanaro did not enter the ghetto. Instead, they circled it, poking their spears between the electrified strands. Their movement sent the dogs into renewed frenzy.

"Control the dogs!" Erich hoarsely ordered the trainers. "They're no match for the Mausers!" Fighting to keep Taurus from charging, he swung the submachine pistol off his shoulder and, the choke chain wrapped around his forearm, lay down on the grass for a clear shot.

Trembling with excitement and fear, he zeroed in on Hempel's heart. He wondered if it might not be wiser to shoot the Zana-Malata, standing with his palm-cupped flames raised like some committeeman welcoming home a household of prodigals.

No, he decided. There was much greater purpose and pleasure in killing Hempel.

"Watch me bring the house down!" a guard loudly bragged, sighting toward the canopy. "See the guy ropes?"

The question momentarily shifted Erich's attention to the ghetto, and what he saw made him lift his cheek from against the gun's cool metal.

Stepping from beneath the canvas, Solomon Freund walked toward a leaping, howling Kalanaro on the other side of the fence.

The African poked at him with a spear from between the wire, but Solomon was out of reach. The Kalanaro withdrew the weapon and hissed, showing his teeth like a baboon, then danced back as Solomon kept coming toward him.

Other prisoners emerged from the shadows, but stayed well out of range of the spears, watching silently as the whitely pulsing African again pranced toward Solomon, feinting, jabbing, shrieking his torment.

The other Kalanaro, apparently sensing a drama developing, drew back. Stamping their feet and spear hafts against the ground, they hooted in derision at their comrade. The guards joined in, pointing and laughing.

When the one at the wire again tentatively stuck his spear between the strands, hesitant to draw closer to the lethal fence, two others rushed toward the wire, spears uplifted and faces contorted, only to retreat as quickly and burst into renewed mirth.

The Kalanaro lunged.

With an athleticism Erich would have thought impossible, Solomon dodged the speartip and grabbed the haft. The Kalanaro tried pulling back, but Solomon clung on and, for a moment, despite the wire between them, Jew and African were pitted like two children playing tug-of-war. The guards and the other Kalanaro roared with delight.

The spearman looked around. His grin remained, but his eyes filled with desperation, making everyone laugh the louder at his predicament.

Erich sighted on Solomon's tormentor. He knew that killing the pygmy would give Hempel an instant to react, but Solomon was one Jew who would not be destroyed unless *he*, Erich, said so.

They were *his* Jews.

Right! And this one fucked my wife, he thought.

His finger tightened on the trigger and he swung the barrel from the Kalanaro to Solomon. He was suddenly stone cold sober.

He fucked my wife, he thought again. Not only that, but she loves the son of a bitch.

Normally an expert and steady marksman, even when drunk, he was trembling. He imagined Miriam arched like a bow, face distorted with passion.

The barrel wavered. He fought to control his aim.

Trying to downthrust, the Kalanaro leaped onto the fence as Solomon let go of the spear.

Sparks jumped from the African's hair, hands, and feet as he hung twitching and spasming, eyes rolled up and head jerking. The acrid odor of burnt flesh mingled with the compound's other scents. With a loud pop, the cable from the generator to the fence exploded. The African's body dropped from the fence and lay tremoring. Erich swung the barrel back toward Hempel, only to find guards standing in the line of fire. Silently cursing his lapse of concentration, he forced himself to relax. And wait.

The camp fell silent. The dogs quieted, noses lifted and sniffing the unfamiliar scent of burnt flesh and hair. As the guards and other Kalanaro approached the body, Sol's face took on a look of disgust mixed with pity. He shook his head once, then turned and walked beneath the canopy.

One of the Africans stooped, ran a finger along a smoldering burn on the body, looked up—and grinned. "*Minihana!*" Light laughter rippled among the guards. Like a master of ceremonies, the black man responded to his audience. "*Minihana! Minihana!*" He looked up again, showing filed teeth as his grin widened. He leapt like a monkey around the body, motioning for the others to do the same. They finally did so, dancing and jumping, racing to the fence and prodding it with their spears as if to re-enact the event.

The Zana-Malata laughed, apparently much amused. Dousing his flames, he padded over to stand near the dead man's head. Hempel joined him, Mann pointed carelessly at the ground. The guards gathered behind him. Like Hitler Youth around a campfire, Erich thought with contempt.

In what appeared to be a benign moment, Hempel bent down and released Misha. The boy sat there, apparently not knowing quite what it was he was supposed to do. Hempel nudged him with his foot and Misha scampered away, out of Erich's line of sight.

More fortunately, Erich thought, out of the line of fire.

He turned to the trainers.

"Zodiac," he said softly.

"Sir?" Fermi had to tug his pawing dog sideways to get close enough to hear.

"Zodiac," Erich repeated, suddenly relieved that he had not executed Hempel...yet. He would send the dogs in; Zodiac was not only their best, and favorite, attack formation, it involved the trainers more than any other maneuver. Unless all the trainers were part of his putdown of Hempel's insubordination, killing the major might prove meaningless. Life after Hempel would never run smoothly as long as the Totenkopfverbände were in the majority, and to rectify that would require all the help he could get.

"Against our own, sir?"

"You call that rabble your own?" Erich eyed each trainer in turn, trying to draw them one by one back into his emotional camp.

"Killing the monkeys is one thing," Holten-Pflug whispered. "But other Germans..."

Erich knew that he could order the trainers to do his will and they almost certainly would comply, but he needed more than that. He needed to be sure of their loyalty.

"You all know that Müller's dead," he said quickly. "The guards killed him, and they're planning the same for the rest of us. Don't you know what's been going on in that goddamned hut over there?"

Though his mouth was open, he stopped speaking. The men would never believe the truth even if he could explain it. He put a hand on Taurus to calm his frustration. When she looked back at him, straining and whining for the kill, he knew what he must say.

"I have known for some time that Sturmbannführer Hempel is a proven collaborator. During the Great War, he collaborated with the Senegalese."

The lie contained enough truth to be believable. The African blacks had been among France's fiercest fighters. After the war, the French had looked the other way when the Senegalese, and doubtless others, raped German girls in the Saar, the region both countries claimed. Hempel *had*, as the trainers knew, been drummed from the army under mysterious circumstances. Perhaps there was a connection....

The trainers' gazes flicked toward the major, and Erich saw that he had touched a nerve. "Goebbels found out the whole truth about Hempel's past a few months ago, and now Berlin wants Hempel forgotten. That's why we were all sent here...to be forgotten."

Anger, shock and despair registered on the trainers' faces.

"Now Hempel's collaborating with French Africans. You know what a pervert he is. He'll kill you and let his little black boyfriends feast on your shepherds."

Fermi's dark brows tugged down in concern, and for a moment Erich wondered if the trainers might also mutiny—in an effort to save their dogs. Then, with pleasure, he saw their faces harden like those of their shepherds.

"Zodiac!" Fermi uttered, and everyone murmured in assent.

"Who'll take one o'clock?" Holten-Pflug asked.

Erich patted his MP38. "*This*," he said, "will take Aquarius' place."

"And the center position?"

"We are all the center. Or else there is no center."

Glancing toward the ghetto, he saw that the Zana-Malata was in that sector, and Hempel was at five o'clock—Taurus' area. How serendipitous, he thought, his excitement growing.

"Spread the dogs wide and let them ease in close so they can attack before too many guards can raise their weapons. When I signal, use your pistols to take out anyone else in your sector."

To hell with saving some of these Kalanaro, he told himself. There was a compound to control. If all the pygmies in the compound got killed, he would find some other way to acquire the pitchblende. Find other Kalanaro.

"Ready?"

The guards nodded. Erich could feel their resolve and the dogs' sense of battle. Just like during those early days at the estate. Unified.

He counted Mausers. Only ten guards were holding weapons, plus Hempel with his Mann. Perfect. Eleven dogs, eleven deaths. Glancing up anxiously toward the sentries in the towers, he saw that they too were watching the Kalanaro sideshow. Once the attack began they would initially withhold fire, he figured, to avoid hitting their comrades.

Taurus would tear out Hempel's throat before the major had time to utter much more than a strangled scream.

Erich smiled to himself as the trainers and dogs moved into position. It was going to be like wolves slaughtering sheep.

He made a small, circular motion with his hand, signaling the trainers to release their charges, then unhooked and patted Taurus. She perked up her ears when he unobtrusively pointed toward Hempel. *Good girl,* he said silently. *Kill him. Kill him for Papa.*

Their muzzles removed, the dogs hunkered down as they spread silently out along the edges of the light. Each is an extension of its trainer, Erich thought proudly, the culmination of years of effort and drill.

He lay down and, savoring the moment as the dogs closed upon the guards and Kalanaro, rested the submachine gun on a hillock of dirt and took aim on the syphilitic. He would shoot the bastard right in that stinking vagina he called a mouth.

He raised his left hand in signal and, as he jerked it down, felt a sense of power surge through him as he squeezed the trigger.

The gun did not fire.

The dogs did not move.

He swore under his breath and worked the action, but no round ejected. He heard another round chamber. If he fired now, the weapon was likely to explode. *Go!* he desperately, soundlessly commanded the dogs as he lurched to his knees and fought with the gun.

Around him, the trainers wrestled with their pistols. Somewhere inside his head he heard the Zana-Malata's raucous laughter, and the gunmetal began to heat in his hands.

"Kill them!" he cried. "Kill them, Taurus!"

He thought he could smell the pungent odor of burnt flesh. He dropped the machine pistol and stared, stupefied, at his palms. The skin was severely burned, yet in his state of somnipathy he felt neither pain nor anxiety. Then he lifted his head and saw the dogs ease down from a crouch to their bellies, tails ticking as they crawled at an oblique angle away from the guards and Kalanaro and toward the ghetto. He tried to call the animals back, but no words formed. There was nothing: not hate or anger or sound, nothing within him save emptiness and a giddy sense of the searchlight's glow.

Taurus and the other dogs rose, shook themselves as if they had been swimming in the Wannsee. Heads down, they meandered around the outer fence until each stopped and lay down, facing the ghetto rather than the guards.

Each in its respective position on the clock. A Zodiac position, with the wrong targets. Watching the Jews.

"*Vahilo minihana,*" his mind whispered. His mouth tasted the way it had after Taurus' surgery, of vomit and flour gruel.

"*Vahilo minihana.*" Softer still. From deep inside. An animal hunger that he could not appease, like the throbbing pain of the dysplasia, somehow transferred to his hip after the surgery.

Slope-shouldered as a dullard, he started forward, holding the MP38 by its sling while the butt bounced along the ground. Grasshoppers sprayed up before him. He thought of stew made of dog meat, fruit bats, insects.

Hunger.

"Sagi?" he heard one of the trainers plead. The man had reached the dog, but the animal, watching the Jews, did not appear to notice. It eyed a prisoner who stepped forth from behind the mosquito netting.

The dog's tongue moved. Two licks, each beginning at the back end of the mouth and moving to the front.

Hunger.

The Kalanaro who had been killed struggled to his feet and steadied himself with his spear. He glanced at the burn stripes across his flesh, and managed a small, crooked grin as Erich strode past him.

Erich kept walking, eyes averted from the Kalanaro. He did not want to continue looking at the pygmy. Did not want to know that the dead had risen.

He reached the ghetto gate. The guard opened it for him. He stood at the entrance, staring, asking himself how he could have been so stupid as to want to save these wretches. He had lost his wife's love, almost lost Taurus, and now he was losing what shred of sanity he had left. And for what?

For *them*?

If they were so important to Hempel that the major would instigate mutiny, then Hempel could have them. He, Erich, would show them—show them all—just how little the Jews meant to him.

"Guard the prisoners!" he shouted at the dogs. "Kill any one of them that moves!"

Head held high, Solomon moved toward him.

Erich shouted again, and pointed, but the shepherds continued to mill, whining impatiently, looking toward the Zana-Malata.

At last, Erich realized his mistake. It was all so simple, that he almost smiled at his own naïveté.

The dogs had never been his. Never been chattels of civilization. They belonged to themselves—and to the syphilitic, who demanded that the only law they or anything else adhere to was that of the jungle.

They too hungered as Erich did. They too felt an anger in the pit of their bellies that made them want to devour their enemies.

The Totenkopfverbände took positions around the ghetto, equidistant from one another, maddeningly precise in their deployment.

As a single being, the guards snapped their Mausers to their shoulders and sighted on the Jews.

Teutonic efficiency, Erich thought sardonically. The German mind so exactly ordered that the nation's children emerged, as if from an assembly line, as perfectly oiled killing machines.

Rather like the shepherds.

Just shoot the creatures that huddle in the ghetto, and save a bullet for me, he thought.

Anything to appease the hunger.

For a moment, he watched the dance of the Kalanaro along the outer perimeter of the fence, then he looked longingly at the gun, wondering if Benyowsky would consider him worthy of suicide.

Chapter 27

When the shadow fell across the camp, Sol suffered the momentary terror of thinking he was losing the last of his sight. He was actually grateful for the reassurance of the searchlights cutting through the darkness. His participation in what followed was as much a function of relief and what felt like a reprieve with his vision, as it was a determination that he would not allow the Jews to be the butt of the Kalanaro's jokes. He did not really care what the little black men thought of them, if indeed they thought at all. But the fact was that the carnival event was put on for the amusement of Hempel and his men.

He cared about that.

To have had to leave Miriam in her fatigued state hurt greatly, and to his surprise seeing Erich so diminished hurt almost as much. It was clear to him, and not only because of the electrification of the fence, that Erich had lost control of the camp. He was drunk or hung over much of the time, he walked with difficulty and most often with a stick, bent over like an old man —or as if he would have preferred to drop to his knees and walk on all fours like his dogs.

Even now, reappearing around the Jewish quarters from the direction of the latrines, he looked aged and defeated.

Solomon looked at the shepherds and guards surrounding the ghetto and wondered if any prisoners would survive if Otto Hempel took full control of the camp, something he feared they would all soon have to face.

He watched Hempel saunter toward Erich, the major smiling suavely. When the two men were less than a meter apart, Hempel halted. Then he took another step forward, as though breaking through whatever aura of invulnerability Erich might think he still possessed, and another step. The men were nearly chest to chest, Hempel with his hands raised as if expecting the formal delivery of a sword of surrender. Even with his fading eyesight, Sol could tell that the smile on the major's lips—and doubtless in his eyes—was one of overbearing disdain.

For the first time in the more than two decades that Solomon had known him, Erich looked thoroughly defeated.

"Your aborted attempt on my life makes you guilty of treason," the major said. "I demand that you hand over your weapon."

Erich did not respond.

The trainers stepped forward, crowding around the officers. They were clearly dismayed and confused.

"*Gefreiter?*" Hempel asked. "*Private?* As of now I am your commanding officer. Obey me, or I will have you shot. You *and* your Jews."

Erich's lips remained clamped shut, but his facial muscles had gone slack; he appeared incapable of lifting his eyes above Hempel's belt buckle. With a shudder, Sol remembered where he'd seen that apathetic, wearied expression before. *Schmuckstück.* Costume jewelry: the living dead—those in Sachsenhausen who had given up hope.

"*Gefreiter!*"

Hempel's face had reddened with wrath. His eyes narrowed like those of a fossa. "Pick your targets," he hissed to the guards, without taking his gaze off Erich. "Choose any who appears weak or without proper respect toward the Reich. Fire in rotation. One round per Jew!"

Turning his head to compensate for his limited vision, Solomon watched his fellow prisoners straighten and draw into a tight circle, facing outward like musk ox to a storm, eyes cold with determination. Gone was the fear and the hope of the past. In place of both was the look of men for whom death held no mystery. Some gripped tent-pole spears—the canopy sagging where the poles had been removed—others had rocks and sharpened sticks retrieved from God knew where, still others held their wooden clogs like spanking paddles.

Even those with bare fists clearly intended to die fighting.

Or in the *pose* of fighting, Sol thought with a feeling of sad certainty. Of what value were such Maccabean heroics against Mausers?

He wondered if a scapegoat could satisfy the need for blood.

Could he trade his life for a reprieve, however temporary, for the lives of his fellow prisoners?

There was only one way to find out, and that was to find out. Bracing himself for the agony of a bullet, he took an exaggerated step toward the gate.

"Sturmbannführer Hempel!" he called out, watching with a kind of raw pleasure as the guard nearest the gate leveled his rifle.

"If you will kill but one Jew tonight—me, their leader, their *rabbi*—I will publicly renounce Judaism and all its evils."

The gasps behind him only served to steel his resolve. They will understand, he promised himself.

They will.

Hempel either did not hear the challenge or chose not to. Abruptly doing a right face, he strode toward Taurus. With his arm stiff, he aimed his Mann toward the dog's neck.

Taurus lifted her head, sniffing the air.

"Don't hurt the dog," Erich said quietly.

"*All* inferiors are to be eliminated," Hempel replied. "Our work here in Madagascar will not be slowed down by those with physical problems."

Erich's head jerked up, and Sol saw him glance around uneasily, as though he had awakened in a strange place. "She's cured," he said in a boyish, petulant voice.

Hempel smiled and shook his head. "My friend the Zana-Malata has indicated to me that the affliction was merely diverted—into you, Gefreiter. Should your death be necessitated, the disorder will seek out its former host, thus again rendering the dog useless."

Sol watched Erich turn toward the Zana-Malata as if for confirmation. The syphilitic gave a slow, regal nod.

After staring at the shepherd for a long time—her tail wagging and her tongue hanging out as she lay panting—Erich lifted the MP38 and held it palms-up across his hands.

"Gefreiter." Hempel clicked his heels together, strode back to Erich, and again clicked his heels. Without any show of emotion, he ripped the colonel's insignia from Erich's blouse, then stepped back and handed the insignia, along with the weapon, to the nearest guard.

Pleshdimer came forward, saluted Hempel, and with theatrical flourish presented the major with a rolled-up paper tied with a black ribbon.

Hempel accepted the roll of paper almost absently, as though deep in thought. "The letting of blood is wholesome," he said, enunciating each word carefully. "It keeps the body politic in balance. The Medievalists knew that, but sometimes lately we seem to forget. Maybe the wound has been opened enough for now. Maybe if...." He allowed his words to trail off, waited, and began again.

"If the men were reassured of your loyalty to the Reich." He paused. Holstering his pistol, he stepped forward and laid his hand on Erich's firearm. "The SS and Abwehr have never been friends," he said quietly. "The German race should be united, should it not, in its quest for its rightful destiny?"

Before Erich could reply, Hempel continued. "I can assure you that the first time you kill a Jew is like your first taste of fine cognac."

Erich took what appeared to be an involuntary step backwards.

"Watch," Hempel said. "I will show you how simple it is."

Once again he unholstered his Mann. Turning to face the Jews, he called out, "Bring one forward. Any one of them will do." A smile crossed his face. "On second thought, bring me Solomon Freund."

"This will stop. Now." Erich's voice rang with fury. "There will be no killing simply to prove a point. Not in my camp."

"*Your* camp? I think not, Gefreiter."

Without any further preliminaries, Hempel removed the ribbon from the paper-roll he had been handed. Holding the document at arm's length, he read in a deep voice: "In the judgment of a special court convened on this sovereign land of the German Isle of the Jews on this the twenty second day of September in the year of our master and Führer, the verminmonger Erich Alois née Weisser has been reduced to the rank of Gefreiter for crimes committed against the Fatherland and against humanity. All semblance of privilege, including that of leading the canine unit he attempted to pervert to his own Jew-inspired principles, has been revoked. He is to continue to serve the Reich and its Madagascar processing center, but he is to be considered by all other personnel, upon penalty of death for acting otherwise, as *persona non grata*. The command of the canine unit shall be placed in the hands of its rightful heir, Sturmbannführer Jurgens Otto von Hempel."

He looked around as if to see if anyone objected.

Pleshdimer hopped around like a child who needed to go to the bathroom. "And me," he said. "You promised."

"So I did." Hempel's voice was benign, his lips turned up in amusement. "The Sturmbannführer shall be assisted by Canine-Commander Rottenführer Wasj Hänkl Pleshdimer," he went on. "Signed, Sturmbannführer Jurgens Otto von Hempel, Commander-in-Chief of our master's and of the Führer's Southeast-African Felsennest Force, on behalf of Gauleiter Franz Josef Goebbels."

He released the lower end of the paper; it rolled upward with a crinkling. His arm stiff, he thrust the paper beneath his left armpit, did a right-face, and surveyed the Totenkopfverbände with a look of fatherly authority. "I will restate the order, so there can be no mistake," he snapped. "Gefreiter Alois is your servant," he told the guards. "Treat him as such!" His arm leaped up in salute. "*Seig heil!*"

Those with the Mausers remained rigid—sighting like pointers on the prisoners. The rest of the Totenkopfverbände sprang into salute and answered in unison. Even the trainers lifted their arms, though their lack of zeal was apparent.

Raising their spears, the Kalanaro shouted, "*Minihana!*"

"Aim!" Hempel ordered the guards with the Mausers.

Mentally bracing for the blaze of a bullet, Solomon lifted his hand, fingers spread against the glare of the searchlights, and stepped closer to the gate. His head was bowed—as if to blunt the sacrilege he was about the commit: the denial of everything he held sacred.

"Sturmbannführer!" he called out to Hempel.

The major looked toward Solomon, diverting his attention from the guards, who grunted with dissatisfaction, having waited too long, heavy carbines in hand, for an order either to fire or to shoulder arms.

Solomon felt strangely apart from the happenings around him, ashamed and alone. *Would Papa have been so quick to deny our faith?* he asked himself.

Outside the fence Erich Alois stood motionless, head bowed, while a swarm of bats descended to feast, as they had done on the day of their arrival on the island.

"Solomon?"

Judith's voice, vague and distant, filtered through the frenzy. Sol dismissed it.

"Solomon...Freund."

Sol fought the buffeting waves of flying rodents as though pushing aside window curtains flapping against his face.

"It's time, Solomon!" Though Judith called his name, she seemed to be speaking to no one in particular. "It's time!"

The dogs pulled back from the fence, tails between their legs. Sol rushed toward the wire, but two of the guards jerked the muzzles of their Mausers in his direction despite the swirling bats, and he was forced back, hating his helplessness.

As if on impulse, Erich beat his way toward Solomon. Gagging on an insect, he stopped to spit it out.

"Gefreiter!" Hempel screamed. Pushing aside a curious Kalanaro, he jammed his Mann against Erich's neck. "Have you my permission to speak to the Jew? You are to stay away from them." He glared with newfound savagery toward the medical tent. "And from the woman."

Erich glared at his attacker. "She's my wife and will soon be in labor!"

"The Jews are all in labor, Gefreiter." The major's mocking tone made it clear that Erich's next word of insubordination would be his last. "Some are merely more productive than others. Now brush these goddamn grasshoppers off of my boots."

Hempel released the safety on his pistol. It made a resounding click in the quiet that had descended upon the camp.

"I said brush me off!"

Heart thudding, Sol watched as Erich backstepped, shaking his head in refusal, and Hempel stiffened his arm. Despite all that Erich had done to him, and to Miriam, Sol could neither sit in judgment nor wish upon him so undignified an end.

"Ready!"

"For God's sake do whatever he asks, Erich!" Sol shouted.

Erich just stood there, as if he had no will at all: neither defiant nor compliant.

Sol sought desperately for any diversion, however temporary. He set his body to launch forward in a run toward the gate.

"Whaaa?" He felt a burning sensation in his throat and was jerked back, the front of his collar cutting off his windpipe.

He tried to sputter his rage. The one thing that remained within his control, the option of suicide, had for the second time in his life been wrested away.

"Look!" Max's voice bellowed in his ear. For an instant, Sol was too disoriented and the aperture of his vision too limited for him to understand.

"There!"

A second person held onto him, yelling in his other ear.

Goldman.

The farmer forced Sol's head around. For a moment Solomon relived another terrible time. Rathenau's assassination; Jacob Freund wrenching his son's head forward to see the death of the statesman they so admired and respected. He heard again his father's hoarse, whispered words, spoken through the ages in times of the death of a loved one: "I wish you long life."

The memory passed, and in its place Solomon saw what Goldman was pointing at.

The Zana-Malata was kneeling before one of Hempel's legs, picking grasshoppers off the major and stuffing them into his vertical mouth-slit, craning his neck and swallowing them like a long-throated bird.

At the other leg, Erich was brushing bugs from the trousers...the pistol still against his skull. His hands moved mechanically, as though connected to arms he did not control.

Hempel was grinning. An orgiastic, satiated face—tightened and twisted with pleasure. In the searchlight, even his hair appeared to shine with the intensity of his emotion, the silver the sheen of alpenglow.

"Now you." Hempel shoved the barrel of the pistol between Erich's eyes. "Just like the Zana-Malata. Eat!—or I'll turn woman and child over to the Kalanaro. Worse yet, to Wasj here."

He waved the pistol and began to laugh.

Erich remained poised for a moment above the trouser crease. Then he snatched at the grasshoppers, stuck them in his mouth, and began to chew.

The syphilitic drew back, chortling and whistling, as he watched Erich glean the major for his supper. Then, with hands that resembled claws, he pushed down Erich's head toward the major's boots.

Erich did not resist. His head remained bowed. As though peering into his own grave, Solomon thought.

What was it that had so separated them, he wondered. A uniform? Religion? Were they really so very different? Did they not love the same woman, and would they not soon earn a similar place in this island's ground, leaving behind...what?

Miriam and the child.

He glanced at his forearm.

37704.

Hölle....Hell.

Hempel had deliberately sought him out at Sachsenhausen. He had chosen the number with care—not because Sol was Jewish, but because of Sol's old friendship with Erich. Hempel's hatred of Erich Weisser Alois went back a long time, to the days when Erich was perhaps the only boy who had refused to go along with the former Freikorps-Youth leader's perversions—the same perversions that had caused Hempel to be drummed out of the army before the end of the Great War. Even then, he had been driven to prey on young boys.

He stared again at the number on his forearm: 37704.

Miriam carried his child, the first-born in this new Jewish homeland. With Erich and Solomon dead, would Hempel brand the child?

In a flash of ugly intuition, Solomon saw:

The number 1.

Chapter 28

The climb up the western hill proved after all too difficult for Miriam to manage alone. Her pregnancy seemed to bear her down much more than its actual weight and she did not resist when Bruqah dropped behind her and propelled her upward, hands flat on the small of her back.

Driven by his strength, she was able to take some note of her surroundings. A variety of growths rose in a dark gauntlet that brushed against her and appeared to block her way, only to open slightly as the two of them rounded each curve. For a while, the foliage almost enclosed the track, then the plant life abruptly gave way to a small, inclined meadow dotted with skinny totems. At its northern end, where the forest fell away, what looked like the ruins of a flat-roofed stone house cut into the grassy incline and stood sentry over the night. Far below lay the glistening sea.

Close to exhaustion, Miriam concentrated on the forward motion of her limbs. She did not look up again until she was parallel to the crypt site. With trepidation she moved toward the edifice, one hand supporting her abdomen. She wondered briefly why on earth Bruqah had brought her here to give birth, here to a place built for death.

"You be safe here," Bruqah said, answering her unspoken question. He smiled down at her as they halted before the stone face of the crypt.

A cold shiver traversed Miriam's spine, like a finger of frozen moonbeam. She glanced back and up over her shoulder.

"Nothing there, Lady Miri," Bruqah said. He pushed open the great stone door with his free hand and, the motion completed, rocked back on his heels. Seeing his tightened features she realized that opening the tomb was at least as troubling to him as it was to her.

The open crypt at once begged and forbade her entry. She drew back from the damp, stale air. She wanted to tell Bruqah that, regardless of the danger that Hempel represented, she would not hide within that place unless all traces of the body some of the men had said had been in there had been removed. If indeed it had been real, and not some trick to scare away intruders. Even with it gone, she was uncertain that she could sequester herself in a death chamber to await the birth of the child.

"It's gone, isn't it?" she asked.

Bruqah craned forward as if listening to the darkness. "It? You mean—?"

"Whatever it is, *who*ever it is...." She held out a hand. "Tell me it is no longer there. That it is gone." She tried without success to keep her voice level.

Smiling, Bruqah shook his head. "She spirit will never be gone, Lady Miri," he said. "Not from our hearts...or hopes, anyhow." His eyes took on a distant, determined look. "But rest easy. Body, *that* be gone. For now."

He started forward, then turned and, hands on her shoulders, eyed her soberly before stepping inside the tomb.

She could hear him rustle around, talking quietly to himself. There was a scratching noise, and a match flared. Through slanting shadows she saw him tilt the glass of a kerosene lamp and light the wick. Almost instantaneously, lazy black smoke curled upward and the tomb was revealed. It reminded her of the tobacco-shop cellar, and she half expected to see a wall lined with shelves holding boxes of cigars and accoutrements, a rust-red seep from between the stones, a sewer grate recessed into the floor. But except for a stone bench, upon which Bruqah placed the lamp, the low ceiling, and the floor of black, tamped earth, the only thing of note in the room were two large eyehooks from which dangled the ends of ragged hemp. The ropes appeared to have been cut.

That, she supposed from the description she had heard, had been where Benyowsky's chair had hung. A corpse a hundred and fifty years old, greeting those intruding upon his grave.

Bruqah wiped the bench with his hand, as if to prepare it for Miriam's arrival. Despite her trepidation, she smiled at the housekeeping gesture. Suddenly mindful of the weight she carried, she walked inside the crypt and allowed Bruqah to help her sit. At first she sat up demurely, feet together and toes pointed, then with the Malagasy's help she lay back, steeling her muscles for the shock of cold stone.

The bench was surprisingly comfortable. There were indentations which seemed to fit her form perfectly. Closing her eyes, she drew in a deep breath and tried to relax. She had reason to be grateful, she thought.

The baby was alive and she was, for the moment, safe from Pleshdimer and Hempel and the Zana-Malata.

Why then did she feel the sense of a corpse within her womb? Why the need to reach for the comfort of Bruqah's hand?

"Tell Solomon that I'm here," she begged in a whisper. She pushed back a sweat-dampened strand of hair from her forehead. "He needs to know. *I* need him to know that I'm...," she glanced around the crypt, "that I'm safe, for the time being." The words emerged with less certainty than she had intended.

"I do not think I should leave you here alone."

"Please, Bruqah. Go, now. Go to come back, as you say. Tell him I'm here and that...and that I love him."

Bruqah brought his lips to her fingers. Rising, he backed from the tomb. She heard him pad several steps across the grass, then the call of a night bird pierced the sound of insects outside and the strangeness of her situation pressed down upon her like a huge hand covering her mouth, trying to smother her. She tried to remember the good times. She with Sol at the shop, in the flat, in his arms.

The contractions began again, the *"...pretend labor"* as Bruqah had called it. A tightness twisted her body, lengthened it, forced her hips upward and her shoulders off her stone couch. Each wave of pain dissipated the memories she was attempting to hold onto so dearly, and she concentrated on making sure she did not crack her skull open when the contraction passed and her head became too heavy for her to hold up any longer.

She took in air hungrily, raggedly.

A form slipped through the entrance. At first she thought Bruqah had returned and, supporting herself with her elbows, she rose up, anxious for assurance that he had spoken to Solomon.

"Bru—"

"*Pour la petite enfant,*" the Zana-Malata said, peering at her from the shadows. *For the infant.*

To her astonishment, Miriam felt little fear. Perhaps, she thought, it was because the Zana-Malata had spoken the longest and most comprehensible phrase she had heard him utter. Or maybe, and far more likely, she was simply too tired to care. Even when she saw that, of all things possible, he held the *Torah* in his arms, she felt only a detached curiosity.

A huge raffia bag hung over his right shoulder. Over his left elbow was what looked like a sawhorse-crib.

He lowered himself to his knees and eased down the *Torah* until one end of the scroll touched the ground. "*Enfant...beau.*"

Happily, Miriam's pains had dissipated, and more happily still, the Zana-Malata appeared to have no intention of harming her. She watched as he lifted the *Torah* and laid it in the sawhorse, unrolling part of the scroll and patting down the paper. She sensed a reverence in his handling of the scroll and felt no affront at his touching it.

"*Enfant...beau,*" he repeated, rocking his arms as if they held a baby.

It was only then that she understood that he had built a crib for the child.

From the raffia bag, he drew out a blood-red *lamba*. With a grand flourish—an upsweep of his arms—he unfurled the cloth and laid it on the dark, earthen floor.

He straightened out the corners with a toe.

Next he withdrew a small human-like skull, a lemur, Miriam figured, after an initial gasp of shock. Smoke spiraled from its eye sockets and filled the tomb with the smell of eucalyptus. She did not find the smell unpleasant.

He set the skull down on the *lamba*'s southwest corner. Additional entries to the collection on the cloth followed: a hoof from the slaughtered zebu claimed the northeast corner; on the northwest, a clump of bristly *savoka*; what appeared to be a dried fruit-pit on the southeast.

At last, the Zana-Malata settled himself onto the dirt in a cross-legged position, smiled his vertical smile, and blew a narrow stream of smoke toward the ceiling. He was acting for all the world, Miriam thought, like an expectant father.

"Lady Miri?" a voice called from outside the tomb.

"Bruqah!" Miriam answered. "I am glad you're back."

For what seemed like a long time there was no answer except for the call of the cicadas and the Zana-Malata's raspy breathing. Then Bruqah said in a hesitant voice. "I cannot enter. Do you not see the Kalanaro guarding the door?"

Miriam lugged herself from the bench and tottered to the entrance. Holding onto the lip of the rock, she strained outward into the starlit night.

She could see Bruqah near the edge of the clearing, a black figure before the dark indigo canvas of sea and sky. Around him, the trees and totems stood like mute, ebony sentinels. But no matter how carefully she squinted toward the brush, she could see nothing more than those and the dark and a covey of fireflies, hovering like guardians at the doorway to the crypt.

Chapter 29

Bruqah pointed toward the Kalanaro who guarded the entrance to the crypt and watched Miriam crane toward the left and right.

"I have company," she said. "The Zana-Malata showed up, with a crib that he appears to have made for the child and all kinds of other things which I suppose make sense to him."

Though he could still not enter the cave, Bruqah felt better. That which he understood rarely caused him fear, and he understood this. The Zana-Malata had left the Kalanaro to guard the entrance to the crypt. Lady Miri could not see them because she did not understand how they could be fossas and men and fireflies, metamorphosing as the whim took them. But he understood. Was he not able, in his own way, to do the same thing? Was he not a traveler's tree for some, capable of giving sustenance, while for others he was at best a man?

Raising his voice but careful not to make his tone in any way threatening, he shouted at the Zana-Malata through the cave opening, asking to be allowed to enter. There were times, he thought, to forego anger. This was clearly one of those times.

"Why is he here, Bruqah?" Miriam asked, making her way slowly toward him.

"He waits for the child he thinks will be the vessel of the soul of Queen Ravalona."

"My child? Oh come now." Miriam laughed. "I've been willing to accept a lot of things you have said, Bruqah, but this is ridiculous."

"Do not laugh, Lady Miri. We must watch him very careful when the birthing time comes. He wishes to be there so that he can take the afterbirth."

"And do what with it!"

Bruqah hesitated before he answered her. He did not want to tell her too much, yet cared too much for her to tell her nothing. In the end, albeit an end that still lay in the far future, the child was what counted—to him, to the Zana-Malata, to Madagascar, and to whatever other future the child's life led her into.

He looked up at the sky and guessed it to be around three or four in the morning. The pains Miriam had experienced were not the real thing. He had induced them to ensure her safety. The actual birth of the child would not happen until the sun had come up and gone down again at least once, which left plenty of time for talk and more than enough time to rid themselves of the Zana-Malata's presence. Soon much would happen to change life on the island. For now, there was little reason why he and his old adversary could not, for a short while at least, declare a tenuous peace.

"I think that you had better answer me, Bruqah," Miriam said. Judging by her tone, curiosity and anxiety were becoming anger.

"He believe," Bruqah said, weighing his words carefully, "that if he eat the afterbirth he will gain power over the soul the child." Which, he thought but chose not to say, was the soul of Ravalona, the soul of Madagascar. He deliberated whether or not to continue. "He believe," he went on, having made the decision, "that same give him power over life and death."

Chapter 30

Released by the nudge from Hempel's boot, Misha wandered around aimlessly for a while, simply enjoying his freedom. Usually when he was not at Hempel's side, he made sure that he stayed within view of the compound, and of the activity around the shack. This time, he played on the beach in the moonlight, built a sand castle, caught one of the tiny sandcrabs that peeked out at him from a pinprick of a hole near the water's edge. He even dared a swim until the proximity of a small barracuda drove him out of the water.

Ultimately, he returned to the Storch to await Hempel, certain that the major would leash him to it like a guard dog. He had grown so accustomed to Hempel's sexual abuse and to Pleshdimer's cruelty, that he at first felt almost neglected. But as the hours passed, he began to enjoy his freedom from pain and to dread its return.

Comforted by the night breeze, he fell asleep under the wing of the plane. When he awoke, dawn had begun to lighten the sky. He lay on the sand until the sun rose, lazily contemplating the recent past. Most of all, he thought about how much Otto Hempel had changed since his, Misha's, voluntary return to the collar and the leash, leaving the boy pretty much to his own devices. He hadn't done the *thing* to him for days, nor had he given Pleshdimer permission to hurt him. This despite the Kapo's constant request that he be allowed to "...beat the little shit."

Rapidly, the sun heated up and crawled under the wing. Misha stood up and brushed himself off. Pretty soon, he figured, Hempel would come to the plane for his morning inspection. What better time than now to do what he had sworn to do, and kill the major? As far as Misha could tell, no one would miss Hempel, except maybe the Zana-Malata and Pleshdimer. Herr Alois would be happy, especially after yesterday. So would Miriam and Solomon. Maybe Bruqah would too, though it was hard to tell what he cared about.

His mind made up, Misha looked around for a weapon. The stones near the mangrove roots were either too little or too heavy. A stick, he decided. If he kept one hidden and at hand, he could plunge it into the major's black heart.

He picked up several sticks and tested them by stabbing them into the sand. The first two broke; the third bent into a bow.

Too tricky, he decided. If he chose the wrong stick, he'd end up not doing the job properly. He was going to have to find something more sophisticated. Something that couldn't miss, like a gun, or Pleshdimer's knife.

He found some shade under the second wing, lay down again, and looked up at the morning sky. He could see a rain cloud approaching rapidly, bringing with it the day's first cloudburst. He didn't mind, in fact he rather enjoyed the momentary coolness that the sudden showers brought in their wake. But a gust of wind diverted the cloud, and it dropped its weather just to the right of him, onto the water.

With no other cloud in sight to distract him, he turned his thoughts to his list. He had neglected it of late because, truth to tell, it had grown a little confusing—what with Hempel racking up points on the plus side just by leaving him alone. That the major deserved to die hadn't changed, only the urgency of it.

The same was not true of Wasj Pleshdimer.

In his mind's eye, Misha walked through multiple possibilities: death by knife—a small boy might not get it through the fat; by bullet—he had no gun. By fire—now there was something to contemplate. Better yet, he would set fire to the Zana-Malata's hut while the two of them were asleep. That way the fat Kapo and the syphilitic could fry together, like the grasshoppers on the fence yesterday—

"You think you can hide from me?"

Misha jumped at the sound of the Kapo's voice, so alive for someone who, in Misha's imaginings, was at that very moment being reduced to ashes. Not only was he very much alive, he held Taurus by a leash, which he slung over one of the plane's struts.

Knotting it firmly, he knelt down and leaned over Misha, his face so close and his breath so acrid that it alone made the boy sick. Misha turned his head to avoid the stench.

With one hand, Pleshdimer turned Misha's face back toward him; with the other he gripped Misha's crotch and twisted.

The boy cried out and the Kapo smiled with pleasure. "Think you can fly the plane and get away, that it?" He released Misha and laughed heartily at his own humor.

Misha crouched in a ready position, determined to make a run for it if the Kapo came near him again. To his right and slightly behind him, Taurus growled and strained at her leash. If he could release the dog quickly enough, he thought, maybe Taurus would attack Pleshdimer and tear off his balls. Despite everything, he grinned at the image.

Then all notion of immediate revenge flew away as Pleshdimer's boot struck hard and accurately into the small of his back.

"I hate you!" Misha screamed, unwilling to control his fury and unable to control the pain. "Hate you, hate you, hate you."

Pleshdimer smiled benignly and let out a satisfied sigh, as if Misha's hatred had momentarily sated him. Then, eyes filled with renewed ugliness, he advanced upon the boy.

"Move it!" Otto Hempel's voice floated up from the beach that ran alongside the lagoon. "I don't have all day for this."

Pleshdimer stopped in his tracks.

Misha looked beyond the Kapo in the direction of the sound. He could see three figures walking along the beach. The major was in the lead. Behind him two men dragged their feet with the apparent weight of the wooden crate they were carrying. As they drew closer, Misha recognized Herr Alois and Herr Freund. The crate, about the size of a small coffin, was marked *MUNITION*" in large black print.

"Over there," the major instructed, pointing at Misha. "Put it down in the shade. Be careful with it, or we'll all blow up."

Sweating profusely, the two men carried the crate the rest of the way and laid it gently on the sand. Herr Alois' face was scrunched up in pain.

"You, Jew, return to the compound. Gefreiter, you stay here."

Solomon's gaze caught Misha's and they nodded slightly at each other in greeting before Sol turned and headed toward the foliage at the edge of the sand. Misha watched him stop once and turn to stare at the group near the Storch. Then, apparently seeing that their attention was focussed on the crate, Herr Freund moved quickly sideways into the greenery.

Chapter 31

Erich stared incredulously at the bomb racks that had been rigged up underneath the Storch's wooden wings.

There were four wire-and-bracket clips on each side. A silver, crenellated cable ran the length of them and connected to eyehooks where each bomb would reside. The intent was clear: as the cable was engaged, the bombs would fall in sequence, beginning with the outermost ones.

Apparently, with forty barely pubescent camp guards, poorly trained for battle, less than a dozen dog handlers who would probably bolt the moment they regained mastery over their charges, and a bunch of Kalanaro who seemed more monkey than human, Major Otto Hempel meant to take the war in Europe onto the mainland of Madagascar—without orders or proper ordnance, and with over a hundred and forty Jews itching to get their fingers around his neck. What could drive even a megalomaniac like Hempel to attempt something so extreme?

It took Erich only a moment to guess the answer.

What better way to hope to have one's ashes enshrined in one of Himmler's holy urns than to almost single-handedly attempt an invasion? Erich would have laughed aloud were it not for the larger picture: he was supposed to be in command; he, not Hempel, would be blamed when the attempt failed. Goebbels would portray Hempel as a hero willing to sacrifice himself for the Reich's Greater Good—and would make scapegoats of the Jews.

He felt as if he were about to explode and clenched his fists, furious at his helplessness. Stripped of his rank, a private, a servant...forced to hand-carry bombs for Otto Hempel. He was hardly in a position to stop this, and yet stop it he must.

A muzzle touched the nape of his neck, making his hairs stand on end. "Straighten up, Gefreiter. You may be a private, but you are a still soldier in the German army."

Hempel stood on the seaward side, next to a growling Taurus. Erich stepped toward his animal, testing her response. The shepherd advanced to the end of her leash, savage-eyed, lowering her head in menace, the muscles along her back evident beneath her coat.

"In a few minutes, Gefreiter, the rest of my men will arrive. You will help them affix the bombs in this crate onto the apparatus we have rigged to the bottom of the wings. Is that clear?"

Erich continued to stare at Taurus.

"Answer me, Gefreiter."

"It is quite clear...Otto."

"Otto?" Hempel's face filled with rage. "*Otto!*"

His features smoothed and he smiled, the old feral smile Erich knew so well. "This is a private moment, so to speak," he said, pleased at his cleverness, "so I will allow your impudence to pass." He took a handmade pipe out of his pocket, tamped it, and lit it. "Not bad, these island leaves," he said, emitting a cloud of foul-smelling smoke.

He puffed for a while, then handed the pipe to Pleshdimer for safekeeping. The Kapo stared at it longingly but did not put it to his lips.

"I have often wondered, Weisser, whether you had any notion of the real mission of this contingent of Nazis and Jews. Did you really think that the Reich would allow Jew and Malagasy to live side-by-side? Are you that naïve?" Hempel looked at Erich with utter disdain. "Do you know what an affront a black Jew is to God? Why do you think the Führer so passionately supported Mussolini against the Ethiopians?"

Erich said nothing.

"We are here to test the effectiveness of tabun nerve-gas on isolated villages," Hempel said. Without waiting to judge the impact of his words, he went on. "As the Madagascar Homeland is implemented, the indigenous population will be eliminated rather than moved. This time, we will operate with real efficiency, against civilian populations, not just against soldiers—as was the case during the Great War."

He gazed dreamily across the water.

"Once I demonstrate how well the nerve gas works in warfare, I will at last, at the age of fifty-eight, realize my goal of becoming one of Himmler's Twelve Lieutenants. I intend to test the weapon on mainland villages immediately, and to use the dogs as perimeter guards to kill anyone attempting escape."

Erich could not even hazard a guess as to why Hempel had grown so expansive. He felt as trapped by the monologue as by the loss of the compound, and stupid for not having guessed that Himmler had intended from the start to sacrifice the Madagascar operation to the good of the Reich by making a martyr out of Hempel. That the Reichsführer had every intention of turning the Jews into scapegoats was no surprise. His method of doing so, however, filled Erich with renewed shock at the depths to which the Reich would descend to achieve its ends.

The existence of tabun, a new, highly lethal chemical weapon, was not news to him. Word of the nerve gas had filtered through the Abwehr's channels and corridors, but along with that had come a warning: tabun was so unstable and so deadly that even the most ardent nationalists among the scientists treated it with wary respect. One miscue, and a commander could wipe out his own force rather than that of the enemy.

Being neither chemist nor physician, Erich did not fully understand the science behind the gas, but he did recall his Abwehr briefing: tabun was an organophosphorous compound which inhibited the action of the body enzyme, cholinesterase, and caused uncontrolled muscular contractions. Apparently, very small amounts resulted in paralysis, prostration, and death.

"After my men have taken body counts to determine gas-kill percentages, the Jews will bury the evidence," Hempel said. "I will get rid of *them* with the final bomb, and radio home to Berlin." He reached again for his pipe. Inhaled. Exhaled. "Yes, it's good enough. But I must confess that more than anything I long for a good cigar."

He removed the pipe from his mouth and stared at it intently.

"I wonder what your father would make of this," he said. "Did you know that he created a limited-edition cigar in my honor? *Rittmeister*, he called it, which of course is what I was at the time. He and I often sat in the tobacco shop, enjoying a cigar, a few cognacs. Reminiscing about the Great War, and about good German boys bewitched by Jewesses." He looked at Erich and shook his head, as if at a favorite but recalcitrant nephew. "It broke my heart to hear him go on about you, Erich. It really did. I told him I'd take care of you. As I do all my boys. There isn't *anything* I wouldn't do for your father." He gave Erich a knowing look. "Or he for me."

The man was deranged, over the brink of insanity, Erich thought. At this stage, killing him would be a kindness to Hempel and to humanity. He could do it here and now. Strangle him with his bare hands.

Why, then, did he not by now have Hempel's neck in his hands?

Because, unless he planned it right, it would be considered murder?

That was part, but not all of it, he told himself. There were other, more profound problems to be solved before dispatching the major. Like regaining control over the camp, and over the shepherds.

In the deepest part of his being, he could feel how torn Taurus was between her bloodlust and her desire to serve her former master. Somehow he had to break the hold the Zana-Malata had over her and over the other dogs.

He would need the trainers for that, as well as Solomon and the rest of the Jews. Until then, the death of the major would have to wait.

Hempel slipped an arm across Erich's shoulders and, contemplative, guided him toward the water's edge. Erich tried not to think of the pain in his hip and mind. Escape and vengeance: those were all that mattered now.

"How lucky we are to live in such a time as this!" Hempel swept an arm toward the box under the Storch's wing. "The day, Gefreiter, will come—and soon!—when *one* man," he lifted an index finger, "will control the world's destiny. One responsible, highly trained individual...," he paused for theatrical effect, "such as myself."

He held up both hands as if begging an enthusiastic audience to cease their applause. "I know, I know. You're wondering if I am worthy of such a challenge. I have asked myself that question many times. I am not always the man of action some people take me to be. In fact I am as committed to introspection and self-evaluation as any other officer of my caliber. Objective analysis—that's what sets men apart from women and Jews! I have assessed this situation with open eyes, and I tell you, the opportunity exists *here* for us to make a major moral contribution, not just to the world as we know it, but to all of history." He peered at the aircraft with an apparent sense of destiny. "The tides of men...you know what I mean." The timbre in his voice abruptly changed and he shook his head slightly, as though having awakened from daydream.

"So you're going to attempt to overthrow Madagascar," Erich said. "Now, *before* base camps are established."

For a moment Hempel appeared nonplussed and then gave Erich a loving, almost paternal look. He glanced around, as though to assure himself that no one else was within hearing range. "Had I fifty men such as myself I would attempt it. The balance of power in a backwater nation such as this could be tipped for the better with such a small fine force—but," he shook his head, "you know what abysmal men Reichsführer Himmler fettered me with for this operation. Not worth the price of the uniforms they wear." The smile, having wavered, returned. "Though they do have endearing qualities, especially the younger ones."

"You have no plans for an immediate attempt on the mainland?"

Hempel either did not notice or chose to ignore Erich's tone. Lifting his gaze toward the larger island, a sense of imperious longing in his eyes, he said, "See where the massif rises to an apex?" He pointed toward the line of beige cliffs that jutted high above the swell of greenery along the shore. "Beyond that, the jungle is broken into small, sunken pockets surrounded by walls of limestone. I've flown over them three times, and each time I'm more impressed with just how cut off from the rest of the world those pockets really are. No way in or out except along narrow waterways—though I understand that a labyrinth of tunnels where underground rivers used to flow is also supposed to exist."

He looked at Erich and again put an arm across his shoulders. Erich stepped away from the embrace.

"That topography provides us with ideal testing conditions," Hempel continued. "Sometimes I think it was divinely ordained that we come here to Madagascar, you and I. Your rapport with the slave laborers, my science...and," he added, "my military strength. Himmler himself could not have created a better melding. So here's my actual plan." He relit the pipe. "We identify a dozen—no, *two* dozen villages in those isolated jungle pockets. I come in low," he made a flying motion with his hand, "barely above the massif. For accuracy, you see. No sense wasting ordnance by neutralizing jungle rather than the Natives. Meanwhile, we station the dogs to block all avenues of escape. We don't want to endanger any of our own people, should the gas drift. After a few minutes, you and your Jews will go in, calculate the bomb-to-kill ratio, and bury or burn all evidence. Pity we don't have anybody around who could perform autopsies on the ones who're still twitching. The results would be of value—"

He gave Erich an amused look and added, "Don't worry. I've enough gas masks for your detail. Except for a few Jews we will dispose of as an example, I don't plan to eliminate any of your slave laborers until the experiment's been completed and I'm ready to report back to Himmler. The Jews and their military dupes may have stayed my hand when we gassed the enemy at Ypres, but this time I'll demonstrate the effectiveness of my ideas *before* we implement them in a crisis. The battlefield's no place for gas warfare...too many preventative measures exist! The *civilian* population—that's where we must hurt those who would harm the Reich!" He crabbed his fingers and pretended to reach for Erich's testicles. "Right down there where their gonads grow." He grinned. "You want a homeland for your Jew friends, Gefreiter?" Hempel pulled himself up straight, his chin set in triumph and his eyes uplifted in proud forbearance. "Fine. After the initial experiment is concluded and the Reichsführer has made me one of his trusted lieutenants for my efforts, I'll eradicate Madagascar of its former inhabitants—and without firing a shot. I'll give you and your Jews a land you can populate without further contagion."

"And your Zana-Malata?" Erich asked sarcastically. "You'll eliminate him as well? I thought perhaps he was the one holding your leash."

"We have an arrangement, he and I. I admire his abilities, and he admires my strength. He helps to further our plans to ensure the progress toward perfection of an Aryan world in the knowledge that he will be provided for, and his enemies eliminated. Our syphilitic is of this land, but he holds no love for the people who have exiled him to this rock. Even a Jew lover such as yourself can appreciate that...or have I misread you?"

"Let me get this straight." Erich fought to maintain a calm posture. "After all the preparation and plans, what you want is to turn Madagascar into Sachsenhausen."

Hempel grinned. "Unless a simpler solution to the Jewish question can be found."

"Such as?" Erich's head was pounding, almost as much from the sun and his hangover as from the effort of keeping himself from making the futile gesture of breaking the major's neck with his bare hands.

"Don't look so distressed, Gefreiter. I will demonstrate how easy it is to kill, even when it is someone you know."

Calmly, he unholstered his Mann, released the safety, and cocked the pistol at Taurus. In the split-second before Erich could react, Hempel swiveled around, leveled the gun at Pleshdimer, and with a, "Sorry, Wasj," shot him through the chest.

An expression of absolute surprise crossed the Kapo's face before he fell. Erich watched the man twitch and the ground around him darken as blood seeped into the sand. Then he heard Misha let out a gurgle that contained more pain than joy and Taurus began to bark.

"Erich!" Solomon shouted, breaking through the bushes at a run.

He had covered half the distance before he stopped. "I thought he...you.... I couldn't see." He stared at Erich.

"Never mind *see*, Jew," Hempel said. He aimed the pistol at Solomon. "The question is, how much did you hear?"

Chapter 32

"Let's go, Jew."

Hempel waved the pistol around in what seemed to Sol to be a far too casual manner. Sol tamed his instinct to duck. It was one thing to be shot by Hempel deliberately, another to be caught by a stray, careless bullet.

He glanced at Erich, who stood beside the Storch, facing Taurus, and wondered if Bruqah had told him, too, that Miriam was safely tucked away in the crypt and close to giving birth. His own conversation with Bruqah had of necessity been brief, and mostly composed of a vehement objection to her removal from the proximity of the corpsman and the medical tent. But that had given way quickly to gratitude that Bruqah was taking care of her.

"Walk!" Hempel prodded Sol in the back of the neck. "And you, Gefreiter, follow us."

Sol turned and trudged toward the path to the compound, Hempel close at his heels and uncharacteristically silent. As they approached the gate, the guards saluted with newfound enthusiasm. Trainers and guards alike looked away as Sol passed. He looked back to see how they reacted to Erich and found that, somewhere between the Storch and the camp, Erich had slipped away.

"Stop here," Hempel said, as they reached the inner gate that led into the Jewish quarters. "*Gef*—" He glanced over his shoulder and reddened as he discovered Erich's absence. Regaining his composure with effort, he said, "I have an announcement to make."

Hempel had uttered no word since his instructions to Sol and Erich. Unnerved, Sol looked at where the Kalanaro had fried himself upon the wire the previous night, and wished that the feeling of horror that had settled into the small of his back would resolve itself. He could see the African among his friends, chattering happily as though having returned from a successful hunt. Searching for a way to make sense of what he'd seen, Sol wondered if the white mud with which the Kalanaro had smeared themselves had something to do with the man's apparent imperviousness to electric shock.

"Gather your Jews over there." Hempel pointed to the open space where the Rosh Hashanah Service had been held and where, tonight at sundown, they had planned to hold a Yom Kippur Service.

While the Jews gathered—those of them who could be found within the compound—Hempel sent a runner for Johann, the wireless operator whom he had apparently pre-selected as his new adjutant. When the young Aryan corporal reached his side, the major assumed the same stance as when he had stripped Erich of rank, and held up his hand for silence.

"Your rabbi here," he pointed at Sol, "has, not for the first time, overstepped his boundaries. I would have shot him on the spot, but a better idea occurred to me. I have heard rumblings of your intention to hold a religious service tonight, with or without permission."

He would have made a fine actor, Sol thought, as Hempel paused.

"Let it be clear to you that I forbid you to hold your Service," Hempel went on, obviously enjoying the drama of the moment. "In order to ensure that you take me at my word, I have my own new tradition to announce. Consider it my way to celebrate Yom Kippur. From now on, for each transgression, no matter how small, at least one Jew will be killed."

He paused again, looked around, and once more pointed his pistol at Solomon. "Shall I, after all, shoot your beloved rabbi, or is there one of you who will volunteer as his replacement? I frankly had other plans for him, but I could be persuaded to change my mind."

No one moved.

"The oldest among you, perhaps? Or the youngest?" Hempel looked around, like a butcher on a buying trip at the local abattoir.

A breathless silence seized the prisoners, during which Solomon heard the major tell Johann, "With so many to choose from it's like being a boy in a brothel, don't you think?"

Johann grinned.

"*Must I repeat myself?*" Hempel screamed.

The circle of guards who had followed the young corporal to the scene raised their Mausers and stood at attention.

"Take me!" someone called out from the back of the group of Jews. "No, take me!" another volunteered, and then another, until a chorus of voices offered themselves as Solomon's proxy.

"Stop this!" Sol shouted. "I will not allow any of you to die for me."

"The choice is not yours, Rabbi!"

David Kupke, a young man in his mid twenties, stepped forward. Sol did not know him well, though people said he was once the finest young wheelwright ever to fire up a forge in Duderstadt, a strapping, happy youth given to swapping bierstube stories of hard labor and easy women. Two years in the camps had transformed him into a stooped husk who rarely spoke and spent every possible moment creating string-art masterpieces between his fingers.

He turned toward the other prisoners and—hands at chest height so the Nazis couldn't see—made a string-art piece which, though imaginary, had a clear purpose. A noose for Otto Hempel.

Angry chin held high, he turned to face the major.

"Do you serve Germany...or do you serve God!" Hempel demanded, a look of humor in his eyes.

"They are one and the same, Sturmbannführer!"

"You serve with every ounce of your filthy Jewish flesh?"

"Yes, Sturmbannführer!"

"Then prove your worth."

Hempel stuck his left foot forward. The prisoner dropped to his knees and kissed the toe of the major's boot.

"You seem to have been well schooled at Sachsenhausen," Hempel said. "Stand up. You serve a master well. From now on, you will serve the Kalanaro. Because your attitude has proved sufficient, you will not be eaten...while still alive."

The major made a sharp left-face as he leveled his pistol and fired point-blank into the young man's face. The body staggered back against the fence, and collapsed.

Solomon stared in horror at the blood. Goldman took half a step forward.

"You want something, Jew?" Hempel said to him. "Aren't you the one who blew the horn and turned my tank into a plow?"

Goldman stared the major down.

Hempel turned. "I'll be back at sundown. Anyone who looks like they're even thinking of a religious service will be fed to the dogs." He spun on his heel and was gone.

"Why, Lucius?" Sol asked. He thought of the child about to be born. Of Miriam and Misha who needed him, as did the others in the compound. "For God's sake, why did David do it?"

"For many reasons." Goldman looked toward the horizon. "They need you here, the others. You have always been there for us." He gazed at the dead man, then into Solomon's eyes. "Whether you wish it or not, I am going to sing *Kol Nidre* tonight."

Solomon began to object, but Goldman held up his hand. "Hear me out, Reb. I know how you feel about risking our lives for a tradition which God will surely forgive us for ignoring. I understand your logic, your reasoning. But what is in my heart is in my heart. Perhaps I have simply had enough of this struggle and this is my way to kill myself. A coward's way—to have it done for me and die a martyr. Whatever the reason, I shall sing *Kol Nidre* at sundown and mourn this young man's death. Should I survive until sundown tomorrow, I will blow the Shofar after *Yiskor*."

"At least let us poll the others," Sol insisted.

"You know very well that they will say it must be my choice," Goldman said.

"I suppose I do." Sol's voice was heavy with sadness. "I suppose I do."

"He will kill us all eventually, Otto Hempel," Goldman said.

Sol shook his head. "I do not think so. Even a madman would recognize that he requires laborers. Besides, we will not let him. This is not Sachsenhausen. There are three times as many of us as them, and we are growing stronger daily." And he needs us to complete his private agenda, Sol thought, but was too weary to say. "Perhaps there can even be *L'shanah habaa b'Yerushalayim*...a next year in Jerusalem," he said instead.

A feeling of exhaustion dragged at him and he put his head in his hands——

——*In a flash of brilliant, cobalt-blue light, he enters the crypt and moves toward Miriam, who holds a blanket-wrapped baby in her arms.* He reaches out for her but she pulls away, staring at his hands. He looks down at them, and they are covered with blood.

"Deborah," he whispers. "We'll call her 'Deborah.'" He wishes he could close his eyes around that thought forever——

The Jews gathered in clusters, talking of choices and the lack of them, and of next year in Jerusalem.

"Before we do either," Max said, "we must bury David and go back to work, or feel Pleshdimer's stick in our ribs."

"Pleshdimer is dead," Solomon said quietly.

In the ensuing silence, he told the others what he had seen, and what he had overheard about Hempel's grand scheme.

"What are we to do, Rabbi?" someone asked.

"We wait," Sol answered before he realized he had spoken.

He focussed on the faces before him. His decisions would come not from himself or from God, but from these men around him.

"They may make a show of strength by killing a few to frighten the many. Those without the brains or balls to be real men have to flex *something*," he said. There was a ripple of nervous, macabre chuckling. He waited until it had quieted before he went on. "The Nazis are madmen, but they are not inefficient. It is out of the question that they sailed the *Altmark* all the way here just to shoot us."

"Unless Hempel wants to end whatever was being attempted here, and have an excuse to go home," Goldman said.

Sol searched for a comeback that would combine logic and hope, but the logical answer was that Goldman was right—and hope wasn't logical.

"We must free ourselves and make a home here," Max said.

"A home*land*," someone argued.

"Jews! Back to work," the young voice of Johann called out, interrupting their discussions. "You think you're on holiday? You have a dock to finish."

Sol and Lucius headed for the wood-milling area. For the most part, it was not a rough detail, but it was noisy, and for Sol there were inherent dangers that caused him more pain than it might have the others. Standing a meter away and cradling a log end in his arms, he drew back as the two circular blades sent woodchips and sawdust flying. The spray beat against his face and invaded his eyes, bringing instant pain.

"Will you conduct the Service?" Goldman whispered, in the momentary silence between cuts.

Sol shook his head and rushed to meet what the saws produced. Shouldering several planks, he walked across the compound, through the gate, and down the steep, rutted trail that led to the beach.

"Will you conduct the Service?" Goldman asked again, coming up behind him. "If not, say so and I shall find another!"

Goldman moved ahead. The two men concentrated on their loads as the trail steepened and their speed increased. When they came out of the forest and into the light, the sea breeze washed against their hot skin.

"It's much too risky," Sol said. But by then the sorghum farmer had pulled far ahead. They did not speak of the matter again until they had returned to the compound for lunch and Sol saw the older man moving from group to group, conferring with the others. Two strides and he was behind Goldman.

"If everyone can seem to be going about their business as normally as possible, I will lead all of you in words of prayer this holy day," he whispered, "but you must pray with me in silence, so as not to attract attention. Even saying one word is courting disaster, so I cannot conduct a full *Kol Nidre* Service. In return for this concession, you must promise not to sing."

"I will do what I must," Goldman said.

Sol continued to drift from one small group to another. As he left each one, they in turn moved among other prisoners. The flicker of lifted eyes was enough to tell him which men were ready to receive whatever joy he could give them. How fine a congregation these men would have made, he thought, seated in the Grünewald Synagogue, wearing the traditional white of the Day of Atonement. How much finer they looked than had those businessmen in Berlin. Even dressed as they were, and enslaved, they were willing to risk their lives for one prayer. These men were indeed the children of God.

Sol walked among them, voice lower than a whisper. "As you know, Lucius Goldman insists upon singing *Kol Nidre* tonight. If Erich Weisser were still in command, we could safely hold a service. We could even, tomorrow, commemorate *Neilah*, and properly close the gates of Yom Kippur by blowing the Shofar after the final saying of *Yizkor*, the prayer for the dead. But he is not. With Otto Hempel in command, who among us does not believe that that one long blast would bring retribution upon our heads? I am sure God sees, and understands our need to keep the horn wrapped in its rag and hidden away this year. Doubtless he will also forgive our lack of prayer shawls, *yarmulkes*, and candles."

He turned away from observing the others and, standing alone, thought about the death of a man and the coming of a child.

Chapter 33

Certainly, Herr Sturmbannführer, I'll follow you to the camp like a good boy, Erich thought, staring at the back of Hempel's head. In a pig's eye, he would. A few minutes later he had sidestepped into the foliage and was watching Hempel and Solomon crest the rise and disappear into the compound area. The only possible reason for re-entering the compound would have been to find a bottle of schnapps. What had begun as general discomfort in his hip now ran like liquid fire up his back and down both legs. Even the last of what was in his flask might have served to dull the pain a little.

Worse than the pain, though, was the debasement. To think, he told himself, that he had actually begun to trail the pair, like a dog skulking after a master, or some pathetic camp follower trying to work her way toward the center of power—a whore sniffing for money.

Cat got your tongue? the hooker had mocked him that Christmas he had stood beneath the street lamp and imagined Solomon and Miriam in the flat across the street, sleeping in one another's arms. *I don't mind pain if the money's right....*

Taurus had shown her pain.

Taurus.

He glanced back at the Storch. All his life he had sacrificed, and for what! All the years of athletic training and toil, only to have his chance for the Olympics snatched away by a scant two centimeters. Climbing the military ladder despite damaged fingers that should have kept him out of the Service in the first place, only to find the platform at the top crowded with the likes of Heinrich Himmler and that clubfooted whoremonger, Josef Goebbels. Here, on an island in the backwater of nowhere, struggling to save the original intent of the mission and salvage what pride he had left, only to be usurped by one for whom service consisted of boys and young soldiers bending over and parting their buttocks.

He felt useless, used up. He had nothing more to give. Solomon could have Miriam; she had never been his anyway. And the baby, who knew whose child that was. Probably not even Miriam knew, he thought acidly. He turned and trundled back down toward the beach, reveling in the pain, wondering if Taurus would greet him, or if it would be like coming home to an empty house.

When the sea and the Storch were in full view, the water like crinkled aluminum in the breeze, he looked at the beautiful dog tethered beneath the wing. In a moment of icy clarity, he knew that there was one more sacrifice he had to make, one more trial he must endure. He supposed he had known it since that first day, when the Zana-Malata reduced the guard dogs to whimpering cowards beneath the hut; certainly he had known it, but refused to admit it, from the moment the pain in his hips was no longer sympathetic, but real.

According to the syphilitic, the transference of the dysplasia from Taurus to Erich was only temporary in that, if he died, it would return to the dog. And unless he regained his command, he was as good as dead. Killing Hempel wasn't enough—and could mean being hauled to Berlin in chains. Rather, he needed the men's acknowledgement, if not acclamation, of his leadership. Hempel might not have him physically leashed, like Taurus and Misha, but he was tethered just the same. When whatever purpose the major had for him was over, he would be discarded as surely and suddenly as Pleshdimer had been.

He touched the knife sheathed at his side and began a jerky hobble-run despite the pain. There was only one way he would have the emotional strength to manage this ultimate sacrifice, he thought. Somehow, he would have to force himself into a mental state that divorced him from his emotional attachment to Taurus.

The answer came to him more easily than he had anticipated: he would bring on an epileptic seizure. Berlin's dance marathons had intrigued him, but he'd had to stay out of ballrooms because of the lights that bounced off the mirrored globes revolving overhead; during his countless hours at the Marmorhaus, Strongheart and Rin Tin Tin flickering on the screen had placed him teetering on the abyss of an epileptic episode.

The pain and the satisfaction of having made a decision burned like a clean flame. He picked up speed, running now, an awkward gallop, winding in and out of the foliage and staring at the sunlight that strobed between the trees.

"Taurus," he said, bursting onto the beach.

Misha, sitting in the sand, looked up at him from near Pleshdimer's body. Taurus strained in excitement against her leash. She was his again, the connection renewed.

Something punched him in the small of his back with such force that he arched and, groaning, fell to his knees. The boy jumped up and started toward him, his face tight with concern.

Erich thought he saw the boy say something, but suddenly he was beyond sound. Instead of an aquamarine sea, he looked down upon a sea of vegetation, hunter green and painted with shadow. The sea rotated, above him now, while beneath him shone a puddled yellow moon.

His breathing returned to normal. He gained his feet and, brushing Misha aside, stumbled to the plane and clung to the prop. Losing his balance, he slid to the ground. Taurus padded forward, straining so hard to reach him that her collar must tear away from her neck. He thought he could hear her barking as, on hands and knees, he fought for air, the world alternately tipping and spinning, light glinting dully off the blade of his knife.

He needed her power, her unthinking desire for vengeance and for blood, and there was only one way to get it. He fell sideways, twitching, her name on his lips.

As abruptly as it had begun, the seizure ended, and he was filled with a calm and a strength. His mind felt clear. He stood up slowly, feeling light yet strong, the air around him sweet and imbued with life. There had been a time, once, when he had believed that he and Taurus together could conquer the world. For a while, he had lost that conviction. It returned to him now, and he felt young again. He and Taurus, merged as one being, would be unstoppable except through the force of God. He remembered the many times that Bruqah had said that, in Africa, believing made it so. He could not believe more fervently than he did at that moment; all that was left was to make it so.

"C-cut the l-leash," he said, handing the knife to Misha, who was peering up at him. "So n-no one can ev-ever u-use it again."

Misha did as he was told, sawing earnestly at the leather. Then he held the knife to his side as the dog, freed not only from the tether but from the Zana-Malata's bonds, bounded toward her master.

Erich knelt, opening his arms, exultant not only from the sense of well-being which inevitably followed a seizure, but also from Taurus' return. She reached him, sliding to a stop, head lifted like a long-throated bird as she licked his face.

"M-my dearest l-love," he said.

He took her muzzle in one hand. With the other he clenched a thick fold of her neck, and jerked with all of his might.

The neck broke with an ease that surprised him.

She toppled with her head across his lap, staring blankly across the water. Her tail slapped once at a wavelet that reached her hind paws, and her whole body spasmed before the last of the air in her lungs was gone.

Misha dropped the knife and backed up so quickly that he bumped into the float and fell against the fuselage. He sat there in the sand, emitting tiny noises of disbelief.

Erich lifted Taurus' head from his leg and set it down gently. A final quiver passed through her. He stroked her, feeling the need to speak but unable to think of the right words.

When he rose, the dysplasia was gone. His hip sockets no longer ground in exquisite pain.

He picked up the knife from where Misha, in his shock, had dropped it onto the sand, passed it across his pants to wipe off the saltwater, and returned to the dog. Almost dispassionately, he wondered if he would be able to tell, now that she was gone, if the disease had again invaded her.

Turning her onto her back, he slit up from the soft, exposed belly to the rib cage, the skin so white in the sunlight it resembled purity itself. Truly the heritage of perfection, he told himself. Grace had mated with Harras, offspring of the German grand champion, Etzel von Oeringen. From her had come Achilles, whom Hitler had killed. From Achilles—Taurus, born during a blood-red May sunrise before the Nazis had come to power.

He could not recall having felt so physically and emotionally strong. He, Erich Weisser Alois, would be the last of the line.

He held the coat away from the flesh and finished slitting up to the throat and beneath the muzzle. Gripping with one hand and paring with the knife, he slid the dogskin backwards, the flesh and tissue white and pink and ropy with veins. He left the paws attached to the skin, sawing through the forelegs at the first joint. Finally he stood, put his foot against her neck, and pulled toward the tail. The dogskin slid free except at the hind legs, which he quickly released.

For the first time since he had embarked on his course of action, remorse and compassion tugged at him as he held up the skin, the inside slick and gleaming. He fought the emotions, laid the skin across her body and pulled off his shirt and boots. Kneeling as if he were bowing before a lord, about to be knighted, he drew the skin over his back, shivering at the first touch of its moist warmth.

He stood up. From the corner of his eye he saw Misha scramble behind the float and stare in fear. The reaction made him feel electric. The skin hung like a cape, with the head hanging down his back. He secured it to himself with his boot laces. He tied it at his shoulders and beneath his biceps through holes he cut in the coat, then fastened it to his waist with his belt. Charged with power, he thought how puny and pathetic were the ways of humans. His eyesight was no longer sharp, but his other senses were keener than he had ever imagined possible. He smelled more than heard the Zana-Malata attempting to command him. The syphilitic's voice, if indeed it could be called that, hung in the oppressive air, before it drifted away on a sea breeze that wafted against the nape of his neck.

Feeling the need for ritual before he completed whatever transformation still lay in store for him, he sheathed the knife and, stooping, burrowed his hands into Taurus' body cavity. Pulling out the heart, the size of two melded fists, he tore it free. He turned to the breeze and lifted the heart to the sun, but said no words; he could think of no God worthy of prayer.

He lowered his hands to his chest and looked down at the heart, remembering Taurus running alongside him as he bicycled. Consciously, he put the nostalgia behind him and tore off a chunk of the heart with his teeth.

He did not bother chewing.

The meat slid thick and rich down his throat.

Screaming—exultant, emboldened—he pitched the heart two-handed into the sea.

Chapter 34

Misha huddled behind the float, comforted by the feel of the warm water of the lagoon moving around him. He stared in disbelief at Herr Alois, who appeared to have completely lost his mind. The thought occurred to him that he might be next; that in his feeding frenzy, the colonel would decide he had a hunger for consuming the flesh of young boys.

To his relief, Herr Alois, or Taurus, or whoever he thought he was, hardly gave him a second glance before he took off at a run in the direction of the encampment.

It was not until he was out of sight that Misha remembered the Kapo. Warily, he moved out of the water and across the sand, in the direction of the dead man.

"Help me. Please, help me."

Misha stopped in his tracks. At that moment, all he wanted to do was scream that this could not be possible. The Kapo was dead. He had to be dead.

Pleshdimer moaned and opened his eyes. "A drink, Misha. A little water." He tried to move, cried out in pain, and covered his wound with his enormous hands.

Automatically, Misha took a step toward him. Then he stopped again. "No!" he shouted. "I want you to die!"

Half-crawling, passing out briefly at irregular intervals, Pleshdimer pulled himself around in the direction of the trail to the Zana-Malata's hut. Keeping some distance between them, Misha followed the Kapo and his trail of blood. Every now and again, when Pleshdimer came across some means of leverage, he attempted to get to his feet. A few times, he even managed to stagger forward for a step or two before falling to the ground.

Finally he tripped, tumbled, and lay still beneath the underbrush.

Misha waited, expecting to hear the Kapo call out or to see him emerge from cover like some lumbering boar. When what seemed like forever had passed in silence, he tiptoed closer. All he could see was the bottom half of the man's inert body.

He felt a surge of happiness, not entirely untainted by guilt at celebrating death—even this man's. Then he took off as fast as he could in the direction of the Zana-Malata's hut, keeping to the jungle so as not to be seen. He did not stop running until he was only a few feet away. He could smell the burning coals from the brazier inside.

Unsure whether or not the Zana-Malata was in the hut, he sat down on the grass and stared at the sunset. Soon it would be dark; soon it would be Yom Kippur.

He sat there unmoving until the onset of dusk. When he heard Herr Goldman's voice singing *Kol Nidre* he listened, recalling, dry-eyed, the last Yom Kippur he had spent with his mama and papa.

"Good Yomtov, Papa," he said softly. "Good Yomtov, Ma—"

He stopped, interrupted by gunshot and the insane barking of dogs. Even on Yom Kippur, he thought, as a plan formed in his mind. He would go inside and steal the Zana-Malata's magic. If he had that, he would never need to be afraid again. He ran up to the zebu-hide-covered doorway, stood still for a second to listen to the silence inside, and entered the hut.

The brazier burned, even in the Zana-Malata's absence. By its light, he looked around the room. Since he had last seen it, it had been emptied of much of its clutter. He felt a transient hope that the syphilitic had moved away for good, but though much was gone, too much still remained.

Tentatively, remembering his plan, he groped for the stack of tanghin pits that the syphilitic kept inside the buffalo skull on the shelf in the corner of the room. The skull was too high for him to reach, so he climbed into the suspended raffia chair and, balancing precariously, grasped one of the pits.

He opened his hand to look at his booty, and cried out as a flame burst into the air. The suddenness frightened him, but he felt no heat from the fire which quickly went out when he dropped the pit. He examined his hand, expecting to see burn marks, but it was fine. He dug into the skull for a second pit and, holding it clenched in his fist, climbed off the chair.

Now what? he asked himself. Figuring he would go back outside and think while he listened for the sounds of the Shofar from the compound, he stepped over the brazier and headed for the doorway. From outside he heard the renewed barking of the dogs. He stood with his back to the zebu-hide covering, wondering if there was anything else he should take. A knife glinted in the corner of the room.

He took a step forward—

Bloody fingers encircled his ankle from behind.

Groaning, using his elbows, the Kapo pulled himself into the hut.

"I want you to die!" Misha screamed like he had at the lagoon, lashing out with his foot.

Weakened by the loss of blood, Pleshdimer loosened his hold on the boy. Misha backed up against the far wall and watched as, impossibly, inch by inch, the Kapo crawled toward him.

Chapter 35

An hour or so before sundown, with the workday almost over, Sol saw Lucius Goldman take off for the spring. The farmer returned with his leather shoes knotted together and strung around his neck.

"I have prepared for Yom Kippur," Goldman told him.

The Hasid, Sol knew, was referring to the ritual cleansing, and to the fact that it was forbidden to wear leather shoes on the Day of Atonement.

"Walking on bare feet is a foolishness on a tropical island where such creatures as centipedes proliferate," Sol said.

Goldman laughed mirthlessly. "If they bite me, it will save the Sturmbannführer a bullet."

Sol avoided the man's eyes, for fear of seeing a mirror image of hopelessness. Instead, he looked at the horizon where the sun was about to be swallowed by the oncoming night.

As he had arranged with them, Sol's fellow prisoners did everything possible to create the illusion that tonight was no different than yesterday.

All except Goldman.

Apparently unable to live with the irreverence of praying with a bare head, he reached into his pocket and extracted a banyan leaf which he placed on the crown of his skull. The gesture brought back memories for Sol—his father, donning his silk *tallit,* touching the Torah reverently with the prayer shawl's *tzitzit,* the soft fringes his mother had attached to the corners with blue thread, bending his head to recite the *Shema.*

"*Shema yisrael, adonai elohainu adonai echad,*" Sol began in a whisper. "Hear O Israel, the Lord is Our God, the Lord is One."

Unable to contain himself, Goldman's voice rang out. The first stanza of *Kol Nidre* coincided with his people's declaration of faith, their affirmation of God's unity.

Almost at once, a shadow fell across the congregation.

"*Manome!*" Hempel shouted, a word he had apparently practiced for the occasion. "*Sacrifice*! You want to pray? I'll give you a reason for prayer!"

Goldman continued to sing. Hempel unholstered his Mann and pointed it at the farmer.

"Leave him alone," Sol said. "This was my doing. You want me, so here I am."

Goldman tugged urgently at Solomon's arm. "Please, Rabbi."

Sol shook his head. "I can't let you die for me."

"Idiots! Now they're fighting to die." Hempel laughed. "You'll both get it eventually. *Ve-la!*" he shouted. "Punishment."

"May the Lord comfort you, together with all who mourn—" Goldman said, as the shot reached its mark.

Dying, he fell to the ground and finished the ancient litany of mourning, "—and bring you peace." With enormous effort, he lifted his head and, gazing at Sol, said, "*L'shanah habaa b'Yerushalayim,* my friend." *Next year in Jerusalem.*

He shut his eyes, shuddered, and lay still.

Hot tears ran down Solomon's face. Looking directly at Hempel, he said, "*May God never forgive you.*"

Laughing, Hempel instructed two of the Jews to carry Goldman's body to one of the pandanus palms, its canopy a luxuriant umbrella in the bright light of the combined searchlights. There, the corpse was stripped naked. His hands were tied together with a length of concertina wire and he was hanged by them from one of the branches.

This can't be happening, Sol thought, looking around at the circle of Jews who had been led out of the ghetto to watch. He wanted to shriek aloud, to protest that he, and not his friend, should be the victim of this barbarism. It was only then that he noticed the continued absence of the Zana-Malata. The trainers had joined the spectacle, along with their dogs, which jumped and yelped around the body, tearing at their leashes and leaving Sol neither the time nor the stomach to speculate about the syphilitic's whereabouts.

"Release the dogs," Hempel commanded, from his favorite haunt beneath the tanghin tree,

The animals bounded forward. In a feeding frenzy, they tore at the bleeding body with savage intensity. Nothing was sacrosanct—head, hands, arms. In minutes, what was left of the legs was bloody and raw. One foot was gone, the other missing toes.

The guards shifted closer to the action, applauding and laughing whenever an animal made a particularly high leap. The trainers stood at the edge of the crowd, eyes expressionless and faces plaster-white in the glow of the moon and the searchlights, apparently unwilling to push past Hempel's men and attempt to control the shepherds.

The killings would go on and on, Sol thought, until the good Sturmbannführer denuded the island of Jews and all blacks except the Zana-Malata and the Kalanaro. Then the bloodlust would turn on itself, like a rabid dog chewing its own leg to the bone. In the end, Erich and the trainers would probably be impaled on sharpened poles, and Hempel would return to Goebbels to report how he had saved the Madagascar experiment from traitors, Jew-mongers, and dog-fuckers.

A dog pirouetted high in the air, tearing off a chunk of thigh as the guards roared their approval. Bright-eyed with self-satisfaction, the animal lifted its head and trotted off into the darkness, wolfing down the prize.

Chortling, a group of Kalanaro appeared. They danced around the body, kicking up clouds of dust and mimicking the shepherds. The dogs backed away, whimpering but persistent—hyenas hungry for a lion to finish with the kill.

"He who consumes his enemy, consumes power." Hempel meandered along the line of guards, smiling amiably. They parted as he came forward. The dogs padded to various points in their Zodiac circle, lay down, and peered up at Goldman.

"So as our friend would say," he put an arm across Johann's shoulders, and pointed toward the Zana-Malata's hut. "*Mihinana!...*Eat!"

Nobody moved to accept the invitation.

"That the strong must cull the weak is a necessary evil." Hempel's familiar, paternal smile had returned. "It is a natural law which our modern society tries to circumvent—to their ultimate dissolution. Darwin and our Führer have shown us a better way. The rules of the animal world, where life is its most pristine, are pure and immutable. Humanity must renew and espouse its beginnings if it hopes to survive."

Sol averted his eyes from what was left of Lucius Goldman. He wanted to walk away, to mourn the Hasid in private, but Hempel had started on one of his monologues, and there was to be no escape from it.

"I am a self-educated man." Hempel waved his cigar and strode along the edge of the circle as he pontificated. "Unlike the effete intellectuals at the universities, I was wise enough to know that I could not read all the books, nor would I want to. I, therefore, thoroughly studied only those tomes beside which all other books pale by comparison. *Mein Kampf, The German Military Arms Manual, The Complete Stories of Sherlock Holmes.*

"Thus I have been spared from the *Bible*. From what I've been told, that novel," this to snickering from Johann and the other guards, "is filled with lost tribes, lost innocents, paradise lost. Also lost minds, from the kind of people I've witnessed fooled by it.

"One thing about it does intrigue me, the fiction about a barefooted runaway named Daniel who calms a den of lions.

"So here we have a Daniel." With his cigar he indicated Solomon, whose heart immediately started to pound. "As a true believer he must know that, should we command the animals to tear Daniel apart, the beasts will be calmed by the power of prayer."

The guards laughed heartily but the trainers, apparently with some sense of what was to come, blanched.

"Like any good story, ours of this modern Daniel has a twist." He held out his hand and Johann placed in it a roll of paper similar to the one Hempel had read to Erich.

"In the judgement of this impartial court," Hempel read, "convened this twenty-third day of September, nineteen hundred and thirty nine, on the German Isle of the Jews, we hereby condemn to death by dismemberment the subhuman known by the slave name Solomon Isaac Freund, prisoner three seven seven zero four. Dismemberment shall occur at the rate of one joint per hour, said body part to be fed to the canine unit while the prisoner watches. Signed, Sturmbannführer Jurgens Otto von Hempel, Commander-in-Chief of our master's and Führer's Southeast-African Felsennest Force, on behalf of Reichsführer Heinrich Himmler."

There was another enthusiastic round of applause. Sol, who had shut his eyes, opened them a slit. He could see only watery blues and yellows, for tears of mourning had obscured what sight the disease had not affected.

"But first, a little sport," Hempel continued. "We work hard enough teaching the Jews to work that we certainly deserve a little play!"

He moved toward Sol. The dogs edged forward, sniffing at Sol's legs and growling. He forced himself to stand his ground and not to look at them.

"That's it, my shepherds." Hempel reached down to pat a dog on the head. "Get a good whiff of Jew stench. Remember it." He took hold of Sol's shoulders, and his lips broke into a fatherly grin. "What the dogs don't eat, my little Jew boy will," he said softly. "We're aware you've a soft spot for him, so we'll save him...."

He seized Sol's genitals, and tugged. Groaning from the pain, Sol lurched forward.

"This will be less satisfying than hanging your father was," Hempel said, letting go. "But then we must take our pleasure where and when we can."

Sol was so filled with hatred at the confirmation of what, in his heart, he had always known, that he felt no more physical pain. He rocked back on his heels.

"This one likes to run at the mouth!" Hempel looked over his shoulder toward the guards, and grinned broadly. "Well, let's see how fast the rest of him can run! Any bettors among you?"

Within moments, he outlined the rules of his game. Sol would have about a hundred-meter head start. Bets were placed according to how far the men thought he would get before the dogs brought him down. The edge of the forest various distances down the path, or the beach below. The *savoka* had the lowest odds at even money, the beach the highest at a-hundred-to-one. At the men's insistence, side bets were also placed according to how many hours they thought Sol would live once the dismemberment began.

Hempel turned his grin toward Solomon. "We'll take your ears and nose—but not your eyes—then carve you down to head and torso before we cut off your jewels and feed them to Misha. Perhaps that will serve to improve his performance."

If Sachsenhausen had taught Sol anything, it had given him the ability to distinguish between truth and idle threat where the Nazis were concerned. He had no doubt that the major fully intended to do exactly as he said. Only by refusing to fight his fear and letting his shoulders sag was he able to remain upright at all.

Hempel pushed his face close to Sol's, his breath hot and rank. "Ever been attacked by a dog?" he screamed.

The ferocity caught Sol by surprise. He started to shake his head and then managed, "No, Sturmbannführer."

"I can't hear you, *Hundescheiss*!" Hempel stabbed his index finger against Sol's voice box.

The attack knocked Sol back a step. Only power of will kept him from grabbing his throat and dropping to the ground. He tried to blurt back the answer, but retched. Hans Hannes had told him about how Hempel had arranged his own Olympics, on the Oranienburg grain fields. A hundred prisoners condemned to death for trivial offenses had been lined up single file while the major stood a quarter-kilometer away, pistol in hand. The men had been made to sprint, tearing off their clothes as they ran. Arriving at the "finish," the naked man would fall to his knees and kiss the major's boots as Hempel checked his stopwatch. The reward for a good run was that Hempel shot the man immediately. A poor time, or failure to treat the major's boots with proper respect, meant the flogging bull followed by death by slow-hanging.

"No, Sturmbannführer. I have never been attacked by a dog."

"How about by ten, then?" The major turned his head slightly and nodded to acknowledge the guards' roar of laughter. "No need to worry, though." He drew a pair of leather gloves from his hip pocket and began sliding them on, the rolled-up paper tucked in his left armpit. "If you fight well, I may even order the dogs away quickly. Lie there like the cowardly Jew you are and I may not be so humane." He touched Solomon's shoulder, almost tenderly. "Run well! Make the Fatherland and our odds-makers proud!"

Sol lifted his chin. If the Nazis expected him to plead or physically ready himself in some way, they were mistaken. He leaned forward slightly, one hand on his forward knee. Eyes keened, he peered into the darkness, his tunnel vision defining for him a running lane to the rain forest. Everything outside that avenue was insignificant. Dodging would waste precious steps and seconds, given the shepherds' ability to change direction instantly. His only hope was to gain enough lead before they were loosed. If he could make it into the water, he might have a chance.

If.

If sharks weren't present—or hungry. Or if the dogs did not elect to follow him into the sea.

"Prepare to release the dogs," Hempel said. Then to the animals, "*Mahlzeit*! Eat hearty! Now run, Jew. GO!"

Sol leapt forward, powered by desperation. For a time, all thought was gone. There was a dreamy quality to his running—an effortlessness despite the terror that squeezed at his diaphragm, draining him of oxygen. His legs pumped in fluid motion as he ran on feet made iron-hard by daily forty-kilometer agonies on the Sachsenhausen shoe-testing site. His breaths soughed from lungs strengthened and expanded by the *Altmark*'s hellish heat. Though his awkwardness and Erich's jeers had kept him off the track team at Goethe, he was naturally blessed with a runner's lithe limbs.

On the wings of adrenaline, he headed for the jungle. Behind him, the dogs were barking, begging to be released, anxious for the chase and the kill. Once, he slowed just enough to glance over his shoulder. The guards and dogs were clustered together, within a blaze of searchlight. It surprised him somewhat that the searchlight was not attempting to track him, not that the dogs needed that kind of help. Other than his hope for the sea, he had no idea how to fool them or escape them, let alone defeat them.

With luck and a stick or stone, he might be able to fight off one or two, but eventually an animal would break through whatever makeshift defenses he might muster, and take him down. That would be the end of it, he thought, trying not to imagine what would come next.

If he only had time, a stone could be turned into a mace, a strip of branch a spear, a length of liana a garrote.

If...

He ran.

The jungle loomed, an upsurge of bamboo and palm trunks intertwined with lianas.

Then came the dogs. Their excited yelps hammered at him, spurring him, his running no longer smooth. He began to claw the air. His breathing raged like a bellows in his ears. When he glanced back over his shoulder, dark shapes with dark eyes bounded out of the light. Thorns tore at his calves and brambles ripped across his abdomen and chest as he raced onward, dodging sideways to skirt the larger, darker clumps, and using his arms to slash and bat away thinner shadows.

The dogs were right behind him, barking as they threw themselves through the stickers.

Sol squinted against the darkness and saw he would not make the forest edge before they were upon him. They would drag him down—here at the edge of the rain forest.

He spun, hoping he could fight hard enough that they would seize him by the throat and kill him. Not such a terrible way to die, he told himself. Hadn't Erich said that a dog bite could be so painful that it caused a form of paralysis?

The lead shepherd bounded out of the brush and leapt, sleek as an onrushing storm, its eyes dark-scarlet as the belly of a black widow. Sol stood his ground and prepared himself for the impact.

Chapter 36

Erich had smelled Solomon before he had seen him, even amid the scent of fear and blood that came from the compound, odoriferous as old peat moss.

Drawn to the meadow by Goldman's voice, he had seen everything from a hunkering position amid ferns in the *savoka*— heard the pistol fire from near the tanghin tree, watched the shepherds leap and tear at the hanged man. What was left of his humanity was sickened, yet the scene increased the hunger in his belly.

Then a silhouette came charging out of the spotlight. He ducked instinctively, only to pull up his head again as the dogs, barking wildly, set off after the running man.

With an odd feeling of emotionlessness, he watched Solomon run toward him and the jungle. It all seemed to be happening outside himself, to some species with which he no longer felt close kinship. Solomon was nearly at the *savoka*, his breaths thundering through Erich's skull, before the dog-man reacted.

Prey, he thought.

A desire for blood coursed through him, along with a vague memory of teeth sinking into a whore's wrist, and his mouth was filled with a hot taste.

He gripped his knife and waited.

The figure came on, legs threshing through the grass. The dogs, released by the guards, bounded after him.

"Sol," Erich whispered, as Solomon stumbled forward several steps, caught himself with one hand as he started to fall, and staggered further into the shadow of the rain forest. He glanced back just as Sagi, first of the dogs, crossed the remaining meters and leapt into the air.

Erich moved.

Without understanding why, he launched himself between Solomon and the dog, taking Sagi's charge full-force, then rolling with the animal and hitting its head with the haft of his knife. The dog pawed desperately, but Erich clung on. The man's mine! he wanted to say.

"Erich?" Sol asked as Sagi rolled off Erich and lay panting.

The other shepherds neared, slowing, sniffing, pacing.

Sol crawled through the *savoka*, reaching out to Erich. For an instant Erich started to back away, as if he were fearful of the man. Then the man's hands were on his back, clutching the fur, and Erich felt like whimpering with relief. He felt the pain where Sagi had bitten his hand and licked the wound, the desire for blood sated not by the taste of it, but by the hands of a friend.

"Erich?" Sol asked again.

The name sounded foreign, not a part of him at all. Sagi lay with paws outstretched, whining. He nuzzled his head beneath Erich's hand, also searching for comfort. The other shepherds moved closer, sniffing the dogskin, pressing their noses against Erich's bare chest.

He put his arms around their heads.

Home, he thought.

A spotlight, sweeping the area, found them. The dogs lifted their heads and looked into the glare, as if questioning what vile light dare disturb their gathering.

Erich looked between the animals to see Hempel and several guards coming slowly toward them, joking among themselves about how unfortunate it was for the dogs to be dining on a Jew.

He gripped Sol's wrist. "Go, Spatz!"

Even his own voice sounded strange to him.

For a moment, Sol did not move. Then the spotlight found him again, and he clutched Erich's wrist. A memory deeper even than the taste of blood seized Erich. He blinked and looked down at their joined hands, clasped in a way he had not experienced in decades. The *Wandervögel* handshake, he realized in a kind of dull comprehension that left him open-mouthed and brought his gaze up to meet Sol's.

"Keep Miriam alive," he found himself saying. Sagi nudged him, again seeking affection. "Keep her safe." He handed Sol the knife, haft first.

Sol took it, half-rising as the Nazis approached.

"Brothers in blood," Erich said.

Sol leaned over to touch Erich's cheek with the back of his hand. "Blood brothers," he said. He reached beneath the waist of his pants and drew out the Iron Cross.

"Here," he said, handing it to Erich. Then he was gone, lurching into the darkness of the jungle.

Let's go! Erich communicated the command empathically to the other shepherds. He darted into the foliage, reveling in the freedom from pain in his hip, the dogs hard at his heels. He could hear Sol crashing through the brush, working his way downhill toward the beach.

You make damn sure she's safe, Erich thought toward the retreating figure, as he worked his way east, along the forest edge.

Spotlights and flashlights lanced amid the jungle. He kept at a crouch, moving with an effortlessness that made him giddy with excitement, sensing his way more by smell than sight. With the other dogs close behind him, he passed the path that led down the steepest part of the hill and up again to the *valavato*. He could smell the odor of sweat—human sweat, the stench left from hours or perhaps even days ago.

Running freely, they explored the island's secret places.

He was one with the pack.

Chapter 37

"I play your glowworm song for you on *valiha*, Lady Miri?" Bruqah asked from his perch at the opening of the crypt. "You look too sad since you hear Farmer Goldman song."

Miriam walked toward him with difficulty. "I *am* sad, Bruqah," she said. "I should have been down there with Solomon tonight. It is Yom Kippur, a very special time for my people." She smiled at him, and he could see the effort that it took for her to do so. "I don't mean to sound ungrateful—"

"You not that," he assured her. "You want to speak to Bruqah of this Yom Kippur."

"You said that very well." She smiled again, more easily now. "But no, I don't really want to talk about it."

"I think you have been with me too much. You hold things inside like Bruqah."

She took enough steps forward so that she could see the encampment. "I heard shots. Now the dogs have gone crazy. What is happening, do you think?"

Bruqah hesitated. He did not have to be down there to know that there were great happenings afoot. The Zana-Malata had rarely left his post inside the crypt, and then only for minutes at a time. They had exchanged no more than a few brief words, yet Bruqah knew that the syphilitic had abandoned his game with the major for things of far greater consequence to him. Soon, Otto Hempel would feel the results of no longer having the sorcerer as his help-mate. As for the dogs, he could hear by their sounds that they were being governed by the smell of blood.

None of this was he willing to tell Miriam, for he knew equally well that within a few hours she would be in labor.

"Come, Lady Miri," he said, wanting to draw her back from her view of the compound. Solomon was in danger, he knew, and he did not want her to catch so much as a glimpse of him. If she guessed that he needed help, she would insist that Bruqah leave her and go down there.

Much as he would have liked to help Solomon, his duty—to himself and his people, as much as to Miriam—was to remain here at her side until the baby was born. He had left her twice since bringing her up here, the first time at her request to inform Solomon of her whereabouts, the second to take a sea bath and change into a fresh *lamba* and to fetch the gold earring which he wore upon ceremonial occasions.

Standing at Miriam's side, he watched the searchlights sweep the compound. Along the edge of the forest, three German guards with pistols ranged the area, as if they were searching for someone—or something. Leaving her, he walked to the edge of the cliff and peered down.

Below, a large pirogue with a lantern attached to a spar on the front was moving toward the island. He could make out half a dozen men, rowing steadily.

"Who are they?" Miriam asked, coming up behind him and clutching his arm.

"*Fokolana*," Bruqah explained. "Big council from tribe at southern part of bay. When Malagash king say, 'All to shave heads smooth as baby's butt to mourn son's death' those peoples say no. Many blood spill because of so, but those peoples keep hair and independence. Bruqah live with them sometime."

"Are they members of your tribe?"

"Vazimba no tribe, as I tell you. One here, one there, one there. So on." He made little gestures as if to indicate places on a map. "We special persons." He put his fist proudly against his chest. "No one walk in Vazimba shadow."

She glanced back toward the compound. "Look!" she said.

He followed her gaze. A Kalanaro appeared, then another and another, moving up the hill and halting behind the *valavato* totems as if they were trying to hide, even though the posts did little to conceal them.

Bruqah chuckled and turned back toward the sea as another shot resounded through the night. The guards had caught sight of the canoe. The second guard fired, and the oncoming lantern winked out. Now the pirogue was only a dark form on the water.

Both guards took aim. "No," Bruqah said quietly.

As he had that day, when Misha fell prey to the pitcher plant, he bowed his head and mumbled words Miriam could not comprehend. As if obeying a command, the guards relaxed and lowered their weapons. One of them lit a cigarette. When Bruqah lifted his head, they moved off toward the compound.

"How did you do that?" Miriam asked. "You stopped them from shooting. Sometimes you frighten me, Bruqah. You're as much a sorcerer as the Zana-Malata."

Bruqah nodded. "I tell you before, Africa she magical. You see. You believe. I am *mpanandro*-Vazimba. Zana-Malata takes power for self and punish people for making him alone. I wish only to preserve my people and she history. She die, I die, for never to return. With Vazimba, so long Germantown men behave, they need be only afraid of smell." He craned his neck around and sniffed an armpit. "Phew! Bruqah *stink*!"

He was happy to hear Miriam laugh.

"You may play 'Glowworm' if it pleases you," she said, "but I must lie down. I'm very tired. Tired of waiting for this baby, I wish it would come, already."

Bruqah looked at her seriously. "Deborah come soon, Lady Miri. We are all children of the dusk on this island, but she will be child of the dawn." He took her arm to help her inside.

She pulled away from him. "I thought you could not pass by the guardians of the crypt," she said.

"Not alone, Lady Miri. They will not harm me if I am with you."

They walked inside together and he helped her onto her stone bed.

He ignored the Zana-Malata who, as usual, was seated in a cross-legged position, smoking and staring expectantly beyond the entrance to the crypt.

Chapter 38

Sol fought to still his noisy breathing and glanced over his shoulder to make certain that the dogs had stayed with Erich.

In front of him, splashed by moonlight, four large rubber dinghies floated on the bay. A fifth boat, half covered with planking that would form a floating dock once the Madagascar project moved to the mainland, was beached on the sand. On it, his back to Sol, sat a guard, his Mauser across his lap. His head lay forward against his chest, but from within the foliage Sol could not tell if the man were sleeping...and, if so, how deeply.

From up the hill, though muffled by the forest, came shouting and barking. By the sound of it, Hempel had realized that something had interfered with the shepherds' human retrieval. If Sol was going to take one of the dinghies and attempt escape, it would have to be now. The knife Erich had given him itched in his palm and he froze for a moment at what he was contemplating— to not only take a man's life, but to do so on Yom Kippur.

More than that, to abandon Miriam and the baby to Hempel, and Erich to madness. For the first time in many decades, he had heard his nickname on Erich's lips. Now, in his mind's eye, he heard the echo of the people in his dybbuk-inspired visions: Emanuel, Margabrook, Lise, all of whom had conspired to stop him from taking his own life at Sachsenhausen by telling him that he had a destiny to fulfill.

Was this that destiny, killing a man to save himself?

The images of David, his face blown away by Hempel's bullet, and of Lucius Goldman, shot to death and savaged, rose to remind him that Hempel had struck without mercy on this Day of Atonement.

Telling himself that only by surviving could he return to free the others, Sol squirmed forward on his belly, elbows and toes digging into the wet sand, fingers around the blade so that it would not glint. The boat guard, perhaps stirred by the noise from up the hill, shifted position, and the Mauser slipped from his grasp. He caught the weapon instinctively and sat up. Then his head lolled against his shoulder, and his snoring joined the other sounds of the night.

Sol released a slow breath, blinked against the assault of insects drawn by his sweat, and kept crawling toward the man's back. Huge, khaki-clad, unprotected, it seemed to be the only object in the universe.

Gripping the knife by the hasp, Sol covered the blade with his free hand and rose to a crouch. Pretend that you *are* Erich, he told himself. One hand over the guard's mouth and snap back the head at the same time you thrust. Now!

The guard's breathing roared in Sol's ears, but he found himself unable to move the final step or to raise his arm. A small cry of despair passed through his lips and he stared down stupidly at his knife hand, wondering if his inability to kill was gallantry...or cowardice.

The sound was enough to awaken the man. Intuitively, he turned toward Sol. "What—?"

Sol's arm leapt up, and as if he were watching himself he saw himself backhand the man across the nose with the butt end of the knife. There was a crack as cartilage shattered. The guard moaned and crumpled into the boat's open half, blood streaming from both nostrils, rifle clattering against the planking.

Hands protecting his skull, Sol hit the ground and huddled beside the boat, expecting a bullet. He lay with his face in the sand, listening to the guard take what had to be his last labored breaths.

The sounds from the hill grew louder. Squinting toward the forest, Sol regained his feet. At this stage it was too late to worry about other guards, so he chose to decide that there were none. Erich had maintained two, and sometimes three guards at the boats; for Hempel the "enemy" was within the compound. He believed that he needed to keep the Jews corralled and the trainers scrutinized, not worry about mainlanders encroaching.

Deciding that for the moment he was safe, Sol straightened up and splashed into the water, moving toward the other dinghies. Staring at the boats and the black metal oars, he asked himself what he thought he was doing. Even if he did make it to the mainland without being riddled by rifle fire, where could he get help? If he found French authorities, would they risk their lives for the Jews when, according to Erich, the French had formulated the original Madagascar Plan?

He could hear people coming down the hill—the longer but easier way, by the path. They were talking and laughing. Taking their time. That meant they felt that they still had him under control.

Which they did, he thought disconsolately.

Unless...

He waded back to the landed boat and threw himself across the side, ready to smash down again with the knife. The guard was either still out cold, or dead. Sol lifted him in a fireman's carry and hustled him to the boat in the water. Cutting loose the lines that tied it to the others, he pushed the boat into the currents. It began at once to drift away from the island. He watched until the guard, sprawled in the bottom, was no longer in view, then he waded back to shore and ran up the beach and into the trees. Treasuring silence over distance, he eased between bamboo pickets and entered the foliage.

By then, he had formulated a plan. Without questioning the odds of its working, he headed for the bottom of the strangler fig which abutted the jungle and whose branches overhung the gunner's station at the top of the limestone knoll.

The huge strangler fig's roots had sought the soil, creeping beneath the leaves of the forest floor. As it took of the food and water there, it killed the tree upon which it had germinated and became a gigantic, chaotic ladder.

There was a lesson there somewhere, Sol thought. He located a vine, tied on the knife, and looped it like a necklace around his head, with the knife hanging down his back. He spat upon his hands, rubbed them in the duff, and began to climb up into the thick overstory.

He had heard of South American Indians and African Pygmies—the latter said to be the greatest tree climbers in the world—winding rope between their ankles to form a brace so that they could shimmy up the slickest trunks imaginable, climbing into the heavens in quest of fruits, insects, and honeycomb. The death wrought by the roots of the strangler fig made the goal more attainable to a city dweller like himself.

Still this was crazy, his trying to ascend the tree. Crazy even if he had daylight or lamplight by which to operate, given the tree's towering height. In fact, his whole plan was crazy. But escaping without trying to free Miriam and the others was crazier still.

In the darkness there was no way to measure distance. He had no way to tell how far he would climb, nor to determine how far he'd fall. Each handhold was a challenge; he could not discern if there would be another above it or if, sliding his fingers up the thick roots, he was pulling himself into a dead end and would have to descend and try another route. He attempted to pick bark off the roots as he went, thinking he might be able to locate the marks and thus better orient himself should he have to go down again, but the process slowed him, so he gave it up and concentrated on moving upward.

He reached leaves, leathery against his cheeks as he forced his head between the whorled foliage and supported his weight by hooking an arm, at the armpit, over a branch. Above the leaves a tiny breeze blew, and he could see a patch of sky. To his right loomed the pale, deeply convex cliff face. Peering up, he saw that the cliff bulged under the top branches of the tree; he had picked the correct strangler.

He took a breath and tried to get his bearings. Though some sounds, like the calling of birds and lemurs, carried remarkably well through the forest despite the natural buffer of the trees, others were evasive. He could hear the chugging of the generator, but it was impossible to tell if he was level with the camp, or if it was above or below him. High up through the seep of moonlight he could sometimes discern the side of the limestone chimney, a ghostly gray-green that bulked above the forest canopy. His goal, the small breastworks that formed the formed the fourth sentry post, lay atop the hill.

Sol moved along steadily, with an agility that surprised him. He could only see his hand clearly when he held it close to his face, yet he felt a sense of comfort in these strange environs. This despite the danger of the climb and the almost deafening hiss of a million insects whose origins were foreign to him. Perhaps, he thought, it was his old friend, darkness, comforting him with the familiarity of his days and nights in the Berlin sewer beneath his father's tobacco shop.

Again, he tried to get his bearings. Toward the bottom, where the sunlight rarely reached, the foliage had been dense; here, higher up, where occasional patches of moonlight filtered through, the shadows formed patterns in chiaroscuro.

Something high in the canopy caught his eye. Face tilted up, for once blessing the tunnel vision that enabled him to concentrate on a tiny area or single object as though through a telescope, he caught the flashing signals of what had to be hundreds, if not thousands, of fireflies. Paul Lincke's melody began to play absurdly in his head.

"*Glühwürmchen, Glühwürmchen, Glimmre, Glimmre,*" he murmured, as he wiped sweat from his eyes and, parting a veil of loosely dangling lianas, struggled to see more clearly.

The moonlight increased, and climbing became easier. Every time he poked his head through the foliage, the fireflies loomed closer. Bright with promise, they blinked above him like the lights at KaDeWe department store during the holiday season. He almost felt as if he could reach up and capture them, and could not but wonder if the winking were a code to prevent just such a happening.

Twenty more meters, he guessed, anxiously peering up past the gnarled roots and foliage, and trying without success to see the top of the knoll. Here, higher than many surrounding trees, the effect of the moonlight was greater. He could see some of the overstory below, stippled in dark green. A fresh breeze blew, sending waves through the leaves like ripples on the surface of a lake.

Hearing a movement above him, he stopped climbing, put his face against the bark and drank in the air. Resting like that, he thought through more of his plan.

It was simple enough in concept.

He would knock out the sentry, secure the machine gun, and...what? Free the entire camp?

He had never fired any kind of gun. Just how many of his own people would be killed or injured by his lack of experience?

What he had believed was an excellent idea became a jumble, and he was almost relieved when something growled above him. He was less relieved when he heard a jaw snap shut and felt teeth graze his fingertips. Yellow almond-shaped eyes with elliptical pupils glared down at him, and he reached for the knife.

The animal drew nearer. A fox-like head entered the weak light, and a fossa padded toward him, down the thick branch.

The knife felt suddenly clammy in his hands. He drew back, trying to get as much trunk as possible between them. The fossas had looked fierce enough on land; they were the largest carnivores on Madagascar other than boars, Bruqah had said. Now it seemed both fierce and comfortable, and in control, here, in its own milieu.

Snarling and hissing, it raised onto three legs and swiped at him with a forepaw. Sol parried, thrusting half-heartedly with the knife. The fossa slashed her claws across the back of his hand and leapt over his arm and onto the trunk, legs outstretched as she clung for balance, one back leg braced against a knot. Again she leapt, suspending herself between another branch and his head, squalling her rage at his intrusion, tearing at his shoulders and face with her claws. Drawing blood.

He twisted in terror, lost hold of the tree, and teetered in space, the rear legs of the huge cat scratching for purchase on his forehead and cheeks as the animal discovered itself in a similar predicament.

He screamed as the knife fell from his hands, and managed to clutch the tree, slamming himself against the trunk with such force that the fossa, spitting and caterwauling, toppled into his arms. For an instant he saw only fur and fury. Then, as quickly as it had attacked, it jumped back onto its branch.

Sol swiped angrily with a forearm at his bloodied face and stared away from the fossa, lest the meeting of eyes provoke another attack. As silent as it had earlier been furious, the fossa stalked along a branch and loped down to what appeared to be its mate.

He looked down into darkness and wondered if returning to the forest floor would not be wiser. Maybe he should, after all, attempt an escape to the mainland.

Both fossas began moving toward him—sleek shadows, upper lips curled back, incisors showing. He steeled himself, thinking that he could punch one hard enough to dissuade both from combat.

The fossas tilted their heads one way and another, snarling in displeasure. Two dozen pairs of eyes peered down from the dim heights. Lemurs. Defending the living coffin they called home against a common enemy.

The fossas glared at Solomon and made off into the foliage. Slowly the chittering declined, and the tiny lemurs, too, pattered away between the leaves.

Sol drew up his shirt tail and mopped his face before continuing. As he pulled himself upward, a pecking began. The vibration ticked through the roots as his hands touched them.

"*Ha-h'aye.*"

Sol saw the creature for only an instant, tapping its skeletal finger against the host tree's rotted trunk and looking for insect life in the dying wood. When it looked up, the eyes—betrayed by moonbeams breaking between the leaves—seemed to Sol as large and commanding as the radio speakers on the Funkturm. He shivered, and before the aye-aye disappeared among the maze of roots and lianas that encased the once vital tree, it pointed at him with its skeletal finger. He began to climb again, faster this time, wondering what there was about the aye-aye's sound that filled him with hope rather than despair. Because the animal reminded him of Bruqah, despite the Malagasy's fear of it? Because he yearned for some foghorn to pipe him through his emotional storm?

What, he wondered, had caused the aye-aye to be branded as a harbinger of ill fortune? Bruqah said that his people believed it brought bad luck or death to any village where it appeared. The only escape was to kill it and if possible to burn down and relocate the village. Even dead, it was powerful magic. The sorcerer who dared to keep its finger gained occult strength which increased exponentially in power if he had the courage to twist or bite the finger from the still-living animal.

The limestone chimney bulked against the tree, so close to the trunk that Sol could touch it. He switched to the other side of the trunk and kept climbing, the going easier now despite the branches delaying him, the night clarifying his limited field of vision as he continued to rise above the surrounding canopy.

He was drawing closer to his goal: the sentry post was just overhead. Someone coughed. He strained to hear if there was more than one sentry, but couldn't tell. He could hear no voices except those that floated up to him from the main part of the compound.

Through the latticework, he thought he could see part of the northeast sentry tower and a section of the kennel area; the chimney of limestone blocked the rest. He heard shouted commands and saw a string of half a dozen lights as men—guards, he assumed—double-timed down the path that led into the forest and toward the beach.

He ascended with increased determination, making sure of his handholds as he moved up through the overstory. A snapped branch might alert a sentry.

Then the chimney appeared to fall away from the tree as though he were leaving the earth entirely, like the one time he had ridden in an airplane. The branches thinned out. Hunching his chest over a crotch of branches, he reached out and parted the foliage.

Perhaps it was the danger of falling and the vertigo—part of him wanted to step out and walk across the overstory, positive the sea of greenery would support him—but for an instant he felt closer to God than at any other time he could remember. Here where bromeliads bloomed like clusters of gemstones, the realm of God seemed more certain.

He moved downward until he reached a thick branch extending out over the chimney, and crawled out as far as he could without being seen. When the broad back of the sentry hunched over the machine gun atop the limestone chimney was directly below him, reality quickly cut him down to size.

Even given the element of surprise—assuming he managed to drop behind the guard before the man noticed him—the Nazi could probably overpower him easily. And even if that were not so, how was he to kill the guard?...throw him off the chimney? Go back and try to find the knife he had dropped?

Now that was a truly stupid idea, he thought, eyeing the bats that flitted around the knoll and envying them their ease of movement in the darkness. His lack of fear of the creatures surprised him.

The guard, apparently, felt differently. When one of them flew too close to his head, he stood up abruptly and waved it away.

Sol seized the moment.

He fell upon the guard, knowing now that he was capable of killing and that he was strong, far stronger than he had realized. He also had the advantage of surprise. Sol landed just behind him. The man turned, eyes registering shock, and swung a fist. Sol ducked, searching for a weapon—anything! He shoved the ammo box, heavy with machine gun belts, at the guard. The man grabbed the box. He stumbled backwards, lost his balance, and plunged over the side of the knoll into the forest below, his cry like that of a bird. The belts, still attached to the gun, uncoiled from the box as he fell.

That's another one down, Sol thought, acknowledging to himself how much easier anything, even killing, was the second time. Feeling only relief that the other man and not he had been disposed of, he gathered the belts and squatted behind the machine gun. Now all he had to do was to figure out how to use it, and how to wipe out the encampment without also wiping out the Jewish contingent.

Leaning on the gun, he stared at the compound until his attention was drawn toward the Zana-Malata's hut. In the glare of a searchlight, he saw Misha's small figure disentangle itself from the zebu-hide. It tore from the door-frame as he fell down the steps and stumbled away from the hut. There was a loud series of pops and within moments the hut was ablaze. A second figure emerged. Sol was shocked to recognize the huge form of the Kapo, staggering in a circle, his shirt aflame.

A siren blared and searchlights swept the area. Misha opened his hands. Immediately, a flame erupted from them. The boy froze like a mesmerized deer. There was a shot. The boy did not move.

"Run, Misha!" Sol shouted. He looked down at the machine gun. "Dear God," he whispered. "Show me how to do this."

And he began to fire.

Chapter 39

Frozen in the beam of the searchlight, Misha heard Herr Freund call out to him in warning from the top of the knoll.

Behind him, the Zana-Malata's hut crackled and roared as the fire set by the brazier sent sparks flying in all directions. Pleshdimer's dead, he thought. Dead, dead, dead! He felt no pang of conscience at having set the shack on fire with Pleshdimer inside it. If anything, he was sorry that it had been an accident, though no sorrier than he had felt when he'd discovered that the Kapo had, after all, not died at the hands of the major.

He could feel in his clenched fist the tanghin pit that had started the fire. Though he had no idea how the sorcery worked, he'd picked up the pit again before darting out of the hut, taking the syphilitic's magic and making it his own.

A shot broke through his hypnotic state. He looked up at the sentry tower, realized that they were shooting at him, and took a running dive into the closest bush.

Now what? he thought. He could go up to the crypt, where Bruqah had taken Miriam, but he had seen the Zana-Malata headed in that direction. The last thing he needed was punishment for having destroyed the syphilitic's home. He knew the major was in the mess tent because he had watched him go in there, but he wasn't about to go to *him*, especially after what he had done to Herr Goldman. As for Herr Freund, who was up there shooting, he was afraid to go to him in case he was hit by a stray bullet on the way.

The first searchlight went out, destroyed by the machine gun fire from the knoll. Crouching there, Misha thought about one of the stories his papa had told him—all about an ancient city somewhere in Palestine, near the Dead Sea. Just like here, the Jews were looking for a homeland. They had found a home in Jericho, by making the walls of the city come tumbling down so that they could go in—even if their enemies didn't want them to.

That gave him an idea; he was amazed that he hadn't thought of it before.

He would go into the Jewish quarters, find the zebu horn that he had given Herr Goldman to use as a Shofar, and blow it. The fence that formed the Jewish sleeping area would tumble down—and the outside fence—and everyone would be free.

He parted the branches and peered at the compound. Ahead of him, and slightly to the left, he could see Herr Alois and the rest of the shepherds. The colonel was still dressed in Taurus' skin. He was hauling a section of the punishment cage.

Ignoring the spray of bullets from the knoll and from the sentry towers, Misha sprinted toward the dogs. As he ran, the American Negro song that his father had taught him rang softly inside his head, and in his mind's eye he saw the walls of Jericho come tumbling down.

Chapter 40

Keeping carefully within the jungle, Erich and his dogs circumnavigated the meadow. When they were near the ruins of Benyowsky's hospital, he found a vantage point which allowed him to observe Hempel without being seen.

The major, probably thinking that the pack was still chasing Sol, was returning triumphantly to the camp. The guards gathered around as he entered with the air of a conqueror. In a group, they ducked into the mess tent.

Erich looked around. The overhang of vermiliads and orchids would afford him and the dogs protection from the knoll and sentry towers, allowing them to get to the compound unseen.

He led the way. With the pack behind him, he dropped to his belly and crawled toward the fence.

The smell of smoke stopped them. Turning around, he saw a spiral of smoke coming from the Zana-Malata's hut, and watched as the shack burst into flames. He didn't have time to wonder who, if anyone, was inside, before he saw Misha run and stop, caught in the beam of the sentry towers' searchlights. He heard Solomon's shouted warning, and a burst of fire from the sentry station atop the knoll.

Misha scooted toward the bushes.

Spatz! His *Spatz!* Solomon Freund...*wise friend*, Erich thought. Who would have credited him with the balls?

As the other sentry posts returned fire, Erich acted. He dragged part of the collapsed punishment cage over to a small natural cavity at the base of the fence. The other shepherds looked at him expectantly as he shoved the lashed bamboo under the fence to pry it up. One by one, they crawled forward as if to be petted, and passed safely beneath. He smiled when he saw that Misha was last in line behind them.

When they were all inside, Erich led the way to the area behind the supply tent, keeping to the shadows as the spotlights swept the compound.

The trainers could join him if they wanted to, he thought. Right now, all they had were empty dog runs. They could all be a unit again until the *Altmark* returned, at which time some if not all them might try to head back to Germany.

He would not miss them.

The shepherds were really the only friends he had left. His true friends.

My friends, he heard the syphilitic call from the top of the hill. My Sagittarius, my Pisces, my Erich....

He put his hands over his ears and listened only to the pounding of his heart. Hempel and the guards had burst from the mess tent and were near the Panzer shooting toward the knoll. Machine-gun fire spat from above them, and they dove to the ground.

Bullets ricocheted off the tank. One man screamed and fell, clutching himself. Hempel rolled behind the tank as another spray of bullets stitched a line toward him. A searchlight shattered. The remaining two swung chaotically from the sentry towers, searching for the enemy and finally realizing it came from one of their own positions. They fired toward the limestone chimney, and Solomon retaliated. A second light went out in response.

Misha and the dogs drew close as the guards opened fire on anyone and anything that moved. Erich put an arm for comfort around the nearest neck. Stay calm, he told them, though he knew he was incapable of taking his own advice.

Solomon fired a burst toward the generator, but hit the water tower, which was in the way. Water streamed from it.

Just shoot the spotlights, Spatz. Don't worry about the power! Erich thought.

He looked over at the Jewish quarters, knowing intuitively that Hempel's boys would have re-electrified the wire around the sleeping area while the major was down at the beach.

What he saw made him want to stand up and cheer.

The Jews had torn down the canopy that he had given them and thrown it over the fence. Four or five of them were beating down the wire with the poles that had held up the tent. Having broken the circuit, they poured over the fence. What was left of it buckled under their weight.

Solomon laid down peppery fire. The sentry towers fired back, and the guards near the tank blasted at the human wave heading toward them. The front line of Jews fell back, their agonized screams filling the night, only to have more Jews rush on.

Turning to Misha, Erich gave him quick instructions. "Go into the munitions tent. Open one of the small wooden crates marked *Granate*. It'll be on the right, near the entrance. Bring me a grenade. And be careful," he added as an afterthought.

Before he had finished the sentence, Misha was headed around the tent.

Erich and the shepherds followed, staying close to the canvas. He could see in the dark far better than his adversaries, and he was surprised to find himself without fear and also without bloodlust. He operated on animal instinct alone, but there was still the hunger with which to contend. He looked around, fearing the Zana-Malata's presence. He could feel the sorcerer's voice calling to him, but it was weak and distant. Then the voice was gone.

The dogs would not obey the syphilitic any more. Will they obey me? Erich wondered. He didn't know, but he had to try. Silently, he gave the command: *Zodiac.*

The dogs fanned out. As if the animals had reversed roles and called out to them, the trainers moved from various points of the encampment to join their charges.

Ready, Erich commanded.

The spotlight sighted the boy at the same time as the guard who had stayed his post outside the munitions supply tent.

"Kill him!" Hempel screamed.

"*No!*" Franz burst from the medical tent, flailing his arms as he ran. "Don't shoot the boy!"

A volley from half a dozen guards caught the corpsman with such force that he left his feet. When he hit the ground, his legs flopped toward his head and down again like a rag doll. His arms splayed out, his head turned at an unnatural angle, and blood ran in a jagged line from his mouth.

As if by silent command, all carbines snapped toward the boy, who stood motionless within the searchlight's glare. He had stretched out his arm. Elongated flames rose from his palm into the night sky.

"Shoot him!" Hempel screamed again, but no one moved. Erich could almost taste the fear and frustration in the major's voice. Where is your precious syphilitic now, he thought sarcastically.

Attack! Erich mentally commanded Pisces and, trusting in the animal, jumped up in full sight of everyone. "Shoot *me,* you bastards! Kill a colonel!" he yelled.

"It's Alois!" someone shouted. "Dressed as a dog!"

Shooting started again. Solomon fired as the spotlight moved toward the new target. No more than a split-second later, Pisces was upon the man. As a rain of bullets took man and beast, the boy tore at the tent-flap ties and dashed inside. He emerged moments later holding two grenades.

"Here! Bring them here!" Erich yelled. "Roll them if you have to! We've got to blow up the generator!"

Misha started forward, half running, half staggering, then stuttery fire kicked up the dirt before him and he was running the other way, toward the power plant. He dropped one grenade and wheeled around to retrieve it, only to see the ground behind him erupt with bullets. He leapt and rolled.

Erich saw him yank out the pin, and then the boy screamed as he charged, arm lifted.

A bullet spun him around before he reached the generator. The grenade fell from his hand, bounced as though striking a rock, and rolled down the incline that Jews in their work had worn smooth of grass. Misha lay in a heap as the grenade came to rest against one leg of the water tower.

The explosion shook the ground, pelting Erich with rocks and debris. When it was over, he rolled onto his back, trying to spot Solomon but instead seeing the tripod topple.

Everything seemed to happen in slow motion. The bottom of one leg of the tower was missing—jagged where it had been blown off—and the whole thing leaned drunkenly, water fountaining from the holes Solomon had shot in it in his attempt to destroy the generator.

Another leg snapped beneath the weight and the structure tipped. Water cascaded as the tower fell onto the generator and the headquarters tent. The generator sizzled—and shorted. There were several sharp pops, then darkness.

No more shots came from the limestone chimney.

Hempel climbed onto the Panzer and entered the turret. There was a growl and a metallic whir, and the tank swung around to face the Jews. Their knot spread out into a line.

Hempel stuck up his head. "I warned you and yours against any insurrection, Rabbi!" he screamed.

In a shower of sparks, the roof of the hut collapsed. The major ducked down again into the Panzer.

Erich looked up, positioning his body. If only Solomon would give covering fire...if he was still alive.

He tensed himself, and felt the dogs tense in response. His years of track and field, their years of training with the Abwehr and then in the specialized program he had set up on the Rathenau estate, it was all culminating here.

Fire spewed from the barrel of the tank's gun. Perhaps a fourth of the Jews were mown down, limbs scattered like tenpins, as the .50 caliber machine gun traced through their line.

The remainder swarmed upon the tank, so close to it now as to render it ineffective. The guards shot them at point-blank range but they kept coming, one or two wrestling the Mausers from the hands of sadistic boys who thought themselves soldiers, and returning the fire.

The shepherds leapt, tearing at throats and testicles. Erich speared his hand into an eye with a satisfaction he would not have dreamed possible; the guard staggered back, falling against Johann, who was wrestling with Max, each ripping savagely at the other. Someone rifle-butted Erich in the back. He went down hard, and glanced up just in time to see the tank swivel toward the melee.

He's going to shoot us all, he thought, even if it means killing his own men.

Hempel popped his head out of the turret to look around. Bullets rang against the armor as Fermi and Holten-Pflug knelt and fired, forcing the major back inside. A wave of Jews reached the tank and began, by force of numbers, to overturn it.

The Totenkopfverbände threw down their weapons and ran toward the jungle, closely pursued by dogs, trainers, and Jews. Those still alive in the sentry towers raised their hands in surrender. The tank growled and lurched forward, spitting clods of dirt as the rocking treads grappled for purchase.

Jews and guards screamed as the tank crushed them in Hempel's haste to exit the camp and save himself.

The machine was halfway to the road leading down the hill when it stalled. Erich ran toward it, leaped on and peered inside, expecting to get shot by Hempel's pistol. He had done what he had set out to do. He had saved the Jews. Now there was only one thing left. Rid himself and the world of Hempel.

A mouselemur, the tank's sole occupant, gazed up at him with doleful eyes.

Instinctively, Erich knew that Hempel was headed toward the Storch. He let Taurus' spirit course through him. Immediately he sensed the shortcut the major had taken. He sniffed the air, consciously attempting to cease thinking in human terms. The world was sapped of all pigments, the jungle a hothouse of orchids gone to gray, but the forest was rich with odors. His hearing was likewise acute. The rumble of a centipede across a leaf; the storm of Hempel's breaths a hundred meters down the hill.

As he dashed among the trees and ferns, Erich could still hear sporadic shooting behind him. He moved laterally along the hillside until the desire to stop seized him and he sniffed the air a second time. He could smell them. The Kalanaro, their body heat aromatic strata he could read like a geological map. Those monkey-men were old, it occurred to him for some reason he could not explain but which he had already begun to trust: old as Benyowsky's diary, perhaps old when it was written. Had they been the ones who stood, three thousand strong, as Benyowsky and the King of the North sliced their own chests with the royal *assegai* and sucked each other's blood?

Ampanzanda-be!

Where was the meaning to Benyowsky's life? The writing of the country's first constitution? the attempt to save Ravalona, only to be betrayed by friends and his own idealistic ambition? What joy could have come to the Count in the cool darkness of the crypt?

Perhaps only the grasshoppers and the centipedes held meaning. Perhaps only footfalls through the woods at the first light of dawn. All else, he told himself, must be nothingness, must be chaos. The only real advice worth listening to was the sound of his own heart, where the voices of dogs dwelled.

"Taurus," he said.

And then: "Miriam."

Sensing her presence within the *valavato* and knowing that if he neared it he might lose all control, he continued to descend the hill, slipping effortlessly between lianas and brambles. With his newfound senses had come surety of foot. At the base of the hill a tidal pond loomed like a moat, but he danced across the line of stumps and sprang to a grassy dune. Digging his hands into the sand he scrambled to the top and peered over.

The Storch, two small tabun bombs emplaced beneath the wings, was turning, taxiing hard, prop wash dimpling the water. He set his sights on the white September moon above the western tree line. Only a low spine of beach ridge blocked the pilot's view of him as he sprinted across the sand, heading for the short spit that arced into the sea at the open end of the lagoon.

Ducking his head, he ran in a half-crouch for the end of the spit. The dogskin slapped against him, the foliage cast crenellated shadows across the sand, enabling him to run in relative secrecy. The last twenty meters, though, was fully exposed, an apron of wet beach studded with sharp, dark stones. He hit the area at top stride, so charged with anger and power that he sailed painlessly across the rocks, laughing as Hempel aimed the Mann.

The plane whipped toward him as the first shot zinged past his ear.

He splashed out into the lagoon. Hempel waved his right arm as he attempted another shot and jerked the craft to the left, revving as he headed into the bay. The floats sluiced across wavelets, spray rooster-tailing behind.

Erich threw himself into a surface dive.

He caught the right float's tail fin. Its force whipped his body out straight. As water pelted over him and the plane picked up speed, he grabbed the strut. The left float lifted off the water and the right, lower due to his weight, followed suit. He saw the major jerk the controls to the left, trying to compensate as the aircraft pitched to the right. The machine yawed crazily and slowly corrected.

Hempel's feet were directly above him, soles against the wraparound window. He looked down, eyes angry.

Erich bared his teeth and grinned up at him.

The major, swearing inaudibly, reached across to the passenger seat and picked up his gun. As he maneuvered in his chair to get a clear shot down through the glass, Erich took a firm grip on the sponson and heaved himself left, caught the strut that ran to the left wing, and pulled himself up toward the passenger hatch. He heard the gun fire—twice, like someone cracking walnuts—but he was beyond fear, beyond caring. Physical action subordinated thought.

He shouted, smashing at the hatch with his fist.

The window splintered into a spiderweb of shattered glass. He wrenched at the door handle so hard that the door slammed open and caught the airflow. The momentum knocked him against the fuselage.

Another shot rang out. "You should have shot me long ago, when you had the chance," Erich shouted, as the plane dipped to one side and the pistol flew from Hempel's hand.

Laughing, Erich placed the arch of his foot into the V of the strut joint and swung up to look the pilot in the eyes.

Hempel threw the plane into a turn. Greenery displaced the blue of the sea as they banked back toward Mangabéy. Erich clutched the top of the hatch frame and, raising and tucking his legs as though he were about to pole vault, hurled himself inside and lashed out with both feet, catching the major squarely on the jaw.

Hempel lurched backwards against the pilot's window. His head thudded twice against the pane and the Storch veered sharply left, bringing Erich fully inside the cockpit. He landed crossways over the seats, legs in Hempel's lap, and snapped his left knee up against the major's chin. Hempel sighed, and slumped in the seat.

The plane nose-dived.

As the ground slanted closer, Hempel came-to with a groan. He squinted through the window beneath his feet, paled—and pulled back on the wheel. The plane began a roller-coaster climb.

Hempel reached for the loop of black wire that ran along the top of the front window and out to the bombs.

Erich seized him by the shoulders, twisting and wrenching as he dug his nails into the man's flesh.

Hempel pawed at the air, trying to grab the wire loop, but Erich shoved him back, hard, into the pilot's seat, driving his full force into him. Without thinking, he leaned forward and sank his teeth deep into the man's neck.

The major gurgled and slammed his fists against the back of Erich's head. "Bastard! You bas...!"

The sound ceased. The resistance stopped.

Erich felt the plane bank—too far. The blue of the bay was framed in the passenger window and the moon showed silver on the bottom front of the nose.

So be it! he thought. Damn them all!

Hempel hit him again but it was like a friend chucking another on the shoulder in greeting. His arms slid down Erich's back and sagged to his sides. His mouth was open and he was staring blankly.

When Erich pulled the Iron Cross from his pocket and put it around Hempel's neck, the major did not resist.

Erich patted the medal once against the man's chest, and smiled. With one hand, he took hold of Hempel's neck, and twisted. The major's eyes protruded. A blood bubble formed on his lips, popped, and meandered down his chin. He slumped in the seat. Erich spat out Hempel's blood and flesh, and laughed again, a cackle that seemed to emanate from outside himself.

The plane had begun to spiral, but Erich made no attempt to gain the controls; control, he realized, was the last thing he wanted.

He lay with the crown of his skull against the window as the plane dipped. The only thing that mattered to him now was the redolent green of the Antabalana River region below. He thought he could hear the voices of thousands of Jews as they unloaded from ships, their cries in his honor like the adulation of tribesmen, hurrahs spilling like tumbling jungle waters into the bay.

He could see the moon, a silver wafer on a velvet sky. Perhaps, he thought, the Bushmen were right and that really was where the soul went. Leni had told him that one parched night as they sat on the edge of an African desert.

He laughed again and the moon spun, melting into madness.

Chapter 41

Chaos reigned in the encampment. In the melee, which he had started, Sol admitted to himself freely, it was hard if not impossible to tell who was winning and who was losing. The compound was no longer guarded against incursion from within or attack from without. The generator had been rendered useless by the collapsing water tower, the fences were for the most part shredded, and the searchlights were no longer operable.

Which meant that Sol no longer had even the vaguest idea of which targets he was hitting.

Having acknowledged all of that, he ceased firing and climbed down from behind the breastworks. His intent was to go down the south side of the limestone chimney, sprint through the clearing that Miriam called the grotto, and emerge well past the camp and the carnage.

From there, a reasonably short and not all that unpleasant run up the next hill would take him to the crypt.

A surge of pleasure reminded him that for the first time in his adult life he would be running to and not from—not away, not between sewer walls, not along the well-laid-out hell of the Sachsenhausen shoe-testing course that he'd had to endure for weeks on end.

Seeing the boy fall near the water tank and not get up had changed that plan. Misha lay somewhere down there, among the shots and the screams and the growling of both men and dogs.

Keeping as close as possible to the limestone chimney, Sol descended the front of the chimney rather than its rear, and climbed down into the camp. Once he was inside the compound, he found that most of the fighting was concentrated in the area near the main gate. He moved between the tents with comparative ease, as long as he kept his head down when he ran to avoid the natural traps of the tent lines. With the exception of tripping once, over a dead guard, he reached the boy without mishap.

Misha lay where Sol had last spotted him, crumpled in a small heap near the water tank. Sol turned him over carefully. Blood had welled up in a wound on the boy's forehead. Sol spat on his fingers and wiped it away. It was no more than a graze.

He touched the carotid artery and, to his great relief, found a pulse.

"Misha," he said in a hoarse voice. "It's Herr Freund. Open your eyes and speak to me, young man."

The boy's eyes fluttered open and he took a shallow breath. "Don't make me go back to the hut," he mumbled. "I don't want to go back any more."

Sol glanced up at what was left of the shack. "I don't think that you need worry about that." He ruffled the boy's hair. His fingers came in contact with a lump. "Try to sit up, Mishele," he said.

Misha sat up with no trouble, but his hand shot to his head and he scrunched up his face.

"Head hurt?" Sol asked.

Misha nodded gently, as if to minimize the movement. "I thought I was dead."

Sol chuckled. "You must have hit your head when you fell, but I am happy to be able to tell you that you are very much alive. Now let's see if we can get you out of here that way."

He started to bundle up the boy in his arms, but Misha shook him off. "I can walk myself, Herr Freund," he said, though he did reach for Sol's hand.

In that way, man and boy together, they walked between the tents and headed for the front of the camp. Everywhere Sol looked there were bodies, many of them dead or almost dead, others being attended to by their friends as best they could. Those guards whom he had seen earlier running for the forest had apparently not returned, nor had the dogs who had chased them. Nevertheless, there were enough of Hempel's men alive and around that the occasional shooting broke out. Hempel and the tank were gone, and Erich was nowhere to be seen.

Worried about Miriam's safety, he hastened his steps. There was no real reason now not to exit through the gate, but it would make him and the boy easy targets for any sniper who might be hiding and waiting.

Apparently sensing Sol's hesitation, Misha tugged at his hand. "We could go out the way I came in," he said.

Sol followed the boy, and soon he was arching his back as he crawled beneath the fence, which was amazingly intact on that side. Misha was already under the wire. They ran hand-in-hand for several meters before machine-gun fire burst from one of the sentry towers. The boy stumbled. This time brooking no argument, Sol swept him into his arms. He did not stop running until they were well up the western track.

He set the boy down and turned to look at the encampment. Dawn had begun to lighten the sky. The hut was little more than a pile of embers, the compound a shambles.

Beside him, the boy began to cough.

Sol crouched down and removed the dog collar from Misha's neck. He pitched it into the bushes and placed his arm across the boy's narrow shoulders. They stayed motionless for a moment, surveying the manmade chaos below. They leaned against each other as if for support—though whether for physical or emotional support, Sol was not sure. He had the feeling that he had escaped not only from the Nazis, but from a life of dread lived on a predetermined road. His belief that everything happened for a reason was unshaken, for God, unlike man, did not roll dice. But how much of a part he was expected to play in God's plan? And how much of *that* was predetermined?

He stood up, brushing off his knees. There was a great sadness in him for those of his fellow Jews who'd had to lose their lives in this battle, but his overwhelming feelings were of gratitude that he was alive, and pride that he had helped to free his people.

"I think that you should tell me a story, Herr Freund," Misha said, once more taking Sol's hand. "Rabbi Freund." He seemed to be testing the words. "I think that you are a much better rabbi than you know."

Solomon laughed. "Better yet," he said, "let us sing."

Misha looked startled. "Sing? Someone will hear us."

"I do not think there are many left who care what we do. But perhaps you are right, so we shall sing softly. "*Da-da-yenu,*" he began. "*Da-da-yenu, Da-da-yenu, Da-yenu, Da-ye-nu,*"

The boy grinned and joined in and they sang the song which, traditionally, was heard at Passover and was everyone's favorite because of its optimism and its happy beat.

Dayenu. Enough. We are slaves no longer. We are free.

When they had stopped singing, Misha tugged at Solomon's hand. Sol wiped away the tears that had formed as he'd remembered sitting at the Seder with his parents and his sister, Recha, vying for who could sing the song with the most ferocity.

"What is it, Misha?" he asked. "Another song?"

"The Kapo," Misha said. "He wasn't dead down there on the beach. I...I tripped over the brazier and started the fire—"

"Slow down, Mishele."

The boy took a deep breath. "I went back to the hut to steal the Zana-Malata's magic. When I was leaving, he...the Kapo...he came after me. I was so scared, Herr Freund. He was blocking my way and then he saw the knife lying there—" He shuddered.

"You don't have to talk about it," Sol said.

"I want to tell you," the boy insisted. "He reached for the knife. That was when I ran. I tripped over the brazier and the coals spilled all over. I knew they were burning, Herr Freund. I did. I knew they would start a fire." The boy was silent for a moment. "But I'm not sorry. I'm glad he's dead."

"I'm glad he's dead, too, Mishele. He was a very bad man."

"I wish I could kill the Sturmbahnführer, too," Misha went on.

Sol squeezed the boy's hand. "Who could blame you for feeling that way? Not even God, I think."

"I love you, Herr Freund," the boy said suddenly. "Not as much as I love Papa, but I do love you."

His thin little face was serious, his eyes held a hint of tears. Sol picked him up and hugged him. "And I love you, too, Misha. Very much."

They had stopped walking and were halfway up the hill that led to the crypt. Sol looked out over the trees toward the eastern edge of the lagoon, trying to keep himself from crying. He heard the thrum of the Storch, and hugged the boy tighter. In an instant the plane appeared, its spray like an elaborate headdress as it moved at a rapid rate past the spit and toward open water. He could see a figure, recognizable only because it was a man dressed in dogskin, running along the sand.

Erich.

Like a champion swimmer he dove, flat out onto a float as the plane passed. The aircraft lifted. Erich dangled for a moment, but quickly pulled himself up.

The Storch came around in a sharp turn and flew overhead, not much higher than the trees. Erich threw himself into the machine through the hatch door.

The plane sputtered twice, banked, and flew on, completing the arc and heading toward the mainland, its drone diminishing as it grew smaller.

Not wanting to lose sight of it, Sol cupped a hand above his eyes. Then he spied its silhouette against the moon.

The Storch fell, spinning like a ride at Luna Park. At first Sol thought that it would pull out, that Hempel—who was surely the pilot—would right the craft and swoop in for an effortless landing.

But the angle of descent was too steep and he watched helplessly as the plane disappeared into the trees.

The boy was looking up at him, knowledge that the plane had crashed evident in his young face.

"I do not think that Otto Hempel will ever hurt you again," Sol said.

Nor Erich, me, he thought, staring at the place where the plane had gone down.

Misha kicked a stone. Smiled. Kicked another. Sol tried to return the smile, but his heart was too filled with tears.

"*Dayenu*," he said softly. "Goodbye, old friend. May you rest in peace."

Chapter 42

Miriam let out a slow breath and chewed down hard on the leaf that Bruqah had placed in her mouth to help her through labor. She could see the pre-dawn sky through the open doorway, cobalt-blue and studded with stars. She could not recall having seen a sky that color, but then she had never really spent much time looking at the sky, she thought, especially not one so early in the morning, especially not during the throes of labor.

"Soon, Lady Miri." Bruqah wiped her forehead with a damp cloth.

"Soon!" Miriam shouted. "I'm tired of hearing you say that. Can't you find something else to say?" She lowered her voice. "I'm sorry, Bruqah. I shouldn't be shouting at *you*. It's not like you did this to me, and if it weren't for you—"

She gasped as another round of pain tore at her. Bruqah signaled the Zana-Malata to hold her by the ankles to steady her until the wave passed. When it had, she swore silently at the sky and everything that walked the earth beneath it. The God who condemned women to this was certainly male and had no sense of humor whatsoever; of that she was damn sure.

"Solomon!" she hissed between gritted teeth, not knowing if she wanted to kill him or have him at her side supporting her.

"We will find Mister Sollyman!" Bruqah said. "As soon baby is here. Chew the leaf, Lady Miri. It will help. It is the way of our women."

She breathed rapidly, hyperventilating as the next contraction rolled from her womb. Arched in agony, she wondered why sex had been invented in the first place—and why she had been so foolish as to partake.

Bruqah put a hand against her cheek. The coolness of his flesh startled her, and for a moment she looked up without pain at his white teeth and shining eyes.

"We have a saying for such times," he whispered, running his hand up across her forehead and gently pushing her hair back, "'Where childbirth blooms, the indri watches.'"

"What's that supposed to mean!"

"Mean, Lady Miri?"

She shook her head in exasperation. "You and your goddamn sayings." Another contraction was coming on; she prepared herself for its fury. "Your people are as bad as..." She released a slow groan, "...the Germans. A saying for everything."

He grinned. "We have one for that too, Lady Miri."

Sitting up, she seized his shoulder. "Solomon!"

He pressed her back down. "In good time. For now you have the baby to worry you about."

"There!"

Sol and Misha stood framed in the doorway, as if by a horseshoe of sky. Fireflies winked around their heads like sequins.

"Miriam!"

She chewed down on the leaf.

"You and the boy stay outside, please, Rabbi," Bruqah said.

Before Miriam could argue, another wave of pain rose through her. She gasped and bit down hard. The leaf tasted slightly bitter, like dried coffee.

"Push!" Bruqah said.

"I am pushing, damn you!"

"Not hard enough. Bite on the leaf."

She bit down again. Suddenly light-headed, she drifted down a stream into a realm where pain existed, real, but apart from her. Solomon and Bruqah stood behind a shimmery curtain, smiling and speaking to her in soundless voices. She attempted to return the smile, to assure them that everything was all right, that she was quite adept at delivering this baby or any other, but her facial muscles refused to respond.

It did not matter. Nothing was important except the child. They knew that, surely; even men could understand such things.

She heard a woman thanking and praising her; and for an instant she was certain she saw several dozen natives, naked and coated with white mud, cheer and lift gleaming spear blades into the air—but it was only a trick of the breeze and the breaking dawn.

And she saw fireflies.

Glowworms...was that Lincke's melody tinkling across her mind? She glanced up at Bruqah. He was cranking her music box, cradled in the crook of his arm. He raised a eucalyptus branch and shook it above her head, then executed an abrupt turn and shook the branch toward the door.

"*Only a moment more.*"

The voice was Judith's. Miriam reached out for her hand.——

——"*I can't help you, Miriam. You must do this on your own. When you see me again, it will be in the flesh. For now, we belong to the child, the others and I.*"——

———One more time, the pain intruded. Miriam braced against the rough surface of the rock wall with her hand and bore down until it seemed as if she would turn herself inside out. Three quick breaths, and she pushed down again. She tried for more breaths but the waves of pain were too close, each one greater and rolling over its predecessor. The agony seemed to rip her groin asunder.

"Solly! Misha! Come! She is here, the baby."

"A...what? You mean the baby's here already? I..."

Bruqah wrapped the infant in a *lamba*. A layer of blue-veined flesh veiled the upper half of baby's face. Plastered from the top of the totally bald head to the nose, it looked like a bandit's mask.

With infinite care, Bruqah cut the umbilical cord and slipped the caul from the child's head. She could see the Zana-Malata behind him, hear him babbling something unintelligible.

"What is he saying?" she asked.

"He praise the spirit child of Ravalona." Bruqah handed the child to her and placed his hand over hers. She felt his sincerity. "Though he praises true, he seeks the afterbirth. He wishes to eat it, for strength—and seeing face of death."

"He wants to die?"

"He wishes to recognize she face so to dance out of she path."

At any other time Miriam might have chuckled at Bruqah's convoluted language. "The man helped me," she said simply. "Give it to him."

"No can do," Bruqah said.

At that, the Zana-Malata darted forward. Grabbing the caul, he began to stuff it hungrily into his mouth. When Bruqah lunged for him, the syphilitic sidestepped neatly and darted out of the crypt.

"Get him, Solly!" Bruqah shouted. But he was too late.

Bruqah veiled the eucalyptus branch in purple gossamer and, sticking his head outside the door and jamming the branch into a crack in the rockwork, struck a match and set afire each dangling cloth-end. Quickly the flames spread; leaves crackled. He re-entered the crypt and, squatting by her side, took her hands between his palms.

"Bruqah inform the Kalanaro. They will help drive demons away."

She wanted to smile but, realizing Bruqah was serious, instinctively put her hand on the child's back. Then she called out to Sol and Misha, for it was time they too saw the child of the dawn.

Epilogue

Because it was so interpreted from the Talmud by some of them, the Jews buried their dead in the four days between the Day of Atonement and Succot.

Because it is written that the building of the *Succah*, the hut which commemorates the season of rejoicing—*zman simhatainu*—must begin immediately after Yom Kippur, they mourned privately and joined together to erect the tabernacle. For this, they gathered the traditional citron, the branches of palm trees, the boughs of thick-leafed trees, and the willows where the spring emptied at the bottom of the cliff. One-hundred surviving Jews, and the two dog trainers, Fermi and the family man, Holten-Pflug.

Having built three walls, they left the fourth one open and began on the roof, using only that which grows from the ground and has been cut off from the ground. They left a space in the roof, no more than ten inches wide, yet large enough to see the stars and let in the rain, thus showing that they trusted in God to provide and to keep them safe.

From the roof they hung decorations of fruit and flowers. In the same way they decorated the walls. A child and a young man named Max retrieved a zebu-horn Shofar from the debris of the encampment and placed it in a position of honor.

At dusk on the fourth day after Yom Kippur, a holiday was declared, and the Festival of Succot began. They sang and they danced, and they expressed joy in God and in their new-found, hard-earned, freedom.

While they sang and they danced, the Kalanaro poled from Nosy Mangabéy to the mainland. In the light of the rising moon, their pirogue looked like it was overflowing with glowworms. The fireflies winked on and off in unison.

A man watched them. In his arms he held an infant, wrapped in a *lamba*, perfectly content.

When he could no longer see the pirogue, he looked down at the beach and listened to the chanting that floated up to him.

Baruch ata adonai elohainu melech ha-olam shesheheyanu v'kee-ymanu v'hee-gee-anu lazman hazeh.

"Blessed art Thou, Lord our God, King of the universe who has imparted His wisdom to those who revere Him," he echoed softly, so that the child would not become alarmed. "Sweet Deborah," he crooned, and stared down at her in the light of the quarter moon.

Swept up by the power of the benediction, he entered the child's mind. There, in the flesh of his flesh, he rediscovered the dybbuk that had been in him for most of his life.

Entering Deborah's consciousness, he found himself back where the dybbuk began: with the nurse, Judith, who was killed by the grenade that took the life of Walther Rathenau. Entering the woman's cobalt-blue eyes, he discovered that Judith could have stopped the assassination through the conscious giving of her own life. Instead, she chose to live—and lost her life and her soul as well.

Unlike the five sparrows—Rathenau, Erich, Emanuel, Margabrook, and Lise, those who lost their lives to help others—Judith was never willing even to risk hers for someone else.

Ironically, though he was once nicknamed *Spatz*—"Sparrow"— this man was not one of them. Unlike them, he had not lost his life. His gift, or curse, was to see into the future. Since boyhood, he has been able to see glimpses of what the dybbuk will bring.

Returning to the present—to the hilltop—he wondered if it were possible to change history so that the dybbuk that was now within his infant daughter had no chance to alter events in devastating ways.

He wrestled with the ultimate moral dilemma.

Staring out over the bay, he made his choice: He would watch over Deborah and make sure the dybbuk was not exorcised. He would teach her what wisdom he could, in the hope that her actions would allow the dybbuk to atone for its sins, and find rest at last.

A woman called out to him from the beach. He did not answer, for there was one more thing he must do before joining the others.

He held the infant against his chest. Her heart beat against his. Though he had promised himself he would never deliberately ask to be shown the future, he invited it to come to him.

"Please," he begged——

——*Please....*

The word snakes from the mouth of a girl of perhaps eight, wreathed in cobalt-blue light. She is tied naked to a carved wooden post by ropes wound among the water buffalo horns nailed above her head. Behind her, the vent of a volcano boils against the dusk. Her face quivers, her eyes are huge with terror. Suddenly her body sags, and only the ropes that bind her fast keep her from slumping to the ground.

Bruqah help me, she mutters, almost as if out of old habit. *Papa help me. I'm here. I'm here.* Then her voice is lost beneath the sputter and pop of red-orange lava fingers crawling among the stone menhirs and monoliths that surround her.

The eight-year-old glances between the saw-toothed leaves of the tanghin tree.

"Leave me alone, Jehuda!" she shouts.

Why Deborah! Do I offend you? You who deny my existence?

The voice comes from inside the girl's head.

In front of her, a thin spiral of smoke rises from black lava, and heat-charred snags smolder like damp torches. Out of that comes a snarling, a growling, and figures appear, men dressed in skins and carrying rifles and axes. Hunchbacked, they moved across the landscape.

Making wide ambulatory crossings along the hillside to avoid a molten area, stopping every now and then to shoot back down the hill, the figures close in. It is almost impossible to tell them apart, for their heads are draped with the heads of dogs.

Squatting, concentrating their firepower on the brush below, the bizarre coven watch in silence as a skin-dressed man emerges from a thicket of thorns. He, too, wears a dog head, but it lies upside-down between his shoulderblades. Around his neck, he wears an Iron Cross.

He sits down and starts to beat a weir drum. The others dance. Slowly. All elbows and shoulders, moving clockwise along the swamp that edges the rain forest. Now counter-clockwise, soundless except for the occasional slapping of guns and sheathed knives against their skin.

The drummer rises. Passing between the others, he trudges up the black pumice and threads his way through the huge gravestones to stoop before the unconscious girl.

Taloned fingers lift her chin. Her eyes blink open and her facial muscles constrict with fear. Whimpering quietly, she tries to work her arms free. The rope scrapes uselessly against the totem and the dog-man raises his head and laughs——

Laughter from the beach and the whimpering of the child who was being held too close drew the man out of the vision.

"I'll be right down," he said, but he did not move. "It is not over yet, is it, Erich," he whispered.

He stared at the Madagascar mainland, toward the rain forest, where four days ago he saw a plane spiral down to Earth.

Afterword

While The Madagascar Manifesto is a work of fiction, the authors strove to remain as true as possible to historical fact where it did not directly impact the decision to send a mission to the island of Madagascar. The authors made an effort to reflect language use and rhythms that were prevalent at the time, but for reading ease did take certain small liberties. For example, "suspenders" and "flashlight" were only then replacing the more common "braces" and "hand torch."

Madagascar's relatively low population prior to World War II, together with its being situated south of the oil-rich lands of the Red Sea and close to the British shipping lanes between India and South Africa, brought it to Hitler's attention. In early 1938, he instructed Eichman to collect material about the island for a "foreign-policy solution" to the "Jewish question."

The idea of expelling Europe's Jews to Madagascar, which was controlled by the French, did not begin with the Nazis; the proposal goes back at least as far as Napolean, who favored it. Between the World Wars, the idea was championed by Britain's Henry Hamilton Beamish and Arnold Leese, and in the Netherlands by Egon van Winghene. The Joint Distribution Committee of the U.S. House of Representatives also toyed with the notion of resettling the Jews to Madagascar. As the obvious fact of the German conquest of Europe grew stronger, France's Baron von Rothchild, the Jewish cognac magnate, even offered to buy the island in a desperate attempt to help save his people.

In 1937, the Poles, who wished to encourage the emigration of large numbers of Jews, received permission from the French to send a three-man investigative commission—two of whom were Jews—to Madagascar to explore the possibility of just such resettlement. In Berlin, the idea was greeted enthusiastically, especially by Heinrich Himmler, who wrote, "However cruel and tragic each individual case may be, this method is still the best, if one rejects the Bolshevik method of physical extermination of a people out of inner conviction as un-German and impossible." It is now accepted that the discussion of the Madagascar Plan by the Nazis was one of many public relations ploys used to buy time while they implemented their true final solution. Where this work diverges from accepted historical reality is in the implementation of the first stage of the Madagascar Plan.

Die Zigarrenkiste is based on a store in what was, until recently, East Berlin. The beating of the Gentile co-owner resulting from the "mistaken identity" and his subsequent robbery of the store really happened. The Jewish co-owner—modeled on Janet Berliner's grandfather—actually witnessed Rathenau's assassination. Except for the second nurse and the grenade that kills her, the assassination is presented exactly as it happened. That Rathenau's chauffeur survived without a scratch was probably due less to good luck or miracle than to a weak grenade.

The assassins went to prison but were released after short terms. One of them, Ernst von Salomon, became a successful novelist and playwright; all his writings are based on his association with the conspirators.

At least one meeting between Hitler and a Gypsy fortune teller really occurred, as did the wild pre-Olympics party at Peacock Island and the winter solstice celebrations by the SS. The Grünewald synagogue, Wewelsburg Castle, Luna Park, and the Wannsee are real places. The Nazi *"Endlösung"* (the "final solution" to exterminate the Jews through the use of poison gas) was decided at Wannsee in 1943.

The El Dorado was real, though Kaverne is fictitious, as is Ananas. Brecht escaped from Germany and, together with his collaborator Kurt Weill, became a wealthy playwright, mostly from the British production of *The Three Penny Opera*. Werner Fink miraculously survived the Nazi regime.

Walther Rathenau did have a niece, though any relationship between her and the character in this book is purely coincidental. "Vlad"—Vladimir Nabokov—did teach tennis lessons in Berlin. He emigrated to the United States and became one of this country's top novelists and critics; he was particularly famous for *Lolita*. Whether he ever met Rathenau's niece is a matter of conjecture.

Prince Auwi was killed on the Russian Front. Juan Perón, who became the dictator Argentina, was emissary to Italy and was in Berlin at the time of the novel.

Leni Riefenstahl eventually produced her book on the Bushmen. Her film about the 1936 Olympics is considered by some to have been, despite its propaganda, the finest documentary ever produced about athletics.

Sachsenhausen and Oranienburg are for the most part accurately described. Flower beds were created in many parts of the camp, and prisoners' blood was sometimes used for fertilizer; the shoe track is also accurately described.

The fictional Doctor Schmidt is a composite of two male doctors who performed medical experiments at the camp. Tabun was a nerve gas developed by the Nazis in 1937.

The existence of the Cushitic Falasha Jews is a matter of public record. That a subsect of the Falashas consisted of refugees from Elephantine, Egypt, is conjecture on the authors' part, but is highly possible. When the Elephantine Jews were driven out of the Egyptian military post and never seen again, they fled southeast—to what is now Ethiopia and the Sudan.

The material concerning the atom bomb is also a matter of public record. In reality, however, Lise Meitner fled her native Austria and went to Sweden, where she and Otto Hahn exchanged love letters and probably scientific notes. A mistake in calculations that resulted in the Germans continuing to use heavy water instead of graphite as a neutron modulator, and the fact that the Nazis' fear of "Jewish science" caused them to fractionalize rather than concentrate research efforts, were the main reasons why Germany did not develop the bomb. Professor Heisenberg, the leading player in the German race to create the bomb, did play Bach fugues in the Haigerloch *Schlosskirke,* where his laboratory was set up.

The island of Madagascar lies in the Indian Ocean, off Africa's southeast coast. It is the world's fourth largest island—the size of the Atlantic Seaboard from New York to Savanah, and inland as far as Atlanta. Having broken away from the mainland a hundred million years ago—perhaps, as some insist, as part of the continent of Lemuria—it developed a flora and fauna as unique as those of Australia or the Galapagos.

Madagascar's northern rain forests, the world's densest, teem with orchids and lemurs; the spiny deserts of the south are home to latex trees, whose sap causes blindness, and harpoon burrs, which tear flesh to ribbons. Until they were hunted to extinction, pygmy hippos roamed the land; there stalked the giant, flightless Aepyornis, the elephant bird known as the *roc* in the Sinbad story and whose rare, semi-fossilized eggs are still found on occasion.

The island, only two hundred and fifty miles from the mainland, remained uninhabited until 500 B.C. Surprisingly, the first settlers arrived not from Africa but from Java (now Indonesia), three thousand miles to the east. These became known on Madagascar as the Vazimba, a race of bronze sailors who island-hopped their outrigger canoes all the way across the Indian Ocean only to drown in a gene pool when the peoples of what are now Mozambique and Somalia crossed from Africa to the rich island the Vazimba had discovered. Inter-marrying gave the skin of many Malagasy a coppery color—though few islanders can trace their ancestry back to the original settlers.

Today the island suffers from overpopulation—especially along the central plateau, whose indigenous plant life has been burned off in an ecological disaster of staggering dimensions.

Nosy Mangabé (to help the reader with pronunciation, the island is spelled Mangabéy in the novel) is a real island in the mouth of Madagascar's Antongil Bay. Few Malagasy set foot on Mangabéy, perhaps because of its history. Involved in a disastrous colony-attempt during the eighteenth century, it was later used as a small but secure base by British and French pirates. Mauritius Augustus Benyowsky built a bamboo hospital on the island during the late eighteenth century. Daniel Defore studied the island as background to his writings, and the English pirate Captain Avery used it as a stronghold, possibly because the northeastern area of Madagascar is the source of numerous rare gems, including apatite, found nowhere else in the world.

The Vazimba and Zana-Malata are real peoples, as are the Betsileo and Antakarana; reports differ as to whether the Kalanaro exist in reality or are a synonym for the Tanal, the legendary People of the Forest. Trial by ordeal, using the pit of the tanghin fruit, is accurately described, as is the ceremony for opening a *valavato* tomb, though no crypt exists on Mangabéy. The Ranavalona legend is a combination of two legends well known in the region.

While aye-ayes were not indigenous to Mangabéy until a modern conservation effort relocated several families, the authors chose to make the supposition that there was at least one. Today, Mangabéy is the world's only official refuge of the aye-aye, a lemur whose supposed powers of predicting death the Malagasy once feared so much that they killed the creature on sight. For the moment, the translocated aye-ayes are safe on Mangabéy.

Under certain circumstances, some fireflies are known to blink in unison.

Finally, readers may be interested to know that Madagascar's rain forest is proportionately the densest, the most definitive, and the fastest declining rain forest in the world.

About the Authors

Sometimes referred to as The Hot and Cold Team, Janet Berliner and George Guthridge have coauthored numerous short stories in addition to *The Madagascar Manifesto*. Many of those stories are collected in *Exotic Locals* (CD-ROM available from Lone Wolf Publications).

Singularly, Janet Berliner is the author of *Rite of the Dragon* (trade paperback available from Wildside Publishing), and coauthor of *The Execution Exchange*. Her mosaic novel *Flirting With Death*, coauthored with Kevin J. Anderson, Matthew J. Costello, and F. Paul Wilson will be published by TOR/Forge in the Fall of 2002. She also created *The Unicorn Sonata*, which Peter S. Beagle wrote. Janet is also the editor of six anthologies, including *Snapshots: Twentieth Century Mother-Daughter Fiction* (coedited with Joyce Carol Oates; David R. Godine Publishers) and *Peter S. Beagle's Immortal Unicorn* (coedited with Peter S. Beagle; HarperCollins Publishers). Janet has also been a journalist, lecturer, teacher, translator, and editor. Further information can be found on the BerlinerPhiles website at members.aol.com/berlphil.

For his part, George Guthridge is the author of the Western *Bloodletter*. His short fiction has earned him three nominations for major awards, twice for the Nebula and once for the Hugo. His stories have appeared in *Isaac Asimov's Science Fiction Magazine*, *Amazing Stories*, *The Magazine of Fantasy and Science Fiction*, and many other magazines and anthologies. George is also an award-winning educator. For twenty years he has taught children in Alaska, where his techniques helped his students, mostly Eskimo children often considered ineducable, to thrice win national Young Problem Solvers competitions. George is currently at work on a book which uses narrative techniques to tell the story of his work, as well as his continued work as a professor in the University of Alaska Fairbanks' Distance Education Progam, working at the Dillingham campus.

Come check out our web site for details on these Meisha Merlin authors!

Kevin J. Anderson
Robert Asprin
Robin Wayne Bailey
Edo van Belkom
Janet Berliner
Storm Constantine
Diane Duane
Sylvia Engdahl
Jim Grimsley
George Guthridge
Keith Hartman
Beth Hilgartner
P. C. Hodgell
Tanya Huff
Janet Kagan
Caitlin R. Kiernan

Lee Killough

George R. R. Martin

Lee Martindale

Jack McDevitt

Sharon Lee & Steve Miller

James A. Moore

Adam Niswander

Andre Norton

Jody Lynn Nye

Selina Rosen

Kristine Kathryn Rusch

Pamela Sargent

Michael Scott

William Mark Simmons

S. P. Somtow

Allen Steele

Mark Tiedeman

Freda Warrington

www.MeishaMerlin.com